A Life Tested

A Life Singular
Book 5

Lorraine Pestell

Paperback ISBN: 978-1-925151-14-5
E-book ISBN: 978-1-925151-06-0
Amazon ASIN: B01DEEJOEQ

Other books in the "A Life Singular" series:
Book 1 – A Life Singular
Book 2 – A Life Found
Book 3 – A Life Entwined
Book 4 – A Life Lived
Book 6 – A Life Loved
Book 7 – A Life After

For the crusader formerly known as Doctor Philip Nitschke,
and for the fundamental human right not to be

The author supports two not-for-profit organisations which provide
invaluable assistance to Australian children in need:

EdConnect Australia (formerly the School Volunteer Program)
*(http://EdConnetAustralia.org.au) "We're harnessing the wisdom
and skills of older generations to enrich the learning experience of
young people who are at risk of falling by the wayside in an often
over-burdened school system."*

The Smith Family *(www.thesmithfamily.com.au). "The Smith
Family is a children's charity helping disadvantaged Australian
children to get the most out of their education, so they can create
better futures for themselves."*

Prologue

Dan's knees buckled under him, heart beating so fast that his ears were ringing. The call disconnected, and as he flopped down onto the mattress, the screen of his mobile telephone reverted to its colourful background. He had downloaded this picture from The Good School's website a year ago, and he gulped when he acknowledged its new significance.

The dazed student needed to tell someone; to share this amazing piece of news. But whom? His mum would be fast asleep at home in Glasgow, as would the mentor who had acted as referee for his application, both five hours in advance of his current location. He stared beyond the window of his shoebox-sized hotel room at the blizzard sleeting across the Charles River to the city of Boston, still having difficulty coming to terms with this superb turn of events.

There was one person who would understand perfectly... What time would it be in Brisbane? Another nine hours ahead of the UK. No.... Eleven hours. It was summer down there, wasn't it? Daylight savings, the strange expression people used in America when they moved their clocks forward. Or back. Which was it? It must already be Thursday afternoon on the east coast of Australia. This time-travel thing always confused him much more than it ought to.

The familiar sound of an arrow being drawn and fired from a longbow swooshed from the tablet computer behind him, synchronised with the vibration of his smartphone against his thigh. The dual prompts jolted the Scot out of his trance. A new e-mail; the one he had been told to expect. So he wasn't dreaming after all!

Dan's fingers entered his four-digit "PIN" code to unlock the outdated device and confirm the message's arrival, just as the Admissions bursar foreshadowed. And to cap it all, there was a text from *her*:

"Heard news. Awesome! So happy 4 u. C u @ dinner.
Freya :-)"

God Almighty! As if the ambitious teenager wasn't excited enough, now his insides churned for a whole different reason. He hadn't the nerve to ring the winner of last year's scholarship yet, noting she had taken the easy option too. He tapped out a quick reply, itching to read the contents of Kierney Diamond's e-mail.

> "Thx. Unreal, my head's spinning. Talk soon. Can't wait to finally meet. DFin"

Was that too obvious? Was it obvious enough? Perhaps Freya meant nothing more than their attendance at the *gala* dinner, where the outgoing leader was to hand over to the next incumbent. She said she was happy for him, that was all. There was probably a line of smart, good-looking guys eager to be her guest that evening, and there was no way he would have the courage to ask her out. Not yet anyway... Not at this stage of his life.

Dan's finger hovered over the unread e-mail, opening it to reveal several short paragraphs with embedded links to four separate documents, the passwords for which had been sent in a text earlier by the friendly Australian United Nations diplomat.

Tap. An acceptance form. No-brainer!

Tap. Details of available accommodation for the first week in January, all expenses paid!

Tap again. Order of Proceedings for the inauguration ceremony, complete with his name printed with "Guest of Honour" underneath.

And one last tap. A certificate for the recipient to print and pin up on his wall, and a logo file to add to his website, LinkedIn profile and *Curriculm Vitæ*. He had done it! After years of dedication to the guiding principles set out in "A Life Singular", the working-classed Partick couple's surviving twin, born with not much more than an entrepreneurial spirit and a curious drive to rock the boat, was well on his way to true greatness. A place at The Good School was the only thing he had ever coveted, apart from having his father shake his hand as the son whose existence had been so far disavowed.

Dan Finley would make the great Jeff Diamond proud. If it took every last breath in his pale, scrawny body, he would take the teachings from the great man's autobiography to the next level. After everything he had put himself through up to this point, he needed to trust destiny to deliver him to his dream girl, so they could take carriage of the work their idols had handed down.

It was their destiny. He had already designed the tattoo.

Leading From The Front

One of Australia's most influential men reached the small suburban boxing club belonging to Alberto Santos Fernandez, in town to lay his murdering father to rest once and for all. His heart was heavy, but his head was clear. The biggest question on his mind was whether he could fly in and out before word of his presence broke among the crime gangs of Sydney's west. It had been well over a year since he had heard from Mark Jaworski, but it was still best not to tempt providence.

In reality, Jeff had no evidence to suggest anyone might seek retribution against him. Did Rough Diamond's demise make any difference? The fortunate son's profile had been plenty high enough over the last few years for the victims' families to claim revenge for any grudges they might harbour.

Nevertheless, the star was as jumpy as a sack of motherless joeys as he locked the driver's door of his rented Commodore and crossed the street to Alberto's club. He smiled and shook his head. No-one had thought to mention that his philanthropic contribution included a flashing neon sign above the door!

The benefactor found the old man and his middle son, Felipe, watching television in the basement. He had visited several times in recent months, having paid for a major overhaul of the facilities and equipment in an effort to promote the club too far into the limelight for the underworld element to bother with it anymore. Striding past a series of rings on both sides, he waved at those who called out to him but chose not to stop and talk. He noticed a picture of himself on the wall behind the bar, posing with Alberto and a number of the older boys who trained here. So he had done some good for his hometown at least, in his rush to change the world. It compensated somewhat for the gaudy signage.

The proprietor ushered his worthy sponsor through to the rear lounge, which had been deemed out-of-scope for the renovation project; a stark contrast to the crisp, new *décor* in the public areas. Jeff placed a brown paper bag containing two bottles of an imported, special vintage Chilean wine, prompting Felipe to spring up and produce four ornate goblets from under the bar.

The anxious celebrity downed his first taste of the rich, red *Carmenere* in only a couple of gulps. Alberto's son reached forward to refill his glass. With nerves easing a little, the former local reminded his hosts that the family's youngest child, Carlos, had been in his year at school, extrapolating that Felipe was closer in age to Madalena. The young man with streaks of peroxide highlights in his hair had spent the last few years working in the Mediterranean for a tour company, leading Jeff to believe him to be one of the few men in the neighbourhood who had never slept with his sister.

A while later, a knock on the door signalled the arrival of Joe Cafici, the owner of the hardware store above which the Diamonds had lived in the nineteen-sixties. Although the old man had retired, so overweight that he struggled to walk unaided, and the shop was now run by his sons, concern lurked at the back of Jeff's mind as to who might belong in the card shark's circle these days.

Since deciding not to sell the Stones Road flat, the songwriter had leased it to a husband and wife team of musicians, who used the space to teach children in the area. They had kept him informed of any suspicious activity, repeatedly complaining that the elderly Italian had a habit of snooping around and asking after their famous landlord's schedule and whereabouts.

Jeff was boxed into a corner this evening however, wondering who else might turn up out of the blue to drink with him on the pretext of paying their respects. He had no choice but to trust Alberto's judgement. None of these men had been friends with his father, so perhaps the occasion was more "good riddance" than "for he's a jolly good fellow."

Once Joe had shuffled into a vacated armchair, the local-boy-made-good began to recount the events of the previous week and explained what he hoped to achieve from this trip. He evaded a number of nostalgic questions about days he didn't care to remember, determined to wait until he and Alberto were alone before checking on any gangland activity currently playing out around Fairfield and Parramatta.

Despite the old man's insistence that Cafici was trustworthy, the celebrity was not prepared to give the grumpy, bow-legged Italian one *iota* of information which could be misused. Moreover, he had forgotten how vile it was to shake the hand of yet another man who had indulged in carnal pleasure at the expense of his sister's youth.

Two bottles of wine and far too many cigarettes later, *Señora* Santos showed their handsome guest to his lodgings for the night. He wasn't at all surprised when they reached the top of the stairs and the door opened into Eva's childhood bedroom. She had since moved to another similar building nearby with her boyfriend, and her former school friend struggled not to laugh when his memory treated him to a few select images from the countless times he had sneaked into this room as a hot-headed colt, right under the nose of this woman who was now breathless and swooning in his presence.

Alberto's wife made sure Jeff had everything he needed, even teaching him how to work the shower in the family's cramped bathroom. As soon as she had disappeared back to her incoherent husband, he closed the door and pushed his overnight bag up against it. Paranoia ripped at the edges of his conscience. Surely no-one would try to break in and attack him in his sleep with the South American couple and their son in residence. Would they?

The walls were most likely paper-thin, the thought of which elicited another *frisson* of embarrassment. The lost boy realised the nocturnal visits of his teenage years may well have been overheard, despite their clumsy efforts to remain undetected! Many a sweat-drenched hour had passed on this bed, while he enjoyed the nubile but mindless companionship of the Chileans' only daughter, sharing minute quantities of weed that one or the other had purloined through various creative means.

The best thing about his current predicament, the world-changer mused as he undressed and rolled his clothes up on top of his suitcase, was the way this salt-of-the-earth and his family had made no effort to pamper him, nor even to apologise for the basic accommodation. They regarded him in the same friendly, compassionate vein to which the poor, fatherless child had been treated fifteen years ago. Tonight, he lay in the single bed once more; this time as a filthy rich, fatherless child.

The songwriter's keen ears tuned in to the sounds of Fairfield's restless suburban nightlife. Women shouted at whoever would listen to their woes, while tanked-up blokes set to, posturing outside seedy bars; the odd dog howling or yelping, babies crying, and cars hooning up and down the streets, tyres squealing on the wet bitumen. His mind still fascinated by Madalena's image of their maternal grandmother dancing in the street at the news of her son-in-law's passing, a song was already moulding itself around this tempting hook and demanding to be written down before it prevented him from sleeping.

Flicking on the bedside light and reaching into his bag for a notepad, Jeff found to his amazement that instead of the bitter ritual the phrase initially conjured up, the composition materialised into something decidedly celebratory. A *fiesta* to exalt the irreversible exile of a spectre which had blighted so many people's lives, never more to haunt them.

The multi-millionaire drifted off to sleep, detached in a surreal yet comfortable way from the community he was trying to avoid. He began to envision how life might have turned out if he had become embroiled in the underworld hierarchy, as his arrogance had taunted his ailing dad. Would he have been capable of setting man against man? And if so, could he have committed his firstborn to follow in his footsteps through the dangerous world, where criminals strove every day to stay one step ahead of each other and two steps ahead of the police?

The boy from Canley Vale's wild imagination soon gave way to a vivid dream, where he and a teenaged Jet, still with curly, blond hair but now tall and strong, were ring-leaders for a job offloading a consignment of drugs from a boat moored in a dark inlet somewhere along the Parramatta River. With a mixture of pride and fear, he watched his boy-child handle a gun as if it were his best friend.

Inevitably, sleeping alone in a strange bed with nothing but an overnight bag and an overactive mind to protect him, the dreamer was soon sitting bolt upright, shaking vigorously in a cold sweat and gasping for air. The nightmare had left his head infused with footage of himself fighting his boorish father and their hardened Polish opponents, weapons drawn and with blood splattered everywhere. Some of this blood belonged to Jet, even though he had no recollection of why or where his son had disappeared to before naked fear pitched him out of the dream.

'Jesus fucking Christ,' Jeff swore under his breath, springing up and tearing at the handle of the small window which afforded a clear view of the industrial warehouse across the laneway.

He directed his cigarette smoke through the opening, as he had done in this room many times before. Nothing material had changed inside him after all, had it? Lodged in his decadent, loved-up new life, the tormented soul from Sydney's south-west had merely learned to suppress the horrific memories.

While his heart rate slowed to a more normal pace, the stowaway acknowledged a perverse, pleasing pride that immeasurable happiness and quantifiably alarming wealth had not displaced his adolescent flaws altogether. He was not really the new Jeff Diamond, in spite of Lynn dubbing him so. Rather, he was the original but tremendously improved Jeff Diamond.

The next morning, well rested yet uneasy, the songwriter shared a rushed breakfast with the Santos Fernandez family, thanked them for their hospitality and departed before sunrise for Her Majesty's Prison Parklea. Paranoid or not, being followed as he drove to the high-security facility that his father had called home for almost eighteen years was a chilling prospect.

Jeff's memory was these days less accurate on the intricacies of the streets running north-south in his former stomping ground, no longer confident in his ability to outsmart a tail. The anonymous, white Holden sedan wove against the thickening commuter traffic, taking the occasional side-road both deliberately and not so deliberately. It eventually turned into the same visitors' car park where his wife and daughter had danced during their previous visit, not long before the old man had coughed his guts up for the very last time.

The Australian hero locked the car doors from the inside and wound the driver's seat backwards, pulling his baseball cap down low. With a long wait until the administration office's fluorescent lights would surge into life, he read the Sydney Morning Herald for an hour before remembering having spotted a public telephone outside the reception block.

What time was it? His watch reported eight o'clock and a handful of minutes. Lynn had taken the children to Benloch to spend time with their grandparents while her husband had been working overseas, and they were guaranteed to be up and about by now. Their exuberance would do more to brighten his day than a roomful of dazzling strip-lights.

'Marianna, it's Jeff,' the rock star announced. 'How're you going?'

'Oh, hello, dear. My condolences. I'm so sorry to hear about your father. How are you?'

'Ah, I'm fine. Thanks. We were hardly close. Could I speak to Lynn, please? I'm in a call-box and don't have much change.'

'Yes, yes... Of course,' his mother-in-law understood. 'Give us your number. She can ring you back. That's no problem.'

'Great. Thanks again,' the caller said to no-one, hearing the receiver clonk onto the table and the sound of hurrying footsteps.

'Dad!' a young boy's voice burst through the telephone within seconds, brimming with excitement. 'It's Jet.'

'No! It can't be. I must have the wrong number,' his father joked, struck by an overpowering sense of relief that last night's bad dream had not come true.

'Dad, it *is* me!' the five-year-old pleaded, laughing. 'It *is* the right number.'

Concerned the call was about to cut off, the traveller steered the boy on to more serious matters. 'OK. I know. I'm only kidding. But hey, brains... Could you do me a favour and write down my number? Is there some paper by the 'phone?'

'Yes,' Jet replied, eager to please after being given responsibility for something which sounded important. 'And I've got a pen.'

'Cool. Good man.'

The musician read out the digits on the vandalised telephone booth, remembering to add the area code for New South Wales, then asked the child to play it back to him. His pulse pumping in his ears, he listened to the sequence echoing his son's transcription.

'OK! Perfect, mate. When I hang up, dial that number, and I'll answer. If nothing happens, hang up again and wait for me to ring back. OK?'

'Okey dokey! Hang up, Dad.'

'*Adiós, amigo,*' Jeff chuckled, pressing the button to terminate the call and smiling as he imagined Jet's short, stubby fingers searching for the numbers one by one.

A few cars had begun to circle the car park, staff arriving to prepare for the day's scheduled visits. The Australian icon kept his face to the wall. Before long, the telephone made a peculiar jangling noise, vibrating the cracked Perspex shelter. He snatched the receiver off its hook and leaned into the hooded surround, speaking as softly as he could.

'Hey, mate. Good job. Is *Mamá* there?'

'Yes. Dad wants to talk to you,' he heard the lad say, the volume of his youthful voice fading as he turned his head away from the mouthpiece.

'Hi, *hombre mío*. How are you?' Lynn's tender greeting melted his heart. 'And *where* are you?'

'Pretty good, thanks. I'm at Parklea already,' he whispered. 'Can't really talk 'cause there's people wandering about. Just wanted to say I miss you.'

'Oh, thank you. That's nice. We miss you too. Was last night alright?'

'Ah, y'know…'

'Oh, right. Nightmare?' his wife asked, the conclusion no stretch for her telepathic powers.

'Yep. Correct. Anyway… Anything happening down on the farm?'

'Of course! All manner of action hereabouts,' the young mother asserted. 'We've been swimming, riding, hunting bees… You name it!'

'*¡Excelente!* Much the same as me then.'

Lynn let out a sunny laugh. 'Oh, good! The boxing club's branched out evidently. Hope it all goes OK today. Not too harrowing. Do you have to see your dad?'

'Don't know. Guess so. Although it's not too tricky for them to confirm his identity in this place, I imagine. I'm prepared for it. Morbid fascination and all that. Tell you later. We can have ghost stories round the campfire on Sunday.'

'Ugh! Do we have to?' the singer groaned. 'Do you want to talk to the kids now?'

'Yeah. If they're there. Thanks, angel. I love you so much.'

'I love you too. Here's Kizzy.'

A vision of his deceased father slotted into a mortuary compartment within this building's cold, grey walls dominated the superstar's concentration in the momentary lapse. The distasteful image was soon voided by the sound of his wife coaching their little girl on what to say, followed by the silky softness of breathy giggles growing louder.

How many prisoners waited for such extra-special calls once a week, knowing this was all they deserved? And for those whose liberty remained unshackled, sweet moments like these made being away from home worthwhile too.

'*¡Olá, Papá! Soy Kierney. Ça va là-bas?*'

'*¡Olá, gorgeousita!*' her dad responded with a lump in his throat. '*Oui. Tout va vraiment bien ici, merci, mademoiselle.* You having fun over there too?'

The youngster giggled. 'We saw bees. Buzzy bees!'

'Buzzy bees? Wow! Fantastic, baby. Were they flying or just sleeping?'

'Flying *and* sleeping,' the toddler explained, her tone most insistent.

'Flying and sleeping at the same time? Isn't that dangerous? They'll buzz straight into a tree or a wall and get a nasty bump on their buzzy heads.'

Kierney's laughter wrapped itself around a long sigh reminiscent of her mother. 'No, *Papá*! Not at the same time. Some sleeping and some flying.'

'Oh, I see. That's a relief. So what else have you guys been up to?'

'Heaps,' she replied. '*Mamá* says stop talking.'

Jeff laughed. 'Right! You'd better give the 'phone back to *Mamá*. I'll see you soon, *pequeñita. Te amo.*'

'*Te amo* too, *Papá*,' the little girl chimed, clearly having the receiver wrestled away by her big brother. '*Adiós.*'

'*Adiós, hjia mía.*'

'Dad!' Jet shouted.

'Mate!' the caller replied, cupping his hand over the microphone. 'Can't talk for long. You have a good day, and I'll see you on Sunday. I've got some cool stories to tell you. Please could you give *Mamá* the 'phone?'

'OK. Bye, Dad!'

'Hello!' Lynn was chuckling at the fast exchanges while re-instituting some semblance of peace between the warring siblings. 'Thanks for ringing. Keep safe. I'll let you go. Good luck with everything.'

'Cheers, angel,' Jeff said, wishing he didn't have to terminate the call and rely on their invisible elastic connection for the gruesome task ahead. 'I'll let you listen into all my stories too, I promise.'

'Great. *Gracias, Papá*,' his dream girl gave her husband one of her best audible grins. 'Look forward to it. I love you. Bye.'

The revitalised superstar placed the receiver on its hook and walked over to the reception office's main entrance, wiping a sweaty palm on his trouser leg. Feeling out of place among his own kind, he held the door for a woman sporting a mouth covered in cold sores and with three young children in tow, all unkempt and whining. Not a word of thanks was forthcoming, and his black trousers narrowly avoided falling ash from her cigarette as he followed the brood inside and up to the Admittance desk.

'Mister Diamond!' a lady behind the counter called out, identifying their special guest in an instant and trying not to sound too excited. 'Welcome back!'

'Thanks,' the famous son nodded. 'Sooner than I thought.'

'Step this way, please,' she instructed, pointing to the end of the barrier, where her colleague had lifted a hinged section for him to enter the office.

Jeff sighed. He was passing into the inner sanctum of Her Majesty's Prison Parklea yet again, hoping this was the last time. At the request of a muscle-bound thug in uniform, he sat down at an interview table. Without so much as exchanging pleasantries, he was offered coffee and told to wait.

The square room's walls were at least freshly painted and adorned with benign landscape photographs, in contrast to the desolate, grey prisoners' conjugal rooms. The celebrity wondered if the guard's austere manner was a deliberate ploy to make everyone feel culpable, or whether his conditioning had caused him to forget there was any other way to interact.

Lighting a cigarette, the songwriter leafed through the paperwork he had so far received about his father's incarceration and demise. The cold, hard facts rang like a crowbar against the cage of his vicarious guilt. He remembered the counsellor, Chris Williams, promising him biscuits as well as coffee, and asked the guard if he could make an internal telephone call. His request was declined without explanation.

Just as the celebrity's patience was starting to wear thin, in walked the governor himself. He was flanked by two other men, one of whom waved as if greeting an old friend. The personality-free duty officer stood to attention.

'Mister Maloney,' Jeff called to mind, standing up and offering his right hand. 'And Larry Shepherd. Good to see you again.'

'You too, Mister Diamond,' replied Tom Maloney, on the defensive, suspicious that his authority was about to be undermined. 'Have you two met before?'

'Hello, Jeff. Good to see you again,' Larry shook the visitor's hand *con gusto*. 'Yes, sir. I was present when the prisoner met his son a few years back. I was just trying to remember how long ago that was.'

''Seventy-six,' the son in question answered. 'Winter, July or August. It was lashing with rain that day, as I recall. How're you going?'

'Good, Jeff,' the psychologist replied. 'And you?'

'I'm very sorry for your loss, Mister Diamond,' the officious chief warden interrupted.

The lower-ranked officer stepped back. It was clear from Maloney's attitude that they were not here to take a trip down Memory Lane. There was quite obviously a process to which prisoners' relatives were expected to adhere, and they were damned well going to adhere to it.

'Thanks,' Jeff acknowledged. 'And also for coming over personally. You must be busy. I'm sure you're not normally called upon for this kind of thing.'

'That's correct,' the governor replied, appearing to relax. 'Please sit down. I'll leave you in Officer Shepherd's capable hands. He can answer any questions you have about the release of your father's body and any *post mortem* examination you may wish to have carried out. There's a full report of the events leading up to his passing, so please take as long as you need to review it.'

A bolt of revulsion shot through the star's head. *Post mortem*? Did he want one? This was all becoming a little too real for the man who had managed to keep his next of kin at a healthy distance for his whole life. Flashbacks flooded his mind of the afternoon he had sat in an almost identical room at Fairfield Hospital, working his way through the same material in connection with his mother's death. No matter how much more mature he was these days, whether actual or perceived, this was still an onerous circumstance. Some of life's responsibilities were just plain difficult, regardless of any mental preparation put in ahead of time.

The rock star was disturbed by how profoundly this experience was affecting him. If this feeling of desolation came in the aftermath of an estranged parent's demise, how awful must it be to clean up after the death of someone special? Children were expected to outlast their parents, although not usually by as long as in his case. Nevertheless, this latest epiphany gave rise to a new level of sympathy for the lines of desperate adults outside the feeding camps and hospitals in the poor African countries he had visited in recent years, let alone for the parents of Amanda Fallon and Mary-Anne Pearce back in Chicago.

Get over it, Jeff scolded himself. *You didn't even like the bastard.* He had no right to compare himself with any of these bereaved folk. He ought to dispense with the bureaucracy as quickly as possible so he could fly home and concentrate on more important people than this murdering Polish Jew who had never dispensed an ounce of charity.

His official duty fulfilled, the governor clipped his heels and coughed, spurring both subordinates into a rushed salute. He left the room exuding military swagger, and the three remaining men sat around the table, staring at each other's collection of paperwork. The younger officer present, who had hung back until this point while in the company of superiors, introduced himself as Lindsay and offered to assist with completing the array of forms. The celebrity had no chance to ask if he were Lindsay somebody or somebody Lindsay.

'So this is all that remains of my dad,' the philosopher remarked, looking from one pile to the next. 'Weird, isn't it?'

'Not quite all,' Larry replied. 'And I'm also sorry, Jeff, although I hear you had a good meeting with him last week with your family. The visit caused a stir among the ladies in the office, I must say.'

'We did,' the superstar nodded, smirking at the quaint allegory. 'Yeah. I bet! Our kids are good value with ladies in offices. My dad almost seemed human compared to the previous time. I remember saying to my sister that it's amazing how staring death in the face can change one's perspective on things.'

The senior staff member laughed aloud, whereas Lindsay tried not to.

'You're right,' the kindly psychologist agreed. 'And young children tend to soften even the hardest of hearts. I believe you met my colleague, Chris Williams, last time too.'

'Yep. That's right. Chris came and prepared us for what we were about to receive,' the comic leaned back into his chair, now much more at ease. 'She was very professional. She asked me to swing by today, so I'd like to do that, if I can.'

'Oh, definitely. We work in the same building. I'll walk you over later.'

Officer Lindsay Lindsay pulled out a sheet of paper from his folder and laid it on the table in front of the imposing figure, who instantly recognised it as a death certificate. Its companion artefact was stored in the filing cabinet at *Escondido*.

'Is that for me to sign?' he asked the prison employee, who had drawn the short straw of *administrivia* for the day.

'Yes, sir. It provides details of the deceased and the doctor's comments as to cause of death. You need to check it to make sure the information's accurate before you sign it.'

'Do I?' Jeff replied, stealing a quick glance at Larry. 'How do I check it's accurate? I wasn't there at the time.'

Shepherd intervened, appreciating the sardonic observation. 'What Lindsay means, Jeff, is that if you can verify your father's personal details, please, and initial to say you've read the doctor's statement, that would be fine.'

The visitor nodded. 'Thanks. Sure. Aren't many personal details I can verify either, to be honest.'

He perused the form, bile rising as confused flashbacks dimmed and then intensified behind his eyes. The medical report asserted that the prisoner suffered respiratory failure after an extended bout of coughing, and that subsequently he had fallen unconscious and was unable to be resuscitated. The cynic wondered if they had made much effort to revive him, but fell short of voicing this view. It was far better for everyone that they hadn't tried too hard.

As Governor Maloney had hinted earlier, the form also contained a small box which the next of kin could tick to request a *post mortem*. The celebrity's pen floated over it for a second or so before leaving it blank. What difference would it make? How often did relatives of such hardcore criminals sue Her Majesty for damages?

'Y'know...' he muttered, as he adorned the death certificate with his lightning-fast autograph, these days as consistent as a rubber stamp. 'I signed one of these for my mum when I was fourteen.'

Larry gasped. 'Really? As a minor?'

'Yep. As a minor. Fucked, huh?'

The greying man let out a low whistle. 'You went through a lot back then,' he stated the obvious. 'I wonder how the law actually stands on that? Your dad was technically her next of kin, but he probably wasn't involved at all. I haven't been around all that long here, but I'm curious to find out.'

'I'm a hundred percent sure he wasn't involved,' Jeff confirmed. 'Please don't worry about it on my behalf. What's the use in finding out? To arrest me for falsifying my mother's death certificate? She's no less dead with my signature than with his! I'd have been more than happy not to sign it.'

'No. Absolutely not. I apologise if I offended you. It just beggars belief that they'd get a young bloke to sign an official document.'

'Yeah. No offence taken, mate. I thought so too, but it made me feel kind o' powerful doing it. The most important thing I'd ever done, up to that point,' the celebrity paused, letting his observation sink in. 'My sister's older than me too, so by rights she should've signed it before me. I can't think of a single ramification from a death certificate being declared null and void. It certainly leads you to question the purpose of all this red tape, doesn't it?

Officer Lindsay sniggered, all three sharing the black humour.

'Now, Jeff... First things first,' the psychologist said, laying his palm on the forearm of the young man's smart leather jacket. 'Can we get you another cup of coffee?'

The friendly millionnaire smiled. 'No, thanks, Larry. I'll wait and have one with Chris. What's next on your list, Officer Lindsay?'

Officer Shepherd stepped in due to a discomfited expression on his younger colleague's face. 'We can accompany you to view the deceased, if you so wish,' he informed their famous visitor, noticing his limbs stiffen too. 'But there's no obligation. One of us can formally identify him if you'd prefer.'

'Jeez. What the hell! I'll do it. It's pretty much the only reason I'm here, if I'm being perfectly honest.'

'Very good. Then we can go through the process for organising a funeral, if you haven't already got your own people in mind.'

Jeff sighed and shook his head. 'No. My people don't do funerals. Their territory normally has much louder audiences these days, if I'm allowed to say that without sounding too arrogant. And hopefully a bit more upbeat too.'

The fawning staff members bellowed, appreciating both the irony and the abject humility which the entertainment industry powerhouse consistently failed to hide.

'And I should see for myself that he's truly gone, in case my sister wants to know how he looked. I might as well take a peek at the old bastard at rest. For Christ's sake, he gave us enough grief. He deserves a final kick in the balls.'

The threesome rose to their feet, Jeff towering above the pair clad in prison blue. Lindsay led the way, still red in the face, sandwiching the plain-clothed rock star between them. Again, he was struck by how all these institutionalised routines made him feel so much like a criminal.

They twisted and turned through several corridors until they reached the mortuary. The smell from within was as unfamiliar as it was obnoxious to the young man's finely-tuned nasal passages. In fact, all five senses battled to take

19

in the austere, cold surroundings, while the clash of disinfectant and formaldehyde threatened to strip his throat of any moisture.

Dressed in white laboratory coats and the type of steel-capped boots more often associated with construction workers, four attendants were milling around examination tables topped with stainless steel. Nursing navvies for deceased wrongdoers, the itinerant minstrel pondered. There was bound to be a song in there somewhere, given a sleepless night here or there...

Two corpses lay out on trolleys, one zipped inside its body-bag and the other with its face and torso exposed. Each had a small label stuck to the coarse fabric with sellotape: name, initial, prisoner identification number and a six-figure date. Any other data were presumably superfluous by this stage.

'How many people go through here in your average month?' Jeff asked Larry, struggling to stop his left hand fidgeting with the lighter and packet of cigarettes in his pants pocket.

'Oh, only one or two. Sometimes none.'

'Many suicides?'

The psychologist stared at the classic mask of impertinence. 'We do our best to prevent it, but yes. Of course.'

Officer Lindsay had sloped off without saying goodbye, his part of the proceedings either complete or temporarily suspended. A female with a white coat over her uniform now stood beside the men, trying not to make it too obvious that she was ogling the tall, good-looking superstar in their midst.

'Jeff Diamond,' he addressed her, extending his hand.

The woman allowed the musician's long fingers to close around hers, performing a sort of curtsey and stuttering over her own name. 'Vi-, V-Vicky Taylor. It's great to meet you.'

Officer Shepherd frowned. 'Mister Diamond's father has just passed away.'

Too star-struck to have made the connection, V-Vicky blushed again. 'In here? Oh, my God. I'm so sorry.'

'No worries,' the songwriter reassured her with one of his sexiest, lopsided smiles. 'I detested the bloke.'

The mortuary assistant giggled after seeking permission from the higher-ranking officer, who also shared the joke. To make the most of the cheerful mood, Jeff produced his cigarette packet, flipped the lid and offered it round, much to the young woman's astonishment. She declined with a flick of her hand.

'Only kidding,' the comic quipped, closing the pack and dropping it back into his pocket.

'You have a great way with people,' Larry chuckled. 'You make everyone feel very comfortable around you. It's a real skill.'

'Cheers. Let's see if I can do anything to make my arsehole father more comfortable, shall we? Can't say this'd be my favourite place to work.'

Vicky smiled. 'Over here, Mister Diamond, please.'

She slid open a drawer and checked the label on the body-bag against her list, coughing in embarrassment. Satisfied that the prisoner number corresponded to the one on her clipboard, she asked the two men whether they wished her to unzip the bag.

Jeff nodded in response to the officer's invitation, inhaling to shore up his internal defences. 'Go for it.'

Paul Diamond's eyes stared straight ahead as his son's met them. Apart from the initial shock at being confronted with a lifeless human being, the celebrity felt nothing. The lined features could have belonged to a total stranger as far as his heart was concerned.

The pallid, corrugated face wore a peaceful expression which was foreign both to the wearer and his son. Still dressed in inmate's clothing, Diamond Senior's greying, wispy fringe had been combed back to reveal a healed wound above his left eye, about five centimetres in length under the hairline.

'I never knew he had a scar up there,' Jeff remarked to no-one in particular, drawing an index finger down his own forehead. 'Doesn't look too old.'

'No,' Larry agreed. 'Probably happened in the carpentry sheds. I could look it up on his medical records, if you're worried.'

The celebrity shook his head and smiled. 'No. It's nothing. I'm pretty sure we can rule it out as a cause of death.'

The mortician gulped, desperate to stifle a laugh, and grabbed onto the bag's zip, unable to take her eyes off this perfectly irresistible specimen. 'Have you seen enough?'

'Oh, yeah,' he confirmed. 'Quite enough, thanks, Vicky. What do I have to do now?'

The older man placed a kindly hand on the visitor's back and steered him towards a desk on the other side of the room. 'We just need a signature to record you've sighted the deceased and are satisfied that everything's in order.'

'And if I'm not?'

Larry refused to be drawn into excessive playfulness, conscious of the fact that he and the mortuary assistant were supposed to be working. This might well be what work was like for someone at the top of the entertainment industry's ivory tower, but it was incumbent upon him to set an example, as the superior officer.

'If you're not, we put things right,' he responded.

Jeff raised his hand to thank the affable psychologist for humouring him. 'I'm sorry,' he said. 'I should show more respect. It's just bloody hard to care what happens to him now he's dead, seeing how little care we had for each other while he was alive.'

'Fair do. I understand. Let's go back to the office. We can discuss funeral details and hand over his belongings, then we're free to share a coffee with Ms Williams.'

The superstar said goodbye to the amiable young lady in the white coat, who had continued to watch his every move with distinct interest, and turned to follow Larry along the maze of corridors. Catching the view through a window into the visitors' reception area, he noticed most seats were now occupied by relatives and friends. A large number of people found themselves in a similar situation to his. He oughtn't to forget how well he was being treated, considering he was, as they were, regrettably linked to a serious criminal.

'Now... Would you like us to arrange the funeral for you?' the older staff member asked. 'A lot of men die in here with no-one willing or available to organise their funeral. It's no trouble. Just a simple service. Was your father Jewish?'

'Thanks,' Jeff nodded. 'It would be helpful. He was born a Jew, but I have no idea whether he considered himself Jewish as a man. Did he sign up to anything when he came in?'

'No, he didn't. I checked yesterday.'

'Then a short, secular service'll be fine,' the son decided. 'Lynn, the kids, my sister and me. No-one else'd want to be there, unless Parklea wants to send the murdering bastard off?'

Neither men saw fit to comment any further, and within a couple of minutes, they had arrived back to the original sitting room. As he had become accustomed in this bizarre, privileged lifestyle of his, the multi-millionnaire sat in the mission brown, Government-issue chair and waited until it was time for the next stop on today's itinerary.

Soon enough, Larry brought in a small box sealed with a label marked "DIAMOND, P.", under which was a series of digits which must have been his father's unique identifier.

'Do I have your permission to open it?' the officer asked.

'No worries, mate. Go right ahead.'

The cover's removal divulged nothing to the son about a man who had shared little more than a surname with his kith and kin. It contained a pair of reading glasses, the photographs and manuscript left with him after the family's visit, and a gold signet ring that had been an eighteenth birthday gift from the reprobate's own father, to whom he had also been a stranger.

Briefly lifting the ring up to the light to verify the engraved initials before dropping it back into the box, Jeff's eyes fell on a heavy stainless steel chain he recognised. His dad would have likely been wearing it when he was arrested. A hairbrush and a wallet containing fifteen pounds and some loose change constituted the prisoner's remaining worldly goods.

'Hey. That's interesting,' the twenty-eight-year-old exclaimed, picking up the obsolete currency. 'Shows how long he was in here for!'

'Yes, indeed,' Larry nodded, pointing to yet another form. 'Just a signature here, please, and you can either take these things away with you or we'll dispose of them.'

'Not much to show for a life, is it?' Jeff sighed, melancholy seeping in at the impending closure. 'I'll take the box with me. At least I can show my kids the sum total of their grandfather.'

The star's autograph was witnessed for a third time by the patient man. 'That's fine. Let's go and get some coffee. Did you want to put that in your car first? We have to cross the car park anyway.'

As the two men marched through the busy waiting room, Larry Shepherd was fascinated by to observe how the volume of chatter dropped to a whisper as the charismatic celebrity passed by, noticing how people's eyes and fingers followed him all the way to the exit.

'Does it bother you, everyone staring all the time?'

'Yes and no,' he smirked, the gust of fresh air dispersing the pressure cloud from above his head. 'It depends who, when, where... Impossible to answer without a beer in my hand.'

The elder cynic slammed the boot of the hired car and chuckled. 'You're a good politician too. Do you ever answer a question seriously?'

'Sometimes,' the visitor smiled. 'When I have a beer in my hand.'

'Ha! Very good. Pity I'm on duty, or I'd share a few with you.'

'Next time I'm here,' Jeff offered, pausing for a couple of seconds before grinning at the amicable uniformed officer beside him.

Larry let rip with another belly laugh, knowing how ridiculous a *scenario* this was. From the plain, rented sedan to the flamboyant signature, and from the cavalier strides through Reception to the vulnerability pasted on his forehead, this enigmatic star was a walking, talking set of contradictions. In a different space and time, he had no doubt they could become firm friends, and he already regretted not being able to see Jeff Diamond again.

***

Chris Williams stood up from her desk and rushed towards the two men as they approached the entrance of the prison medical centre's psychiatric wing. Grinning from ear to ear, she motioned to a room off to one side, furnished only with armchairs covered in bland, hard-wearing upholstery and a coffee table which had seen better days.

'Hello again, Jeff,' the motherly woman said, arms outstretched. 'Welcome. I'm so sorry for the loss of your father.'

With no appetite for public intimacy and still queasy after their detour, the superstar took a diagonal step out of her path. Chris followed his lead, unperturbed, until they reached the doorway and out of plain sight.

By way of apology, he placed a conciliatory hand on her shoulder and pecked her cheek. 'Now don't you start!'

'Aw... Don't be like that,' she moaned, winking at her colleague who had not waited to be asked to sit down. 'You only just found him.'

Jeff nodded, dropping heavily into one of the armchairs. 'That's true enough, but it was too late. To feel anything, I mean.'

'Oh, well... It wasn't too late for him,' Chris countered in all seriousness. 'He was deeply affected by your last visit; seeing you with your beautiful family, and how you look after your sister. He asked to see me the very next morning.'

'Ah, yeah?'

Officer Shepherd shifted in his chair, unsure whether he should be party to these confidences.

'Larry, it's fine,' Jeff said, sensing the man's discomfort. 'No secrets. There's no point, is there?'

'I suppose not. If you're sure...'

Chris disappeared to the kitchen on the other side of the corridor, soon returning with three mugs of coffee on a tray. She offered round the sugar and milk, first sniffing the jug to verify it was fresh. Chuckling at more homely traits so infrequently bestowed upon him, the superstar took three spoonfuls of sugar and whisked them in before chancing the milk.

'Cheers, ma'am. Bloody hell!' he groaned, taking a swig of the hot drink. 'Thank Christ this is nearly over. I'll be glad to get home tomorrow. Where are those bickies you promised?'

The counsellor scrambled to her feet and fetched a bumper pack of biscuits from a shopping bag which sat on a shelf by the door. Along with the supermarket snacks, she produced a white envelope and handed it to its addressee. Jeff flinched, unsettled by the conspicuous act. This second offering must contain his father's last documented thoughts.

'I'm so sorry,' Chris laughed. 'I fully intended to give you this when you first came in. And the biscuits too! Help yourself. Eat them all because I shouldn't have any.'

Watching the plump lady pat her hips critically, all in a dither, the others tucked into the simple fare without such reservations. Her guest slipped the envelope into the inside pocket of his jacket, whence it immediately began to emit "Read me" signals.

'Thank you,' Jeff said, sipping his coffee and feeling more relaxed. 'So Chris, how long've you been working in this weird environment? Both of you,

24

I guess... There must be heaps of easier types of patients to devote your time to.'

The two members of staff exchanged knowing stares while the counsellor answered. 'Don't you want to know what your father told me during our last couple of meetings?'

'Don't know. Do I?' the distracted man turned her question around like a pro'. 'Will it make me remember him differently?'

'Yes. I think it might. Or you could just open the envelope and read about it instead. I thought it might do you good to discuss it while you're still here.'

Jeff exhaled, sweat prickling the skin on the back of his neck as his shirt collar rubbed against it. The atmosphere created by this concentration of experts in human cognition was fast brewing stronger than the instant coffee, with the odds of surviving unscathed stacked against his inner child. This woman knew as much about his *modus operandi* as he did. Probably more. It was her job after all.

'Jesus Christ! Of course it would. Sure. I'm shit-scared, if you hadn't guessed already. I got blamed for everything when my parents were around,' he hazarded, feeling his ribcage tighten and a headache began to throb in his temples. 'Everything. That's why I'm stalling.'

Both sages nodded in true psychologist's style, making the entertainer chuckle.

'I finally reconciled all that shit, after I'd grown up and met someone interested in the real me,' he went on. 'So I'm scared that if I open this letter, I'll start liking him and conclude that I *was* to blame all along. Or else, he'll appeal to me so much with his dying words that I'll blame myself for letting him die alone. Or both, knowing me.'

Larry leaned over and clattered his empty mug down onto the coffee table. 'To me, it sounds as if you're coming to these conclusions whether you read what's in the letter or not.'

The philosopher directed a long index finger at the man sitting to his right. 'Spot on, mate. So what good would it do to read it? That's what I meant about remembering him differently.'

Chris smiled, captivated by the young leader at his most personable. 'You're very intelligent, Jeff. I've read a lot about you and have seen just as many interviews on TV. I don't think I've ever met someone who understands the world as well as you do. And someone who understands himself too... I don't mean to interfere or invade your privacy, but I'm guessing you must've overcome significant obstacles to get where you are, and I can completely understand what you just expressed.'

Jeff felt tears stinging at the back of his eyes. 'In other words, my fears are grounded?' he asked, resigned to an unpalatable answer.

'Yes. Absolutely. But you *will* read the letter because you already know how it's going to affect you. It's a good idea, I assure you. It'll bring you some closure, even though it might take some time to come to terms with your own feelings.'

Wiping his face, their guest sniffed. 'Great! Just when you think it's safe to cross the street, along comes a semi-trailer with no brakes.'

With a hearty laugh, Larry took this opportunity to make another round of coffee, leaving the star in the custody of his hypnotised female colleague. Spooning sugar into over-full mugs, he looked from doctor to patient, wondering whose turn it was to impart the next insightful piece of advice.

'Can I tell you something only Lynn knows?' the young man launched forth.

'Most certainly,' Chris responded. 'Completely confidential, of course.'

'Thanks. Oh, that's not important,' he said, taking a deep breath and lifting his mug to his lips to hide his uncertainty. 'I don't know whether you read about it here, but while I was performing in Chicago last year, two female med' students were crushed to death in the crowd, right next to the stage.'

The older man shook his head, deferring to his colleague.

'No! I didn't hear,' she gasped. 'I'm surprised I don't remember that. I call myself a big fan. Was it on the news?'

Jeff smiled at her endorsement and prepared to fill in the blanks. 'Cheers. Sure was on the news! The story did die down pretty fast though, *Allah* be praised. It was horrendous for a while; first having to confront the families, and then making sure they were taken care of. But it was like retribution for me, y'know what I mean? An eye for an eye almost, because what did it turn me into?'

The dumbstruck pair shook their heads. They watched a thunderous expression spread over the songwriter's erstwhile smiling face.

'I killed two people, just like my fucking father. But much worse... At least he took out two low-life scum wankers like him. I killed two innocent women.'

'Oh, come on... That's nonsense, mate,' Larry insisted. 'You didn't kill them. It was an accident.'

'Oh, I know,' the tormented soul corrected himself, the hems of his trouser legs flapping as his muscles quivered inside. 'I do have a tendency to over-dramatise, in case you'd never noticed! But at the end of the day, there are two families out there who lost loved ones because of me. It comes to the same thing.'

Eyes filling with tears, Chris was rendered speechless by the genuine guilt and grief on display. 'Now listen, Jeff...' her professional side resumed control. 'I understand how you might think that way, but no-one's blaming you for the death of those young girls.'

'Aren't they? Are you sure?'

'Well... No. I'm not sure, obviously,' the red-faced woman contradicted herself. 'I've no knowledge of these families. But it'd be very wrong of them to blame you, if they do.'

'I agree,' Jeff replied, standing up and shaking the cramp out of his legs. 'And by the same token, I also think it was very wrong of my father to blame me for not protecting my mum and sister from being raped by the fuckers he ended up stabbing to death. It didn't make any difference what I thought, or even what the truth was. As far as he was concerned, I'd let 'em all down, and he died before I could get him to change his mind.'

'Oh, right. Yes. I see your point,' Larry muttered, the puzzle's various pieces beginning to fit together. 'Bugger! We never know the whole story, do we, Chris?'

Jeff took his seat again, feeling better for having the confession off his chest at last. 'Those girls... I went to their funerals. Paid compensation to their families. I visit them whenever I'm over there, and even sent them cards on the anniversary of their daughters' deaths. It's human nature to want to blame someone, even if it's only secretly. You have to admit their easiest target is me.'

'And you have to live with this knowledge. I hear you. What about the staff at the venue?' Chris asked. 'Surely they're more to blame than you? Stadium ground staff, security guards or whoever they are?'

'Maybe,' the musician nodded. 'We all tried to stop it. I got a message from security that the crowd was pushing forwards. Shit! I even got them to do this stupid dance move to take several paces back, but it wasn't enough to save those girls' lives, nor stop a few more from getting injured and suffocating.'

'Mister Diamond, sir...' Larry's stern voice interrupted. 'You didn't kill those young ladies in cold blood. What you need to get clear in your mind is that your father pre-meditated the murder of two men known to him for many years, and men who were hardly pillars of society. His wasn't a spur-of-the-moment crime of passion, or even an accident that went badly wrong. He intended to do exactly what he did. You cannot put yourself in the same category.'

'No, mate. Thanks. And I don't,' Jeff assured him. 'And I have the most beautiful woman in the world sitting at home, who knows me inside out and is just as good a therapist as you guys... no offence... who'll tell me the same thing over and over again.'

Chris smiled, swooning. 'Oh, you should have seen them, Shep! Lynn and the children. They're adorable, the little ones.'

'Thanks again,' the proud parent chuckled. 'They're very cute, even if I do say so myself. Anyway... I'm not bothered about me. I know I'll get through any more nightmares, and the uncontrollable anger's pretty much gone. It's more the guilt at not being able to help my dad change like I did. I had this wild idea that I'd somehow avenge those girls' deaths by abetting his repentance.'

'What makes you think he could've changed?' Larry issued a gentle challenge. 'Let alone wanted to change?'

''Cause that's what I do,' the intellectual asserted, not with conceit but with a modest audacity which was both endearing and disarming. 'I help people behave differently towards other people. That's why I'm on this Earth. Dad said to us last week that he never got past the teenaged anger. I mastered that skill, so I could've helped him do the same.'

'And you wanted to help him even after everything he put you and your family through?' the spellbound counsellor asked. 'Perhaps you just didn't want it enough?'

'Who knows? That's a good point,' Jeff nodded, pausing to weigh up this latest offering. 'And I do still hate his guts for all that. It's like the whole lung transplant question we'd started to debate: does a murdering smoker deserve to receive a new pair of lungs ahead of a law-abiding person who never smoked in his or her life?

'Or does a selfish bastard who gave up his wife's dignity as payment for botched heists deserve to have his life rebuilt, in advance of a community of farmers suffering ethnic persecution in Africa? I can't do anything about Dad now, so I have to hope I get another opportunity to redress the balance later on. But hey? Where *is* the list handed down from on high that tells us what our accountabilities are? Whose sins do we inherit if they're not atoned in their lifetime?'

'Gee. Can't say I've ever thought about that! Something else for you to work through with your adorable wife,' Larry answered, his tone laden with empathy. 'As you say, it's what you do. You're more than capable of making the right decision. Either you do nothing, which is an option you'll never be comfortable with, or you just have to learn to deal with the after-effects, because you can't be all things to all men.'

'Christ Almighty! You're damned right, mate,' the world-changer raised his voice, smiling. 'The legacy I can't bloody shake. I can never repay a debt that stems from becoming so unbelievably successful either. And it's been so long, I don't even remember whom it's owed to...'

Jeff exhaled, laughing along with the others and levering himself up from the low armchair. 'Whatever... I can't stay here chatting all day. You guys've got a prison to run. Thanks for everything you've done for me, both of you, and mostly for Dad. I hope he said some nice things about you too the other day, Chris.'

'Oh, yes. He did,' the woman confirmed. 'He was quite gentlemanly in those closing hours. Your influence had rubbed off.'

'Whoa! Is that right? That's good to hear,' the showman said, shaking both their hands in turn. 'Larry, cheers for arranging the funeral and for making sure we followed all the right protocols. I'm off to downtown Parramatta now, to see if I can track down my wayward sister. Oh, and I totally forgot to ask... Was there a will?'

'No, there wasn't, mate. At least not lodged with us. He might've had one outside we didn't know about. Did he mention one to you, Chris?'

The counsellor shook her head.

'The only reason for asking was that I wanted to know whether to bury him or cremate him,' Jeff clarified. 'And if I find out he's got millions of bucks' worth of treasure stashed away somewhere, I'll send it to you.'

'Oh, great! That'd come in handy!' the middle-aged woman exclaimed.

Larry chuckled. 'You never know with these buggers. We'd recommend a cremation, if you have no preference. It's easier for everyone.'

'Takes up less room,' the irreverent superstar joked. 'Right. That's what we'll do. Thanks again.'

'I'll ring you early next week to let you know when the service will be. So I will see you again after all,' the middle-aged psychologist smiled. 'We might even get a chance to go for that beer?'

'Absolutely,' Jeff nodded, shaking his hand once more. 'I'll ask my office to think about a place we can all go afterwards. Somewhere kid-friendly. You're welcome too, Chris. A quiet lunch somewhere'd round things out well.'

Jeff Diamond left the Parklea prison complex for the final time, spinning the car's rear wheels on a patch of damp gravel which had been spread to fill in a widening ditch between the bitumen of the car park and the concrete driveway. He felt free and content that the morning had finished on a positive note. He couldn't wait to hear Lynn's opinion on the topics he had shared with two fine psychoanalysts.

Farewell To A Stranger

The rock star found his sister at home and very busy indeed. In fact, when he reached her landing, there were two other men hanging about, pretending they weren't in line for a good shag. He descended to ground level again and walked to a nearby public telephone, wondering if the street-girl had replaced the broken answering machine with the new one sent up by his office manager.

A resounding negatory! The bemused brother heard the strident warbling in Madalena's apartment from all the way across the road, calling through the wide-open windows. He secreted himself in his ordinary car to scribble a note, then climbed the stairs once more and slipped it under her door. It crossed his mind that the press would have a field day if "The Australian Elvis" were to be spotted coming out of a known prostitute's place of work in the western suburbs. Almost worth giving them a tip-off...

To kill some time, Jeff drove back to Fairfield, turning into the park where he and Lynn had sheltered under huge oaks from the Christmas Day sunshine to share hopes and dreams for their trip to wintry London; the day before he had confronted his greatest fear.

Climbing the hill and sitting down on a lichen-clad bench under one of the trees, he opened the letter Chris Williams had given him. He had expected the blood to rush to his head in anxiety's nauseating pall as the envelope's tear grew longer. Peculiarly however, he felt nothing.

Inside was a single sheet of paper adorned with the same neat handwriting that had provided the corrections on a previous letter penned by his father.

"Dear Jeff,"

Good start, sarcasm rose from his inner child.

"I think this is the end for me. I am in a lot of pain and have decided not to get treatment. It was grouse..."

The word "good" had been written first but crossed out.

31

"…to see you, your family and Madaleine too. Nice to see you were all so happy. I was jealous but grateful you haven't ended up like me. No hard feelings."

The orphan son exhaled and bit back the tears, unable to bring himself to banish his own hard feelings. Not yet anyway. The ignorant man hadn't even known how to spell his daughter's name, requiring Chris to take a guess. With increasing bitterness, he read the next paragraph.

"Your little girl is so like your mum that I can't get her out of my head. I know you will give them a good life. Perhaps they will have a better life in some way because I gave you such a bad one. That's a good ending for me, after all the bad stuff, like you said."

Bloody cheek! Was his father taking the credit for making his son a good parent? Jeff cursed out loud, mainly because he would have said the same thing in his father's place. Begrudgingly, he admitted to an element of truth in the old man's statement.

"I read some of your book. Powerful stuff, mate. Too rich for me, but I get what you mean. I did waste my life, except I gave you to the world by accident. Beats me how you ended up like you are. Me and your mum said that when you were a kid, but that's nothing to how you turned out."

Whoa! So the self-centred criminal had been paying attention in those early days after all, the lost boy realised. It was a surprise to read about his parents discussing the topic of their children. The last paragraph was a short one, its backhanded compliment well meant.

"You and your sister keep well. And finally, love that classy, sexy woman of yours long and hard for me. She is good for you, so be good to her, for me.
Good luck,
Dad."

The initial "D" of Dad had an extra-long tail, exposing this last, important correction as an afterthought. Nevertheless, reading the letter for the second and third times, Jeff was satisfied with how his relationship with his father had concluded. He was damned if he would be good to Lynn as a tribute to the abusive bastard. This was way beyond the call of duty.

'I don't need any additional inspiration to love her long and hard,' he murmured to the piece of paper in his hand. 'Thanks all the same.'

A modicum of pride seeped into the humble intellectual's brain, knowing he had managed to nudge his father in some small way towards finding his heart. The old codger had also reaffirmed his place in their so-called family. He wondered if a similar letter lay in store for Madalena too. Chris hadn't mentioned one. At least the father had met his maker with a better idea of who his children were, which gave the young man an odd sense of accomplishment. He didn't view these small positive steps as a victory by any means, since the prisoner was dead and gone.

The vindication the celebrity had felt when leaving the maximum security facility after their last meeting was no longer apparent, yet it hardly mattered anymore. Proving himself to his father was irrelevant now he was the head of the family, such as it was. Time to wipe the slate clean.

Looking at his watch, the driver wondered whether diverting back to Madalena's flat might be another total waste of effort. It was coming up for two o'clock, and he was hungry after an early breakfast. Should he don his cap and sunglasses and join the line outside her door? At least this should guarantee him half an hour out of her working day…

***

Lynn and the children left the Dysons' Benloch homestead on Saturday afternoon, keen to be home in time for Jeff's return. She had found the excitement in his voice infectious the night before, when he recounted the day's events with much more cheer than she had expected. Jet and Kierney were asleep in the back of the car, allowing her to sing the finishing touches of a new melody into a cassette recorder sitting in her lap while she drove.

This was the raw material for a perfect Tex Fletcher song, and the masterful composer was intending to send a tape to the British songwriter to have him improve on it. Ideally, she would have liked to ask him to record a version before she gave it to her favourite stallion, but time was of the essence for the upcoming occasion. She planned to celebrate the fact that he had come through the trials of recent weeks stronger and happier, having almost shaken off his last remaining ghouls.

Driving down the outside lane of the Nepean Highway, the young mother became aware of lights flashing in her rear-view mirror. Checking her speedometer, at first she feared a police car had picked up her speeding tail. Looking over her shoulder for a clearer picture, she made out a familiar regal *bête noir* bearing down on them. She pulled into the left-hand lane at the next opportunity, and husband and wife exchanged muted greetings through their respective car windows.

The pair of luxury vehicles cruised in convoy for the rest of the journey, meandering the last few kilometres along the tranquil, undulating Mount Eliza roads until they reached the gates of *Escondido*, which pivoted open in front of them on command. Merak, the six-year-old German Shepherd whom the family shared with one of their drivers, bounded alongside the cars on their way to the garage, where Greg was busy working on a restoration project.

Waving to the friendly former Air Force engineer, the couple embraced without inhibition at the rear of Lynn's BMW. The children were still asleep inside, giving their parents a rare opportunity for the type of impetuous, red-blooded reunion they had always shared as new lovers.

After a drawn-out kiss, Jeff held his wife at arms' length to stare into her welcoming eyes. 'Jeez, angel! What a fantastic way to arrive home, escorting each other back to base like that.'

'Yes, it was. How are you? You look much better than I expected,' Lynn pressed against his eager body. 'And feel great too!'

'Cheers, you tease! It's so good to see you guys. If I wasn't already the horniest man on the planet, that was one hell of a way to get me going. Thanks for coming home early. I'm stoked at having this extra night together.'

'No worries!' the woman giggled, leaning back and gazing into his smiling face. 'Your eyes are so alive, even in this light. I think you dropped a few years.'

The happy man loosened his grip and patted his various pockets. 'Nope. They'll be here somewhere. You can't miss 'em. They come in packs of ten.'

The young mother opened the door next to Kierney, taking care not to frighten her. Her husband went around to the other side of the car and did the same for their son, who was already stirring. He gave his dad a wide smile as soon as his eyes focussed, too excited to regulate his volume setting.

'Hey, you're back! Are we home? I didn't know you were here.'

'Shhh!' Jeff hissed. 'Kizzy's still asleep. I was following you for the last twenty minutes, and you didn't even twig, Batman. How're you going?'

'We're having a barby tonight,' the boy couldn't wait to spill the beans. 'We brought the meat from Grandma's.'

'*Excelente*,' his father replied, pressing a finger to his lips. 'Grandma-burgers. *¡Muy sabroso!*'

The young boy doubled over with laughter, almost wriggling his way out of Jeff's grip. 'Mum! Dad said "Grandma-burgers"!'

'Jetto, shush, please,' Lynn raised a finger to her mouth too, her eyes pointing out the sleeping toddler in her arms. 'Yum! Lovely. Looking forward to trying them. Go indoors, please.'

Once inside the house, the patient sportswoman stretched Kierney's limp body out along one of the sofas in the lounge room while her husband unloaded the rest of the luggage from both cars. Jet did his best to keep quiet around his little sister, but as usual, failed with consummate flair. The little girl woke up and rubbed her eyes, slid off the couch and wandered out to find her parents.

'Where's *Papá*?' she asked her mother, wandering past the bottom of the stairs and into the kitchen.

'Upstairs. Go and find him. He needs a big cuddle.'

The two-year-old climbed the staircase and trotted towards the master bedroom at the far end of the corridor. She found her special friend lying on the bed, staring at the ceiling and on the verge of sleep. Feather-light footsteps and excited breathing gave her away, but he pretended the friendly ambush was a total surprise.

'*¿Papá, qué tal?*' she whispered. '*¿Estás dormido?*'

'*Sí. ¿Has despertado?*'

'*¡Sí! No me* sleepwalking.' Kierney giggled at his statement of the obvious, holding both arms out straight in front of her and marching from one side of the bed to the other, there and back until it made the horizontal comic feel quite sick.

The little girl stopped and pivoted on her heels. 'Granddad died.'

'Yeah, baby. Sleepwalking *es somnambulismo. El abuelo murió. ¿Estás triste?*'

'*Un poco.*'

'*Yo también,*' her dad agreed, slotting his hands under her armpits and elevating her lightness over his legs to set her down on Lynn's side of the bed. '*Bueno, pequeñita. Muy bueno.* I need a big hug from one of my two special ladies.'

The dark-haired pair, both descended from a departed prisoner and somehow tuned to the same wavelength, grieved together. With no desire to curtail this inexplicable process for fear of disconcerting the pensive youngster, Jeff let his opinions be known.

'It's good that we feel a bit sad, Kizzy. Granddad was a bad man who could've been a good man. Now he's gone, he won't ever be a good man. That's what's sad, isn't it?'

Kierney nodded. 'We can be good for him.'

The bereaved son opened his eyes and gaped at the tiny soothsayer. 'You said exactly what Granddad said. Did *Mamá* tell you?'

'No,' she shook her head, mystified by the question.

'Then that's what we'll do,' the philosopher cuddled the precious child into his chest, kissing her forehead. 'Do we have a deal?'

'*Sí,*' the vibration of her breath answered. '*¿Y Jetto y la mamá?*'

'*Bien sûr, ma petite.* D'you know Granddad thought you were as beautiful as *mi mamá, tu abuela*?'

'Am I?'

'Well, *I* think you're even more beautiful,' the romantic insisted. ''Cause you're like *tu mamá* too. Beautiful on the outside and on the inside.'

'How? You can't see me on the inside,' she challenged, pouting.

'Oh, yes, I can,' her dad objected, bouncing the clever-clogs up and down on his midriff. 'I'm the *papá*. I can see everything, remember? I can see your thoughts are beautiful, just like your pretty face. Know what I mean?'

Kierney sat upright and nodded to her smiling hero, who caught his breath as his mind pondered their profound connection. It was an entirely different bond from the one he shared with Lynn, and noticeably more intense than his feelings for his son.

The intellectual had learned not to be too critical of this heartfelt affinity, although some guilt and shame were destined to endure. His wife had no complaints about his devotion to their boisterous firstborn, understanding only too well that this tiny female clone was his carbon-copy. Indeed, Jet exhibited many more Dyson traits than the Diamond equivalent at his current age.

The three-year-old unravelled her arms from her dad's embrace and stretched them around his chest, squeezing hard. 'You're beautiful on the outside and inside too, *Papá*.'

Jeff sniffed. '*Gracias, pequeñita*. That's kind of you. Shall we go down and help get the barbecue ready? *Mamá*'ll be missing us.'

'OK,' his eager sidekick agreed, rolling off his stomach and careening all the way down to the floor in a single, uncoordinated fling.

'Hey! Careful,' the concerned man cried out, seeing the youngster pick herself up and affix a sweet smile to her face. 'You're like those bees of yours, flying and sleeping at the same time.'

Daughter and father wandered downstairs hand-in-hand, the little girl following him as he paced down several steps and then back up a few, then down a few more, and so on and so forth. Dancing from the sweeping bannister on one side to the handrail attached to the curved wall on the other, they eventually reached the bottom in fits of laughter.

'What are you two doing?' Lynn asked, hearing the giggling conspirators coming towards the kitchen.

'Taking an awful long time to come down the stairs,' Jeff answered, planting a tender kiss on his wife's cheek. 'What are you two doing?'

'Waiting for you to light the barbecue.'

'Right you are, ma'am. That I can do,' he said, saluting with the tongs he had been handed by his accuser and shaking them at his son, who had arrived at a run to present for duty. 'Mate! Barby time. Man's work.'

***

'I vote let's all go up to our room and watch the stars,' Jeff suggested after their tasty, carnivorous feast.

It was eight-thirty, and all four were tired from the day's excitement. Thankfully, the parents hadn't needed to fend off a discussion about "grannibalism" at the table, which Lynn had feared after her son's inquisitive mind had latched onto yet another of her husband's dangerous plays on words.

Merak had returned to his master earlier for his own dinner and evening walk, leaving the foursome to their own devices. Kierney had dozed off once or twice on her mother's lap while pretending to be a kitten. She awoke again when the strength in Lynn's Olympian limbs lifted her off the couch and carried her upstairs, soon followed by the others.

The children cleaned their teeth and dressed in their pyjamas. An unusually mild, cloudless night for the end of July allowed for the two heavy shutters behind the French windows in the main bedroom to be opened before the family climbed under the quilt. The soul-mates linked hands over their babies' heads, currents of love zipping from heart to heart along their arms.

'Y'see all those stars up there?' Jeff asked his sleepy bedfellows. 'Well... Imagine they're all the people who've died, like Granddad, who didn't do all the good things they wanted to, or should've done.'

'OK,' his wife replied on behalf of them all.

Kierney had no trouble recalling her last conversation in this room, sitting up proudly and pointing with both index fingers. 'Yes, I know! Granddad wanted me to be good for him, so how 'bout we're all good for the star people?'

'Yeah!' her brother agreed with equal enthusiasm, reaching his hands towards the open window as well.

'Which one's Granddad?' the little girl pondered aloud.

'Which star?' Lynn prompted.

'Yes. Which star? And which is *Papá*'s *mamá*?'

'Any stars you like, *pequeñita*,' her father suggested. 'That's between you and them. Pick whichever ones you like the look of.'

Jet's right arm extending as far as it could, he waved into the heavens. 'I pick that one for Granddad and that one *para la Abuela*.'

'Good man,' Jeff said, placing a weighty, approving hand on the lad's forehead.

His partner turned to the drowsy toddler. 'Which ones are you choosing, Kizzo?'

'I'll choose tomorrow,' she whimpered, eyelids drooping as she scanned the distant lights. 'I don't know yet.'

'Fair enough,' her father replied, cocking his head towards his amused lover. 'Perfectly fine, in fact.'

'In that case…' Lynn suggested, stroking their daughter's hair. 'How about tomorrow you guys draw a picture for Granddad's funeral, showing him which star you picked and what you're going to do to be good for him?'

The songwriter squeezed his dream girl's forearm, unable to put his feelings into words. Both children were as keen as mustard, and he couldn't wait to see the results of this endeavour.

'And now you two have to get into your own beds, because it's far too squashy in here,' Lynn announced, cuddling Kierney in close.

The parents decamped with the youngsters to Jet's bedroom and read them a quick story, again all crowded onto the boy's bed. Father and daughter were both fast asleep by the time the sportswoman closed the book. Waking at his wife's touch, Jeff transported the little girl into her own room and turned out the light.

'*Hasta mañana, Jetto,*' he waved, passing the door. '*Te amo.*'

Back in their inviting king-sized bed, with windows sealed but shutters open, the blonde beauty wrapped her arms around her melancholy husband and kissed his lips. 'So, *Don Corleone*,' she opened with a cheeky smile, running tantalising fingernails down his chest and stomach with enough force to rekindle his latent fire. 'Are you going to make it worth my while to stay with you, now you're the head of the family?'

'Sure am. Every fucking day, lady,' he enunciated syllable by syllable, tears gathering in the corners of his eyes. 'Every fucking day.'

'Thanks,' Lynn gasped as he began to caress her all over. 'I know you would anyway, despite what was in the letter.'

Sex between the homecoming lovers was as intense as ever, rendered all the sweeter by several days apart and the renewed commitment both felt towards each other after the latest major milestone in their life singular. Jeff was in full control of his destiny, and therefore that of the whole family, and his dream girl wouldn't have had it any other way.

'Before you go to sleep…' she whispered.

'Yeah?' her husband murmured, on the edge of slumber.

'I've written a song for you, from your dad. Can I play it to you now, or would you like to hear it tomorrow morning?'

The rock star chuckled, turning over and propping himself up on his elbow. 'If you wanted me to hear it tomorrow morning, you wouldn't have mentioned it now.'

His wife shrugged. 'Sorry. I didn't plan this very well, did I?'

'Do we have to go downstairs, or can you play it up here?' Jeff asked, his interest in this novel angle well and truly roused.

Delighted, the lithe musician sprang halfway across the bedroom in one bound and switched on an electric piano which lived in the far corner. Often caught in such songwriting emergencies after lovemaking had inspired their creative juices, the six-octave instrument was put to regular use. Balancing it on her knee, she played a progression of pronounced opening chords and was soon giving her most favourite Prince Charming a taste of the tender melody which would hit the charts all over the world in a month's time.

'Are you OK?' the singer asked as she powered off the keyboard and lowered it onto the floor beside the bed. 'About the way you feel, I mean.'

'Yep. Why? Are you ready to go again?' the larrikin teased. 'Jesus! You're insatiable. And I love it.'

Fending off rapturous arms, the young mother yelped. 'No! I'm just glad you're feeling better.'

'Damn!'

The traveller's firm grip closed around his wife's waist, climbing on top and smothering her mouth into a deep kiss. He knew she was powerless to resist him this way, the muscles of his heart taut and as fit to burst as his balls.

'OK, so I'm horny too...' Lynn gasped. 'Come here, you gorgeous hulk.'

'Well, I'm not,' a hundred kilogrammes of sexual chemistry dropped sideways onto the mattress, facing away from his abandoned bedfellow. 'I'm officially in mourning. See you in four weeks.'

The tennis champion groaned, sitting up and reaching for her pyjamas. 'Four weeks? Wow! OK. Leaving me in the cold. Winter'll be nearly over by then... I'll have to outsource.'

'You do that,' Jeff held his ground, stroking his aching penis and wondering how long his playmate would be able to maintain the *charade*. 'Let me know how it goes.'

The couple fell silent, losing themselves in their marriage's irresistible emotional rollercoaster, both knowing neither could hold out for much longer. "I'm still your father. You're still my son." The simple sentences at the core of Lynn's new lyric ran through her mind over and over again. Her man was bearing up admirably in comparison to previous crossroads, and her heart glowed.

'*Je t'adore, mon ami,*' she whispered, brushing his shoulder with loving fingertips.

'Oh, *je t'adore aussi,*' the boy from Canley Vale cried. 'Jesus, angel. I'm so confused. Seeing him in that bloody morgue was like being kicked by a shoe with no foot inside.'

The caring woman spooned in behind her exhausted husband, her hand drawn into his. 'Ugh! What a horrible analogy. What do you mean?'

'Like it hurt, but I knew there wouldn't be a second blow.'

Neither lover moved for the longest time, grief tumbling from the world-changer's core. Cradling his substantial, quaking frame as best she could, Lynn traced lazy kisses over the heaving expanse of muscular shoulders and stroked her warm feet in a slow rhythm up and down his calves.

Jeff moaned in pleasure. 'You make me so happy.'

'So happy that you're sad?'

The orphan sniffed at the conundrum. 'Yeah. That's me.'

'I s'pose so,' the sportswoman sighed. 'It's fine, and I love you all the more for it, my beautiful black stallion. Together, forever, wherever. That's us.'

Twisting around to face his dream girl, overjoyed with the imagery these three words conjured up. 'Jeez, I don't want this to end.'

'It won't end,' she promised. 'Why would it end? I'm as happy as you are. Let me sing you the song again. Can I? Then I'll force myself upon you.'

The keyboard's lights flashed for the second time as the singer prepared to reprise her poignant composition. Keeping the volume lower this time, in case she disturbed their slumbering gnomes, the tune carried its message around the room. After she had played the final cadence and removed her fingers from the keys, Jeff lay for several minutes in virtual silence, his deep breathing the only sound.

'It's beautiful,' he said at last, relishing the sensation of soft lips against his tear-stained cheek. 'I think that's the most beautiful song ever written in the history of time. Thanks again.'

Lynn smiled, dismissing the exaggerated compliment. 'I don't think so, but I hoped you'd like it. I wanted to say how good it was to see the two of you together the other week. You were so impressive with him after what he did to you. How you reunited us all before it was too late, and how well you are now you're home and king of the castle. Masterful, magic man.'

As much as the musical tribute, this touching testament did nothing to stem the peacemaker's tears. They were the expression of pure euphoria rather than loss. As usual, his soul-mate understood him perfectly. Introducing the generation before to the generation after had indeed happened just in time. He wouldn't want Jet and Kierney to spend any more time with their Granddad even if he had survived. The old man didn't deserve it, no matter how much it had warmed his heart to witness the bastard fighting with his own, under-used humanity.

'I do kind o' miss him,' he confessed, after another few moments of silence.

'It's probably the grieving process kicking in,' Lynn offered. 'Do you think you'll sleep without nightmares tonight?'

'Hope so. When I was at Alberto's, I dreamed Jetto and I were involved in the old gang, and he got stabbed. Our son's blood on the ground. Jesus! Not being able to find him woke me up, I think.'

'Oh, my God. That's horrible too. Another dream where you wanted to save someone but couldn't,' his wife posited. 'That's the recurring theme, isn't it? I bet you were relieved to see him this afternoon, loud and clear as ever.'

Jeff turned and kissed her, emotions overflowing. 'Got it in one, gorgeous.'

'Well, we're all safe and all together in our own house. Let's hope it's enough to let you sleep peacefully.'

'Yeah. Thanks. But can I just tell you one more thing that came up while I was talking to Chris and Larry? Then I promise I'll leave you alone.'

'Of course. I want to know.'

'Larry made a comment that I needed to realise I can't be all things to all men,' the philosopher explained.

'That was brave of him,' his beautiful best friend checked, a broad grin on her face. 'Based on what?'

Her husband sniggered at the snide retort. 'Yeah, yeah... I mentioned we'd been talking about whether Dad would've deserved a transplant if he'd lived long enough, and posed a question about how we're supposed to find out what we're accountable for... You know, by which rules do we choose who deserves something more?'

Lynn frowned. 'I don't understand the connection, but tell me anyway.'

'No. Well... *No importa*,' Jeff replied. 'I told them the reason I'm compelled to do as much as I possibly can, and that it looks like I'm trying to solve every single problem in the world, is because I'm stuck with this debt for having become so successful and so damned happy.'

'Hmm...' the young woman nodded, none the wiser as to her intellectual's point.

'And I said that I'd been carrying this debt around for so long that I've forgotten whose it is.'

Blue eyes widened in the darkness, reflecting the full moon streaming in through the French windows. 'Right! OK. Do you mean now you *are* free, you still don't feel free and don't know why?'

Kissing her forehead, Jeff was stoked at this lateral deduction. 'Exactly, genius!'

'And it's definitely not a debt to me? Didn't it used to be me?'

'Yeah. No. It's not you any more,' the boy from Canley Vale confirmed. 'I learned to believe you.'

Lynn stroked his face. 'Good. Well, tell you what?'

'What?'

'Stop the standing order and wait for someone to complain,' she suggested. 'Just do what *you* think is right, and figure out if anything changes. If it does, you'll know what's left to deal with. And if nothing happens, you really are free.'

Jeff rolled over onto his back and stared at the ceiling, processing this new plan handed down by his trusted adviser. 'That'll do nicely. Now go to sleep and leave me alone.'

'Sorry,' his dream girl laughed, giving his lips one last kiss for luck. 'Anything you wish, boss.'

'Hey!' the rock star objected, rolling over and enveloping her in his arms. 'That's enough of that. I'm not in mourning anymore, I've decided. You couldn't do without me for four hours, let alone four weeks, could you?'

'Goodnight. *Hasta la vista.* You're the Ace of Diamonds now. Make it count.'

***

The funeral of Paul Diamond was, as predicted, a simple affair. Madalena agreed to forgo some appointments and had made an effort to don appropriate attire. She stood tall in a floral skirt with a black background, long enough to cover the unsightly, bruised thighs and knobbly knees normally on full view. She had borrowed a dark green top from her flatmate and rounded out the mutation with a formal black jacket which Lynn had packed as a contingency. The wind blew icy cold, blustery and damp, as befitting a cremation ceremony.

Jeff toyed with the idea of wearing a suit and tie, deciding against it at the last minute. His father only knew him in the leather jacket given to him by his guardian angel on his twentieth birthday. The bitter son couldn't work out if he chose to put it on because his dad had coveted it, or whether he simply wanted to remind the old bastard that he was the only one permitted to wear this well-travelled item of clothing.

His wife looked as elegant and sophisticated as usual in a black pencil skirt and figure-hugging coat, with black stockings and high-heeled shoes which elevated her almost to her husband's height. The children were also smartly turned out, causing Chris Williams to breach protocol and ask if she could take a photograph of the stylish celebrity family.

Jet and Kierney had each drawn a picture of their Granddad's star, and their parents helped to place them on top of the pine coffin. The boy had asked to see inside many times, fascinated to the point of obsession that a dead body lay right next to them. Lynn had needed to reprimand him quite forcefully before he agreed to keep quiet.

The youngest Diamond held her father's hand through the short service provided by Parklea's chaplain. The two parents exchanged glances, coming to realise how empathetic their little girl was becoming. When the time came to say his few rehearsed lines, Jeff spoke from where he stood rather than moving to the front, not wanting to break the spell for the diminutive angel.

The record producer had invited a promising Melbourne Academy musician by the name of Rod Germany to record the special song, backed by her piano accompaniment. Although neither could articulate why, both musicians considered singing live at the murderer's funeral as inappropriate. The plaintive rendition moved everyone to tears, even the hard-hearted Madalena.

Lifting Jet up in her arms as the coffin slipped behind the sliding doors into the crematorium, the young mum noticed he was shivering. The simplicity of the service was perfect to emphasise to their children the importance of recognising people for the significance they bore on one's life, and she hugged her son close as the polished brown casket disappeared. With Kierney also hoisted high enough to watch, the abandoned child put his arm around the blond half of his family, and they all whispered goodbye to Granddad.

Lunch had been arranged at a pub about five kilometres from the prison, in a small function room leading out to a beer garden. Too cold to sit outside, the kids were given a chance to let off steam while the adults shared a meal and a few drinks. Larry Shepherd was utterly awestruck by the intelligent and personable Missus Diamond, sharing a private confession with his colleague that he had been somewhat cynical about the match-made-in-heaven portrayed for the cameras. He was delighted to prove his suspicions wrong, conceding that the two high-achievers from such different walks of life were harmony personified.

After lunch, the family said farewell to Chris and Larry and headed off to the cemetery where Lucy Diamond was buried. The urn containing her husband's ashes was placed in a box and into the rear luggage compartment, amid much curiosity from both children. Jet's reckless enthusiasm again became impossible to quell when he was told the container would be opened at some point, to scatter the chundering old jailbird's remains into the air.

'Mate,' Jeff growled, taking his son by the upper arm and shaking him still. 'This is not a game, OK? We need to show respect for Granddad now.'

'Sorry, Dad,' the boy replied, climbing into the car without another word, only turning round once every ten seconds, checking with his x-ray eyes to make sure the small box didn't vanish from the boot.

Madalena hadn't visited her mother's grave a single time since the desolate woman had been interred fifteen years earlier. Her brother remembered stopping by at least twice before moving to Melbourne, yet neither sibling knew how to find the location without resorting to the street directory.

'Shameful, huh?' the songwriter said. 'What a sad indictment on how we felt about our *mamá*.'

However, once in the graveyard, the troubled adolescent's memory came up trumps, and he guided his relatives almost straight to the simple headstone for which he had saved six weeks' wages after the drug addict's funeral. He informed them all of this fact for the express purpose of shaming his disinterested sister, yet the obvious hint zipped by unnoticed by its intended recipient.

'Come and look at this, kids,' their mum invited, crouching down beside them and pointing to the words carved into the moss-eaten stone. 'This is your grandmother, *Papá*'s *mamá*. Luciana, her name was. She died in nineteen-sixty-six. See? Ten years before *Mamá* and *Papá* got married. She died on *Papá*'s birthday. Isn't that sad?'

Kierney nodded, gazing at her mother and then at her father. Her bottom lip quivered as the statement hit home.

'How d'you know that, angel?' the Sydney native asked, putting his hand on his daughter's head and stroking her hair. 'I sure as hell didn't tell you.'

'No, you didn't. I saw her death certificate once,' Lynn confessed. 'Remember, on the plane to London? You handed me the folder with all your exam' certificates in?'

Jeff fended off a hostile glare from his sister before nodding. 'Yeah. Whoa! That's right. It is in there.'

'I didn't know it was your birthday,' Madalena remarked, momentarily saddened for her brother. 'Was it really? Shit birthday!'

Lynn gave her husband a sympathetic smile, both disappointed that their youngsters were subjected to more foul language. Instead of lambasting the hapless aunt, they shared a telepathic private joke. Compared to other childhood birthdays spent alone and tortured by mental scars, this was an apt enough description for the day that kicked off his fifteenth year!

Meanwhile, Jet drilled his finger along the headstone's sunken lettering, reading out each letter one by one before reciting his grandmother's name. 'Luciana Moreno Diamond.'

'That's it, mate. *Muy bien*,' his dad praised, sinking down on his haunches and embracing his son. '*Es tu abuela*.'

Madalena was still clutching the small brown urn, initial disgust giving way to annoyance. 'When are we going to do this?' she asked, shaking it as if she were collecting coins for charity. 'And where?'

Jeff stood up and laced an arm around his beautiful best friend, reeling from the discovery that she had been in on this secret for some time without letting on. 'Well... You and I need to make a choice,' he told his sister. 'Do we get another headstone and put them side-by-side, thereby reuniting our parents? Or do we take him somewhere else because they've been apart for so long.'

'Do you think they still loved each other when your mum passed away?' Lynn asked the siblings.

Her sister-in-law screwed her face up. 'Na. Doubt it.'

The rock star nodded. 'Yeah. I tend to agree, to be honest. You'd like to think there was some romance to be had in leaving them together in death, but I'm with Lena. It doesn't sit right with me either. Their love got lost in the general crap of life. Good point, angel.'

Smiling, his wife shrugged, pleased to have been useful. She sensed a new plan being formulated on the fly, almost able to hear the cogs ratcheting around in the deep thinker's mind as he searched for a suitable spot to release Paul Diamond's remains into the elements. The others followed his gaze too, tracking full circle over the cemetery grounds. Kierney ran to her dad and asked to be carried.

'Hey, *pequeñita*,' the tall man said, hoisting her up into the air and kissing her lips. '*¿Estás OK?*'

The little girl nodded and hugged her daddy's neck. The wind had picked up, causing the trees' boughs and branches to sway with frightening, supernatural whooshes and crackles. The ghost stories they had dreamed up at bedtime the night before were about to be acted out for real.

'Here's what we'll do...' Jeff announced, staring into a pair of deep blue eyes.

'What?' Jet shouted, fired up by the prospect of more excitement.

'We're going to take this little tin of Granddad home with us, and when we next go to New York, we can find out where he was born and scatter him there. How does that sound?'

Lynn nodded. 'Sounds perfect. Good thinking.'

'But what about me?' Madalena whined. 'Why don't I get to see it?'

'You can if you like,' the multi-millionnaire contradicted his older sister, who had never grown out of her childlike fear of missing out. 'You'd like Auntie Lena to come to New York with us, wouldn't you, guys?'

Both niece and nephew gave their wholehearted support to this idea, as did their uncouth relative. The compassionate blonde read her husband's thoughts. Only the previous week, his sister had bade good riddance to their father and questioned why they should even go to the trouble of arranging a funeral. Jeff caught her eye out of the children's field of vision and winked, before his attention was summarily snapped back to more disrespectful overtones.

'Can I?' she shrieked. 'Yeah. Take me to New York. Wow! I always wanted to go.'

Her brother winced, an injection of acid wrath boiling his blood. 'Sure. Why not? As long as you can get the time off work...'

Madalena hit his arm hard and uttered an incomprehensible Spanish expletive at the top of her voice, much to the kids' astonishment.

'That's settled then,' Lynn laughed. 'Shall we go? These guys are getting cold.'

'Sure,' the world-changer agreed. 'We all are.'

Over the following weeks, the couple hatched a plan for an unusual type of memorial service for the double-murderer on the Stones Road, coinciding with the launch of a revitalisation project The Fellowship had been incubating for a few years. While the philanthropist was overseas on another African negotiation mission, the rear-end of the Diamond pantomime horse used her political connections in Sydney to help paint the vision of a procession through the streets to commemorate the city's favourite son. He was the ideal role model for the current generation of teenagers and young adults, his early life spent among people who had fallen victim to the poverty, apathy and lack of opportunity so typical in the western suburbs.

Local councils had been hesitant at first, doubting the level of support they would garner from residents and the business community for an event which might be perceived as glorifying the stand-over tactics of the criminal thugs still operating in the area. Also worried about reactivating some of the old feuds, the millionnaire had sided with the officials initially.

As they often did, the eternal collaborators worked through their differences in the recording studio, emerging with a hit song to be released as a single in the months leading up to the anniversary of Diamond Senior's passing, the scheduled date of the parade. Education sessions at local high schools were to be provided by staff at Parklea and other prisons, to warn students of the dangers of becoming involved with the underworld and to convince them that school was a much better solution for staying out of trouble.

Gerry's tax specialists assisted the Diamonds to create two annual university bursaries to be offered at Fairfield High School, to be granted in Jeff's name to one boy and one girl from disadvantaged families who had succeeded against the odds.

The deceased and latterly infamous character who had started out in New York and who was soon to return there in a rather different form, courtesy of the family he abused, was to have his pathetic, good-for-nothing life honoured far more highly than he deserved. This disproportionate tribute inflicted only a fleeting blight on Jeff's conscience, soon rationalising it by projecting forward. In reality, the celebration was meant for those who managed to rise above.

As his gorgeous lover reminded him from time to time, the neglected son had turned bad to good. No-one else had sought to end the Jaworskis' *vendetta* against his family, and it had not been Pavel Diament who secured his daughter's release from the prostitution ring and set her up in a modest apartment in Parramatta. The rock star with an overpowering sense of true justice was in the process of providing hope and opportunity to neighbourhood schoolchildren with backgrounds like his. He gave them something to believe in: themselves.

So the deadbeat father's character had been written out of the skilful artist's life-story. With his dream girl by his side, and their two inspired and enlightened beings, Unity and Liberty, sprouting up before their eyes, Jeff

Diamond left the burden of the pretender behind. He was the chief now; free to be whoever he wanted for whomever he chose. And so far no creditors had come forward to call in his debt.

Best Holiday Ever

Wiping tears from her eyes, Kierney closed the book and sat it carefully on her bedside table. She was but a toddler when her paternal grandfather had passed away, with the vaguest memories of the one and only time they met. She didn't remember scattering his ashes in New York, but the family had spoken about it often enough for her to piece together an accurate picture.

The eighteen-year-old was humbled by her dad's stories. She was about to start the second semester of her undergraduate degree at Sydney University, delayed for twelve months when her mother had succumbed to the fatal bullet. Throughout the harrowing aftermath the Diamond family endured during nineteen-ninety-six, the young woman's plans to work at the United Nations had never faltered. And now, reading the autobiography's uplifting themes, she was even more certain that "The Big Apple" was where her chosen career should take her.

Kierney Lynn Freedom Diamond was the daughter of a Catholic Argentinean Polish Jew, with a substantial amount of Dutch Australian blood mixed in. Her brother's genetic composition was in inverse proportions to her own, yet they were both the same deep down; bound together by a heritage steeped in broad-ranging wisdom and moral sustenance.

How hard her parents had worked! And what a happy family they had made! The teenager's nerves remained raw after a full year of their new world order, and sometimes the sense of unfairness was truly unbearable. She cried to her chosen constellation for a few minutes of escape, tears of hope and tears of loss running down the sides of her face and into her ears, pressing her head back onto the pillow.

Why did their blissful family existence have to end this way? Why weren't her mum and dad on hand to see her complete her degree, meet the love of her life and one day give them grandchildren? They had planned to watch her being installed as the first female Secretary General of the United Nations. What an occasion this would have been for the fabulous foursome!

Five more pages before lights-out, the student decided, picking up her father's final offering again. Having got this far into it, she no longer felt strange reading about her own life. She was excited about the next chapter, looking forward to his account of the family's first notable European adventure; the one which had always held such a special place in her parents' hearts. Over the years, the famous dynasty learned to maximise their enjoyment from holidays and the togetherness they engendered. Leisure time for the Diamond youngsters had become a premium commodity at a young age, and even more so once their individual sporting and educational challenges began to command more and more of a commitment.

The dark-haired beauty was under no illusion that the memories she would soon revisit on paper represented the first of many amazing trips around the world her parents found so fascinating. They promised to give her greater insight into the journeys each family member had taken into self-discovery.

Kierney smiled at an amusing reference to her big brother, hearing her *papá*'s peculiar but always apposite turn of phrase sing out from the page.

***

The Melbourne summer of nineteen-eighty-one and –two spent its *dénouement* in a month of virtually constant rain. Lynn Dyson Diamond had arrived back at *Escondido* after a week promoting her latest album in the UK to find the rest of her family huddled together on the balcony of the master bedroom, all five senses being bombarded by the wild weather coming in off the bay.

All three had jumped out of their skins when the French windows creaked open behind them, their wooden frames caught by the eddying gusts and flung closed again, slipping clean out of the jet-setter's fingers. She had laughed from the inside at their scared expressions, threatening to lock the doors and leave them outside all night.

Jet rushed down from his dad's lap and began to bash the glass, his other hand grabbing for his hood as the wind did its best to rip the coat off his back.

'What's the matter?' his mother asked casually, opening the door a mere crack and bending to the lad's eye level. 'Don't you want to sleep out there tonight?'

'No!' he yelped. 'It's howling like a werewolf out here.'

'Is it? And who taught you that expression, I wonder?'

Jeff twisted around, revealing tufts of black hair belonging to a small, dark-haired girl who was wrapped in his jacket. She hadn't been able to hear the conversation between mother and son until now, and her eyes stared up at her dad. They both listened to the four-year-old baying to the moon, his head thrown back to hurl into the night sky, and Kierney freed her hands to clamp them over her chilly ears.

'Let's go inside,' the evening's chaperone decided, levering his tall frame off the deckchair and turning to the French windows. 'Brrrr! *Sésame, ouvre-toi, Mamá.* It's bloody cold out here.'

The doors opened for the magician, and Lynn took their daughter from his arms and kissed her frozen cheek. Droplets of spray shone like tiny jewels in her hair, but she was toasty-warm otherwise. Jet ran into the huge bedroom, flipped both shoes off without breaking stride and leaped onto the bed.

'Welcome! Home! Mum!' he chanted in time with each bounce. 'Welcome! Home! Mum!'

'Thank you, darling,' she replied, catching him on the rise. 'It's lovely to be home.'

While the vociferous boy was smothered in kisses, much to his disgust, his father fetched a towel from the *en suite* bathroom to dry Kierney's face and hands before doing the same for himself. The little girl giggled to hear her brother's protestations go unheeded.

'Help me, Dad!' the youngster yelled. 'I hate kisses. Help me! No kisses. Stop!'

Lynn desisted after some coaxing, allowing the breathless boy back onto his feet. Still grumbling about being wet all over, he sprang off the bed with a heavy thud and sprinted away to the sanctuary of his own room. Seizing his chance, Jeff leaned into his wife's arms, and their mouths met for the first time in seven days.

'I don't hate being kissed,' he stated for the record. 'Although I resent having to make do with tired, hand-me-down lips.'

His lover shrugged. 'Beggars can't be choosers. How long were you out there?'

'Fifteen minutes. Maybe a bit more,' the guilty babysitter answered, glancing over at the bedside clock despite having no idea what time they had climbed the stairs with this latest hare-brained scheme of his. 'It's pretty spectacular, right in the jaws of nature's wrath. How're you going, angel? You look hot, hot, hot!'

Her grin swallowed by another, equally complimentary kiss, Lynn's attention was distracted by the insistent tapping of a tiny fist on her thigh. The couple broke away from their intimate embrace to find Kierney with a picture to show her mother. In the half-light shining in from the hallway, the young woman had trouble making out its subject.

'I can't see it properly,' she said, holding out her hand. 'Let's go downstairs and make some drinks, and I'll look at it carefully down there.'

'*E' il Colosseo et la Tour Eiffel*,' the proud little linguist declared. 'I copied them from the book.'

'*Oh, bravo, cariña. Excelente.* Very clever. Come on... Go and get Jetto, please, and let's go down.'

Placing four mugs on the table, the blissful mother found a whole gallery of pictures left on display for her return. Jet had drawn Buckingham Palace and another building she thought might be *le Château de Versailles*. Her heart soared, realising their dad had been schooling their children on European landmarks while she was away.

'You have been busy,' she said. 'What's brought on this sudden love of architecture?'

'We're going on holidays,' her son informed her. 'Everywhere.'

'Everywhere? When?'

Her sheepish husband turned tail as soon as he sauntered through the kitchen doorway, pretending to invent an important errand. Lynn flicked a finger at the energetic boy, instructing him to fetch his father to come clean. David returned victorious, dragging his Goliath by the hand.

'Yep. Guilty as charged. I've selfishly decided the only way we're going to be in one place all together for more than a few days is if I whisk you off on holidays. That way, you can't escape.'

The popular record producer's mouth dropped open in mock alarm. 'Wow! Who'd want to escape? That's fantastic. When? Can I re-pack first or do I just turn around and load my case back into the car?'

'I don't give a flying...' Jeff chuckled. 'As long as you're there with us, you can wear the same clothes for three weeks for all I care. Or not wear 'em? Entirely your call, *mon amie*.'

Jet cackled, always grateful to be served a new slogan on a plate. 'Mum's going naked on holidays! Mum's going naked on holidays!'

'Only if you do too,' Lynn teased her son, who huffed and puffed in indignation at such a ridiculous suggestion.

'No way!'

That night, after the little ones were tucked up in bed, the wine-infused sentimentalist described the five-week expedition across western Europe which he and the children had planned out. Many hands had made light work of a thousand-piece jigsaw puzzle, leaving a lumpy *montage* of famous eighteenth- and nineteenth-century edifices on the coffee table.

Jeff had also written a passionate song about the correlation between maturity and his ability to handle separation, providing these heaven-sent evenings continued. His spellbound wife caressed her crooning husband at the piano while he sang to her, his blatant heart sitting proud on his sleeve once more.

***

Jeff Diamond turned thirty, in Earth-years at least, on the second of June nineteen-eighty-two. In the eyes of the world, he and his perfect, photogenic family could do no wrong. He had written and recorded the "Terrors and

Triumphs" album during his performing sabbatical, and it had shot to Number One in over twenty countries within a few days of release.

The album's signature single also topped the charts for several weeks, inspired by the songwriter's tongue-in-cheek interpretation of the recent Steven Spielberg movie about a boy, a bike and an extra-terrestrial with a robotic command of the English language and a neck which measured his level of anxiety. He had taken his son to see the film; their first trip to the cinema together, peppered with detours to the toilet and lolly bar.

Soon to turn five, Jet couldn't wait to re-enact his favourite scenes in the garden at *Escondido*. Enlisting his father's help with interpreting some of the themes he was too young to understand, the budding director cast the rest of his extended family in various roles until, one-by-one, they found excuses to return inside.

Wheeling round at a certain point, the youngster realised he was alone on set and unleashed his artistic fury on the world. 'Dad!' he hurried across the grass, pretending to grip imaginary handlebars.

'What?' Jeff shouted back from the kitchen deck.

'Where's Mum?'

'She's gone inside. What's up?'

Still in character, the lad threw his invisible bicycle down onto its side on the *patio* and ran closer to the house. 'Why's everyone gone?'

'Things to do, mate,' his dad explained. 'Things to do.'

Guilt sprang from the rock star's conscience, seeing the boy stamp his foot. His face was contorted, desperate not to cry. The millionnaire continued turning pages in his pile of overdue correspondence, signing on dotted lines for the next stage in each of the Diamonds' projects.

'Why?' his son carried on whining. 'Hey! Please, thank you, how are you? I don't care. Just someone come and play with me.'

The busy celebrity couldn't help laughing, even though he identified far more strongly than he should with the heartfelt plea beneath the surface of his son's frustration. He fought to counter a rush of nausea at images of his own father taunting him with food at about Jet's age. Anxious to spend time with the man he so seldom saw, he remembered being encouraged to follow the mean-spirited criminal onto the landing, only to have the door slammed in his face.

Putting his pen down, the lost boy from Canley Vale placed his empty coffee mug on top of the paperwork to prevent them from taking flight on the stiff sea breeze. No child of his would be rejected in such a hurtful way. None of their good causes was worth this much.

Even as a toddler, Jet had always held an inbuilt fascination for life on other planets, and when "ET" brought his dreams to life on the big screen, a perennial seed had been sown. Like Eliot, Lynn and Jeff's little boy had a bicycle and a younger sister, leading him to believe he too could promote love and friendship between his fellow Earthlings and their interplanetary buddies. If only he could figure out how to make his bike fly...

Australia's favourite musical couple had been married for six-and-a-half years, with barely a cross word spoken in that time. Stronger together, they always said. And they meant it. Friends' marriages started and ended around them, but none seemed as connected as Lynn Dyson and Jeff Diamond.

Neither lover questioned each other's movements and associations when they were apart, such was the faith they held in their partnership. If anything, going their separate ways with voracious *paparazzi* hounds hiding round every corner proved their confidence rather than threatened it.

The successful *duo*'s frontman had revealed the secret ingredient in their relationship to an interviewer, minutes before the curtain went up on his birthday concert; an event billed as Lynn's way of thanking the man who had shown her what real life and real love were all about.

'We make love,' he emphasised. 'And by that, I mean we create it, wherever and whenever we can, with whomever we can. Most often with each other, of course. Goes without saying! Then, when our kids came along, Lynn and I wondered if we had enough love to spread across all of us, but it just keeps getting more and more intense. It's amazing. I wouldn't change a thing.'

The flourishing family continued to invite the cameras into their house as part of a regular television series. There was even talk of a dedicated cable channel to show a constant stream of music videos, their movies and these documentaries, such was the demand for all things Diamond.

One early episode showed the happiest scene at home at *Escondido* on a bright summer's day, with Jet and Kierney playing in the front courtyard, which had been designed to resemble a Mexican village square, complete with cobblestones and a tiered fountain.

Jeff spoke to the camera about how the two children were developing their own distinct characters. 'They're both extremely inclusive, but in different ways,' he said, seeking and receiving a smile of confirmation from their mother. 'Jet'll come in and collide with you. His world gobbles yours up 'cause he's so keen to get going. Your grey, adult world's suddenly awash with the brightest primary colours for the first few minutes, until everything settles down.

'But with Kizzy, she'll sidle up and wait beside you while her pastel-coloured world gradually seeps into your grey one. Only when the melding's complete will she assume control. It's fascinating to see them at work.'

This was the kind of inside information of which the Australian public never tired. It wasn't so much the fast cars, the picturesque *hacienda* or the high-profile lifestyle that kept the photogenic family so welcome in the country's living rooms. Rather, it was their extraordinary ordinariness which was infectious. Parents frequently spoke about dynamics between their children, but only Lynn and Jeff Diamond made it sound so meaningful.

Another back-office bright idea, in her capacity as chief organiser of their life singular, was to agree a palatable theme for the Sydney memorial parade. This feat required careful positioning with the local council since Diamond Senior's time on Earth was not worth celebrating in and of itself; he was a confessed and convicted murderer who had given his children one of the worst starts in life she could imagine. The loving wife and mother longed to stage a pageant to show the area's downtrodden population, not to mention the more privileged ones around them who seldom cared to find out, that her husband had shown it was possible to avoid falling victim to a life without prospects and prosperity.

The rear-end of the famous pantomime horse managed to keep the whole event secret for long enough to arrange a route beginning at the flat where Madalena and Jeff had grown up, proceeding past their high school and their paternal grandparents' home, and ending up at Alberto's boxing club. While the philanthropic gipsy was overseas, she had even flown up to meet with the ailing Chilean, along with her befuddled sister-in-law. It had felt clandestine and deceitful, but her intentions were honourable. She wanted her miracle-worker to be able to commemorate his dad's life by making it a day for recognising people's good qualities.

The parade was to consist of pupils from high schools in the area, the New South Wales Police Band, sporting teams and representatives from the closest regiments of the Army, Air Force and Navy, together with the many charity employees and volunteers supported by the Diamond Celebration Foundation. Outside the thriving training centre, universities and trade colleges were to set up stalls for students to obtain information about careers and options for further education. And lastly, a group of nurses and social workers would be on hand to speak to young people, especially girls, about the importance of contraception and not using pregnancy as a way to escape taking responsibility for their future.

With only a raw but eager collective of voices, the soulful *contralto* recorded and released a single within a week. Radio stations all over the world pounced on it, generating substantial interest from the news media too. Its optimistic theme hit home, with the star's universally identifiable trademark. An abundance of money or fame was not required for one person to walk with another towards a better future.

People arrived in their droves, from far and wide, keen to support their favourite superstars, but more importantly to stand up for their fellow man, woman and child. This inherently simple idea had inspired people in all walks of life, and the thirty-year-old was proud of his silver-spoon lady and her cavernous heart.

The night after *La Grande Marche*, Lynn and Jeff made sweet music again all alone, staying in a family suite at the Intercontinental with the children and their nannies next-door. They were confident Paul Diamond had been given an appropriate send-off and that his sorry legacy would live on in a positive and hopeful light.

The golden-haired beauty turned to her contented black stallion, verging on sleep after indulging in some exquisite carnal fulfilment. 'Let's not let our love get lost in the general crap of life.'

'Seconded, angel,' he smiled, as his words came winging their way back to him in the dark.

And if the memories of that day weren't sweet enough, a week later, Cathy Lane delivered an envelope received by their publishing company, hand-addressed to the couple and with "PLEASE DO NOT BEND" in large lettering on both sides. It contained a simple note saying, "Thought you might like this," and a photograph of the loving mother leaning down to talk to her son at his Granddad's parade. She was stroking his cheek while the youngster bit his lip and put on a brave face for the crowds.

This priceless *memento* from someone of generous spirit took pride of place on the office wall at *Escondido*, admired by all who set eyes on it. Yet despite taking out a full-page spread in the New South Wales, Queensland and Victorian daily newspapers to thank the anonymous photographer, the young parents were never to find out who had sent the gift.

***

Suitcases packed, nannies dispatched to their respective destinations and peaceful *hacienda* prepared for lockdown, the Diamonds were off on their European voyage. It was to be the last family holiday before the Dyson sporting induction started in earnest for young Jet, committing him to spend the majority of the next ten years' school-free days in training. A similar plan was also in store for Kierney the following year.

Jeff had been impatient for the children to be old enough to appreciate the beauty and culture of Europe. The family's itinerary was to originate in Rome, whence they would gain a subtle and gradual appreciation for the true meaning of the word "classical". Although Aboriginal relics had been dated back tens of thousands of years, they bore few recognisable hallmarks of a historic period. Modern-day settlers in Australia were wrong to consider the mid-eighteenth century as the beginning of time; positively infantile when compared to most of the developed world, which of course was but a juvenile next to Egyptian and other middle-eastern cultures.

The perennial student promised his offspring, and therefore himself, that it wouldn't be too long before they had the opportunity to come full-circle and honour the indigenous version of the same concept. A whole lifetime of educational holidays lay ahead of them, the knowledge-hungry father mused. Leading up to their departure, he and his ambitious wife had read their little sponges several stories about Roman times and brutal gladiatorial conquests to turn even their grandpa pale.

After Rome, the travellers planned to take a train to Lake Como, to tackle the second phenomenon: geographical boundaries. How was it possible to climb a mountain whose base was in one country and its summit in another? Then on to Dijon, France, again by train winding through The Alps, where they would meet up with Junior, Julie and their two boys.

They would also encounter a third special exhibit here: plants which had been growing in the same place since the tenth century *Anno Domini*. It was imperative, as the intellectual had explained to his enchanted pupils, that all adults sample the fruits of these venerable vineyards.

Paris, without question, would be the everlasting lovers' preeminent destination, excited to treat themselves to the abundance of pleasurable sensory experiences that the French capital had to offer. Lynn also looked forward to celebrating her twenty-seventh birthday in the romantic location with her loved ones and her elder brother's family, before the Dyson *troupe* headed home to the farm. Their addition to the trip had been last-minute, when Melbourne Football Club had made an unexpected exit from the finals season!

And so to London, back to the scenes of the first blissful year the star-crossed couple had spent together in their small flat, surrounded by friends and without a family member in sight. These had been happy and carefree times, during which many of the projects these days consuming hundreds of hours every month had been merely the pipe-dreams of two idealistic humanitarians lapping up the wisdom of intellectuals and libertarians alike.

In the car on the way to the airport, the parents tested the youthful brains for various phrases in the languages they would soon be using with natives who hadn't been imported to Australia to help raise them. Both passed with flying colours, receiving a special treat of chocolates thrown over the driver's shoulders. Jet and Kierney laughed so hard that they could scarcely hold themselves upright against their seatbelts.

'Where do you want to go most?' Lynn asked the excitable siblings. 'Not including you, *Papá*.'

Jeff pulled a sad face but stayed compliantly quiet. He checked out the children's expressions in the rear-view mirror. Their *mamá* had posed a tough question.

'I'll like the mountains,' Jet decided after a few seconds, before backtracking from the idea. 'But there won't be snow, will there?'

'No. Most likely not,' Lynn confirmed. 'But they'll still be impressive. Much higher than Falls Creek.'

'I want to see the chariots on top of the building,' Kierney joined in.

'In which city?' her dad challenged, turning round and giving her a wide smile.

The youngster took a deep breath and prepared to roll her "r"s like a native, as proud as punch. '*En R-r-r-roma,*' she giggled.

'*Si, signorina!*' the linguist replied, repeating the little girl's effort in a much louder voice than she could muster. '*En R-r-r-r-roma.*'

'And who's on those chariots?' Lynn asked.

'We are!' her son answered. 'Unity and Liberty. Ryan and Kierney.'

'Good stuff, mate. D'you remember those two, *pequeñita?*'

'*Sí, Papá. Me acuerdo.*'

Aeroplane travel was humdrum for the Diamond children, at ease with the protocol when they reached their rows. Both climbed into their seats and looked out of the window while their parents took care of hand luggage filled with amusements for all ages. Most of the time, they flew for an hour or two around Australia, which was no big deal for anyone. The prospect of spending a whole day in the same spot filled Jet with dread, as it did his mum and dad.

'You can swap seats with Kiz every now and again,' Lynn suggested with a smile.

Pretending he wasn't listening, Jeff watched the indignant lad put hands on hips at his mother's ridiculous idea. 'Kizzy's seat's just as boring as mine,' he whined.

'No, it's not,' his little sister was offended. 'I like my seat.'

'I like your seat too,' the father told his tiny, easy-to-please neighbour, 'because you're in it.'

Kierney grinned at the tall handsome man next to whom she was installed, leaning against his side with heavy eyelids. The young mother ruffled the songwriter's hair in appreciation from the row behind, and he reached a long right arm around to locate a convenient body-part to squeeze in return. The flight attendants fussed about them as usual, surprised to see the family travelling in the Economy section.

'It's better with the kids,' Lynn explained. 'It's not fair when people have paid extra for a seat in what turns out to be Kindergarten Class.'

Arriving in Julius Caesar's domicile was a relief for all four, despite no major incident on the journey. Despite Jeff's Italian having a definite Spanish flavour, the taxi driver had no idea at first as to the identity of his passengers. However, the penny dropped as soon as they mentioned Australia, causing him to go into a typical Latin spin. Jet gaped at his mother in amazement while the man's hands gesticulated, his voice becoming louder and louder.

'Is the driver telling Dad off?' the boy asked in a confused whisper.

Australia's darling chuckled. 'No. I don't think so. He's excited to be taking us to our hotel, that's all.'

'*R-r-r-r-roma,*' Kierney rolled from her mother's lap, pointing at an overhead traffic sign. '*R-r-r-roma, Papá. ¿Lo que ves?*'

'*Sí, bambina mia,*' Jeff nodded. '*Fantastico! Siamo in vacanza!*'

The family spent the next three days walking the length and breadth of the ancient and modern citadels, devouring *pizza* and *spaghetti* and drinking some of the best coffee they had ever tasted. They had booked into a bed and breakfast run by a retired banker and his wife. Off the main tourist track, Lynn had received the suggestion from a friend of her parents. Their host made a huge fuss of the children whenever she saw them, much to Jet's revulsion. He was not a baby anymore, as he kept reminding his mum and dad, and old ladies were only supposed to kiss babies.

'Sorry, mate. I don't like it much either, but Silvana just wants to be friendly. Italian people love a good snog.'

His daughter laughed. 'So you and *Mamá* have to live in Italy all the time.'

'Good idea,' Lynn said, cupping her husband's stubbly chin in both hands and planting a big kiss on his lips.

Wide-eyed, the vacationing sex-god grinned at the youngsters. 'Whoa! That was amazing. Can you say that again, please, Kizzo.'

'You and Mamá must live in Italy so you can kiss all the time,' the happy child obliged.

Nothing happened.

Sister and brother stood waiting with their mouths open for a repeat performance, only for the blonde beauty to carry on unpacking as if she had lost all interest in the dark-haired Adonis by her side. Then, with their little hearts about to implode with disappointment, the joker leaped on his wife, almost knocking her over. Jet and Kierney sprang up, not wishing to miss out on a ferocious cuddle, and pretty soon everyone was in a heap on the floor.

'We love being on holidays, don't we, guys?' Lynn laughed, pulling each child up by the first arm she caught hold of, leaving Jeff with no-one left to kiss or tickle. '*Chi vuole il gelato?*'

'Me!' Jet exclaimed, bouncing up and down.

'*Scusi?*'

'*Io!*' the boy translated. '*Per favore, Mamá.*'

'*E io, per favore,*' Kierney added, tugging at her mum's skirt.

'*Grazie due. E tu, Papá?*'

'OK. If I must,' he teased, leaning in for another kiss, which was declined overtly this time.

The following morning, the family were up and out after an early breakfast, psyched up and ready to visit the statues of Unity and Liberty atop the Vittorio Emanuele war memorial building. Jeff embraced his beautiful best friend as their two living emblems gazed up at the sculptures after which they had been named, in awe that they were seeing them up close at long last.

Their dad had often brought these monuments to life in stories or through pictures in various books, but the parents were delighted that, even at their tender ages, a sense of identity and distinct purpose were emerging in the little people they had created.

'This is you two in the olden days,' their father told them, crouching down and putting a hand around each. 'People had to fight for what they believed in back then. Real fighting. Battles, y'know...'

Both youngsters nodded, mesmerised by the bronze figures carried in chariots on massive wheels and muscular horses with flared nostrils. The tennis champion glided past the *trio* to photograph the special moment. The intense young philosopher had been looking forward to sharing this sight ever since their boy-child had first arrived.

Their next stop was the Colosseum. The MCG of Rome, the sportswoman joked, much to the artistic authority's disapproval. Again, Jet and Kierney listened to their parents' description of gladiators who fought with lions and bulls, and how ordinary people would gather under the stage to wait for their turn. The five-year-old had found it particularly funny when his mother likened Grandpa Dyson and Uncle Junior to gladiators, unable to imagine them dressed in short skirts and strange, feathery caps.

'Just shows how stadium design hasn't changed much in a millennium,' Lynn thought aloud, leaning over one of the walls to the multiple tiers of seating below.

'Yep,' her husband nodded. 'Except for snack bars and women's toilets.'

They had planned to visit the Vatican and the Sistine Chapel, but had been told by some American tourists at a nearby table over lunch that the queue snaked almost to the banks of the Tiber. Not expecting the children to tolerate such a long wait with only priceless art and sculpture as their reward, they changed their plans. Instead, they took a taxi northwards to the old part of town, where the narrow streets were steeped in history and graced with designer boutiques.

'D'you know where we're going next, *pequeñita?*' the ecstatic globetrotter asked his daughter, who was beginning to fall asleep on his knee with the stop-start motion.

'No, *Papá?*'

'*La fontana di Trevi.* Remember what it is?'

'*Agua pura,*' the girl recalled.

'Trevi Fountain,' her brother joined in. 'Where we can throw some money in and make a wish and give poor people some food.'

'*Exactamente,*' Jeff smiled, hugging his son with his spare hand. 'A wish for the sandwich shop.'

Lynn chuckled, familiar with the story behind her husband's quirky interpretation. He had told them the day before that the word "*panini*" translated to sandwiches, and the man who sculpted the last few statues at the Trevi Fountain was named Giuseppe Pannini. The know-all had gone on to teach them that in recent years the city council of Rome had been using the money tossed in to the water by romantic tourists to run a discount supermarket for needy people.

The taxi dropped its passengers off in a dead-end street a couple of blocks from the fountain. Huge crowds thronged, snapping photographs of each other and marvelling at the magnificent architecture. Many a disbelieving double-take greeted the iconic Australian family as they tried to slip into the scene unnoticed. They had no choice but to strike poses with strangers for a good fifteen minutes, signing autographs and answering the same questions over and over again.

The children, although bored by all the fuss on such a warm day, remained patient and doled out blithe smiles on demand. Their sympathetic mother grinned, letting them know it wouldn't be long before they could continue their walk. Jeff brought the *impromptu* media call to a close, requesting some privacy while they visited the fountain.

'*Quante monete vi gettano nella fontana, figlia-issima?*' he father asked Kierney, who was enchanted by the brilliance of the marble masterpieces, with the sunlight reflecting off the water.

Jet was equally impressed by the flow cascading into the curvaceous trough, amazed at how he had been able to hear its thunderous volume increasing from several streets away.

'*Due, Papá,*' his sister smiled, unable to stand still with such excitement.

'*Perché solo due?* Isn't the song "Three Coins In A Fountain"?'

The rock star crooned the well-known lyric, much to the joy of those around. Kierney repeated the lines back to him, bringing tears to his eyes. With Lynn's hand on his shoulder, he felt her kiss the top of his arm through his T-shirt.

'I only want to throw two,' Jet agreed. 'I don't want to get a divorce.'

'You're not even married,' the thirty-year-old joked, dealing him a playful nudge. 'Are you? Did I miss your wedding?'

'No!' the lad sneered in disgust. 'Course not!'

'*Due è storia romantica. No, Papá?*' Kierney reminded them. '*Tutti dobbiamo gettare due.*'

'*Buono. Perfetto, bambina,*' her dad laughed. 'It's a deal. *Andiamo allora.*'

Plundering the contents of Lynn's purse and Jeff's pockets, the family rustled up eight identical coins. They edged their way to the rails, making space for the diminutive pair to squeeze in front of their parents' legs to secure a clear view of where to cast their romance tokens.

Later on, the quartet had dinner outside, sitting at a restaurant table not far from the fountain. Most of the waiters were American students, also pumped to meet the famous couple. The children were tired, and soon occupied a parent's lap to drift off to sleep, allowing the lovers the opportunity to enjoy the rest of their bottle of wine while soaking up the serene atmosphere and unhurried service.

'I'm having the absolute best time,' the Olympian announced, blowing her husband a kiss.

Stubbing out his cigarette and directing the smoke over the top of Jet's blond head, he took his wife's outstretched hand and kissed it. 'Me too, angel. I love you, *signora.*'

'*Grazie mille.* I love you too. This is a very special time. The kids are so inquisitive, and you seem to get such a kick out of encouraging them. I hope it lasts for a long time, this phase.'

'Me too, angel, *di nuovo,*' Jeff repeated, his impish smile setting her heart racing. 'I love you, *signora bellissima.*'

'*Grazie mille, di nuovo!* And I want to rip your clothes off and roll around in our uncomfortable bed as soon as possible,' the golden-haired songstress added, placing gentle hands over Kierney's ears.

Jeff feigned surprise but made it his duty not to object. 'Me too, angel. Be my guest.'

Why on Earth were they still sitting in this restaurant when such an offer was on another, more insubstantial table? He wasted no time in gathering their son up in his arms and signalling for the waiter to bring their bill. Lynn peeled out several notes from his wallet, for which her hand had plunged suggestively into his pants pocket, almost letting her precious load slip down to the ground in the process.

The little girl moaned as her feet touched the hard stone, thinking she would have to walk. Her mother hoisted her onto her hip, whence she drifted straight back to sleep. Once inside the dark hallway of their accommodation, Jeff's right hand fumbled along the wall until it found the light switch, and both adults stifled laughs.

Jet awoke and rubbed his eyes, realising they were already in their bedroom. 'Are we here?' he murmured. 'Is it night time?'

'Yes, son,' the father confirmed, slipping the boy's pyjama top over his head. '*E domani ci andiamo a Lago di Como.*'

'*En el tren?*' Kierney asked from behind their tour guide.

'*En treno. Si,*' he translated her Spanish into Italian. '*Eccitante, no?*'

'*Si,*' Lynn laughed, sighing. '*Tempo a letto, papá.*'

'Of course,' Jeff winked at the siren silhouetted in the doorway. 'D'you think I'd forget?'

'Are you going to have sex?' the innocent three-year-old asked.

'None of your business, *pequeñita*,' the doting dad kissed his daughter's scalp, whispering in her ear. 'I hope so.'

The little girl giggled and put her hand in front of her mouth as if she had heard something she shouldn't have.

'What did he say?' her mum enquired, suspicious.

Kierney shook her head.

'Nice work, Kizzo,' the conspirator chuckled. '*Tempo a letto*, guys.'

With the children locked into the bedroom next-door, the world's greatest lover closed their own door. Curling one hand round the back of his wife's neck and pulling her towards him, he leaned leftwards and laid the key onto a small table in the corner.

Lynn slipped her fingers around his waist, sweeping down until they found the points of his hipbones. As his breathing quickened, the pair of sensual palms travelled up and down his back before heading to undo his belt and trousers. There was most definitely something about *R-r-r-r-roma* that brought out the Latin in both of them…

Their lips locked and tongues searching, Jeff unbuttoned his beautiful best friend's dress and peeled it over her shoulders, caressing the firm mounds beneath her bra. His right hand clamped her buttock, lending extra resistance as she writhed with the sensation of his fingertips inside her panties. She moaned in his ear, and it turned him on further.

'*Tempo a letto, Mamá*,' the charmer repeated, bringing her to orgasm.

The couple lay down as the overworked mattress objected, and the wrought iron frame rocked and jolted in response to their steady motion. The songwriter smiled whenever his wife tensed up, scared they were about to end up in a pile on the floor with an embarrassing confession to make to Silvana in the morning.

'This is Italy, angel,' he whispered in her ear. 'Everyone's at it. Silvana'd expect nothing less.'

Lynn let out a long, slow moan, and her eyes filled with tears of joy as rapture overtook her for a second climax.

He kissed her mouth with deep-seated passion. '*Ti amo*, baby.'

'*Ti amo, amore mio.*'

Como's scenery was a picture postcard brought to life for the touring party, who checked into their lakeside hotel in double-quick time to jump aboard a tourist boat across the mirrored water. The children's incessant chatter flitted from their passage through dark mountains with snowy caps and steep, tree-covered sides, described by their resident poet as "unshaven cheeks", and flying over the spectacular highs and lows in a tiny bi-plane they had spied tracking alongside the train as they trundled into the station.

Their eyes popping out of their heads at the sight of a funicular ready to take them from Italy to Switzerland for a single upward fare, both little ones were lulled into a stupor in their seats by Jeff's romantic quotes from F. Scott Fitzgerald's "Tender Is The Night".

'He wrote something like, "Mountain-climbing cars are built on a slant like the angle of a hat brim of a man who doesn't want to be recognised."'

'That's funny,' Jet giggled.

The children fell asleep on the padded benches while they waited for the carriages to fill up. The Europhile songwriter beguiled his adult companion with more quotations from the same novel, reeled off word-for-word with little effort.

'Angel, this one's for you... "She crossed and re-crossed her knees frequently in the manner of tall restless virgins." How evocative is that?'

Lynn smiled, one hand stroking her husband's back in idle semi-circles. 'It's lovely. Like you, he must've been regularly in the company of tall, restless virgins.'

'Indeed,' Jeff cocked his head. 'Why not? No point leaving the US for Europe and not partaking in the luxuries of life, huh? How about this? Talking about the beauty of the lake. "Upon it floated swans like boats and boats like swans..."'

'Is this thing electric?' Lynn asked, staring outside at the mechanism of wires and greased cogs. 'I can't hear any engines, and those cables look pretty thin to pull us all the way up there?'

'It's water-powered,' the intellectual shrugged, 'which may not make you feel any more secure!'

'Water?'

'Yep. Look up, guys...' the wise man ushered their roused offspring to the opposite side of the carriage, whence Jeff explained how the car above was in the process of having its tanks pumped full of water to make it heavier than all the people in theirs. Gravity would then cause it to sink to the bottom while they rose to the top.

'*Yin* and *yang*,' Kierney chanted, swinging her father's arm in increasing and decreasing circles. '*Como la mamá y el papá.*

***

The small town of Dijon, famous for its mustard even though the seeds hailed from Canada, nestled in the rolling countryside of the Burgundy region of eastern France. With vineyards dating back to the tenth and eleventh centuries, the buildings and landscape had remained untouched for much of that time. Away from the hillsides where the best wine grew, small towns and villages housed the more modern aspects of life, leaving the higher ground for perfecting *les Grands Crus* and *les Premiers Crus* for which the region was renowned.

The Diamonds arrived in their hotel, named after Philippe le Bon, one of the district's most significant founders, after another train journey which had seen the family wind through formidable mountains and beside the lakes of Switzerland. Jet and Kierney had spent the first hour with their noses glued to the window, marvelling at the type of scenery they would never find in Australia. After a while however, spectacular began to bore them, and they reverted to cheating at silly card games with their parents.

Junior, Julie and their boys had arrived a few hours earlier and were already checked into their rooms at the same hotel. Quite by chance, the two Australian mobs bumped into each other in the centre of town, both being stalked by a number of fans, who couldn't believe their luck when all eight coincided in the narrow streets. The sets of cousins were over the moon, galloping in circles in the manner of military horses around the square where they decided to stop for an afternoon coffee.

Luckily for the adults, one of the nannies whom Lynn and Jeff had employed to look after much tinier children was now a qualified primary school teacher in Strasbourg. The young mum had rung Nadine when they had first planned their holiday, hoping she could help them out on their arrival in France. The Frenchwoman had jumped at the chance of seeing *les petits diamants* again, and the four parents were gifted a ready-made childminder.

In the courtyard of their hotel, the holidaymakers and their willing helper gathered to schedule their forty-eight hours in Dijon. Jeff drew a matrix on a sheet of paper and started to list all the places they wanted to visit down the left-hand side.

'Lynn has taught you well,' his brother-in-law teased.

For the headings of the other two columns, the tour guide wrote "JuJuSoBr" and "JeLyJeKi".

'What's "ju-ju-sober"?' asked Jet, who by now thought he was the best reader in town.

'It's this lot,' the wordsmith replied, waving towards the other family.

'Ju-ju-sober? Is it French? What does it mean?'

'Mate, it's a secret code,' his dad said, putting his finger to his mouth. 'So nobody knows who we are.'

Nadine laughed, unable to resist her former boss' contagious playfulness. 'But everyone knows who you are.'

'Yeah. That's true,' the rock star sighed before raising his voice again. 'Hey, kids… Who knows what an abbreviation is?'

All four shook their heads.

'*Mamá*, do you know?' Jeff smiled, seeing his dream girl raise her hand.

'Or do you just need to be excused?' Junior chuckled. 'Go on, Lynn. Show us your education wasn't wasted.'

The usually elegant woman stuck her tongue out at her brother, making the children laugh. 'An abbreviation's what you say when you can't be bothered to say the whole word or set of words,' she told the eager youngsters. 'Like "breckie" instead of breakfast, or "RACV" for the Royal Automobile Club of Victoria.'

'Oh, I know,' her son piped up. 'Like Kiz instead of Kierney?'

'Perfect, mate,' his father gave the lad a high-five. 'But not Jet instead of Ryan because they're different names. Anyway, "JuJuSoBr" is my abbreviation for these guys, so we don't have to always say Junior, Julie, Sonny and Bruce.'

'You could always just say "the Dysons",' the footballer's wife suggested.

'Too easy,' the comic responded, lifting his beer bottle to the subdued woman. 'Have another drink, Jules.'

His sister-in-law was pregnant again, therefore denied alcohol on their epic holiday. She clearly didn't enjoy watching the others having so much fun, frowning at the handsome musician.

'"Jelly-jeeky",' Sonny laughed at his cousin, reading the top of the right-hand column on Jeff's sheet of paper. '"Jelly-jeeky"? That sounds funny.'

'So does "ju-ju-sober",' the indignant five-year-old replied.

'OK, OK,' Lynn stopped the boys from getting too silly. 'I think we've found some good names to call ourselves while we're together. 'They're the "Ju-ju-sobers" and we're the "Jelly-jeekies". *Merci beaucoup, Papá!*'

'*De rien, ma chérie*,' Jeff winked at his wife, who cradled a drowsy Kierney on her knee.

Pretty soon, the excursionists had fine-tuned their schedule, and the two mothers showed Nadine up to their bedrooms. The dads took all four kids to a nearby park to run their batteries down before the parents were due to hit the town's sights.

'This was a great idea,' Junior said. 'The boys are so looking forward to spending time with you guys, and we're desperate for adult company.'

'Is Julie OK?' the peacemaker asked. 'She seems pretty quiet.'

'Shit, yeah. It's been a tough few months, to tell you the truth. We're not getting on that well, and I don't really know why. Perhaps because we're stuck up at Narrandera. Jules gets bored. I've tried setting stuff up for her to get involved with, but she's not interested, even though she knows it'd be easier to make friends if she was.'

His brother-in-law frowned. 'Do you have to live up there?'

'For the moment, we do,' the footballer nodded. 'I'd like to get things ticking over for another two years or so. She was happy with that timeframe initially, but then it became a bad idea all of a sudden.'

'When she got knocked up again?'

'Maybe, but probably even before that,' Junior confessed. 'Julie's not like Lynn. She can't immerse herself in things like Lynn and I can. And you too, obviously. She needs to be entertained, and there's just not much entertainment for someone like her in Narrandera.'

Jeff chuckled. 'Nope. Well... Have to admit I agree. I couldn't live that far out. Is she OK with having the kids around? She's not sick of being a mum, is she?'

'Yes, a bit. That's part of it too. You're always so damned perceptive. These two are go-go-go all the time, and she gets tired of the noise and constant fighting, *et cetera*. You know how it is. And now with Number Three coming along, it's going to be rough on all of us.'

'Bummer, mate. Can we help?'

'You are already,' Junior smiled, turning to walk in the opposite direction. 'This holiday's helping heaps. That's where we started, before I spewed out all my woes. This trip'll make a big difference, I think. I want Jules to observe how you guys are around each other.'

'Really?' the musician exclaimed, frowning in jest. 'Have you put cameras in our room?'

Junior punched his brother-in-law on the upper arm. 'No, you idiot. As a family.'

'OK. Cool. Not sure how it'll solve the boredom problem though, but we're happy to oblige. Does Lynn know any of this?'

The sportsman shook his head. 'No. I'm embarrassed to tell her. You know what our family's like. No-one's allowed to have problems.'

'Dyson eternal denial strikes again!' the amateur psychologist sighed in consternation. 'That's not how life works, mate. Jesus! You beat the world at its own games, and yet you can't speak honestly with each other? Just goes to show that nobody's perfect.'

The man many Australians called "Bigger D" shrugged in defeat. 'I s'pose so. You're right. That's what I mean by observing you guys. I need to too.'

'Can *I* tell Lynn?' Jeff asked. 'She might have some bright ideas. It happens a lot.'

'Ha! Yeah, I've noticed. That's embarrassing too. Sure. You can tell her, I guess.'

Kierney and Bruce came running up to their fathers, brandishing a collection of fallen flora.

'*Papa, regarde!*' the little girl shouted from about ten metres away.

'*Plus proche, pequeñita,*' her dad yelled back, beckoning the children to come closer to prevent their shrill voices from cracking the windows of a nearby greenhouse.

The two men sat themselves down on a long bench and prepared for their natural history lesson. Kierney emptied an armful of stuff into her dad's open palms.

'*Qu'est-ce que vous avez là?*' the polyglot asked, leaning forward to kiss the little girl's pink forehead.

'*Les feuilles et d'autres choses. Je ne sais pas ce que c'est.*'

'*Ce que ces sont,*' he corrected, holding up a sample of the specimens to remind Kierney to use the plural part of the verb. '*Moi non plus*, gorgeous. D'you know what these are, Brucey?'

The younger Dyson son shook his head and proceeded to throw all his bits and pieces on the cobblestones in frustration. His cousin pouted at the petulant behaviour, as if she were about to cry. Jeff lifted Bruce onto his knee while ruffling his daughter's hair. Given the fractious behaviour their young ones were displaying, he suggested to Junior that they adjourn to the hotel.

'Kizzo, please run and get your bro' and Sonny?' he requested, clutching all her treasure into his ample fist.

The two younger kids scuttled off to round up the whole gang for their return trip. They whooped in delight to find four beds had been prepared in the same room, a cruel challenge for later on. Nadine welcomed *les gosses* and reverted to ordering them around like the old days in Melbourne. She had always had a good way with them, Lynn assured Julie.

The sights of Dijon seen to their fullest extent, and after an excellent tour of some of the town's oldest vineyards, the families climbed aboard a train bound for Paris. The Dyson boys had picked up quite a large vocabulary of French words, and everyone had got on famously. The Diamonds were sad to say farewell to their old friend, who promised to visit them the following year.

While the children snoozed to the clangorous rhythm of metal wheels rolling over innumerable sleepers, the two Dyson siblings discussed their younger brother's failing health and wondered what the future held for him. Stigma was still rife in the media, particularly in the popular press, and some cruel commentary had taken an additional toll on his resilience as he found himself running defence against endless aspersions concerning the reason for his immune deficiency. Their conservative father remained awkward and intolerant towards Sandy's relationship with Jason, and Marianna was beside herself with worry.

Lynn informed her elder brother that Jeff had been told in no uncertain terms by Bart not to interfere, which had made her blood boil much like it had in the years before they were married. Junior agreed that the more allies Sandy had the better at this stage in his life. Still, neither saw fit to criticise their parents or Australia's sporting bodies. Since there was no sign of a cure once full-blown AIDS took hold, everyone was doing everything they could to make him as comfortable as possible.

'Mum's preparing to lose a child,' the sportsman rued. 'Dad's not. It's as if he's drawn a line under him, like Sandy's no longer part of the family, if you listen to the way Dad talks about him. He's just some sick, gay bastard without a name.'

Jeff sat back, hands cradling his glass of *Côte de Beaune* and keeping his opinions to himself. A few motivational words in a French park had inaugurated a new tradition. Lynn leaned into her steadfast stallion with tears in her eyes, reminding him of those first, tentative conversations they had shared at Benloch ten years ago. She and Sandy had always been close; the big sister preparing to lose someone too.

'At least he's been able to be his own person for the last while,' the tennis champion added. 'And he's been happy too, with Jason and all their friends in San Fran' and New York.'

'Do you think he wishes Dad was more forgiving?' Junior asked.

'Yes. I'm sure he does, but he also understands how hard it is for someone like Dad to come to terms with a son who's turned out so different to him. Even Mum thinks that way, I think. Like they failed somehow. Like Sandy's "not quite right".'

Again the songwriter said nothing, grinning while his wife drew quotation marks in the air. Now was not the time to compare his own relationship with Big D, even though he suspected this to be at the root of his lover's allegation. No-one was past papering over the cracks in his or her perfect world every now and again, when it suited them. He was no exception.

Once installed in the busy metropolis, in a small hotel Jeff had discovered several years earlier near *la Sorbonne*, the two families settled down for the next phase of their European adventure. Ecstatic to return to his favourite city without a punishing work schedule, the lifelong student could scarcely wait to immerse himself in more intellectual pursuits. Boasting magnificent university bookshops around every corner, the narrow, cobbled streets were littered with eccentric-looking academics and fresh, fashionable undergraduates awaiting their opportunity to become eccentric-looking academics.

The *cafés* teemed with customers at most hours of the day, but were at their quietest at the sort of breakfast times the young parents were forced to keep. Although forgoing a sharp nip of *Armagnac* with the day's first dose of caffeine and a sample of the many *anises* the bars displayed on their shelves, the old soul did his best to soak up the atmosphere and pass on its mystique to his fellow travellers.

'"Paris always shows her teeth, laughing when she does not scold. A cluster of mud and stone if you like, but above all things a moral entity."'

'"*Les Misérables*",' his wife told her brother and sister-in-law. 'He knows it off by heart, cover to cover.'

Jeff chuckled at the row of blank stares his quotation had met. '"Daring is the currency of progress." The lady speaks the truth. When I read about

Gavroche, I read my own story. Plain and simple. Being here always makes me want to become a perennial student,' he said, grasping at the air with his fingers. 'There's knowledge swirling all around us. Can't you smell it, guys? This place re-orients people. It's why I want to bring these two... They need to be able to find True North so they learn to set and reset their moral compasses.'

The children watched this strange behaviour in a mixture of wonderment and sympathy. They could smell their parents' strong coffee and Nutella spread on warm, crusty rolls, but they had no idea how their noses might discern the presence of knowledge.

'Let's move here when we retire,' Lynn promised her animated partner, reaching to grab one of his expressive hands and kiss it. 'I can just see you holding court here, with your *cravatte* and long hair, smoking slimline cigars and surrounded by muses of every shade. They'll hang off your every word, *monsieur le* magic man.'

'*Merci bien,* angel,' Jeff smiled, leaning forward to connect with her mouth. 'Sounds perfect. Although I can't help but think you're taking the...'

Jet stared at his father, hoping to be treated to a rude word. He wasn't rewarded this time, much to his disgust.

'I thought your preferred seat of learning was Boston,' Junior said. 'Isn't that why your company's investing so heavily in MIT?'

'From a business perspective, yeah,' he affirmed. 'But retirement's not business. Hope not anyway! Purely to feed our own desires. Our personal development plans, in Dyson terms. MIT's going to change the world on a truly practical level, but learning here's more about the attainment of spiritual and philosophical wisdom. For me, this place is for fixing the next world.'

'The next world? What on Earth are you talking about?' Julie sneered. 'What next world? Heaven or another planet? Are you going to colonise the Moon? Delusions of grandeur or what!'

'He means for when our souls come back next time,' Lynn was quick to advocate for her husband's ardent quest, yet with no clear evidence to support it either.

The former marketing adviser scoffed. 'Oh, right! You're just as fanciful as he is. You guys get into enough trouble fixing today's problems, let alone trying to change the future.'

'Don't mock it 'til you try it, Jules,' the ambitious man shrugged, catching his brother-in-law's eye. 'You might like it. Smoke a joint with me tonight, and we'll see what that does to your flights of fancy.'

'I'm pregnant!' the indignant, short-tempered mother reminded him. 'My child'll get high. I'll wait until I get to the next world.'

The handsome songwriter raised a hand as if he were inviting her to continue. 'See?' he smiled, taking hold of another imaginary bubble of knowledge and throwing it Julie's way. 'Paris is working for you too. You're already thinking more broadly. But seriously… Only focussing on this week, next month or even the next twenty years isn't enough. We won't be prepared to take advantage of what's on offer.'

Junior nodded, taking his wife's hand. He had to admit Jeff Diamond was an impressive man, and matched with his farsighted sister, their partnership was formidable. This charismatic rock star was an expert at teaching people who thought they already knew enough, whereas Lynn specialised in teaching those who wanted to know more. Maybe Julie needed a bit of both, but he wasn't game to suggest it. He too elected to rely on Paris to do its wondrous thing.

The blonde chart-topper had booked an outing on their first evening in the city of lights, for which the children would be staying up beyond their normal bedtime; even later than their special holiday bedtime, in fact. They were all hysterical about such a treat, especially once they found out about the open-topped bus. After huge piles of *spaghetti Bolognese*, the famous octet caused a predictable *furore* at the tour company's offices while waiting for the double-decker to arrive.

Each tourist was given a set of earphones to be plugged into sockets on the vehicle's side walls, causing great hilarity among the boys as they attempted to walk down the aisle, stretching the cords to their limit and having them ping off of their ears without warning. When the novelty of this trick had worn off, their new game was to tangle each other up as tightly as they could with their earphone wires, until Bruce's neck was constricted a little too far by his older brother, at which point Junior called a halt.

All the while, three-year-old Kierney sat on her father's lap, content to leave the spirited shenanigans to her cousins. Clearly, this city suited her too. It wouldn't take long for their thoughtful girl to outgrow whiskers on kittens and bright copper kettles. Given half a chance, Lynn was sure, *café cognac*, *Pastis* and cannabis joints would soon count among her favourite things.

The intuitive mother had rendered Jeff speechless with this analogy earlier the same evening, and they had spent an hour before dinner teaching both children the Mary Poppins song, being creative with the lyrics while staying within the bounds of minority.

Once all the passengers were on board, the tour set off, the illuminations of *Paris par nuit* awaiting them. The commentary was available in English, to Junior and Julie's relief, and the bus negotiated frenetic evening congestion and the many other tourist coaches quite well, with only a single track of irate horns blowing as size won out at certain tight junctions.

At the enormous, star-shaped roundabout around *l'Arc de Triomphe*, the adults were apprehensive as their carriage made a beeline for eight or more lanes of fast-moving traffic. From his cabin down below, the driver had figured out long ago that the only way to break through the endless stream was to drive straight into the middle. Thankfully, a path opened up, allowing the nervous passengers an up-close-and-personal view of the carved names commemorating French battles through the ages.

The next stop was the Eiffel Tower, which they approached from the north of the River Seine. Bored with the historical aspect of the tour, the three boisterous playmates began to jump around, bouncing on the slippery plastic surface dangerously close to the low railing. For the first time since JuJuSoBr had joined JeLyJeKi, Jeff's ire was released.

'Hey, Jetto! Stop jumping on the seats, guys. Right now, please.'

His deep baritone was scarily firm as he grabbed Sonny and Jet by the arm and dragged them down hard into a sitting position. His eyes drilled into young Bruce's to encourage him to do the same.

'Either stand on the floor or sit still. One or the other.'

The two Dyson boys were shocked to hear their fun-loving uncle sound so menacing all of a sudden, with Jet snapping an immediate apology. He too recognised something serious must be afoot, given the abnormal show of anger directed at the *trio*'s antics.

By no means finished berating the youngsters, and doing his best to shield them from a deck full of nosey onlookers, the thirty-year-old shuffled all three boys to the edge of the bus, instructing them to look over the side.

'Can you see how far down the ground is? If you fell out, you'd hit the pavement bloody hard.'

Certain his message had been understood, the teacher persisted. 'We don't want to spend our holiday visiting you in hospital,' he said, this time a little calmer and with the city lights revealing colourful tears glistening in his eyes. 'Or worse, taking you home in a box. Understand, guys?'

'Yes, Dad,' Jet responded, giving his father's legs a sincere hug before walking around to the seat behind, where his mother and sister were sitting. 'I'm sorry. I'll be careful. I don't want to be in hospital or in a box.'

'Good man. Thanks. Me neither,' Jeff smiled his forgiveness, tapping each boy's head with his fingers like a set of outlandish altar bongos. 'That's OK. Just stand and look out as we drive along. The tower's going to start flashing in a second.'

Sure enough, the light show transformed all three hundred metres of the iconic spire, starting right on cue to a chorus of "oohs" and "ahhs". There must have been six or seven tour buses all crammed into the same vantage point.

From the row behind, Junior slapped his brother-in-law's back. 'Well said, mate. Stay calm now, boys. No more jumping around.'

Fortunately, the illuminations had distracted their fellow passengers from the celebrity *fracas*. Kierney shuffled across to sit on her mother's lap, and she too leaned over the rail to gauge the long drop to the stone paving below. The little girl didn't like to hear her *papá* shouting. It happened so rarely and only for a genuine reason. Cuddling her in close, Lynn donated one of her earpieces so she could listen to the rousing piped classical music completing the sensory symphony.

With the boys now well and truly under control, Jeff put his arm around his wife's shoulders and kissed her hair. Rubbing his daughter's coat sleeve, he apologised for scaring them. Clapping and cheering echoed from the battalion of buses when the tower was plunged into darkness, and the children's excitement soon transferred to the next point on their itinerary, as the vehicle jerked forwards and joined the line of traffic bound for *la Place de Pigalles*.

The famous windmill on the roof of *le Moulin Rouge* was a landmark well-known to the Diamond children. The Can-Can now played through their earphones, and Kierney giggled with delight as her mother took hold behind her stockinged calves and kicked a pair of floppy legs in the air in time to the music. She tapped the heels of her shoes alternately on the metal wall of the bus and then on her daddy's knee.

Not wanting to be outshone by the little girl, the three terrors sat on their seat and invented their own dance, lifting imaginary petticoats with all sorts of vigorous and suggestive moves. Junior slid around from two rows behind to take their photograph.

Tired at the end of another long day, the boys climbed one-by-one onto an available lap and settled down to listen to the soothing music which accompanied the commentary. They learned about *la Place de la Concorde, le Louvre, la Cathédrale de Notre Dame* and *l'Isle de la Cité*. The adults were amused to find the explanation so rivetting as to put their charges to sleep, and gazing around the open-topped deck, the same opportunity to sit and enjoy the historic setting in the cool autumn air had been afforded to most sets of parents.

Back in the hotel and with the children knocked out until morning, Junior and Julie took their leave a few minutes before midnight. Lynn thanked her husband for ensuring the youngsters had understood why he was so cross, and for not remaining a monster for longer than necessary to reinforce the lesson.

'That reminds me...' Jeff grinned. 'Your brother was the spitting image of your dad earlier, when he was talking about the kids larking about.'

'Was he? I didn't notice.'

'Yeah. D'you remember the time when your dad used the expression "larking about" to refer to horses humping?'

The former farm girl laughed. She had no memory of this occasion, but her father had often used such euphemisms in front of his children and grandchildren. Typical Victorian reserve was the Dysons' staple diet in the nineteen-fifties and -sixties, to protect sensitive ears and eyes from stark reality. No insulating veneer had been applied to the Sydneysider's childhood, as she well knew. This lack of inhibition had cast Jet and Kierney into the cold, hard truth, cushioned by an inspiring layer of imagery instead.

'That's funny. June said he learns how to be a good father from you,' she chose to reply. 'I think he quite likes finding out how not to be like Dad nowadays.'

Compassionate blue eyes reinforcing the sincerity in her words, the philosopher chanced a quick trade of favours. 'Angel, what would I need to promise to get your permission to go out again?' he asked, kissing her questioning mouth. 'I'd like to make the most of being here. Just walking around and soaking up the atmosphere, y'know...'

'Shhh, you idiot! You don't have to promise anything,' Lynn replied, stroking the side of his face and scratching his two-day-old beard. 'How could I refuse? I know how much you love it here. You're so gorgeous, Jeff. Just go and have fun.'

'Christ! That easy? I love you so much,' he sighed, clasping her hands in his and kissing their fingertips. 'Thanks. And you are too. You don't know how happy you make me.'

'As happy as you make me, I hope. Be home before dawn, please, 'cause I said I'd go for a run with June,' his wife requested, pressing her wanton body against his groin. 'Now go before I drag you to bed.'

The reprobate groaned at the wicked dilemma she had so delicately inflicted on him as he made for the door. Twisting the black jetstone ring on the middle finger of his right hand, he turned back in agony, only to be rejected out of hand.

'*Non!*' his *regala* laughed. '*Allez! La Bohème attend son vieux ami.* Enjoy!'

The songwriter blew a kiss to the sexy woman on whom he was a fool to run out. How sweet it was to be married to Lynn Dyson, he thought, skipping down the narrow, spiral staircase and lunging at the fire escape door. In her own inimitable style, she had turned him on and let him loose; no better state to be in when roaming around *le quartier Latin.*

The *cafés* and bars were crammed with exquisite intellectuals, both men and women, who recognised the newcomer and welcomed him into their midst. A party of stylish students called out for him to join them from their seats on the pavement, tempting him by waving their half-full bottles of wine and champagne. It was well-known among his fans that Jeff Diamond loved Paris, and the local population adored him all the more for this.

The bewitched, red-blooded male headed for a small basement bar where he had spent many an hour as a single man, arguing facts and disputing theories with professors and students alike, balancing girls on aching thighs and rolling fresh, young marijuana leaves into cigarettes, while the meaning of life was rendered more and more distinct yet ever elusive. Fortunately, time appeared to have stood still in the years between his visits, with even a few familiar faces to pick up where they had left off.

Paradise beckoned, and the wanderer did not hesitate. With his beloved family tucked up in bed and the prospect of another lazy day of sightseeing tomorrow, he succumbed to these most basic of guilty pleasures. A blues pianist played in one corner, nodding to him every now and again, and he was soon laughing along with the spicy, left-wing satirical humour for which this district was famous.

The night passed all too quickly. Before he knew it, the musician's watch told him it was past four o'clock in the morning. Remembering his Cinderella *caveat*, he took his leave from the easy company which had relaxed his body and stimulated his brain. He walked the kilometre back to the hotel, undressed in clumsy silence and slipped into bed, cuddling Lynn's warmth.

'You been smoking something exotic,' she whispered, turning around towards him with a sleepy smile. 'Your skin even smells bohemian; oozing through your pores.'

'Yeah? Sorry, angel,' her aroused lover answered, pushing strands of wayward hair away from her face and placing tender but insistent kisses on her cheek and in the corners of her eyes. 'D'you want me to take a shower?'

'No,' came a husky reply, her lips sweeping over his chest and stomach until they found the enlarged and throbbing penis which had woken her.

'Good. I don't have time for any of that. I have to be inside you. I want you so much. I could hardly walk home, the anticipation was so enormous.'

Under the covers, Jeff's searching hand held onto his wife's breasts, massaging them while he rubbed the hair covering her pubic bone. With words of love rasping in her ear, deft fingers swept up her spine and on towards her mouth, coaxing her to turn and face away from him. His muscles felt as if they were aflame as he pulled her ever closer, releasing hot, smoky breath against her neck. He loved how she responded to his every desire, and his expert touch found her moist and open for him.

Lynn twisted her head as far as she could to smile at the wanderer's humorous expressions, and their lips met. By the time they broke for air, both were on the brink of climax. She pulled away to delay gratification for a tantalising moment, causing him to thrust even harder into her, the delicious rush of abandon rising from her own insides. His left hand cupping her breast, he stroked the sensitive skin underneath the nipple and tipped her into a vat of ecstasy.

'Oh... *Je t'adore, mon ami*. You are the world's greatest lover.'

Her dashing French knight's orgasm was so powerful that he couldn't utter a word in reply. The substances he had consumed during the night had unleashed a complex chemistry which allowed him to pace himself to perfection. The sensation was sublime, seeming to last forever.

'Wow!' the young woman whispered, kissing the hairs on his forearm over and over. 'That was *magnifique*. You're on fire!'

Jeff's speechless lips covered the tanned skin on his wife's neck and shoulders with intense kisses, his heart begging the feeling not to subside. Together, they were undoubtedly the world's greatest lovers, and sharing this *Parisien* paradise was the icing on the cake.

There were no romantic phrases adequate to describe the extent of his love, so the poet remained silent. Lynn would understand. She always understood his statements, even when he didn't quite get around to making them.

Making Amends

At six-thirty in the morning, Lynn slipped from her noble scholar's crushing grip to prepare for her run through the streets at first light. He didn't stir as she let herself out of the bedroom to check on the children, who were wide awake and full of questions about what the new day might hold. The athlete requested they leave their *papá* to sleep for another hour at least. Thankfully, Julie was on hand to supervise while the Olympians caught up on lost training time.

Jet and Kierney jumped for joy when the clock's hands ticked over the sixty-minute mark. All four little ones formed a line at the door to see if their dark-haired playmate was awake. The room smelled of smoke, alcohol and sweat; a rich, adult odour the Diamond children had come to associate with their father but which the Dyson boys found particularly foreign.

'*Papa, lève-toi,*' the half-pint whispered in his ear, slotting her foot between the frame and the mattress and heaving herself up the side of the bed to reach his chin.

The slumbering giant didn't move. A small left index finger reached towards his lips and brushed them, relishing the change in skin textures along his parched lips. Three statues in the shape of young boys stood behind her, holding their breath and watching for the smallest sign of life to be pounced on.

'*Papá, dors-toi encore?*' the determined messenger asked slightly louder, her mouth within a few centimetres of a hairy chin.

Still nothing. Gritting her teeth and trying not to overbalance, the little girl glanced back to her brother, who had grown tired of the softly-softly approach.

'Dad, wake up!' he shouted, banging his fist on top of the mattress. 'It's time to get up.'

'Shhh,' Kierney hissed. 'That's too loud.'

His daughter having looked away again, Jeff took the chance to check the lay of the land, squinting to allow his eyes to focus. By the time she turned back to stroke his face again, he had resumed his former, inanimate state. To the little mite's joy however, a long tongue curled out of her daddy's mouth, and his front teeth gripped her fingers. She squealed in delight when one eye opened and winked at her.

With no hope of defending himself once the songwriter had confirmed his ongoing sentience, mayhem erupted in the bedroom. All four children leaped up onto the *duvet* and began to wrestle each other. Shielding his gipsy girl's more delicate frame from the kicks and punches, the umpire did his best to prevent anyone from injuring themselves.

So loud was the *brouhaha* that it brought Julie to the doorway, jaw dropping in amazement. 'What's going on?' she exclaimed, witnessing a stack of writhing bodies, some under the covers and some on top. 'Ugh! It stinks of cigarettes in here.'

Sonny and Bruce paused and swang around at the sound of their mother's voice. Jet and Kierney cuddled into their father, pleased to have him to themselves for a few seconds.

'Sorry, Jules. I had a late night. That bloody wife of mine. She sent me out smoking and drinking until all hours.'

'What? You two went out again after we went to bed?'

'No,' Jeff laughed, thinking how disgusted Julie would be to think they had left the children unattended. 'Just me. Come on, kids. Jump down. I need to get the windows open and have a shower. *Est-ce que vous avez faim?*'

'*Oui!*' Jet yelled at the top of his voice. '*Je vais prendre cent croissants.*'

'*Cent?*' his dad repeated, turning to the other boys. '*Combien de croissants voudriez-vous, les garçons?*'

'*Deux cents!*' the Diamonds' elder cousin answered, much to the adults' surprise.

'Well done! *Très bien*, Sonny,' Julie joined in. 'Two hundred *croissants* is a wee bit excessive. You'll be bilingual by the time we get home though.'

'Yeah,' her brother-in-law scoffed. 'Just in time to forget it again. Kizzy, *gorgeousita*, please go with Auntie Julie to get dressed while I jump in the shower with Jetto.'

The other children scattered, and Jeff beamed his energetic son up off the bed and over his shoulder, dumping him in the bath. He instructed him to remove his pyjamas before water soaked them. After their lightning-fast ablutions, the pocket dynamo ran out of the bedroom under a fluffy, white towel, pretending to be a ghost, tripping over the corners and nosediving straight into the carpet.

As the superstar selected the day's clothing from the crumpled pile he had extracted from his suitcase and attempted to make their environment presentable, he could hear renewed hilarity on the other side of the door. He also picked out Lynn's voice like the homing beacon it had become. What could be better? They were together for another perfect day in paradise.

At breakfast, the two older boys accepted the challenge of demolishing their third *croissant* but were forced to admit defeat. The task of picking a small number of attractions to visit had also proved difficult after spying so many interesting spots from the top floor of the bus.

Catching himself daydreaming several times while their plans took shape, the romantic rock star relived the last twelve hours, still unable to believe how lucky he was. Lynn fed off his introverted mood and leaned in to plant an affectionate peck on his cheek.

'Is it my imagination, or are you especially amorous this morning?' he grinned.

'It's your imagination,' the dismissive Olympian shot back, making the others burst out laughing with her comic timing.

'Damn,' her husband shrugged. 'Tough gig, isn't it, Kizzo.'

His tiny sidekick didn't understand the subtleties of her father's complaint, but the innocent nod he received in return warmed his heart further. The two mums suggested they all retreat to their rooms and ready themselves for the day out. Jeff stood to attention, swallowing down his remaining coffee in a single gulp.

Placing her hands on the handsome man's shoulders, his beautiful best friend shoved him back down onto his chair. 'Kids, we're going to leave *Papá* in peace today. He's going to have a thinking day.'

'What's a thinking day?' Sonny cried out.

'Am I?' his uncle asked in disbelief. 'Why do I deserve a thinking day? I'm happy to come with you guys. Really.'

'No,' Lynn refused, kissing the top of her husband's head, where his thick, black hair was still damp from the shower.

The Dyson boys groaned, pretending to vomit at the sloppy gesture. They were dismayed to receive an abrupt scolding from their father, who wheeled his brood round and out of the dining room. Left to make their peace in private, the intellectual rose to his feet again, laced one hand around his dream girl's waist while drawing their children into a bear-hug too.

'Whoa! Your *mamá* is the absolute best in the whole wide world,' he told them. 'Isn't she?'

'Yes,' the angelic pair answered in unison.

'Well... *Merci*, angel,' the grateful man said. 'I can't quite believe this second amazing opportunity, but I'll take it gladly if you're sure.'

'I'm sure,' the sportswoman ran her fingers down the side of his cheek, remembering how tight his jawline used to be and confirming this was no longer so. 'Very sure. I know how much being here means to you.'

The band called JeLyJeKi wended its way back to the stairs and ascended to their rooms, where the JuJuSoBr collective was nearly ready to go. Jeff wished them all a happy day, making no attempt to wipe the broad grin off his face. He toyed with the idea of inviting Junior to join him, but thought better of it. A period of cerebral contemplation wouldn't have been his cup of tea.

The blond Adonis dreamed of farms and football, the world-changer smiled, neither topic likely to figure on the agenda he had in mind.

'*Est-ce que je peux aller avec toi, Papá?*' Kierney asked in her sweetest voice. '*S'il te plaît?*'

'*Non, pequeñita,*' her father shook his head, the walls around his heart constricting at the lugubrious request. 'Not today. You'll be bored. I'm only going to chat, smoke and drink. Nothing else, I promise. You'll have way more fun with *Mamá*, Jet and the others.'

The three-year-old's lip began to quiver as she tried to stop herself crying, and so did Jeff's. Lynn took the little one's hand and led her over to the boys, talking up the assortment of exciting things they were planning to do.

'When we come back to Paris in a few years' time, I'm sure *Papá*'ll take you with him,' her mother added. 'When you're a little bit older. You can wait until then, can't you, Kizzy, darling?'

Kierney nodded, and her father blew her an extravagant kiss.

'*C'est un promis, pequeñita.* Have a great time, you guys. Take heaps of pictures.'

'*Amuses-toi bien, Papá,*' Jet shouted.

'*Merci bien. Et vous aussi.*'

Jeff blew his son a kiss too, expecting and receiving a grimace and a groan for his trouble. He got both in spades, laughing as he waved the touring party off. A lone tear slipped out of the corner of his eye as the image of the dark-haired miniature sparkler floated across his mind again. She would be fine after a couple of minutes with her *mamá*.

Dressing anew in black from top to toe, as befitting a bohemian rock-god with delusions of grandeur, he combed his hair back off his unshaven face. 'You're the luckiest bloke in the world, Jeff Diamond,' he informed his reflection. 'Don't ever forget this day. *Es un regalo de tu regala.*'

***

Entering a spacious lecture theatre with ornate architectural features off *la Rue Saint Jacques*, the famous figure chose a spot in the back row. Several students gasped as they noticed who had sneaked into the room, and he put his finger to his mouth and smiled.

Not long afterwards, one of the nubile young nymphs he had encountered in the bar the previous night slipped into the seat beside him. They kissed the French way, twice on each cheek.

'*Ça va?*' he asked.

'*Oui. Et toi?*' the skinny, nameless *dilettante* responded. '*C'est ennuiant, celui-là. On va prendre un café?*'

The visitor shook his head. He wasn't here to play this game. That was the old Jeff Diamond's territory. Without doubt, the new Jeff Diamond was here to enjoy himself too, and to take liberties galore, but not to the extent of abusing this windfall privilege. The young woman's silent protest was animated but light-hearted, and she soon reverted her attention to what turned out to be a fascinating lecture. Two hours went by in a flash, losing himself in the multitude of ideas and images collected in his greedy brain.

When the class was over, the multi-lingual Australian excused himself from last night's friend and crossed the street to the office of an Anthropology professor he had met the last time he was in Paris; a like-minded individual who wrote regular columns and opinion pieces on topics of social justice. Alain Verdot grinned from ear to ear when he saw Jeff's familiar face at his window.

The men shared a few beers and cigarettes over a late lunch, along with detailed and ofttimes exaggerated accounts of their respective bodies of work. As soon as Stonebridge Music had notified the academic of the family's impending northern hemisphere expedition, he had invited the respected champions of human rights for dinner with his wife. Today, Jeff declined the offer with an overt apology, for this also would be a bridge too far for his good fortune.

Finding no other lectures to capture his imagination, the old soul spent the afternoon browsing in bookshop after bookshop. He bought three weighty *tômes* and headed to a *café* on *le Boulevard Saint Michel* to wade through them until his loved ones returned to claim him.

One of these volumes had been bought with Lynn in mind, as an alternative to her father's autocratic learning methodology. Shinichi Suzuki, a Japanese educationalist, had published a new method the previous year which purported to be a philosophy for creating "high ability and beautiful character" in its students through a nurturing environment.

Using music as its main example, the songwriter read about this so-called revolutionary teaching style with interest, since Suzuki had modelled it on a concept of early childhood education which focussed on factors observed in native language acquisition. Immersion, encouragement, small steps and an unforced timetable for learning material based on each child's developmental readiness, it taught them to imitate examples, internalise principles and contribute novel ideas.

"High ability" and "beautiful character" were apt descriptions for two traits of prime importance, according to Lynn Dyson, mother and teacher *extraordinaire*. As her wise husband read the case studies, he couldn't help but supplant the faces of his own, unblemished babies into the *scenaria*, losing himself in their futures and wondering who they might become on attaining the ripe, old age of thirty.

Seven squashed cigarette stubs languished in the ashtray by the time the doting father was broken out of this *rêverie* by the dulcet tones of a fractious five-year-old waving the French flag and singing *"La Marseillaise"*, or at least a valiant attempt thereof. An equally weary three-year-old followed, clambering up onto his lap and nuzzling into his black shirt as if she were trying to disappear into the camouflage.

Lynn bent down to kiss the man who loved her so much, and he signalled for a waiter to bring them some drinks.

'*T'as passé une belle journée?*' the tall, stunning blonde asked, winding her legs around his under the glass-topped wicker table.

'*Absoluement,*' Jeff nodded, leaning over and stealing another kiss. '*Et vous?* What did you do with JuJuSoBr, mate?'

'They've gone back to the hotel for a sleep,' Jet replied. 'But we said we'd come and find you first. And here you are!'

'Thanks. And here I am. I bought some books.'

Already having spotted the Suzuki Method, its intended recipient began to leaf through it. The waiter brought a couple of glasses of *Pastis*, some water in a *carafe* and a jug of orange juice for the children. The mother requested more water and made sure they all drank a glassful after their long day pounding the streets.

'Did you smoke all those ciggies?' Kierney asked, pointing to the full ashtray.

'No. That wasn't me,' her dad lied without conviction. 'It was the man next-door. He swapped the ashtrays when I wasn't looking.'

The youngsters chortled at the sight of their mother rolling her eyes. She was ecstatic to find her partner more relaxed than she had ever known. It had been a good idea to leave him to his inner self today. She could see how much of a tonic it had been.

'*Demain, nous allons à Versailles,*' Lynn announced.

'*D'accord,*' Jeff smiled. '*Magnifique.* That'll be our first time together. *Encore des trains?*'

'Yes! Yes!' Jet jumped up and down in his seat. 'It's more than fifteen stops. I saw it on the map.'

'You're correct, mate,' his father confirmed. 'It's a long way, *mais c'est formidable.*'

'*Formidable!*' came an echo from the philosopher's lap. '*Il y'a de la musique dans les jardins.*'

'Is that right, *pequeñita?* How d'you know this?'

'*Mamá* told us a story. *C'est un très grand palais avec les plus petits palais dans les jardins, comme chez nous.*'

The intellectual smiled and cuddled Kierney in close. This was true enough, although quite by chance. *Escondido* had smaller palaces around its boundaries, not unlike *Versailles*, scale notwithstanding.

'So what did you do all day, *Prof' le Noir*?' Lynn asked. 'Expand your brain?'

'Yep. Can't you tell?' he frowned, turning his head from one side to the other.

'No. It looks the same to me,' Jet giggled, 'but your chin's hairier.'

The celebrity pouted. 'Spoilsport. You're supposed to say how clever I look.'

Meandering through the web of backstreets *en route* to their hotel, the happy family sauntered through *les Jardins de Luxembourg*, taking time to smell the roses, both real and metaphorical. They came across an old-fashioned *pissoir*, where the youngsters were most amused to see the tops and tails of men who had need of the facility.

'D'you wanna give it a go, mate?' Jeff enticed his son inside. '*Mamá* can film our feet while we pee.'

Lynn's video camera obliged, training on one large and one small pair of shoes standing next to each other, facing outwards like two true *Parisiens* and doing what came naturally against the curved, wrought-iron wall. She panned up to the top edge to catch her husband's mischievous grin, filming his hand reaching above before pointing downwards to indicate their son was somewhere way down below. Laughing into the microphone as he lifted the boy up against his will, she continued to capture for posterity the frantic screams and thrashing shoes hitting the metal. The child rose higher and higher, in fear of having his private parts exposed to the waiting world.

Their visit to *Versailles* was a huge success. Julie's mood had ameliorated every day as the vacation progressed, much to Junior's relief. While the two families traipsed through the palaces, both grand and less grand, the children listened to stories of wealth and power from the man whose memory never let him down. Gruesome accounts of Marie Antoinette and *les guillotines* hit the spot with the bloodthirsty boys, and Kierney lost herself in a series of cute fantasies among the antique children's furniture, dolls and toys in the staterooms.

Their last evening in Paris was soon upon them, and the following day they were to cross the English Channel to their final holiday destination: Tex Fletcher's house in Windsor Great Park, to the south-west of London. Before this however, the celebrity entertainers had promised to attend the grand re-opening of a *cabaret* club bought by the rocker eight years earlier to save it from bankruptcy and forced closure. Newly refurbished, the venue was about to launch a whole new class of show, as yet another complementary competitor to *les Folies Bergère*.

The Wild Horses Saloon had provided inspiration for the extravagant bucks' night Lynn had helped Gerry to organise. Located in the prestigious *Avenue Georges V*, well away from the seedier clubs near *Montmartre*, the ostentatious club had built a solid reputation from local and overseas visitors alike. It also attracted acclaimed artists as special guests, fronting the obligatory statuesque, leggy *danceuses*.

This particular night's high-classed show had sold out months ago, such was the demand for this type of entertainment, so the Diamonds slipped into a booth in the shadows where they could remain invisible. A brief slither of time to themselves without the children was *manna* from heaven, cementing the profound intimacy they had gained so far in their holiday.

With his arm around his beautiful best friend, the nightclub's current owner leaned back into the sumptuous velvet *banquette* while two rows of tall, lithe exotic women disrobed and floated in flawless formation. The aesthetics of their show appealed to the artistic couple's every sense, yet despite their glamour, the pouting red lips and their bodies' gyrations, he took genuine pleasure in reporting that these women offered no sexual attraction whatsoever. Everything he could ever want in a lover sat wrapped in his arms right here.

'I'm going to go all Scott Fitzgerald on you again,' Jeff said, taking his dream girl's left hand in his and rubbing the smooth white gold of her wedding ring between thumb and middle finger.

'Are you? More tall, restless virgins?'

The poet chuckled, having his bluff called not for the first time this evening. 'No. Just you. Perfect, one-in-a-trillion Lynn Dyson Diamond. "The *gourmandise* of a tingling curry eaten with chilled white wine," is how he described an acute, pleasurable sensation. That's where I am right now. You are delicious. I've never been so happy as these last few days.'

After the show, the affluent Australians were ushered backstage to thank the cast and to share a few cocktails. They posed for photographs with the entire production crew, who were full of questions and keen to unearth valuable secrets from showbusiness stalwarts at the pinnacle of their professions.

'Angel, *digame…*' Jeff asked once the couple had taken their leave, now strolling back towards the river and the nearest *Métro* station. 'I can't possibly be making you as happy as you're making me.'

'Why not?' his wife replied. 'You constantly make me happy. I'm having such an amazing time. I doubt I'm capable of being any happier.'

'Yeah? But you do so many special things for me; go out of your way to give me pleasures I don't deserve. Seems like I'm always being spoiled with licence to feed my desires. What can I give you in return?'

'This,' Lynn answered, patting him on the chest, her fingers rubbing the tattoo over his heart.

'My shirt?' he laughed, unfastening it without delay. 'Sure. You're welcome. You're way too easily pleased!'

The Olympian tutted, hurrying to do the buttons up as fast as they were undone. 'No. What's under the shirt, you dag! And under the skin and bones too.'

'Ugh,' the exhibitionist grinned. 'Why would you want that? My smoke-filled lungs ain't no good to no-one.'

'True,' she smiled, 'which is why you're limited to only two cigarettes a day once we get home.'

Jeff grimaced and nodded at the same time. 'Hmm...' he mused. 'Tough but fair. But seriously... What can I do to make up for all this fantastic happiness you're giving me?'

'Just what you're doing already,' the beauty replied, standing on tiptoes to kiss his sensuous lips. 'I feel completely loved every minute of the day, which is all I could ever need. The kids adore you, and you adore them. I don't want anything else. Honestly.'

'Na. I don't buy that,' the philosopher insisted, guiding his lover until her back was pressed up against the promenade's blackened wall. 'Promise you'll let me know the minute I'm not giving you what you want?'

The couple kissed, their bodies squeezing together from chest to groin and their legs entwined, relaxing into each other as their temperatures rose. Agreeing to her side of the bargain between Jeff's stubbly cheek and the palm of a possessive right hand, Lynn succumbed to his insistence again and again. For a fleeting moment, it was as though they had been transplanted back into the first few heady months of their relationship, he a nineteen-year-old nobody and she a starlet of sixteen.

'God, you're so sexy. What are you trying to prove, you beast? It feels like...' Lynn's voice trailed off to a pained whisper as her ardent accomplice's hand released its pressure on her breast and travelled down her ribcage until its palm came to rest on her abdomen.

She caught her breath, tears pushing through her eyes and falling in streams of strange, rekindled emotions. 'We've stood here before,' she muttered, her mouth still kidnapped by the fevered lips of her black knight. 'Jeff, I love you. I can see your face and hear you right here, but in my mind you're wearing different clothes. And so am I.'

Her lover's other hand paused on her hipbone, with no intention of loosening his grip. 'Yeah. I know. I feel it too.'

'Am I pregnant? Is that what you can feel?'

'No. You *were* pregnant. A long time ago,' Jeff sighed, easing the pressure and wrapping apologetic arms around his wife.

'What's going on?' Lynn sobbed. 'I don't want to let you go. I felt some sort of weird constriction in my stomach, and it's still there. Have you got this same thing in your head?'

'I reckon. But no, angel. We never knew this child. That's the sense I get, as clear as day,' the true romantic sniffed back tears and stroked his beautiful best friend's damp cheeks.

The champion athlete's legs weakened as if she were about to fall. 'Oh, my God. That's so tragic. That's what Paris is trying to tell us. Are you OK?'

'Don't know yet. Jesus! Not totally,' her husband's voice was shaky, as though he were determined to be strong for her. '*Je t'adore, Regala.* You're right. It's why we needed to come here and have this amazing holiday.'

'But what just happened? A flashback to our former incarnations or something?'

'Maybe, yeah. It felt like that to me too. I got you pregnant. That's why we couldn't be together... 'Cause you belonged to someone else, I think. I couldn't get you out of wherever you were. Together, forever, wherever.'

The crazed eyes of Lynn Dyson's beautiful black stallion had returned, staring into the starry heavens while his vice-like hold tightened with greater strength than she had ever experienced before from her tormented lover.

'I think you died for me, angel. Because of me.'

'Oh, my God! Do you really believe that? Well, we're here together again now,' she shivered. 'Whatever happened here all those years ago was not Jeff Diamond's fault.'

'I cost you your life,' the old soul wept. 'They may even have put you to death in those days. Christ, I don't know. Am I making all this shit up?'

His guardian angel stood tall, having forgotten how powerful these anxiety attacks used to be. 'It's OK. It doesn't matter if it's real or not. Something happened that we both have distant memories of, and this is how you've interpreted it. Just think how things've changed though. It took me a minute to figure out how to help you, it's been so long.'

Seeing a half-smile spreading across her tortured soul-mate's face, Lynn broke away, these flagrant fears now usurped by an air of triumph. 'Now I know what you can promise me!'

The peculiar atmosphere bloated with yet more intensity as the songwriter's eyes seized hers. 'Anything, angel.'

'Please don't ever, ever leave me. The current me, that is... Lynn Diamond.'

'Leave you?' Jeff exhaled, leaning his torso backwards as if this were the most preposterous idea he had ever heard. 'Why the fuck would I leave you?'

'I hope you won't, but you asked what I need from you,' the young woman whispered. 'And I promise I'll never, ever leave you.'

Another profound and consummate kiss sealed their present-day promises. She unzipped the fly of her breathless partner's trousers, slid her fingers inside his underwear to make contact with the skin stretched over a heated erection, all the time watching his eyes flash with anticipation. Similar to the early days, the troubled adolescent's mood had swung one hundred and eighty degrees in an instant, his left hand returning to massage her breast while sybaritic lips nipped at her neck.

'We'd better get back,' the rock star hissed. 'Unless you want me to take you right here.'

The furtive celebrity scanned their surroundings. A large contingent of night-owls, tourists and locals alike, were still promenading in the balmy air, and the river bank offered no suitable cover for a clandestine outdoor *liaison*. Even in libertarian Paris, there were levels of *decorum* one must maintain, especially when the whole world knew Lynn Dyson and Jeff Diamond were in town. *Paparazzi* might well have been secreted behind a parked car or in an embankment alcove, ready to snap their money-grabbing shutters at the slightest inkling of impropriety.

The eager *lothario* coughed in amusement as the pair straightened each other out and headed eastwards along the south bank of *la Seine*. 'I've got a new song in my head,' he announced.

'The "I'm trying to walk normally with a stiffy again" song?' his wife giggled, noticing his uncomfortable gait.

Jeff gave her a scolding glare, grabbing hold of her waist and tugging her sideways until she was walking in front of him, which only made things worse as fantasies took flight, such were the pleasures to be found where those two long legs joined.

'This isn't helping one bit,' he told her, raising his eyebrows at an elderly couple who scrutinised them with frumpy suspicion. 'I bet that old bloke's thinking, "I could have her, if only I were forty years younger."'

'Be quiet!' Lynn laughed. 'You're a visitor in their lovely city. You can't say things like that. We're supposed to be responsible citizens.'

'Fuck that!' the showman shouted. '*Nous sommes tous libres à Paris.* We can say whatever we damned well want. The song's called "Firebrand Soul", and it's about independence from people who held us down. My mind's also telling me I'm ready to go back on the road. It's an "up yours" to Gravity the Troll.'

The blonde bombshell paused, sliding in beside her man, whose former hot-blooded passion had been interrupted by a sudden bout of angry hindsight. These episodes of oscillation were rare these days, yet she knew that feeding them had a habit of yielding an even greater creative power.

'*Dites-moi, monsieur Hugo,*' she smiled, her eyes wild with love. 'What's the theme?'

The lost boy inside reared his lonely head for the first time in months. 'My mum used to use the phrase "He's independent" to mean "I don't give a fuck where he is."'

'Oh, wow,' the young woman murmured, gripping his hand. 'Where's this come from?'

'Jesus, angel! I don't know. Being thrown back to those times when I never thought I'd see you again, I guess. Still unable to believe you cared about this worthless shit of a man who'd stolen into your life.'

'I didn't care about a worthless shit. I don't remember a worthless shit.'

'Yeah. I knew that afterwards. Well, I dare to know it. Y'know, sometimes I was scared to touch you because of the triggers it unleashed in me, and that we'd end up having sex again when not even I wanted to.'

The couple's pace had slowed to a stroll, as if the world-changer's legs now weighed a tonne. His dream girl let go of his clammy hand and threaded her arm across his kidneys, slotting her thumb inside the waistband of his pants.

'It was almost too much for you too, wasn't it?'

'Ah, pure heaven, baby. *Merci*. Yeah. Back then, I had no idea you could touch someone without it being sexual... just for affection... until you came along. The need never figured in my life, and I certainly wouldn't have recognised it in the girls I went with.'

Lynn flinched, references to prior girlfriends still smarting, even after years of faithful married bliss. 'Didn't your parents hug you?'

'Nope. Not that I remember. Not once I could move myself around, I s'pose. Only my grandmother, and that was more like being smothered, suffocated... A bit like Jet's reaction. But I do the same to the kids now, don't I?'

'You do, but they love it, Jeff,' the caring woman answered. 'Don't feel guilty for expressing how you feel. It's beautiful. You do it to me when we haven't seen each other for a while, and I love it too. Shows we love each other, and need each other. Now what were you saying about getting back on the road?'

If this new song the megastar had written signified exorcism of Mary-Anne Pearce and Amanda Fallon's ghosts at last, this was music to Lynn's ears, knowing how much positive energy he derived from performing on stage to a live audience. Overcoming the fear of history repeating would be no mean achievement, since his audiences were only likely to be larger and more frenzied upon his return.

'This is another excellent birthday present you'd be giving me,' she shouted over the noise of a train arriving at the platform from the tunnel's blackness. 'The perfect way to end our stay in Paris. I'd love to hear it when we get to Tex's?'

'Yeah. Definitely,' the musician agreed. 'In fact, it's one for him and me to record together.'

By the time the Dyson-Diamond pantomime horse had traversed the station tunnels and surfaced to road level at *les Jardins de Luxembourg*, the two halves had formulated a skeleton tour schedule for the coming year. He would start with some small, intimate venues and work back up to the forty- and fifty-thousand-seater stadiums where the Jeff Diamond spectacular could soar to its theatrical heights.

Both families were up early the following morning for their drive through northern France to Calais and the ferry across to the south-eastern coast of

Great Britain. Two right-hand-drive Range Rovers, one silver and one black, had been parked in the hotel's rear courtyard beneath the Australians' rooms, and their children were excited at the prospect of riding in a car again after the last few weeks spent in a series of aeroplanes, trains and taxis.

Lynn suggested the youngsters might craft a few signs to help them with communications between the two vehicles during their journey, and it had been the cause of high drama.

'You have to write the meaning of each letter on the back, or we'll get very confused,' she told her son, who held up a piece of stiff card on which he had written the letter "P". 'What does "P" mean?'

'Parking!' the boy shouted, trying not to laugh when he cottoned on to the other possibility.

'Are you sure it's not "Need a pee"?' his dad challenged. 'Better to have "S" for stop.'

'That could be "S" for sh...' Jet nudged his cousin, whose eyes almost popped out of his head.

'Jetto!' both parents exclaimed. 'Be quiet!'

'No! "T"'s for toilet,' Sonny bleated, holding up the corresponding sign.

'But isn't "T" for tea?' Julie whined in response, miming drinking from a genteel cup and saucer.

'That makes you want to use the other "T" sign. Or the "P" sign,' Lynn added, watching all four kids exchange horrified glances.

'Let's just have one sign,' Jeff suggested. 'Whatever we need to do, we'll need to stop, won't we?'

'Oh, Dad,' Jet grunted. 'We haven't got an "S" for stop. Now we have to start again.'

'No. This'll do. We'll just use the "P", mate,' the kind man smiled, pointing to their original artwork. 'Come on... Let's get this show on the road. We need to get to Calais by lunchtime, or else the "B" for ship'll go without us.'

The rev-head was also glad to be back behind the wheel. Junior was less experienced at driving on the opposite carriageway, happy for his brother-in-law to exact his control-freakiness from the lead car in their short convoy. The tour party had saved the previous day's coins for the French motorway system's new tolling machines, the feeding of which would fall to the passenger while travelling in British cars.

Within three hours, the English Channel rose grey and foreboding on the horizon, and the tourists soon pulled up at the rear of a long line of vehicles ready to board the next ferry. The children were most relieved to discover they would not be forced to stay inside the cars for the duration of the crossing, but the weather was freezing and squally on deck. Everyone rugged up for their trips out into the raging elements.

'This is fun, *Papá*,' Kierney chimed as her father lifted her up to experience the full spectrum of sensory input from the choppy waves.

'Anyone feeling sick?' Lynn checked.

'No!' Jet shouted, accentuating the ship's yawing and rolling. 'I love it! It's like riding a huge horse.'

Satisfied her brood would survive the four-hour trip without upset, the young mother cuddled into her husband's tall frame and sheltered from the main thrust of the breeze. Jeff again took stock of where they were, relishing the sights: wind blowing long, golden hair back off the unusually ruddy complexion on his beauty queen's face, coupled with their offspring's vitality and broad smiles. He put his arm around his cherished travelling companion and kissed her cheek hard.

'I love you guys,' he shouted. 'This is such a fantastic holiday. I love seeing you so happy.'

Twenty minutes spent examining every lifeboat, having their ears battered by the noise of gigantic engines echoing through the funnel's steel panels and feeling the spray from turbulent waters kicked up at the stern by the ferry's twin propellers, the two families adjourned to the relative peace and quiet of the cafeteria.

While the wives joined a lengthy queue for drinks and snacks, Junior sat back to receive another lesson on mastering the finer side of life, encircled by their customary ring of admirers. Football and farming skills he possessed in extreme quantities, yet somehow he had matured to the stage where this charismatic songwriter's ideas now presented untold wisdom to the successful sporting hero.

'It's about achieving something greater than the sum of its parts, mate, in my humble opinion. A journey shared is a much more moving experience than a journey taken alone,' Jeff mused aloud, being lulled to drowsiness by the ceaseless thrum of the motors vibrating the bench seat. 'Statements are shaped by context and enriched by sharing. When there's no sharing, there's no art and therefore no beauty. When it comes down to it, the job of the artist is to uplift our souls.'

'Man!' Bart Dyson the Third moaned. 'All that sentimental mush sounds meaningful coming out of your mouth, you pretentious arse. In my not so humble opinion... I'd sound like a fraud if I tried it.'

The songwriter chuckled. 'Cheers, I think! Sentiment's not only the slushy, gushy stuff of love songs and rallying cries. For me, sentiment equals humanity. A "sentient being" is the same as a "human being". We all feel, and it's not superficial. It's the basis of life itself. No point living if we're not in the moment. Letting everything pass us by without leaving an impression is superficial.'

Kierney and Bruce appeared as the first to return with a tray laden with packets of biscuits and savoury snacks for the group. The little girl giggled as her father scooped her up and hovered her over the table so she could deposit the spoils in its centre. Taking his cue from a pair of dark, prompting eyes, Junior replicated the deft move for his younger son.

'People have so much intellect that they become stupid,' the wise man dared, tearing the packaging of a few items and tucking into a handful of salt and vinegar crisps. 'Mmm... *Gracias, pequeñita.* Yummy. All for me! Some folks never look beyond what they already know. Or often just what they think they know, 'cause they've become so damned clever that they've lost the ability to test their theories against reality. Sentiment is common decency; stuff that makes us proud.'

'Yeah, sure,' his wife's elder brother nodded. 'Of course, mate. I appreciate what you're saying. It's logical, but isn't there a danger of overanalysing everything?'

'Ha! Damned straight there is, and I'm one of the worst for overanalyzing. But it tends to come full circle on you if you're honest with yourself. Cry, hurt, ponder, love... It's all really the same thing. Love makes the main building blocks of humanity. It builds bridges. Figuratively speaking, that is...'

***

The interviewer paused, hearing Ryan Diamond catch his breath. 'Are you OK? Did you want to take a break?'

Ten years had passed since the ancient soul had left his teenaged children and gone in search of his felled soul-mate. To commemorate the milestone, the Australian Broadcasting Corporation had commissioned an hour-long documentary focussing on the couple's legacy.

The producer had interrupted the young man's rehearsal to run some footage of his sister's commentary, which was to be superimposed over scenes from the industrious partnership's treks through geographies ravaged by disasters. Kierney had conducted some thorough research which was further crafted by ABC statisticians into a bunch of powerful graphics charting their family's contribution to recovery efforts.

'No, Matt. Thanks, but I'm fine. Hearing Kiz express how much she misses them brings it home to me every time,' the cricketer chuckled. 'It's still sad and a little bit painful. More than anything though, this stuff makes me so proud to be descended from them.'

The cameras rolled on, conversation skewing to Savannah, who stood off-stage, enjoying a casual chat over *espressi ristretti* with the family's former manager. Today was the first time Gerry Blake had met the sportsman's latest and hottest girlfriend, and it was obvious that the retired playboy hadn't lost his touch!

'Dad was always keen to drive the lesser-known aspects of each issue; things the general public might not have heard about or understood clearly. Often, he hardly touched on the stuff that'd already been covered in the media, if you think about it. In the beginning... And even with "A Life Singular", it was all about the backstory for him, 'cause he believed that's where the real truth about a person or a situation lives.'

Matthew Gregory, a rising star in prime-time current affairs programming, smiled. 'Perfect *segue*, Ryan. I'd like to turn our attention to your parents' autobiography, which has sold more copies in the last decade than you've scored runs for your country.'

'Tens of thousands more!' the self-effacing twenty-nine-year-old affirmed. 'Sure. My dad hated the thought of his writing insulting readers' intelligence, which is why he worked so diligently to summon the right image. He and Mum wanted to change people's opinions subtly, not solely by demonstrating the cold, hard facts. It's why the end of Act Two and Act Three are really a series of parables. Lessons in life, learned in the swamp during the various projects we were involved in at the time.

'Mum and Dad perfected a formula during their life together. People act through a combination of the mind, the heart and the body. "IQ", "EQ" and "PQ", in today's parlance,' the famous son continued. 'Therefore, whenever the 'papers or the fans had heard enough about charitable or world-changing topics, they'd release a new album or go on tour or something. Or win some more tennis titles, *et cetera...*

'And if they reckoned people needed a reminder about how to love each other, they'd make some huge romantic gesture, such as the "Together, Forever, Wherever" campaign. Then when they got the impression they'd saturated the press for long enough and no-one ever wanted to hear from them ever again, they'd counter the media hype by disappearing and popping up at school for a while, to annoy the heck out of Kiz and me!'

The tall, lanky television presenter laughed out loud, himself having attended Melbourne Academy in Kierney's class. 'I remember that! Not quite in those terms, but we did tend to think they'd moved into the gatehouse on a permanent basis at certain times of the school year. If we can digress for a moment, I'd like to refer you to a piece of film I found a few days ago. If I may, Ryan?'

The director cut the action, and the two former schoolmates relaxed back into their armchairs. At this point in the finished programme, a video clip was to be shown of a pathologist going on record after Jeff Diamond's autopsy. For a man who consistently denied his body a fighting chance for good health, as a result of the never-ending cocktail of poisons he had ingested since childhood, the Coroner's *post mortem* examination had revealed a constitution that bore not one shred of evidence of such prolonged maltreatment.

Furthermore, the most surprising finding was that the songwriter's vital organs dwarfed those of a normal human male by a ratio of almost two to one.

Several hypotheses were put forward at the time, both by eminent physicians and less well-respected zealots, to suggest his larger-than-life *persona* and corresponding habits had forced his internal functions to expand to accommodate this capacity. Yet his children were more comfortable with the version of the truth that saw him surviving his own substance abuse unscathed precisely due to a set of oversized body parts commissioned by a soul who knew what to expect of its latest life-form.

'I remember our mum saying one day,' Ryan spoke into the camera, 'when Dad was struggling to sleep after another harrowing conversation about some crisis or other, "This heart of yours, it's too big. Too much spare room to deal with other people's problems." Mum always said he had extra dimensions to take on the whole world's issues, but those took their toll too. Dad maintained it was an old soul thing, accumulating life lessons in a giant brain and a giant heart.'

'And did your father think he could fix all these issues?' the interviewer almost teased.

'Of course not, Matty,' the protective son scoffed. 'But he sure as hell wanted to fix everything. Mum used to tell him to put up the "car park full" sign as a joke. He never quite bought into this joke though.'

'Sorry, mate,' the good-looking media man frowned. 'I was just kidding. I idolised the bloke too. Going back to "A Life Singular" again, you mentioned it had three acts. Can you describe your dad's intentions with structuring it this way?'

'Probably not,' his friend grinned. 'Act One, as the exposition, was setting up how their relationship had come about, and why the world needs more people like them. A call to arms, if you like... His role was to show people what could be accomplished when great minds and strong hearts work together, by mixing some handy hints in with the romance and sex.'

The young man noticed his girlfriend's hand give a wave of appreciation at this latest piece of truth. Savannah was the love of his life, a Spanish-speaking woman who had been through the ringer in her past and wore physical and emotional scars to prove it. Prior to making this stunning nymph's acquaintance, he had remained cynical about his father's prophesies of returning souls. Yet these had been tossed upside down over the preceding three months, leading Paragon Holdings' Chief Executive Officer to eat his words.

'Act Two is devoted to all the brilliant work Mum and Dad did in their life together: the music; sporting achievements; the businesses and charities; and of course, me and my sister! Dad's clear message to us when he was writing was that the climax which was to have topped out Act Two of their life singular never materialised because the whole "JL" tattoo thing came crashing down. So the idea of a traditional Act Three to bring the story to a natural conclusion became null and void.'

'Could you explain this a little further, please?' Matthew pressed for more.

'Well, given the circumstances, there could hardly be a *dénouement*, could there?' the handsome young man turned to the audience to enlist their support. 'We shared way too many jokes about faked climaxes back at the tail-end of 'ninety-six. After Mum was shot, everything unravelled much too fast for us all. Especially for Dad, of course. There was no *dénouement* to their life singular in reality. He didn't write much about the last few months, except a raft of philosophical debate with himself about whether his suicide was truly rational. Just a factual account of a truly horrible time, mixed with a smidgen of hope for an unknown future.'

The interviewer sighed, hearing the imposing but humble chip off his parents' blocks express himself plainly and without pathos. 'Did you and your sister agree with your dad's plans for suicide?'

'"Agree"'s not quite the right word,' Ryan shook his head. 'I can't speak for Kierney, but neither of us wanted to see him die. Goes without saying, I hope. He was the best father anyone could have; the absolute best in every way. We did support him in his decision though. We'd always spoken about their desire to move on into the next life together, ever since we were old enough to listen.

'Personally, I'm not yet entirely convinced on the whole reincarnation concept. Particularly any conscious knowledge of who we were and are going to be, or that it's possible to influence the future. But I do understand the depth of love Mum and Dad had for each other. He lost the one person he existed for, and the life he was left with held no appeal. As his kids, heaps of our friends and even some family members were angry at him that we seemed not to count on the "plus side" of his cost-benefit analysis, as he lamented to Kiz and me several times.'

'But how could anyone take it any other way?' Matt had trouble containing his own bias. 'Two children at university, who'd only just lost their mother... Didn't you feel like he'd abandoned you? Betrayed you somehow?'

'No. Never,' the film-maker insisted. 'We did fight back from time to time, and questioned how confident he could be to end up with Mum again. E.g. was that worth giving everything else up for? But he prepared us so well for what happened. We knew we'd be fine, and we are fine. More than fine, in fact. Thriving and eager to extend their legacy.'

Ever the romantic like their father, Kierney was convinced her parents had nudged destiny from their ethereal vantage point, while Ryan remained more than sceptical. Savannah Jordà had fled the lawless rapists of her *Basque Catalán* brotherhood to study acting in California, changing her surname to "Jordan" to aid assimilation. Jeff Diamond's autobiography had brought the young lovers together, whether accidentally or on purpose, softening the cricketer's resolve in the process.

Nevertheless, since the moment he had clicked on a three-minute video *résumé* which the dusky, hot-headed hopeful had sent to his Colorado hideaway, the boss of Monterey Films hadn't been able to imagine himself with any other woman. Only now was he beginning to appreciate the power of love, knocked head-over-heels by its overwhelming force.

'My sister and I are on a mission to stop people or corporations or governments… anyone in a position of so-called authority… taking advantage of the ordinary individual. She's doing it via the United Nations and on a global scale, whereas my work's more targeted through Paragon's lobbying and activism and also through the independent film-makers we're working with.

'The effects of abuse and neglect stay with people forever,' he winked at his gorgeous girlfriend, who had moved closer to the set when the subject changed. 'There's one specific story from when I was about five years old that's stayed with me ever since and continues to motivate me. My dad had been away overseas for a few weeks and started to muck around with me when he came home.

'It struck him when we were there, in *Escondido*. He was carrying me like a sack of dog food along the narrow hallway from our kitchen to the recording studio, bumping my head and feet deliberately into doorframes and walls. "Oops! Sorry, mate," he kept saying, over and over again. I remember being consumed by a fit of uncontrollable giggles and my fists pummelling Dad's chest and arms to let me go. When he finally did put me down, I had to leg it to the can 'cause I'd been laughing so much.

'Apparently, Dad crumbled to the floor and bursts into tears while I was gone. Our happy family was sometimes hard for him to handle. The scars were too deep. Memories of how cruel his own father had been, and the fact that his mother did nothing about it… just looked on impassively… were often too much of a contrast. I remember Mum comforting him and me together, saying "Dad cries because he's happy and sad at the same time." Kierney and I learned heaps from those lessons, and we're committed to helping others to escape such mental torture by not having it happen in the first place.'

***

The ransom of Range Rovers made safe passage through Kent and into Surrey, pulling into the mediæval town of Windsor on Greater London's south-western fringe by early evening. Responding to an instruction of "P" from the excited communications party in "Batmobile Number One", the cars stopped one behind the other next to a callbox in the high street to obtain detailed directions from Tex Fletcher's housekeeper.

The children could scarcely believe their eyes when around the following corner they came face-to-face with the eleventh-century castle's Round Tower, which had been described to them in minute detail on their way across the Channel. Their enthusiasm for venturing inside waned at the sight of soldiers with guns, and then more so when Junior sowed seeds of turrets haunted by visitors who tried to defy the sentries.

The fading light caused the lawns and gravel pathways to blend in a layer of low-lying mist, triggering plenty more ghostly noises and spooky tales. By the time the two men returned from their telephone call and were ready to drive on, all four kids had turned ashen-faced and reticent.

'What's been going on in here?' Jeff asked.

Jet obliged with a loud, ghoulish moan and some tickly fingers up the driver's neck. His dad shivered, shaking his shoulders, which crackled and crunched with the residual tension of the last few hours of concentration.

Lynn requested the boisterous trickster stop scaring his sister, only for Kierney to pipe up to say she wasn't at all frightened. 'Well, I am,' their mum smiled. 'The castle'll look much friendlier in the morning. Do we know where we're going?'

'I do,' her husband replied. 'Do you?'

The feisty blonde slapped his knee. 'Drive on, James.'

Dealing her a salacious wink, the joker saluted and lifted his left hand to the rear-view mirror to signal their departure to the car behind. The luxurious but lumbering roadliner lurched forwards on the wet pavers.

'Onwards to Castle Tex Flex. Hungry, kids?'

'Yay!' both yelled at the tops of their voices.

'Is Gudrun coming tomorrow?' Jet asked. 'She can come to the castle with us.'

This twenty-four-year-old Dane whom the Diamonds hoped to recruit as one of their nannies for the coming school year was due to join them the following day for a trial period before they all committed to her passage to Melbourne. Jet and Kierney had been sad to say *au revoir* again to Nadine, but always looked forward the next batch of childminders. The regular turnover had helped them deal with change, and their parents were happy to see them showing the right sorts of emotions at each parting or new appointment.

'Good idea, mate,' Jeff agreed. 'It'll be a good way for us all to get acquainted. Can she cope with this much lunacy for a whole year?'

'But what if she's scared of ghosts?' Kierney wondered, putting on a terrified face.

Her mother laughed. 'Then you'll have to take care of her. Hold her hand. She'll be fine. They have ghostly castles in Denmark too.'

'Perhaps she lives in one,' the five-year-old offered. 'Maybe she's already seen a ghost and can tell us what they're like.'

'Quite possibly,' the patient woman nodded. 'Do you think she knows all the songs from Hans Christian Andersen?'

'She might be a mermaid,' Jeff suggested, sending them all sliding sideways as he made a sharp turn down a narrow, unlit lane.

Kierney gasped, such an eventuality not occurring to her before. How perfect would it be to have a mermaid to talk to! And what a good swimming teacher...

'We'll know soon enough,' Lynn grinned at her husband's quirky suggestion. 'If she's wearing jeans, we'll know she's not a mermaid.'

The little ones giggled, their hands impersonating a mermaid's scaly tail trying to walk around the castle. Within a few minutes, the two cars pulled off the road and were now approaching an enormous, wrought-iron *portico*. The Diamond children wound down their windows and yelled back to the Dysons that there were ghosts here too, not realising their cousins had fallen asleep. The tennis champion jumped out and announced their arrival into an intercom' system, and a few seconds later, the gates began to part.

'Mister Frankenstein will see us now,' the fun-loving mother poked her head through the rear passenger window, using her deepest, scariest voice and making the kids jump.

'Turn the lights off, Dad,' Sergeant-Major Diamond commanded. 'They might shoot at us.'

'They're not going to shoot at us,' Jeff laughed. 'They're too busy making our dinner to shoot at us.'

The British singer-songwriter's domestic staff met their guests at the ostentatious covered entrance, mercifully unarmed. They made a huge fuss of the children.

'Meet Sleepy and Grumpy,' their employer's chief collaborator told them when the two Dyson boys clumped their way through into the hallway, having objected to being woken up and subsequently finding themselves in a strange place. 'And these are our dwarves, Dopey and Dopier.'

'I'm not dopey,' Jet whined, holding out his right hand to their welcoming committee. 'I'm Doc, or Jet really. Pleased to meet you.'

The celebrity couple had visited this historic, rambling mansion several times before and were familiar with its layout. The housekeeper informed them that Tex had commissioned a few alterations, before showing them upstairs to a brand new suite of bedrooms. The long corridor, every spare surface cluttered with priceless *objets d'art*, was lined with nude statues, boggling the children's eyes. Julie feared the high likelihood of breakage resulting from her boys' exuberance, grabbing Bruce's hand and ushering them into their room.

The Diamonds were taken to a separate wing across the landing from the Dysons. In a simultaneous backwards motion, after their tiring day, both mother and father slumped down onto the inviting bed and groaned. The kids took this as a signal to leap up and join them, and a huge tickling match ensued, punctuated by much screaming and shouting.

Before too long, Junior's large frame appeared round the door. 'Excuse me,' he said in an officious accent, walking in and picking Jet up by the collar of his jumper. 'Keep it down, please. We're shattered.'

Having dropped the young boy on the rug, their superhuman uncle then lifted Kierney off and dangled her above her parents' bodies, her short, squirming limbs dangling in mid-air. With a flick of his strong wrists, the little girl landed on top of a pile of designer pillows.

The final fortnight of the family's fabulous *fiesta* fair flew by. Gudrun settled in without a hitch, the children delighting in her bubbly personality and sense of fun. This allowed the recording artists to focus on preparing their catalogue of new songs for Tex Fletcher's return, spending hours in the studio working on orchestral arrangements.

The swashbuckling master of the house arrived at the Windsor mansion to huge fanfare and in a foul temper, taking his airline grievances out on everyone. Feeling awkward that their presence might only add to the temperamental artist's tantrums, the Dysons took the decision to fly back to Melbourne a few days early, leaving the Diamonds to pick up the spoiled man's pieces.

'This has been the best holiday ever,' Jeff told his children in a quiet moment away from their host.

'Me too,' agreed Kierney.

'You too? But you're only three!' her dad chuckled, lifting her up into his arms and kissing her nose. 'How could you possibly know, gorgeous? It'll be good to be home though, in our own beds, won't it?'

The little girl nodded. 'And see Merak and Janey.'

'And the donkeys,' her brother added. 'And going back to school to see my friends.'

Jeff agreed. 'Yep. All that, mate. It's nice to go away but also nice to come home. The hallmark of happiness. Just you remember that, OK? How 'bout we do *Mamá* a favour and start packing our cases?'

Inspired by their homeward journey and an energetic new task, the starlets trotted off to find their empty suitcases and dragged them into their bedroom. Hanging out for their father's next instruction, the playful pair sensed a game about to kick off.

'OK! Cool. Here's the deal,' he began, deathly serious. 'First, you need a layer of clothes you've already worn, spread over the bottom of the case.'

The children scurried to do as they were asked, laughing at their father counting down in a multitude of languages. Pint-sized pairs of pants, tops and swimsuits were tossed around between them, being used as weapons when necessary, and soon the lining fabric of both bags was covered.

'Good job,' their captain praised, not even raising a smile. 'Now go and get a towel each from the bathroom.'

Jet's eyes tracked from his sister's to his dad's before obeying with a shrug of amusement. They hurried back and spread the towels over their dirty clothes, standing to attention at the foot of the bed.

'Now get in, please,' he pointed to their cases.

'Get in?' Kierney echoed. 'Are we going home in here?'

'Yep,' their father couldn't hide his smile this time. 'Go on. Get in. I need to see how heavy you are. No arguments.'

The tender tyrant crouched down and began to zip up the suitcases, first with Jet inside and then his kid sister. Overcome with emotion at how far these two special beings trusted him, he left a small gap unzipped and stuck a hand through to tickle them.

Right on cue, Lynn walked into the room, opening her mouth to tell the others some news. Jeff raised his palm for silence, his head encouraging her eyes downwards. The bulging pieces of luggage were breathing heavily, also uttering the occasional stifled sniff.

'Wow! Thanks, *Papá*. This all looks much tidier now. Coming for dinner?'

With a muffled cry drifting from the far side, Jeff tapped the left-hand suitcase. 'You're welcome, angel,' he responded. 'Right, Jetto! You ready for your weight test?'

'Uh?' came a tiny voice. 'Oh. Yes!'

'When's my turn?' the other bag asked in the sweetest tone.

'Thirty seconds, Kizzy. Start counting. Jesus Christ!' the tall celebrity groaned as he lifted the first *valise* off the ground, stretched to his full height and began to walk around the bedroom. 'You're too heavy, mate. I don't know if we'll be able to take you home after all.'

The young lad sneezed and sniggered simultaneously, yelping every time his dad bounced him across the carpet. Both adults laughed as the second case wobbled, imagining their daughter anxious to take a turn.

'Me! Me!' Kierney was yelling from inside the other piece of luggage, having found the opening through which to poke her tiny arm.

'Hey! Who's this?' Lynn asked, taking hold of the wiggling fingers. 'Who put a little girl into a suitcase?'

'*Mamá!*' the toddler shouted through the gap, her lips scratching against the zip's teeth. '*Papá* put us in.'

The tennis champion flexed her muscles and fell in with her joyful husband to march from one side of the room to the other, spinning round at the opposite wall and goose-stepping back again. She knocked her lighter load into Jet's levitating chariot as she stood on tiptoe to kiss the love of her life.

'Stop! Put me down! I'm 'phoning Childlight,' the five-year-old complained, sounding breathless. 'Cruelty to children!'

Hit with a new ploy, Lynn tapped her partner-in-crime's arm, eyes pointing towards the quilt. 'Here we go!' she cried. 'Prepare to fly, guys!'

The strong-armed parents took synchronised inward breaths and swang their encased loved ones onto the bed, amid much screaming and whooping from inside. The cases slid along the silky surface of the *duvet* until their momentum dissipated and they came to a standstill near the stock of pastel pillows at the bed's head.

'Open me up, please!' Kierney panted, forcing her arm as far out of the hole as possible, grappling for something to get hold of.

'Open you up? Why?' Jeff queried, crouching down to nibble at her pink fingers. 'It's much safer in there, *pequeñita*. No-one can tickle you or eat you.'

'*Papá*, I want to come out,' the little mite persisted. 'Please unzip me.'

'OK, baby. Jet, d'you want out too, mate?' the father asked, his voice deafening when aimed through the gap in his son's dark container. 'You're very quiet. Maybe he fell asleep, *Mamá*. Oh, well... He obviously doesn't need any dinner.'

Deriving as much enjoyment from their silly game as their offspring, the grown-ups grinned at each other on hearing stifled giggles from the lad. While her husband's wicked fingers penetrated the gloom and located their target, the young mum unfastened Kierney's suitcase and let the light in bit-by-bit.

'Ow! Jeez, son!' Jeff howled, snatching his hand out to examine his wound after receiving a sharp bite. 'That's not fair. Payback time! You're *gonna* be sorry you did that, kiddo!'

The boy's bag was rolled over and over and over on the bed, at one point narrowly avoiding being tipped onto the floor by the songwriter's size twelve foot spinning to its rescue in a deft martial arts move. Meanwhile, their daughter had been lifted out of her mobile prison, in paroxysms of laughter while nestled in her mother's arms. She tried to smooth the waves of dark, unruly hair which had become tangled during their antics, her angelic face flushed and glistening from being in a confined space for so long.

'D'you *wanna* come out?' the musician blared through the narrow opening, still sucking his bitten finger.

'Yeah! Set me free, Dad! Please.'

'What? You want freedom after exacting your revenge so wilfully? Well, tough,' the strong man fought back, spinning the case around for good measure.

'Dad, no! Let me out!' Jet shouted. 'I'm sorry I bit you. Let me out!'

'Why should I? You're a dangerous animal.'

The gargantuan, testosterone-fuelled tussle between father and son was allowed to continue for a few more seconds before the blonde referee called a halt. Reluctantly, her husband slid the zip from one end to the other, the lid lifting to reveal its triumphant occupant, who stood up on shaky legs, rubbing his eyes before dropping onto his backside as dizziness overtook him.

'Can I see your finger?' Jet asked, his face a picture of apology. 'I didn't mean to hurt you.'

Jeff wrapped said digit in his other hand, shaking his head with a terrified expression. 'No way,' he moaned, the corners of his mouth drooping. 'You'll only do it again.'

'I won't. I'm sorry, Dad. I didn't mean it.'

'You did absolutely mean it,' the wounded soldier countered, enveloping the open-hearted youngster in a hug and kissing his warm forehead. 'But I still love you, champ. Heaps and heaps.'

Five weeks away from both families' highly abnormal version of normality was the perfect length of holiday, and they were all looking forward to arriving home and settling back into a routine.

Cultivated from the brown-tinged landscape of northern Victoria, with its endless rolling paddocks peppered with livestock and its patchwork of different crops, both Dyson settlements were expansive, imposing and fit-for-purpose; fertile earth at its best, extending as far as the eye could see.

Their blond-haired, patriotic owners wouldn't have had it any other way. It reflected how their lives were led. Faster, further, stronger each year, the all-Australian sporting dynasty's *motto* held true into its fourth generation.

By happy contrast however, the *hacienda* welcomed back its tired *posse* like old friends. In the three years since they took up residence, *Escondido* had been turned into a bohemian paradise which promised its owners a world of hedonistic repose replete with creature comforts to feed the soul. It represented a worthy compromise for a pair who worshipped the four pillars of fulfilment: freedom, beauty, truth and love; an eclectic, romance-infused mix of cultural harmony.

Jet settled into the local primary school with no trouble at all, replacing his cousins' *camaraderie* with a handful of friends from the neighbourhood. His sister was enrolled in a *Kindergarten* playgroup three mornings a week, mainly because Lynn and Jeff had taken the decision to delay their children's start at the feeder school for Melbourne Academy for a couple of years.

It was important to the liberal thinkers that enough time be devoted to learning how to mix with all abilities and backgrounds, rather than restricting their inculcation to the exclusivity of Melbourne's *élite*. This move had met with a cool reception from their high-society grandparents, more than negated by the delight shown by the Mount Eliza community and Mornington Peninsula newspapers.

'We'd like our children to benefit from the best education for their individual personalities,' the famous mother had told the television cameras which flocked down from the city to capture her little girl's first day at school. 'So does every other decent parent. If we were to send Jet and Kierney to high school in Frankston and then slip it a *squillion* dollars to educate our kids, guess what? It'd turn into an *élitist* school. Raising the standard of universal education is not a problem we can solve in the time needed to educate one generation of kids. It doesn't mean we'll be taking our feet off the gas on the campaign while they're at MA though either…'

Staying local also meant parents and nannies would not wear out their tyres by driving on a daily basis between *Escondido* and the CBD, allowing them to take full advantage of their splendid, tailor-made domain for unusually long periods. An extra buzz always filled the air when both superstars were in residence at the same time, since their electrifying compatibility infected the rest of the household.

The photogenic couple had written, directed and starred in a zany romantic comedy released at the end of November, presenting another round of *premières* to attend and an ever-growing platform of fame and adulation for speaking out on the issues they supported. The charities, *Enseignants pour la Paix*, Childlight and The Fellowship, reaped enormous benefits from their patrons' exposure, causing Gerry and Cathy ongoing recruiting headaches while trying to cope with the Diamond Celebration Foundation's phenomenal growth rate.

With the festive season approaching, Lynn was her usual knee-deep in concert preparations both in Sydney and Melbourne, with several other recordings taking place for television stations in multiple countries. Their many discussions around the breakfast and dinner tables about rousing performances which kept the fire alive for his talented wife also served to reinforce Jeff's determination to return to touring after the holidays. Recovered from the Chicago tragedy, he was his own man again, recharged and primed to conquer the world.

The purveyor of the finest steamy choreography and inflammatory rock music chose Melbourne's Festival Hall as the venue for his first live show in two years. He opened with one of his oldest and best loved hits, its driving beat lifting the crowd to its collective feet before the composer had even set foot on the stage. All it took was the change of a single lyrical reference from talking to singing, and he had the audience eating out of his hand from the outset.

Both ends of the pantomime horse rejoiced in having the great Jeff Diamond unquestionably back in town. A boom camera panned down to show his partner in the second row, overflowing with joy to see her husband up where he belonged. With a classy lightshow and regular bursts of comedic banter, celluloid images beamed across the globe, followed by the inevitable invitations for concert gigs pouring into Stonebridge Music's offices again.

Under increasing pressure to perform together, entertainment's golden couple resisted the temptation and reserved these for special fundraising opportunities. This was for two reasons: firstly, they knew their marketing machine needed to retain something up its sleeve for the future, should the pace of their popularity ever slow; and secondly, the mystique surrounding their off-air relationship depended on *not* being seen together every minute of every day.

Regular spurious articles surfaced in women's magazines and on gossip shows the world over, informing their adoring public that all was not rosy in the Diamonds' garden. Fuelled by speculation of rifts and affairs from all quarters, some had a tenuous link to reality and others were complete and utter fantasy. Lynn and Jeff were careful when choosing which of these fairy stories they shared with the children as part of their education on how to maintain the integrity of their young public profiles, while providing a continual source of amusement behind closed doors.

Several months into his tour, photographs appeared of the handsome musician in the arms of a sultry minor celebrity whose career could only be helped by such publicity. Maya Philippe, a Mauritian swimwear model with connections in French political circles, had in fact been shooting a commercial with the multi-lingual rock star to raise awareness for poverty and human suffering in war-ravaged Cambodia after Pol Pot's tyrannical and bloodthirsty *régime* had been toppled. The Australian media hounds seized on the picture, taking it out of context and heralding the breakdown of his marriage to their favourite daughter.

Despite having overcome his old insecurities, the scarred addict continued to struggle whenever these baseless stories broke while he was so far away from home. The next morning however, he had been relieved to catch an interview Lynn gave to another over-zealous reporter who had broken ranks and caught her while training in the Sportsdrome.

As he had hoped, the showman's beautiful best friend was all smiles in the clip comprising a single comment from an untroubled woman. 'It's rubbish. We've never been closer. I hope people ignore these assumptions and stick to the important causes Jeff and Maya are supporting.'

Even so, the devoted family man couldn't help but worry, remembering the many times when faithfulness had been overtly tested on the road before his sabbatical. Might his wife begin to wonder if there were more to these suggestive poses than met the eye? Indeed, as she confessed later over the telephone, she had admitted to Michelle to being more than a little concerned that he had been up to his old tricks. It was a healthy warning sign, but stressful nonetheless.

'It *is* rubbish, angel. Complete fabrication. I don't know how I can prove it, but I love you so much and can't wait to show you.'

'Jeff, I believe you,' his dream girl replied. 'Of course I don't like the pictures, but it's work. I understand that. I'm sure the roles'll be reversed at some stage.'

'Hmm...' the humble man murmured. 'That I don't want to see either. Point taken.'

***

Richard "Sandy" Dyson passed away in April at just twenty-three years old, after succumbing to the AIDS virus and enduring six months of steady but relentless deterioration. Jason, his partner of half a decade, and also HIV positive, was devastated in spite of the inevitability, preparing himself for the media onslaught.

During the brief adult portion of his life, Lynn's brother had flitted between Sydney and San Francisco, enjoying relative anonymity while he pursued his athletics and show-jumping goals and devoted time to coaching other queer sportsmen through the difficulties of dealing with their sexuality in such gender-stereotypical cultures.

Having championed gay and lesbian rights for the last few years as part of their social justice agenda, Lynn and Jeff were at pains to help Bart and Marianna through the tough period. After an initial denial of all links to AIDS and the homosexual community in general, they finally managed to convince the big man to acknowledge his younger son's true identity.

Accepting homosexuality was as much of a gargantuan struggle for the Dyson parents' generation as wrestling off the blame for his mother's death had been for their impoverished son-in-law, making the necessary actions of support clear to their vital link. Her patience with the old-fashioned elders earned a draught of eye-rolling and foot-stamping from the liberal and incontrovertibly teenaged Anna.

Sandy's funeral was a low-key affair attended by close family and friends in the burgeoning Sydney suburb of Newtown. After a respectable mourning period, Jeff made the suggestion of inviting the grieving mother on a speaking tour of Europe and the United States, assisting him to spruik the African AIDS crisis. The middle-classed curious turned up in droves to see the hot-shot musician appear with his glamorous mother-in-law. He drilled home to the stately former ballerina and her peers that each affected family member spent over a year's salary treating the immunodeficiency disease.

Dubbed the "Standing Room Only" circuit, the unlikely pairing climbed rickety staircases, in stuffy halls and open-air *auditoria* in towns small and large, to explain how the medication's prohibitive cost often meant families were left with heart-rending choices: if a husband and wife were both HIV positive, they were forced to pick who should receive treatment. And whom did they invariably choose? The father by default, since he had greater earning capacity, with the invariable by-product of leaving their offspring to fend for themselves when their unfortunate, ailing mother passed away.

On and on their message went, Marianna Dyson's spirits soon restored by the landslide of adoring fans who accosted them. Fan-mail thanked them for educating people about situations where HIV-infected children of African families also fell victim to horrendous lotteries, the parents only able to apply their scarce financial resources to either treatment or schooling. One *or* the other, Jeff would stress to the spellbound audiences.

'Vaccination or education,' his seductive, dark-brown baritone insisted, weighing the invisible choices in his hands one by one. 'And who gets the education? The boys, of course... Surprise, surprise!'

The more the philomath learned about the inequalities of life, the more determined he became to reduce the gaps. He found his life's public ramifications embodied in the mysterious dark-haired gipsy growing up in their house, and the ambitious parents would prognosticate long into the night on the future awaiting their children; especially for a girl due to come of age at the turn of a millennium.

What sort of world might Kierney inhabit as an adult? A level playing field that would allow her aspiration to soar to its full height, or a misogynistic boy's club which preferred its young women in submission and subjugation, limited to carrying out the bidding of her male superiors? And what type of change was the Midas couple likely to influence if they were to start now?

For her husband's thirty-first birthday, Lynn invited a number of prominent feminists and academics to dinner at the Grand Hyatt's restaurant. With the ambition of spurring on the equal opportunity movement with their public weight, the guests and their hosts met each argument head-on. Initially agreeing rebuttals as to why a person's gender should not dictate their contribution to society, they moved on to brainstorm campaigns and publicity stunts for the Diamond pantomime horse to champion from their position of privilege and power.

The philosophical songwriter had taken so much inspiration from this outrageously successful and licentious evening that the characters and plot for a new musical had already crystallised in the creative partnership's brains by the time they reached the steps of their apartment building. Its hook leaped out at the intellectual as soon as he had stretched out naked on the balcony sun-lounger with a glass of malt whisky in his hand and a quilted blanket ready to warm his wife's body when she joined him outside.

'Big sky,' he announced, relishing the feel of lean thighs, chilly from the winter's night air, brushing against his hot-blooded body.

'Big sky?' the bemused woman repeated, accepting a kiss from the man whose mind never stood still. 'Yes, it is. Pretty big. Wow! How come you're so warm already?'

Reaching his free hand around the beauty's shoulders to pull her closer, drunken arrogance mixed with romantic charm as Jeff searched for a suitable response. 'One part gratitude for an amazing birthday, one part alcohol infusion, two parts inspired by an overload of good ideas and ninety-six parts in love with you. Feeding my anticipation as to what that might buy me.'

'Oh. That's gorgeous. It buys you anything you like, my beautiful black stallion. What about the sky though?'

Smothered into an ardent embrace, the nubile blonde heard the tumbler's heavy base click onto the tiles and watched as her generous measure of Baileys was harvested from her fingers. How she loved this giant of a man! And how he loved her too... Giving into the delicious taste of his tongue in her mouth, she slipped her empty hand under the cover and clutched his erect penis, chuckling at the deep and desperate groan her touch educed.

'You remember last week, on the balcony at *Escondido*,' he breathed between kisses, 'when Kizzy was thinking out loud about not being able to see much of the sky?'

Lynn nodded, recalling the moment with unfailing clarity. The habit of spending quality time with their gorgeous little ones between dinner and bedtime had become a tradition, come rain and come shine, all four piling onto deck chairs and usually accompanied by the dogs. Since the family had taken in a rescued white, cross-bred German Shepherd to keep Merak company, Greg had all but surrendered the shared dog to his new lady-friend.

'I'm going to dedicate this film to "the girl who asks",' Jeff stated, rolling over and exerting dominion over his muse, who sighed with a mixture of physical and emotional pleasure. 'I want the score to contain anthems for women's rights and the unfettered pursuit of reason. Jesus! That felt good, angel. Damned good.'

The self-nominated sex-god's jaw tightened as a rush of insecurity shot like an ice-shard through the heat of his arousal. His wife smiled in sympathy at the predictable response, reaching her hand round his neck, where her fingernails scored the muscles at the base of his skull. Neither cared whether their cries of ecstasy could be heard above the rumble of Melbourne's early morning traffic.

Kierney had been fascinated by the fact that only a small section of the wide, blue universal backdrop was visible whenever she gazed out of her bedroom window, and how she could see a lot more from the balcony. How big was the whole sky? The toddler's insightful observation captivated her dad's imagination. Within a month, he and Lynn had written almost an entire *libretto* under the working title of "Laura's Light", named after a character in the little girl's favourite book.

In June nineteen-eighty-three, soon after Jeff's birthday, he and his dream girl announced a partnership with the Massachusetts Institute of Technology, Paragon Holdings and The Good School, whereby gifted students would have the opportunity to spend a gap year at the hallowed seat of learning between finishing high school and attending university. The chosen few would work with postgraduates in the Technology and Innovation fields of computer science, biotechnology and engineering, emphasising the value of strong leadership around the moral and social impacts of progress.

In the press conference which launched the programme, the philanthropist delivered one of his more stirring motivational speeches. He told the assembled media representatives that he would have made sure he was at the front of the queue for a course such as this, stressing the importance of resisting the temptation to rush into wide-reaching technological advances without developing appropriate ethical frameworks to regulate their application to real people.

Jeff spoke of the widening gulf between those who were in a position to take advantage of technology and those who would never be. The Diamond Celebration Foundation promised to tackle this important issue as a matter of priority, citing it as a one-way ticket to democracy's collapse if all the power were to rest in the hands of the very few.

The Diamonds' hegemony period had no end in sight. The treadmill turned faster and faster with each passing month, both superstars in high demand for all sorts of extra-curricular assignments, in addition to those generated through direct endeavours. The extended leave of absence with their young children soon slipped away into the dim and distant past, the number of days and nights the couple spent under the same roof reducing in lockstep.

'At least we're never going to get bored with our own company this way,' Lynn laughed, sitting down with her transient husband for an express dinner at Melbourne Airport *en route* to the US Open tennis tournament.

'I look forward to that day,' Jeff replied, having recently arrived back into Australia after a thirty-hour flight from South Africa. 'I still remain unconvinced that absence makes the heart grow fonder, but we're certainly its most dedicated lab' rats, gorgeous. And its best advocates, I add with reluctance.'

His wife shook her head. 'Agreed. Three weeks together at the end of this month though... It's hard not to wish the time away when I'm alone, I miss you so much. I can always feel you with me in some way. Sounds ridiculous, but I can.'

'It's not ridiculous at all, angel, 'cause we're connected beyond Lynn and Jeff. Way beyond. Doesn't mean I won't miss you too, by the way. I shall, without doubt. And here's another open question for us to ponder in our separateness: what if the physical absence is more acute because we're still together spiritually?'

The tennis champion's eyes filled with tears. 'That's a beautiful thing to say. I love you.'

As Jet and Kierney settled into their daily routines of school, music lessons and sports, the blonde star began to crank up her own songwriting output once again. Inspired by the eternal optimism of their son, she released a single with the unforgettable hook of "I'll give you tomorrow if you give me today. Your heart beats my name, and your eyes lead the way."

With the *doyenne* of Australian musical royalty's skill of layering sexy sophistication with a galvanising motif, the upbeat dance track shot to the top of charts on every continent. The record from which this hit was taken also sold multi-platinum quantities everywhere, sparking a hurriedly organised tour to reinforce its success and leaving Lynn Dyson's parental leave balance as bankrupt as her husband's.

For the singer's birthday in September, Jeff commissioned a professional photographer to create a new batch of souvenirs for the family album. He had recovered from a brief crisis of conscience the previous year, after three pictures of the photogenic quartet fetched over a million dollars in a race for exclusive rights, instead imagining the good deeds they could pull off with such easy money.

The celebrities posed one behind the other for a composite pair of photographs to capture the world's attention; the left-hand portrait showing mother and daughter and father and son craning round to smile at each other while trying not to fall over, while the right-hand depicted them all standing at ease and gazing eyes-front. Spontaneous for the latter, the handsome comedian had lifted his foot between the other three pairs of calves, causing Kierney to laugh very naturally, knowing she wasn't supposed to move.

Magazines and television shows all around the world clamoured for more, and their wish was granted in the form of the next series of documentaries set at the familiar beachside *hacienda* in the spring. The opening episode began with an off-the-cuff comedy sketch during which the man of the house offered his good lady wife the top of a banana as she emerged from the gymnasium after a hot and sweaty training session.

'This is a family show,' he reminded her, before she accepted the first bite with a salacious smile.

The opening credits rolled over Jeff's pained expression, cross-eyed as he feigned agony.

Off the back of this outrageous popularity, at the end of the year, Lynn launched the "Walk Away" program. A departure from their usual charities, this initiative was aimed at desperate parents of young children, in response to research findings which suggested new parents may be driven to cruelty as a result of sleep deprivation and post-natal depression. A natural symbiosis between The Fellowship and Childlight, it worked on the premise that temporary neglect was better than permanent damage through abuse if desperation arose.

Nineteen-eighty-four rolled around, seeing the Dyson-Diamond partnership on yet another Jumbo Jet, bound for Los Angeles and the Academy Awards, where they picked up Oscars for Best Music Score, Best Song and Best Screenplay for "Laura's Light". Shortly beforehand, they had also received Golden Globes for Best Director and Best Motion Picture. The children and nannies joined them afterwards in Florida for a trip to Disneyworld to celebrate their first fortnight of uninterrupted family fun since Europe over twelve months earlier.

Their familial bond grew stronger than ever during this time of acute togetherness. Jet sprouted a newfound degree of independence as the months went by, undergoing his initiation into Grandpa Dyson's wondrous ways, and the friendly child couldn't wait to start his first year of city-based primary school after the summer holidays.

With Jeff's travel schedule as manic as ever, and the blond dynamo cached in the Thomas Parfitt School's dormitory five nights out of every seven, mother and daughter were free to play girls-at-large during the week, before collecting an exhausted tyke after sports on Saturday morning and escaping to *Escondido* for the rest of each weekend.

In stark contrast to her brother's happy-go-lucky demeanour, the personality inherited by the couple's second child was brooding and unquenchable. At only five years old, she had become a force to be reckoned with in any debate around fairness. She was endowed with her dad's uncanny ability to see all sides of an argument, along with infinite patience and sufficient fortitude to outlast any dissenter.

The world-changing traveller returned from another overseas trip after hearing reports of one such intense interaction with a neighbour's fourteen-year-old while he was away. Lynn had described how Kierney had dug her heels into the lawn and rammed her hands on her hips, scoring point after point against a young girl who dared to issue a challenge on a matter of right *versus* wrong.

However, before he was allowed a debrief from his wife, who had observed the entire dialogue from the open kitchen window, he was ushered into the playroom to be serenaded. His two most favourite women had collaborated on a new song, "Papa's Girl", to thank the proud man for giving her these valuable gifts.

Total Immersion

'Dad, look!'

Bart Dyson's eldest grandchild came haring across the cobblestones towards his father, having difficulty taming an unruly bundle of clothing under one arm while brandishing a manila folder in the other hand. Making the most of an unseasonably tropical December evening, Jeff had adjourned to the courtyard for a cigarette and an ice-cold beer after several hours cooped up in the office on the telephone.

'Hey, mate! *Whatcha* got?' he yelled back, watching his son's last-minute navigation of a rise in camber around the Spanish colonial fountain reconstructed at their sacred secret hideaway. 'Where've you been?'

The six-year-old barrelled into his dad's legs, excitement overruling his ability to slam on the brakes in time. 'At the Sportsdrome,' he panted, 'with Grandpa and Fraser. Look at my whites!'

'Very cool, Jetto,' the songwriter responded, eager to hear what his son had made of this new entity destined to figure heavily in his young life. 'Who's Fraser?'

'My coach. He's going to help me play for Australia.'

Extinguishing his cigarette in the ashtray, the affectionate celebrity covered Jet's head with the palm of a huge hand, ruffling his hair hard enough to make him wobble right down to his feet. The boy grabbed his father's legs in a rough rugby tackle, hauling him off the iron seat. After scant resistance, his opponent complied, and they began to wrestle on the unyielding flagstones.

'Careful, mate. You're getting too strong for me,' Jeff complained, receiving a parry of painful blows to his right thigh and stomach. 'I need a coach too, to keep me stronger than you.'

'Yeah. Good idea,' the youngster agreed, ceasing their battle without warning in order to open his new file on the table and spread out the pieces of paper for examination and due sanction. 'Look! Here's my summer program.'

The intellectual snaffled a proud smile, hearing his son enunciate each block of text aloud, as if practising a speech. After every sentence, as his parents had taught him, he paused to take a steadying breath and made eye contact with his audience. The negotiator leaned back on his chair and took in the news, already convinced it wouldn't be to his liking.

Regardless, for the sake of the bouncing bowler impatient for his big break, Jeff resisted the temptation to betray his emotions. Jet was about to be sucked into the Dyson machine, the redirection of which would require tact and diplomacy of the highest order.

'From New Year's Day 'til you go back to school?' he deduced from the *pro forma* stapled to the folder's inside cover. 'What d'you think about that?'

'It's nearly the whole holidays,' Jet admitted. 'It's what you need to do to be captain of Australia. Dedication. Grandpa told me I'm going to be very tired and need to eat heaps.'

The amiable retort hid the truth, its dealer poking the boy in the stomach and squeezing his right biceps. 'You already eat heaps, muscle man. Is Sonny doing this too, d'you know?'

The lad chortled, twisting round to squeeze his dad's arm. Jeff flexed his knees, straightened his spine with a deep groan, and the small frame levitated clean off the ground. After thrashing his helpless legs, dangling in mid-air above the chair, Jet let go and dropped back down, landing a barrage of punches into his opponent's taut abdominal muscles.

'Hey, mate,' Jeff grabbed his shoulders more roughly than he intended before recoiling out of guilt. 'I asked you a question. Is Sonny doing this too?'

'No. Next year,' the lad answered, still shadowboxing at anything he could reach. 'He's too young. He's not going to do cricket anyway.'

'Shame,' the celebrity growled, grabbing the frustrated little boy and hugging him in close. 'Calm down, Jetto. It'll be better next year when Sonny's doing at least some of the same training. You're going to be able to show him what to do, so you'll still be the boss cousin.'

The child was pacified by his father's beneficent advocacy, inhaling and puffing his chest out at the prospect of overshadowing the second Dyson grandson, who was fast closing the gap in both height and weight. It was also clear to Jeff that the idea of spending the whole summer holiday at a training camp even overawed the Crown Prince of Australian sport.

'Which sport's Sonny focussing on?'

'He doesn't know yet,' Jet frowned, climbing onto his dad's knee as if seeking safe harbour. 'Football or tennis.'

The supportive counsellor worked the usual magic. 'Yeah. Well, you'll still be able to kick his butt at tennis for a while, I reckon. Are you happy with cricket? Honestly?'

'Oh, yeah! I love it,' the boy cried straightaway. 'And you can come to school and watch me. With Mum and Kizzy too.'

'We shall indeed,' his dad nodded. 'Don't want to miss a single run or wicket, mate. Wherever you're playing, all over the world: The Ashes, the Windies, India. Everywhere.'

Jet laughed. 'What's the Windies?'

'Too many baked beans,' Jeff responded with a straight face. 'Didn't Fraser tell you about that? I'm sure you're going to find out about them soon enough.'

'Baked beans! Like farting, you mean?' the blond larrikin giggled, swinging an impatient foot. 'I don't believe you. What's the Windies really?'

The boy's handsome and hairy hero shrugged, feigning disappointment. 'What? You don't believe your own *papá*? Why would I lie to you? *Mein Gott!*'

''Cause you didn't smile,' the seven-year-old slid off his father's knee and landed like a lead weight on the ground, indignant hands held aloft. 'I always know when you're joking because you pretend it's not funny.'

'Ha! Good man,' the intellectual laughed. 'You're good at reading people. I mean the West Indies, kiddo.'

'Oh!' the youngster exclaimed. 'West Indies. I know who they are. Viv Richards and Joel Garner. Tall, black players.'

'*Exactamente,*' Jeff nodded. 'You'll never play for the Windies 'cause you're short and white with blond hair. They'd never have you.'

Shoulders lifting in defiance, the champion in the making's reply was nonchalant. 'Who cares? I only want to play for Australia, so it doesn't matter. I'm going to beat them. And I'll be as tall as you soon, won't I?'

'Yep. 'Xpect so. Maybe even taller. And you'll be stronger and faster and cleverer too.'

'Why?' his son asked, leaning on his dad's long legs and nuzzling against his shirt. 'Will I be stronger than you?'

'Undoubtedly, mate. Mum and I are going to make sure of it,' Jeff replied, giving the end of the boy's nose an affectionate press. 'It's what parents are for. No point having kids if we don't teach you how to be better than us.'

***

'He's a little kid, angel,' the songwriter moaned. 'Seven years old. When does he get a chance to enjoy the school holidays like a normal boy?'

The children were in bed, and Lynn had emerged from the office, after taking up where her husband had paused: on the telephone to her agent in London for the last hour. A short European tour was about to kick off, and they needed to organise the last remaining items on her busy schedule.

'But Jet's not a normal boy, is he?'

'Why not?'

'Because we want him to achieve great things,' she smiled, sinking down onto the rug to leaf through a workbook which Kierney had brought home from school.

'Yeah, OK. But not at seven years old,' Jeff persisted, tapping the open pages on her lap with the bulb of his bare big toe. 'Can we talk about this, please?'

The young woman closed the book and replaced it on the coffee table. She had been expecting a backlash at some stage, knowing her husband was uncomfortable with their son's heavy training program. This issue was coming to a head, his agenda given away by the extra, earnest edge to his voice.

'It was just the same for me. I enjoyed it at his age.'

The philosopher let out a long sigh. 'I know. You made good friends, and it didn't do you any harm. I know all that, and you're perfect, so how can I dispute it?'

'But you *are* disputing it,' Lynn laughed.

'Shit! Please take this seriously,' he continued, unsettled by their rare difference of opinion. 'This is our son we're talking about. He's got a little sister. When do we get to take our next family holiday? Are you going to do the same to Kizzy next year?'

'Jeff, *I'm* not doing anything to them,' his wife fought back. 'We agreed they'd go into training when they turned seven.'

'I know, angel. But all day, every day?'

'It's not all day, every day. You're exaggerating.'

'Not by much,' the rock star shook his head, jaw set and eyes fixed on hers. 'Five full days a week and half of every Saturday. That's not far off a full-time job. More than an adult's typical working week.'

Lynn sat forward on the couch. 'So what do you want me to do? Pull him out? I can't do that. We agreed they'd be part of the Dyson world, and this is how it starts. He'll love it, Jeff. Really love it.'

Because he doesn't know any better, the child inside sneered. Was this the juncture at which he ought to remind his dream girl of the anger she had directed at her parents when they removed her choices as a teenager? Yes, their son was half Dyson, and the bigger half at that... And he certainly didn't seek to snooker the lad's blatant sporting ambitions.

'But why total immersion?' he asked, feeling dejected but determined not to let it show too early. 'Look at what it did to Anna. She's a robot.'

'What? That's not fair,' the Olympian objected. 'Anna's not a robot. She loved every minute of it too, and she's been extremely successful.'

'Doubtless,' Jeff snapped, springing off the couch. 'Sorry, angel. I don't want to argue like this. I'm going for a drive to sort my head out.'

Raising herself to her knees after the angry man, Lynn reached out to catch his hand but missed it by a few centimetres. He kept walking, and she decided not to follow. It was the first time she could remember him leaving her without a kiss, setting off alarm bells in her mind.

How much had he drunk over dinner? Should she ask George or Greg to shadow him? Was the former hot-headed tearaway even in a fit state to drive? As the son of a violent criminal, he was usually so responsible when it came to mixing alcohol with automobiles, but she hadn't seen his mood this turbulent for many months.

In the old station-wagon the family had bought for transporting their canine companions, the Ace of Diamonds snaked around the coast towards Dromana and onto the peninsula proper, with the two excitable dogs panting and slobbering in the back behind the *grille*. His thoughts wound in ever-increasing circles. This was shaping up as a sticky mess to dissect, even for someone with such refined negotiating skills. What did he always advise his clients? Keeping one's emotions out of the equation was never a good strategy. Depersonalising an issue risked losing the fundamental will to reach a resolution.

Yet faced with her unswerving belief in the Dyson champion-building methods, Lynn was not prepared to bring the argument back to a personal level. Jet was not only her firstborn; he was also Bart's eldest grandchild.

The clever minx had been right to point out that both parents had been complicit in signing their son's destiny over to forthcoming Australian sporting glory. They had promised him to the cricket squad slated to win the Ashes in the nineteen-ninety-four and –five season. So far-fetched and futuristic had the goal seemed at the time, Jeff hadn't given the subject of training *régimes* much consideration, and now he was about to face the consequences of this rare oversight.

Pulling into a lookout car park near Rosebud, the thirty-two-year-old switched off the ignition and opened the driver's door. Like a video clip on mute, he smiled at the dogs bouncing and barking through the station-wagon's windows, before lifting the rear hatch and letting them gallop down to the rocks below.

Leaning on the bonnet and staring out across the still water of Port Phillip Bay, the confused celebrity lit a cigarette and cursed his beautiful best friend's uncharacteristic obstinacy. How far might she go to uphold the Dyson dynasty? How vague a memory was her own metamorphic rebellion?

And, more to the point, what would he do to make his case? What was going on here? Why did this mean so much? The forever lover had stormed out of their marital home for the first time in nine years, feeling more strongly about this than any other issue they had faced before. Was it he who was being unreasonable?

As greatly as it pained him, the wise man had to accept that his instincts could well be wrong and this intensive induction to the dedication required to be a world-beater was indeed the best option. The miniature live-wire had demonstrated a heroic heart and an aptitude for strategy, so it was little wonder he latched onto the complexities of the ancient and idiosyncratic sport. Jet had set his sights on winning The Ashes from the moment he developed sufficient hand-eye coordination to belt leather with willow, and there was no denying his love for all things cricket, over and above anything else in his youthful life.

No, Jeff thought, dropping the end of his cigarette on the gravel and twisting it under the toe of his shoe. The exact problem in a nutshell... Of all people, he, the promoter of broadmindedness and exposure to wide-ranging sources of knowledge, must never compromise his principles so far as to support the loving of any one thing to the exclusion of all else.

Devoting almost forty hours each week for ten years' worth of Australian summers to a single objective was not what was best for their son. This type of total immersion hadn't done the other Dyson prodigies any real harm. Yet he had, during a decade of family gatherings, listened to many regrets of holiday activities which the grown-up siblings had forfeited in favour of their punishing training schedules.

Scaling and slithering down the cliff via a set of rickety, weathered wooden steps covered in damp moss, the songwriter found himself on a small, deserted beach. The moon hung bright against a cloudless sky, and the lights of Melbourne twinkled in the distance off to the right. His canine charges were pleased to have their master join them, jumping up and barking, willing him to throw an object of flotsam or jetsam into the surf for them to fight over. He obliged, relaxing as he facilitated their carefree game.

Somehow, the concerned father concluded, he must find the right angle to convince Lynn to give their son some latitude. Attaining the status of "Greatest Cricketer of All Time" to please his grandfather should not prevent him from developing into a well-rounded, cultivated human being during the striving years.

His mind's eye pictured without difficulty the contrast between the bright and positive view of hereditary rights and privileges as seen by this happy Aryan child of imperial stock and the daunting, ugly future the self-styled father had perceived as a mixed-race seven-year-old in the slums of western Sydney. Ryan "Jet" Diamond saw a wealth of promise waiting right around the corner, whereas the young Jeffrey Moreno Diamond had only encountered obstacles separating him from opportunities way out of reach.

Yes, the struggle required to achieve one's goals was a lesson worth learning, and Australia's future leaders needed valuable exposure to situations which would never occur in their aristocratic station without unnatural interference. With his philosophical roots firmly planted in eighteenth-century French literature, the concept of *"La Lutte"* underpinned his very ethos.

There was no doubt the lost boy from Canley Vale was recouping his own stolen innocence through his children, so perhaps his reaction stemmed from losing a summer of vicarious enjoyment from a purely selfish standpoint.

Lynn and he had discussed this many times over, and she had not once begrudged his indulgence, going so far as to recommend it as a vital part of the healing process.

Maybe Bart Dyson's elder daughter had decided enough was enough and that six years was ample time for a full recovery. The compassionate husband couldn't blame her for diverting their offspring away from the romantic childhood ideals he espoused and focussing them on more serious, world-beating objectives.

Two hours hence, Jeff returned to a worried family. The children had been roused from their beds by car tyres on the loose shingle, followed by the sound of dogs barking and the creak of the courtyard door. Their mum had retreated to the studio to rehearse for her European trip later the same week, trying to put his unexpected exit out of her mind. She was also relieved to see him return.

'Where did you go, Dad?' Jet asked. 'You were ages.'

'Nowhere, mate. Just drove Merak and Janey for a walk on the beach,' the disconsolate man answered, crouching down to hug both youngsters to his chest. 'You don't have to worry about me. That's not your job.'

'Go back to bed, please, guys,' Lynn requested, pointing to the top of the grand, sweeping staircase. '*Papá*'s safe now. You'll see him in the morning.'

The reluctant *duo* climbed the stairs, disturbed by the unusual atmosphere which had descended on their home since dinner. The mysterious traveller grinned and blew them both a kiss, encouraging the four obedient little feet to patter up the last few steps and shut their bedroom doors.

Husband and wife faced off for several seconds in the vast, vaulted hallway, under a veil of silence, before the magnanimous intellectual gestured towards the lounge room door. His beautiful best friend responded with no more defiance than the children, and he blew her another grateful kiss in return. They both let out an awkward chuckle, the air still dense with confusion.

'So what now?' Lynn asked, sitting in the same spot she had occupied when Jeff had walked out on her. 'Why did you leave?'

Her multi-millionnaire husband perched on the arm of the couch, determined not to lose his cool again. 'Shit, I don't know. Because I was too angry to talk to you sensibly, I guess.'

'But why has this suddenly become such a problem? You knew Jet was going to have intensive coaching this summer. You've had months to object, but we've barely talked about it.'

'Yeah. I know,' the negotiator admitted. 'I haven't got a leg to stand on, but I'm not stupid... I can see where you're coming from. I just can't support what we're committing him to. I can't, angel. *Ça y'est!*'

Lynn's tone began to harden again. 'But you have to. We agreed.'

'Why do I have to? Isn't there a middle ground?' Jeff tried not to absorb his wife's growing frustration. 'I'm not saying cancel the whole thing, but I'd like to have our son around for six of the best weeks of the year. And I don't want him to bruise his spirit by too much of a good thing. Remember you told me how you longed for freedom and to manage your own life? But now you're doing the same thing to our kids. Don't you remember how you felt?'

'Yes, of course I do. But I was in my teens by then,' the talented beauty replied, acknowledging the truth in her man's well-chosen words. 'Jet's at the prime age for learning, and you know it.'

The father's anger got the better of him, both at her tactics and at himself for not having a ready response. 'Damn you, Lynn. Don't keep reminding me of things I already know. Jet's also at the prime learning age for reading, for making friends, for studying, for music, for every fucking thing except sex, drugs and rock'n'roll. So why just cricket? What's so important about bloody cricket that takes up a whole summer's worth of prime learning time?'

'I'm sorry,' his wife insisted, apparently as embittered as her husband. 'He's not only learning how to be a good cricketer. He's learning self-discipline, leadership, teamwork and time management.'

'No, he's bloody well not!' Jeff snarled, slamming his fists down hard on his knees. 'He's having those things rammed down his throat at an age when he's not ready to think in those terms. Let him be a kid a bit longer, for Christ's sake. Please? Sorry, angel. I need to get out of here. I'm going to spend the night in the city, if that's OK?'

Drawing himself up to his full height, the musician stared down into the Olympian's disappointed eyes and resisted the overwhelming temptation to forget the whole thing and take her to bed. Even his fine-tuned, irrepressible *libido* was not so rampant as to ignore a seemingly minor detail which was in the process of morphing into a point of principle for both parties.

'Why are you running away?' Lynn asked, springing to her feet and reaching for his left hand. 'This isn't like you.'

The conscientious objector took her hand and brushed his lips across it. 'Jeez, I don't know that either. 'Cause I can't deal with it? With you, maybe... I don't want to spend all night arguing about this, but I'm not willing to let it go.'

'Then stay here, please. You'll disturb the kids again. We can talk about it in the morning.'

Jeff's jaw was set in absolute recalcitrance. 'No, angel. I can't stay. Even if you're able to park it 'til the morning, I shan't be able to. I can't quite believe I'm saying this, but I need to get away from you and think things over. The power of what I'm feeling's doing my head in. I hate the very thought of walking out on you guys, but I feel so damned strongly about this. I'll ring you in the morning, OK?'

The young woman exhaled, reining in her emotions. 'Yeah, alright. If you're sure. Drive safely. I'm sorry you're doing this. For the record, I don't understand either.'

'G'night, angel,' her husband muttered. 'Sleep well.'

The songwriter picked up his car keys and left home for the second time that night. Lynn presumed he had forgotten her flight for France was due to leave the following morning, which made her all the angrier. Perhaps a period of physical separation was the right way to deal with the painful novelty of opinions poles apart; the first time they had ever been so hostile towards each other. She was also a little concerned at how driven she was to win this argument.

She felt a strange betrayal, as if her closest ally was denigrating her heritage. Bart Dyson's daughter had made as many compromises as her renegade lover on the way they were bringing up their children. Any tough decisions taken before today had been no big deal, on reflection, but she wasn't prepared to jeopardise Jet's opportunity to become a truly great cricketer. She was a truly great tennis player. Her whole family were truly great sportspeople. Greatness tended to go hand-in-hand with the surname, yet the fact her son was a Diamond and not a Dyson hardly made him less entitled to experience the type of success she and her siblings had experienced.

***

'I can't believe how immovable you are,' Jeff said over the telephone the following morning. 'It's like I'm talking to your old man.'

The downhearted musician risked this overly flagrant comment, having resolved overnight to stand his ground. He had waited until the children would be outside in the pool or playing in the garden before ringing to continue their unfinished conversation. As predicted, Lynn saw red at the comparison with Big D, especially when she reflected on some of the titanic clashes fought by the two most important men in her life.

'That's so unfair. You had me agree to some pretty extreme things when we first got together. You're a fine one to accuse me of being immovable.'

The rock star took this one on the chin. 'I know, and I'm sorry,' he responded. 'I would've accepted you changing your mind though, if you'd told me why.'

'Oh, would you?'

'Yes, angel. I would've.'

His wife sighed. 'So where does this put us then?'

'The kid's half mine, Lynn,' the negotiator launched into a speech he had prepared while unable to sleep. 'I'd like a say in the decision that sees an end to long summer holidays at the age of seven.'

'There are several people who should have a say, as dramatic as you make it sound... Especially Jet himself. I'm sure you agree with that.'

'Sure,' the patient man replied. 'Perfectly fine. So have you asked him if he wants to spend the whole summer holiday training?'

'No,' she admitted.

'Well, I did,' Jeff informed her. 'And he couldn't give me an answer, to be honest. Doesn't know yet, I guess. And since you're the only one of us who does... Christ! This is all so unnecessary. Although he did get very edgy straight afterwards. I want us to ask him again. Together, if you're OK with that?'

'No, I'm not. Don't make it worse for him,' the exasperated mother pleaded. 'Don't put him in the position where he has to choose between his dad and his grandpa.'

The superstar sighed. He disliked having any type of serious conversation over the telephone, unable to see the expression on his wife's face or her body language while sitting through this ordeal. Worse still that he was aching for her after a stressful night alone, and the image of her flawless figure glowed like a beacon in the part of his brain controlled from elsewhere.

'OK. I won't put pressure on him, angel,' he vowed, 'but we need to know how he truly feels.'

'Yes, alright. Ask him whenever you deign to reappear at your home.'

Jeff laughed at her latest caustic remark. There was something incredibly erotic about his dream girl using sarcasm to taunt his craving carnal mind.

'Yeah. Cheers. We all deserve a slice of the action, baby, when it comes to this kind of decision,' he continued. 'Even Kizzo. She won't want to spend the holidays as an only child either.'

'Kierney'll be involved in something similar from next year too,' Lynn tossed in a casual reminder with uncharacteristic malice. 'I'm not going to change anything. We agreed this before they were even born.'

'Fuck! That's bullshit,' her husband cursed into the mouthpiece. 'So what does it mean? We can't agree to disagree about our kids? Is this big enough to break us up?'

'I hope not,' the sportswoman's toned softened.

'Good. There must be some middle ground then.'

The peacemaker's request was met with silence from the other end of the line. He let the dead air hang between them, hoping his beautiful best friend would yield first. It was a dangerous plan, and one in which he wasn't the least bit confident.

'This is our son's future success,' Lynn spoke after a lengthy hiatus which saw his heart rate surge.

'Yep. I know. And his future happiness, don't forget,' her lover replied, managing to conceal his relief that the conversation was not over. 'I know what this means to you, angel. Believe me, I know. I want him to be successful too but I also want him to be happy.'

'He will be happy. He is happy.'

Jeff stuck to his guns, sensing a degree of vulnerability to be exploited to the full with any other negotiating party. 'After sixteen years of single-minded determination?' the cynic in him couldn't refrain. 'Like you, you mean? You didn't like it.'

'I did like it. Really liked it... I only grew out of it when I fell in love. Jet and Kierney can do the same. They can make their decision when they're old enough to have one to make.'

The man of unfailing empathy shook his head. 'Yeah. That's what I'm afraid of. What if he gets to twenty-five and thinks, "Fuck! What happened to my prime?" How d'you know they won't rebel and go off the rails? They could end up like some of the other next-gen' celebrity sons and daughters we know.'

'They won't!'

'Won't they? You sound very sure of something we have no idea about...'

'Because they've got us as parents,' Lynn insisted. 'We wouldn't let that happen to our kids. I know you wouldn't, and I hope you know I wouldn't either.'

'Of course I do, angel,' he relented, hearing another trace of fear in his wife's tone. 'But it's possible. Jet's got more of you in him than me, it's true, but I'd hate to trigger some latent, inherited depressive gene. Plus, every generation needs something slightly different, and I'm concerned your dad's approach might not be the best option the second time around.'

'Argh! Well, you'll just have to trust him, Jeff,' his wife reverted to her previous hard line. 'Dad knows what he's doing and he's very successful. Jet idolises him almost as much as you. You know that.'

'Jesus, Lynn! I can't believe you won't even give an inch,' he moaned in tearful irritation. 'What the hell's got into you? Is this thing going to wreck our relationship?'

'Maybe it is. You're making this thing much bigger than it needs to be. It's only a summer of cricket training. Why don't *you* give an inch?'

The negotiator scoffed at the woman's obduracy, even though it cut him to the quick. Long-forgotten insecurities began to creep out of the darkness behind his eyes, and his blood pressure climbed as he fought to halt their incursion.

'Right. Let's start the bidding... Eight out of nine weeks is your starting position, or do you want all nine with only a few hours off to visit us on Christmas Day? Is that still what you want? Will you even drop to seven?'

'No,' his offer was turned down flat.

'Fucking hell! Move, damn you.'

'I don't see you moving,' Lynn challenged.

'What are you talking about?' her angry husband returned. 'I'm prepared to move. I told you I wanted a say, not that I wanted to dictate.'

'And you think I'm dictating?'

The young man exhaled. 'Yes. Quite honestly, you are. I understand we had an agreement, and I won't try to bail out of that. But you haven't offered me any concessions whatsoever.'

'Hey!' Lynn yelped. 'Hang on a minute! I'm not some operative at your negotiating table.'

'And I'm not some Joe Public do-gooder sticking his nose into the life of someone else's child,' came her husband's automatic rebuttal. 'Jet's my kid as much as he's yours. Just because he's got blond hair doesn't mean...'

'Oh, for God's sake! I know that, but his future's mapped out.'

'No, angel. It isn't. No-one's future's mapped out. No-one's... It's up to each of us what we make of our life, and it's up to you and me to give our son the best start to his. The rest is up to him. I don't believe this is the only way.'

'Jeff, I need to get to the airport,' the tennis champion cut the conversation short, without even acknowledging his point. 'I'm sorry, but I have to get off the 'phone now. I'll ring again as soon as I'm in the hotel, providing it's not a stupid time.'

'No. This is more important than catching a bloody 'plane! I'll drive out and meet you at Tulla', if necessary,' her husband allowed his voice to sound dejected for the first time during their arduous discussion. 'Did you even hear what I was saying?'

'Yes, I did.'

'And you're happy to leave it there? Don't you have *anything* further to say?'

The young mother sighed, belying the churning in her stomach. 'Only that I think we should take some time to work out where to go next. I don't like arguing like this any more than you do. It's horrible, not getting on. But it looks as though we've found something we can't agree on, and it's a real shame it affects our kids too.'

'Even more reason to keep talking,' Jeff begged. 'Please, angel. Don't do this.'

'I'm sorry. Let's think about it while I'm overseas. Then hopefully, we'll have reached some more conclusions by the time we're back in the same place.'

'Jesus Christ! I just don't believe this. It's like someone else's taken over your brain in the last twenty-four hours. You know what? Whatever you want. Have a good trip and say *bonjour* to *la belle France* for me. I love you.'

'Thank you,' her voice was solemn and resigned. 'I shall. And I love you too.'

'Do you? You don't sound very sure.'

'I'm not sure actually,' Lynn whispered. 'But I hope it passes.'

'Shit.'

Silence whistled down the line between the city and the peninsula suburbs. Scarcely recognising themselves, both lovers knew how deep this admission would pierce the world-changer's restored outer shell, and yet neither denied her honest opinion needed airing.

'Whoa, Lynn,' he murmured, desperate to remain calm while Gravity laced up his hobnail boots after a long time hibernating in his cave. 'One disagreement, and our burning hot love's washed down the drain? Where's the depth?'

'No, of course it isn't. Listen,' his indignant wife replied. 'Forget Jet having to choose for a moment... You're making *me* choose between you and Dad again.'

'I'm not!' Jeff bleated. 'Jeez! This isn't nineteen-seventy-four anymore. I'm no longer the scum-of-the-earth street kid your dad wanted you to steer clear of. You've taken my side over his heaps of times lately, and I'd like us to steer our children's lives a bit differently on this subject. That's all. It's not a love *versus* hate matter.'

The rock star heard a sharp breath and paused.

'I don't hate you,' his dream girl had been wounded too. 'And arguing like this must change the way you feel about me... Or else it's just a night without sex talking.'

'Fuck, angel! That's a pretty cheap shot,' the angry tearaway's nostrils flared. 'No way. You're so wrong about that. I do still feel the same way about you. Just bloody disappointed that we can't work this out without doling out petty insults.'

'Who's doling out petty insults?'

'A night without sex talking?' a sardonic tone repeated into the telephone. 'You know me better than that. At least, I hope you do. My balls've been running low-level interference ever since I left, screaming at my conscience to give in and wrap you up in my arms... Make you come like a breached dam.'

The young woman sighed. 'I'm sorry, Jeff.'

'I know, and so am I. We're not animals, angel,' the new and improved multi-millionnaire crooned. 'We're sophisticated human beings. We should be able to work this out, for Christ's sake. We're worth a try, aren't we?'

The caller thought he heard his wife crying but made no concession, steeling his heart against the demoralising sound. He had said what he needed to say, and now it was up to her.

'Yes. We are. And I'm sure we'll figure it out when I get home,' she faltered. 'I need some time to think about everything. OK?'

'Sure. I can wait. I waited two years once upon a time,' the relieved romantic quipped. 'I'll see you next week. Safe flight, angel.'

Pressing down on the button to cut off the call, the perturbed peacemaker massaged his locked jaw. He was filled with desolation that Lynn appeared so determined to win, even to the extent of doubting her love for him. He hoped it was a kneejerk reaction made under pressure, similar to the initial callous rejection she had given him on her return from the Dyson-engineered American *sojourn*. Nevertheless, he couldn't help wondering if this time it might be for real.

***

The couple known for its windbag tendency didn't speak for a full week. A long, vexatious seven days at home with the children only reinforced Jeff's foreboding, putting on a brave face and trying not to labour over what the future might hold. The diminutive Diamonds were sensitive to their dad's sadness, no matter how hard he tried to disguise it by playing games and telling jokes. At first, they refrained from prying into their parents' unhappiness, but after a few days, underlying anxiety overcame them all.

One lousy row in over eight years, the songwriter sat at the grand piano and waited while his daughter carried a mug of coffee with love and care in pigeon-steps from the kitchen to the lounge room. She was angry with herself for slopping some over the edges. Placating her with a grateful kiss, he took the vessel out of tentative hands and lifted the empathetic girl onto his knee.

One serious family dispute was nothing to worry about by normal standards, yet it spelled disaster for the insecure half of the world's most unbreakable partnership. His own plight was aggravated by the youngsters' distress, then further heightened by his own fears into an unsavoury spiral of doom.

'Why did *Mamá* make you sad?' Kierney asked, having earlier run full pelt into his waiting embrace after a trip to the beach with Ashley, the latest nanny to arrive from New Zealand.

'*Mamá* didn't make me sad on purpose,' Jeff reassured her. 'We made each other sad, *pequeñita*. We had an argument. Sometimes it's hard for us to agree on everything, 'specially when she's not here.'

'Was it about me?' Jet piped up from his seat at the other end of the room. 'She said last night you think my cricket training's too much.'

The tousle-haired bundle of energy had given his dad a subdued greeting when the *trio* reunited, as if unwilling to be drawn into conversation. Having brought a jigsaw down from his bedroom after showering the sand and salt off his tanned body, he had marched towards the furthest corner of the cavernous space, cleared the games table and tipped out the puzzle pieces without a word.

This atypical introversion had prompted the concerned father to request Ashley's temporary absence while he revived the boy's flagging spirits.

'Yep. I do, mate,' he responded, encasing his son's entire shoulder in a reassuring hand, 'but it's not your fault. *Mamá* and I want you both to be the greatest at whatever you want to do. At the moment, we don't agree about how to go about it. We'll figure it out though. Just give us time, OK?'

'So what's going to happen?' Kierney pressed. '*Mamá*'s making us all sad.'

'No, she's not. The situation's making us sad,' the philosopher countered. 'I'm sorry you feel sad too, guys. Hopefully, it'll all be over by the time *Mamá* comes home.'

'Are you getting divorced?' Jet asked without lifting his eyes, his tone as casual as if enquiring about what his dad had had eaten for lunch.

A metaphysical dagger plunged through the songwriter's heart, the troll's aim staying true during his period of retirement. 'No! Did *Mamá* talk about divorce with you?'

'No,' the child shook his head, casting a sideways glance at his sister. 'Kizzy's teacher from last year asked, didn't she? We met her at the ice-cream shop with Ash.'

The little girl nodded, her lower lip quivering. Jeff's eyes filled with tears, and he hugged both children in close. *Fantastic.* They were long used to the world placing bets on how long their marriage might survive, yet this time the odds had plummeted. The penalty of proclaiming themselves as the perfect public pair was that their dirty laundry was fair game to be run up the flagpole for all to see.

'I don't know why she asked this question,' the furious father answered in a measured tone aimed to not quite underplay his disquiet at such gossip-mongering. 'I haven't said anything to anyone. I don't know how she knows there's anything wrong, *pequeñitos*.'

Watching Kierney's wide, brown eyes flash over his shoulder towards the hallway as if afraid of being overheard, Jeff lowered his voice to prompt his daughter. 'Did Ashley talk about us to Ms Faulkner?'

He received a surreptitious nod in reply. Transforming a gloomy frown into a broad smile, he was placated by his ability to introduce some lightness into the atmosphere when the little imps followed his lead and giggled at their piece of espionage.

'Yes,' Jet confirmed in a whisper. 'She heard you swearing at Mum on the 'phone.'

'Shhh, mate,' the celebrity warned. 'I don't want you to repeat what Ashley said, please. I'll ask her to keep her opinions to herself from now on. That's the best idea, don't you think?'

'*Sí, Papá*,' two angelic voices sang in unison.

'*Me encantáis, tanto tanto,*' their father declared, planting emphatic kisses on each child's cheek. 'How about some dinner? *¿Tienéis hambre?*'

The threesome strolled into the kitchen to find Ashley and Usha cooking up a storm, a pungent, exotic aroma of turmeric and peppers permeating the ground floor. The kids ran to the cutlery drawer, eager to help set the table for their evening meal. Jeff was glad to have settled them down for now, despite his own insides being far from stabilised.

'Smells good, guys,' he smiled, rubbing his hands together and smacking his lips. 'How long have we got?'

'About fifteen minutes,' the rotund Indian medical student answered. 'I hope it's not too hot. Tell me if I put too much spices in.'

'It'll be great,' their boss replied. 'Ash, please could I have a word with you in the office?'

The more senior of the two new childminders blushed a deep pink, reaching for a tea towel to dry her hands. Diffident in full view of her charges, she followed the handsome musician along the corridor to the Diamonds' nerve centre, as the room had become known. Off duty earlier in the day and immersed in her studies, Usha was bemused to see the children exchange furtive glances and a few nervous titters.

Once out of earshot, Jeff invited the Kiwi to sit down. Crossing her long, slim legs, she masked her nerves with a valiant attempt at flirtation, a poor choice of tactic for her encounter with one of popular culture's most charming men. She had only been with the Diamonds since the previous November and was still technically on probation.

'Relax,' the man of the house opened, resisting the temptation to eye off the woman's underdressed figure. 'Do you know what I want to talk to you about?'

'No. But it must be bad if you have to talk to me on my own,' Ashley's attitude turned defensive.

A wry smile spread across the poster boy's face. 'Yeah. Valid assumption. I'm not happy, that's true enough. Jet told me Kierney's teacher asked them if their mum and dad are getting divorced. I'd like to know how she came to be asking such a question, please.'

The nanny fidgeted in her chair, and her face paled from red to ashen grey. Educated at one of Wellington's prestigious private schools, she had come close to blowing her opportunity to work for Lynn and Jeff Diamond once before, when she and a boyfriend had walked out of a restaurant without paying.

Her father had disclosed this indiscretion during Stonebridge Music's interview process since an arrest without charge had shown up on the applicant's police record. She had been amazed that they hadn't rejected her out of hand at this point, left to assume the songwriter's own blemished past had prompted him to give her a second chance.

126

Pondering the thoughts running through the student's mind, said former petty criminal watched her clench and release her palms. He regretted making the student so uncomfortable.

'It sounds like you already know,' Ashley shot back, her attitude a little too rebellious for her boss' liking.

'Yes and no. I know what the kids told me, but now I'd like to hear your side of the story,' he answered, staring into the woman's frightened eyes.

'I didn't say anything much. What did they say I said?'

Jeff's temper was fast fraying with the surliness the twenty-year-old ought to have outgrown by now. 'Who? The kids?'

The aspiring advertising creative nodded and coughed, guessing the flick of her employer's hand meant he didn't intend to respond. 'Usha told me I'd be in trouble if I said anything to anyone,' a less defiant voice uttered. 'I just said I heard you on the 'phone to Lynn and that you were having a blue.'

'Ah, yeah?' the seasoned peacemaker sniffed and grinned at the typical down-under euphemism. 'Is that so unusual? How did you get from "blue" to "divorce" so quickly?'

Ashley shrugged, tears welling in her eyes. 'Sorry. I don't know. What did the kids tell you?'

'The same, pretty much,' Jeff half-smiled, cocking his head, 'so thanks for being honest. You signed a confidentiality agreement, Ash, d'you remember?'

The contrite nanny nodded, tugging at her mini-skirt in an effort to rise to the more formal part of the discussion. Again, the lonely husband discerned a dose of coquettish body language from the chair opposite, dismissing an instinctive response without delay. He gave her the benefit of the doubt, knowing it was equally likely to be his own plebeian, lustful reaction to being up close and personal with a nubile, attractive female after a week of abstinence.

'I thought we explained what the confidentiality agreement was for,' he carried on. 'Do I need to explain it again?'

The South Islander chuckled. 'No. I get it. Am I fired?'

'D'you want to be fired?'

Ashley burst into tears, all attempts at flirting abandoned. 'No. I'm sorry, Jeff. I really am. I really want to keep working for you.'

'OK. Cool. You're not fired. It's alright,' Jeff's bruised heart bled some more for the distraught young woman, leaning back in the leather office chair and picking up a batch of envelopes. 'Just keep things to yourself from now on, please. If you're asked any questions, say "No comment," or "I don't know," or defer to us as to how we'd like you to respond if you get asked the same thing in the future. Though, if it happens again, the end result might be different. D'you understand? Let's be quite clear: "confidential" means "confidential" and "agreement" means "agreement," but "blue" does not mean "divorce". You OK with that, Ash?'

'Yes. Thanks,' Ashley's laughter turned into a noisy sigh of relief. 'Thanks very much. It won't happen again, I promise.'

The superstar rested his hands on his knees and straightened his legs before encouraging his employee to do likewise. 'You're welcome. Subject closed. Let's eat.'

Jeff collected his unopened post and a couple of folders of correspondence which he knew were overdue for attention, then ushered the New Zealander out of the room. Hoping the armful of documents would serve as a distraction for the evening while Miss Irony taunted him that "blue" was closer to "divorce" than he might think, he gritted his teeth and requested the information he hoped would provide an additional antidote to his nagging doubts.

'Out of interest, and I know I said the subject was closed,' he hazarded, 'but how did Kizzo answer her teacher's question?'

Ashley cackled, throwing her arms in the air. 'She shouted "No!" really loud and turned away in disgust. It made us all laugh, even her.'

The sunken hero was satisfied enough with this news, and he broke away to collect his precious gems to wash up before dinner. By the time the Diamonds loped down the wide staircase and sat up to the table with the others to enjoy a rather hot curry, their combined mood had reverted to jovial and carefree. Watching the two women exchange surreptitious glances, he smiled inside. With any luck, they had all learned a valuable lesson.

***

Once Jet, Kierney and their caretakers had retired to bed, Jeff sat at the piano and went over the day's events, idly playing with some melodies which had been brewing for the last hour or so. He needed to bring things to a head with Lynn somehow. There was no way the family and its *entourage* could tolerate this standoff for much longer.

Checking his watch and then removing it from his right wrist, the musician calculated the time difference between Melbourne and Stockholm, where his gorgeous *cabaret diva* would be entertaining her ardent fans that evening during the brief concert series. They had compromised about this, hadn't they? Their management company only committed the young mother to whirlwind tours these days, neither parent wanting her to be too long away from the children, despite colossal demand for her performances.

Cathy Lane, the public relations manager at Stonebridge Music, had faxed over a review from a French newspaper describing a triumphant three-night stint in Paris. Reading it both delighted and annoyed her proud boss that the cessation of diplomatic relations had not appeared to affect Lynn's ability to woo her admirers.

Why should this temporary glitch make a difference to her star quality? The rock guitarist chastised himself for his pointless jealousy, having taken to the stage himself at various levels of distress during his early career. And Lynn was a Dyson after all, bestowed with sufficient inherited grit and determination to enable the segregation of expendable feelings from pre-defined goals with minimal application. It was a trait she had always possessed and one her husband was comfortable not to share.

'Hey... It's me,' the despondent Australian spoke into the receiver when the call connected.

'Jeff, hello,' his wife's sultry, post-gig voice answered, casting him into the depths of fantasy. 'How are you? Are the kids alright?'

'Yeah. We're all fine, thanks,' he replied. 'You? Awesome notices from Paris. Congrats, angel.'

'Are there?' the modest star checked in surprise. 'Oh, thanks. I haven't seen any.'

'They're great. Cath sent them to me. Where are you going next? *Deutschland?*'

The sound of papers shuffling was faint from the other side of the world as Lynn retrieved her itinerary. '*Ja, sicher.* Frankfurt and Munich. Then home.'

'*Gracias a Dios,*' Jeff sighed. 'It's all around Mount Eliza that we're getting divorced.'

'What? Divorced? How come? How do they know?'

'So it's true?' the comic chided, his chest constricting with dread for what may be to come. 'When did this happen?'

'Shut up. Of course it's not true,' his dream girl's reply was upbeat until she recalled how they had left their relationship in *limbo*. 'Sorry. That's not what I meant. I meant how does anyone know we're fighting?'

'We had a security breach,' Jeff admitted, seeing and raising her misplaced *badinage*. 'Ashley heard me talking angrily on the 'phone to you. Put two and two together with Kizzy's former teacher and made twenty-two.'

'Oh. Did you challenge her? How did you find out?'

'JeKi dobbed her in,' the songwriter explained. 'They didn't say outright, but Kizzy's eyes gave it away, and then Jetto blurted everything out.'

'That sounds like him,' the nervous woman chuckled. 'Were they shocked?'

Again Jeff clenched his jaw, afraid of what his mouth might say if it were given free rein. 'Yeah. A bit. They're fine now though. Usha cooked up a flaming beef *bhuna*, so they're probably floating thirty centimetres above their mattresses as we speak.'

'Euch! That's gross!' Lynn laughed again. 'So how are you?'

'I thought you'd never ask,' the comedian continued as if everything was normal between them. 'D'you care?'

'Yes. I do care. I've been doing a lot of thinking.'

'Good,' Jeff said. 'Me too. Did you come to any conclusions?'

'No. Not yet,' his wife confessed.

'How much more thinking do you have to do? What's left to think about?'

'I don't know.'

'Jesus. Here we go again. Is this the best we've got?' her husband implored, tired of the stalemate.

'I've got, you mean?'

The intellectual inhaled, dragging on a cigarette and swirling his fifth tumbler of whisky. 'No. I mean is it the best we can do?'

'Yes. Quite honestly.'

Jeff's heart sank yet again at the apathy in his dream girl's attitude. What was happening to their perfect world? What had become of the pantomime horse which never stopped talking? It was hard for him to believe they were in such an all-or-nothing dilemma over their personal life when they had pulled off so many sophisticated business deals and established their fair share of non-government organisations to make a noticeable positive impact on the global stage.

'So d'you really mean to tell me you'd trade our marriage for total control over our kids? Where's the scale in between?'

'No. I'm not sure there is one on this issue, to be honest,' Lynn replied. 'I'm sorry this is so hard. I just don't feel like I can compromise on the plans we have for Jet.'

'Angel, can I tell you how ridiculous this is?'

'You just did.'

The thirty-two-year-old smirked, the Scotch allowing him to see the funny side. 'Well, don't you agree?' he persisted. 'We're supposed to be the ones who work things out. I fly all over, encouraging people to compromise on matters of huge significance, like peace and genocide, cruelty to women and children, HIV tolerance, *et cetera*. And yet I can't even persuade my wife to give an inch about a boy's cricket training. Why is that, baby? At least tell me this much?'

The Olympian's dilemma was palpable half a world away. 'Oh, I have no clue. I'm sorry, but I can't tell you why, except that I made a commitment to Dad. *We* made a commitment to Dad.'

'Yeah. But he's got three perfectly good candidates with the right surname waiting for their chance at greatness,' Jeff continued. 'Can't we do a little of our own experimenting with greatness? I don't want Jet or Kierney to miss out on the Dyson influence altogether. I've never said that. All I want is to have some balance in their lives while they're dependent on us for decisions. Not total immersion, Lynn. That's all I ask.'

'Alright. I'll think about it,' Lynn's answer sounded too cool, almost cursory. 'I don't want to fight anymore. I'm sorry, Jeff. I have some interviews to do this morning. I need to get ready. Hope you have a good night.'

'Yeah, right. G'night,' her husband replied, at a complete loss as to what to make of her casual assurance. 'I love you. Don't forget.'

Replacing the telephone receiver, the intellectual took one consolation from their unwelcome exchange: Gravity was now nowhere to be found. Had he learned to live without the persistent troll? Was his resilience robust enough to have made the bastard think twice about going on the offensive after all these years?

Up yours, you dwarf arsehole! You can't touch me now. I can handle this without your interference, thanks very much.

Jeff couldn't fathom why, but the lost boy inside was incapable of blaming himself this time. This dispute was all Lynn's doing, and he simply needed to exercise patience. The wisdom he had gained in recent years on the subject of human nature had equipped him with a weird fascination to see how far his golden-haired princess might take the situation. One thing was certain though: he would be in significant strife if their relationship were to reach the point of no return; the harbinger of doom would be upon him, flanked by Gravity and Miss Irony riding arm-in-arm into the sunset.

Stuck in Stockholm on a freezing morning and intending to pound the icy pavement between her hotel and the river, following the *concièrge*'s instructions south down the *Scheelegatan* to the strand and along the banks of the *Ridderfjården*, Lynn ended the call and wept from the heart. She knew her wise man was right. He saw through her obstinacy these days, and she had expected him to capitulate rather than lose her.

The father of her gorgeous little ones didn't deserve another dose of all-Australian hubris. This tireless, benevolent genius, whom she admired and respected so much for his dedication to causes for the benefit of so many others, rarely asked for anything for himself, so what right did she have to shut him down? Their love had first fashioned a neglected child into a steadfast sex-god, and then transformed him into a devoted and skilful parent beyond even her high expectations. His only request was to participate in Jet and Kierney's summer spontaneity to make up for the childhood he lost to vice and violence.

She had never put him to the test when the shoe was on the other foot, but judging by his level of devotion to her, the children and everything else in his busy life, she had no reason to doubt his word. And now they were each asking the other to give up a deeply held belief in order to stay together as a couple and as a family. That wasn't fair. He was absolutely right.

Yet on the other hand, the alternative for the much-loved athlete and musician would involve diverging from the Dyson master plan. What would the patriarch of Australian sport make of Jeff's interference with his grandson's training? A rivalry still simmered under the surface between the two successful men, and the odds were stacked in favour of Bart taking offence if his son-in-law presumed to know how best to build a champion.

The next morning at *Escondido*, the philanthropist had risen early to make several telephone calls before the others awoke, intent on avoiding being overheard by either nanny. He had tossed and turned all night, marvelling at how strange this phenomenon was to him these days.

As ever, the most peaceful sleep arrived too late to be enjoyed, and the first conscious thought to accompany the alarm's intrusion was both reassuring and sickening in its familiarity: *I owe it to myself to force the future's hand.*

Jeff dragged himself downstairs to the gymnasium to blast away the morning doldrums before showering and throwing a few nights' worth of clothing into a suitcase. On a mercy mission through Changi Airport for the second time, he smiled to himself as he tucked his passport into the inside pocket of his leather jacket. He had to dig deep in his memory to compare the respective success forecasts between then and now.

After using the giant map of the world on Jet's wall to point out the aeroplane's route to its frosty European destination, the superstar prepared to leave the children in their pyjamas early on the bright summer's morning. 'I'm going to winter to bring *Mamá* back. We'll all be friends again, I promise.'

Kierney clung to the traveller's legs, sobbing her heart out. Her wailing upset her brother too, both wanting their parents home together and for life to return to normal, but also reluctant to let their father out of sight in case neither returned. Leaving an anxious Ashley in charge of picking up the pieces, he sped off in the Aston Martin.

And not an hour later, with a deep layer of snow on the ground outside her hotel room window, the rear half of said powerful imitation animal lifted the receiver and dialled *Escondido*, suddenly struck by a strange sense of unease.

The New Zealander answered the telephone. 'Jeff's left,' she let on, the hesitation in her response metered out as rudeness, unsure how much information she should divulge. 'He said he was flying out to meet you.'

Thanking the student who had set the cat among the pigeons the previous day, the sophisticated songstress hung up and cried. She had been so busy running through her schedule of interviews, rehearsals and performances that her innermost feelings had been kept at bay. Now however, with a morning to herself, the seriousness of the situation began to perforate her staunch conviction.

Were her priorities all wrong? For none too noble a reason, she had fallen short of true commitment to their marriage and all it represented in the face of its first real ultimatum. The family's happiness and the love affair to top all love affairs was worth far more than an archaic game where the players dressed from head to toe in white and slugged it out in fierce sunshine, stopping for rain, lunch and tea, all for the prestige of lifting a tiny, wooden trophy. This gentlemen's ritual was all rather trivial when considered next to the elimination of sadistic military *régimes* or saving whole communities from starvation.

Her husband, in his own inimitable yet modest omniscience, had detected a chink in her armour and clearly planned to throw his full charismatic weight behind this argument in much the same manner as he approached obstinate government agency officials and self-righteous corporate executives.

In fact, this behaviour was no different from the way the born charmer had manipulated his flaxen-haired quarry in those early days, convincing her he wasn't the risky prospect implied by his lineage. The brutal and unforgettable pull to be together that gripped the young lovers in the nineteen-seventies had surrendered to a serene synchronicity in the current decade, where life's uncertainties were no less challenging but much easier to surmount as a united force.

With the lost boy's mental dogfights and monstrous doubts far behind them, Lynn had no desire to dwell in this erratic pyre again for longer than necessary. Neither did she care to live without her enigmatic and passionate frontman. She could conceive of nothing worse.

A Meaningful Life

Let loose in Germany's industrial heartland, Jeff Diamond made heads turn as he strode into the concert hall in the city of *Frankfurt-am-Main* and took his seat in a box above the stalls. The cultural capital always celebrated his presence, people all around pointing and whispering to each other as he dispensed trademarked half-smiles, provocative winks and sly waves in liberal measure.

When prompted to pay attention by the orchestra tuning to "A", Lynn Dyson Diamond's audience resumed their respectful and adoring silence, appreciating the musicianship of the band members, some of whom had toured with her since their university days.

The celebrity philanthropist had arrived by taxi towards the end of the first half and had sunk a couple of refreshing *Dunkelwiezen* in the bar with Christian Johansson, Lynn's European tour manager and publicist. Rather than waiting until the tumultuous reception died down and the stage emptied for the intermission, the two men had secreted themselves to one side, between banks of throbbing speakers and racks of guitars.

In awe as ever, Jeff tapped into the familiar electric thrill which passed through the fans and musicians alike, nourished by the mix of well-known hits and new material. The sights, sounds, smells and vibrations of a stadium gig never failed to energise him, and he and his wife's tour party stared out through particles of dust floating through the air on criss-crossing multi-coloured beams of light.

Ticketholders revelled in the evening of classy entertainment, on their feet dancing for some and sitting with their eyes closed for others. The singer's smooth *contralto* voice was becoming more soulful as time went by, her voice a little deeper and expert in the application of colour and texture to every melody. Indeed, she often engaged in light-hearted banter on the subject, blaming the change of pitch and the mellowing of its tone on the last ten years of passive smoking, for which her husband was somewhat ashamed to accept responsibility.

In a lame effort to assuage his guilt with affection, the songwriter had reassured his dream girl that the occasional ragged edge gave her voice an even sexier quality. Here tonight, with jetlag threatening to overtake his disquieted mind, he listened to copious wolf-whistles from the large, lascivious male contingent and issued a silent prayer that his ring would still be on her finger at nightfall.

Jeff took his seat with the rest of Stonebridge Music's northern hemisphere team in the third row of a balcony overlooking the performers. With the ever-popular "Feels Like Yesterday" wrapping up the second half, the band left the stage for the final time after three *encores*. The crowd was about to cease their cheering and foot-stomping and begin the mass exodus when Lynn and a solo 'cellist walked back across the wide expanse, resuming their places at the grand piano.

To a hushed audience ecstatic to prolong the show despite the late hour, the musician sat down and started to play the introduction of a song which no-one recognised. The superstars' invisible elastic connection slackened in a heartbeat, and by the end of the first verse, the lyric had transmitted a secret code to its recipient. Her sincere rendition told him she knew the love of her life had flown in tonight and was sitting in the audience. While everyone cheered and gazed around in anticipation, he stayed motionless and anonymous, waiting for the reparative statement to run its course.

Lynn Dyson Diamond's heart had never felt so full and in need of purging its sins. She spilled her hopes and dreams for little faces left pressed against the window at home, watching their father follow an errant woman into the wide, blue yonder. Double-octave bass notes thumped in anger at her own stubbornness, sweeping *arpeggios* launching her words from defence to retribution and back again, as the singer's emotions carried to the handsome man, somewhere out there in the darkness.

On and on went the broken chords in *sonata* form, trickling out in rhythmic beauty then splashing on the floor like tears in a confessional. Crystal clear *vibrato* floating to the auditorium's rafters, the singer deliberately ran her lungs beyond empty, gasping the last syllable of every line in anguish. All around sat mesmerised by the unexpected injection of chamber music as it metered out her march to the gallows. The debt was hers all along, not his…

The fluidity of the pianist's right hand duelled with the strict, leaden beat of her left, while intimate phrases brought her dreams to life by virtue of one man alone. A man she loved more than anything in the world.

The relief flooding through Jeff's veins acted like a powerful drug hitting his nervous system. Everything would turn out alright, he guessed, unable to wipe the stupid grin off his face. Twenty-four hours ripe for much better use by not spending them at an altitude of eleven thousand metres had yielded the most productive day's labour in a long while.

The object of this soulful penance fought back tears as the 'cellist's impassioned counterpoint chased along with the last few melancholic piano chords, raising his bow in a tasteful signal for the crowd to rise. Clearly exorcised, Lynn stood to acknowledge the rapturous applause, searching eyes having no hope of catching those of her beautiful black stallion from such a distance.   She thanked the audience in German for coming to share her enjoyable evening and exited the stage for the final time.

The representatives of the couple's management company were none the wiser as to what had brought on this spontaneous addition to the night's set, and the star's husband offered no clues either. He underplayed the almost deranged attack of joy, anticipating a similar reception as soon as he could break away from the group.

If it came to it, Jeff reflected, a champagne cork popping close to his right ear, life without his dream girl would mean nothing, despite the multitude of good fortune which had been bestowed upon him in recent years: his inordinate wealth; his ever-lengthening and multifarious list of achievements; and even the kids…

Faced with a make-or-break decision from the prodigious siren on whom he had staked his star-struck claim, the old soul was under no illusion that he would snap and fold like a delicate Japanese fan. Jeff Diamond belonged with Lynn Dyson. This was an incontrovertible truth, and all that mattered in the end.

It took a few minutes of quiet deliberation before the handsome man noticed all eyes now fixed on him, subliminal expectation seeming to have transferred to their adoring public. He decided to flee the auditorium in case eager fans trapped him, keen to uncover the story behind Lynn's heartfelt apology. Yet his feet had stuck fast, rooted to the spot, his mind reprising the deep stringed instrument's haunting theme, urging the lyric to spring forth again and again.

Sensing the uncontainable adulation fermenting as the seconds ticked by, the rock musician shook himself out of his dreamlike state and proceeded downstairs towards the labyrinth of backstage corridors well known from his own concerts in this town. Refusing to be waylaid by the hordes of fans streaming in his direction, most armed with pens and programmes, he picked out a young female stagehand and commandeered her assistance.

'*Guten Abend,*' he said to the startled worker. '*Kann Ich herein gehen?*'

'Jeff Diamond!' she gasped. '*Jawohl. Moment, bitte.*'

The special visitor was allowed through a door labelled "*Kein Eintritt. Personal nur*", and he thanked the woman with a broad smile, hoping she would take her leave after granting him access.

She coughed, standing her ground. 'Mister Diamond… *Bitte, kann Ich…?*'

To the impatient celebrity's consternation, she too had produced a pen and a programme out of nowhere and now begged for his autograph. Without delay, he scrawled his signature across a dazzling picture of his wife, and they parted company, both energised in much the same ways. He heard the familiar sounds of post-concert celebrations, clinking of glasses over raucous conversation and adrenaline-infused laughter, all emanating from a room at the end of the corridor.

Lynn and her band were busy entertaining a number of special guests and radio station competition winners in one of the rehearsal rooms, part of the customary obligations which kept goodwill and charitable donations flooding in. Her husband decided to wait to see his beautiful best friend on her own. He didn't want to steal any limelight from tonight's main event by making a grand entrance.

Locating the singer's dressing-room, Jeff tried the door. It wasn't locked, and the sight within was all too recognisable; organised, tidy and professional to the last. Most unlike his own dressing-rooms! He slumped down into the make-up chair and stared at his reflection in the mirror before glancing around at the occupant's personal effects.

His eyes alighted on a photograph of himself and the children, housed in a small, plastic fold-up frame that bore the scars and knocks of thousands of kilometres travelled. Jeff pictured the young mother looking at this picture while she had written her wistful *encore*. How many of his own heartfelt ballads had been given life while staring at the photographs which roamed the planet in his wallet?

The philosopher pondered what Jet and Kierney would have him say to their mother on his mission to put the pieces back together. Forcing his thoughts to the present, he remembered he was here to represent all three while jet-lag clouded his mind and sexual urgency escalated in his body. The innocent little mites didn't want their blissful existence to dissolve any more than he did. Was Lynn truly prepared to risk this? Surely not... Far more than intensive sports training, their gorgeous children deserved and needed a stable, happy environment in which to grow up. And so did he. This was why he was here, plain and simple.

Shrieks of laughter and chatter from across the hall suggested the lively gathering showed no sign of coming to a swift conclusion behind the closed door. Visualising a familiar scene in full swing, Jeff picked up the copy of Lee Iacocca's autobiography he had given his wife for Christmas, pleased to find the bookmark inserted close to the end. He looked forward to discussing its messages with her after this unfortunate *fiasco* was over.

Flicking past each chapter with idle fingers, the multi-millionnaire's thoughts drifted back to the lonely figure serenading him from the piano in the dark. What had changed since they last spoke? Was this a genuine change of heart, or had she admitted defeat to save their marriage? He hoped for the former, yet would settle for the latter. There was no doubt he would do the same if faced with the catastrophic alternative.

Nodding off in the warmth of the stuffy, windowless dressing-room, the stowaway became aware of his fellow musician's voice in the corridor. She was thanking her musicians and arranging to meet them again in an hour for a late dinner. Springs inside the door handle resisted with a metallic twang as it turned, followed by an audible sigh as the beauty entered, clutching a bouquet of roses and a half-full pint glass of water.

'Hey, angel.'

Alarmed to find someone in her private quarters, Lynn stopped in her tracks on seeing the long-legged frame lounging in her chair, his dark, handsome features ringed by naked light bulbs. As she was to share with her diary much later on, the weight of control in their marriage underwent an irrevocable switch at this precise moment. Jeff felt it too. Their eyes met, both stars blindsided by the realisation that the choice of what to do with this power lay fairly and squarely in the hands of the nobody from Canley Vale.

Would he take it or share it?

Blood drained from Australia's most influential woman's head as she digested the startling view. The man sitting in front of her was relaxed and assured, dressed in pale denim jeans and a black shirt with a faint, woven, self-coloured silk check. She was simultaneously shocked and overjoyed, for the first time seeing someone in complete command of his circumstance. It took a few seconds for this pivotal moment to register in her psyche, and moreover to recognise its true importance. The final step in her lost boy's lengthy transformation declared its precipitate, absolute and unequivocal completion, now squaring up to the regal thoroughbred who had always been his destiny.

'How did you get in here?' Lynn asked, her voice breathless.

'Through the door,' the comic shrugged, rising to his feet. 'Come here, you exquisite creature.'

Extending his arms and grinning at his poor joke, Jeff's arousal coursed through him at breakneck speed. His dream girl's soul was screaming for his, and he had waited long enough to touch her. No longer able to bear the suspense either, the singer lurched forwards, collapsing into his embrace in a flood of pent-up tears.

The intensity of their shared passion locked the couple's lips together, and they stood pressing into each other as if they had been apart for an eternity. Inching his sobbing wife back to the door through which she had entered only two minutes ago, the interloper turned the latch to shut themselves away from the rest of the world until they had reunited once and for all.

'I can't believe you flew all the way here for this,' the grateful woman cried. 'Thank you. You're amazing.'

'No worries, gorgeous. And thank *you*. For the song, I mean. I'm not going to let this beat us, angel,' he kissed his beautiful best friend's moistened cheek and cupped a wanton left hand under her breast.

'Jeff,' his wife breathed across day-old stubble.

'Shhh. I need you and I love you,' he told her. 'We're too important to be allowed to fall apart.'

The thirty-two-year-old manœuvred the female form he could hardly bear to touch for fear of losing all control, and she followed his lead without objection. It had ever been so, and by all indications, would continue ever to be so. Her eyes red and bleary, she sat down in the seat where she had found him waiting.

The visitor leaned on the bench table and picked up the book he had been leafing through. 'Have you enjoyed this?'

The Olympian smiled at this authoritative intellectual whose charm was melting her heart as easily as he had as a nineteen-year-old student. The combination of kindness and strength seduced her then and now, and with persuasive power unrivalled by anyone she had met in between. In comparison, even her own omnipotent father paled into the scenery, case in point...

'Do you really want to talk about Lee Iacocca?' she chuckled, relaxing a little.

'Nope,' Jeff smiled back, expelling the stale air from his lungs. 'I'm trying not to rape you.'

'Oh,' Lynn murmured, a sudden jolt transporting both lovers to the same juncture in their complicated history.

Here in Frankfurt in nineteen-eighty-four, their second Moment of Truth had come to pass. The memory of the first still managed to make them shiver, codified in their private chronology as "the tennis skirt episode", was the night when the innocent schoolgirl had reduced an aggressive predator to her crawling, desperate prey. Tonight the tables had been turned, and the significance was lost on neither of them.

Back in the original, delicate era of tentative togetherness, an unknown quantity from Sydney's west had offered his soul on the altar of undying love, faced with the vision of attractiveness he had coveted all his young life; in equal parts saviour and sorceress. And now here, in a classic dungeon cell in the pre-war industrial *Festhalle* concert venue some twelve years later, he had bargained for its safe return as a revered and respected leader.

The superstars knew the result of this imaginary trade lay in their hands, eyes transfixed in the tiny space, surrounded by costumes and greasepaint, instrument cases and manuscript books. It was as if their two ancient souls had taken flight side-by-side to steer their current incarnations towards a second defining crossroads. Would the rebellious world-changer reclaim his soul from Lynn's keeping and acquire hers along with it, just because he could? Or would the refashioned nobleman agree to bank them both, never to be traded again?

The songwriter stocked his lungs full of air, ready to put the world to rights. 'So... Where are we?'

'Together, I hope,' the awestruck blonde replied, moved to tears again. 'I'm so sorry, Jeff. I mean it. I was wrong, and you're completely right.'

A strange mix of satisfaction and relief rendered the philosopher unsteady, and he shook his head to stave off the vertigo. Of all the myriad *mots justes* darting around his mind, not a single one made it past his vocal cords. The couple stayed motionless for a few seconds, as if two paintings of the same landscape were fusing together from different perspectives.

Breaking the spell, Jeff leaned forwards and kissed his wife's chilled lips. '*Merci, mon amie.* Y'know, I don't think there's anything else to be said, is there? Let's get out of here and leave all this suffocation behind. What did you arrange with the others?'

Lynn pulled back in surprise, smiling eyes shooting downwards from his face to his crotch. 'Don't you want to go to the hotel?'

'Angel, I'm not nineteen anymore,' the red-blooded star scolded, wagging his finger at the preposterous suggestion. 'Give me credit for an attempt at self-control at least, will you?'

Giggling, the compassionate woman stood tall and hugged her larrikin husband, wrapping her arms around his torso. Belying his previous statement, he secured her lithe frame with hungry hands while his mouth smothered the grin from her mouth, relishing her relaxing into his strong grip.

'But what about my self-control?' she asked, running her fingers along the swollen front of his jeans. 'Am I allowed to want to take you to bed?'

'Oh, yeah. Absolutely you are,' Jeff snarled, 'but first there are *dos pequeñitos preciosos* back home who'd give anything to hear us smile.'

Tears of guilt welled up in both pairs of eyes at the poignant phrase which had slipped so nonchalantly out of the poet's mouth, and the conjoined parents clung to each other in desperate deliverance. The wise man stroked his dream girl's long, golden hair as she sobbed on his shoulder, a dainty knock on the dressing-room door ignored while they enjoyed this sublime interlude. The delightful image of the children hearing their parents smile was far too powerful to dismiss too soon.

'Let's go back to the hotel anyway,' Lynn decided, pushing herself away from her husband's chest and kissing him on the lips. 'We can ring the kids, get naked and then join the others for dinner.'

Jeff nodded. 'Sounds great. Starkers for dinner, eh? I'd pay to see that. What are we waiting for?'

The pair rustled together Lynn's belongings and tidied what was left for the stagehands to pack up, the dust in the air crackling with the circulating electricity. The singer's chief roadie met her and her mysterious diversion in the doorway, startled to discover the reason for her long absence.

Shaking the hand of each musician in his wife's band, the respected rocker merged into their party to leave the concert hall to its dark and eerie weekend.

'That's something you and Dad believe in equally as much,' the twenty-nine-year-old songstress opined as they walked out into the humid summer's night.

'Which something?' Jeff answered, unable to prise his hand from her shoulder.

'Personal responsibility,' she clarified with a chuckle. 'Sorry! Didn't realise your telepathy was switched off. I was just thinking how he always used to say, "We're all in total control of what we say and do. No-one else."'

'Unless you've been drugged or hypnotised,' the defensive comic countered.

'Oh, shut up. I'm serious. I never really knew what this meant until we got together and I found out where you came from. You know... Like someone might push us to great lengths, but in the end we always have a choice: to behave like we'd like to be treated or to compromise our moral standards.'

'Yep. *Absoluement, mon amie.* Your point being?'

Lynn sighed. 'God, Jeff! You're going to be intolerably smug until you've got your rocks off, aren't you? I mean you taught me this. It's all up to us.'

'Did I? That was clever of me. Shall we go back to your dressing-room? I can only do intolerably smug for so long...'

In the early hours of the following morning, Lynn and Jeff Diamond arrived at the hotel after a slap-up meal at Medici, on the edge of *der Altstadt*, having celebrated another satisfying night of musical entertainment with her band and a number of German guests. Weary beyond measure after the last ten days' intensity, they fell into bed, wrapped in each others' insatiable arms.

'Let's never do that again,' Jeff muttered, lips caressing his companion's closed eyelids. 'Let's agree never to get so far apart before rescuing ourselves, OK?'

With one hand kneading the knots in her man's neck and shoulder muscles and the other flexing his growing erection, the singer nodded. 'OK. Agreed. I'm so grateful you came here like this. It reminds me of the night in Singapore when you left so suddenly. Don't leave tonight.'

'No chance,' the romantic chuckled. 'That was a ridiculously principled thing to do. I regretted it as soon as I did it.'

'Did you? You should've come back. I don't deserve you; not now and not then.'

'Crap! Utter fuckin' crap, lady!'

'No, it's not,' Lynn insisted. 'You've always been the one who understands what's really important. Your colours are brighter than mine, your volume's louder and everything in life means so much more to you than to anyone else.'

'Why, thank you, ma'am,' her husband replied in a languid Louisiana accent, doffing an invisible cap. 'I'd like to think so, and I'm glad you noticed.'

'Out of interest...' the young woman changed her tone. 'Why did you come to Singapore that night? I mean, what was at the heart of it? Didn't you trust me?'

Jeff inhaled, remembering all too well the paralysis which had hit him listening to the cry for help his dream girl had left on the answering machine following her parents' bizarre insertion of an alternate love-interest into their relationship.

'No. I trusted you,' he replied, drawing her body in closer. 'It was like it took me back somehow to when we couldn't be together, in a life gone by.'

'Oh, wow,' the singer murmured. 'Like we were about to go through another life apart?'

'Yeah. Exactly. Then, when we were in the lobby of the Raffles with Jean-Charles, I got an overpowering sense that I couldn't let history repeat itself.'

Lynn kissed his bare flesh. 'It's making me shiver again. That wasn't the only reason you did it though, was it?'

'Absolutely not,' the red-blooded male chuckled. 'I wasn't about to let some other bastard steal my woman. Whether you liked it or not.'

'Hey!' the blonde beauty slapped his chest. 'Caveman. Whether I liked it or not?'

Jeff kissed her pouting lips. 'Of course. Did you ever think you had a choice in the matter? But seriously, it's weird, angel. I can't explain how I feel the past and the present mix together, but there's something going on.'

Australia's princess levered herself up until she sat astride her majestic lover's hips, letting his penis fill her to the limit. 'Why is that?' she asked, clenching her muscles and rising up until the tip almost came free before plunging back down again. 'How come life's so much more meaningful to you than it is to the rest of us?'

'The rest of us?' Jeff echoed in disbelief. 'Christ, that feels so fucking good! My ego's only too happy to hear you tell me I'm special, but I'm sure as hell not *that* special. There are others who feel like me, and you're one of them. That's why I fell in love with you in the first place. You're a kindred spirit, Ms Dyson Diamond. Well and truly.'

Moving together in shared pleasure, Lynn sank down to lay along her husband's piping-hot body and rested the side of her head on his collarbone. She relished the sensation of his strong right hand pressing into the small of her back as the fingers of his left wove their magic on her engorged clitoris. The *savant* was convincing in his assurance, yet she was unable to count herself in the same league after the last few days had shown her to be so uncooperative.

Breakfast was served in a quiet corner of the hotel's dining room the following morning. With a few hours to kill before they needed to check in at the airport, the Antipodean celebrities talked through the alternatives to their son's total immersion like mature, open-minded and equal individuals and arrived at a revised master plan for both children's path to sporting glory.

Under no illusion that these alterations would pass muster with her father, the tennis champion requested, in the spirit of personal responsibility, that she should be the one to present it to Jet's grandfather.

'You spend so much time with Kierney,' she insisted to the reluctant control freak over a second cup of coffee. 'You're all over her.'

'All over her?' Jeff exclaimed. 'Jesus Christ, angel. You make me sound like a pædophile.'

Lynn grimaced, giggling. 'Oh, my God! No! That's not what I meant at all. I'd never accuse you of that.'

The doting dad reached across the table and grasped his wife's nervous hand. 'I know you wouldn't. It's true though... There is a greater affinity between me and Kizzo. We look the same, think the same and feel the same, but it doesn't mean I love or care about Jet any less. It's just more of a stretch to relate to him.'

The sportswoman nodded. 'Of course. If you loved or cared for him less, we wouldn't even have had this argument.'

'*Exactamente. Gracias*, angel. OK. I'll commit to spending more time with Jetto as my half of this pledge of personal responsibility. Let's spend a week each summer training together, all four of us, and then another week me with him, you with Kierney. I know I'd benefit from that too, and it'll satisfy my separation anxiety, which is probably at the root of all this anyway.'

The young woman smiled in sympathy. 'Alright. I like that idea. Not sure how it'll fly with Dad, but I'll suggest it.'

'Cheers, gorgeous,' Jeff responded. 'Shall we get out of here? I like getting to the airport early. It kids me into thinking we'll get home sooner.'

Throwing her husband a roll of her quizzical blue eyes, Lynn pushed her chair back and tossed her linen napkin onto the table beside the empty coffee cup. At Reception, she paid the bill for the group's entire stay and dropped her remaining *Deutschemark* coins into the tip saucer. The couple collected their luggage and wandered across the lobby, where the rest of the tour party prepared to leave for the day-long homeward leg.

'I did speak to Jet yesterday,' the young mum confessed as they took their places on the bus. 'Just so you know...'

'Great. Thanks.'

'And you were right there too,' she sighed. 'He does think his training hours are too much. He admitted he was tired, which he would never normally do, would he?'

'Nope,' the imp smiled. 'I won't say, "I told you so."'

'Won't you?' Lynn laughed, slapping him hard on the arm. 'Thanks. How kind of you!'

But her words were swallowed into an *impromptu* kiss which raised a chorus of whoops and whistles from their fellow travellers. When their eyes re-opened however, Australia's darling found a lost boy pleading from the multi-millionnaire's shining gaze, and the pulsing currents sparking between them took her breath away.

'*Sin tu amor, no soy nada,*' he whispered. '*Te amo.*'

'*Mismo, mismo.* Together, forever, wherever, Jeff.'

The soul-mates reached home after a brief stopover in Singapore and made their peace with a pair of pumped-up jumping beans who didn't want to hit the sack that night. Finally alone in their own bed at *Escondido*, Lynn voiced her epiphany both to her husband and to the day's journal: that in the preceding forty-eight hours of their relationship, their respective roles had reversed. It was she who now worried about losing him and having to taking the blame, whereas the former bundle of anxiety and paranoia was in charge of reassurance and placation.

'Ah, yeah? Jesus! That's not how I see it,' Jeff responded with a wry grin. 'This doesn't feel like a win to me. I've already written a song about it, but it's going to be a while before I can sing it to you. Way too painful to play just yet. I need to think of someone appropriate to record it.'

'Oh, OK,' Lynn answered, feeling guilty for falling back into the *status quo* so readily. 'It's a hit then? Can you even tell me its title?'

'Hmm… It's a hit. Massive. At the moment, its title's "Love Is Not Victory". It expresses my fear of our love dying in this lifetime and how nothing would ever be the same afterwards. Beyond the here and now. How precarious this life is, y'know…'

'Wow. Can't wait to hear it,' his beautiful best friend gasped and cuddled in closer, fine hairs prickling on the back of her neck. 'I promise I'm never going to let this happen to us again.'

'Me neither, angel. You have my word.'

Full of gratitude for their marriage's safe return, the pair drifted off into its individual sleepy thoughts. The occasional percussive squeak from a fruit bat passing their windows broke the silence, prompting a comforting stroke of a finger against naked flesh.

'I was shit-scared,' came another confession, accompanied by a soft kiss on his dream girl's forehead.

'Of losing us? Me too.'

'Yep. But much more than that… Scared I'd end up surrendering to stay together. And then I might start to resent you and end up hating myself 'cause I'm dependent on someone I don't respect. It'd destroy us eventually, for this time around.'

Lynn shivered. This notion mirrored her own thoughts. Perhaps history had threatened to repeat itself again, and valuable lessons learned in another lifetime had saved their star-crossed souls. Was this what was meant by "a fate worse than death"?

***

'Tantric sex is a form of meditation.'

'Oh, really?' his son's eyebrows raised in amusement at the joke at Gerry's expense. 'How does the other person feel about that?'

The widower chuckled, filled with a perverse pride at how worldly the young man sounded in the company of two such seasoned campaigners. '"The spiritual eyesight improves as the physical eyesight declines," if I can cite Plato.'

'I wish I could stop you,' the steadfast manager groaned at yet another *à-propos* quotation from the grand master of literature. 'Is that right? There's hope for short-sighted, old bastards like me in the afterlife then?'

'Doubtless, you numbskull, but that wasn't what I meant,' Jeff scoffed. 'Ry?'

The teenaged sportsman, who had been drafted in to organise the Irishman's extravagant send-off from *singledom*, swallowed a mouthful of salted cashews and chased them down with the finest James Boag's Premium. The Diamond men were on their own tonight, while Kierney solved world hunger on the Melbourne University campus.

'He means the beauty within becomes a lot more attractive when we can no longer see the outside so well. In other words, he thinks you're less superficial than you used to be, now you're completely decrepit.'

'Fucking cheek!' the Diamonds' manager guffawed. 'God Almighty! You are definitely your father's son.'

The musician feigned innocence, denying all responsibility. 'I have no control over his independent thoughts. Probably a better one for the occasion is, "Your heart is capable of showing you where the treasure is," mate.'

'It is?' Ryan sniggered, punching his dad on the shoulder and emptying his beer bottle. 'What are you talking about now, old man? I'm not sure I'm up for any more wise words tonight. What say you, Gerry? Another?'

The groom-to-be stood up, bidding the young buck to stay seated. 'My shout. Carry on, mate. I like the sound of more treasure.'

Jeff winked at his son. His longtime friend had turned into a bit of a softie after all. Despite all attempts to pin his descent into marital bliss on pressure from his *fiancée*, it appeared the old soak was serious about hanging up his party clothes and settling down.

'It's from "*El Alquimista*" by Paulo Coelho, the Brazilian writer I met up with again last year. Remember, Ry?'

'"The Alchemist",' the cricketer nodded. 'Yeah. I remember you talking about him.'

'Marriage is an outdated institution these days, I think,' the billionnaire continued, lighting a cigar and passing the lighter to the strapping sportsman. 'It was beginning to be so even when Lynn and I did it.'

'So why did you get married?' the lad asked.

'Because it was nineteen-seventy-six, mate, predominately. It'll be interesting to see if you and Kiz even want to get married when you meet your soul-mates.'

'If, you mean?'

The songwriter shook his head. 'No. I mean when, you cynic. You'll never meet her if you convince yourself you won't. Marriage was beginning to lose its meaning even when your mum and I did it.'

'So then… Why *did* you guys get married?' Ryan asked again.

'Yes. Why did you get married, mate?' Gerry joined in with backing vocals, setting three chilled stubbies onto the table and accepting a lighted cigar. 'Cheers. I'd like to think it was because you'd given me such a hard time about not marrying Heather, but not even I'm vain enough to believe that.'

Jeff sniffed, his half-smile these days no longer exuding the same disarming *puissance*. 'Sadly, you're right. I did it, first and foremost, so Lynn'd feel I'd given her the greatest commitment. As perceived by everyone else, that is... I needed it too, as it turned out, but I never understood why. It's like the *premier* level of allegiance two people can give each other. Like the New Year's Honours List from the Queen.'

'Or the Brownlow,' the lad quipped. 'Best and fairest. For services rendered to further corporal pleasure.'

'Yeah. Something like that. But that time's gone. Or passing anyway, I reckon. You may be one of the last, Gezza.'

The threesome had arrived for a logistics meeting for the accountant's bucks' party, which was now only a week away. They were waiting for two other grooms' men to join them, having received a text message to say they were running late. A great many things remained to organise, but the night was still young.

'So where do I have to go to find this treasure,' the long-suffering manager asked.

'The Pyramids, according to his book,' his client replied, 'but I prefer to tell this bloke he needs to explore the depths of his own ambitions. I don't know where the quote comes from, but it's something like "One dies of thirst just when the palm trees appear on the horizon." In other words, keep going until you find it, rather than settling for an easy option. The toughest decisions'll always be your best.'

The nineteen-year-old gasped, seized by a deep sense of admiration for the man across the table who had given him life. His dad's passage into the unknown was now a surety, with less than a month left to elicit these veritable pearls of wisdom. Some he uttered freely and unencumbered by the effects of excess alcohol or drugs, and others had to be prised out of him as if they were life's secret passwords.

147

'Thanks, Dad. Tell me though... What did Mum say when you asked her to marry you? Was she expecting it?'

Jeff chuckled. 'No. Her first response was, "Are you serious?"'

'"Are you serious?"' Gerry yelped. 'Are you serious?'

'Parrot-face!' the pair of Diamonds blurted out, feeding off each others' heightened emotions.

'Shit!' Ryan laughed. 'Did she hesitate?'

'No. Why?'

The young man smiled. 'Nothing. Only it'd be bloody disconcerting to pop the question and then see doubt in your partner's eyes. It'd make me want to retract it until I could be sure both of us want to.'

'Jesus, mate!' his father raised his voice. 'I thought I was the one who overthought everything.'

'He's been hanging around you too long,' Gerry interjected, pointing out the arrival of their two remaining committee members. 'There they are, at bloody last. I saw doubt in Fiona's eyes, but she came around pretty quickly. I put it down to shock, Jetto. And it has to be a shock... Catch them at a weak moment, otherwise they'd turn us down if they had any sense.'

'"What force is more potent than love?"' the musician expounded again.

'Smack,' his son sneered.

Stubbing out his cigar, Jeff leaned back in his chair and frowned. 'Nope. Stravinsky this time, I believe. He said something like "Knowing others is intelligence but knowing yourself is true wisdom." Strong people can control others. Like you, mate, on the sporting field. But knowing oneself is truly valuable. If you're sure of what you want, it means you've already subconsciously purged yourself of any lingering doubt. It'll be the right time.'

Ryan saw tears bead in the corners of the great man's eyes. 'Thanks. I hope so. I just want what you had, and to be able to do good with it all.'

'Cheers,' the celebrity angled the lip of his beer bottle towards the sincere teenager. 'You will. If you're in the mood for more inspirational quotes, I think it was Edmund Burke who said, "The only thing necessary for evil to triumph is for good men to do nothing." This, I predict, shall be the chief crime of the next few decades, while the human race's priorities shift from general advances in wellbeing to short-term material gratification.'

'Oh, fuck,' the executive sighed, waving over his two business associates and pulling out a spare chair for them to take their place at the table. 'Join us, gents. Lord Sparkle here's about to go off on one of his rants. Save me and talk about today's round of golf, if you would!'

The philosopher continued undeterred, primarily for his son's benefit. 'That sentence is flawed in its application though, because evil's power is inevitably farther-reaching and more destructive than good folks' ability to wield humility. Humility has to be exercised as a pre-emptive strike against the power of evil.'

Roger and Tim, two of Gerry's cronies from among Melbourne's self-made gentry, the first an investment banker and the second the owner of a sports physiotherapy practice, took their seats at the bucks' party planning table, shaking the Diamonds' hands with typical exuberance.

'I saw an old interview of yours on SBS last night, Jeff,' Roger opened. 'Just caught the last five minutes or so. Did you know it was on?'

The celebrity shook his head, bored already and hoping he would be able to fend off this undesirable attention. 'Nope. When was it from?'

The trader whistled. 'Not sure. Must have been at least ten years old. Your good lady wife was in it too, looking as stunning as ever. Something about coffee commercials and how some people thought you were queer.'

Ryan and Gerry exchanged furtive glances as the outspoken man realised he ought to have finished his sentence without adding the final phrase. The patient superstar's outward calm didn't waver however, the mention of Lynn enough to deflect the crass comment.

'Yeah? We did do some coffee ads for Nescafé a while back. You guys came with us, mate. Remember?'

His son nodded. 'Antigua?'

'Correct. We always looked forward to those assignments, Rodge. We filmed a series of different scenes, including some that could be classified as soft porn', I seem to recall.'

'Hey!' the cricketer yelped. 'Not in front of the children!'

The others tittered like schoolboys, eyeing off the youngest man at the table, also the largest and most robust by a country mile.

'You'll get over it, mate,' his father smiled. 'It was a lot of fun: exotic locations, sexy and sophisticated poses, a strong coffee in my hand and my favourite lady by my side. Hardly what you'd call work.'

Jeff paused, resisting the temptation to rub his shirt, under which the "JL" tattoo sang a familiar, sweet song. 'It was also when your mum and I had the producer in stitches. D'you remember that too, Ry?'

'No? Which producer?'

'I asked Lynn to dinner, while we were on camera, but she wasn't concentrating. Not expecting the question. Jesus, it was funny!' the forty-four-year-old waxed lyrical, paying no mind to the four pairs of eyes drilling into his. '"Dinner?" she murmured, all dreamy. "Yes, dinner," I said. "You might also know it as the evening meal. They're quite common, and I'd like to share one with you for a change."'

His audience laughed.

'Lynn eventually responded, "Oh, sure!" Once she floated down to Earth again... I could hardly keep a straight face. "You know... Otherwise known as eating socially." But yeah, I've been accused of being gay all my life. It never bothered me. The other blokes at school used to call me "pooftah" or "queer-boy" whenever I went to music practice or danced at parties, and my usual retort was that I was fine with those nicknames, 'cause it showed I had more class than them. They never knew how to answer back, strangely enough. I'm not queer. I just like music. And they should've tried it, since I was the one surrounded in girls!'

The billionnaire reached down to the vacant seat beside him, where he had placed the folder containing Gerry's bucks' party plans. 'We need to change the subject, guys. Things to do, decisions to be made, *et cetera*. I was occasionally interviewed about something worthwhile actually... Such as our business and education ventures.'

'You're right, mate,' his manager affirmed. 'We're not trying to needle you. Let's focus.'

'Sure, but why's all that domiciled overseas?' Tim asked. 'I always wondered why you and Lynn Dyson, of all people, set up most of your "R & D" and venture capital in the US.'

Jeff fended off the accountant's best efforts to shut the physiotherapist down. 'Two main reasons, mate: one, this country's not big enough to have its own Silicon Valley; not enough people, not enough large corporations, and we can't give people the huge tax breaks a large economy can afford; and the second factor is our Tall Poppy Syndrome. If you're *out there* and you fail, you're fair game. We have a very low tolerance for failure; yet failing's an integral part of learning. I have no idea why, but the US capitalises on this, whereas the rest of the world doesn't.'

***

'D'you want to know what extreme wealth is?' Australia's most successful rock musician responded to the interviewer's opening challenge. 'When you can fart in your *en suite* bathroom and your partner sleeps through it?'

The live studio audience erupted in laughter, clapping Jeff Diamond's earthy wit. He and Lynn were in Sydney for a fundraising telethon in aid of Childlight, and found themselves on a panel of celebrities and forced to justify their lifestyle to a rather green upstart of a journalist. In reality, the couple weren't many years older than the feisty brunette; a point the intellectual was determined to communicate as tangentially as he could get away with.

'All humans are basically the same, Anita. Truly.'

'That's a ridiculous claim,' the woman jeered. 'How can you say that, when you've been filmed so often in your mansion on the bay? Your lifestyle and wealth are well known.'

'Come on, please,' Lynn piped up, resting a loving hand on her husband's knee, knowing how short a fuse he had for such parallels. 'We have the same needs as anyone. It's just that we satisfy them differently sometimes. I still shave my legs and armpits, for example.'

The handsome man's head flicked sideways, complete amazement plastered on his face. 'Do you? Jeez, don't tell 'em that!'

''Fraid so, mate,' the blonde beauty chuckled along with the crowd. 'And am I allowed to say we still have to cut our toenails every now and again too? I guess some may think we have people who do these things for us, and I suppose we might... But get real!'

Anita Smith continued, the wind knocked out of her sails. 'Jeff, you've often admitted to suffering from depression and other mental illnesses.'

'Yeah. That's true.'

'Do you ever get asked what could you possibly have to be depressed about?'

'Sure. All the damned time,' the thirty-two-year-old answered. 'There's no point in arguing if they're not prepared to believe me, but I normally remind them there's no choice involved. D'you really think anyone'd choose to be unhappy? Why would they? It just doesn't make sense to me why it's even a mystery to some people. Then when they criticise us for fighting back against all the famine relief *aggro*... It's a hailstorm of bad feeling no-one needs when they're trying to do something good for the world. Knock it off.'

Both women shook their heads. It did sound most illogical when expressed by this master communicator, causing the audience to lapse into an embarrassed silence too. Sensing the panel's momentum dwindling, Lynn picked up the mantle by promising their fans that they would be hanging around after the show for some "As" and "Ps".

'"As" and "Ps"? What does that mean?' the interviewer was quick to grab the olive branch.

'Autographs and photographs,' the rock star replied, looping an arm round his beautiful best friend. 'It's a shorthand we coined a while back. Or "the 'graphs". The more money you guys donate, the more "'graphs" we'll do.'

Another round of rapturous applause sprang forth, prompting Anita to return to her previous, assertive stance. 'Why, Jeff, now you devote so much time to charity and you have two kids too, do you still drink so much?'

'What's "so much"?' the addict shot back, shaking his head. 'To fight complacency mainly; to keep in touch with reality. I was born an outcast and I'm driven to remember what it was like. I'm over eighteen and I enjoy the taste of Scotch, brandy and fine red wine. Alright with you?'

'What's the quote you use?' Lynn interjected. 'Something like it's not what a man puts into his mouth but what comes out of it that we should be afraid of...'

Again, the journalist could think of no comeback and moved on to the nude scenes the sportswoman had recently shot on location for her latest starring role. 'How do you feel about Lynn's naked body on the big screen?'

'Cool! The bigger the better, as far as I'm concerned,' the proud man grinned. 'As long as it's only my eyes that have to share the bounty... To be honest, I get more jealous of blokes she has dinner with. They get to drown in her smile and get whipped senseless by her sharp tongue.

'There's also a brilliant quote I read out to Lynn on our tenth anniversary actually... from "One Hundred Years of Solitude" by Gabriel García Márquez. It goes along the lines of "They enjoyed the miracle of loving each other as much at the table as in bed, and they grew to be so happy that even when they were two worn-out old people they kept on blooming like little children and playing together like dogs."'

'Like dogs?' the interviewer yelped. 'Is that a euphemism?'

'Not for me. But you're right, Lynn didn't warm to that bit either! There's no substitute for the real thing though, and neither of us is into sharing, are we, angel?'

In January nineteen-eighty-five, Jeff Diamond was presented with two more accolades to confirm he had reached the pinnacle of his career, much to his partner's delight: the coveted "Songwriter's Guild Award" in New York and "Australian of the Year" back home in the capital city of Canberra. These were humbling moments for the man from such lowly stock, to be recognised among his peers for what was now over ten years of ground-breaking success.

Both ends of the deserving pantomime horse flew to Los Angeles early in the New Year to accept the first award at a grand ceremony, leaving the children in the care of their grandparents. The young mum stayed on in California afterwards to record a new album, bidding a reluctant goodbye to her partner.

After a quick stopover in Brussels for some meetings and to check in with the "Teachers for Peace" team, the solo father landed back in Melbourne, keen to spend some quality time with Jet and Kierney between school terms. He couldn't wait to return to *Escondido*, where the kids' shrill voices juddered as they raced around on their scooters over the uneven surface of the courtyard cobblestones.

Jeff collected the excitable bundles of energy from Benloch on Saturday afternoon. The six-year-old boy was excited to tell his dad about the new techniques he had learned from his cricket coach. The traveller paid careful attention and made appropriate noises of approval at polite intervals until every last, minute detail had been elucidated.

This summer, his little daughter had been enrolled in a training program too, as premature as this seemed to her father. Her Dyson destiny was to be a world champion at one or more racquet sports, and she was already demonstrating precocious ability for both badminton and the Australians' staple of tennis. This pleased her *papá*, hoping that in years to come the two dark Diamonds would be regular squash partners, his own racquet sport of choice.

The depleted family chose not to take the hour-long road trip to Mount Eliza on this occasion. Instead the car pulled into the basement of their city apartment building, where the architects of the couple's dream home, Don and Sue Jenner, were hosting a party. They had invited their celebrity neighbours, not for a single moment expecting they might be inclined, or far less available, to attend.

Sue had never been so thrilled to receive an acceptance, even though the prospect of entertaining such world-famous guests sent her into a spin. What a perfect opportunity to show off to their work colleagues and other friends!

Lynn had let their host know in advance that she would be flying into Melbourne the same evening, but that Jeff planned to be in town. The two mums had arranged for Sue's children to spend the night on the sixteenth floor to be babysat by the Diamonds' nannies in exchange for plying the tall, dark, handsome man with food and drink until she got home.

With Dawson and Mairi Jenner installed in their close friends' secure apartment, under the watchful eyes of Ashley and Usha, the songwriter stepped into the lift, looking forward to an enjoyable evening. It had been the longest time since he and his soul-mate had been invited to a normal party thrown by normal people in a normal home.

As the levels clicked by on his descent, the superstar recalled fond memories, relishing such simple pleasures before the blonde bombshell and her bohemian wannabe had shipped out to London. He conjured up with consummate ease the intense therapeutic effect of feeling her lean back against his rapturous body while standing glued to each other as they talked, smoked and drank their fill with ordinary folk. These low-profile events demanded no airs and graces, no grandstanding and no special treatment; simply a guy and a girl out for a good time.

The new arrival, clad in an old pair of jeans, a midnight blue, long-sleeved collared shirt and thongs on his feet, pressed the Jenners' doorbell with his elbow, grappling with two bottles of wine, a six-pack of beer and a gift purchased by his wife in California. A boy of about twelve or thirteen opened the door, with the shrieking homeowner hot on his heels.

'Thanks, mate,' he said to the young lad, chuckling at the *crescendo* of female voices which greeted him in the hallway.

'Hi, Jeff! I'm so rapt you could make it,' Sue cried out, ecstatic to receive a kiss on the cheek in front of her friends.

'Get out of here!' the musician shook his head, struggling out of a violent hug while still clutching his armful. '*I'm* so rapt I could make it. I haven't been to a house party forever! Thanks for inviting us. Hey... And this is for you from us.'

The dizzy host swooned at the small, carefully wrapped gift that was placed into outstretched palm. 'Oh, thanks so much! You shouldn't have got me anything.'

'I didn't,' the charmer laughed. 'Lynn did.'

'Well, thanks anyway. This is Christopher, by the way,' Sue turned to the boy. 'He's going camping with your two next week. He's our friends' son. Anders and Cat, the South Africans.'

'Cool! These are for you then,' Jeff went to hand the beers over, swiping them away before the youngster could grab hold. 'Well, maybe not. Enjoying the holidays, mate?'

The boy nodded, speechless at having a real-life celebrity standing right next to him. And calling him by the most manly of nicknames to boot. It made him feel grown up.

'Come on in,' Sue beckoned, accepting the wine along with her gift. 'Thanks. You didn't have to bring all this stuff.'

Her guest declined to respond, following his clamorous reception committee into the kitchen and depositing his offering into the esky. Its contents had overflowed onto the floor, rendering it wet and slippery, so he helped himself to a stubby and turned around. Every single conversation in the room lulled on cue, drawing an inaudible sigh from the man himself. It was clearly too much to hope that he could dodge becoming the centre of attention altogether. He downed the first beer within five seconds, picked a second out of the ice and twisted its top off, tossing the serrated disc towards the bin and scoring a direct hit.

'Well done!' Sue praised her special guest. 'Can I get you anything to eat?'

'Please. I'm starving,' Jeff replied, keen to put an end to all the fuss. 'I'll have a lobster Thermidor, followed by steak and chips. And then...'

The architect and her friends exchanged furtive asides, enchanted to be the butt of the star's gentle humour. This man's larger-than-life *persona* was no less magnetic in person than it appeared on the television screen. A born flirt, her demeanour turned decidedly girlish whenever she found herself in his company, much to her husband's annoyance.

'OK, I get it. Sorry, Jeff. Don's in the lounge room. Go and find him, and I promise you're on your own from now on. Is Lynn coming later?'

The joker nodded, putting his arm around his embarrassed neighbour and kissing her cheek again. Glowing with pride, Sue scanned the route to her kitchen to check how many people were on hand to witness her fifteen minutes of fame.

'Cheers,' the new arrival smiled, helping himself to a third bottle of beer from the overflowing vat. 'I appreciate it. Lynn'll be home around nine, if all goes to plan. She's going to ring here.'

'Oh, good. How are Jet and Kierney?'

'Fantastic, thanks. Ready to play up with your guys all night, I imagine.'

In the large living room with the same floorplan as his own, several floors above, Jeff spied Don Jenner on the other side, talking with a bunch of city slickers; smartly attired professional men on their days off. One was a fellow architect whom the celebrity recognised as having worked on the drawings for *Escondido*.

'Mister Diamond!' Don shouted, grabbing the outstretched hand and shaking it with vigour. 'Welcome. Great of you to come. Did you see Sue? She's been in a bloody flap all week because you guys accepted our invite!'

'Oh, yeah,' the famous guest scoffed. 'I've been here for an hour already. She only just let me escape from the kitchen press conference.'

The ring of onlookers chuckled too, knowing how keen their wives had been when Sue announced she would be showing off their extra-special neighbours. One-by-one, they introduced themselves to the charismatic man, receiving his presence with much less commotion but no less awe. After a few obligatory questions about his recent awards and the couple's high-profile activities over the festive season, the conversation soon returned to cricket and the astonishing probability of Australia drawing three test matches with Pakistan.

At last, Jeff rued, accepting a cigarette and fishing a lighter from his pants pocket in reciprocation. Not before time, a semblance of normality had descended on the setting. The only thing separating this from pure *nirvana* was the company of his beautiful best friend, who would be along in a while to put the icing on the sweetest of cakes.

After a while, the celebrity became aware of young Christopher having wheedled his way through the throng to end up at his side. He was tuned in to his idol's every word. Jeff possessed no off-switch for his Pied Piper attributes, so he made a valiant attempt to involve the lad in their adult discussion.

Beer, wine, cigarettes and easy conversation did their best to inoculate the star against the disappointing demise of anonymity, finding himself holding court with almost the entire guest list. He succumbed to endless probing enquiries about his music, his charities and even his wife's favourite aphrodisiac, alleviated by the praise heaped upon him from all sides. Grandstanding again, he chastised himself with a certain resignation. Every time he asked a digressive question of one of the others, discussion invariably switched back to the celebrities and their enviable lifestyle before too long.

His diminutive sidekick's father provided a welcome temporary distraction by describing their Great Ocean Road camping trip planned for the lead-up to Australia Day, before spoiling the songwriter's retreat to the chorus by declaring the Diamond progeny were to accompany them. This blatant crack at seizing the limelight was rewarded by the esteemed celebrity, who added that the couple themselves would also be tagging along for the last few days.

Sick of resisting the temptation to check his watch every thirty seconds, Jeff rejoiced when a telephone rang at the other end of the room. He tugged extra-hard on their invisible elastic connection, rewarded not long afterwards by the sight of Sue jogging towards him, gesticulating behind her as if fire had broken out.

'Lynn's on the line!'

'Thanks,' the performer replied over the large circle of hangers-on, emptying his wine glass and thrusting it into the stunned twelve-year-old's hand. 'Excuse me, folks. Tell 'em about Childlight, please, Chris.'

The guests swooned at the typical, benevolent gesture, while the special guest was ushered into the Jenners' study. He lifted the receiver on the desk, slumping into the chair as relief threatened to knock him off-balance. The sound of his wife's soothing greeting provided its usual medicinal boost.

'Hey, beautiful. How're you going? Are you coming down?'

'Hi! Depends on whether you're coming up,' came her response.

'As we speak, baby,' Jeff quipped, with no need to lie.

'Then I'd better not come down,' the Olympian answered in a prim and proper tone. 'You come up, and afterwards we can both go down together.'

The red-blooded lover inhaled, reckless anticipation rising inside after their few days apart. 'OK. No objections here. So if I'm coming up, will you go down?'

'*Bien sûr, mon ami.*'

'Nice,' Jeff smiled. 'On my way.'

In his eagerness, he almost slammed the receiver down, hoping no-one had eavesdropped on their private conversation from other telephones. What did it matter? Bidding a temporary farewell to Sue, the man from upstairs jumped into the lift and entered the code for the penthouse floor.

All was eerily quiet when Jeff stepped onto the landing, the children and their nannies ensconced in the southern half of the apartment. He spied a crack of soft light where the door to the master bedroom had been left ajar, and with his heartbeat quickening, he pushed it open and prepared his senses for their familiar, favourite feast.

Sure enough, there was his very own goddess, languishing in black satin *lingerie,* her long, blonde hair shining in the glow from the bedside lamp. Her lips had been painted the same enticing colour as her nails, reflecting her man's raging desire. Looking up from her book, she grinned at his breathless reaction and swang her legs sexily off the bed, walking round to greet him.

The couple stood together in silence, moving in an instinctive slow dance to a cool East Coast soul album they had been gifted on their recent trip to New York. Items of clothing were shed one-by-one from the partygoer's eager body, Lynn's tantalising hands and lips traversing around its every contour, intent on keeping her promise.

'Christ, angel! You have to stop. This is way too one-sided.'

Anxious to prolong their lovemaking too, the young woman did as she was told. She gave in to the warmth of the expert's caress and allowed herself to fall gracefully onto the mattress, her mouth never diverting from its passage from his rock-hard erection to the hairy torso until it reached the tattoos on his chest. His breath deafening in her ears, he encouraged her chin upwards until their tongues intertwined. Within moments his penis was inside her, his fingers massaging her clitoris and leaving her no choice but to orgasm with wild abandon.

The lovers slowed everything down once safe behind a locked door, playing with each other's shared state of heightened arousal. When no leeway remained on the powerhouse's fuse, Lynn straightened her back and rode them both to climax. Even though his eyes were shut tight, he could picture the broad smile on her face, and it made the moment all the more sublime. The beer and wine he had consumed earlier in the evening had slowed his reflexes to perfection, and the euphoria laced through his body took its time to subside.

'Hey! Have you fallen asleep?' the athlete asked, tapping her finger on her motionless husband's forehead.

'*Sí. ¿Y tú?*'

'No,' she giggled. 'I should know better than to ask you that question.'

'You should,' Jeff's mouth broke into a half-smile, still without opening his eyes. 'Come and join me.'

Lowering herself onto her black stallion's chest and feeling him reach to pull the sheet up, Lynn revelled in beguiling thuds from a slowing heartbeat against her breasts. They remained still in the dark until both were on the verge of sleep.

'What time did you say we'd be back?' the young woman asked, raising her head to read the luminous digits of her bedside clock-radio.

'I didn't. We don't have to. They'd understand. Long flight, irrepressible urges, *et cetera, et cetera.*'

'No. We should go,' his wife chuckled. 'Tempting as it is, we can't let them down. I know Sue was looking forward to showing us off.'

'Mmm... She did a good job at that already. Did you eat on the 'plane? There's some posh nosh down there, unless it's all gone by the time we get back.'

'Oh, yum,' the blonde beauty smiled and rubbed her belly, climbing off and heading into the *en suite*. 'I am pretty hungry.'

'Yeah. You were,' Jeff shrugged, moaning as if she had used up his every last drop of energy.

The noise of the shower droned behind the bathroom door, lulling the satisfied man back into a half-sleep. How amazing could this life get? Their kids and their overnight buddies were fast asleep under the watch of two trustworthy young women, his dream girl had treated him to the ultimate sexual experience yet again, and he was about to return to the party brandishing a metaphoric First Prize rosette. Star-struck neighbours were a tiny price to pay for this brand of happiness.

The door opened with a creak which startled the drowsy musician awake, only for his eyes to meet the vision of a tall, lithe frame silhouetted against the harsh backlight. He blinked and faked a yawn.

'I so need a self-satisfied fat cat moment,' he announced, rolling up to a sitting position and stretching in pleasure.

'You do? Why?'

Her normally humble husband exhaled in frustration, his shoulders and spine cracking as he twisted from side to side. 'Jesus! Those guys haven't let up on me all night. To go back to that party post-coitally would be just the most gratifyingly triumphant feeling. Where would that put me on the self-indulgence scale?'

'Nudging the bell, I'd say,' Lynn giggled and reached out her hands to pull him up. 'I'd be allowing you to break your own cardinal rule.'

'That's what I mean. So are you going to?' Jeff frowned, drinking in her laughter without opening his eyes. 'How're you *gonna* stop me?'

A kiss arrived on unsuspecting lips, causing its recipient to lift his arms and make a grab for the nubile form. Knowing neither prospective fat cat would ever be sufficiently self-satisfied to renege on a deal with friends, his puny protests mutated into a low growl on his way to the shower, following an angel's siren call.

'Your wish is my command,' she whispered. 'It's so good to be home, and I love you so much.'

'I love you too. More than ever, every day.'

Washed and spruced up again, the eternal couple was soon on its way to the tenth floor. The rock star whistled at his wife's reflection in the lift's mirrored wall, hugging her close and biting her neck until she squealed. It was as if they had been transported back in time by a decade, behaving like teenagers bound for a house party on a Saturday evening. She wore no make-up for their casual night out, her skin radiant in the aftermath of their romantic *liaison*, and her hair was scrunched into a lazy style which was a favourite with her greatest admirer; a look perfectly positioned on the scale between formal and informal.

The sportswoman's graceful, idling gait made her calf-length Thai silk skirt brush against the leather of her boots, swaying in a fluid motion as she stepped out of the lift in front of her mesmerised date and walked towards their friends' apartment, her black and olive top cut on the edge of decency.

Frenzied screaming began anew as soon as the bell rang. One of Sue's workmates opened the door, bundled aside by the host in her hurry to welcome the famous couple again. True to form, Lynn linked arms with the young mother like a long-lost friend, while her amused chaperone watched the shoal of women drift into the kitchen. Taking his leave from the tipsy group, he poured himself a generous goblet of *Shiraz*, hoping he would be able to reclaim his trophy once the excitement had died down.

Catching his wife's eye, the self-assured man held up a second, empty glass and received a grateful nod for his trouble. He filled it from the same bottle and turned to enter the lounge room. Reaching the doorway, Don immediately called him over, and he headed towards the bunch of drunkards, wearing a wry smile.

Here we go again...

'Greedy,' one of the others remarked, seeing the celebrity with a glass in each hand.

'Yep,' Jeff agreed. 'Stops me smoking though.'

Everyone within earshot burst out laughing. Out of the corner of his eye, he saw Lynn being led through the room, already allocated a white wine. They both shrugged at the oversupply of alcohol, and her fingers brushed his thigh as she passed by, sending his pulse through the roof.

Nineteen all over again, it was the nobody from New South Wales' turn to be proud he could show his date off to new mates, ashamed for the silent scorn he had heaped on the other guests' exaggerated reactions. He was no different. Here was the world's most beautiful woman, for whom he held on to a spare drink in the hope she might return to boost his ego that little bit farther...

'Lynn looks hot,' Don hissed, leaning into the tall musician. 'Very hot.'

Jeff's dark, expressive eyes flashed a gentle warning in reply. 'What can I say, mate? Can't disagree.'

Six more hungry males also tracked the famous entertainer's progress through the room as she was guided towards a small group of women near the balcony doors. She exuded serenity at every step, shaking the hands of some and kissing those she had met through their children's play-dates. Every now and again, she glanced over to where her husband had become involved in a loud political debate, buoyed by each small wink of appreciation.

Sue introduced the famous mum to a woman whose daughter was due to start at Jet's primary school next year. It was difficult to secure a place at the main feeder for Melbourne Academy, and the gushing South Yarra resident wanted to make this fact known to the crowd. The patient star chatted with the collection of over-ambitious parents, all the while angling for her chance to escape into her man's arms.

'Where are your little ones tonight?' another of Sue's friends asked in the same accusative tone to which Lynn was accustomed from the middle-classed set of conventionalists.

Why was it such an issue for the Diamond adults to be seen in their hometown without Jet and Kierney in tow, even though most disapproving parents were quick to admit to yearning for time to themselves with the next breath?

'Upstairs,' Sue interjected. 'Ours are up there too, in Lynn and Jeff's apartment.'

The host's answer cancelled out the pointed question, proceeding to tell the haughty mothers how well the quartet got on. The tennis star trotted out the same tired lines she always used to explain how valuable it was for her precious youngsters to have friends so close by, especially now that Dawson and Jet would be at school together.

Jeff was right, the travel-weary superstar mused. As parties went, this one was a hard slog.

As the clock's hands clicked towards Sunday, and the flow of alcohol had mellowed the evening out, the celebrities managed to reconnect at the food table. They stole a quick kiss while charging their plates, knowing all eyes were on them, while also exchanging a telepathic sigh of mutual frustration.

The rock star gestured to the vacant end of a long couch, where the *duo* sat down to eat. Anders, the leader of Don's camping fraternity, plonked his stout frame down on the coffee table opposite, his rowdy South African banter shattering the moment of quiet togetherness the couple had sought.

'So! Your kids still coming out to Lorne then?' asked the overweight architect with the crimson complexion.

'Oh, yes. Definitely,' Lynn answered. 'They're really looking forward to it. Jet's been practising in the garden at home.'

'Excellent,' Anders laughed, enjoying the attention of this stunning blonde whom he had met only once before. 'Anything we need to be aware of? Allergies or anything?'

Both parents shook their heads, their mouths full.

'Just treat them as you would your own kids,' Jeff suggested, swallowing his mouthful down in a hurry. 'They're very independent. If they need something, they'll ask for it. If they ask for something you don't want them to have, say no, and you won't hear another word.'

The forthright engineer nodded, filling his own large orifice with a piece of sausage roll. 'Like it. Good way to be. Nice to know you're not spoiling 'em. It crossed my mind they might be a little too well-protected.'

Lynn jumped in, frightened that such a comment would be too red a rag for the bull sitting on her right. 'No,' she smiled. 'No need to worry about that. Jet's a handful 'cause he's so into everything. He'll want to try his hand at any new skill, but he's pretty sensible with it. Kierney's often quiet. She's like her dad: a big thinker. But don't think she's not enjoying herself, because she will be, I'm sure.'

As the conversation progressed, Anders' wife joined them, along with a few of the men with whom Jeff had been fixing the federal and state governments' problems a while ago. In another deliberate but largely futile attempt to blend into the background, the crowd-pleasers introduced neutral topics of conversation. This tactic worked for the most part, enabling them to relax and unwind at last.

'Are you talking about kiddie-fiddlers again?' Sue cried, arriving at a raucous point in the group's discourse.

'Sue, please!' Lynn pleaded, seeing the compassionate activist's eyes darken at the vile word. 'Don't get him started. That's such a horrible term.'

Nevertheless, her husband prepared to answer the previous question, asked by a high-ranking public servant in the Victorian legislature with whom they had been dissecting the various Childlight programs launched since they had last heard any second-hand news from the Jenners.

'There are two types of pædophilia, in my opinion,' Jeff sighed, accepting a lighted cigarette from the rear half of the pantomime horse. 'Some wankers get off on pictures of kids... or worse, videos... simply perving on the fact they're under age. And then there are those who exploit children for actual sex but probably don't even consider them as kids. The victims in the second category are just objects to be fucked, if you pardon my crude language.'

The women around the crowded coffee table whined, while their partners coughed their disgust. Lynn leaned sideways into Jeff's shoulder and squeezed his tense thigh, understanding only too well that he spoke from personal experience in addition to considered analysis of the research they funded.

'They're both just as wrong as each other, in my opinion, but very different behaviours psychologically,' the intellectual continued. 'That's why we've got the two parallel campaigns. We're not going to stop it. We're not that naïve. However, we are aiming to give kids the skills to recognise each type of pædophile, and also what's perfectly innocent behaviour, so they can take evasive action if they need to. The plan is to have the two campaigns intersect at the end of March for a huge blitz. Need to take things one step at a time though, 'cause these are pretty sophisticated messages to put out into mainstream consciousness.'

As usual, Lynn Dyson's parasitic frontman had the spellbound audience eating out of his hand. She acknowledged their tentative applause and praise on his behalf, checking off one of his self-satisfied fat cat conditions in the process.

Placing his empty dinner plate on the floor by his feet, Jeff draped his left arm around his wife and coaxed her back into the couch with him, where they ignored their onlookers and indulged in a deep kiss. Using his free hand to egg the inebriated men on, he smothered his wife's giggling protestations until the caterwauling attained fever pitch. The evening was perfect at last.

Sue and Don were over the moon to find their special guests in no hurry to leave, half expecting them to make an excuse as soon as the first few who were paying for babysitters dispersed. Instead, they accepted *liqueurs* and coffees, remaining glued to the same spot for a further two hours.

'You guys are really the best of friends, aren't you?' Cat sighed to the tennis champion, stealing a quiet moment while the others pre-empted the next weeks' sporting outcomes. 'It's like electricity. I almost expect to get a shock if I try and sit between you.'

Having overheard the comment, the rock star chuckled but decided not to interrupt the female confessions. He was curious to hear how Lynn would deal with this observation, notwithstanding his wish to respect their privacy.

'Yes, we are,' the softly-spoken celebrity agreed. 'We're best friends who also spend a lot of time apart, with all our various engagements. It fuels the fire, that's for sure.'

'Bet you had to put out his fire earlier...' Don interjected. 'You were gone a long time, mate.'

An assortment of awkward utterances whisked full-circle around the group. Even the *lothario* himself was a little shocked by such a direct sexual *innuendo*, catching his dream girl's eye. By the expression on her face, the architect's remark was taken as overly intrusive. The devil inside got the better of him, as it often did, and he resolved to play along and beg for forgiveness later.

'What d'you mean exactly, Don?' he chided. 'Of course I was a long time. What are you insinuating? You're ex-Army, aren't you, Anders? Tell this desk-jockey how important it is to thoroughly debrief after every mission.'

The portly South African rocked back and forth, his guffaws drowning out all other chatter. The Diamonds' downstairs neighbours both blushed at the rebuff which made their friends snigger.

As the practised exhibitionist calculated, his stooge came to their rescue. 'He's always a long time actually.'

'Oh, really?' Don gave a relieved laugh. 'Is that right? Can I take that to the 'papers?'

'If you like,' Lynn put on an exhausted tone.

Jeff nudged his wife, shrugging in mock modesty. 'I do my best. No point leaving you wanting.'

Sue could no longer contain her mortification at this latest suggestive lead. She sprang up and stuttered something about making more coffee. To her surprise, the roguish showman declared his intention to help out.

'Great idea. You OK there for a few minutes, angel?'

The gorgeous singer's smile masked a trace of melancholy, warming the old soul's heart. As usual, he had been forgiven before he had the chance to make amends.

In the kitchen, their host fussed around, collecting mugs and jugs. Her multi-millionaire assistant couldn't help but laugh at her determination to keep the show on the road. Reminded of Celia Blake's stiff-upper-lip stoicism in the face of her family's depravity, he filled the kettle and prepared the coffee

162

pots while waiting for the water to boil, while listening to some inane background topic manufactured to rescue some *decorum*.

Content that she hadn't forgotten anything, the busy woman let out a long sigh. 'Jeff, thank you so much for coming tonight,' she gushed. 'It's been amazing to finally introduce you to everyone. I think most of our friends reckon we make up the fact that you're our neighbours.'

'It's fine, Sue,' Jeff replied, hugging her and planting a kiss on her forehead. 'It's been an easy gig. We'll leave our invoice on the counter when we go.'

'Oh, don't say that,' the woman whined. 'Has it been an ordeal?'

'No. Absolutely not,' he insisted, feeling guilty. 'It's been fun. Really. We're having a great time. It's just that I have this entirely unrealistic fantasy that we can blend into the background like I used to. Y'know... Just go to a party to get drunk and talk shit.'

'But you have got drunk and talked shit,' the feisty host countered.

'True,' he laughed, 'but someone else's shit would be far better. Not ours all the time. It's our fate always to be front and centre, I guess. Goes with the territory. I should be grateful but I'm not, shameful as it sounds.'

Sue frowned. 'Well... Then you shouldn't have such interesting lives. People love what you're doing. Good things for ordinary people. That's why they want to hear all about it.'

Their host's comments were well-intentioned and designed as a figurative slap for being so precious, yet they angered him more than they should. Deep in contemplation, Jeff flicked off the kettle before it reached boiling point and poured the hot water on top of the coffee grounds, stirring the steeping liquid with the handle of a long knife he found lying on the bench-top.

His host gave an exasperated laugh. 'Men!'

'Indeed,' he smirked. 'I have to take issue with what you said though, with respect, 'cause most conversations tonight have been about us and not about what we're doing.'

To the star's surprise, the householder let his argument fly right over her head, as if caught in a childlike pretence. The disease of the middle-class was stubborn in the face of his desire to eradicate apathy, even among his so-called supporters.

Instead, Sue tossed her hair over her shoulder and angled her head towards the kitchen door, picking up the tray and signalling for the statuesque man to exit ahead of her. 'Well, I'm still glad you could come. And thank you for looking after Daws and Mairi too.'

Jeff scoffed, turning round. 'You're welcome, but I haven't lifted a finger to look after your kids, lady,' he teased. 'You can thank Ash and Ushy tomorrow morning when you make the long trip up to collect them. Or afternoon. Whenever's fine by us.'

The babble in the lounge room was brash and *staccato*, each voice seeming to compete with the next in direct proportion to the quantity of alcohol consumed. To complement their beverages, Don had brought out the cigars, and the smaller group of die-hards shuffled out onto the balcony to finish the evening in the cool night air.

The thoughtful songwriter beckoned for Lynn to sit on his lap, and they sat drinking their mugs of coffee while he puffed on a ripened Cuban stogie. Exchanging a series of furtive kisses while the others weren't looking, he recounted the gist of his conversation with Sue to his patient muse.

'We'll be able to make our getaway soon,' she said, watching him curl smoke past his tongue until it spiralled on the breeze. 'You are so gorgeous.'

'*Toi aussi, angelissima,*' he responded, pressing smoky lips to her cheek just as the attention turned back to them. '*Je t'aime*, Lynn Dyson. Will you marry me?'

'Ahh! That's so romantic,' cooed Cat, twisting round to her husband. 'Why don't you ask me to marry you again?'

'Eh? Why the hell would I want to marry you twice?' Anders shouted at the top of his lungs for the benefit of his hen-pecked cronies. 'What do I get in return?'

Everyone laughed except the Diamonds. The introvert rested his forehead on his dream girl's arm and sighed. He should learn to keep his opinions to himself in these situations. It would be far safer for all concerned if he saved such utopian notions for later, once the forever pair was alone.

Safer but not genuine, the philosopher changed his mind, since Lynn would be deprived of the open affirmation she deserved. For better or for worse, the success of their public life had been built on a series of impulsive acts and outrageous statements. Sue was right. This was what people wanted to hear, even though those who craved it often ended up being burned as a result.

Jeff grinned at the gregarious South African woman, who hadn't appeared to take her husband's remarks to heart. Lynn noticed the conciliatory glance and took the initiative on cue.

'You'd get more of everything, Anders,' she stated, receiving another kiss from her delighted stooge. 'Wouldn't he, Cat?'

Leaving those around them to adjudicate on the rights and wrongs of this idea, the songwriter changed the subject yet again. 'Where's Chris, guys? I never saw him leave. Which hot chick did he go home with?'

Peals of laughter rang out. Christopher Wedderburn was a studious, nerdy child, most unlike his father. No-one could imagine him doing anything remotely naughty.

'He's asleep in Dawson's room,' the boy's mother dispelled the myth. 'Thanks for taking him under your wing earlier. He eats, sleeps and breathes Jeff Diamond.'

'At least, we think he's in his room,' Anders added, more subdued this time. 'He may've picked up some Jeff Diamond tricks tonight, so beware all who sail in her. And speaking of children, we'll be leaving from here as early as we can on Tuesday, to miss the worst of the traffic through Geelong.'

'That's cool,' Lynn piped up. 'We'll have ours down here by eight, if that's early enough. They're all kitted out. Well, as far as I know, they are.'

'What time will we expect you on Saturday then?' Cat asked. 'Just so we know whether to wait around or go for a swim beforehand... If the weather's hot, here's hoping!'

'Good question,' Lynn answered, stifling a yawn. 'I need to work out our itinerary. I'll 'phone you on Monday.'

'*Excelente.* We should go, angel,' her husband suggested, stretching his numb legs. 'If you're having trouble remembering our itinerary, you must be tired. Come on, wench. Stand up, so I can get the blood flowing again. Let me take you to bed.'

A mix of whistles and groans from the men mingled with the jealous whining of their female partners. By all accounts, they had a lot to live up to tonight.

'Again?' the singer's feeble *rejoindre* made their friends laugh.

'Yep. Of course, again,' the comic snapped, stretching his arms up to the ceiling and yawning. 'Move it, woman. We've got a long way to go, and I can't stay awake too long either.'

The couple bade their goodbyes and thanked the hosts for their hospitality. They refused to allow Don to escort them off the premises and issued an open invitation for the group to gather at *Escondido* for a weekend in the not-too-distant future.

Lynn almost dozed off in the lift during their six-storey journey, and the happy pair stumbled into their bedroom and closed the door. Silence reigned in the apartment's southern wing, the best remedy for a taxing evening.

'So?' the caring woman asked, cuddling in close to her man. 'Did you achieve self-satisfied fat cat status tonight, my magic man?'

Jeff smiled and kissed the nape of his lover's neck, tightening his grip around her body. 'Fleetingly,' he murmured. 'Yet another aspirational goal.'

'You'll need to fish out the "Built to Last" T-shirt, if you've still got it,' she giggled, referring to the one he had worn on their first weekend at Benloch, way back in nineteen-seventy-two.

The drowsy superstar chuckled at the fond memory. 'Good idea. *Dors bien, Regala.*'

What seemed like ten minutes of peaceful slumber was infiltrated not by a nightmare, since these were a rarity these days, but by the determined tone of a small boy trying his best to be subtle. Both parents awoke straightaway, inwardly imploding and outwardly concerned. Jeff extended a long right arm to prevent his wife from pushing the sheet away.

'Stay there,' he whispered. 'I've got it. Go back to sleep.'

The master bedroom door opened, letting in enough light from the impending sunrise to paint a glowing outline around their son. The father's feet found the carpet, holding his weight while he fished for his boxer shorts. Standing tall and pulling his underwear up at the same time, he heard Lynn stifle a gentle laugh.

'Come on, mate. What woke you up?'

'There was a loud noise in my dream.'

'And you forgot Dawson was in your room, didn't you?'

Lifting the youngster up by the armpits and cuddling him, the musician pulled the door shut behind them. Jet struggled to break free and dropped to the floor, stopped from bursting back into the bedroom by lightning paternal reflexes.

'No! I want Mum to sit with me.'

'Well, sorry, mate,' Jeff stood firm, 'but it's me this time. We take it in turns. You know that.'

'I want Mum,' the boy insisted.

'So do I. She needs a break, son.'

The young mother relapsed into unconsciousness a second or two later, envisaging the six-year-old squirming in his dad's tight grip. The next thing she remembered, the mattress sank down to the left, surrendering to her husband's mass. Hearing a long sigh, she turned over to thank him for taking the load tonight.

'Did you say, "It's my turn to love you this time"?' she giggled. 'How far into your cheek was your tongue at that point?'

Jeff kissed her. 'Right down my throat.'

'If it's any consolation, Kizzy does it to me too.'

'I know,' the emotional man whispered. 'It's OK. Go back to sleep.'

Lynn lay still in the dark with a firm suspicion as to the state of her beautiful black stallion's mind. The years facing and expunging the scourge of his childhood had taught her not to labour the point, even though it ripped her heart to shreds every time he encountered a reminder. In the silence, she reached over and brushed his cheek, confirming her conclusion.

'I'm sorry it makes you feel so wretched,' she said. 'He does love you.'

'I know. Thanks. I'm OK.'

This little white lie was as effective as headlights in a thick fog. 'We all love you, Jeff. You'll be chuffed with what he wants to do for your birthday. You're the best dad, and the best husband.'

The lost boy turned towards the soothing words and enveloped his therapist in loving arms. 'And you make everything better.'

'Even if it doesn't feel like it?'

'Yeah. Exactly,' he smiled. 'Why doesn't it drive you crazy that you can't make me feel better? It drives me crazy when I can't do it for you.'

Lynn cupped his tense jaw in her hand and kissed his damp lips. 'Because I don't blame myself, and neither should you. I can't fix what I didn't break. Just like you.'

Australia's most influential contemporary leader threw back his head and cried the day's emotions away, rocked back and forth like an infant by his saviour. 'Sorry to monopolise you tonight.'

'You didn't.'

'I just have to touch you constantly,' he stressed. 'You're a drug for all the other shit.'

His wife kissed the bare flesh of her husband's shoulder. 'Yeah, I know. It's lovely.'

'I crave your touch,' Jeff needed to roll out his whole raft of excuses.

'Do you? Well, that's good, because I crave touching you.'

A renewed flood of gratitude surged through the old soul's senses. 'Perfect,' he murmured. 'I love you.'

'I love you too. At least getting this out now will mean you're happier in the morning,' the wise woman promised. 'That's one thing we don't need to worry about now. Goodnight.'

Feast And Famine

A couple of months later, the same crowd from the Jenners' party were to meet again at an afternoon fundraising concert at the Melbourne Academy junior campus. The collection of well-to-do, high achievers had staked out a spot near the stage for their picnic, each extolling their children's accomplishments since term began.

Jet had integrated into his new school with ease and already enjoyed celebrity status among his classmates. He idolised his many male role models, eager to try everything they suggested, and his joyful positive energy was infectious and inspiring to his parents. Ideas for an offbeat musical was germinating in their minds and in the recording studio at *Escondido*, depicting their son as "The Boy Who Would Be King", a youthful hero looking forward to a bright future. Several early lyrics soon appeared from the prolific songwriters' collaboration, and the developing theme suited the rambunctious human cannonball to a tee.

Not to be outdone, Kierney also started in the first grade a few days before her fifth birthday, soaking up the endless variety of adventures and loving every one. Her teachers were amazed by the quantity of information such a young brain could absorb and how quickly she grasped quite complex concepts; so much so that the Diamond parents had been advised to accelerate their daughter by a year.

Lynn and Jeff opted not to accept the school's recommendation after several hours of discussion. The decision to widen their son's horizons rather than push him faster and further in a single direction had paid dividends within months. Even his grandfather was forced to admit to the startling results.

And with their wounds from the previous year's splinter still not fully healed, the young mother had made it clear to her all-knowing husband that she was prepared to accept his adjudication on this latest conundrum too. Throughout her own schooling, the tennis champion had always been two years younger than her classmates, and harking back to those tender teenage times reminded them both how the emerging star had been forever locked in a battle for levels of freedom to which she was not yet entitled.

Jeff also recounted his own experiences by contrast, whereby inadvertent freedom had been handed to him on a plate when his drug-addled mother fell victim to a fatal overdose. His own push for autonomy had been thwarted by the Sydney state government education system, before he had eventually been allowed to enrol in additional classes over and above the regular syllabus.

'Put Kierney's future in her own hands, angel. You know how like us she is.'

'Like you, you mean,' Lynn corrected him.

'No. Like both of us,' the scholar insisted. 'You wanted control too, remember? And we're here to give her or at least point her in the direction of all the advice she needs. Advancing to Grade Two would be fine, but she'll still have the same narrow curriculum. Just more complicated sums and longer words to read.'

'Maybe,' his wife deliberated, smiling at the simple imagery.

'It's later on when she'll find it stifling, just like we did,' the rock star added. 'It's a foregone conclusion she's going to be way more responsible than the average girl, and way more enquiring. Look at her...'

Slender fingers pressed on the adamant man's mouth to silence him. 'Alright, Mister Conscience! Enough already. You've convinced me,' she laughed. 'I agree with you. Kierney stays with her own age-group, and we'll feed her stuff independently.'

Thus, this particular thirty-five degree Sunday afternoon in March, warmer than average for Melbourne, saw the road warrior arriving mid-way through the concert. He had flown back from Africa unheralded, due to the potential danger resulting from his travel plans being publicised. Dumping his bags in the hallway of the apartment, he drove straight over to the Toorak Road reserve which the school had commandeered. Still dressed in dark grey suit trousers and a white business shirt, he hadn't wasted time on getting changed, such was his hurry to return to his precious family.

Parking the car nearby, the great Jeff Diamond turned all heads, as he always did, marching through the cordon monitored by excited school volunteers, delighted to see the generous patron stuff a wad of notes into the collection box. Scanning the irregular pattern of picnic rugs and the various *cliques* of children playing games on the lawn, he soon spotted Jet and Kierney involved in a well-organised cricket match.

The doting dad stood on the sidelines while his offspring played on, oblivious of their new spectator. When the over finished and the hapless fielders were prompted to change ends by the budding cricketer, the local icon realised he had been rumbled.

'Wait!' Jet's shrill voice rang out, shouting to the bowler. 'It's my dad!'

The match was summarily suspended, and both teams broke ranks and ran towards the striking celebrity. Ecstatic to be mobbed by the friendly crowd, Jeff gently nudged away the bigger kids to allow his own to reach him. He scanned the sea of languishing parents until his eyes spied his beautiful best friend, their eyes meeting over the idyllic scene. His heart soared, making him catch his breath. Life was sweet. So unbelievably sweet.

'Carry on with the game, guys,' the father urged, cuddling them both close. 'I want to see you bowl, mate. You too, *pequeñita. Te veo en un minuto.*'

The girl's bossy brother was already herding the others into their positions, putting a protective arm around his little sister. 'OK,' he agreed. 'Can I bowl next, Scotty?'

Scotty, the songwriter discerned, must have been appointed as today's captain, all of ten years old. The taller lad nodded and began to marshal everyone back to the makeshift wicket. With a last kiss from her beloved *papá*, a cheerful Kierney trotted after her brother to take up a fielding position somewhere near mid-off.

He smiled at the youngsters' willingness to play by the accepted rules and wondered how long this innocence would prevail, before it became every player for him- or herself. He wound his way through the colourful bags and eskies until he reached the spot where he had picked Lynn out in the crowd on arrival. She raised her hand as he slipped behind her, and he gripped it tightly. Their friends shuffled along to make room for the heroic peacemaker while his wife introduced him to those he hadn't met on a previous occasion.

Before the blonde beauty could even offer her husband a cold beer or a bite to eat, he dropped to his knees, encased the back of her head in one huge, strong hand and lowered her flat onto the ground. To the others' dismay and without any trace of inhibition, Jeff rolled on top of his gorgeous angel, smothering her with kisses and holding her against the whole length of his body.

The women swooned once again at the romantic statement. There was no doubting this was his forever girl, more than pleased to see her after spending too long apart. Their lips separated after a minute or so, and they sat up together, still lost in their own world. Tears glistened in the larrikin's eyes as he rolled his shirt-sleeves over a few times and straightened his pants, winking at the row of gawping mouths.

Having recovered their equilibrium, the select group of parents relaxed and enjoyed the next few concert numbers. The new arrival accepted a chilled stubby from Don's stock and dug into the delicious spread they had assembled between them. While he was eating, Lynn turned and tapped his arm, pointing to their right, towards the roped-off aisle dividing the picnic area from the playground.

Their dark-haired gipsy girl stood waiting to be noticed, melting her dad's heart when her face broke into a broad smile. The patient child would have waited forever, his thoughts jumbled, but she should never have to. He hooked his index finger, giving her permission to join the adults. She didn't need to be asked twice, seizing the invitation with glee.

Kierney sat on the grass between her daddy's long legs, leaning back onto his stomach without a word, content to let her parents and their friends chat away over her head.

'Is she OK?' one of the mothers whispered.

'She's fine, aren't you, Kizzo?' the tennis champion answered. 'You just want to reconnect with your *papá*, don't you?'

The child nodded, twisting round to look straight into her mum's eyes.

'Me too, *pequeñita*. Like I needed to reconnect with *Mamá*,' Jeff added, stroking his daughter's hair. 'It's what we do, isn't it, *mis amigas*.'

The rock star's arms swept down from above, half-empty beer bottle still in one hand, and scooped Kierney clean off the ground until she was upside down with her nose only a couple of centimetres from his. They kissed each others' faces and rubbed noses, the little girl giggling through the whole rigmarole.

'*Te amo, KLF*,' the love-god whispered into her ear.

'*Te amo, Papá*.'

This was how fathers were supposed to behave. How this man had learned such skills never ceased to amaze his wife. It must be instinctive, she decided, and somehow these impulses had remained dormant in Jeff's parents. He was marvellous with Jet and Kierney: at every step, he held their hands to lead them towards tomorrow, building their confidence by encouraging them to try everything.

The nobody from Canley Vale buried his lips into the child's sweet-smelling hair. Their boy would be king, if it were in his power, and their gipsy girl would grow up in an environment where women were no longer second-classed citizens. Lynn's eyes welled up as she listened to the two dark Diamonds exchanging news in a mixture of Spanish and French, giving thanks that their tight-knit family was flourishing through thick and thin.

***

In mid-July nineteen-eighty-four, Paragon Holdings posted its earnings for the preceding financial year. Jeff was overseas of course, promoting both a new album for the continental European market and a Childlight crisis centre opening in Glasgow, Scotland. Gerry had telephoned to break the news, as excited as Lynn had ever known him.

'You guys've got to slow down,' the couple's ebullient manager bleated. 'These are insane numbers, Ms D. He's going to go ballistic when he hears. Be afraid, good lady. Be very afraid. That's all I'll say on the matter.'

This statement was only partially true however. Although turnover and profit from the innovation seed-funding arm of the business were gigantic and the money their partnerships attracted from investors continued to flood in from all over the globe, the outgoing side of the conglomerate's ledger was of equivalent *largesse*.

That night, over a crackly telephone line, the rear-end of the intrepid pantomime horse warned its forward half about the following day's market announcement. As expected, the revelation was greeted with mixed emotions. With intense pride for what they and their loyal employees and partners had achieved, the celebrities also knew only too well how much more needed to be done.

'You can afford to *buy* Africa if you want,' Gerry had joked.

'I would if I thought it'd solve anything,' Jeff lamented on hearing a passable rendition of the accountant's remark. 'Which bit would you like, angel? Kenya's nice. Botswana too. House prices in Somalia are dipping a little lately, so not such a good investment.'

All bitterness aside, the traveller congratulated his dedicated program manager on her significant but wholly-understated contribution to the fantastic financial results. One of the year's biggest money-spinners had originated from an idea of hers to write and record multiple songs with the same title, and to release them at the same time in aid of different causes.

Needless to say, the simultaneous launch caught the imagination of the international record-buying public. The competing titles jostled for superior chart positions for many weeks, netting the Diamond Celebration Foundation close to fifty million US dollars. Awards and accolades kept pouring in, as did the money, making its redirection their biggest problem.

'I don't want to see the stats,' the passionate philanthropist yelled into the telephone, standing up and waving a three-page report in the air.

The youngsters stared at their mother in consternation, and in turn at the cameraman and producer who had arrived that morning to film the latest episode in the ongoing documentary series. Lynn shrugged and grinned, also taken aback by the sudden change of tone after what had started out as a friendly introduction to the new recruit in their Ethiopian feeding camps' taskforce. The ground staff had been informed of a rapid escalation in the volume of refugees, especially children, arriving malnourished and on the verge of death in the war-torn country, disturbing the couple a great deal.

'Mate, don't give me all these executive excuse tools,' the effort's commander-in-chief continued, flapping the papers on the table as if they were meaningless. 'Project plans, risk registers and logistics reports. This doesn't cut it, Jamie.'

The tennis champion stood up and suggested to the children that it might be a good time to make *Papá* some lunch. Kierney growled, impersonating the angry man, who waved back and mimed biting someone's hand. He grinned and blew a kiss as his family took the sensible step of leaving the office to reverberate with these turbulent forces. The camera continued to run regardless, and the indefatigable campaigner focussed on the tough conversation he needed to have with the Diamond Celebration Foundation representative who had been sent as an advance party to witness the devastation as it unfolded in Africa's north-east.

'Listen, Jamie, please,' Jeff implored, calming down. 'I don't mean to take it out on you. Sorry, mate. I know you guys are doing your best, but people are still fucking dying. It's the only thing we're here to stop. Remember that? We need a communications strategy to direct those with food and medicine to the hungry and sick. Simple as that. Tell me how many people you need, where to send them and what we need to be saying to whom. The stats are back-office dramas, mate. Getting the number of arrivals to go down is my job. Yours is to get the number of survivors to go up.'

The sting taken out of the discussion, the philanthropist settled down for a protracted call, and the cameras were requested to pause their filming due to the unsavoury subject matter. It was mid-October, and *Escondido*'s comfort provided a veritable sanctuary for the family to drive their African mission. Although still writing and recording, the charities and relief efforts were taking up more and more of the couple's time, barely keeping pace with the critical situation in these countries.

Looking out of his office window at the swimming pool and the gardens leading down to the cliffs' edge, the millionnaire racked his brain about how to rationalise his involvement with famine relief and refugee care with the surroundings wherein he now luxuriated. He had so many different roles these days: songwriter, performer, composer of musicals, actor, director, rally car driver, squash player, company boss, charity figurehead and spokesperson for any number of worthy causes, not to mention husband and father. Was he spreading himself too thinly to be effective at anything?

Lynn told her doubting doomsayer every day that he deserved everything he had achieved, and most of all because so much of the pair's income found its way into someone else's hands sooner or later. She shuddered to think of their lifestyle's opulence if they were to spend every cent they generated on themselves. Quite apart from their inability to comprehend how such a large amount of money might be disbursed, this cold, hard fact helped him make sense of where he was and how happy he ought to be with his lot. Jeff Diamond was learning to recognise his own worth.

October rolled around before the Midas couple succeeded in mobilising a film crew in Korem, Ethiopia. There were scenes of jubilation at *Escondido* when the diligent project manager broke the news to her husband, who proceeded to lift her up and swing her round in circles, much to the children's amusement. He knew it was largely due to his wife's tireless efforts that they had managed to clinch this deal, and by her meticulous planning that their insurance company had eventually agreed to cover the whole tour contingent, including the frontman himself.

The intent of the forthcoming documentary was purely humanitarian at its core, yet the authorities in Ethiopia and several other neighbouring countries remained paranoid about the possibility of a political sub-agenda. Jeff spent hours negotiating with all parties, flying twice around the world in the process, scarcely having set foot in his home in three months.

And while the jet-setting celebrity did what he did best, in front of the cameras and hordes of reporters hot for more theatre, his gorgeous wife was again rallying support from the music world's greatest stars to back him up. In London and in the USA, songs were banged out and laid down in huge warehouses, to be released in time for Christmas.

Over the course of the next few months, more than a hundred and thirty million US dollars were raised, and the trend of those horrendous original "numbers" for which the philanthropist had lambasted poor Jamie began to turn downward. Everywhere the hard-working couple went, they were hailed as heroes, and they made sure the fire continued to feed itself by never missing an opportunity to highlight the plight of those still starving and suffering in north-eastern Africa.

Immediately after Christmas, the children settled into another summer sports program, allowing Lynn the headspace to plan an extraordinary popular music event with likeminded artists that would simultaneously unite entertainers and fans in every part of the world. Off the back of the success of various charity records at the end of nineteen-eighty-four, the Diamond Celebration Foundation's "Feed Africa" campaign joined forces with the British and American stars who had schemed up a concert *extravaganza* to keep everyone's attention focussed on the desperate plight. Most top names signed up, keen to jump on the bandwagon. Indeed, some who overestimated their status as a top name had to be turned away, having failed to respond to the call in time.

Billed as the "Global Jukebox", large-scale events were to be held on each side of the Atlantic Ocean, one in Wembley Stadium in North London and the other in Philadelphia's John F. Kennedy Stadium. For the same day, concerts inspired by the initiative were organised in many other countries too, including Australia's cultural capital, Melbourne. The LiveAid phenomenon took off as one of the most ambitious satellite link-ups and television broadcasts of all time, with an estimated audience of almost two billion people.

In parallel, their own high-profile campaigns for famine relief and building refugee camps spiralled Lynn and Jeff ever upwards in terms of popularity, accompanied by untold levels of exhaustion and even longer separations. In the months leading up to her thirtieth birthday, the sportswoman's peak physical condition became her greatest asset as she flew in endless circles around the world, sorting out venues, sound systems, playlists and running sheets. Her partner too had precious little time to play his usual party-animal tricks, often finding his diet limited to rice, water and a colourful handful of precautionary pills while filming in medical tents and feeding stations.

Jet and Kierney were excited to be met at the Sidney Myer Music Bowl by their parents on the thirteenth of July. Nine hours ahead of London and almost a day ahead of the United States' east coast, the eve of the huge event saw unprecedented crowds staking claim to valuable patches of grass all across the gardens. Melbourne Academy's winter school holidays having been brought forward by special permission, the youngsters and their friends pitched tents and gathered round portable stoves to prepare for a concert hosted by the city's tireless ambassadors.

'Seventy-two thousand people in Wembley,' Lynn gasped, putting the telephone down after a last call to Cathy in the Stonebridge Music offices. 'Wow, Jet! What do you think of that?'

'Wow!' he echoed.

'How many in JFK?' his dad asked. 'More?'

'Not sure. About a hundred, I think.'

'Only a hundred people?' Jet's irritation rivalled that of his father. 'Why?'

The songwriter smiled. 'A hundred thousand, mate. Does that sound more like it?'

The youngster huffed and puffed, annoyed that he had taken his mother so literally. His dad scooped him up into the air and wrestled with him to get rid of their excess nervous energy, even a little apprehensive himself. What if the forty-odd-thousand-strong local audience were to end up too squashed in, especially when excitement pushed everyone ever nearer to the stage? The last thing he wanted to happen was a repeat of the fatalities in Chicago four years earlier. He was in the business of saving lives these days, not losing them.

The seasoned performers had engaged crowd control experts in the venue and planned for every eventuality. Between the production staff and stadium management, exit drills were prepared, along with rallying messages to be flashed up on the large screens; the same screens which would enable those in the far reaches of the gardens to feel more involved with the action, and therefore removing the temptation to storm the floor. In true Dyson tradition, nothing had been left to chance. Jeff hoped not anyway...

From tomorrow in Australian Eastern Standard Time on the morning of the concert, as the first few ticketholders entered through the barriers and found their preferred vantage points on ground level, the Diamonds chose to wander around and soak up the rarefied atmosphere. Such a unique experience was not to be missed, and even little Kierney traipsed along with her eyes wide and mouth permanently open at the sheer enormity.

People clamoured to have their picture taken with the celebrity family, who were happy to oblige as long as each photographer reached into his or her pocket and threw coins into the donation buckets which followed them wherever they roamed. The children had been issued with noise-cancelling headphones for when their caretakers ferried them backstage during their parents' performances. Jet failed to see why he had to wear them, but his little sister was glad of the muffling effect as soon as the sound-checks began.

The audience swayed and cheered through sets by all the greats with the summer sun beating down, while the honoured family thrilled the crowd again halfway through the afternoon by appearing unheralded at the rear of the stadium floor, enjoying the music among the throng with their nannies and a security contingent.

During another set later on, from his position behind the wings and still obsessed by the possibility of fans being stampeded to the ground, Jeff found himself staring into frightened eyes belonging to a young woman facing this exact fate. The venue's staff had not noticed her and ignored the performer's plea to lift her out at first.

While the band's lead singer carried on unaware of the drama below, the songwriter jumped off a speaker and landed in the mass of bodies to save the panicked fan himself, picking her out from the *melée* and dragging her into free space between the barrier and the stage. Once out of danger, the pair danced until the song finished, in full view of the cameras and to cheering fans. No-one was any the wiser until days later, when the lucky fan told her story to the country's media, soon corroborated by television footage of the unsung hero's actions.

Musical and comedy acts were interspersed with moving videos from Ethiopia during the marathon line-up in each location, causing the trajectory of donations to shoot ever upward. At a certain point, one of the richest men in Dubai called into the telethon centre and asked to speak with Jeff Diamond. The sheikh was patched through to his celebrity wife instead, with the film rolling, soon discovering his pledge was worth a million dollars to the cause.

The forever couple saw the end in sight nearly sixteen hours later, after having performed, compèred, interviewed and encouraged donations all day and well into the evening. When British band, Genesis, had finished their set in Wembley, their lead singer headed straight for Heathrow, whence he boarded a flight that detoured over the London crowd on its way to New York. Phil Collins landed at JFK Airport before tracking further west by helicopter through the skies to the stadium named after the same former president.

By far the most memorable moment came at the conclusion of the UK proceedings. Paul McCartney and a whole host of others gathered around for a rendition of the Beatles' "Let It Be", encouraging the crowd to belt it out with no less *gusto* than at the start of the day.

Back in the Australian Sunday's fading light, even the hardest heart melted as the amazing concert experience was drawn to a close with the figure of six-year-old Kierney Lynn Freedom Diamond standing on the grand piano and singing the opening lines of the show's closing number in a mixture of English and French. Her sweet voice rang out as clear as a bell, with no sign of nerves whatsoever. Her brother joined her for the second verse, vaulting onto the closed lid and harmonising without effort, the tired audience re-energised when their mother also appeared to sit next to her husband at the majestic black instrument.

With the chorus of "Feed the world. Let them know it's Christmas time again" chanted by the entire crowd as they cleared the stadium's perimeter, the stage emptied and the stars vanished behind the scenes to be ferried to the after-party. The Diamonds chose not to join them. Instead, they waited in a deserted dressing-room until the coast was clear before venturing out to the litter-strewn area.

All energy expended, the chief fundraiser sat down on the ground and peered through the dusty dryness, taking in the magnitude of the day. The concert in Pennsylvania was still in full swing, as were smaller ones in Chicago, San Francisco, Rio de Janeiro and Los Angeles. Three scheduled interviews remained for the famous couple, and he wondered if they could summon the strength to do them justice.

Lynn crouched down beside her inspiring partner while the children ran this way and that in the open space. 'Happy?'

'Numb, more than anything,' the husband admitted. 'Totally numb, but happy too, yeah. What about you?'

'Very happy,' his dream girl answered, kissing his mouth hard. 'You are the most amazing man. Do you know what you guys all did today?'

Humility oozed out of the rock star's every pore. 'No. What we did, angel. You've worked harder than me on this. You're the architect of "Feed Africa". I'm only the parasitic frontman, remember?'

'Yeah, right,' she sneered. 'And I'm the arse-end. I know my place.'

Moulding the loose gravel chips to the shape of his reclining body, Jeff pulled his wife down and enveloped her in his arms. The private moment was soon discovered by their children, who came running over and bundled on top of their parents, screaming and yelling.

Without warning, every single light went out in the music bowl, plunging the Diamonds and their pared-down group of retainers into total darkness. Low clouds gathered overhead, adding to the spectral mystique and obscuring the moon from lighting their path to the concourse. The whites of their children's startled eyes were the only source of illumination.

'It's the end of the world,' the philosopher whispered into his lover's ear, not wishing to scare Jet and Kierney any further.

'What a way to go,' the smiling mother quipped. 'Come on, everyone. We'd better get to the hotel. We've got that cross with Wembley for the ABC's breakfast show.'

Groaning, the songwriter hauled himself to his feet and held his hands out to the youngsters. At a snail's pace, and with heavy legs and hearts, they all made their way to the waiting bus. They knew the night had to come to an end, yet in truth it wasn't ending at all. Elsewhere around the globe, people continued to die. Plenty of work still required.

***

'What does "DNA" stand for?' Jet asked his father, poring over the newspaper.

'Deoxyribonucleic acid,' Jeff rattled off without a moment's thought.

'Deoxy-what?' his son laughed. 'How do you remember things like that?'

'Don't know,' the philosopher answered, almost asleep. 'Because it interests me, I guess. I bet you remember the things you want to too.'

The eight-year-old shrugged. 'S'pose so.'

It was such a relief to be home. Another long three weeks away, and the youngsters' summer holidays were nearly over. Dog-tired, underweight and bruised all over from his basic means of travel on the sub-Saharan plains, the world-changer laboured to afford the lad the attention he deserved.

'What're you reading?' he asked, heaving himself out of the armchair and plonking himself down next to the boy on the floor in front of the coffee table.

'About this man who murdered a girl from Blackburn. That's where Thomas lives, isn't it? They found his DNA on her clothes. Does that mean he really killed her?'

The exhausted celebrity scanned down a four-paragraph summary of the Coronial inquest which had caught the curious student's imagination. He remembered reading about the same case before he left for Africa. The victim was only eleven years old and had been strangled and sexually assaulted. This was hardly suitable material for a primary school child, but for some reason both his children had inherited their father's fascination for morbid topics.

'Only he and the girl know the answer to that question, mate,' his dad responded. 'And unfortunately, she can't tell anyone. It's likely he did do something to her if they found his DNA on her body, but it depends what else they find and where they find it.'

Jet fixed his father's eyes in his, ready to detonate another blast of questions. 'What do you mean? Where they find the DNA?' he enquired. 'What does it look like anyway?'

'You can only see it with a microscope, or do scientific tests for it,' Jeff explained. 'It comes from tiny pieces of skin or a hair or something. Or saliva, if he touched her with his mouth.'

'His mouth?' the boy yelped. 'Ugh, really? Like he kissed her or something?'

'Well, yeah. Or it could be from a sneeze, or just touching her t-shirt or other clothing... Think of it this way,' the patient teacher continued, dragging his innocent son backwards to sit between his legs. 'Hey, I missed you so much, Jetto. I love coming home and spending time with you guys. Imagine if that man... the accused, he's called... had been walking along, minding his own business. Out for a walk with his dog, maybe... And he suddenly spotted a girl lying in the bushes. If he bent down to take a look, touched her face to see if she moved or was still breathing, for example, then picked her up to carry her to hospital or to the police, her DNA might easily get on his clothes, mightn't it?'

Jet craned his neck around, a broad grin on his face. 'Oh, yeah! I didn't think of that.'

'That's why we have to be careful not to jump to conclusions,' the intellectual smiled. 'However... What if the man had lifted the girl's skirt up and put his hand inside her undies. Some of his DNA could transfer to her body, and in a place where adults shouldn't touch children.'

Jeff felt his son's shoulders droop and imagined the smile vanishing from his youthful *visage*. He oughtn't to go too far. There was a threshold he couldn't cross without damaging his child's optimistic view of the world, but it was also his duty as a parent to take him right up close to this boundary in a safe environment.

'See what I mean?' he prompted, tapping the top of the lad's head. 'Now do you think he did it?'

'Yes,' the response was more enthusiastic this time, before a second thought set in. 'Well... Not killed her, but he shouldn't do sexual abuse. He can go to prison for that too, can't he?'

'Absolutely. You're spot on, mate. Not necessarily a murderer, but still guilty of a serious crime. *Complicado*, isn't it? Can you imagine what it'd be like to be sent to prison for the rest of your life when you didn't kill anyone? It'd be terrible for everyone you know to think of you as a murderer when you're perfectly innocent.'

Jet's head gave a solemn nod. His dad could sense the telling message had been received loud and clear by the coldness radiating from rigid limbs.

'When people see your picture in the newspaper or on TV, you can see them saying, "Hey! There's that nasty Jet Diamond. Did you know he killed sixteen people last year? He must be an arsehole."'

The boy turned around again, laughing at the expression of disdain on his father's face. 'Stop it, Dad! I'm not going to kill anyone ever, ever, ever. It's terrible. But I don't want to be a judge either. Judges have to decide when they don't know what really happened.'

'Exactly right, brain-box,' Jeff smiled, raising a high-five. 'That's why they collect all the evidence, and the judge doesn't have to make the decision on his or her own. D'you know what a jury is?'

The curly, blonde head shook from side to side underneath his dad's chin. These brief moments in time were so precious for both. The musician's busy mind no longer felt so tired, distracted from its political obsessions to dispense some life lessons to the king-in-waiting.

'When there's a serious case, like murder or violence of some sort, or when someone sets a building on fire or plants a bomb... And when it looks like the person should go to prison for a long time if found guilty, there are always twelve ordinary adults just like *Mamá* and me, who have to sit and listen to the whole case in the court, and then make a decision at the end. They're the jury. And if all twelve people can't agree whether to vote "guilty" or "not guilty", they have to sit there and sit there and sit there and sit there...'

Jet slapped his father on the arm, snorting and joining in the endless sentence. 'Sit there and sit there and sit there, and then what?'

'Sit there some more,' the teacher carried on, 'until they finally agree, "guilty" or "not guilty". After that, the judge tells the accused what the jury's decided and figures out how many years he or she should go to prison for.'

'Oh,' the eight-year-old mused. 'But what other evidence can they collect? Like a knife or a gun?'

'Yep. The murder weapon,' the storyteller affirmed, hissing venom into his son's ear and making him giggle again. 'But it can't be just any knife or gun. The solicitor who's trying to convict the accused, who's called the prosecution, must prove it was *the* knife or gun that was used to murder the victim. Or skin from the bloke's hands if the victim was strangled, and not someone else's hands.'

'How?'

'DNA again, maybe, or fingerprints? Or if it's a gun, the bullet found in the body has to be the right type for that gun and must've been fired at the right time. They can do all kinds of tests to find out how many hours ago someone died, and then how long ago the gun was fired. If the timing's not right, they can't say for certain that the person committed the murder, can they?'

Again the boy's head shook. 'No. But what if the man had two guns?'

'They'd test both, I guess. But better for the bloke to get rid of the gun altogether, so the police can't find it and test it.'

'How?'

'Heaps of different ways, mate,' the father answered, aware that some of these educational nuggets of dubious value should be saved for future years. 'Throw it in a river, somewhere a long way from where you live, or bury it somewhere...'

The sound of the front door opening and footsteps of the rest of the family returning home diverted the schemers from their grisly conversation. Kierney was calling their names, her high-pitched voice becoming louder as it closed in on the lounge room door.

'*¿Papá, estáis aquí?*' she shouted, breaking into a run as soon as she found them.

Pleased the fabulous foursome was once more together after the girls' trip into the city, Jeff scooped his son up and carried him like a sack of potatoes on his hip towards the others. 'Hey, angels,' he said, struggling to maintain his grip on the squirming dead-weight, whose arms thrashed about in an effort to free himself. 'I found this lying around, so I was going to throw it out. It's just making a mess. Do you have any use for it?'

'No! No! No! Let me down! Let me down!'

'Oh, I don't know,' Lynn answered, happy to play along. 'It is sometimes useful. We shouldn't throw it out just yet. Put it in a box upstairs for now.'

With protestations ringing loud and clear from the unfortunate lad, the handsome superstar's lips locked on his lover's with a full complement of potent longing. After a few seconds, the strength in his arms began to give way due to the barrage of kicks and punches he was receiving, and he let the offending object drop onto the carpet.

Jet jumped to his feet and waved triumphant fists. 'See?' he declared, 'I can beat you now. You'd better not try that again, Dad.'

'Oh, yeah?' his six-foot four-inch opponent retorted, lunging again with a loud roar.

But his son was too quick. Jeff's fingers could only grasp at thin air while the lithe imp vanished into the hallway and up the stairs. Kierney almost lost her balance, laughing at the *duo*'s antics, having waited for the right time to show her beloved *papá* the spoils with which she had come home. Her mother's talkative eyes urged him to turn around.

'OK, a*lors! ¿Lo que has comprado, pequeñita?*' he asked, seeing two shopping bags at her feet.

'My bridesmaid's dress *y unas botas.*'

'*¡Fantastico!* Can I see, *por favor?*'

'*Papá está muy cansada, querida.* Show them to him quickly, then you can try them on later, *después de la cena,*' Lynn rattled off the family's special brand of Spanglish like a native.

'*Muy bueno, Mamá. Gracias. Estoy muy cansado*, you're right, angel. Especially after fighting with *su hermano horible.*'

Kierney trotted forwards into her father's open arms and hugged him. His knees buckled underneath them, and the two dark-haired Diamonds ended up on the floor. Pretending to be fast asleep, Jeff lifted her on top of him until she straddled his torso, before laying her down on his chest.

'*Te amo, Papá,*' she whispered against his bristly neck.

'*Te amo también. A las dos, a los tres.* A bit more than yesterday and not as much as tomorrow.'

The little girl sat up straight, smiling at one of her favourite phrases, and Jeff's heart glowed when Lynn's loving hand ruffled their daughter's hair. Christ, it was so good to be home! These last three weeks away had been the hardest yet, both in terms of the challenges their famine relief efforts had faced in North Africa and because he missed these perfect beings so much.

Purged of all physical and emotional resources, the traveller had plunged into a deep depression during the homeward flight, the like of which he hadn't experienced for many years, further deepened by the dispiriting prospect of another similar month ahead.

Lynn lifted Kierney up off her daddy, requesting that she take her purchases upstairs. Having succeeded in dispatching both underlings to their bedrooms, the canny parents rejoiced at their limited time alone in the lounge room. Sitting down on the white, deep-pile carpet next to her husband, who was dressed in his customary head-to-toe black, she leaned forwards and kissed his enticing lips.

'*Te amo, Papá,*' she mimicked the child about to turn seven. 'You look terrible. Why don't you get some sleep? I'll cook up something tasty for dinner in the meantime, and then we can all start again when you've balanced out a bit.'

Jeff closed his eyes and inhaled a long, slow breath. 'Nice idea. Sorry I'm not better company, angel. I'm so unbelievably happy to be home, but the message's not getting through to the outside, is it?'

'Don't worry about it,' the compassionate woman dismissed the downbeat observation, feeling him jump out of his skin at another kiss on the lips. 'Oh, my God! Sorry to scare you.'

The songwriter groaned. 'Jesus! I'm so wound up. My mind's racing two hundred miles a minute, and I'm all doom and gloom. I can't seem to snap out of it this time.'

'I can tell,' Lynn chuckled. 'Give it a few days. You'll get through it. You always do, and we're here to ensure you make the most of this break. But first, please stop apologising. What you've been doing over there is huge. It's bound to take its toll. Give yourself a pat on the back for a change!'

'Yes, ma'am. I love you,' her husband smiled and opened his eyes. 'You're so good to me, and the kids are awesome. You're growing them into very special people while I'm swanning around all over the place, baby. I just want you to know how grateful I am.'

'*We're* growing them into special people,' the sportswoman countered. 'They don't forget you while you're away. They talk about you all the time. They ask about what you're doing in Africa, what you're eating and what the weather's like. It's not all *Mamá, Mamá, Mamá.*'

Jeff lifted his left hand, his index finger pointing at his head. 'It is in here,' he said, before moving his hand to his chest. 'And here, and here...'

Tutting like a schoolteacher, his wife grabbed the roaming digits as they trekked towards his crotch, only to place them on her breast. The sex-starved hero wasted no time in fondling his prize. Sitting across his abdomen, as Kierney had done a few minutes earlier, she stroked the dark outer shadow on her husband's face. It masked a still darker inner shadow which was her job to diffuse.

'Thank you,' she said. 'And you're in mine too. Let's not do three weeks again for a while. It's too long for all of us, isn't it?'

The sad man nodded. 'Can we go upstairs and lock ourselves in the bedroom?'

'No,' Lynn scolded. 'I told the girls they could have the night off. And anyway, you're too tired. You have to get some sleep, Mister Diamond. I insist.'

'But why?' he whined like their son. 'I'm not tired. You always tell me when you think I'm tired, and I'm the only one who knows if I'm tired or not.'

Before his guardian angel had a chance to respond to such a childish tirade, the comic began to emit loud snoring noises. With a haughty laugh, she levered her tall frame to its full height and left the room, leaving her inanimate partner lying on the floor with a feeling of contented arousal permeating the deep crevices of his mind.

This woman was dynamite! She had managed to lift the melancholy musician's mood enough for another few hours, until a good night's sleep could supplement the remedy. After a few seconds spent in lurid fantasies, he rolled over and hauled himself to his feet too, tracking his dream girl down in the office, where she was collecting messages from the answering machine.

'You are perfect, Ms Diamond,' he whispered, nipping the delicate skin on the side of her neck while his eyes scanned down the list of people whose telephone calls they would be returning the following day. 'Whoa! This is not going to be fun. Where did they all spring from? I've reluctantly agreed to take your advice, even though I think my idea's far superior. I hope you'll be more amenable to physical gratification when I wake up. As you mentioned, three weeks is a bloody long time.'

Lynn smiled. 'I'm sure you'll be able to persuade me. Get upstairs right now, or else I'm out of bounds until Thursday.'

'Thursday?' the spurned man exclaimed, stepping back from Lynn's body *post haste*. 'Why Thursday? What's today anyway? I have absolutely no clue what day it is, but Thursday sounds like a ridiculously long way off.'

The Olympian laughed out loud. 'It's Monday. *Va t'en*. I've got work to do.'

Muttering under his breath, the jilted lover turned and skulked out of the office and down the corridor, hanging on to the curved bannister as he dragged leaden limbs up the stairs. On his way to the master suite, he knocked on his son's door, pushing it open to find him constructing some weird and wonderful spacecraft out of a construction kit he received from the Blakes for Christmas.

'Dad, go away,' Jet moaned, running towards the door and trying to shut his father out. 'I'm making something that's a surprise.'

Feeling guilty, the intruder did as he was told. 'Sorry, mate. Thanks heaps. I promise I didn't see anything. I'm going to bed now, so I'll wait for you to show me when it's ready.'

Satisfied that his secret was safe, Jet shouted out his wishes for a peaceful sleep, and the wanderer moved on to Kierney's room, hoping he wouldn't be spoiling any grand plan here too.

'*¿Kizzy, puedo entrar?*'

There was no reply. Jeff pushed the door open, his eyes settling on his daughter's bed. She had fallen asleep while reading a book, waves of dark hair weaving through the words on each page. It was an enchanting sight, and his inner camera stood still while it stocked up with a full reel of memories for his next trip away.

So all was well with his family... Nothing else needed immediate attention, giving the world-changer nowhere else to go but to bed. The French windows leading onto the balcony were wide open to let in the stiff sea breeze, and the sun glinted on the bay in the distance, stretching its rays all the way to the horizon. He closed the shutters to darken the room, but left the doors untouched. A cooling stream of air drifted past, guiding his pacified soul towards the king-sized bed. Within minutes, he was out for the count.

Ten Years On

The Diamonds held a full-scale shindig at *Escondido* on the first Saturday in February, marking both Kierney's seventh birthday and the couple's tenth wedding anniversary. Their hectic post-Christmas travel schedule had forced them to postpone their customary New Year's Day celebration, but it had worked out better for everyone in the end.

With the children developing their own special friendships through school, arranging a get-together during January was increasingly difficult due to the number of families vacating the city for annual summer breaks. Hosting an event to coincide with the little girl's birthday even enabled Junior and Julie to leave the Narrandera homestead safe in the hands of a full complement of revitalised staff.

Over the worst of his depressive lapse, Jeff had spent the last few days writing the *libretto* for another new musical he and Lynn were developing with the violin *virtuosa* and composer, Kiley Jones. The idea had come to the French literature *aficionado* a couple of months earlier, having revisited Honoré de Balzac's *"La Comédie Humaine"* series while circling the Earth for the umpteenth time.

Translated as "The Black Sheep", *"La Rabouilleuse"* plotted the interplay between two brothers; one a swashbuckling soldier who fulfilled everyone's ambitions, and the other a quiet artist destined for invisible poverty. It presented the social justice advocate with the perfect platform to demonstrate how true reality seldom resembled that which life's *façade* exposed.

The hot summer's afternoon had been spent by the pool, supervising ten whooping and splashing water-babies who had been invited for the weekend to share the birthday fun. Parents and nannies alike hoped the extra energy supplied by gooey chocolate cake and ice creams would work its way through their systems sometime before nightfall.

Unable to prevent the party dividing along gender lines, Jeff watched as the boisterous boys turned to soccer with Kierney's big brother while the gregarious girls dreamed up a theatrical production of their own. While it came as no surprise that Jet had taken charge of the fierce competition metered out on the lawn, it was fascinating to see their daughter exerting a contrasting brand of persuasive influence on the more complex and troublesome interactions between the actresses.

'What are you smiling at?' Lynn asked, returning from the kitchen with bottles of beer for the three men.

'Cheers, angel. How much Kizzy reminds me of me.'

'She's much prettier than you, mate,' teased Doug, the father of one of the gipsy girl's classmates. 'I look forward to an invitation to her sixteenth birthday party.'

The stockbroker's pasty, imported skin already showed signs of having been exposed to plenty of direct sunlight, mirrored by a distinct slur in his pompous accent which failed to endear him to the locals round the table. He had offered to drive the city-based school-friends out to Mount Eliza and home again, prizing an afternoon in the company of Melbourne's hottest celebrities.

'Undoubtedly,' the songwriter frowned. 'And I'll thank you not to air any further thoughts of perving on my daughter and her friends, one of whom happens to be your own. If you don't mind.'

'Hmm,' his wife murmured, shaking her head in disapproval. 'But why, Jeff? What's she doing that's so like you?'

'Ah, not much. It's more wishful thinking and beer, I expect,' he replied, raising the new bottle to his beautiful best friend. 'I got a school report when I was about the same age which said, "An unexpected class leader, never assumes control but we all know he's in charge," and Kizzy's just the same. Don't you think?'

Lynn nodded. 'Yes, I do. You never told me about that report before. One to be proud of.'

The scholar shrugged. 'I'd forgotten until just then. It sort of got lost in the annals of time. My parents took exception to the remark 'cause they thought it was criticism. I remember being stoked with it though.'

'The shape of things to come,' Sue Jenner piped up. 'I wonder if that teacher ever thinks about her premonition?'

'She was a bloke, I think,' Jeff countered. 'But yeah, it'd be interesting, if a little self-serving, to find out. Long time ago. Teachers never lasted long at our school. At least, not those who were any good... I most likely negated any brownie points this behaviour scored by getting into a fist-fight in the playground or being caught smoking. I was hardly the model student.'

A few minutes later, Kierney came running over to the poolside table and stopped short to gauge the adults' conversation. She breathed a deep sigh of relief when her mother allowed her to interrupt, moving straight in to pose a secret question into the tended ear. Apparently, one of the girls was refusing to take part in their burgeoning thespian masterpiece, and the youngster had come to suggest she might prefer playing football with the boys. Hilary was a tomboy who was far more active than the average student, and Lynn had engaged in several discussions with her parents about joining a Dyson sports program at Melbourne Academy.

'I think that'd be fine,' she whispered, stroking the birthday girl's scorched, shining hair. 'Go and ask *Papá* for some help. He'll know the best way to include her into the boys' game. And then you all need to put your hats on, alright?'

Overhearing a demand on his presence, Jeff turned his alcohol-impaired attention to his gorgeous gipsy girl. '*¿Qué pasa, pequeñita?*' he asked, standing up and walking over to the other side of the table. 'What will I know what to do how with hats?'

His daughter giggled. '*Papá*, that doesn't make any sense.'

'Yes, it does,' he refuted, hands on hips. 'It's just you've had too much birthday sugar to understand me properly.'

'Be serious, please. *Nesso tu ayuda*,' the seven-year-old stamped her foot.

'Sorry, baby. *Digame.*'

The empathetic man of the house smiled at the girl's stern attitude, crouching down and brushing the ball of his thumb across her sweat-drenched forehead. Again, she leaned in and whispered her idea into his ear. Long arms wrapped around the featherweight body and lifted it high into the air. This request would be a useful learning experience for the children, not to mention an interesting experiment for him.

Edging away from the other parents, the peacemaker shared a quick checkpoint with the budding negotiator. 'Are you sure Hilary doesn't want to be in the play?' he asked, putting her feet back on solid ground.

'Yes, I'm sure,' Kierney answered. 'But she's too scared to ask them if she can play football.'

Taking his daughter's hand, Jeff nodded. 'OK. Here's the go… I'll come and referee for a few minutes, you go and get Hilary and tell her what we're going to do, and we'll make a substitution when everyone's ready. Is there someone over there who you want to be your Prince Charming?'

The young girl landed a playful slap on her dad's thigh. 'Why? What are you suggesting?'

Jeff's eyes widened. 'What am I suggesting?' he echoed, laughing hard. 'Lynn Dyson Diamond, you've swapped bodies with your daughter. There are far easier ways to get birthday cake than that, *mon amie.*'

'I don't want any of those boys for my boyfriend, if that's what you're suggesting, *Papá.*'

'*Bueno*,' the incurable romantic replied, kissing the adamant maiden's hand. 'They're all too young for you anyway. Just checkin'. Now go talk to Hilary.'

Kierney ran back to her friends at the poolside, where a multi-coloured assortment of towels had been rigged up on the rotary clothesline as theatre curtains. In the meantime, her dad positioned himself on an imaginary sideline, watching the boys passing the ball to each other and executing sliding tackles quite skilfully for a bunch of under-nines. Jet waved to the new referee, unwise to the solution concocted by the rest of his family.

Scanning the field from one goal to the other, none of the players appeared tired or uncommitted, much to Jeff's *chagrin*. His original plan was likely to end in angry tears and temper tantrums if he wasn't careful, not dissimilar to early rounds of peace talks. Short of picking someone at random, there was no fair way to complete his assignment.

Kierney and Hilary were already walking across the *patio*, deep in conversation. A surge of relief flooded his veins, clashing with the angst generated by his current task. The initial concern Lynn and he had harboured for their solitary and contemplative daughter was dispersed by the delight of seeing her at ease when surrounded by her peers, behaving like normal, fun-loving girls and boys.

'Hey, Jetto!' the scheming father shouted to the other end of the pitch, having spotted the ball going wide of the net and off into the bushes. 'Can you come over here, please?'

The boy ran at full pelt towards the house, always eager to help. 'What, Dad?'

'You know Hilary?' he asked, bending down and holding out his arm to encourage Jet in close.

The boy's face was a picture at the thought of having to integrate a girl into his team. Anxious not to offend his dad by refusing, the valiant effort couldn't quite hide his disgust. However, the youngster was quick to admit that Hilary was a good footballer, having seen her in action several times at school.

'D'you want to trade someone?' Jeff enquired, stoked to secure one half of the deal.

'To play with the girls? No way!'

'Why not?'

''Cause that's girl's stuff,' Jet yelped. 'They'll hate me. Anyway... It'll be time for dinner soon, won't it?'

The musician wasn't wearing his watch and had consumed too many beers for his body-clock to be anywhere near accurate. 'I don't know what time it is, mate. But if you're hungry, chances are dinner'll be up soon.'

'Can I trade something instead?' the boy asked.

Kierney and Hilary had arrived at the sideline pep talk. Jeff winked at his co-conspirator, who looked as if she were about to float away on a white, fluffy cloud of elation.

'Maybe... What would you like to trade, captain?'

Jet took a deep breath, puffing his chest out on hearing his new rank. 'After dinner, when there's just Dawson and Mairi and us left, please may we play Twister? And I promise I'll spin the arrow for twice as long as the others.'

'Deal!' the father held his right hand out to his son, who seized it with authoritarian vigour. 'Good man. Now, please take Hilary into the middle and give her a chance to warm up. Kizzy, what'd you like to say to your brother?'

'Thanks, Jet,' the birthday girl was ready. 'And Twister would be really fun.'

Jeff nodded. '*Excelente*. That's settled then. On *ya*, mate. Do you mind if I watch you play for a while?'

'No, Dad,' Jet yelled, jogging towards his suspicious teammates with their extra player in tow. 'Guys, Hilary's going to play with us. She's on your side, Daws. Where do you want her to play?'

Having dispatched his daughter to resume her directorial duties with the remaining cast, the world-changer glanced over to the poolside table and gave Lynn a sly thumbs-up. He lay down on his stomach in the short, thick grass, stretching jet-lagged legs out behind him and propping his chin up on his hands, pondering how long their children would be so compliant.

If only the favour of warring adults were so easily curried by a game of Twister after dinner!

***

Later that same evening, while the caterers prepared for the select gathering of grown-up party guests, Lynn produced a box containing the Twister kit. Seven gleeful children bunched around, Jet and Kierney, their friends, Dawson and Mairi, and the three Dyson cousins, Sonny, Bruce and Jazz. With their mothers as adjudicators, each child took a turn at spinning the dial and shouting out the positions into which their playmates had to contort themselves.

The menfolk had retired outside to the verandah for an after-dinner, pre-party drink and a round of cigars. Raucous laughter rang through the ground floor, and Jeff gave thanks that his fabulous family had helped him dissolve the fog of disillusion yet again. Life couldn't be better for this nobody from Canley Vale: his mates around him, sitting dead-centre in a house he had designed as a home for the world's most beautiful woman and their pair of thriving human treasures.

While beer after beer slipped down his throat, the multi-millionnaire did his best to ridicule the ever-present gloomy feelings which hung over him like a damp, dilapidated ceiling. Why did his ungrateful mind refuse to accept his amazing good fortune? After all the work he had done with Sarah Friedman and the talented people at The Fellowship on beating the scourge of depression, his insecurities still found him out even on such a joyful day.

Gerry slapped his absent-minded client on the back. 'Excuse me, Einstein,' he scoffed. 'Are we boring you? Wake up and drink up.'

The dreamer shook his head. 'Sorry, mate. I'm knackered, but I'm warming up, I assure you. Too much fairy bread earlier obviously.'

Blowing a long plume of smoke from his cigar, the stalwart campaigner tried hard to banish disturbing mental images of African children as they rushed to form a veil across his eyes as soon as he let his guard down. Gravity and Miss Irony had directed their ire to politics of late, no longer able to chastise him with footage from his childhood.

Junior was seated across the table from his brother-in-law and the affable accountant, surrounded by a number of the Diamonds' Mount Eliza neighbours, all claiming to be awestruck Australian Rules Football fans. He asked when Jeff's new album was to be released, receiving a bemused shrug in return.

'Not for a while actually. I haven't written much for ages. Not for me to record, I mean. I hardly ever get time to craft anything beyond its bare bones, so I've taken to sending people fractured, half-baked ideas and letting them make something of them.'

'Still lucrative though,' Gerry added, tapping numbers into an imaginary calculator.

'Jesus! Shut up, Blake-san,' the songwriter groaned, slamming inebriated fingers down on the back of his manager's hand. 'Let's go inside and join the others. Everyone else'll be arriving soon, and I need to rehearse my fucking speech.'

The hardened drinkers jeered as one, complaining about having to sit through a batch of cheesy family reminiscences. Their host chuckled, knowing full well that the format of the evening did not contain any such arduous segments. Stubbing out their cigars and picking up their empty glasses, the group adjourned into the house to reconnect with their kith and kin.

Stopping on the way back from the toilet to take a sneak peek inside the decorated function room, Jeff stood and gazed up at the banner which Lynn had requested be strung above the stage. "Together, Forever, Wherever" was the three-word catchphrase the couple had adopted for their tenth wedding anniversary, along with a plethora of fundraising events for their charities.

Tonight, the globetrotting superstar appreciated the sentiment more than ever before. 'You're an ungrateful arsehole, Jeff Diamond,' he muttered to himself, before waving to the catering staff and giving them an appreciative round of applause. 'The room looks amazing, guys. Thanks heaps. What time are we starting?'

The downhearted frontman had an hour of relative leisure up his sleeve. He needed to disperse the blues in the next sixty minutes and exchange his clown face for one pasted with genuine gladness for being the centre of attention at a party dedicated to celebrating a decade of married bliss. So where was his dream girl, for that matter? It was high time he challenged his Olympian bedfellow to a game of Twister!

Back in the lounge room however, Gerry and Pia had beaten him to the board, cheered on by a ringside row of children. Quite an X-rated sparring match had begun, causing the mothers to distract their young ones. Junior and Don were preparing to go three rounds next, impatient to enter the lion's den with its spots of primary colours.

'*Papá*, you missed us playing Twister,' Kierney gasped, running into her father's legs. 'It was so much fun.'

'Sorry, gorgeous,' her father replied. 'I'm sure it was huge fun, and I'm glad you've had such a good birthday party. You too, Jetto. Thanks for doing so well with the footy. You're a true captain. Are you guys going to bed?'

Lynn nodded, stealing a quick kiss from her knight in dulled armour as she passed by. 'Come up in ten minutes,' she invited, receiving a heart-jolting wink for her trouble. 'You know what I mean...'

Jeff gave his precious progeny a hug before they loped and jostled up the stairs to get ready for bed. Behind the noisy bunch, his wife, his sister-in-law and the nannies took bets on the likelihood of settling them down in a hurry, well aware that dreaming about their fun-filled day would be the last thing on their minds.

Having wished each child goodnight one-by-one, the man of the house strolled outside to take a seat next to Sue Jenner. 'Is the party over?' he asked with a heavy sigh.

'You need another drink,' the architect laughed. 'It's not like you to wimp out.'

Clasping his hands together as a sign of good intent, the host rose to his feet again and checked who else needed their drinks replenished. He downed a pint of cold water while filling the order and paused in the doorway on his way back from the kitchen, inhaling several deep breaths in an attempt to kickstart a more positive outlook.

Jeff savoured the malt whisky's smooth finish as it coated the inside of his mouth, chuckling at his brother-in-law and a city neighbour tangling their legs and arms on the smattering of coloured circles on the floor. Thank Christ his sister hadn't come down from Sydney for this event!

Again normal clashed with abnormal in the philosopher's mind. He assumed the employment lawyer with his left hand on yellow had never before imagined this brush with stardom, courtesy of his daughter's friendship, would include spending time staring at Junior Dyson's spread buttocks while they swayed and wobbled on a slippery plastic sheet.

The fading light gave the scene a surreal, glowing backdrop, and the distant sound of waves pounding the beach helped the musician to relax somewhat. He checked his watch and confirmed with a *frisson* of anticipation that the time had come to steal the mother of his children from her bedtime stories and into his arms for the rest of the evening.

The superstar slid his empty crystal tumbler onto the table and left the guests to their shenanigans. On nights like these, he congratulated his own forethought in soundproofing the children's bedrooms, since barely a trace of merriment was audible from down below. The three droopy girls were crowded into the bathroom, each smoothing down a mass of tangled long hair with one hand while cleaning her teeth with the other. He smiled to himself, the sight of their oversized nightdresses recalling a throwaway remark by his better half, suggesting they buy clothing options on the futures market to hedge the regular growth spurts.

The boys' room was a whole different matter, resembling a warzone littered with trip hazards rather than landmines. The level of tiredness rivalled that of the girls next-door, judging by the ill-tempered struggle to reach the washbasin taps, yet their natural competitiveness would never allow a similar display of drowsiness.

Leaving Julie to focus on her sons, Jeff distracted the others by asking for more funny stories about their Twister game, soon eliciting fits of giggles at the amusing sights they had witnessed downstairs. 'You guys are way too grown up,' he frowned at his son and his sleepover roommates. 'Leave it behind for the night, boys. Get some sleep and you can play again in the morning. Except very quietly, because we're all planning on a late start.'

Everyone knew the promise dealt by the *trio* of nodding heads would be impossible to keep. It was as if the oxygen was being sucked out of the room as the devils held their breaths, eager for their parents to turn out the light and leave them to their mischief.

As expected, the Dyson cousins dissolved into more laughter in the short time it took for the door to swing shut. Lynn burst in and switched the light on again, catching two guilty brothers climbing out of their beds. Suitably reprimanded, the fearsome foursome fell silent once more, managing to hold in their excitement until the three adults reached the top of the stairs.

'Shut it, guys!' came the deepest, most sonorous voice Jeff could summon while doing his best not to laugh. 'Go to sleep. *Silencio.*'

Neither mum was any the wiser as to whether the reluctant general's order did the trick. Parting company with Julie, who was eager for a glass of champagne, the Diamonds made their getaway, vanishing into the master bedroom. An endorphin rush orchestrated by his guardian angel was a sure-fire tonic to turn the heavy-hearted campaigner into Lord of the Manor for the duration of their party.

Hand in hand and skin still tingling from their rapid interlude, Lynn and Jeff smuggled themselves into the function room to check everything was ready for proceedings to kick off. The disc jockey had primed the sound system by running a medley of disco' hits at a low volume, entertaining the caterers while they made the last few finishing touches to the table decorations.

'Time for one game of Twister?' the larrikin dared, escorting the beauty across the wide hallway and into the lounge room to join an inflated number of grown-up friends and family members.

As if they were about to dance the Anniversary Waltz, husband courted wife with flamboyant grace towards the glossy square of plastic. Throwing inhibition to the wind, the stars of stage and screen went head-to-head over the coloured dots.

Relishing a chance for dominance, Gerry commandeered the spinner and took it upon himself to amend the rules in the most outlandish way. The contestants stretched their flexible, well-trained limbs to their limits for maximum entanglement, determined for their mouths to connect regardless of how precarious their balance became.

Jeff groaned, having been challenged with yet another near impossible manœuvre. 'Come off it, Blake-san! It's bloody hopeless trying to play seriously with this woman,' he sniggered, close to landing ninety-two kilograms of lean skeleton on the athlete's sturdy frame. 'She just can't concentrate. Her mind wanders way too much.'

'Oh, it does, does it?' Lynn refuted, making sure her right arm on red rubbed tantalisingly along the upper reaches of her opponent's left leg on green. 'We wouldn't want our minds wandering, would we?'

'No, dear,' the man gasped, breathless not only for effect.

'OK! Listen up! Jeff, right hand on left breast,' the executive commanded, paying no attention whatsoever to where the spinning arrow pointed.

'Mine or hers?' his client checked, adjusting position to free his hand, ready to pander to an audience doubled up in hysterics.

'Lynn's, of course,' Gerry jibed. 'Unless you'd like to feel yourself up in front of your friends.'

The performer smiled. 'Not particularly. My pleasure, angel. D'you mind?'

'Do I have a choice? Go right ahead,' the tennis champion chuckled as her husband's wrist twisted to fondle her curves through a translucent silk top.

The Irishman coughed, losing his place along with the rest of the room's male contingent. 'Your turn, Lynn. Right arm on green.'

'What? Are you sure?'

'Absolutely,' the *compère* guffawed, with a deft flick of the arrow to tally the dial with his suggestion. 'See?'

'Hey!' Jeff exclaimed, receiving an elbow in the testicles as a slender forearm nudged his left leg outwards to allow her fingers to reach the slippery emerald circle beyond. 'Watch it, lady.'

'Sorry,' she giggled, grabbing for his shoulder as the pair rocked back and forth a couple of times. 'Next? Gerry, hurry up!'

'Ahem,' the accountant fumbled, far too interested in the visual spectacle. 'Yes, ma'am. Of course. Where were we? Jeff! Middle leg on blue.'

The cheering crowd dissolved into more peals of hearty mirth. A substantial number of new guests had arrived during the gladiatorial championship, and the volume of chatter and sporadic applause intensified as suspense mounted. Who would be first to plunge to the floor?

Jeff looked up and caught the eye of his nineteen-year-old sister-in-law. 'Right,' he winked. 'Hey, Anna. I'd come over and say hello, but I doubt I'll ever be able to walk again at this rate.'

Lynn tried to crane her neck around to acknowledge her family's arrival, and the duelling pair rocked in a precarious lover's *limbo*.

'Jeff!' Sue cried out. 'You haven't completed your move.'

'That's what you think,' the handsome rock star teased, glancing down towards his crotch and thereby embarrassing their friend further. 'OK! Middle leg on blue. Might be a good idea actually. Get some nifty tripod thing going. That'll mean we can pause for a ciggie. Could you get that for me, honey?'

Tantalising their friends' imaginations, Australia's darling reached her free hand towards the zip of her husband's fly. Jeff let out a long moan, licked his lips in mock ecstasy.

Spotting a doubting expression on Marianna Dyson's face, Gerry span the wheel again. 'Lynn! Left tit on red.'

Sighing, the gracious woman prepared to shift her weight leftwards. 'When's the damned party starting?' she asked, looking up into a pair of shining, dark eyes.

'Steady up, mate,' Jeff warned his old friend. 'From here, it looks like the party's already started, angel.'

'Happy anniversary,' his wife whispered, accepting a kiss blown through the air. 'Is this what you had in mind?'

To another round of applause, her ardent lover leaned down and kissed the closest piece of bare flesh. 'Not quite, but it's pretty bloody good,' he hissed, lifting his gaze to find Gerry and the others. 'Look and learn, kiddies. Look and learn.'

A wild glaze formed cataracts in her husband's eyes; mania the compassionate woman hadn't seen for some years. She knew how hard he was fighting with his mind to enjoy this celebratory occasion, worried by traces of old troubles returning.

'Let's stop now. We need to move into the other room. They'll be ready to serve cocktails. It's been an absolute pleasure, Gerry.'

'Woohoo!' Sue chanted. 'We have a draw! How appropriate for an anniversary.'

The forever lovers flopped down onto the plastic sheet, their limbs still laced together. After a few seconds of heavy breathing to ensure a fitting climax, Lynn freed herself from underneath, stood up to straighten her clothing and threaded painted toes into her shoes.

'Hello, everyone,' she announced, raking her blonde locks away from her face. 'Welcome to the mad-house. We're so glad you could come.'

Mustering sufficient energy to spring to his feet behind his co-host, the rock star rested his hands on her shoulders and surveyed the scene. There would have been fifty or sixty people crammed into the entrance of their capacious living room, with many more milling about in the hallway. Waiters mingled, each laden with a tray of drinks and nibbles. The party had started without them, he realised with some shame, wandering around to greet the various groups of revellers.

Lynn lifted two glasses of a favourite *Tempranillo* from a salver, passing one to her husband. 'You OK?'

'Sure, yeah. All good,' the charmer nodded, kissing luscious painted lips. 'You are the best. Wonderful show, I reckon, but I'm sorry things got so out of hand.'

'It's fine. Just harmless fun. I'm just concerned you're trying too hard. You need to calm down a bit.'

Jeff frowned. '*Whaddya* mean? I'm perfectly calm,' he hissed through gritted teeth, clenching his free fist.

'Good,' Lynn shook her head. 'That's alright then. Let's move everyone through.'

The Diamonds went their separate ways to conduct a thorough sweep of the lounge, requesting their guests take their drinks and conversations into the function room. A cheesy mirror ball cast its spangles around the space, and upbeat music was drifting through the speakers. A bank of tables adorned with food lined the windowed wall, and three men in black waistcoats staffed the bar on the opposite side.

'Hey! We should have these guys here all the time,' the man of the house joked to their closest neighbour. 'What can I get you, Stew?'

After everyone had filled their plates and glasses and were either propping up the bar or seated at one of the circular tables on three sides of the dance floor, Lynn called for their attention. 'Thank you all for coming to share our "Ten Years On" party,' she opened. 'A few weeks late, but for good reason.'

'Yep. Thanks from me too, folks,' the front-end of the pantomime horse added, a broad grin plastered on his face. 'Now, can you believe it's ten years? Jesus, I can't! Ten years since I did this woman a favour...'

The sophisticated singer shot her husband a dubious stare, wondering how far he might stray from political-correctness tonight, for once behind closed doors and among friends. Despite her fear for his sanity, the heartfelt words he had uttered earlier in the day stirred her heart until the pressure of tears built up in her eyes.

'Now, I'm a nice guy,' the orator continued, 'and I couldn't bear to see Lynn Dyson stuck on the shelf; gathering dust, untouched and unsatisfied...'

His wife's eyebrows dipped to a steely frown, daring him to keep going. Jeff let out a smoky laugh, backing away briefly with his hands at chest height.

'And my guess is it'll be me who's untouched and unsatisfied if I keep this up much longer!' he confessed, scanning the rows of familiar, smiling faces. 'But I'd like to say a very public thank-you to this sensational woman and our gorgeous kids for the happiness they've brought me over the last decade. They're every reason I get up in the morning. And that's the truth, no matter how you might choose to interpret that statement, Gerry Blake...'

The guests clapped and cheered their good friends, who had indeed accomplished so much in the period between their wedding and the present day. It seemed to all except the celebrities themselves like the blink of an eye. A poster-sized photograph of the couple, taken on their honeymoon, had been framed and was now displayed on the grand piano, and Jeff inched his stunning wife stage-right until they stood alongside it.

'Do we look ten years older?' he asked the assembly in jest, standing tall and mirroring the pose, hugging his quarry against his side.

A spattering of responses, some supportive, some otherwise, drifted back towards the low platform, making the assembled throng laugh.

'Hmm...' Lynn mused, resuming her speech. 'Mixed reviews, mate. I suppose that's fair. Anyway... We didn't want to stand on ceremony tonight. Please just enjoy yourselves, and we'll do our best to get around to everyone for a chat and plenty of dancing. It's fantastic that so many of you were able to join us out here beyond the 'burbs, and I can't wait to find out what you're all up to.'

Formalities over, the expert dancer escorted his bride to the centre of the *parquet* flooring, giving the disc jockey a cue to start the next track. A swinging jazz accompaniment faded up, and the expectant crowd gaped at the famous showbusiness personalities.

'Don't panic,' Jeff's voice rang out over the music. 'We're not going to sing. I'd just like to echo what my stunning wife said, and to invite you all to share this track with us. These last ten years've been an even more amazing ride than we expected. A real rollercoaster, to tell you the truth. We've got the two most adorable children upstairs with their friends; hopefully sleeping, but I doubt it... I have the world's sexiest, most inwardly- and outwardly-beautiful woman right by my side, and some of our best friends here in front of us.'

The speech paused as the star's voice cracked with emotion, prompting a peck on the cheek from his partner-in-crime.

'I'd like to say thank-you to all of you for having faith in us,' he continued. 'To Bart and Marianna, for giving birth to this glorious creature; to Gerry, Cath and all the crews for making our life run as smoothly as it does, despite my every attempt to cause chaos; to Irina, Jackie and Tina, our trio of childminders; and to George and Greg, our transportation consultants... i.e. drivers... Yes, that's you, guys...'

Australia's richest man pointed to each nominee in turn, with his unswerving partner nodding her own appreciation and clapping along with everyone else. The volume of a slower, bluesy version of their nineteen-seventy-four hit, "Everlasting", slowly built up over the applause, and Jeff dipped his hip and swept his soul-mate off her feet for an anniversary waltz to remember.

'That's it,' he threw some final words over his shoulder before turning back to his partner and anointing her forehead with a mark of his love. 'Let's dance.'

Lynn followed her husband's confident lead, gliding across the floor on love's magic carpet, as she had on New Year's Day a decade earlier. She leaned in and stole a kiss from his lips, which he refused to give over for quite a number of seconds.

'Ten years, baby,' he hissed, breathing hard. 'Next stop twenty.'

The lithe dancer nodded, shaking her long hair behind her shoulders and letting the mirror ball cast her body in glittery light for her favourite man. 'Don't know about you, but I'm going for gold.'

'Fifty years,' Jeff repeated, closing his eyes and spinning themselves full circle. 'Whoa! Sounds way better than twenty. Count me in!'

***

Their workout served as a thorough warm-up for the Diamonds, who weren't given a single opportunity to rest their feet for over an hour after dinner. The disc jockey soon had everyone up and dancing, with partners swapping with each other regularly as the evening wore on. Oldies, new songs, favourites and lesser-known inserts were greeted with equal enthusiasm by all ages.

With the doors closed, the noise from the function room was but a faint hum when Lynn managed to sneak away to check on the children, whom she found dead to the world after their busy day in the fresh seaside air. Leaning against frame of her son's bedroom door, she drank in the sight of his curly blond head, a slight smile evident on his face. She wondered what the future might have in store for their close-knit family unit now this ten-year milestone had passed.

Her deep-thinking lover was right. Their first decade as a married couple had been one hell of a rollercoaster ride, and the start of their second foreshadowed more theatrics in the coming twelve months alone. Longer trips to Africa for Jeff, meetings after meetings in Europe and the United States for her; all part of the concerted effort to equalise the world's riches across populations and to eliminate the persecution of innocent victims. She doubted the world-changer who shared her bed would ever in his wild, teenaged dreams have guessed the extent to which these global issues might usurp their life singular, almost to the exclusion of their original goals.

The grateful woman took this break from merriment obligations to take stock of her situation, enjoying a rare snatch of solitude. She ought to do this more often, she realised. Her philosopher in residence called this "acknowledging the moment," and boy, what a moment it was! Casting her mind back to their wedding ceremony, and how starry-eyed she had been as a twenty-year-old, she pictured herself dressed in an ivory gown and speaking the ambitious vows which bride and groom had pronounced with the utmost sincerity. She promised a confession to tonight's diary entry that even in the frantic lead-up to the main event she had never paused to consider the shape and size their new life was set to assume.

Both superstars had been surprised by how much they enjoyed the role of parent, and their own relationship had strengthened as the months and years went by. Not a day passed for either lover in second thoughts about their marriage, except for the awful fortnight spent arguing across the miles over Jet's cricket training. This dreadful hiatus now seemed such a long time ago, and the rear-end of the Diamond pantomime horse had never felt more comfortable or content with her dedication at this very moment.

Breaking out of her daydream, Lynn became aware of someone standing behind her. Marianna had come upstairs to leave something in the guest bedroom and noticed her daughter looking lonely and pensive.

'Hi, Mum,' the younger woman turned and smiled. 'Sorry. I didn't know you were there. Are you OK?'

'Yes. I'm fine. Are you? Are you crying?'

'No. Well, not really. An opportunity for emotional reflection. Taking stock, as Jeff would say.'

'Oh, alright, dear. That's good,' her mother was relieved. 'I didn't like to think of you crying during your anniversary party. That's not a good sign.'

'I'm not,' Lynn chuckled, following the grandmother into Jet's room. 'It's a fantastic night, and Kizzy's birthday party went well this afternoon too. I'm really happy, Mum. Unbelievably so. Please don't worry.'

'So why are you standing here on your own?' Marianna persisted.

'Oh, no reason. I came up to check on these guys, and it was so peaceful watching Jet's chest rising and falling, wondering what he's dreaming about, *et cetera*. Counting my blessings, I suppose you'd say.'

Lynn closed the door on the sleeping boys, linked arms with her mother and walked the short distance along the landing to Kierney's room. Both women smiled at the three little angels crammed into the space, one carrying the dominant blonde Dyson genes, one brunette and unrelated and one dark-haired gipsy, the spitting image of her father.

Like the rascals next-door, the girls were in a deep slumber after such an exciting day. Mindful not to forget Mairi Jenner, the young mum brushed the hair off her daughter's face and lifted the sheet higher to cover her shoulders. She watched Marianna do the same for her other granddaughter without even the faintest murmur.

'Are you coming back to the party now?' Lynn whispered, trying to close the door without the latch clicking too loudly.

Mother and daughter headed towards the wide, sweeping staircase. At the far end of the hallway down below, the doors into the function room opened for a waiter to pass through with a fresh batch of drinks, allowing the thumping bass of disco' music to resonate and amplify across the marble tiles.

'How long's Jeff home for?' the former ballerina enquired, pausing on the last step. 'You've been left on your own about as much as I was when you lot were little.'

'I know,' the daughter responded, knowing her mother was fishing for a complaint about her husband's selfishness. 'He's here for almost a month this time, barring a few day-trips. It's going to be fantastic to have some time together while the kids are at school. We've got so much half-finished music to work on. I can't wait.'

'Does he really need to travel so often and for so long?'

'Unfortunately, yes. At least over the next few months. He gets sick of it. More than I do, in fact. It's harder on him than on me, Mum, because I've got Jet and Kierney around me, and I can come and go as I please. He's taken a long time to settle down after this last adventure. It's so tough on his mind, not being able to see things come to fruition more quickly. He often thinks about chucking it all in and staying at home, but neither of us'll make that choice until there's an alternative. It's no different to you and Dad in those early days of building the Sports Institute.'

'Oh, no. I don't agree, darling. What Jeff's doing is considerably more dangerous than your father's situation ever was,' Marianna contradicted, annoyance invading her normal, high-society intonation.

Lynn recoiled, knowing she had found the nub of her mother's issue. 'That's true,' she acquiesced. 'Sorry, Mum, but we're fine with it all. Gerry does a fantastic job of managing all the risks and security stuff. And I can't believe how well our life's turned out. That's exactly what I was thinking about when you found me. We love each other more than ever, and our marriage is a hundred times better than I ever expected. Jeff's the most wonderful husband, the kids are gorgeous, gorgeous, gorgeous.'

Still the stateswoman stayed rooted to the bottom stair.

'I love this house and our lifestyle,' her daughter carried on, concentration flitting towards the music. 'Of course we're worried. Jeff worries I'll get bored and run away 'cause he leaves me on my own too much. We both worry for his mental state, and I worry for his safety. Well, no. We both worry about safety, but we take plenty of advice and precautions. The security guys follow a strict protocol every time, otherwise we couldn't get insurance. But other than that, we're perfectly happy. Honestly!'

The pair of determined matriarchs returned to the party arm-in-arm, stopping to talk with Bart and Anna for a while. The younger wife knew her mother had the family's best interests at heart, also presuming her own reactions would be much the same in twenty or thirty years' time, once Jet and Kierney's intrepid lives were regularly generating security risk *memoranda*. Thank goodness her father was upbeat and full of news regarding the Seoul Olympics and the year's tennis season!

Itching to rejoin her husband and wondering how he was holding up amid all the attention, Lynn let the Dyson clan monopolise her for half an hour or so. She glanced around every now and again, trying to locate her very beautiful and very, very black stallion. He was nowhere obvious. She imagined him sitting in the courtyard in front of the house, glass of a reserve *Rioja* in hand, lost in private turmoil about what to do next for Africa, smoking a cigarette and burying his fingers in the soft ruff belonging to Merak, the floppy German Shepherd with the longest tongue in the world.

Her attention diverted for a few minutes by a fascinating piece of gossip imparted by her brother, the patient woman jumped for joy at a sudden pressure from firm, familiar fingers fondling her neck. On instinct, she raised her shoulder to her ear and squeezed Jeff's hand.

'Have any of you good people seen my wife?' the handsome stranger asked the blond sportsmen and -women. 'She's about so tall, sexy as all hell. You can't miss her.'

Lynn craned her neck round, staring up into loving eyes, their black rings commonplace, which drilled into her heart without so much as a flicker of facial animation.

'I haven't seen her for so long. I doubt if I'll even recognise her,' Jeff lamented, bending down and placing a kiss on the blonde head beneath his nose. 'What the heck! You'll do. You look sexy as hell also. I'll stay with you 'til she comes back, if that's OK?'

The clown dropped down onto the empty seat to his new friend's right, and she shuffled her chair closer to cuddle into his taut, welcoming frame, which felt somewhat bonier than usual. His left arm locked over her shoulder into its favourite position, and the lovers' legendary world righted itself again.

Two blue eyes asked their question of their brown counterparts while the table's animated discussion pressed on, the wiser pair giving her an answer that made her overflow with joy. The quartet of talkative eyes had honed their messages, with few words necessary after ten years sharing the same life singular. But then again, she smiled, words would always be a staple in their relationship.

'Mum was comparing you to Dad just now,' Lynn changed the subject when the conversation lulled.

'Ah, yeah? Suave, sophisticated...'

'Not exactly,' the older woman chuckled. 'I was reminding her of the times when Bart used to leave me alone with the children for weeks on end.'

The hard-working activist shook his head and fought a strong urge to push his chair back and absent himself from the table. 'I see,' he managed to remain courteous. 'It's tough on all of us, Marianna. I agree. I expect you found that too, sir?'

'For sure,' Bart affirmed. 'Going to bed in a lonely room night after night's not that glamorous. Waking up in a hotel's not all it's cracked up to be.'

Jeff nodded, thankful for Big D's support. 'Precisely. Yeah... Without question, I do heaps of interesting things and enjoy some amazing perks, but you're right, sir. It all comes down to a series of 'plane trips and stark, square boxes, peppered with a whole bunch of long, drawn-out conversations with people who often don't give a toss about what we're trying to do.'

'So why do you keep going?' Julie's high-pitched voice interjected, only to receive a glare from Junior.

'Because I believe in what we're doing,' the world-changer answered, as he had rattled off a thousand times to journalists and politicians in every corner of the globe.

'*We* believe in what we're doing,' Lynn insisted. 'It's the right thing to do. It's Jeff's odyssey, just like promoting Australian sport's yours, Dad.'

The singer felt her ribs being squeezed so firmly that she nearly overbalanced on her chair. A sideways glance confirmed how chuffed her mystery man was with this parallel. Indeed, he hadn't heard her describe his life's work as an odyssey before, yet the term was about as *à-propos* as a term could be.

Jeff Diamond hadn't chosen to advocate for the starving people of Africa. They had singled him out in the same inexplicable directive that had driven him to pick Lynn Dyson to help him navigate his charmed life. Why him? Why her? The soul-mates had often discussed whether they would ever find out if destiny had issued these altruistic aspirations, or if these concepts were nothing more than hare-brained schemes conjured up by an excess of mind-altering substances. Either way, the proud husband was more than prepared to live with the "odyssey" label, especially if his beautiful best friend was too.

'And you were happy to let Dad continue, weren't you, Mum? You didn't ask him to stop?'

'Not entirely happy,' Marianna hesitated, her child-rearing years well and truly behind her. 'But no, I would never have asked him to stop.'

'Well, then... It's exactly the same for me,' Lynn persisted. 'We're the ones who stand by our men while they do whatever it is they need to do.

That's just how it is. Exactly what I signed up for ten years ago, and I love the fact we're even more involved with things than we set out to be. That's fair, isn't it?'

'Abso-flaming-lutely! Fine by me,' Jeff exhaled through pursed lips, buoyed by his wife's verbal conviction in full view of her family. 'But what I don't like is you having to pick up the pieces when I get home, which is far less pretty. That's the part I'm not comfortable with. The rest we can adjust.'

The determined champion dismissed these concerns with a swat of her racquet-wielding wrist. 'We cope well with the stresses overall. More than cope... We're imperfectly perfect together. I'm married to a veritable heartthrob, the kids are inspirations and I'm doing fine with everything. It's no problem to re-calibrate every now and again.'

'Jeez! *Muchas gracias*, angel. Heartthrob, eh? That's a moniker and a half! We'll do much more than cope. We'll get stronger. This is only the ten-year mark. Just wait for the twentieth episode of this bloody soap opera.'

Lynn's chair twitched with her man's shifting weight. She responded to the subtle signal by standing and announcing a sudden imperative to mingle with their other guests. The Dysons and their claustrophobic discussion left behind, the boy from Canley Vale led his dream girl onto the floor as if they had been thrown back in time to their first dance as a married couple. He waved to the disc jockey, hoping he would select something suitable as the next track.

While the current song worked towards its final chorus and fade, the young woman's skin tingled as strong arms pulled her close, leaning her cheek against his chest. Her right hand rubbed the fabric of his shirt over the "JL" tattoo, and he kissed the top of her head. They moved from side to side in no apparent direction, regrouping after yet another telling moment in time.

'You don't seem the worse for wear for drink,' Lynn smiled, using one of Gerry's ostentatious expressions.

'Affirmative. Indeed I'm not, dear lady. I stopped drinking about an hour ago. Maybe longer.'

'Really? Why? Are you OK?'

Jeff laughed out loud, amused that the love of his life thought him incapable of combining sobriety and sound health. 'Yeah. And I want to stay that way, that's all,' he explained. 'I want to wake up early with you and the kids tomorrow morning, make breckie for whomever's still here and enjoy several good coffees with the most beautiful woman in the world, all without feeling like the shutters won't open.'

'Oh,' his wife sighed, appreciating the imagery. 'That's really nice. That works for me.'

'I love you, Lynn Dyson Diamond,' he whispered in her ear, as the familiar strains of "Every September" drifted from the speakers. 'I want to thank you for what you said over there.'

'Argh! You're welcome,' she replied, standing on tiptoe to kiss his lips. 'I took exception to Mum's tone too. I felt you seize up.'

Smirking, the dancer twisted his partner round in an easy circle under his left arm, pushing her away from his body and then inviting her back towards him with his inimitable Latin flair. 'I did,' he confessed. 'See? It might not have been so pleasant if I'd been drinking, so there's another benefit. Saved my mother-in-law's feelings... I guess that counts. I'm learning, angel. Slowly, but I'm learning.'

Lynn giggled. She knew the romantic rebel had a soft spot for the elegant stateswoman, seldom meaning half the terse words used to describe such invasive discussions.

'I've written a song I'd like to play you tonight, before we go to bed,' the musician revealed. 'If we've still got the inclination once everyone's departed.'

'Oh, yes? I'd love that. I haven't got anything to play you though.'

Jeff swallowed her implied apology with a deep kiss. 'So what? And besides, it's a dark-hearted song, as you might expect. I need to sing it to you because it's perfect for tonight.'

'A sad party song,' Lynn teased. 'Novel.'

'Sarcasm, eh? You ungrateful bitch,' came the songwriter's brusque retort, while he whipped the unsuspecting athlete round fast and almost letting her fall. 'I'll dump you in favour of my old wife, if you're not careful.'

Forgetting she was only the substitute, the blonde bombshell fluttered her eyelids. 'I'm sorry, sir. You know I can't wait to hear it.'

Again, the sex-god's mouth locked with hers, his tanks refuelling fast since their surreptitious tryst. The transfer of power made Lynn swoon, helpless to refuse even if she had wanted to. While they kissed, her thoughts turned back to the adamant conversation she had shared with her mother, upstairs outside the children's bedrooms.

No, she had no qualms about her chosen path through this life. Their marriage was more rewarding after ten years than it had been in the first, and that was saying something! Jeff had the ability to melt her heart in no time flat, whichever the circumstance or mood, and butterflies took flight in her stomach yet again as his tongue devoured hers.

The morning after the night before broke over Port Phillip Bay before five o'clock. Its soft, white light adopted the technique of a certain small person who slept next-door, by sidling into *Escondido*'s magnificent corner suite. The French windows had been left open all night, and a dewy chill roused the master of the house. He rolled over to find Lynn curled up in their sheet next to him, without the heart to disturb her.

Getting to his feet and pulling on a pair of shorts and last night's shirt, which lay crumpled on the floor at his bedside, Jeff stepped out onto the balcony and leaned over to monitor the sun's progress as it rose over his kingdom. The spectacular coastal view was accompanied by an even more remarkable private outlook, since he had awoken clear-headed, positive and excited to start the day. The decision to stop drinking early may well have contributed to this phenomenal turnaround, but receiving his dream girl's vehement support and her unrelenting encouragement for his quest had given him an invaluable leg-up out of the doldrums.

Frightened that too much introspection might reverse the transformation, the thirty-three-year-old meditated on Merak as he wandered around, sniffing each tree and bush on the perimeter of his property for traces of uneaten intruders or discarded party snacks. Janey, the *albina* Shepherd-cross the family had taken in as a rescue, sat on the *patio*, supervising from afar while her mate attended to his own life's work.

Did everything follow a pre-defined order? The multi-millionnaire had learned an important lesson last night: something which was clearly second-nature to patient, intelligent and instinctive women like Lynn. Perhaps conflicted, impulsive and bloody-minded men like him weren't privy to this secret, lest its enormity cause them to abandon their goals and settle for an easy life. Another fold of obfuscation had been peeled back, opening a whole host of new avenues for his overactive mind.

In his atypical early state of high energy, Jeff had two habitual choices for letting off steam: the first and his infinite preference was lost in peaceful slumber and deserved to stay this way, so he scribbled a quick note on a piece of paper and embraced the second option. He picked up one of their son's teddy bears, which had been planted face-down on top of the chest of drawers, and leaned it on his pillow against the headboard. He propped up the torn-off page in front of the soft toy, its message plain: "JIM" followed by a winking smiley face.

The frequent flyer pounded the last few weeks' negativity out of his legs, with the treadmill set to an impressive speed. It didn't take long for his muscles to free up, soon settling into a comfortable rhythm. Even though his eyes stared out of the window and along the south coast of mainland Australia, his mind had teleported back to his beloved Africa, where it had him talking to another batch of senior government operatives who insisted on turning a blind eye to the many acts of corruption or misappropriation which continued to beset their aid distribution efforts.

The peacemaker needed to find some other avenue of appeal to his delegates' familial sides, reminding them of the wisdom in their wives, mothers and daughters. All but the most evil of men wanted their children to grow up safe and happy, and the way to deliver on this ambition was by capitalising on the strength of their women.

Jeff planned a detour to Adama during his next trip to the diverse continent. Talks between the Ethiopian government and the leaders of the Tigrayan People's Liberation Front were fundamental to winning over the rank and file. He had crossed paths with Jemal Mehretu twice the previous year, when they had both been guest speakers at the Kwabe conference in Zambia, impressed with his resolve and apparent compassion for the African people as a whole. It was worth a telephone call tomorrow at least, to sound his new ideas out with his trusted advisers in Addis Ababa.

He was onto something with this novel angle, the star's mind whirred along with the belt under his feet. In the fast-moving latter half of the twentieth century, human beings had rushed headlong into a technological gold rush which promised growth and prosperity in ever more sophisticated lifestyles. If his company was responsible for most of this momentum, it must also take accountability for any adverse side-effects. Redefining sophistication as the antonym of simplicity would prove flawed as soon as one scratched the surface.

The runner tapped the speed button and reduced the pace to a steady ten kilometres per hour. He scolded himself for being so short-sighted. How had he missed this indisputable conclusion, especially considering his foundation's voluminous analysis into the human race's basic needs? People would never know true happiness unless progress gave them simplicity.

Guilty for intruding on something so inconspicuous, Jeff's thoughts turned to his guardian angel and the explanation she had provided to their daughter only two days ago concerning dress sense, make-up and jewellery. Lynn's motto had always been "less is more" when it came to her outward appearance, having taken a leaf out of her own mother's book.

You don't have to spend a million dollars to look a million dollars, the father recalled her prudence, *because you're already worth the same million dollars simply by being you.*

He had crept up on Lynn standing behind their little girl at the mirror, where they had been choosing an outfit for her birthday party. With anthropology in action in his own home, the intellectual had watched the pair trying out different hairstyles and posing for an imaginary camera, giggling as they pulled faces at their reflections. Kierney soon understood that every single combination of clothes and hairstyle was enhanced whenever she wore a smile and made direct eye contact with people. Could there possibly be a more convincing personification of peace than this?

The further he searched for clues, the more the humbled humanitarian appreciated the elegant but simple sophistication which surrounded him every day, and yet he had never consciously considered its power to upgrade and reboot his soul. He had spent such a large proportion of the last few years away from the mother-ship that he had more-or-less abdicated all household duties to his wife, which was no great loss to anyone. The nannies, drivers and gardeners were all familiar with their roles in the Diamonds' serial drama, as were the children; so much so that whenever the captain was back aboard, all he was required to do was relax and regenerate in preparation for the next scene in the epic play to which he would now always refer as his odyssey.

Jeff terminated the program on the treadmill and jumped off, while the belt continued its cool-down minus the resistance of his heavy strides. Crossing to the mirrored wall, he picked up a pair of twenty-kilogram dumbbells and began to lift them in slow, steady movements. His ribcage stood out from bare skin, and the muscles on his arms were noticeably weaker since Christmas. He followed the smooth rhythm of the weights, upwards at speed and downwards in strict stages. It would take him no time at all to rebuild his strength as long as he remained in this positive frame of mind.

As the jet-setter's workout continued, he heard the door to the gymnasium swing open behind him. Experience predicted the new arrival as Bart or Junior, but he hoped for Lynn in their place. He was ecstatic to have his wish come true, seeing the slender figure of his dream girl approaching, wearing tight exercise clothing and with her hair tied up in a messy ponytail.

Losing count of how many repetitions he had completed, the red-blooded male pretended not to be distracted. '*Buenos días*, gorgeous,' he grinned at the mirror. 'Sleep well?'

With the reticulated sprinklers spattering against thirsty leaves as a backdrop, quenching the parched garden, the sportswoman's hands gripped her husband's waist, and her lips pressed into his sweat-drenched back, triggering spasms through both shoulder blades. All probability of remaining focussed and impassive flew out the window as his blood pressure spiked.

As excited as he had been at nineteen years of age, when their relationship was brand new, Jeff's *libido* crashed through red-alert. He collapsed against her forthright touch, seeing no point in struggling to disguise his desire.

'Yes, thanks,' the nymph-like temptress answered, 'Jim.'

Her husband laughed, having forgotten about the teddy's private message, so busy had his mind been in the last forty-five minutes.

'You're up so early,' the Olympian said, running her fingernails up and down his sides while offering no defence against his wandering hands, 'and you look amazing.'

'I feel amazing,' the re-energised man agreed, resting the weights on the bench and spinning round, an erection prominent in his shorts. 'Your fault, angel.'

They kissed, and Jeff tried not to lather his sexy training partner with stale sweat. She broke away after a few seconds and sauntered over to the running machine just as her brother pushed the door open. With a wave, Bart Dyson Junior selected an exercise bike and started his warm-up, sitting tall in the saddle to stretch his back and twisting from side to side.

'Good morning,' the massive sportsman shouted. 'You guys are up early. How are your heads?'

'Fine, thanks,' Lynn shouted in response, without turning around from her own travail. 'Yours? Is Julie still asleep?'

'Yeah. *Sparko.*'

Pleasantries over, brother and sister set about their usual *régime*, as they had done for years and years. Disappointed their *liaison* had been curtailed, Jeff leaned on the console of his wife's running machine and gazed into her radiant face. He longed for an hour alone with her to explain the plan he had cultivated during his solitary run, temporarily pushed to one side to simmer away in the back of his mind. For now however, he needed to content himself with playing host to their overnight guests.

'You're extremely edible,' Lynn told him, the thrum of the treadmill's belt acting as a damper pedal on her confidences. 'Your hair's gone really wavy, and you're all pumped and slick. You look happier than I've seen for a while; especially compared to yesterday afternoon. It's like a layer of your face has been peeled off, and it's exposed something brand spanking.'

The adoring puppy blew hot air through pursed lips, darting sideways to avoid a demonstrative slap. 'Give it a rest, lady. Very perceptive though. That's about how it is. What you said last night, about supporting me through my odyssey... It acted like a drug, *Regala*. I woke up feeling so effing fresh and revitalised this morning, so thank you.'

Smiling, the singer held her hand out towards her grateful husband. She knew how dangerously close to the schism he had been sailing in the last few days and was overjoyed to see his debilitating depression decamp. Although she meant every word she had said to her family, she still held serious reservations about the toll their tireless peacemaking efforts took on her parasitic frontman.

'I'm so glad. I love you so much.'

Jeff shook his head. 'Christ Almighty, I love you so much too, but I'm going to have to get out of here soon 'cause if I look at this...' the middle finger of his left hand ran down one side of the athlete's skin-tight top, skipping from flesh to Lycra and back to flesh again, '...for much longer, it's going to get very embarrassing very fast. So I'm *gawn outta here.*'

His wife chuckled at the forced Texan drawl, her eyes drifting downwards to the front of his soaking shorts. Sure enough, her insides flipped at the welcome rise under loose fabric. Gipsy eyes again warned her off, flashing from the space between them to Junior over his shoulder. She gave him a playful shrug and focussed back on the machine's controls.

'Not fair,' he moaned, grabbing a towel from a pile against the adjacent wall and looping it over one arm so it hung low enough to hide his arousal. 'Not fair at all.'

Alone again, the inspired visionary crossed the wide hallway and bounded up the stairs two at a time. Not a single sound issued forth from the children's rooms, so he disappeared into the master suite to shower and dress. Within five minutes, he had descended to ground level again and put on two pots of coffee, amazed to discover it was not yet seven o'clock. Taking a pair of large glasses of water outside to the deck, the changed man stood and inhaled several lungfuls of the newborn summer day.

The rest of the Dyson adults were soon up and about, tailgated by Don and Sue. Their host was certain no-one would see hide or hair of Gerry for hours! Keen to boost his mood yet higher with some childlike dynamism, he made seven mugs of Milo and carried them upstairs on a tray. Bruce was the first to stir when his favourite uncle entered the boys' room. Junior and Julie's second son cried out in excitement at the offer of a steaming, chocolaty drink, sounding out Jet and Sonny. Only Dawson slept on, programmed differently to the sporting strain.

Next-door, Kierney was sitting up in bed reading, unconcerned with waking her roommates. '*Papá!*' she whooped, seeing her father open the door with his foot.

Jeff smiled and winked at the studious girl, who was nearly as beautiful as her mother and twice as cute. Placing the tray with the remaining three mugs onto the desk, he perched on the end of her bed, leaned forwards and exchanged morning kisses.

'*¿Estás OK, pequeñita?*' he asked. '*T'as bien dormi?*'

She stifled a giggle. '*Sí, oui. Y toi?*'

The polyglot transferred a mug into his gorgeous daughter's hands and nodded. '*Sí, oui!* Hey, Jazz, Mairi… Time to get up.'

Four-year-old Jarradie Dyson sat up with a start, forgetting where she was. In a heartbeat, Jeff swapped to sit on the floor beside the girl's pillow and rested a gentle hand on her shoulder to stem her panic.

'Morning, gorgeous. We're in Kizzy's room. D'you remember? You slept through our whole party.'

A smile formed on the youngest child's lips, and she reached out to hug her uncle Jeff. He accepted her affection with a glad heart, realising that his own kids no longer needed such reassurance. On his other side, Mairi Jenner opened her eyes and let out a happy yelp, declaring his mission accomplished.

'It's a warm, sunny morning, *chicas*,' he announced. 'Why don't you get into your bathers? We could have a swim before breckie. The lads are getting up too.'

All three girls nodded, springing out of bed and delving into their respective bags to search for their swimming togs. Their naughty playmate stood up to steal Mairi's mug of Milo to a chorus of wild objections, then turned to pick up a few small items of clothing off the floor. He tossed them to each screaming pawn at random, causing great hilarity.

'Drink up, get your kit on and come downstairs when you're done, please,' the songwriter instructed. 'Your bathers are downstairs already after yesterday, so no point looking for them up here. Your dad's in the gym', Jazzy, but Mai's mum and dad are being *lazyboneses*.'

The littlest Jenner broke ranks, deciding to go after the rest of her sleepy family. His nefarious plan executed, Jeff waved a cursory *hasta la vista* to the two remaining girls and left them to their own devices.

Not long afterwards, the ear-splitting cacophony emanating from the swimming pool was sufficiently raucous to wake every neighbour within a five-kilometre radius of Mount Eliza. Lynn joined the happy bunch after her training session, jumping straight into the water while still wearing her workout gear, much to the children's amusement.

With only the indomitable accountant and his latest leggy conquest left upstairs, the rock star volunteered to supervise the youngsters' drying off. He kept them warm by looping round in circles through the gardens on an unscripted treasure hunt, giving his wife and mother-in-law time to help the nannies cook up a hearty breakfast.

'You are fantastic,' Jeff whispered in the tennis champion's ear, leaning in to steal a kiss while everyone took their seats at the poolside table. 'Can't wait to get you on your own.'

The golden-haired beauty tutted like Marianna, loud enough to make the rest of her family turn around. Most out of character, her husband didn't mind the romantic moment being spoiled. This auspicious morning was brightening by the minute, anticipation in his loins rivalled only by a foreign optimism in his head. A plan was crystallising at speed between and behind the superficial breakfast conversations.

***

By the second week in February nineteen-eighty-six, Jeff Diamond's show was back on the road, both physically and emotionally. After a quick stop in London to promote another major international event to mobilise large-scale fundraising, the couple's paths forked. Lynn flew to Los Angeles to make music, while her husband boarded a flight to Addis Ababa to make peace.

The Tigrayan People's Liberation Front had rejected the superstar's initial invitation to hold local talks in their stronghold areas, but continued pressure persuaded the political party leaders to meet a low-profile delegation in the township of Sebeta. The charity figurehead met his assigned driver in a deserted warehouse district, the deal requiring the lone pair to leave the camera crew and security staff back at base. A few kilometres into their journey, as arranged, a second vehicle pulled up alongside them.

His heart in his mouth, Jeff twisted the black jet-stone ring with the pattern of four diamonds off his finger and thrust it deep into his jeans pocket. He repeated the process with his wedding ring, furious with himself for agreeing to this measure. His was a plain, gold band like thousands of others worn by married men all over the world; far less likely to identify him than the prominent symbol he wore on his right hand.

The passenger climbed into the back of the van and tugged some sacks and blankets over his head, hiding both from government-backed militia and from any rogue elements of the TPLF who had been kept in the dark about his presence in the district as premeditated subterfuge. Significant scepticism remained over the celebrity's motivations, despite his express wish not to endanger the delicate process in play to free Ethiopia from the Derg once and for all.

The sun-scorched dirt road had the van's worn tyres skimming and slithering across its camber to avoid the many potholes. Jeff lost count of the number of times his head crashed into bare metal and then back down onto the thin vinyl floor covering. He drew a breath of hysterical laughter when the vehicle hit yet another obstacle, his substantial mass suspended momentarily before dropping and sliding backwards in response to renewed acceleration.

Here he was, one of the world's richest men, being transported like livestock to the knacker's yard. The horrified face of Gerry Blake flashed into his mind's eye. If only his business manager could see him now... There was no finer illustration of the two friends' differing levels of commitment!

After what seemed like a few hours, the driver slammed on the brakes, and his human cargo heard the back door being yanked open. Recognising the voices, he pushed the covers off and sat up, blinking as his eyes adjusted to the light again.

'Welcome, Mister Diamond,' Mabuza smiled. 'You travel First Class, I see.'

'Nothing but the best,' Jeff nodded, swinging his legs out of the cramped confines. 'How're you going, Vusi?'

The two men embraced in full view of two strangers. The van had pulled up in what appeared to be an almost empty car park, less than thirty metres from the barbed wire fence which served as Sebeta's city wall. Beyond stretched the squalor of an overpopulated shantytown, with displaced refugee children milling around, some kicking a football and others kicking up only dust.

'We have approximately hundred people coming,' the party official explained as the group ambled towards a large, single-storey building with a tin roof. 'Mister Mehretu will not be coming, but he has sent a message of support. We have his sister here, and her family. They are well respected in Sebeta.'

'Good,' the negotiator replied, disappointed his main man had failed to show. 'Where is Mister Mehretu then?'

'I don't know,' the friendly operative lied, though poorly. 'He will meet you the day after tomorrow.'

Jeff saw little point in pressing the issue. Fishing the secreted rings from his pockets, he graced each with a quick kiss and screwed them back onto their rightful fingers. He wondered what innocent games Jet and Kierney might be engaged in while he walked to his unknown fate. Lynn and he had agreed before their latest separation that, whether this trip was a success or a failure, this should be his last year spent making commando forays into dangerous territory. Indeed, after the uncomfortable journey he had recently undertaken, the prospect of being grounded now held considerably more merit than when the subject had initially been raised in the opulence of Stonebridge Music's offices.

Inside the large community hall, the visitor was handed a glass full of a cloudy, yellow drink ladled out of a primitive punchbowl. Knowing that sniffing it prior to tasting the first sip would offend his guests, he pegged it as some sort of fermented fruit concoction, most likely containing a near-lethal quantity of impure alcohol. No matter. He had been known to ingest one or two *boissons inconnues* in his time... Taking a generous swig and swallowing it down, he let the sweet nectar slip into his dust-filled lungs.

'You like it?' a young woman asked.

'Yeah. Thanks,' Jeff smiled. 'Very nice. What's in it?'

She laughed. 'Are you sure you want to know?'

The operative's accent and vocabulary indicated she was well-educated; in her mid- to late-twenties, the musician guessed. She must have been one of the organisers, judging by the fact that his minders hadn't tried to corral him away from her, as opposed to their apparent paranoia about other people filing into the hall behind him.

'Yeah. I do want to know,' the only white man in the room affirmed, extending his right hand. 'I'm Jeff. Are you involved with setting all this up?'

'Yes,' she replied. 'I'm Aminah. I'm Jemal Mehretu's cousin. Vusi and I work together here in Sebeta. I am a big fan of yours.'

The superstar gripped her small, bony hand and grinned. 'Cool! Thanks. Great to meet you, Aminah. Thanks for inviting me in here. I know you're putting yourself in danger, so I'm grateful.'

The young woman frowned, her eyes darting from side to side as they made polite conversation. She held her hand out again, this time for her guest's empty glass. He allowed her to refill it, vowing this to be his last dose.

'Thank you,' he replied. 'Where did you study? You have an American accent.'

'Oh, really?' Aminah sounded surprised, adopting a more kittenish tone. 'I don't know why. Too many movies perhaps! I studied in London. A few years after you, as a matter of fact. With John Francis.'

'Did you? Jesus! Small world, eh? Are there many women involved in the campaign?'

'Yes, a few. But not high-profile,' the activist answered. 'And neither am I, except for today. My husband doesn't like me being here, and I have my children's safety to think of.'

Jeff smiled, his thoughts flitting to Lynn at home with their little ones, a safe distance from this neighbourhood rife with knives, guns, kidnappings and petrol bombs. 'Yeah. I'd probably be the same. We're too protective sometimes, we men.'

Aminah's natural laugh cut off, her eyes betraying action over the rock star's right shoulder. He turned to see Vusi walking towards them, accompanied by three tall gentlemen dressed in western-style clothes. The rally was about to get underway.

'D'you know Pieter Engelbrecht?' Jeff leaned over and spoke into the woman's ear.

A brief nod of her head confirmed this piece of sly intelligence.

'Does he still come up here at all?' he continued, running out of time.

This time, the woman shook her head, the proposition apparently implausible. The handsome man winked his thanks before stepping forward to greet the *trio*, introduced to him as TPLF representatives from Adama. They each shook hands without smiling or uttering a word. Jeff was learning fast that it didn't pay to confer trust too readily in this environment, although he wasn't too sure he understood why.

'Ladies and gentlemen,' one of the visiting officials began to address the crowd in a *patois* with French as its base. 'Quiet, please.'

A ponderous silence descended from the ceiling of the packed hall, and all eyes looked past Phathu Babanjida, today's moderator, and concentrated on the obvious foreigner. For each question scalding his own conscience, the philanthropist assumed they had at least an equal number. Why had this Catholic Argentinean Polish Jew come to their township? What business of his was it to interfere in their politics? What could he possibly offer to stop the violence and repression perpetuated by their government? How on Earth might "The Australian Elvis", a songwriter who made millions from prancing around on stage, convince feuding tribal gangs to lay down their weapons?

Jeff's brief conversation with Aminah had reinforced his resolve to focus on the safety and security of families. As Phathu continued his introduction, a song he had written and performed with Lynn the previous summer drifted into his head, sent with perfect synchronicity by the internal force he had come to rely upon for inspiration.

Before handing him the floor, the TPLF leader explained to their audience that the pale-skinned guest was visiting Ethiopia to continue his humanitarian work. This news received a lukewarm reception. The gig was turning out to be even tougher than he had predicted.

'G'day, as they say where I come from... *Bonne journée!*' the charismatic international hero began, hoisting an arm in the air before accepting a microphone. 'Thanks a lot for coming out today, and thanks to the organisers: Vusi, Mister Babanjida and everyone. And to Aminah for the fire juice.'

A ripple of laughter looped round the room at the star's apt description of their local brew, further accentuated by a hand fanning his open mouth. The personal approach always worked best, he figured, his nerves starting to subside. He counted only two white faces other than his in the sea of dark skins, also noticing he was the only one dressed in black, surrounded by every shade of earth-coloured clothing.

'I know you're all wondering what the hell I'm doing here,' he chuckled, assertive eyes taking a quick survey of the front rows. 'And so am I.'

Again, muted chuckles slipped from a few nearby nodding heads, swallowed into the oppressive atmosphere in seconds.

'Firstly, I need to tell you that I'm not a supporter of the TPLF, but then neither am I a supporter of any other rival group or your government.'

Despite sensing the tension mount, the celebrity was not alarmed. In fact, as usual, he had hit his stride within minutes. He caught Phathu's eye, but as before, no emotional cues were forthcoming, and with people still drifting in through the rear doors, the audience shuffled their feet, anxious to hear more.

'But I do wholeheartedly believe in what you're fighting for,' their visitor raised his voice. 'I believe in freedom for everyone. Hey! I even gave my daughter the name Freedom.'

All heads turned to find the origin of several muffled wails of delight, tracing them to a group of young women who had squeezed in to rub shoulders with the well-known chart-topper at the last minute.

'Thanks, ladies!' the joker cocked his head towards the fuss before taking a deep breath. 'As you know, my beautiful wife and I've been involved with Africa for more than ten years. I love your continent and all of its peoples. Your countries can teach the so-called developed world many important lessons, yet there are also things going on here that I'm mighty glad aren't happening in Australia.'

A metaphorical electric fence buzzed around the front of the stage again. Men muttered to each other while the speaker carried on unfazed. He had endured physical pain in coming all this way, and he had the bruises to prove it. He wasn't about to waste the journey by diluting his message.

'There are some talks taking place in "AA" and beyond over the next few months which we'd like all you guys to support. We're seeking to bring an end to the Derg's dominance, but a non-violent end. Non-violent, I stress again. We want your political prisoners out of jail 'cause they don't belong there. But I assure you, killing and maiming other people isn't going to help any of us.'

Jeff's gaze found Aminah in the audience, now carrying a boy of a similar age and size to Kierney. The same anthem which had entertained him a short time earlier rang through his brain like a musical *aide memoire*.

'Have some of you heard our song, "Stronger Together"?' he asked the restless crowd, pausing to gauge a modicum of recognition amid the overwhelming level of suspicion. 'We released it last year for the holiday season, to celebrate the miracle of ten years married. It's a song about love conquering everything else, and this message applies to us all. None of us wants our kids to grow up in the middle of violence and bloodshed. No-one wants our daughters to get raped or attacked coming home from school; or to see our sons holding guns or getting caught in the crossfire. Do we?'

'No!' a chorus of female voices responded to his visceral appeal. 'No, no, no!'

'And no-one wants to lose a child, whether they're ten years old or thirty years old. None of us wants to leave our kids as orphans. Do we?'

Seeing a few cautious male heads shaking, the orator's attention was drawn to another cry from a woman at the back.

'*Merci bien!* What I'm here to do is to encourage all tribes, groups, political parties to get round the table and sort out a future where all African kids can achieve what they can and want to achieve. I want to ask you today to stay away from the riots, looting and burning and concentrate on building that peaceful, integrated future. A constant food supply, fresh water on tap, education for everyone. Then jobs, music, sport, whatever… That's what we should all be aiming for, isn't it? Not stealing, rape and arson in your neighbours' backyards just because they have the wrong religion or they live in the wrong village.'

A round of applause sprang from nowhere, growing in volume until most of the room had joined in. Jeff smiled a little and nodded, anxious not to take undue credit for this positive reaction. The rally's hosts remained stony-faced however, which stirred anger inside the world-changer. These people's current leaders were failing to set a good example, an omission he must address if this initiative was to enjoy any momentum after he climbed back into the rickety van.

'So give your leaders your support, please, ladies and gentlemen,' the Australian drew his speech to a close. 'They're working for your future. Tell 'em what you need. Tell 'em what'll make the difference for you, and then listen to how they'd like you to support them. What sort of Ethiopia do you want to spend the rest of your life in? If you don't work together to change your country, those who can will migrate overseas and progress here'll be even slower. That's reality, OK? Right or wrong, that's reality.'

Several hundred rapid heart rates amplified the applause this time. Jeff's face broke into a wide grin, prolonging the response with enthusiastic gestures. Dozens of pairs of hands were clapping above people's heads, and frantic wailing assaulted his eardrums. Enough was enough. Inciting blind fury would be counterproductive, particularly with the ample quantities of fire-water circulating.

To bring the meeting to an end, he took two or three steps backwards and raised a long arm towards the organisers. 'Thanks! That's a good sound,' he shouted. 'Thanks very much. It's up to you now. Thank you for your hospitality and for listening. Think about it, talk about it… You know what to do.'

'Sing about it!' yelled a teenager from a few rows back.

'Yep. You can do that too,' the superstar laughed. 'Works for me! You guys know Youssouf Elhadji? Support him. They're doing amazing things through music. The more people working for peace and prosperity for all Africans, the more likely we are to secure it.'

Jeff shifted sideways towards his hosts, who had seen fit to participate in the final round of applause. Passing Phathu on his way back to the microphone, the seasoned performer raised him a high-five. The awkward man's effort to reciprocate was tentative, gleaning a renewed bout of clapping and cheering nonetheless.

After a short pause to let the ovation die down, Vusi ushered the popular Australian out of a side door, where they were met by his driver. Aminah followed them out, eager to say goodbye to the friendly, handsome man who had mesmerised her. She hoped another opportunity might transpire, since her heartbeat had never raced with such passionate expectation before.

Pausing once again, the musician turned and gave his new fan a bear-hug, much to her delight. 'Thanks, Aminah,' he said, standing back to shake her hand. 'Keep those kids safe, and yourself. Hope we get to meet again, maybe with your cousin next time.'

'Oh, yes,' the young woman's breath had quickened. 'I'd like that very much. You're an excellent speaker. You got their attention today. I didn't think you would, but you did.'

'Cheers,' the peacemaker grinned, knowing her sentiments were at least in part fuelled by physical attraction, such was his unfathomable gift with the fairer sex.

How had Lynn described this trait in a recent interview? That his body exuded animal magnetism, he recalled with bemused gratitude. How he had inherited this invaluable trick was a complete mystery, yet it was proving to be one of his greatest assets on this particular quest. She had gone on to say that even when her husband was supposed to be waiting well away from the limelight, his aura insisted on making its presence felt.

'Let's see what happens now. Good luck,' the multi-millionnaire bade farewell to the spellbound young mother.

Know Thine Enemies

Jeff, his driver and Vusi darted behind the meeting place with its tin roof and mud-daubed walls, slipping through a gap in the fence and jogging down a street towards their waiting vehicle. Grateful to his helpers for their diligence in planning his *exodus* from a different spot, the celebrity forced a rueful smile when the van's rear door was opened for him to climb under the blankets once again.

'First Class on the way back too,' he joked. 'You guys are too generous.'

'Nothing but the best, Mister Diamond,' his representative repeated. 'See you in Adama. Stay safe.'

'Cheers. You too, mate.'

No sooner was the superstar's famous head obscured from view, than the engine turned over and sprang to life. From his cramped position and with a single, blinding shaft of light penetrating where the vehicle's dented door no longer fitted snugly in its frame, it felt as though the *incognito* mode of transport was leaving Sebeta at a much faster pace than when they had arrived. For a second time, he removed his rings and shoved them into his pocket. Who was he trying to kid? As if removing two pieces of jewellery made identifying him more difficult, especially after standing centre-stage in front of over a hundred men and women, not to mention having challenged some of their longest-held beliefs?

'Jesus Christ!' he yelped from beneath his camouflage, as the van veered over the road.

Hearing no apology from his driver, the star brushed two fingers across his forehead, where it had slammed against the edge of a box travelling with him in this salubrious accommodation. Licking his finger, he tasted blood and groaned in a mixture of amusement and frustration. No matter… He would return home boasting a new scar and a damned good story to share with his son. Assuming he were lucky enough to return home…

The attentive passenger detected a change of road surface and the whipping sound of resistant air around roadside telegraph poles, guessing the fast-moving vehicle had reached the outskirts of the city. He sat up in the confined space and banged on the metal partition separating the cabin from the rear cargo area.

When the driver's ear appeared at the small window, Jeff asked to be dropped off at the airport. He had decided to catch the next flight to Cape Town, an off-the-cuff alteration to his schedule after the conversation with Aminah. Setting his mental course for Stellenboch University, he intended to seek an audience with an old friend who had since become a senior academic.

The timing worked in his favour, and within an hour, the traveller found himself in a hospitable Economy row with an empty seat beside him. Relieved to be able to stretch his legs, the engines' droning soon hypnotised him into a welcome slumber. Before he knew it, the aeroplane was in a steep descent towards the large city on South Africa's west coast, some three-and-a-half hours later.

A dead-ringer for Indiana Jones but adopting James Bond tactics, the dishevelled man jumped into a taxi and began the fifty-kilometre ride through the suburbs and into the wine-growing region of the Western Cape. With a mountain range in the hinterland, the genteel suburb was green and lush, the well-travelled star finding a certain similarity to northern California and no similarity whatsoever to dusty Sebeta.

Ducking into a gents' toilet in the university's administration building, Jeff examined the cut he had sustained on his forehead. The blood had dried over a gash about three centimetres long, fortunately covered by his fringe. Fighting to suppress a flashback of his deceased father from coalescing in the mirror, he splashed water on his face and dabbed the wound dry with towels composed more of sand than paper. His clothes were sweat-stained and crumpled, and he was in dire need of a shower. Time was of the essence however. He was due to leave for the Sudan the following day, not wanting to miss this opportunity to enlist the help of someone he held in high esteem.

At first, the lady behind the reception desk refused to assist with locating Professor Engelbrecht. She relented after one of her colleagues almost fainted on setting eyes on the tall, dark-haired visitor who had arrived without an appointment, failing to make the connection between Jeff Diamond and this unshaven reprobate who had walked in minutes before home-time. After signing autographs for both women and posing for a photograph or two, he was given directions to the Faculty of Humanities, where the professor's office could be found on the ground floor.

Jeff pressed an ear to the door and knocked. A man was speaking in Afrikaans, either on the telephone or conversing with another person inside. He had no idea where Engelbrecht's sympathies lay these days with regard to the escalating campaign of violence waged by the Ethiopian government.

Tread carefully, he reminded himself, once more thrown back to the image of the innocent young boy on Aminah's hip.

'Come in.'

The songwriter twisted the doorknob. The professor's room was larger than he had expected, with a low ceiling and a bank of bookshelves behind a substantial mahogany desk. It was difficult to imagine a place more true to his ideal of an academic's bolt-hole! On a table to one side was a kettle and several mugs and spoons, with a layer of sugar granules scattered around them and a carton of milk sitting open to the stuffy air. Screwed-up pieces of paper were scattered all over the carpet, and a case of red wine beckoned to the exhausted alcoholic.

'Professor, it's Jeff Diamond,' the unheralded caller announced. 'Sorry to intrude.'

'Oh, my God!' the rotund and balding man stood up from his desk. 'Jeff Diamond! I haven't spoken to you in five years. Come in, come in! What brings you to Cape Town?'

As they scanned the room, Jeff's eyes met those of a pretty female student. White, of course, and most likely of Dutch or Boer origin, she had shining blonde hair, and her attire suggested parents with plenty of money. The young woman gasped in astonishment at encountering a global megastar during her weekly tutorial.

'Shall I come back later?' the new arrival asked, transferring his gaze from the wide-eyed student to her mentor. 'I don't want to interrupt.'

'No, no. We were about finished anyway,' Engelbrecht said. 'Would you mind leaving us, Odette? Please drop by tomorrow if there's anything we didn't cover. Thank you, and pass on my regards to your father.'

'That's fine, Professor,' she replied, staring up into her idol's face. 'I can't believe you have Jeff Diamond in your office. I'm a huge fan, Mister Diamond.'

'Thanks, Odette. And I'm a huge fan of your prof'. Sorry to cut your meeting short.'

Smiling at the student's clumsy rush to collect her belongings and disappear, the ladies' man wondered how close these two were. A friend of the family? He oughtn't to leap to conclusions, but she was young, pretty and keen to learn, and the Pieter Engelbrecht he remembered from London had always been ready to teach.

Odette exited the room with no more than a smile, with her tutor shutting the door after her.

'Let me offer you a drink!' shouted the man whose old-fashioned clothing was unkempt and ill-fitting, striding back behind his desk, sitting down and opening a drawer to his left-hand side. 'I have some malt whisky in here that I always bring out for visiting Australians.'

'Ah, yeah?' Jeff smiled. 'In that case, how can I refuse? And Jesus, after the day I've had, it'd go down a bloody treat. How are you, Piet? Still providing a well-rounded education, I see.'

Frowning in mild contempt, the professor looked up from pouring two glasses. 'Ice?'

'Yeah. Thanks,' the intellectual chuckled, raising a hand in apology and heading for the refrigerator to refill the ice bucket. 'How's life? Enjoying it here?'

'Yes, Jeff. Indeed I am,' Pieter replied. 'And you guessed well, by the way. I have to be extremely careful. Her father's a prominent judge on the circuit. Very influential, if you understand my drift.'

'Sure do,' his former partner-in-crime grinned at the display of *macho* pride. 'Cheers! *Prost!* Whatever's appropriate here.'

'Down *ze* hatch,' the lecturer chortled, accentuating the European accent he had almost grown out of during his globetrotting career. 'I have an easy life here. Easier than yours, I'd wager. And how goes the lovely Lynn?'

'Lovely as ever. In the extreme, in fact, thanks. Never better. And Mathilde? How old's your daughter now? Fourteen?'

'Fifteen in November. Catherine's doing well. She's the spitting image of her mother. And Mathilde's well. We're happy enough. She's very active in the university social scene, so again, I have to be careful.'

Jeff shook his head, filled with the tiniest pang of jealousy merely for old times' sake. 'I expect you are, my friend. Good times in old Londinium town. D'you remember those four days we spent in Paris too? Y'know, I went back to that dingy bar a couple of years ago. The same whacky prostitute was there... Mireille... completely spaced out on something. She still knows all the answers.'

'Christ!' Pieter burst out laughing. '*Mireille la foue!* I haven't had that vision in my head for an awfully long time. Mireille must be in her seventies by now.'

'Yep. She looks it too,' the nostalgic musician agreed. 'She's had a hard life, taking money off all those poor young, wannabe *separatistas* hooked on fucking byzantine rubbish. Nothing's changed along *la rue Saint Jacques*, I'm pleased to report. Have you been back recently?'

'To Paris? No,' the well-heeled South African replied. 'To be honest, I'm content to stay put. Only another five years, and I can retire and write books at my leisure. I'm looking forward to it.'

'Sure. Good on *ya*.'

It was the Sydneysider's turn to mock his own base culture. He was getting the distinct impression his old friend had lost the desire to change the world, which would render futile his impulsive detour. Never mind. It never hurt to ask.

'*Und so, Herr Doktor* Angle-grinder... Are you still connected to any of the peace movements?' he asked, crunching a block of ice.

'No. Not at all,' the professor replied. 'There's no such thing as a peace movement anymore. They're all run by militant thugs. It's not safe to be seen to sympathise too much.'

'But do you?' Jeff pressed.

'Sympathise?'

'Yeah.'

'Of course I do, but they're going about things the wrong way,' the lifelong scholar explained. 'There's no strategy. It's tit-for-tat. A bit like Northern Ireland.'

'Yeah? That's what I feared,' the peacemaker nodded. 'I guess you're right. But does it have to be this way?'

'Listen. Are you doing anything for dinner, my Antipodean mate?' Engelbrecht changed the subject.

The singleton-about-town hadn't devoted a single thought to nourishment. Now the idea crossed his mind however, he realised he was ravenous. The professor's hand settled on the telephone, presumably intending to contact his wife and invite this former student buddy for a home-cooked meal.

'Nope,' the younger man answered with enthusiasm. 'Hadn't planned anything.'

'Well, that's easy fixed. You'll be our guest, sir,' Pieter informed him, furious fat fingers dialling fast.

The call connected, and another conversation in Afrikaans ensued. Jeff understood the gist, including the muffled scream which reverberated through the receiver at the mention of his name. He was prepared to prostitute himself yet again for Missus and Miss Engelbrecht if it increased the probability of the professor helping him out.

The punctuated exchange came to an end, and the academic rose to his feet, as tall as the amiable celebrity but these days overweight and unfit. He had aged well overall, Jeff considered, for someone whose corporal conditioning had never been a priority. The Australian wasn't feeling too energetic either, after having spent the day being tumbled around in the back of a van like a load of soaking laundry.

Collecting a khaki raincoat from the stand in the corner of his office, Pieter urged his friend to finish his drink. 'I have much more at home, and better ones too,' he offered. 'The girls are very excited to see you. Catherine has all your records, and your posters on her bedroom wall. She never believed me before when I used to tell her we were friends in London.'

Strapped into Engelbrecht's ageing Mercedes station-wagon, Jeff recounted various highlights from the last eleven years of his spectacular life. He glossed over the showbusiness pomp and circumstance, using the excuse that such gossip column fodder was bound to be the main topic at the dinner table. He was keenest to relay the conflict resolution subject matter to his old sparring partner, who had somehow shed his former irrepressible passion for peace in the comfort of his complacent, prosperous lifestyle.

An imposing house in a leafy suburban *boulevard* matched the type of home the superstar had in mind, complete with yappy terrier and a stereotypical black housekeeper. A woman opened the front door and trotted out to meet them as soon as the old car pulled into the driveway of the Engelbrecht residence. He hardly recognised Mathilde, who had clearly become rather too involved in the university's social life, judging by her figure and rosy cheeks. Nevertheless, he kissed his host's wife and thanked her profusely for the last-minute invitation.

Their teenaged daughter sat awestruck, observing an obedient silence in the adults' company with a glass of lemonade in hand. She hung off the songwriter's every word while he brought concerts and recording experiences to life for her and her mother. Mathilde, conversely, was a veritable geyser of compliments and gushing pride, thankful her husband had taken charge of the *braai* and left his guest at the women's mercy.

'I can't believe it's ten years since I've seen you,' the Johannesburg native crooned. 'Catherine would've been just a toddler. You don't remember that far back, do you, dear?'

The girl shook her head.

'It's eleven years actually,' Jeff corrected her. 'Our kids are eight and seven already, so you're not the only one to have time fly by.'

'Eight and seven,' the plump lady repeated. 'How cute! I hope you've got some pictures?'

The rock star allowed himself an inward smile. A spontaneous invitation after an undercover operation in a foreign country, and he was expected to have a photograph album on hand? Reaching his wallet from the back pocket of his jeans, he pulled out two small and rather creased photographs: the first of the children taken on the beach almost a year ago; and the second of his beautiful best friend, whose welcoming *visage* made his heart flip, not to mention the all-too-predictable reaction from somewhere lower down.

'You remember her,' the Australian smiled, handing Mathilde the one of Lynn, soon followed by the other, 'and these two you don't know. That's Ryan and Kierney, or Jet and Kiz to their friends. It's out of date, but you get the idea.'

Catherine leaned over her mother's shoulder to catch a glimpse of the famous family, both swooning while the housekeeper set a table on the verandah. Jeff gave the native Zulu woman a sly smile, which was returned with apparent glee. He wondered what she might think of his grandiose scheme to marshal battling tribes *via* their womenfolk's common sense. Was she quite content being in the service of a well-to-do, left-wing academic's family, or would she rather have been a philosopher or a scientist herself? Engaging her in conversation would be seen as an insult to his hosts, so he chose not to pursue the gratuitous research.

'Oh, Lynn's so beautiful,' the shy teenager blurted out. 'She's my favourite female singer.'

'Mine too,' the proud guest replied. 'I'll ask her to send you something when I talk to her tonight. She'll remember you, I'm sure.'

The girl blushed, slipping back into her shell. Her mother fussed over the children's picture, cooing at how clever the Diamonds were to have produced two such different offspring. The focus on his family having elicited an attack of extreme loneliness, the traveller wallowed in the plump, homely woman's indulgence until dinner was served.

After their meal, Catherine bid her parents' alluring and altogether fascinating visitor a good night and disappeared to finish her homework. Pieter and Jeff left Mathilde to the television and some embroidery, taking their seats outdoors for the last half-hour of dusk. After they had polished off the second bottle of red wine, a selection of malt whiskies were brought out, and the pair began to work its way through these too.

The real reason for his unscheduled southbound diversion nagged at the celebrity's mellowing consciousness. He opened with care, needing to hit upon a compelling message straightaway in order to convince the worldly professor to sign up. He reminded them both of one or two earnest discussions they had shared with John Francis during their post-graduate studies: those concerning Nelson Mandela's ongoing fight with the government; and also how the tide had begun to turn on the ruling Caucasian parties in the southern half of the continent.

'That was a whole decade ago, mate. Can you believe it? We can't let things lurch and limp on like this for another ten years. Hundreds of thousands more people'll die while these bastards just get richer and richer.'

Pieter coughed, resting a heavy cut-crystal tumbler on his chest. 'I can't argue with that,' he admitted. 'But seriously, what do you think you'll be able to achieve? People are suspicious of outsiders telling them what to do. Fuck! I'm suspicious of you, and I like you! Why exactly are you in South Africa, Jeff?'

The intellectual took a deep breath and poured two more glasses of Glenlivet. As he had learned through his tough adolescence, there was no progress without trust. Still unsure as to whether his previously incorruptible friend's teaching income might be supplemented from other undisclosed sources, he prepared to share his master plan.

Raising his drink in a mute toast, he explained. 'I've rented someone's country seat in France,' he began. 'Miles from anywhere, acres of gardens, proper security... I'm inviting the various leaders to fly in for a few days, to sit down together and thrash out a deal to unseat the Derg.'

'Over *croissants* and *café au lait*?' the sarcastic historian let out a belly laugh. 'How very Jeff Diamond!'

'Yeah. And why not?' the multi-millionnaire saw the sarcasm and raised it, flicking the lip of his glass with a robust, guitar-player's fingernail to educe the clear ringing sound of quality lead crystal. 'Or fine wine and whisky.'

'A cheeky *Bordeaux*?' Engelbrecht harked back to the puerile student banter of their yesteryears. '*N'est-ce pas?*'

'*Absoluement, mon brave. Ça y'est!* Mehretu's in, by the way. Spoke to him three days ago. And I was hoping to meet him today, but he didn't rock up, so now I have to try again at the end of this week. I've found an awesome mediator; a Jewish American, funnily enough. No axe to grind! The TPLF wants to know who else is in before they'll throw their public weight around it, which is probably wise, given the power deals going on around arms supply.'

'Shit! You do know how dangerous this is?' Pieter whispered, his ruddy complexion paling audibly under the cover of darkness. 'Those guys don't always have control over their field ops. I believe they want peace, Jeff, don't get me wrong... But at what fucking price? They don't think twice about blowing another black brother to smithereens if they can't get their way.'

The negotiator leaned back on his chair and lit a cigarette; the first for several hours. Nicotine penetrated the nether reaches of his numbed brain in a matter of seconds, delivering him a dose of much-needed clarity. He lifted a section of his long fringe off his forehead to show the professor the spoils of his unpleasant journey earlier that day.

'D'you see this, Piet?' he asked, receiving a nod in return. 'That was my head hitting a metal box, probably a gun case, hidden in the back of a TPLF truck this morning. It may be hard for you to believe, sitting here in leafy suburbia with your tenure and your stipend, and Odette for a rainy day, but there are people who are willing to be brave for this.'

'Oh, piss off! You never change, do you?' the academic scoffed. 'And thank fucking Christ for that! I thought ten years as a family man would soften you, but you've still got the same incisive vocabulary you always had. I take it you think the government's full of spineless wimps.'

Having succeeded in riling his former debating partner into taking the bait, the songwriter took his foot off the gas. 'No. Not necessarily. But they do need to overcome their shyness about meeting face-to-face with the TPLF. Sure, Mengistu's dangerous, but I believe Mehretu's genuine. D'*ya* reckon?'

'Hmm... I like to think so too. What about the intelligence corps?' Engelbrecht asked. 'Elfadil will have heard about what you're doing, and I don't trust that guy. He's open to the highest bidder, I'm sure.'

'Maybe, yeah. I talked to him a few months ago. He was in Zambia for a conference. Surprised you weren't there, on reflection. He didn't inspire me either. Mate, I'll cut to the chase. I'd love you to join us in the Dordogne for these talks? Four days should be enough.'

'Me?' the professor exclaimed, cowardice and false modesty both impossible to hide. 'You don't need me.'

'Yes, I do. You'd be perfect. You have the background, you're an African native, you're white and you're an opponent of *Apartheid* everywhere. Plus, and most important, you know how to develop an argument and see it through. I need you, man.'

'But why does it have to be in France?'

'Neutral. It's the only way to guarantee safety,' Jeff answered, 'or as much as anyone can guarantee safety. Anonymity too. And frankly... full disclosure... I couldn't get insurance for myself anywhere in Africa except Nigeria, and I'm pretty sure no-one wants to go there for peace talks.'

Pieter guffawed, slapping the table as he lost his balance and tipped forward. 'Ain't that the truth!'

'So will you do it, mate? Please?'

The professor scraped his chair backwards across the decking and stood up to let out a bellowing fart, murmuring about a need to relieve himself. His guest watched him disappear into the house and presumed an honest answer were too difficult to deliver. It was a lot to ask of someone who had left political activism behind. This particular middle-aged man wasn't searching for lost youth. He was looking forward to retirement. He had said as much, hadn't he? Word-for-word.

Dog-tired, Jeff poured himself another glass of whisky and threw it straight down his gullet. Ten o'clock; exactly twelve hours since he first entered the community hall in Sebeta. Now he was at the other end of the continent with only the clothes he wore and a couple of hundred Rand in cash. Wandering around the manicured lawn behind the Engelbrechts' house, the day's bruises were tender under his "JL" tattoo, and he longed for Lynn's healing hands on his body.

If Pieter didn't return from his opportune call of nature with a change of heart, the visitor resolved to check into a hotel nearby, to make sure he caught the first flight back to Addis Ababa the next morning. This would give him enough time to collect the rest of his belongings, which languished in the silence of his original accommodation, and make his way to the airport for his trip northwards to Khartoum. With the prospect of five more stressful days, the easy life of a self-satisfied fat cat became almost irresistible.

His host's lumbering frame loomed out of the darkness, one foot steadfastly planted inside the doorway. He issued an invitation to share a cup of coffee and some cake with Mathilde, a clear sign that the subject was closed.

'I can't do it,' Engelbrecht insisted, resting his hand on the musician's shoulder. 'I have to think of my family.'

The Australian frowned. 'But that's exactly why you should do it, Piet. Jesus! It's the only fucking reason I'm doing it, and I'm not even from Africa.'

Jeff regrouped, lingering on the *patio* and hoping the professor was willing to listen to one last shot. 'You've brought your daughter up to accept all humans as equally worthy, haven't you?'

'Oh, please,' the academic snarled. 'Of course we have.'

'And you have a black housekeeper.'

'Everyone does. What's that got to do with it?'

'No, mate,' came an angry retort. 'Not everyone does. Most people keep their own house, for fuck's sake. Your housekeeper keeps two houses. What's her name, by the way? It's fucking rude of me not to have asked earlier.'

Pieter leaned on the table and rocked back and forth, displaying a certain amount of impatience. 'Nandi. Come on in, *mein Freund*. Join us inside. It's getting cold. Don't try and tell me you don't have help at home too.'

The determined negotiator jabbed a defiant index finger into the tabletop's timber surface. 'Hell, yeah... That's what I mean,' he tried not to shout. 'Help at home. Yes, we have help at home. We have black ones and white ones, and brown, and even the occasional yellow one. They're paid well to do a job well. They don't have to help at home, and they don't have to work for us. They choose to work for us. In fact, they effing well queue up, but the people who work for us are free agents. Nandi could be too.'

'We treat her perfectly well,' the older man objected. 'She likes working here.'

'I know. Apologies, mate. I realise that. But she hardly had her pick of careers, did she? Not like the girls and boy looking after our kids...'

'Boy? You have a male babysitter? Now I've seen everything,' the old stager chuckled.

Jeff shrugged. 'Yep. We do have a male childminder at the moment, which is so much better for Jetto, and our drivers are ex-military. They have choices, and they chose us. The guys we employ work for us for a year or two, then they'll go to uni' and become a graduate something, and go on to have the career they want. Nandi might've wanted that shit too, and I'm damned sure she wants it for her kids and grandkids. You know all this, Piet. We talked about it *ad infinitum* back in the late 'seventies and early 'eighties, but nothing fucking well happened.'

'It's too dangerous, mate,' Engelbrecht was exhausted too, mid-week alcohol slowing him down. 'I'm not sure I can afford the time, for one thing, and I doubt if I've got the energy that something like this needs.'

'The process gives you energy,' the arbitrator rebuffed, lighting another cigarette and offering his old friend the packet.

'No, thank you. I gave up.'

'Good man. Just imagine what Catherine'll think of her dad when she finds out he's part of the machinery that releases the TPLF's political prisoners and sees the Derg come crashing down. An autographed photo' from me or Lynn's nothing compared to that, and you'd have the chance to give her something bloody significant as a legacy.'

The cynic had heard enough grandstanding and waved his hand at the passionate man across the table. 'OK. Come in. Mathilde's made up a bed for you upstairs. I hope you'll be our guest tonight.'

Stubbing out his cigarette in the ashtray, the *mirage* of a comfortable place to rest his bones a cruel temptation indeed. 'No, thanks. It's very kind of you to offer, and I appreciate you giving up your evening for me. I need to be back in "AA" early, so I'll get a cab back into the city and find a hotel.'

'You absolutely will not!' the professor countered. 'Bullshit! I'll drive you to the airport in the morning. Stay here tonight.'

After batting a few more refusals and insistences across the table, Jeff found himself in the study dialling a taxi. He drank a cup of coffee and dished out more asinine conversation with Pieter and his subservient wife while waiting for it to arrive, announced by two blasts of a horn from the driveway.

'OK. That's him now. Thanks heaps for the awesome dinner and the chance to catch up, guys. I'll ring you when I get back from up north. Think about it, please, Piet. And thanks again, Mathilde. It's been so cool to see you and Catherine after all this time.'

'Oh, yes. It's been such a delight. Goodnight, Jeff,' the housewife said, giving him a hard squeeze which his bruises didn't need. 'You really should stay, you know. It's no trouble.'

The celebrity thanked the woman for her hospitality, at pains to dispel the opinion that his exalted status rendered suburban domesticity beneath him these days. Beyond the front porch, the two doctoral fellows shook hands without a word, and Jeff gave his old friend a last slap on the back before climbing into the taxi's rear seat.

'Hello?'

The sound of Lynn's sleepy voice at the end of a long day was more satisfying than any of the expensive whiskies the traveller had sampled in recent hours. He had asked the driver to drop him at the hotel nearest the airport, where he performed a hurried check-in and made straight for the telephone as soon as he was locked inside the small, musty room.

'Angel, it's me,' he said, tears of relief stinging his eyes. 'Sorry it's so late.'

'Hey! That's alright. What happened? Are you OK?'

The world-changer chuckled, at a loss as to where to start. 'Yeah. I guess so. I am now anyway, but I don't want to keep you awake. I'll tell you about it tomorrow at a more reasonable hour. I just needed a fix of your voice before I hit the sack.'

'I'm awake now,' Lynn tried to sound lively. 'What's so funny?'

'Ah, *nada nada*. Hysteria's setting in after a bloody weird string of events. I've had the most bizarre day, topped off with a frustrating evening. D'you remember Piet Engelbrecht from London Uni'?'

'Yes. Of course I do. I didn't know you were meeting up with him. How are they?'

'Fucking hell! He's turned into the archetypal pig in shit,' her husband laughed aloud, coughing as he dealt with the physical side-effects of his mixed-up emotions and inflamed muscles. 'You wouldn't believe how docile he's become. I'm bloody disappointed in him, I have to admit.'

'Wow! That's a shame. He'd be fifty by now, wouldn't he?' Lynn mused. 'What's he doing?'

'Y'know what, baby? Not now. You go back to sleep,' Jeff opted to change the subject instead of burdening his saviour with the day's woes. 'We can talk about this some other time. I need to tell you I'm in Cape Town, in case anything happens.'

'Cape Town?' the singer exclaimed. 'Why? No, OK. I won't ask. Your flight to Khartoum's from Addis, but I'm guessing you have a plan.'

'Not a hope, angel,' her parasitic frontman sniffed, brushing bittersweet tears from his cheek. 'Christ, you make me feel so good. I'm as hard as a rock sitting here in some pokey bedroom that stinks of stale smoke. I wish you were here.'

'Hmm...' Lynn replied. 'Doesn't sound very appealing, the way you describe it.'

The aroused man laughed, removing his clothes while they spoke. 'Very funny. If you were here, I'd have checked into a far nicer place than this. The 'planes are leaving tyre tracks on the roof.'

'Oh, my God! You're not making it sound too safe either, but I'm glad I can make you feel better regardless. Are you going to sleep now or are you wired?'

'I badly need some sleep,' Jeff groaned, 'but I've got a date with your shadow first. You don't have to stick around. We'll be fine without you.'

The blonde beauty sighed. '*Comme d'habitude...* Redundant again. Ring back in the morning if you need me to change any flights or anything, or if things don't work out with my shadow. I love you. Be careful.'

'*Gracias, mon amie.* No effing substitute for the real thing, I assure you, but needs must. I love you too. So much. Mathilde sends her love too. Their girl's nearly fifteen already. Anyway... I shall be careful, angel. I'll call you tonight and tell you everything. You're the best, Lynn. I mean it. Can't wait to be home so I can use my senses on you for real.'

'Oh. That's a lovely idea. Me neither,' his wife's voice sounded enticingly drowsy, exactly like home should sound. 'Goodnight, gorgeous. *Dors bien.*'

'*Toi aussi,* angel.'

***

The next three days played out as humdrum in comparison. To the superstar's delight, he discovered considerable progress had been made within the aid distribution centres in Ethiopia and the Sudan. Even more encouraging, he was beginning to meet more survivors than victims, giving rise to a wealth of positive photo-opportunities and many more hopeful interviews than he had squared up to when last on the ground in his charity's North African camps.

With his injuries healing, and determined to steer clear of dysentery and other bacterial infections this time, the celebrity hero rushed from place to place, hounded at every location by a growing international press contingent. Whenever he stood still for more than a few minutes, children and adults alike flocked to him, earning him the nickname of "Pied Piper of Africa" in the headlines and editorials.

If any of these refugees or aid workers had listened to a Jeff Diamond recording, no reference was ever made to his stellar music career, a by-product which pleased him no end. Registering his only connection with these people as the life-affirming and large-scale humanitarian effort with which his brand was inextricably associated helped to diminish the deep psychological debt he still bore.

However, the philosopher was impatient for his priorities to move up the clout chain. It was no longer enough that he was the people's hero in the micro-world, as his better half often said. Lasting change was only possible if he could convince governments and non-government organisations to work together, as he had accomplished at home in the realms of mental health issues and children's welfare. Policy changes were the minimum he would accept as a success measure these days, driven in the main by Lynn's wise schooling as to the right way to influence the macro-world.

Jeff had received word that Jemal Mehretu was prepared to meet him the following day, and he lost no time in firming up the necessary travel plans to make this happen. It was not without scepticism that he arranged for the same driver who had taken him to Sebeta to collect him from Bole International Airport, battling with an obscure instinct he deemed unfounded.

The anonymous vehicle sped along the dusty roads to the south-east of Addis Ababa until they were clear of urban sprawl. Travelling in relative comfort this time, in the passenger seat, Jeff engaged the man to his left in conversation in the hope of hearing some concrete examples of how citizens would like their ancient civilisation to head into the future. As expected, the basics were the most important: land rights, infrastructure, free trade and jobs; schools and hospitals for everyone; and an end to poverty and inequality in a country which boasted a rich cultural history in comparison to other Saharan countries.

The smooth-talking rock star soon noticed Dennis' eyes flicking up to the rear-view mirror every few seconds, as if he suspected they were being tailed.

The door mirror on Jeff's side had snapped off, and each time he went to glance over his shoulder, the nervous man would shake his head.

Just when the songwriter could resist no longer, two vehicles passed them at speed before slamming on their brakes ahead. The driver had his wits about him, retaining control of the car and swerving to avoid an impact. In only a couple of hundred metres or so however, both had overtaken them again.

'Who are they?' the passenger asked, peering inside the other four-wheel drives, unable to discern the number of occupants due to the amount of dust and dirt kicked up.

'Not TPLF,' Dennis answered, his voice monotone and agitated.

'Friendly?'

'Not friendly.'

Right, the world-changer thought. *This could be interesting...*

One of the other cars slowed to a crawl and waved them through. Imagining for a moment that he was on a movie set, the Australian's mind was doused in an uneasy surrealism; quite the most inappropriate reaction for their current circumstance. The truck which had dropped back previously tore past them once more, and he could have sworn he spied rifles held by at least two of its passengers.

'You OK?' he asked his companion, whose forehead and upper lip were dotted with bulbous beads of sweat.

'Yes, boss. We must keep driving.'

Jeff took this to mean the TPLF operative would rather not be distracted, so he kept all further thoughts to himself and concentrated on the road. Their car careened towards the ditch at the side when the one in front nosedived on its brakes for a second time, before veering into the centre to evade a collision, having passed within a few centimetres of each others' doors.

This game of cat and mouse continued for several more kilometres. One or other of the chasing vehicles would drop back to reveal faces hidden in homemade balaclavas, showing only staring, white-rimmed eyes and mouths full of yellow-brown teeth. Brandishing their weaponry at every chance, their threatening antics escalated as the fraught minutes went by.

'Do they want us to stop?' Jeff asked, sweat collecting on his own brow by this time.

'Yes. I think so. But it's not a good idea.'

'Sure, but how long can you keep this up?' the experienced rally driver checked with the frightened man. 'Don't keep driving just because of me. Let's not be heroes about this, mate.'

Dennis gave no response, engaged in another round of dangerous overtaking manœuvres. This time, the other vehicle's windows had been wound down, the gunmen releasing several rounds of gunfire into the air.

'Jesus Christ!' the star shouted, the invisible director adding a whole new dimension of sound to this action movie. 'They're fucking serious. We'd better stop. Pull over, Den, eh?'

'They will kill us,' the driver shook his head, eyes bloodshot with fear. 'Better to keep driving.'

'They won't kill us,' Jeff contradicted, although he had no idea why his voice was so confident.

It was now evident their escort was becoming bored with the hunt, since the next volley of shells was aimed at the TPLF car's tyres. Spinning around in his seat, the songwriter saw a series of dust plumes puffing up from the ground behind them.

Preparing to overrule his driver and urge him to stop, the Australian's neck slammed against the head-rest as the four-wheel drive flipped onto its roof and then its side, and then its roof once more before skimming across the loose gravel at full pelt.

The sound of metal scraping along the road at speed was thunderous, unlike anything Jeff had ever heard before. The car continued to slide for at least another hundred metres, with its passengers and luggage tumbling around inside. It eventually came to a standstill against an unforgiving boulder, creaking as the bodywork bent like tinfoil with the sudden burst of negative energy. Issuing a last-ditch scream, the engine cut out, and the vehicle pitched a further ninety degrees to leave the passenger door pointing upwards into the blazing sun.

The multi-millionnaire braced himself again, intense pain radiating through his shoulder as it bounced off the windscreen. He was flung against the back of his seat by the opposing forces, convinced he would have been strangled had he not removed his safety belt when the chase commenced.

Glancing downwards at Dennis, he saw his slight frame had become wedged between the dashboard and the driver's seat, which had snapped free of its bolts in the crash. Blood dribbled through thinning hair where his head had smashed against the glass.

Through the shock, Jeff became aware of shouting from outside. He thought better of turning around to face his captors. Instead, he reached down and began to lever his companion's shoulders out from behind the steering column, checking his neck for a pulse. There was one, albeit faint, and the man's eyes opened to slits as he regained consciousness.

The songwriter felt no panic, though he sensed Gravity the troll not too far away. 'Mate, hang on. We'll get you out of here. Just breathe deeply, OK?'

Breathing deeply was no easy feat for either man. The car's windows were all broken, filling the cab with dense, hot dust. Jeff coughed hard and pushed on the buckled door. After shifting his weight underneath the twisted metal, he managed to prise it open and found himself staring into bright blue sky and two gaping shotgun barrels.

'Lynn, I love you,' the old soul muttered under his breath. 'If this is it, you guys know I love you. See you soon.'

The smell of diesel fuel stuck to the hairs inside the city boy's nostrils, masking the overwhelming odour of man-on-man enough to convince him it was worth putting up a fight. Grabbing hold of Dennis' shirt, he cleaved the limp body with all his might until it came free.

Again discerning shouts from muffled male voices, the passenger was unable to decipher their words. He concluded his hearing must have been impaired by the impact of the crash, concentrating instead on freeing himself and his driver from the upturned vehicle in the correct number of pieces. Hooking his hands underneath Dennis' armpits, he found superhuman strength from hidden reserves and began to lift themselves out into the open to meet their fate.

A joyful pictorial catalogue of his precious children ran headlong into each other in Jeff's mind, interspersed with three-dimensional images of his *regala* lying naked next to him in their favourite spot on the Dysons' Benloch settlement. As he wrenched the driver's arms and legs skywards through the cabin, Lynn's tanned, slender body teased him in a fast-forward action replay.

Was this what was meant by having life flash before one's eyes? Was he about to die? In another strange twist of irony, he felt no fear; only a tumultuous rush of sensations, no doubt fuelled by adrenalin and an extraordinary desire to stay alive. What a contrast to the teenager who would have done anything for a chance to die...

Dennis' head flopped forwards and clashed with his rescuer's clavicle, jarring him back to reality. Jesus, that was sore! He hoisted the injured man as high as he could and gave him a gentle jolt.

'Stay awake, mate,' he yelled into the gaunt face, taking his first look at those at the other end of the trained guns. 'What're you going to do? This bloke needs help.'

One of the *guerrillas* sprang onto the front wing of the vehicle and grabbed the inanimate body by the hands. As gravity took hold, Dennis sunk back into the cabin, his feet hitting the cracked fascia with a clatter.

'Hey! Careful!' the angry traveller yelled. 'He's badly hurt. Take it easy.'

Between them, captor and captive managed to extricate the driver from the wreckage. Hoisting his legs clear of the passenger doorframe, the musician dropped down to the ground, relieved to feel the unconscious man's breath on his hand as he cleared his airway. For a moment, he lost his balance and fell against a spinning tyre, guessing the numbness in his own right arm and the shooting pain across his upper chest were the result of a broken collarbone.

Jeff crunched the soles of his boots in the rough road surface to stem the dizziness. Within a second or two, he felt the slim barrel of a rifle jab him between the shoulder blades. Instead of seeing his family's faces again, he was surprised to encounter images of Clint Eastwood and John Wayne pointing shiny Smith and Wessons at each other in a *spaghetti* western setting, and his nerves calmed as a result.

'Stand up!' a terse voice behind ordered. 'Move away from the car.'

The superstar did as he was told, watching two other men attempting to rouse the driver. So far, it appeared these rebels had no intention of killing their prey. Not yet anyway. He kept walking until ordered to stop, which was next to one of the other four-wheel drives.

'Turn around, Mister Diamond,' the gunman barked.

Mister Diamond? Jeff couldn't help but smile at the sudden ill-suited level of respect. It was incongruous in the extreme that someone with the power to snuff out his very existence should choose to be so formal. He turned to face a man of about his age, clean-shaven and well-dressed, apart from the covering of brown dust they all had in common.

'It's Jeff,' the peacemaker responded without changing his expression. 'Is the driver alright?'

'He want to know if driver is alive,' his guard called over to his companions.

'He's alive,' an older man shouted back, annoyed by the interjection. 'Get him in the car.'

The gun barrel now dug into the flesh between the celebrity's ribs. As the pair circled each other, the eyes of his captor focussed over his shoulder to a nearby car. Jeff moved to one side and waited for the rebel to open the door.

'Are you bringing him with us?' he asked, fearing for Dennis' safety. 'You're not going to leave him here, are you?'

'Why do you care?' cursed the man in front of him.

''Cause he needs to get to a hospital,' the prisoner answered, summoning as patient and humble a tone as possible. 'He deserves that. He's my driver. He hasn't done anything wrong.'

'Where are you going?' asked another *guerrilla*, in a distinct British accent.

'To meet with Mister Mehretu. It's where we *were* going, that is... Where are we going now?'

'You come with us now,' the original gunman replied, prodding the insolent prisoner in the back with his rifle butt. 'Get in the car.'

Jeff held his ground, for some reason unafraid. He had escaped this encounter with minor injuries so far, and his priority was clear right at this moment. It was his duty to protect his fellow traveller.

'I want to see the driver in the car first, please,' he stated, standing firm. 'Lift him in, give him some water, and then I'll get in.'

To the negotiator's surprise, the group obeyed his instructions. Dennis was lifted by his ankles and shoulders and tossed like a sack of rice into the rear compartment of the designated four-wheel drive. They even offered the troublemaker a drink from a dirty canteen, throwing Jeff's mind back to Coldwater Creek and how Lynn and he always stocked up on water before trundling across the paddocks for a little light relief in their private paradise.

The current situation seemed to indicate the Diamond frontman had scant likelihood of making it home for their eleventh wedding anniversary. It occurred to him that time and healing had not bestowed a fear of death upon him. If these gunmen blew him to bits, he would meet his demise with a certain familiarity and acceptance. He did not want to die however. After years of wishing his life away, he was more than willing to fight for it today.

The philosopher's watch told him it was three o'clock in the afternoon. He had no idea where he was, nor how long it might be before he found out what this surly bunch of blokes planned to do with him. Drinking in large gulps from the water bottle when it came his way, he contemplated his alternatives.

Running would do no good. He would enjoy less than thirty seconds of freedom before they turned a car around and caught up to him. Even if he managed to sneak away, he would be stupid not to stick to the road, sure to become far more lost than he already was. And if he were to make a break across country, he had no doubt the terrain would present little difficulty for his captors' vehicles, with their high ground clearance and wide, deep-tread tyres.

All these ridiculous escape routes were worthless though, since he couldn't bring himself to abandon his driver, by now surely in a serious condition. The poor man had cried out in pain when the *guerrillas* had bundled him into the car, and an occasional low moan continued to drift from his direction every now and again. The injured African was in the rock star's employ, which in his mind lent him the responsibility of keeping him as comfortable as possible.

'Where are we going?' Jeff asked a tall, lanky youngster who was waiting for the return of the canteen. 'Where are you taking us?'

'Safe-house,' one of the others responded with a cackle.

Safe for whom? the musician replied under his breath. Sheltering from the fiery mid-afternoon sun would be a good start, then maybe a chance to make a telephone call, and even some food. He was beyond starving, and the prospect of bouncing around in a car for another few hours rendered him queasy.

'Do you mind if I take a piss?' the celebrity asked, his eyes travelling from one rebel to the next.

The man who appeared to be in charge nodded to his comrade, who snapped to attention and raised the barrel of his gun until it made contact with their prisoner's stomach.

'Walk,' he barked, flicking the end of his weapon to the left.

The leader was laughing again, pointing to the scene and goading the others on. 'You see?' he jeered. 'Even the great Jeff Diamond needs to pee. So he's not a god after all!'

'Yeah, well...' the millionnaire raised his eyebrows and smiled. 'I don't normally, but it's my day off.'

Facing away from his armed guard, the captive shook his head. A god? Perish the thought! He unzipped his fly and emptied his full bladder onto the ground in front of him. The lessons he had given his young son on how to use public toilets like a man, when all eyes were on his illustrious back, paid off for him in one bizarre hit. As it turned out, he had started a trend, soon aware of a semi-circle of men to his right, all urinating in the desert. It was a shame there were no cameras, the amazed celebrity thought. This scene was worthy of "Blazing Saddles" for its comedic value.

Having been deposed from the deity's pedestal, maybe now the renegades would see fit to kill their famous quarry. Who were they working for? If Dennis' assumption was false, meaning these were TPLF operatives, their intelligence clearly wasn't the best. Or perhaps Mehretu wasn't as trustworthy as his sources gave him credit for...

Climbing into the rear seat of a white Toyota, the master communicator began the long path towards a negotiated conclusion. The man who had slid in next to him had slung his rifle across his thighs and was rolling a cigarette. Jeff envisioned the smoke curling round his own mouth and nose until the nicotine entered his bloodstream, almost believing in the desired effect. His brain relaxed, and he directed his shoulder and back muscles to do the same.

'How come you guys speak to each other in English?' he asked as a benign opener, sneaking a quick glance into the cargo area.

'It is the only language that we have in common,' the driver replied with a grin.

'Really?' their captive smiled too, seeing the furious reaction the man's openness elicited from his boss. 'So where are you all from?'

'Be quiet,' the leader snapped, turning round and scowling at the friendly Australian.

Daring to make eye contact with the rebel in the passenger seat in front of him, Jeff's head gave an infinitesimal twitch. He said nothing. These extras must be hired help, he figured; mercenaries to bolster the group's firepower. They weren't your everyday North African peasants pushing for a better future. These blokes were well-educated, paid soldiers of fortune from Nigeria or countries south of the Equator; Zimbabwe, Botswana or Namibia, and even South African perhaps.

His companion on the rear seat continued to enjoy his cigarette, jumping when his superior officer spoke. He snatched the rifle into his right hand and wavered it in the general vicinity of the hostage's chest. Unflinching, Jeff turned his attention back to his driver, whose breathing had steadied. His eyes were closed. It was important to find out if he was conscious or not.

'Dennis, you still with us?' the empath enquired, staring his neighbour down. 'How's the pain?'

The invalid tried to peer out through a tiny sliver, letting out a groan. It was as if daylight was too much to bear. His mouth moved, but no sound came out.

'Good man,' Jeff replied. 'Headache, huh? Can you give him some more water, please?'

The gunman's gaze flicked across to his leader, who nodded and passed over a water bottle from the passenger footwell. To the celebrity's surprise, the skinny local with marked, blue-black skin presented it to him almost like a gift. What was their game? Was this their idea of fun for a bunch of mates on a Saturday afternoon?

'Cheers,' the brave musician said, raising the canteen to drink the health of his captors.

'Be quiet,' the leader in the front passenger seat barked again. 'Shut the fuck up.'

'Ha! Now you're talking Australian. That I understand perfectly.'

The pair of gunmen broke into laughter, stifling it as their boss grunted his displeasure. Trying not to lose his balance as the vehicle drove on the rough road, Jeff twisted round on his knees and reached over to lift Dennis' head. The wounded man drank a few sips before groaning and spitting out his last mouthful. The caring helper made sure the patient's mouth was empty before laying his skull down flat on the filthy carpeting.

'So are you going to tell me what you're planning to do with us?' he began again, slumping down onto the vinyl upholstery.

'We're going to our safe-house,' the leader repeated. 'It is all you need to know.'

The celebrity nodded, sitting back and resting on the window. Despite how much his stomach churned inside, he was determined to do his best to act carefree, as if he were enjoying their outing in the countryside. The lack of information was frustrating, but at least they hadn't tied his hands and feet and were showing no aggression towards him. Moreover, he no longer feared for his life. Perhaps naïvely, he reminded himself.

Imagining being back home, at Kierney's birthday party, the young father closed his eyes and replayed the piece of childish, amateur theatre to which the girls had treated them. He pressed his spine further into the seat as an imaginary Lynn sat in front of him, leaning against his chest. She put her hand on the inside of his thigh, like she always did. The aroma of shampoo in her hair all but masked a faint tinge of chlorine, and the engagement ring only worn on special occasions glinted in the sunshine. Ten years, he remembered. Ten fantastic years.

Jeff's daydream unfolded as the miles echoed through the tyres, and his eyes blinked in an attempt to relieve the pressure of his own migraine. Returning to his imagination, one arm moved from behind his wife's body to hook his right thumb into the waistband of her mini-skirt, gliding its fingernail backwards and forwards to stroke her hip. He felt her snuggle in closer, turned on by the familiar fire.

A persistent alarm counteracted this cute time-wasting technique, reality imposing thoughts of how worried his dream girl would be if they didn't speak for more than a day or two. The forever couple was fastidious to the point of obsession when it came to nightly telephone calls, unless they happened to be in transit and several thousand metres in the air. Quite apart from the compassion and remote pleasures they gave each other in the process, daily check-ins also formed part of their security checklist and was a condition of their life assurance policies.

If her husband didn't make contact this evening as planned, his wife would raise the alarm without hesitation. Such was the trust between the lovers, neither was likely to jump to infidelity as a reason for missing a *rendezvous*. In his current state of confusion, Jeff was uncertain as to the actions this distress signal was supposed to trigger. From memory, the plan stipulated alerting the official security agency of whichever country the jetsetter was located. He figured he was still in Ethiopia, given the speed they were travelling and the distance to the nearest border. And since they were driving across rough, scrubby bush-land, he also assumed the landscape would challenge any search party.

There was no point in worrying about the technicalities, so he refocussed on the comfortable *scenario* with which he had been amusing himself beforehand. Lynn knew he was on his way from Adama to meet Jemal Mehretu, and that he was due to fly to London in two days' time. Any details between this pair of scheduled milestones would be sketchy at best, so *ad hoc* had this trip turned out to be.

'So, Mister Diamond,' the rebel leader asked out of the blue, distracting the songwriter from his wandering thoughts. 'Why are you not shitting yourself now?'

Involuntary consternation must have spread across the captive's face, because the gunman snatched up his rifle and gave it a menacing rattle. Their hostage refused to bite, choosing only to gaze back at the man in the seat in front.

'How d'you know I'm not?'

The arrogant soldier smiled. 'Because you are almost sleeping.'

'No, mate. I'm not,' Jeff objected. 'Far from it. But I do spend a lot of time in cars and on 'planes with total strangers. I'm used to entertaining myself for hours on end, and I was just enjoying some quality time with my wife and kids.'

'I see,' the snide man chuckled to his driver. 'He is clever. So you travel with men who carry guns?'

The intellectual cocked his head at the firearm grazing his left leg. 'Yep. Sometimes I do, but they're usually pointing away from me rather than at me.'

All three occupants laughed at this quirky retort. Never had he been more fortunate to be born a smartarse! At least he was doing a reasonable job of pretending that self-defecation wasn't on the cards...

'What are your names?' the celebrity asked, seeking to capitalise on the lightened mood.

'This is not important,' the gunman retorted. 'Shut up, Jeff Diamond.'

The thirty-three-year-old raised an apologetic hand. 'I know. Shut the fuck up. Fine. I'll go back to where I was. No worries.'

Stretching his legs under the front seat and shuffling his backside as if settling down for a nap, the man with Mediterranean guile teased his misgiven, dark-skinned captors into believing he was returning to blissful familial dreams. He was not going to let on that the agreeable fodder had vanished from his mind. His objective had been achieved, and the leader began to bark orders at the driver, who nodded and stepped on the accelerator. It appeared they were nearing the end of their journey.

***

Back at *Escondido*, Lynn opened a window to admit a stiff sea breeze. She had been on-edge for the last three hours, with no idea why. She had checked and rechecked all the locks, the children were safe in their bedrooms, and their contracted security firm had run two perimeter checks as a precaution.

The strange feeling had started during dinner, at around seven o'clock, when an inexplicable tension had gripped her chest. At first, the athlete guessed she must have eaten something which didn't agree with her. She spent the next hour waiting for it to pass, but if anything, the sensation only became stronger.

Having ruled out food poisoning, the young woman then sought to blame her menstrual cycle. This didn't add up either. It even crossed her mind that she might be pregnant, and the prospect of a third little Dyson Diamond in the house filled her both with joy and trepidation. What would Jeff say? They had toyed with having another baby many times, always reverting to two being the right number.

The sportswoman was confident her husband would warm to the idea of an unplanned child. She, on the other hand, had not enjoyed being pregnant and looked forward to supporting Jet and Kierney while they grew up in the public eye. She hadn't anticipated having to start again with another set of nappies and bottles.

A nagging doubt persuaded the busy mother that her current symptoms had not arisen from anything as pleasurable as sex. Procreation's early telltale signs were nausea, lethargy and an out-of-kilter metabolism, whereas this evening's peculiar internal pressure appeared to stem from her nervous system and her heart.

Had she fallen ill? There were few healthier people in the world than Lynn Dyson, with her whole family undergoing such regular medical examinations and assessments of physical and mental strength that any illness would be detected at its earliest stage. Ticking off the various ailments which might bring about this type of affliction, her anxiety began to amplify... Cancer? Heart disease? Parkinsons? None was likely, but all were possible.

The Olympian immersed herself in some of her recent correspondence, carried into the lounge room from the study to tide her over another evening on her own. With their childminders off duty and Janey snoozing between the front of the couch and her mistress' calves, she managed to slow her pulse sufficiently to concentrate on a letter the couple had received to confirm a six-month season for their forthcoming musical at the Drury Lane Theatre in London's West End. Jeff would be ecstatic to hear this! He was so proud of their new *œuvre*, and its upcoming *première* was already generating an insane amount of publicity in Europe and the United States.

The thoughtful woman dug her bare toes into the dog's warm fur and checked her watch. What time was it in Addis Ababa? Late afternoon, she calculated; four or five o'clock. The precise time difference eluded her, but she recalled Jeff's itinerary including his long-awaited meeting with the Director of Communications of the Tigrayan People's Liberation Front.

The Diamond machine's back-office chief knew Jemal Mehretu vaguely through their work in northern Africa, and remembered reading that he had lost a son in a recent armed conflict. She also knew her husband considered this man's presence critical to the talks he was planning to hold in France, imagining him being hounded incessantly until he buckled under the rock star's inimitable powers of persuasion.

Still Lynn's nerves continued to jangle as if she had drunk too much coffee too late in the day. She opened the office door to check the facsimile and answering machines again, but found nothing. Standing and staring at a favourite print of her man crouching in the surf, the original having featured on an early album cover, his whereabouts preoccupied her more than usual. This sense of foreboding increased the longer she gazed at his handsome face until, in the end, she had to look away.

Something untoward had happened. She wasn't sick, and the children were fine. The invisible elastic connection she shared with her wandering minstrel was cautioning her, with no way to get hold of him. It took a few minutes of searching through travel documents to find a telephone number for the hotel into which he was booked for the night. Dialling the long series of digits while quite convinced he wouldn't answer, her expectations for peace of mind were low.

'Good afternoon,' she spoke into the mouthpiece. 'I'm wondering if you can help me. Are you able to tell me if Jeff Diamond has arrived back yet?'

'Madam, I am very sorry,' the lady on the switchboard replied in a strong, nasal accent. 'I'm unable to give information about our guests.'

'Oh, yes. This is his wife, Lynn Diamond,' she tried again, running her fingertip along the notes she had scribbled the previous night, as if the written words' indentations held new clues. 'I spoke to him there yesterday evening. He's in room number one hundred and twenty. Please could you put me through to his room?'

Lynn heard the woman sigh, followed by a ringing sound. She stood listening to the repetitive tones for ten or eleven bursts, fixing her eyes on the enlarged photograph again. There was neither answer nor answering machine, so she replaced the receiver. All she could do was wait, too soon to invoke any special procedures.

Piecing together the hardworking negotiator's movements since their brief conversation the night before, the bewildered wife consoled herself that he wasn't expected back in his room until the early hours of the morning, Melbourne time. And if he had been successful in meeting with Mehretu, the pair would likely be out drinking in a bar, coated in girls and sampling exotic drugs until such time as the master lobbyist secured the commitment he sought.

'Are you OK?' Lynn asked of the oversized, framed portrait. 'Hope so. I love you, Jeff. We all love you.'

Hostage

The rebels' so-called safe-house was a rambling farm compound in the middle of nowhere. Jeff watched as two of his travelling companions enlisted the aid of a third man to lift Dennis from the four-wheel drive's boot and carry him inside, while the ringleader remained with their valuable hostage. A pistol had been pulled from the glove compartment, its matte finish scratched from the road's endless battering.

The Australian listened to the clean, clicking noise of well-lubricated bearings as the mercenary loaded his weapon with six slim cartridges and spun the housing. Where the hell were they? By now, he was in a far less humorous mood, concerned for his driver's health and for their combined safety.

No doubt about it however, the years spent persecuted by his father's gangland mates had taught him how to disguise fear. Even though he had left that torturous world behind, his practised survival instincts soon came flooding back.

Grunting, the gunman leaned against the car's passenger door. It swang open, and his boots thudded onto the sandy driveway. Without turning around, he gripped the handle of the rear door and wrenched it towards him, motioning to the prisoner while wielding the loaded firearm in his hand.

'Out, Diamond,' he barked.

Jeff pivoted his long legs out of the footwell and felt his shoes touch the ground. Levering himself to a standing position, he was a good twenty centimetres taller than his captor, who sported several gold teeth and a wide scar on his pockmarked cheek. Their celebrity kidnap victim recognised this type of blemish from his childhood too, likely caused by a knife wound never stitched. Three such souvenirs sat above his own right hip; his dad's idea of a lesson well learned.

The two men crossed the yard to the farmhouse porch. The latest stop on the superstar's tour was an impressive and spacious homestead, with a verandah stretching all the way across the front and down the side, visible from his vantage point. Four women of varying ages sat on wicker chairs near the main door, leaping to their feet at their approach. No matter how or why he arrived anywhere these days, there was always at least one curious female eyeing him up and down.

Tired and sick to the back teeth of the whole experience, Jeff mustered a smile and a wink for his welcoming committee, who immediately went into a huddle and giggled to each other. They ran off into the house as soon as the gunman at his shoulder growled a few words in what could have been any one of the eighty-odd languages spoken in the expansive African desert country.

'Go inside, Mister Diamond,' the leader ordered. 'And to the left.'

The hallway of the colonial dwelling had once been grand. Its high ceilings were adorned with fancy cornices and roses, and a tarnished but impressive *chandelier* hung in the middle. The home, at odds with its surroundings, was doomed to rack and ruin when this group of barbarians had taken possession.

The musician paused in the lobby, imagining the fate of the former owners of this imposing property. 'What is this place?' he asked, turning to face his escort.

'Nowhere. Sit down.'

'Will you at least tell me your name?' Jeff asked. 'This'll be a whole lot easier if I know what to call you. You know mine.'

'Very well,' the wild-eyed rebel responded. 'My family name is Rasul, but my English name is Andrew.'

'OK. Thanks. Which would you like me to use? Today are you a messenger or the patron saint of Scotland?'

Rasul chuckled. 'You are a clever man, Mister Diamond.'

'Jeff.'

'You are a clever man, Jeff. You take the time to learn about us. You have a good name also.'

'Jeff's a good name?' the Australian feigned ignorance.

'Stop now. I don't want to make jokes with you,' the humorous interlude was clearly over. 'Sit down. I have asked the girls to bring you water.'

'Cheers. That'd be great,' the taller man nodded, sinking down into an old couch with weak springs that voiced their disquiet at his considerable mass. 'Where've you taken my driver?'

'He is dying,' Rasul answered without emotion. 'They make him comfortable.'

Furious, the celebrity sprang up again. He couldn't stomach the idea of another innocent person losing his life while at his service. How many more people would be sacrificed while he lived out this extra-large existence of his?

'No way,' he objected. 'We can't let him die. He needs medical attention. A brain scan or something, and some painkillers. Is there a 'phone here?'

'Leave him to us,' Rasul insisted, raising the pistol to Jeff's chest. 'Sit down, Mister Diamond. We keep you here for a few days, then we see how much are you worth to your fans. How much do they pay for your release? Can we expect your wife to agree to our demands?'

The captive's blood turned to ice, and he feared he might pass out. Anticipating such extortion claims as part of Gerry's judicious risk mitigation meetings, he and his beautiful best friend had written agreements which they had both sworn to uphold under any circumstances, never once expecting them to be enacted. Poor Lynn. How dare he put her conscience to the test like this?

Faced with the prospect of bringing Jet and Kierney up on her own, the sensible woman would honour this covenant to the letter. He pictured her slumping back into a chair, distraught and tearful after hearing the breaking news from a uniformed officer.

'Don't you know I'm working towards the same goals as you are?' the activist enquired, summoning a dispassionate voice. 'One of your country's greatest freedom-fighters is expecting to meet me for dinner tonight. We're going to get Mengistu to step down and go to an election.'

Rasul perched himself on an arm of another chair and began to twirl the bullet chamber of his pistol. The rock star saw him processing this information, wishing he could read his mind.

'This will never happen,' the rebel leader shook his head. 'You haven't stopped the war in Ethiopia. What makes you think Mehretu is interested in negotiating with Mengistu?'

''Cause it's the right thing to do,' Jeff replied without hesitation. 'He lost his own son in the fighting. He wants to find another way. Mehretu wants a peaceful Ethiopia. All territorial disputes settled and your prisoners free, famine over and a fair, democratic government in power. I want that too. Your country's inalienable right; the whole population deserves it. And we're not that far away, mate.'

The superstar had issued this rallying cry countless times in recent years. This trip was not a flash in the pan. It was the latest event in a program of sustained and systematic negotiations which had ebbed and flowed, driven by genuine political ambition in the cities and by the tide of violence in open country.

'With all due respect, Jeff Diamond,' Rasul sneered, 'I do not believe you. The TPLF is to sit around a table and negotiate with the Mengistu government, you say? But we are EPRP. We are enough people to succeed alone.'

The peacemaker sat on the edge of his seat and fixed his opponent with a steely stare. 'With all due respect, Rasul Andrew,' he matched his opponent's inflection, 'you need to give the pioneers more credit. Look at South Africa, for example… Nelson Mandela's a well-respected lawyer. Oliver Tambo also. These guys know reason when they hear it. Mandela's already renounced violence. You know that. Your fight needs to renounce violence too, to save your countries' populations. Yeah?'

The wily renegade sniffed. 'I don't care about South Africa. No more magic words, Mister Diamond. I bring water. Are you hungry?'

'No, thanks. Water's good though. And a cigarette, if you have any.'

Rasul walked over to a desk at one end of the large drawing room and prised a drawer open. He pulled out a blue, plastic disposable lighter and a packet of cigarettes, peeling back the lid to present its contents to the Australian. The force of his craving made the smoker's hands jerk and judder as he placed the brown filter between parched lips.

'Cheers. And the lighter?'

Old addictions died hard, Jeff cursed. He had shown weakness, and his captor had not missed it. The merciless *guerrilla* leader toyed with his desperation for a few, exaggerated seconds before tendering the critical implement. Unable to hold his breath any longer, the singer's lungs exhaled as he pressed the lever to ignite the gas. A five-centimetre flame almost singed the hairs inside his nostrils.

Rasul cackled as the famous man's startled reaction gave way to relief, watching him drag hard on the cigarette. He lit one for himself and sat back to enjoy it, having parked his handgun on the desk.

With his nerves more under control, the songwriter's heartbeat relented. He hadn't spotted the brand of tobacco his host had offered, knowing only that it tasted rather more like wildebeest dung than he would have preferred. He needed to find a better way of dealing with this situation. If they were serious about keeping him here for several days, his dependencies were sure to perpetrate their own misery if he couldn't rise above them.

His bemused guard shouted for some water. After a short while, a woman bustled through the door with a heavy ceramic jug and two glasses. Slopping as much on the filthy carpet as into the vessels, she handed one to each man. Jeff accepted his and drank it dry in a single draught. It was refilled without a word, and he repeated the process, relishing the cool sensation in his stomach.

'So is it possible for me to make a 'phone call, please?'

'Tomorrow,' Rasul replied with a smirk, 'or the next day.'

The prisoner shook his head, smacking his empty glass down on the arm of the chair. 'No. That's not on, mate. Mehretu's expecting me. Dennis' family'll be expecting him home, and so shall mine.'

The gunman seemed surprised. 'You don't worry about your driver's family, Mister Diamond.'

'Why not?'

'Is your wife in Addis?'

'No. But I need to contact her,' Jeff answered. 'My manager'll need to know where I am too, and it's not fair to have them worry about me.'

'She will not worry about you,' Rasul teased with a knowing sneer on his face.

'What d'you mean by that?'

'Your wife thinks you are working. She does not think of you while you're away.'

'You know a lot about us,' the Australian said. 'Or did you study psychology? Is that your aim?'

'Yes. I do,' white-rimmed eyes danced in their dark sockets. 'And I know your history. I know what makes you tick, Jeff Diamond. Your past is well-known, even in Africa.'

Reaching for the ashtray and stubbing his cigarette out, Jeff leaned back into the couch. He mustn't take the bait. The past was the past. The bastard had his measure, but he was a different man now. If he let these mind-games worm their way into his psyche, the next few days would see a triumvirate battle of wills unfold between the peasant warrior, Gravity the troll and half of the world's richest and best loved pantomime horse. One vital ingredient was missing, to only the frontman's disadvantage.

'So how much do you want? What are you planning to request?'

'We issue a statement tomorrow.'

'I'll have another cigarette, please,' the star forced a smile. 'What do we do 'til then?'

'I'm going to make love to my woman,' Rasul teased, tossing the battered packet and his lighter at the captive with hostile indifference. 'And you just sit here and enjoy your fantasies. Like in the car. And then we see.'

Jeff seethed inside. This cool and calculating character must have been handpicked for the job. Rasul's attitude reminded him of the way he had spoken to his father when he met him in prison. He had used the same angle, wondering whether it would hurt. Both were correct. It hurt alright...

***

Lynn woke with a start, peering through the darkness at her alarm clock: four in the morning. It felt as though she had done the exact same thing only a few minutes ago, but it had been three o'clock at last count. Drained and listless in spite of several bouts of fitful sleep, she tried Jeff's hotel again. Such a futile exercise, she rued, hearing the telephone ring and ring and imagining an empty room.

Her mind no longer doubted her husband was in danger. With his childhood fears of abandonment and the memory of the desolation this betrayal created, he always managed to find a way to contact her. She meant too much to him not to try, regardless of which corner of the globe he was visiting and how far his hosts' hospitality extended. He had never let her down before, and she had no reason to believe things would be any different this time.

The couple had spoken for over an hour the previous night, spiced with their own expert brand of remote sexual chemistry. The young mother remembered dissolving into giggles several times, hoping not to wake Kierney in the room next-door.

Indeed, the tennis champion had never felt closer to her beautiful black stallion than over the last few weeks, with more than a decade of intimacy now behind them and another crazy year ahead. She was also certain her devotion was reciprocated, point-blank refusing to entertain the thought of him being unfaithful or dismissive of his obligations to let her know he was safe. It wasn't who he was.

Lynn decided to wait until nine o'clock, when she would contact their security company and raise her concerns. They would advise her on what action to take, even though she didn't care to contemplate the conclusions to which they would encourage her to jump. What if the worst had happened, and Jeff were already dead?

With the shock of this sudden terror sending tears rolling down her cheeks, the thirty-year-old held her hand over her mouth to prevent any sign of distress from emerging. Before too long little Kizzy would be awake, her acute perception sure to detect something amiss.

The sportswoman sat tall against the headboard, wiping her eyes with a tissue and sipping from her water glass. *No. Don't overreact...* The father of her children had not died. His enormous heart was still beating loud and clear. The odd sense of foreboding wasn't nearly strong enough for this to be the case.

So what were the possible *scenaria*? A car crash? Maybe her man was languishing unconscious in a provincial hospital, perhaps injured to the point where people couldn't recognise him. Horrific images flashed across Lynn's mind, making her cry again.

Or were they facing a hostage situation the like of which Gerry's risk management meetings had workshopped? This was more probable, given the fact that the prominent peace advocate was planning to meet a high-ranking member of a militant group. Despite all indications to the contrary, Jemal Mehretu may not be as honourable as Jeff thought.

Don't be stupid. It's not the movies, the intelligent woman chastised herself. Exhaling to counter another wave of fear, she blocked out a picture of her impressive lover tied up in a tiny cell with windows too high even for such a tall man to see out. What was going through his mind? He would be at his wits' end too, knowing the panic the absence of contact might spawn.

What an ignorant state to be in! How long did it take for security agencies to scour a landmass as large as Ethiopia for missing foreign nationals? And how hard would they try? There were few more valuable personages than Jeff Diamond these days, yet she couldn't expect authorities to pull out all the stops. He wasn't royalty, a prime minister or a president. When it came down to brass tacks, they were only musicians meddling in other people's business.

Adama was not too far from the borders of Djibouti, Eritrea and Somalia. If the traveller had been captured by one of the many disorganised but determined armed gangs, in which direction would they head? Moreover, given his unscheduled stopover in Cape Town the previous day, he might even have been spirited out of the region altogether...

There was little point in speculating. The rear-end of the pantomime horse had no real idea, and in truth, neither would anyone else. If Jeff had been taken hostage, those who remained several thousand kilometres away simply had to wait for his captors to issue some sort of ransom demand. She dressed in sports gear and made her way downstairs to the gymnasium, where she ran solo and powerless, anxious to tame her wild imagination.

The Diamond family's protection squad responded as any professional outfit should, with considerable urgency to Lynn's telephone call the next morning. She had placed three more calls to the hotel in Adama, after which the receptionist sent someone to confirm Jeff's room had lain empty all night. The key had not moved from the front desk, and the bed sheets and his luggage were untouched.

Gerry convened a meeting at *Escondido* straightaway to invoke the agreed action plan. Within an hour, his BMW crunched across the gravel towards the three-metre high, wooden courtyard portals.

Jet and Kierney had been driven to school by Dave, the new male nanny from Manchester in the UK, none the wiser of their father's apparent evaporation. It was fortunate that their dad was away so frequently as a matter of course, meaning neither child batted an eyelid whenever he failed to show up for breakfast.

Their mother, on the other hand, was beginning to buckle under the strain. Even their happy-go-lucky manager couldn't avoid noticing the stress written all over her face.

'How are you bearing up?' he asked, giving his mate's wife a firm hug and kissing her cheek. 'He'll be fine. There'll be a logical explanation.'

'Thanks, Gerry,' Lynn nodded, at pains to sound grateful for these ineffective platitudes. 'I hope you're right.'

Three security consultants arrived about half an hour later, all uncomfortable in dark suits, ties and stiff collars. They introduced themselves to the lady of the house, providing awkward rehearsed scripts of their credentials as former serving defence force personnel. Their clients sat through the laboured introductions, slinging each other the occasional furtive smile at the solemnity these men were keen to portray.

Channelling her husband's love of the absurd, the film star amused herself with the impression that their nominated security experts were primed and ready for action, sprung like racing greyhounds with a fake rabbit in sight. They were almost salivating at the prospect of being released from their desks to launch themselves into genuine operational duties. Methodically, she walked through the sequence of events she had pieced together, combining facts from Jeff's official itinerary with assumptions based on his usual *modus operandi* while overseas.

'He's impulsive,' the patient woman smiled. 'If he wants to do something, he'll do it, regardless of the plan.'

Gerry choked on his coffee at this comment, thereby reinforcing her understatement well. He received a scowl from his favourite charge, who went on to explain the reason for the rock star's covert mission and that he preferred to retain scope for discretionary diversion during these trips, ever one to take advantage of opportunities as they arose. She recounted his *impromptu* flight to the city on South Africa's western coast while omitting its purpose, having understood the need to maintain radio silence until the target individual's participation was secured.

The advisers remained attentive, jotting down the occasional note. Gerry admired their ability to ignore the fact that they were sitting opposite one of the entertainment world's hottest female bodies, hoping they were at least struggling to disable their x-ray spectacles in her presence.

Mike, who had risen to the rank of Captain in the Special Air Services and had seen action in Vietnam and the Middle East, asked a set of probing questions, the answers to which Lynn and Gerry could only guess.

Was Jeff carrying much cash?

A few hundred US dollars and the same in Birr, his wife hazarded. The typical places the peacemaker had frequented over the last few days were not yet ready for the flexible friend he used in cities. Informants tended to be more forthcoming whenever cold, hard cash was on the table. He knew better than most how this worked, having grown up in a similar feudal environment in Sydney's western suburbs.

Black mark Number One.

Was Jeff carrying sensitive documents?

'Definitely not,' came the unanimous reply.

The streetwise traveller never carried any identifying artefacts apart from his passport, if he could avoid it. He preferred to keep everything in his head, the only exception being a handwritten list of telephone numbers coded to help him remember which was whose.

Gold star this time!

Lynn laughed in exasperation, prompting the stalwart business manager to take over. He ran the consultants through the couple's last six months' worth of security alerts and threats, dismissing the majority as unlikely to result in a militant ambush. The three experienced soldiers agreed. Their working assumption remained intact: that the current *scenario* was the work of a splinter group linked to the Tigrayan People's Liberation Front.

The young mother sighed, amused to hear one of her husband's well-worn expressions coming out of her own mouth before she had a chance to stop it. 'I'm not sure I wouldn't have been able to come to this conclusion on my own.'

The executive sympathised. 'Good point. So gents, if my client's been captured by such a faction, where do you think they'd hold him?'

The Englishman put both hands on the table and flexed his shoulders. 'That's where we need to establish contact with people over there, Gerry, Lynn,' he proffered. 'We're so remote in Australia. None of us knows our way around Ethiopia, and we've got precious little intel' about the TPLF or any other active groups over there. This has to be our first priority when we get back to the office.'

'What about Canberra?' the singer interjected, springing off her chair and heading towards her desk. 'We've spoken to the South African and the Nigerian High Commission officials several times. Or the Ethiopian Embassy in London? I'll find you some names. In the meantime, what do you want me to do?'

'Not worry,' one of the also-ran consultants piped up. 'I'm sure your husband'll turn up safe and well, especially if he changes his plans on a regular basis.'

The Olympian ignored this patronising remark and focussed her attention back on Mike. Such conjecture wouldn't advance their cause in any way. She was the only one to determine how much she worried.

'I mean more around speaking to the press,' the skilled coordinator explained. 'The journoes track our movements inside-out. Our office'll receive 'phone calls galore on Monday morning, looking for updates on Jeff's latest trip to the feeding centres and refugee camps. If he's not available to make a statement, we have to have a plan in place to provide one. I don't want to raise unnecessary alarm, because the story'll take off like wildfire at any mention of hostages or ambushes, *et cetera*.'

The Diamonds' manager nodded. 'Absolutely. I rang Cathy at Stonebridge after we spoke first thing, but she wasn't available. Before I head back into the city, let's ring her together.'

'Sure. What do you suggest?' Lynn referred to the chief consultant again. 'Blackout for now?'

Mike spluttered, out of his depth with such high-profile communications requirements. 'Well... Up to you, Missus Diamond. There's also the risk of information falling into the wrong hands. If your husband *has* been taken hostage, and they're planning to make some demands, an explosion in the media might derail them and force the issue, which we don't want.'

'Exactly,' she agreed. 'That's what I needed to hear. Please call me Lynn. If that's how these people work, which is my definite suspicion, then we want as little as possible in the public domain. Good. Thanks, Mike. Shall we schedule another meeting, just over the 'phone? Tomorrow morning? Is that enough time to contact whomever you need to in Ethiopia?'

'Yes. Ample time, thanks,' the Oxbridge accent responded with renewed enthusiasm. 'This is our highest priority today, and one of us'll get ready to fly over there this afternoon. We need someone on the ground in Addis Ababa tomorrow. Is that something you'd consider too?'

'No,' Gerry answered on his client's behalf. 'Certainly not. Media circus material, mate. Quite apart from being dangerous and potentially inflammatory to the people Jeff's trying to get round the table. No go. Lynn?'

'You took the words out of my mouth!' the singer chuckled, proud of the right-winged accountant's rare display of sensitivity. 'Besides, once Jeff's found, he'll still want to go on to London to carry on with the normal schedule. We wouldn't want to show they've scared us off, or that he's running home to Mummy. We're serious people playing a serious game. We have to live with the consequences and move on quickly.'

The dumbstruck executive gaped for a second before pulling himself together. He curled an arm around the steadfast woman's shoulder and squeezed it tight. No doubt about it, she was courageous in the face of such adversity.

The telephone rang behind them, providing a welcome distraction. The householder lifted the receiver, hearing only the thump of her own heartbeat in her ears. She now had a much better idea of what her lost boy had endured when seized by a panic attack. It was most debilitating.

'Hello?'

'Oh, hello, darling. It's only me,' a female voice spoke.

'Oh, hi, Mum,' Lynn replied, the corners of her mouth turned downwards as she shared her disappointment with their manager. 'How are you?'

Seeking to respect the women's privacy, Gerry ushered the visitors out of the Diamonds' office, waiting with them in the hallway for their client to finish her call.

'Nice house,' one of the juniors commented, spinning full circle on the marble tiles and ogling the ample width of the staircase as it curved between storeys. 'How long have they been here?'

'Eight years or thereabouts,' the manager replied. 'It is a nice house, but you were never here.'

Mike nodded for his colleague to keep his opinions to himself. 'Of course, Mister Blake.'

Lynn's footsteps soon came from around the corner. Full of apology, she shook each man's hand and showed them out through the front door, pleased to see the Irishman escort them all to their car. A strange nostalgia hit her, thrown back to the three *amigos* who had welcomed her into their tight-knit circle in nineteen-seventy-two. How life had changed for them all!

Within a couple of minutes, the indomitable one reappeared at the door. 'Was that alright?' he checked, holding both arms out. 'Would you like me to stay?'

'No. It's fine, thanks,' the tennis champion shook her head. 'I've got heaps to do. Twelve session musicians are due to arrive in the next hour, and that'll keep me busy for the rest of the day. Evening-time's hardest, once the kids have gone to bed.'

'Well... How about I come back tonight? We could 'phone for takeaway and watch a video, like the old days.'

'Don't you have anything better to do?' the music producer chided.

'As it happens, no. But what could be better than spending an evening with you anyway?' the distinguished businessman shrugged. 'Missus D, you know you're very important to me, even though I might not behave that way. Plus, I owe it to your lucky conjugal bastard.'

Lynn raised her eyebrows in dismay, concerned shoulders drooping. 'Please, Gerry. I don't imagine he feels very lucky at the moment.'

The family's oldest friend winced at his poor choice of words but stuck to his guns. 'You know what I mean,' he moaned. 'You know how jealous I am of him when it comes to you. It would be my pleasure to keep you company, and I might even be here when he rings.'

'OK. I'm sorry. I don't want the kids to suspect anything, so can I reserve tomorrow evening instead, please? In case he's still missing...'

Gerry walked forwards and put his hands on her shoulders, leaning down to leave a chaste kiss on the lips of his best mate's wife. 'If you insist,' he mocked. 'Have it your way. You are perfect for him, you know. I can't believe you're so calm. You let him get away with murder, and nothing pisses you off. Brave and loyal.'

'Yeah. Like a lovesick puppy, I know. Role reversal, isn't it, compared to the old days? It's all an act,' the beauty admitted, backing away. 'I'm not calm inside. I felt like I was about to collapse when the 'phone rang. And then it was only my bloody mother.'

The accountant chuckled. 'Did you tell your bloody mother what's happened to your bloody husband?'

'No, I bloody well didn't!'

'Why not? She wouldn't grass to the media, would she?'

'No,' the indignant woman answered. 'I don't want to give her any more ammunition to complain about Jeff leaving me on my own. She's determined he's treating me poorly, and this palaver would only fuel the fire. Wow! Look at that... We've got our own solar light show!'

Nodding, Gerry turned towards the front door, which had been left open since the security consultants departed. A shower had covered the courtyard flagstones with a glistening spray of rain, now ignited by the mid-morning sun into myriad aerial rainbows misting their view of the fountain and the wall beyond.

'Oh, I see. And yes, it is rather *specky*. Did Aristotle Archimedes design that too? Anyway, ring me if anything happens. Or if nothing happens. Either way.'

Lynn laughed aloud, grateful for the humourist's parting embrace. 'I shall. Thanks for coming all the way over here. Don't work too hard.'

***

There were still no news by four-thirty, when Dave and Irina returned with the children after school. Kierney had another tall tale to tell her mother, who wallowed in the distraction for the first half-hour. She had been nervous that her downhearted demeanour might give the game away, but neither child reacted as if they suspected anything. After a quick snack, a suggested trip into Frankston to see a movie met with whoops of approval.

Mid-week evenings in the coastal town were quiet during the school term. Summer was drawing to a close, and the sea breeze whipped up a dust storm along the *promenade*. The three Diamonds had the small cinema almost to themselves, with the exception of an elderly lady trying to control three fractious granddaughters who would have benefitted from more discipline and far less sugar.

Lynn tried her best to mimic her little ones' ability to submit their powers of concentration to the film's plot. She failed, yet two hours passed by without adding to her heartache. Never had she been more thankful for the couple's hectic travel schedule, since Jet and Kierney were quite content to wait for their father to return, promising to make a list before bedtime of all the things they had to tell or show him.

Evening turned into night with a growing sense of dread for the young woman, the dull pain in her chest ever present. She fetched her sewing box from the laundry, filled with a sudden urge to mend Jeff's leather jacket. She had convinced him to leave the twentieth birthday gift behind this time, after its lining tore when being tugged from between two heavy suitcases in the back of a taxi. She remembered teasing her *renaissance* man that it had become too much of a comfort blanket for a world leader whose son had recently turned eight.

His lucky charm defence now rang in the guilt-ridden therapist's ears, taking a seat in the kitchen under the bright fluorescent strip. Had it been keeping the wanderer safe for all these years? The rip along the side seam had spread to almost ten centimetres in length; large enough to hide his wallet on crowded European streets, she could hear him say.

The treasured jacket had clocked up some miles; an interesting holiday project to set the children, the resourceful mother decided, imagining their enthusiasm for delving into past calendars to calculate the distance it had covered. She threaded a needle with dark brown cotton, as close a match in

254

colour as her stock offered the bronze *crêpe*-backed satin, before setting the sharp point down onto the table and picking one of her business cards from the box on the marble worktop.

Pausing for a moment to compose a message for the secret consignment, the adoring woman rested the end of her pen on her chin, bouncing its spring like a pensive child.

> "You are deep inside me. Hurry home soon. *Tu me manques, mon ami.* I love you, and *bon voyage.* JL - together, forever, wherever. Lynn, 14 Aug 1986, xxxx"

Smiling through her tears, the devoted wife slipped the card through the hole and nudged it down until it rested against the lower ribbing, between leather and lining. She stitched the two edges together in tiny cross-stitch, meaning this too as a statement of love.

'How long will it take you to find this?' she whispered to her faraway lover.

Working in the recording studio until after midnight, the mute telephone was beginning to torment the composer. It had only rung once since her checkpoint with their management company, sending her into a spin for no reason. She had narrowly avoided snapping at an innocent employee of their UK agent, whose only crime was to seek confirmation of some details about the upcoming *première* of "The Black Sheep".

Where was Jeff? What condition was he in? How was his fragile mental state holding up? All manner of disturbing images floated across the lonely woman's mind, ranging from the frightening to the sickening, and then to some forced delirious memories hand-picked from the last ten years to rescue her spiralling spirits. She refused to entertain the prospect that he was no longer alive, but what on Earth was preventing him from finding a telephone?

The security consultant who had visited *Escondido* this morning had faxed through an action plan which was cobbled together after conferring with various African contacts. Specifics were sparse notwithstanding, causing Lynn to push the flimsy curling paper to one side after a single read. Their preliminary conclusion was that the traveller was likely to be well outside the city by this time, held hostage somewhere in the vast *hinterland.* The fax also confirmed that no agency, newspaper or television channel had received reports of militant unrest or any ransom demands.

The Diamonds' personal assistant had been the absolute personification of rational discretion while she and Lynn updated each other on their daily agenda items, right up to the point of saying goodbye, when the poor woman burst into tears. Cathy had ended up being comforted by her boss, and not the other way around as intended. Gerry had also called four times during the evening, which both consoled and unnerved his client due to the increasingly worried tone she detected in his voice each time they spoke.

At shortly before two o'clock in the morning, the exhausted wife climbed into the king-sized bed and reached over to her husband's side, rubbing her hands across cool, smooth sheets. Wide awake, she could hold in the tears no longer, his photograph sandwiched between her chest and the sheet.

Lynn was woken by the telephone some four hours later. Making a frantic grab for the receiver in case the urgent sound interrupted her children's sweet dreams, she hoped with all her might to hear the molten, dusky tones of her missing man. There was a slight delay before the line activated, and optimism lit up her soul in anticipation.

'Hello?' she said for the second time.

'Missus Diamond?' a strong South African accent asked. 'Am I speaking with Missus Lynn Diamond?'

Her heart sank. No way would Jeff play tricks on her after this long. Rivulets flowed from her eyes as she gathered her composure.

'Who's this, please?' she replied, cupping her hand over the mouthpiece while she sniffed to clear her nose.

'Ah, hello there,' the man began again, awkward and officious. 'My name is Matthias Hendriksen. I'm calling from Addis Ababa, from BH Consulting. My agency has been engaged by Michael Maynard from Lion Security in connection with your husband's apparent disappearance.'

Lynn gulped down the lump in her throat. The words "husband" and "disappearance" in the same sentence chilled her to the bone. At least they had been kept apart with the word "apparent", although there was little doubt by now that said husband had well and truly disappeared. As if by magic, as her son, in his silly *"Comprendo* the Marvellous" act, often proclaimed with exaggerated flourish.

'Hello, Mister Hendriksen. Yes, it's Lynn Diamond here. Thanks for calling.'

'You're very welcome,' the caller replied. 'I'm afraid I don't have any specific news for you. I'll say that first up.'

'No,' the Olympian sighed. 'I thought as much. What's been going on over there?'

'Alright, now... We understand your husband... May I call him Jeff?'

'Definitely. And it's Lynn, please.'

'Good-oh. Thank you, Lynn,' Matthias continued. 'Our firm has spent several years investigating and conducting covert operations involving the Tigrayan People's Liberation Front. We have a great deal of expertise and intelligence about the cells operating in the region, and my men are currently using every means at our disposal to find out whether these groups are likely to have taken Jeff as a hostage.'

'Thanks very much. I'm familiar with the TPLF. Is this something they do regularly?' Lynn asked, calmed by the extra authority conveyed by his clipped, matter-of-fact accent.

'From time to time, yes,' Matthias affirmed. 'There aren't many high-profile people who come here, you understand. Jeff Diamond would be a huge prize for them.'

Again, the stalwart sportswoman's blood froze. 'What does that mean? Prize in what sense?'

'A bargaining tool. I apologise if I sound overly brutal. I've been in this business a long time. I tend to lose sight of the fact that my clients have not. I'm sorry.'

Switching on the bedside lamp and reaching for a notepad, Lynn held back tears. 'It's all good. I understand. Please carry on.'

'Well, let's see… We know of a few safe-houses that the TPLF keeps. We can make some enquiries today, if you give us the say-so,' the consultant continued. 'Nothing too obvious. As you'll understand, the TPLF has several factions. They also enjoy the sympathies of many other African countries' rebels in terms of their goals. However, their methods are not generally approved of.'

'Yes, I know,' the longstanding campaigner responded. 'That's pretty much why Jeff's over there. He's looking for a peaceful solution.'

Her emotions welled up inside, and her chest tightened. Had they been too naïve to assume a peaceful solution were possible? Did this distant goal warrant such sustained personal sacrifice? Had they bitten off too much? She had been comfortable all known risks were mitigated to their fullest, yet this illusion of preparedness now seemed pretty unreliable. The cause was noble, and a solution greatly needed, but was it worth losing her soul-mate over? What did they owe the African people that they had to donate their lives?

'Can you hear me, Lynn?' the monotone voice asked over a line which clicked and crackled as if a hundred electronic ears were tapping in. 'Are you still there?'

'Yes. Sorry, Matthias. I'm here,' she cleared her throat. 'Anything you can find out would be fantastic. Do you need me to authorise anything?'

The South African coughed. 'Actually, I do. If you can give me a number, I'll send you through a fax for your signature. It's an indemnity form.'

'Right,' Lynn muttered. 'Of course.'

She rattled off *Escondido*'s fax number, which the caller wrote down and then read back. Regardless whether BH Consulting found their multi-millionnaire rock star or not, their arses were covered. She would pay their fee for their target's return, either vertical or horizontal.

The patient woman imagined how Jeff's blood would boil at this unnecessary piece of *administrivia*, but there was no point in objecting. Any form of assistance was invaluable after more than twenty-four hours with no news, and amid both actual and metaphorical darkness, a new team of qualified and indemnified consultants was her best hope.

'Before you go... Please could you tell me,' Lynn started, heart thumping. 'No, well... Maybe I don't want to know...'

'What's that?'

'In your experience, if Jeff *is* being held hostage somewhere, what are the chances of him being returned alive?'

Matthias stifled a pompous chuckle. 'Oh, I can't possibly answer that to your satisfaction, m'lady. Quite good, I would hope. It all depends on whether they make any demands you're not prepared to meet. And we have no idea what those demands might be as yet.'

'Money, obviously?'

'Yes. Or passage through certain land divisions; release of their prisoners. Or a combination of all these. One thing I can tell you is that someone such as your husband would be treated well. If they're going to use him as exchange... currency, if you will... it's in their interest to protect him, feed him, *et cetera*. I very much doubt they would've harmed him at this stage.'

An impulsive and premature slither of hope migrated from the young wife's heart towards her brain. At this stage... These three innocuous words held so many troublesome possibilities.

'Thank you. We just have to wait then, I suppose. Either for them to contact us, or for your intelligence to turn something up.'

'Indeed,' the consultant affirmed. 'I'm sure we shall... And rest assured, Lynn, we'll be in touch as soon as we have anything to report.'

By now even more worried, the Australian thanked the man again, entertaining herself by selecting a face to match his voice. 'Thank you again. Do you have our business manager's name and number? I'm booked to fly to Sydney and back today, so I'll be out of contact at various points in the day. Gerry Blake?'

'I do,' the South African confirmed. 'You need to carry on as normal, I assume, given your standing with the general public. A good idea, madam. Any sniff of unease filtering through will strengthen their resolve. I don't have to tell you these things. You have been well advised by Maynard, I'm sure.'

A wry smile spread across Lynn's face. How little this patronising man knew about the type of people whose payroll he was about to join... He was not dealing with teenybopper pop stars with more money than sense. He was being tasked with repatriating one of the planet's most effective catalysts of peace, prosperity and progress.

'Thanks,' she said once again. 'I'll speak to you later, at some point. Thanks for calling, Matthias.'

'My pleasure, m'lady. Have a safe trip. Stay positive. Goodbye for now.'

Lynn placed the receiver back on its hook and headed for the *en suite*, where she jumped into the shower and opened the water jets to full bore. Reflecting on the serious conversation, she was surprised by the extent to which Jeff had influenced her own mind. Perhaps she oughtn't to risk orphaning their children. How ironic it would be for him to be found alive and well, only to discover that she had perished in the first ever Qantas air crash!

Stop it, she urged her vivid imagination. *It won't happen.*

Jet and Kierney's little hands waved nineteen to the dozen as their mother left through the school gates the following morning. She climbed back into the car, taking a deep breath to steady her conflicted heart. Persecuted by the remote likelihood of coming to grief between Melbourne and Sydney, she had considered cancelling her flight and staying at home.

Also haunted by her need to avoid arousing suspicion, she had stuck to the original plan and dropped the kids off on her way to the airport. As she had done countless times before, she would pick them up again at the end of the day, having flown almost two thousand kilometres while they crammed their minds full of new learning.

The nocturnal call from Ethiopia still played on the star's mind, but Matthias Hendriksen had given her some hope. She agreed that her husband was too precious a gift to squander, even for the most disorganised and anarchistic of bounty hunters.

***

'What the fuck?' Jeff shouted, receiving a sharp jab to the base of his skull from something solid and angular, which he surmised was the butt of a shotgun.

'Wake up, Mister Diamond,' sneered a man whom the captive had not seen before. 'It's breakfast time.'

A chipped plate was wafted under the Australian's nose, covered with an unsightly mound of fried eggs and cured meat, two hunks of white bread and a bent fork. It smelled delicious! Damned wonderful actually, he thought, acknowledging his hunger after a restless night.

Watching the cheerless deliveryman storm out of the room, the hostage stretched and sat straight, fed up with sleeping in stale clothes. He lifted his fork and began to eat, monitored by his gun-toting companion, who had cowered in front of the bad-tempered waiter.

'Cheers, mate,' Jeff smiled. 'You had any yet?'

The young man shook his head. The pair had become well acquainted during the dark hours. An engineering student from Namibia, Thomas had been recruited into the Ethiopian Peoples Revolutionary Party after failing to secure a real job after graduating. Joining a low-grade terrorist troop was a common way to earn easy money, the celebrity had been told, not to mention the free supply of women and copious quantities of alcohol on the rare occasion when he wasn't at the leader's beck and call.

By contrast, the group's special guest had been asked few questions, consequently saved from divulging too many details about his mission in Ethiopia or his profusive lifestyle. In consequence, his first night in this hostile environment passed in relative tranquillity, and the spectre of Rasul's mind-games had receded enough for him to snatch the odd bout of sleep.

His watch said seven-forty; three-forty in the afternoon in Melbourne. No... Sydney, Jeff corrected himself. It was Thursday, and as far as he could remember, his wife would be recording a show and two separate television interviews in his hometown.

How was his dream girl bearing up? What was happening in *Escondido* while he was away? It seemed like an eternity since he left. What had she told the children? And everyone else, for that matter? As worrying as it was for him to be ignorant of his fate, ignorance on top of distance must be far, far worse for Lynn. He knew his half of their stupendous partnership wasn't dead, but did she?

During the night, at each change of watchman, Jeff had issued a request to see Dennis or to use the telephone. His persistent appeals were denied at first, but as the hours ticked by, his guards' responses became less hostile and even a little sympathetic. It was only a matter of time, he assured the voices in his head, although patience had never been their strong suit.

The boy from Canley Vale consoled himself with the knowledge that challenges endured early in his life had turned out to be the perfect preparation for his current status. These men, even Rasul, couldn't mess with his mind anywhere near as well as it could mess with itself.

The guard had fallen asleep several times overnight too, with his ridiculous, toylike machine gun still resting atop long, splayed legs. In the dim light from an antique standard lamp, Jeff used these brief opportunities to stretch his limbs and search for any items which might prove useful later on. He found no telephone in the room. However, he did come across a directory and set about flicking through for a listing of local hospitals. He had torn the relevant page out millimetre by silent millimetre, folded it in quarters and hid it inside his shirt.

Where was he being held? The throbbing in his right shoulder had given way to a dull ache, and his fingers pressed the tender area in an effort to determine if the bone might knit back together in roughly the proper place. He gave thanks for his sexy personal trainer's diligence in ensuring he maintain full fitness for his punishing schedule, since the muscle control in his upper body would save this temporary injury from becoming a permanent disability.

The musician had no idea how far they had driven and in which direction. What he hoped to find was a sheet of letterhead for the old farm or a utility bill, if they even had this sort of metering in Ethiopia... On reflection, the place was more likely to be powered by generators. Local newspaper, in that case? Anything to give him a reference point. It might be days before these blokes decided to make their demands known, and he couldn't be sure his injured driver still had days to play with.

Again harking back to his misspent youth, where he had honed his stealth by creeping in and out of girls' bedroom windows and around his own flat when trying to avoid his stoned parents, the prisoner opened every drawer in the old mahogany desk. The sum total of loot was a few packets of cigarettes and a plastic bag of disposable lighters. He slipped a couple of each inside his shirt for safekeeping and continued his plunder, at least confident of staving off one of his addictions in the short term.

His last circuit came to an abrupt end when the lid of the discarded piano stool complained with a noisy squeak, waking Thomas with a start. The rifle fell to the floor with an even louder clatter, which brought two other bug-eyed rebels shuffling into the room. The Oscar-winning actor straightened up and looked them in the eyes, having shovelled the small pile of manuscript books from the top compartment of the stool into the crook of his right elbow. He pretended to investigate their contents, his body language declaring an artistic innocence.

Embarrassed, Jeff's guard jumped to his feet and sprinted across the room, snatching the items out of his prisoner's hands and tossing them on top of the upright piano. 'What are you doing?'

'Just snooping around. Professional research, Thomas. Y'know…'

The others cackled, diffusing the tension in the air. An eccentric scene unfolded in the old manor house, miles from nowhere and in the middle of the night, as the superstar songwriter took a seat at the piano and brushed a thick layer of dust off the keys. Sneezing three times in quick succession, he reached for the sheet music again. This time, no-one stopped him.

What a peculiar situation; a chance to be grateful for his superficial showbusiness career! If he were an accountant like his old mate Gerry, which excuse could he have used for being caught spying in an EPRP safe-house? Something else to tell his family once he made it back to Melbourne.

So now, in the bright light of morning and having polished off a rather tasty breakfast, the determined performer returned to the keyboard to resume his quest. He leafed through each book one by one, unsupervised and undetected, until a veritable gift jumped out at him. *L'Ecole de Saint Jacques*, Wonji, he read from a music certificate belonging to a certain Daniel Dibaba. Wordlessly, he congratulated the youngster on his achievement and conveyed his sincere thanks for leaving such a vital clue among his collection of sheet music. Shivering a little at the spooky circumstance, he wondered where this boy might have gone and how old he was, hoping he was still capable of playing an instrument.

Another swift examination complete, he selected one of the books and creased its spine back on the music stand. His brain's memory was much stronger than that of his muscles, the fatigue of physical stress like a long-lost friend despite having been consigned to his mind's furthest shelf for some years. His fingers were stiff from three days of atypical inactivity, and the piano echoed chords which were distinctly out of tune.

When the musician looked over his shoulder, he found that Thomas had left the room. Strong cooking smells wafting through from the hallway suggested his kidnappers were partaking of their own piles of Ethiopian-style bacon and eggs. His audience now comprised Rasul and another man whom he recognised from the day before.

Unbeknown to his uncouth crowd, the tunes Jeff picked out were not written on the staves in front of his eyes. Rather, they were old favourites which came to mind as he imagined his wife and children sitting at home, waiting for him to make contact. Desperation and longing coursed through him like torrents until he was forced to stop, unwilling to alert his captors to another deep-set vulnerability. The men clapped with enthusiasm at the music's abrupt end, even calling out for more.

The star bowed in jest but closed the lid over the keyboard with an emphatic slam. 'Not today, gentlemen,' he said. 'These are not circumstances conducive to my best performance. I hope you understand.'

'You will play,' the man who was not Rasul let out a menacing laugh, lifted his weapon and trained it on their minstrel.

In defiance of the stupid gesture, the Australian carried on walking until he reached the couch where he had spent the night. The gun sight tracked his path for the first few steps, before the rebel leader raised his arm and brought an authoritative hand down on the long, slim barrel, pointing it towards the floor.

Jeff kept his eyes fixed on the scuffed boards, saying nothing. The cigarette packets and lighters loose inside his shirt now came to rest against the waistband of his jeans. A post-breakfast nicotine hit would do wonders for his constitution.

'How's Dennis this morning?' he asked, fixing Rasul with an imperious frown. 'And any chance I can have a shower, please?'

The man with the golden teeth dealt his famous hostage a blank stare, giving the impression that the concept of personal hygiene was new to him. Judging by the pungent aroma permeating the room, this omission might well have been widespread among the EPRP membership.

However, to the multi-millionnaire's surprise, Rasul nodded to his subordinate. 'Take him,' he grunted. 'Wait outside. Ten minutes only.'

'Thanks. And Dennis? Can I see him, please?'

'Up!' the mean-looking man ordered again, unwilling to enter into a discussion about the driver.

This reaction induced an instant violent headache for the Australian, a mixture of sadness, anger and fear blending in his heart. Perhaps the poor guy had died after all... If so, this was a terrible by-product of his fight for these people's freedom, and yet another ghost he was destined to cart around for the rest of his life. Further proof that there was no such thing as a benevolent god. Nonetheless keen to clean himself up, he rose to his feet and followed the guard's instructions.

Out of the top dog's earshot, Jeff questioned his new minder about the wounded driver's condition and whereabouts.

'He is alive, Mister Diamond,' the young man's reply was tentative, dropping his former surly *façade*. 'It is good that you care for him. I will tell him.'

Very relieved, the thirty-four-year-old gave the man a wide grin. 'Cheers, mate. What's your name?'

'Femi.'

'From Nigeria? Olufemi?'

The lad nodded. The Afriquofile had identified him as more representative of western African tribes than his gang-mates. A good five years younger than the rest; taller and thinner too. Another gap-year mercenary making some fast cash for his village.

The pair climbed a majestic single-flight staircase and passed four bedrooms, all of which were littered with dark, military style clothing and other personal effects. At the far end of the corridor, Femi pushed a door open to reveal a large bathroom with old-fashioned cast iron fittings. A selection of towels were scattered in damp piles. Jeff presumed it wasn't worth asking for a clean one, so he thanked his guard and entered for his allocated ten minutes of solitude.

Once alone behind a closed door, the hostage's first thought was to check the windows. Of course they were nailed to their frames in several places, offering no avenue of escape. After checking the latch was shut firm and in the process of undoing his shirt buttons, he noticed a two-centimetre opening between the bottom of the door and the floor tiles.

With immediate and striking clarity, Jeff was transported back in time to his adolescent days in his family's pokey western-Sydney rented tenement, when taking a shower or a shit were the only times he ever had to himself. No lock here either, meaning he might be interrupted at any moment; a further reminder of those precocious teenage years. He was no longer surprised at how his life took him in constant circles.

Bundling his jeans and shirt together and shoving them into the aperture to prevent any disturbance while he did what boys did in the shower, the tearaway was once again up to his old tricks. If anyone tried to push the door, the bulky clothing would become wedged, making it harder to slide and giving him extra valuable seconds to cover himself.

Jeff's penis hardened as soon as the cool water humidified the air around his body, a temporary distraction from the man waiting on the other side. His balls had been burning for the past twenty-four hours with the insistence of an overdue ejaculation. After all, he had spent the night lost in thoughts of his dream girl in various states of undress and many passionate embraces, attempting to relax and pass the time.

Selecting four cigarettes and a lighter from his secret stash, the celebrity stepped into a tiled stall dating from the same vintage as his childhood home. He turned the taps as far as they would open and became thirteen again. In the days between his father's longest and last prison sentence and his mother's lonely, lingering death, the lost boy's routine used to unfold this way every morning and every evening as an unending effort to snap out of the deep depression which had gripped him for as long as he could remember.

Hearing nothing from outside the bathroom and relishing the weak stream of lukewarm water running down his back and over his shoulders, he was treated to a fond memory of the time he tried to smoke three cigarettes at once and had nearly fainted! Today he would light only two at once, in honour of those days best forgotten.

The aroused man pursed his lips around the pair of bent, white sticks of tobacco and lit them with an elongated flame, beginning to stroke his shaft in a firm rhythm. He didn't have much time to waste on enticing fantasies. The drug raced to his brain, and the thirty-three-year-old mind's eye glanced downwards at Lynn's smiling face, imagining her mouth swallowing his erection, red lipstick smeared along its size. Her tongue caressed its tip, speeding up and slowing down at will and in response to his every tell-tale murmur or movement. Her hands crept up his buttocks and across the small of his back, before sweeping past his hip to grasp him hard while she straightened up to enjoy a kiss.

'Hey, angel. Christ, I wish you were here,' Jeff said into the shower's stream. 'We're both still alive. I'll be out of here soon. I love you so much.'

***

'I'm OK, Gerry. Really!' Lynn smiled, pushing the insistent man off the doorstep in fun.

'Whatever you say, Missus D,' her husband's oldest friend agreed with reluctance born of several sources. 'But you'll never know what you're missing.'

The lady of the house kissed her visitor's stubbly cheek. 'Whatever indeed,' she giggled. 'I'm sure I won't. Drive safely. See you in the office at nine-thirty.'

The Diamonds' manager waved and let himself out through the courtyard door. He was amazed at how well his mate's wife was coping, given that three days had passed since the great man had gone missing. He had arrived at *Escondido* for dinner while she had been in the throes of breaking the news to the children. Then they had all held a similar meeting with the family's drivers and nannies, stressing the importance of keeping their collective mouths shut. Luckily, the approaching weekend afforded the young mum much better control over the children's interactions.

'But how can we find out where Dad is?' Jet had asked.

'That's the problem, Jetto. It's a big country with heaps of open space, where you can drive for ages without seeing another person or car. It's very easy to hide people in a place like that, just like in the bush here. But he'll be alright. We just need to stay as patient as we can.'

Kierney had jumped onto her mother's lap, determined not to cry. Even Uncle Gerry, the emotional agnostic, recognised the little girl struggling with the fact that her daddy might have been taken prisoner. The sight of Lynn comforting each child in a different way evoked surprising jealousy for their closeness at a time like this, along with gratitude for her constancy during the last few harrowing days.

The *trio* of childminders were shocked, to say the least. They were full of questions too, most of which neither their employer nor her manager had the means to answer. Clear on the consequences of any leaks to the press in terms of losing their jobs, they had promised not to breathe a word to anyone, before disappearing to their accommodation in a huddle of whispers.

With the youngsters in bed, the staff off duty and her chaperone departed after much protestation, the Olympian headed back into the office to check for any inbound *communiqués*. Nothing. Increasingly though, she realised she no longer had such a feeling of dread. Either she was learning how to deal with the uncertainty or the couple's famed invisible elastic connection was trying to tell her that all was not lost.

She hoped for the latter, but expected the former; a trait she had picked up from her wise, old soul-mate.

In part, Lynn was also sick and tired of imagining Jeff in ways described by their security consultants. Mike and his colleagues had recounted kidnapping cases where the hostages had been beaten, bound and gagged, left for days to lay in their own bodily fluids. She failed to appreciate the value of going into such graphic detail, expecting their son to derive considerable grotesque pleasure from this information once their ordeal were over.

Of greater concern to the loving wife were the probable psychological effects of incarceration: the interminable speculative hours, not knowing what fate was likely to befall him or when. Even these days, languishing in relative stability, the traumatised youth still occupying the world-changer's deeper recesses would find the loss of control difficult to withstand. Despite a decade of practice having taught him to widen his circle of trust outside his saviour and their manager, this situation would present as a substantial test.

Without doubt, the tortured nineteen-year-old Lynn had met all those years ago had changed almost beyond recognition since they had been together, to the point where she often forgot the obsessive-compulsive behaviour he had fought to hide and the horrific, violent nightmares which used to plague them night after night. Might the door demons return with him to *Escondido*, or would imaginary gun-wielding kidnappers take their place?

How quickly could the lovers' meticulously cultivated healing process be undone? The compassionate sportswoman wondered how this interruption would affect her ambitious partner when he arrived home, and how they might deal with its aftermath now they had a family too? The depression which had engulfed him over Christmas and the New Year had been manageable, but this current episode had the potential to change her cavalier intellectual back into the unpredictable and angry neurotic they had succeeded in leaving behind.

Stop with the drama already, Lynn scolded herself with a well-worn expression of her gorgeous husband's to decry the overreactions of his past. This may not be a hostage situation at all. There were numerous other possible explanations. Had he been in a car accident and lost his memory? Was he in a coma? Try as she might, these less sensational *scenaria* remained incredible to the intelligent, broadminded woman. Jeff Diamond's face was recognisable almost all over the world. Even if he no longer knew who he was, it was likely that those around him would.

Therefore, the most plausible eventuality was that the superstar, along with anyone else with him at the time, had fallen victim to an accident or illness somewhere isolated and inaccessible. His itinerary had included a long drive in a lone vehicle with an unarmed driver over remote country roads. The stay-at-home half of the Midas couple was yet to hear from the Ethiopian government or the TPLF headquarters as to whether her husband had arrived at his pre-arranged appointment with Jemal Mehretu. If he hadn't, it ought to be feasible to mount a search based on a straight-ish line between Bole International Airport in Addis Ababa and wherever the group's stronghold was located.

The only thing about which the devoted wife was unequivocal was that her man was still breathing. Somehow, she convinced herself, she would know if he were not. She left their children with this positive thought at bedtime, clinging to the same friable twig while she settled down for her third night as the sole occupant of their king-sized bed.

Tomorrow was another day. A Saturday, in fact. Such a day filled with sporting and music activities for the kids normally flew fly by in no time, and the busy mother would be afforded scant occasion to dwell on her mysterious misery while ferrying Jet and Kierney between one event and the next.

Lynn must have fallen asleep soon after she turned the light out, not stirring until dawn. Another sign, she figured, that everything would turn out alright. She became aware of someone looming large at her bedside, staring at her face. The soft breath was willing her to wake up.

'Hey, Kizzo,' she smiled, pulling a hand out from underneath the sheet and running her fingers across the little girl's tear-streaked cheek. 'What's the matter? Are you scared for *Papá*?'

The seven-year-old nodded, her lip wobbling. With loneliness tugging at her own heartstrings, the compassionate parent invited her to climb into bed, and Jeff Diamond's two angels lay side-by-side to shed their tears together. After five minutes, Kierney had calmed down enough to agree to make breakfast while her lazy brother slept on, racing down the stairs after her mother, full of beans.

As predicted, staying busy helped everyone's day go faster. Granted their freedom, the nannies had taken the train into the city, with only two planning to return for dinner. Anxious for news, Lynn rushed into the office at the first opportunity, having been struck by another, fresh batch of nerves. Had something happened while they had been out?

The light on the answering machine flashed in earnest, sending the tennis champion's heart into her throat. Before listening to the message, she closed and locked the door, not wishing the children to burst in and hear anything she was not prepared for them to hear. Her finger pressed the "Play" button, her mind racing while the tape rewound.

'Missus Diamond,' she recognised the voice of Matthias Hendriksen. 'Good afternoon. It's Saturday morning here in Addis Ababa. Afternoon with you. I trust you're well.'

'Get on with it,' the young woman cursed at the machine in the manner of her impatient *paramour*. 'Enough with the niceties. *Gimme* some goddamned information.'

He did. 'Firstly, there are no reports of any deaths in the area. With the TPLF, we would expect to be alerted fairly soon if anyone had been killed, which suggests your husband's still with us.'

Excellent, Lynn thought. Good start, at any rate.

'Secondly, Jemal Mehretu's assistant confirmed his appointment with your husband was not kept, although he was somewhat cagey when asked if he knew the reason why it didn't take place. We're looking further into this now. Our colleagues in the local police force have furnished us with a list of buildings that affiliates of the TPLF have used in the past, and our avenues of enquiry are leading us to a few of these.

'But Lynn,' the message continued, 'our most concrete piece of intel' is that a burned-out vehicle has been found on the side of the road branching off the main highway going south-east from Addis. It's possible this was the car your husband was travelling in.'

Engulfed by a sudden nausea, the blonde superstar dragged her office chair across the floorboards and sat down, pressing "Pause" on the answering machine. Burned-out vehicle? This didn't sound too promising. Maybe her instincts were off the mark after all. She released the button to restart the tape and listened to the rest of Matthias' message again, scribbling down the salient points for Gerry and Cathy.

'The police are examining the vehicle as we speak, and I'll be checking back in with them very soon. It's not clear whether the fire happened as a result of a collision or through running off the road somehow, or if the vehicle was set alight afterwards. And it'll be some time before we know. I'm sorry not to be more definite. That's all we've got so far. Call me anytime. Talk soon. Thank you.'

Lynn remained seated with her head in her hands for a few minutes, digesting the various snippets of information. Would she ring the man from BH Consulting back first, or bring their loyal manager up to speed? Or neither? Why bother Gerry further if there was no certainty that the incinerated car and Jeff were linked? She dialled the security consultant's number.

'Hendriksen,' the voice at the other end snapped.

'Matthias, it's Lynn Diamond.'

'Oh, good, good,' he responded. 'Nice to hear from you, Missus Diamond. How are you? I assume you've listened to my message.'

'Yes, I have, and I'm well, thanks. Thank you for the update. Have there been any developments since?'

'No. Not as such.'

'What do you mean by that?' she asked, thinking this reply sounded rather cryptic. 'Not as such?'

A pause and a sigh drifted through the tiny speaker, and again the nervous woman's heart began to beat faster.

'Lynn, we now think there's a very good chance the car on the side of the road... just off Highway One, which is a new road still under construction in many sections... is the one Jeff was travelling in.'

'OK,' she sighed. 'How can you tell?'

'The vehicle's licensed to a man by the name of Dennis Negatu. We believe he was your husband's driver.'

'Mmm...' the singer murmured. 'The driver he had at the beginning of the week was called Dennis. You're right about that. Jeff always makes a point of using people's first names. So do you know any more about the accident?'

'Yes, we do,' Matthias was nervous too. 'Is there anyone with you, Lynn?'

Ominous words indeed... The loving mother pictured the small angelic creatures who were busy helping the nannies to make dinner, a tear escaping from her right eye.

'Our children and their childminders. Why?'

'What about Mister Blake?' Hendriksen pressed. 'Have you been in touch with him lately?'

'No. I was planning to ring him after I spoke to you,' Lynn answered, feeling more and more like a child on the receiving end of a parental lecture on self-preservation.

'I suggest you might appreciate some adult company tonight,' the snobbish voice was doing its best to sound comforting. 'There were several bullet holes in the bodywork of the four-wheel drive. While there's no sign of the passengers, it's possible they may have been injured.'

'Oh, my God…' this shocking revelation hit the caller squarely between the eyes. 'I see. And no clues as to where they might've gone? If they were by themselves or taken somewhere by someone?'

Aware she was rambling, the supreme organiser's heart was as heavy as her son's cricket bag. She had no reason to believe the consultant's advice was anything but sound.

'No,' Matthias affirmed. 'I'm sorry. We assume the car must've rolled over. The roof is severely dented, and the windscreen's smashed. My gut feel is they weren't alone, and whoever was there with them set the vehicle on fire afterwards, to disguise what happened. That's our best guess at this stage.'

'OK. Thanks. At least they didn't burn to death. I couldn't think of anything worse.'

The ingratiating South African whistled. 'I agree, but you can breathe easy. Your husband didn't suffer this fate.'

'So if this does turn out to be the car he was travelling in…' Lynn thought aloud. 'We still don't know that for sure, do we?'

'No, madam. Not at this point anyway. We'll carry on working here. You need to contact Mister Blake and stay near the 'phone. As soon as we have any more news, we'll be in touch.'

'Thank you, Matthias. I'll do that. Thanks for all your help. To your team too.'

'You're most welcome,' the consultant said. 'Good evening.'

'Good evening,' the young woman lied, pressing the button to terminate the call.

The distraught wife checked the clock, her fingers already dialling Gerry's Toorak residence. To her relief, he answered.

'Hi, Gerry. It's only me.'

'Hello, only you. How are things? Is there news?'

'Sort of,' Lynn replied, her mind scrambling to reconstitute the story in the correct sequence.

The account of Matthias' information transferred, the Diamonds' business manager insisted he cancel his Saturday evening plans and join his Very Important Client *post haste*. She issued a strong objection, but the couple's longstanding caretaker refused to entertain any other option. He had been due to meet some mates at the MCG for a Sheffield Shield cricket match before adjourning to a nightclub, in typical party-boy style. On any normal weekend, Jeff would more than likely have joined him if he happened to be in the country.

Instead, the swashbuckling schmoozer swapped a night of drunken womanising for dinner with Lynn and the kids, all four eager for a happy ending and each expressing it in their own way. Jet was excitable and full of outrageous but optimistic scrapes from which his dad must escape, whereas Kierney was more concerned about what her father was thinking and whether he knew how much they missed him.

'Oh, he does know, darling,' their mother assured her husband's precious little gems. '*Papá* knows we miss him even if he's only gone for an hour. He'll be really missing us too. And we'll have heaps to talk about when he gets home, won't we?'

'Yes!' the boy yelled. 'He can tell us about what it's like for a car to roll over and over. And if the men had guns...'

'Shhh,' the patient teacher smiled. 'That's enough guesswork. It's not a war game, Jetto. Dad didn't want to be caught up in any fighting. You know he doesn't agree with that. We'll just keep hoping he can tell the security men where he is. Then they'll be able to get him out safely.'

'And Dennis the Menace,' Gerry added, waggling his finger at the boisterous eight-year-old.

'Yeah! Dennis the Menace,' Jet agreed with an evil laugh. 'I love Dennis the Menace!'

'No! Dennis the driver,' Kierney corrected her brother, seeking confirmation from Lynn.

'That's right, Kizzy. Although Uncle Gerry means Dennis the Menace, the cartoon character. So you're both right this time.'

Play To Your Strengths

The evening dragged for adults and children alike, so desperate were they to hear from anyone. They played board games and watched videos until they were bored with entertainment, at which point the youngsters cuddled into their mother and the volume of noise in the lounge room plummeted as they tuned in and out of the adults' conversation. At nine o'clock, Lynn took Jet and Kierney up to bed, all three sending best wishes and love to their doting dad, wherever he may be.

Downstairs, the accountant waited for his friend's stunning wife to return, leafing through the newspaper. Scanning the walls lined with a row of Omo tribeswomen whose paintings had been commissioned by the humanitarian couple, he pondered how it would feel to be kidnapped and to be kept away from everything one held dear. Although envious of the sense of belonging Jeff had acquired from creating a family, try as he might, the fun-loving executive couldn't envision himself in the same domestic bliss.

The successful businessman had avoided commitment all his life, with no real intention of changing now he was heading to the latter end of his thirties. The teenaged friendship struck with Jeff Diamond had its origins in chalking up as many drinks, sports and girls as they could claim, and not necessarily in that order.

The unlikely pair of students, one rich and one poor, had egged each other on and bailed each other out on occasions too numerous to mention. Yet since the one-and-only Lynn Dyson had disrupted the field of play, the North Sydney native had been relegated to the lone bachelor position. And now, sitting in the sumptuous *salon* which was home-sweet-home for this happy, successful and settled brood, the thought of never seeing his old mate again loomed calamitous on the horizon.

A feeling of impending loss overtook the party animal, who caught himself staring vacantly at the couple's wedding photograph, in pride of place on top of the polished, white grand piano. What a day that had been! The happiness which had erupted in and around the Dyson Administration building, and for weeks afterwards too, had been infectious and alluring, notwithstanding the pressure his own mother and sisters had heaped on him to follow suit.

271

In truth, the only woman Gerry ever saw himself loving was located upstairs in this very house. Lynn Dyson Diamond was quite the most adorable female specimen from every aspect; not only because she rendered his best mate so rapturously fulfilled, but also because she personified in equal parts angel and devil, an observation with which he and the ambitious Catholic Argentinean Polish Jew had enjoyed endless fantasies over bottles of whisky and brandy procured from his father's drinks cabinet in their mid-teens. Should anything terrible happen to the brilliant *lothario*, could he allow himself to think she might seek solace in his company?

'They're asleep,' the sportswoman announced, returning to the lounge room and breaking the spell.

Of course she wouldn't, the Irishman sniffed. There could be no other man for this woman, and her steadfastness only added to the attraction. Each as besotted as the other, Lynn Dyson and Jeff Diamond were the perfect match in every way. How dare he even entertain the sacrilegious idea?

'Good stuff. How are you going?'

'Oh, I'm OK. Dazed, I suppose, more than anything. I don't know whether to feign optimism in front of everyone here or just keep quiet and wait it out. It's horrible, isn't it, this not knowing? What about you? Where's your optimism metre pointing now?'

'Same,' Gerry agreed. 'Hard to know what to make of yesterday. I almost wish someone would come out of the woodwork with specific demands. At least then we'd have more to go on...'

'Yeah. Exactly. I'll fetch caffeine,' Lynn proposed. 'Put the TV on. A programme for adults and *sans* annoying, repetitive songs preferably.'

The executive chuckled, reaching forward to pick up the remote control from the shelf. His gorgeous host disappeared and returned five minutes later with a tray laden with hot coffee, milk, sugar and the all-important liqueurs. They sat watching the news and sipping their drinks for an hour, conversation growing sparse and stilted with each fruitless hour, peppered with random conjecture about the invisible man's predicament.

'He'd pay his own ransom, wouldn't he?' the couple's manager asked out of the blue.

The superstar looked up in surprise at the strange comment. 'What? I'm going with "Nope". That's nuts though anyway. Don't the people who extort money in this way want the publicity just as much as the money? If all we do is write them a cheque, and Jeff walks free, what do they gain?'

'Five years' supply of weapons and ammunition,' Gerry mused, 'or funds to create fake passports or whatever else they need to infiltrate and cause mayhem.'

'Hmm... Do you think Mister Mehretu knows what's happened?' Lynn wondered aloud, not expecting her companion to have an answer.

'No clue. I know nothing about the man. Yours respects him, but even he's been known to be wrong. Someone's got to break it to him one day, the arrogant prick.'

'Yeah,' the singer giggled. 'Bags not me! At least he's an arrogant prick with the best of motives. And from Mehretu's perspective, perhaps he's trying to find out if he can trust Jeff.'

Gerry gave her an incredulous look. 'By shooting at his car and setting it on fire? How does that work, pray?'

'By what he or we do in response to geopolitical acts,' the experienced diplomat expanded her theory. 'If we make a huge media splash, the TPLF might think twice about participating in the negotiations. But if we keep quiet and bide our time, they can assume our goals aren't self-serving.'

'Nice work,' her friend nodded his approval. 'Certainly a reasonable assumption. You're a smart woman, Missus D.'

She smiled. 'I'm honoured to receive such a gratuitous oxymoron from you, Mister B.'

The tall, curly-haired man scoffed, scooting across the couch to kiss the blonde's cheek. '*Touché*, you gorgeous thing. I've said this before, and I'm sure I'll say it again before long, but that good-for-nothing you married's a lucky, lucky bastard.'

'Thanks,' Lynn grinned, leaning back to avoid any further amorous advances. 'Let's hope his luck continues then. More?'

They refilled their coffee cups and shot glasses, and Gerry helped himself to a slimline cigar from his clients' sideboard treasure trove, also noting the bag of dark green *marijuana* leaves. If this vacuous situation were to continue into its fourth night, he resolved to garnish these illicit goods to assist with relaxation. Lighting the *cigarillo,* he offered the athlete first puff, which was accepted gladly. They discussed various other topics which had been sidelined by the day's horrors, having run out of constructive commentary relevant to the crisis at hand.

At five past midnight, both jumped out of their skins at the shrill warble of the telephone sitting on the table beside the visitor. The tennis champion opened her eyes and pounced on it.

'Hello?'

'Missus Diamond?' a familiar South African voice asked.

'Yes, Matthias. Lynn, please. What's new?'

The security expert sounded upbeat. 'We're not sure, but we think we may have stumbled across a clue.'

'Great,' the sportswoman paused, giving her guest a bright smile. 'What's that?'

'A man's been brought to a hospital in the Adama district,' the caller explained. 'He has head and ribcage injuries and a broken ankle but nothing life-threatening, as far as they knew. The staff say he was dumped outside the Emergency department, in a driveway for ambulances to offload patients.'

'Is it Jeff?'

'No,' Matthias replied in a more solemn tone. 'He's a black man, forty or so years old. He's incoherent but had two pieces of paper tucked inside his shirt.'

'Oh,' the dejected woman sighed. 'The driver?'

'We think so. One was a page that'd been torn out of the 'phone book, listing the local hospitals, and the other was some sort of child's music award from a school in Wonji, which is in the right direction from where the burned-out car was driving.'

The businessman, who had disappeared into the kitchen to pick up the other telephone, butted in on the conversation. 'Mister Hendriksen, this is Gerry Blake, the Diamonds' manager.'

'Oh, good evening, Mister Blake,' the consultant acknowledged. 'I'm pleased the lady has some company. Did you hear what I was saying?'

'Most of it, yes,' the executive affirmed, imagining the capable woman in the room next-door bristling at the patronising attitude. 'So you think my client may be somewhere in this Wonji district, wherever that is?'

'Possible...' Matthias became more forthright now he was speaking to someone a little more removed from the situation. 'It's grazing country, low-lying. We're still talking about a large radius, and it could be spurious of course. But we have assumed this man is Dennis Negatu, Jeff's driver.'

'Isn't he carrying any ID?' Lynn interrupted. 'You can't tell for sure?'

The security agent took a deep breath. 'No, m'lady. His pockets are apparently empty. The good thing is his injuries are minor, and the hospital believes he'll regain consciousness after they hook him up to a drip. He's severely dehydrated and probably hasn't eaten for a couple of days.'

'And Jeff?' Gerry asked on behalf of the lonely, selfless woman sitting in the other room.

'I bet he hid the pieces of paper in Dennis' shirt,' she ruminated. 'It's something he'd do. Perhaps he's in the same place. This Wonji? Is that possible too?'

'Yes, Lynn. It is indeed possible,' Matthias agreed. 'We've sent our men to the area right now to conduct a search. We can't make too close an advance however. They could do something rash if they think they're being watched. Do you understand?'

Australia's darling shook her head at the caller's demeaning manner but said nothing. Fortunately, she didn't have to.

'Lynn understands,' the indomitable one stated for the record. 'Please, Mister Hendriksen. This is no ordinary woman you're talking to here. Lynn, are you OK?'

'I apologise, Missus Diamond. I'd hate to have any misunderstandings or convey unrealistic expectations. The situation may get volatile and...'

'I understand, Matthias,' the patient wife insisted. 'It's fine. And I'm good, thanks, Gerry. So what now?'

'Sit tight,' was the consultant's simple piece of advice. 'As soon as there's anything further to tell you, I'll be back on the line. Be prepared though... We only have a few hours of daylight left.'

The call terminated, and the accountant jogged into the lounge room to find his client pacing around in circles. He moved to embrace her, and they stood together to absorb the news, wondering what to do for the best.

Before they had the chance to come to any conclusions, the telephone rang again. Gerry pointed to it with one hand and to his own chest with the other.

'No,' the blonde shook her head, pointing to her guest's unfinished brandy on the coffee table instead. 'I'll get it. Hello?'

'Yes. Good evening. It's Matthias again, Lynn.'

'Hi.'

'A ransom demand has been made,' the curt South African announced.

The Olympian repeated the short sentence to her companion, who turned tail and retreated to the kitchen extension. Anxious, she sat down on the couch, her head spinning with the prospect of having to make the ultimate tough call. Throughout their married life, Jeff and she had remained adamant that they shouldn't bargain for each other if any such circumstance were to arise.

In her present state of despondency, Lynn failed to recall why on Earth they had come to this decision. 'How?' she asked, delaying the inevitable. 'By whom?'

'Not clear, but we think it's an affiliation of the Ethiopian People's Revolutionary Party, a paramilitary off-shoot of the TPLF,' Hendriksen clarified. 'They've splintered away from the main political, anti-Derg movement in recent times.'

'What do they stand for?' Lynn asked. 'This Ethiopian People's Revolution... whatever you said?'

'Why do you need to know that?' the family's manager yelled from the kitchen. 'It doesn't matter what it means, surely?'

'People's Revolutionary Party,' the South African humoured his client. 'They're a Marxist rebel group. They have a history of small-scale bombings and random attacks mainly, but from time to time they engage in *guerrilla* warfare. They don't necessarily see eye-to-eye with the mainstream TPLF. My view is they've found out your husband was meeting with Mehretu and decided to sabotage it.'

The young ·woman sighed. 'That's good information, thanks. For what reason, I wonder? Guys, I'm going to try to ring Mister Mehretu now. I've met him, and we have a telephone number for him here. I can see if he's aware of what's going on and ask him to step in.'

'Lynn, are you fucking crazy?' Gerry exclaimed, all normal protocols abandoned. 'What if they're on the same side and not on Jeff's? What if Hendriksen's intelligence is flawed?'

'Is your intelligence flawed, Matthias?' the headstrong champion challenged.

'Well, no. I'm at least confident of these facts,' the consultant hesitated, laughing at the unexpected tangent on which their three-way conversation had veered. 'Do you really think you could get through to him directly?'

'Probably not, but it's worth a try. Unless you think it's too risky.'

'No. On the contrary. I think it's a very courageous thing to try,' Matthias replied, with genuine appreciation. 'I'll get off the 'phone and look forward to the next time we speak.'

This second call finished, with both wife and business manager setting off from their respective telephones and running down the corridor to the large office. Gerry gazed around at the complicated array of technology in the domestic study, having not set foot in this room for a year or so. He tapped the surface of the desk while Lynn searched for the rebel leader's number.

After a minute or two, she unclipped the metal rings which bound the file's documents together, removed a sheet of paper and waved it in the air.

'Here goes!' she shrugged, eyes wide open. 'Nothing ventured… It's what Jeff would do in the same position. I need to take action, Gerry. I can't hold off in the hope someone else'll come up with a better plan. It's the only plan we've got.'

Dumbfounded, the executive was full of admiration. 'You're amazing! Brave as… I'm just a lowly accountant, Lynn. I add up numbers, take them away and then write a report. You guys are the ones who know how to live. I only hope you're right.'

'Me too,' the thirty-year-old pulled a scared face.

The line connected without issue, and the rear-end of the most powerful pantomime horse in the world heard it ringing in a series of modern beeps. Four cycles later, a woman's voice repeated the telephone number in a garbled accent.

'Good afternoon,' the star began, her eyes informing the awestruck manager that contact had been made. 'Is this the residence of Mister Jemal Mehretu?'

'Who is this calling, please?' the woman enquired in return, polite and less hurried.

'My name is Lynn Diamond. I'd like to speak to Mister Mehretu about a meeting my husband was supposed to have with him on Thursday. Jeff Diamond, from Australia.'

Gerry sank down into the soft leather cushions beside his old friend's wife. "Jeff Diamond, from Australia," she had said, as if she were the dry cleaners' assistant wishing to notify a customer that his suits were ready for collection. These two successful celebrities were made of the same stern stuff, he concluded. They would stop at nothing to achieve their goals.

After a protracted span of dead air, the practised diplomat discerned a man's voice in the distance, approaching the telephone.

'Hello? This is Mehretu.'

'Oh, Mister Mehretu,' the caller almost sang, unsure whether she recognised the accent or not. 'How are you? This is Lynn Diamond. We met in Zambia last year.'

'Yes, Missus Diamond. That is true,' a friendlier tone continued. 'It was my absolute pleasure. And how are you?'

'Well… We've had a distressing few days, to be honest. I need your help to find out what's happened to Jeff. He didn't attend your meeting the other day, I believe.'

Another long pause stretched across the miles. Despite her measured intonation, Lynn's nerves clanked and clashed in her ears. She sensed the blood draining downwards from her brain and the palms of her hands moistening. She refused to make eye contact with Gerry, fearing she might be reduced to a blubbering mess.

'That is also true,' Mehretu responded after a lengthy pause. 'I was disappointed to hear that the *guerrillas* have demanded a ransom.'

'So you know he's been taken hostage?' the young woman asked. 'Do you know this group, sir?'

'I know *of* these men, yes,' the high ranking TPLF official stated. 'I was downhearted to discover this. These men are opportunistic. They only want to make money and see their pictures in the 'papers. Your husband can give them both these things.'

The man's mild vocabulary suggested he desired a peaceful outcome, but the astute campaigner vowed to reserve judgement for the time being. This man also had a well-catalogued history of violence and bloodshed to his name.

'Are you able to help secure his release, please? Are you still in favour of the negotiations Jeff's organising in France?'

'Missus Diamond,' the freedom-fighter explained. 'I am ten years older than your husband and have followed a similar educational path. We have much in common, and I respect the chap a lot also. I believe in what he is trying to do, and I hope the time is right for these negotiations.'

Lynn listened carefully, wondering if this series of compliments contained an answer to either of her questions. She concluded they had not, and so she asked the first again, maintaining the same conciliatory tone. This technique was straight out of the respected negotiator's handbook. Cringing at the quaint term of endearment which would grate on humiliate her husband's cool outer shell, the fact that he was held in such high regard boosted her confidence at least.

'Are you able to help secure Jeff's release, please, Mister Mehretu?'

'I would like to. I have little influence over these men.'

'You mean the EPRP?' Lynn recited, referring to the the abbreviation she had scrawled when Hendriksen had suggested it. 'Is that who's holding him?'

'Yes. Your information is accurate, Missus Diamond.'

This time, the caller lifted her eyes from on a speck of fluff on the rug, on which they had been hypnotised for the last few minutes, and glanced over at her husband's best mate. 'Are their goals similar to the TPLF's? What do they want? Only money?'

'I don't know,' Mehretu replied. 'They haven't made this sort of high-profile move for many years. As I said, it is purely opportunistic. They found out he was in the area, probably after the township meeting in Sebeta, and decided to try their luck. I would not expect them to have a master plan.'

'Are you able to contact them?' the dogged champion ask her question yet another way, unsure if she had heard a chuckle at the end of his last sentence. 'The children and I would like to have Jeff home soon.'

Gerry held out his hand to the impressive woman beside him, having trouble believing what he was hearing. Aware he was only catching one half of the conversation, this seemed akin to asking the President of the United States to abolish the death penalty. The educated man gave the impression of being in favour of securing Jeff Diamond's freedom, but the political will and influence required was far too overwhelming to contemplate.

'My dear Lynn, I shall try,' Mehretu muttered, 'but I cannot guarantee anything. I don't know this group, and I have no idea where they stand with regard to the party. But yes, I will try. You have my word on this.'

Relief surged through the tennis player's tense limbs, and she felt her cheeks flush. 'Thank you so much, sir,' she whispered, closing her eyes. 'Fantastic, and very kind of you to help out. I'll leave you in peace.'

'Thank you, Missus Diamond. And I shall be taking part in the round-table in France. I shall make sure I'm there. I trust you will receive some good news very soon.'

'Many thanks to you, sir. Jeff'll appreciate your participation a great deal. He values your opinion. Please give my regards to your wife.'

'Thank you. Goodbye. I must go now. Goodbye.'

The diplomat sat welded to her office chair with the telephone cradled in both hands. As she replayed the odd exchange, she stared straight ahead and began to slap a pendulous rhythm with the end of the receiver in the palm of her left hand. She had no basis for believing her actions would bear fruit, but at least she had seized the nettle and the Ethiopian had taken the time to listen. This was all she could ask for under the circumstances.

Gerry pushed his body off the desk, dazed and tired, and placed an expansive arm around her shoulders. 'So,' he said, drawing breath in for the next round. 'That was positive. Well done. What next?'

'Ring Matthias back,' Lynn responded, looking at the clock on the wall and thinking aloud. 'Wow! It's past one o'clock. Sunday morning here, but still pretty early on Saturday evening in Addis Ababa. Let's go back into the lounge room. Or did you want to go to bed? It's pretty late. I don't mind.'

The chivalrous man smiled, flashing mischievous eyes before deferring to his host. 'Well... I can now die a happy man,' he quipped. 'The lovely Lynn has asked me if I want to go to bed, and that she doesn't mind if I do.'

The singer groaned. 'That's terrible! I should know you never miss a trick. I'm very flattered, kind sir, but forsooth, you have the wrong end of the stick. What would your best mate say?'

'Career-limiting move, I'd wager! But there was a time, I'll have you know, when we used to trade girlfriends,' Gerry confessed with a reminiscent sigh. 'But that Mullarkey all stopped when you came on the scene. Our Mister Diamond became unusually territorial at that point. I never understood why...'

Lynn chuckled and slapped the affable accountant's arm, opening the office door and ushering him out. 'Be quiet,' she said. 'We've still got work to do.'

Hendriksen picked up on the first ring. The celebrity recounted the call with Jemal Mehretu in detail to the speechless security consultant, before asking his advice as to how best to respond to the demand her husband's captors had issued.

'They've asked for thirty million Birr,' Matthias told her.

The young woman raised three fingers on her left hand and flashed both hands three times to the family's numbers man.

'Thirty mill'?' he mouthed, thinking they had escaped quite lightly. 'Dollars? American or Aussie?'

Lynn shook her head, still listening to the pedantic messenger. Political demands accompanied the required donation, aimed at the Mengistu government. The Diamonds had no direct influence over such petitions as freedom for incarcerated rebels or the forced resignation of several prominent politicians and judges. One-by-one, she wrote them down on the notepad in front of Gerry, his face growing longer with each appended item.

The diplomatic woman asked Hendriksen to excuse her for a few seconds while she and her right-hand man discussed the conditions of Jeff's release. It was evident that the group was not quite as disorderly as Mehretu had led her to believe, within its rights to link the kidnapping of their famous peacemaker with such fundamental ambitions originating out of the conflict in northern Africa.

The Diamond Celebration Foundation's social justice machine had known this fact for several years, ever since her husband set out to engineer the downfall of the Derg on behalf of the Ethiopian and Eritrean people, for whom he exhibited an esoteric reverence. It was naïve to presume he could do this without playing with the big boys, and without accepting big boys' rules of engagement.

The reluctant accomplice nodded, realising they had little choice but to go through the motions. In fact, Jeff had articulated much the same *mantra* several times during their many risk management and insurance coverage meetings.

'Are you there, Matthias?' Lynn spoke into the mouthpiece, which was warm from being pressed into the palm of her hand.

He was.

'The money's not a problem,' she began. 'Thirty million Birr we can get to you within twenty-four hours, but the rest we obviously can't do on our own. Have government representatives issued a statement?'

Hendriksen coughed. 'I expect they're waiting to hear from you tomorrow morning.'

'It *is* tomorrow morning,' the woman let out a caustic laugh. 'Whom do I need to contact over there? I don't want to waste another day of Jeff's life for the sake of being polite and not ringing until a less anti-social hour.'

Again, Gerry sighed in consternation, although there was no excuse for his astonishment. Smiling up at him, Lynn was already noting down names and numbers. Perhaps he would go to bed after all. He was adding no value to this process. She was in control of the whole shooting match, driven by a strong desire to share personal space with someone other than him as soon as possible.

While the security operative spoke, his client became aware of a set of repeating tones in the background. Three soft bleeps, then a pause. Three more bleeps, then another pause. Call waiting. Might this be Jemal Mehretu with some answers? Would he be that gracious?

'Excuse me, Matthias,' Lynn interjected. 'I'm sorry. I think someone's trying to ring this number. Would you mind hanging up, please? I'll try a few of these people to see what I can find out, and then I'll come back to you.'

The South African wished his tenacious client luck, and she pressed the button on the telephone again. As she suspected, it immediately came to life in her hand. Releasing the same button, she juggled with the tools of her new trade in an effort to lift the receiver up to her ear.

'Hello?'

'Hey,' said a deep, syrupy voice over a poor line.

'Jeff,' she gulped. 'Is that you?'

'Yep. Sure is. I love you. You OK?'

Gerry's eyes met hers, and they both dissolved into a flood of tears. The young woman leaned back in her chair and clutched the telephone's base unit to her chest, unable to speak for relief. The executive lunged from the other end of the couch and took the telephone from her trembling hand.

'Mate, am I stoked to hear from you!'

The rock star laughed. 'Gez? What the fuck are you doing in my house at two in the morning?'

'I wish, mate,' his manager complained. 'I did suggest I seek comfort in her ample bosom, but my gallantry was callously rejected.'

Lynn signalled for the receiver, which was transferred without delay. 'Jeff, I love you too. Sorry I couldn't speak just then. I was overwhelmed by the sound of your voice.'

'That's OK, angel. I'm happy to hear it. I'm not exactly *blasé* about this either.'

'We're all fine,' his wife continued, sniffing back the last few teardrops. 'Now anyway... But how are you? The kids miss you so much, and I miss you even more. Where are you?'

'Oh, it's all good,' he crooned, unable to hide the croak in his voice. 'It's so unbelievably amazing to talk to you. I'm OK. We were involved in some vehicular epilepsy a few days ago. The driver and the car came off way worse. Not so bad now, but my collarbone's stuffed, I think. I'm being held at an old farmhouse, though I have no idea which direction we went in. Can't talk for long 'cause I'm still trying to negotiate my way out of here.'

'Oh, thank God. Are you in pain? I'm really sorry the line was busy. I was...'

'Later, gorgeous,' Jeff cut her off. 'I have to go. You're the most beautiful woman in the world, Lynn Dyson Diamond. Tell Jet and Kizzy how much I love them and that I'll speak to them as soon as I can. And say hello to that Blake bastard too. I'm glad he's there with you, in a fucking jealous kind o' way.'

His wife heard a sudden scuffle and a cacophony of angry voices in the background. 'Jeff...'

'Baby, I have to go. Don't worry about me. I'll be fine. I love you, angel...'

The line cut out, leaving the two adults at *Escondido* staring at each other like startled rabbits. No question, it had been Jeff. No-one else was capable of impersonating his quirky turn of phrase or his soulful, smoky vocal elixir. But no sooner was he there than he was gone. It had been a blessed relief to hear from him, but now their minds were overflowing with a raft of different questions.

'Well, praise the Lord!' Gerry broke the silence. 'He's alive. That's the main thing.'

Lynn nodded, washed-out and weary. 'Yes. And holding it together pretty well. Compared to me anyway!'

'Rubbish. It was a shock for the call to come out of the blue. And he sounds healthy. Obviously not too badly roughed up in whatever happened on the road.'

'No, thankfully. I didn't like the sound of the background noise. Do you think they were holding a gun to his head? Oh... I have this image in my mind of them allowing him to make his one 'phone call before tying and gagging him.'

'Who knows?' the senior partner shrugged. 'I'd like to think not, but it's a possibility. I don't want to paint the whole thing any worse or any better than it is, because we have no bloody idea. What did you want to do now?'

Checking the clock, which said two-fifteen, the musician figured she would find it easier to sleep now that she knew her man hadn't perished in the car accident. They both had avenues to chase down his freedom, even though she hadn't had the chance to warn him about Mehretu's involvement. For the moment at least, the unstoppable pantomime horse was back in the race.

'What a weird day,' Lynn mused. 'Is it wise of Jeff to enter into negotiations with his guards? I suppose he thinks he's got nothing to lose.'

The couple's manager wasn't so sure. 'Except he might push them too far... If he tries his luck once too often, they might get nasty. It's not like dealing with pen-pushing civil servants this time. These aren't necessarily the rational, law-abiding sort.'

'I know, but he's pretty good at reading situations. He'd change his tune if he thought someone was likely to react badly. He does it all the time, even with the kids.'

'Hope you're right,' Gerry said, a yawn revealing a mouthful of expensive dental work subsidised by the Diamonds' royalties. 'I'm fucked. Don't know about you. Should we try and get some sleep? What more can you do now?'

Lynn sighed, scanning down the list of telephone numbers again. 'You're probably right,' she admitted. 'It's Saturday evening in the Ethiopian capital. Tomorrow's a normal working day for them, and people here should be in bed. I'll start again after breakfast. It's a relief that we have some goodish news to pass on to the littlies in the morning.'

The Human Touch

Rasul blasted out an order which Jeff didn't understand, except that its outcome took the form of Thomas pointing his gun at the captive's chest.

'Get up!' the scrawny young man blustered. 'Back to the other room. No more 'phone calls.'

Content with his progress thus far, the multi-millionnaire didn't object. He had been given two minutes to talk to his wife, and the deal had been honoured. It was a start, and at least Lynn now knew he was alive and well, which amounted to a successful day in the life of a hostage, all things considered.

Earlier, the skilled negotiator had managed to convince Rasul to drive Dennis to a hospital, also being allowed to see him before he was taken away. In a lucky break, he had even slipped some valuable clues to him, unseen by the heathens who planned to use them both as human capital.

As far has Jeff could discern, five or six rebels resided in this house, plus the two women. It was the African version of a commune, but with a serious arsenal. The group ran the household for each other, not unlike a bunch of students in university digs, and then from time to time they mounted *sorties* to ambush cars and take hostages for no apparent reason.

Back in the grand lounge room, on the couch he now called his own, the songwriter engaged the group's leader once again. With the initial focus on where he had grown up and how he had come to be part of this operation, the bizarre reverse interview transitioned to the reasons why the EPRP had decided to kidnap him and what they intended to accomplish as a result.

'You were in Sebeta talking to our people,' Rasul sought to remind the celebrity.

'Yeah. Were you there too?'

'No. I was not there,' the Gurage psychology graduate answered, 'but my brother was there, and many of my friends.'

'So what about that rally made you do this? Didn't you agree with what I said?'

The man whose side-on profile rendered him practically invisible laughed like a marauding crow. 'Oh, yes. We liked some things you said, but we don't like you going to bed with the government to make a deal with the TPLF.'

The patient intellectual leaned in, moving as close to this enigmatic bounty hunter as he could without leaving his uncomfortable couch. 'But that's the wrong spin, mate,' he said. 'I'm not in bed with anyone, more's the pity. The intelligence agencies are as suspicious of me as they are of you, and Babanjida and Mehretu and all the others. I bet they've got a fatter file on me than they have on you.'

Rasul snorted through his nostrils, signalling disapproval. A dash of *macho* competitiveness was sure to get a rise out of the youngbloods, the man from Sydney's south-west guessed, providing he didn't go far enough to cause anyone to lose face. No-one could confirm or deny this particular dubious fact.

He carried on, sitting back and stretching his legs. 'Mate, I'm simply trying to set up some conversations between people who count, so they gain a better understanding of each other's point of view and work out how to transition Ethiopia and Eritrea into truly representative, democratic nations. Tell me those aren't things you guys want, my psychologist friend?'

'Of course we want this,' the man dismissed the attempt to reel him in. 'We think Mehretu is not sincere. Why do you target him and not Andom or Abate?'

'We're not targeting anyone,' Jeff was quick to correct this misconception. 'You can all come to my party. It's open house. You can come too, if you like, but you must be unarmed and ready to sit down and talk. Mehretu and I went to the same university in London, although ten years apart. We've had a few useful discussions lately. I don't doubt his sincerity, but tell me more if you have evidence. I'd be keen to hear it.'

Rasul had lost interest in the conversation, yelling without warning for one of the others to supervise the prisoner while he left the room. The philosopher smirked. There was no substance to the ringleader's objections after all, and he was content to have him depart. His new playmate was Femi, with whom he had developed an affinity the day before.

'How's the ransom coming along? Have they responded?'

'Are you nervous now?' Femi smiled. 'I don't blame you.'

The boyish response took the thirty-three-year-old by surprise. Up until this moment, he had been anything but nervous. Should he be? He had learned a few disturbing facts during the course of his third day of incarceration, but he had been so eager to pursue his private negotiation strategy with the individuals in the house that he had temporarily lost sight of the deal out in the public domain. Who knew about the ransom demand? And who was in charge of the official reply?

The showman winced. He ought to have made wiser use of his two minutes of intercourse with Lynn. Did she even know the terms of the rebels' demands? How stupid of him not to find this out. He had been so preoccupied by the sound of her voice and the prospect of peace on the Mornington Peninsula tonight that he had not taken best advantage of their brief contact. He didn't expect the hired sidekick to explain the details, and it was not something to be discussed with a junior operative at any rate. He needed to build trust with Rasul, now regretting having undermined his authority.

Jeff changed the subject. 'Femi, when do you next get to go home? To see your family?'

'I don't have a plan to go home. My family is all gone.'

'What d'you mean, all gone?' the Australian detected some sadness in his words.

'My brothers have fled to different countries,' the defensive Nigerian told him. 'And my parents are no longer living.'

'Whoa, that's tough. How long ago did they die?'

'When I was a boy,' Femi replied. 'Your parents are dead too. I read much about you. You have come from nothing.'

Acknowledging this simple truth, the poet smiled. 'You're right about that. And I'll go back to nothing. It's what happens in between that's important.'

The mercenary slouched, embarrassed. 'I like to hear about Jeff Diamond all my life.'

'Yeah? Thanks a lot.'

Jeff felt strangely protective towards this lanky lad with the power to extinguish his very being at a moment's notice. He supposed the rifle was loaded, even though this was an assumption he was in no rush to validate. Not unlike the gangs in Sydney's west or in the slums of other so-called developed cities, anti-Derg foot-soldiers were either lost boys from broken homes or disillusioned immigrants denied equal opportunity. Indeed, he mused, most countries' armed forces depended on much the same demographic, their rank and file recruited from the poor, ragged edges of town, where knowing how to kill and die was the best skill a young man had to offer.

'You are like Rasul,' Femi continued. 'His father in prison for murder.'

'Is that right?' the hostage frowned at this useful morsel which had landed in his lap. 'My father's dead now. He was a piece of shit.'

The Nigerian straightened up, laughing aloud. 'A piece of shit!' he repeated. 'I hear this words on American television. I know what it means. Rasul's father is also a piece of shit.'

'Ah, yeah? Sounds like it! Is that why he joined the EPRP? To escape from his dad's influence?'

The younger of the two clammed up. 'I don't know. It's better not to talk about it. You need to talk to him of these things.'

'Sure. That's fair,' the empath frowned. 'I'm sorry. I don't want you to break confidences. You're a good man, Femi.'

'No. I don't think so. I can tell you that they agreed to pay the money for you.'

'Is that right? Who? How do you know?'

The guard recoiled. He shouldn't have been giving away these secrets, and Jeff shared his internal conflict of interest. One half of his conscience warned of the immorality of making the gunman compromise his values, yet the other half said, "What the hell?" It was Femi's choice where he drew the circumference of his trust boundary, and the rock star was no stranger to people's inner circle.

If the quietly-spoken mercenary identified with his hostage closely enough, the Pied Piper would be a fool not to take full advantage. It was every man for himself when it came to overrun farmhouses in the catchment of Saint Jack's primary school. As a free man, things would be different, but with everything the Australian valued out of reach at present, bring it on!

'I hear that your wife will send the money on Monday,' the sheepish informant continued. 'But please, you must let Rasul tell you.'

Jeff grinned, extending his right hand. 'No problem. I'll act surprised, don't you worry.'

The amenable enemy's fingers clasping his, a *mélange* of emotions swirled around the musician's head. He remembered when he and Lynn had drawn up various binding agreements for the "Feed Africa" campaign the previous year. They had sought reams of legal and philosophical advice, and cogitated long into the night on the rights and wrongs of relenting on blackmail demands, coming to the final position of "Don't give them the satisfaction. See you in the next life." Their causes were bigger than either individual, or so it had seemed at the time…

The revelation a year later that his soul-mate had gone back on her word was humbling in the extreme. At home in Melbourne and faced with a situation to which they only related via books or from the movies, her ordinarily judicious mind had changed. She had decided that the man she loved, with all his idiosyncrasies, addictions, sins and general recklessness, was worth more to her and their children than a peaceful African future.

So the young mother's head had lost out to her heart through this process, and by consequence, it was a welcome lesson for Jeff too; a perverse and pleasing slap in the face. He imagined his wife working towards her courageous decision alone, having bounced ideas off a trusted friend such as Michelle or Gerry, while the fabled Hungarian pugilists, Dogma and Pragma, slugged it out in her mind's boxing ring.

Lynn Dyson had always been the stayer, taught from a young age to pick a course and follow it through to its bitter end. Her black stallion, on the other hand, was the one with the death-wish, whose existence was cheap and squanderable, changing tack whenever the unpredictable winds and currents of life delivered him evidence to modify his opinion. He had learned to value this latest human lifeform, if only for what it meant to everyone else, but he had never counted on the exorbitant price it might fetch from the girl of his dreams.

Today's unexpected and unsolicited validation nourished the frustrated hostage's soul, and he lay back to stare once more at the ceiling in stunned silence. Thomas arrived to take over from the Nigerian, who seemed relieved to be out of the deep water into which he had waded. Jeff wished him a good night, and the sentiment was mirrored.

Dinner was served at dusk, unrecognisable but tasty. Although his accommodation bore no resemblance to the five-star luxury he was used to, the billionnaire rocker couldn't complain about his treatment. Not since the first day had he been woken by a rifle butt to the back of the head or felt the pressure of a weapon trained on him wherever he went. These lost boys did not intend to kill him. His utility was far greater alive than dead, even for petulant knuckleheads like Rasul.

Tired and preoccupied with the sketchy account of his ransom deal, the prisoner lay across the lumpy couch and smoked the single cigarette on his meal tray, a substitute for dessert. How many more days like this would there be? Next to the separation from his loved ones, boredom was his biggest challenge. Yet for an introvert whose whole childhood had been spent trying to ignore the world around him, this was not insurmountable.

'Sunday tomorrow,' Jeff muttered to his night-time companion, a full stomach on top of another twenty-four hours without exercise rendering him drowsy.

'Yes. The day of rest.'

The songwriter laughed, blowing a long plume of smoke straight up towards the ceiling. 'Are you a Christian, my friend?'

'Yes. Are you?'

'No. I'm a confused agnostic who could become a born-again atheist.'

It was the African's turn to chuckle. 'What is that? What confuses you?'

'Why people believe in religion in the first place, I guess,' the hostage answered. 'Especially people who say they do things in God's name. Did God send you to kidnap me, for example?'

The gunman shook his head. 'No. It is my job.'

'So who's more powerful, God or the person who pays your wages?'

Thomas' gnarly fingers closed around the handle of the gun, his frame shifting on its chair. After seventy-two hours in the company of this exalted but enigmatic celebrity, the dynamics of the rebel cell were changing. The mercenaries grew restless and unsure.

'I pray to God that he will help me, and now I have this job,' the young man explained. 'I hope someday that I can do another job, but for now God wants me to do this job.'

'Is that what you believe?' Jeff sat up, planting his stockinged feet on the floor. 'Truly? In your heart, I mean? Or in your fine, educated head?'

'Mister Diamond,' Thomas stiffened. 'You have the most fine, most educated head, and even you say you are confused. I am confused but I want to believe in God. Do you want to believe in God?'

His captive inhaled and exhaled to steady his nerves, wishing he could slip his hand inside his shirt and help himself to a surreptitious second helping of dessert. Instead, he rubbed the inked skin over his heart. Did he want to believe in God? What a pertinent question this was!

'Mate, I don't know what I want to believe in, to be perfectly honest. I know I don't subscribe to formal religion, with its eight o'clock mass and its eleven o'clock Holy Communion. All these artificial observances, like not eating pork or only eating fish on Fridays... Or worshipping cows and letting them hold up traffic in some of the world's most densely-populated cities. Y'know what I mean? India... The man-made stuff people think will take them closer to God.'

Thomas, his eyes wide with amazement at the richness of the musician's response, lifted the gun off his knees and placed it down on the floorboards at his feet. The heartwarming statement was not lost on the empathetic Australian. Like his "JL" tattoo, it was a symbol of equality and respect.

'Thank you,' Jeff muttered, extending his hand.

'I believe to see God you must get closer to him,' Thomas leaned across and completed the gesture. 'My mother fears God very much. She never lets us miss Sunday in the church because she thinks God make us sick or some terrible thing to happen.'

'And did it?'

'Oh, yes,' the tall rebel grinned. 'Sometimes it rains when her clean washing is outside. That is God's fault.'

The showman laughed aloud at the kid's gift of comic timing. 'Very cool, mate. I like your sense of humour. My good friend at home, who's also my manager... Gerry, his name is... his mother's the same. She told her kids they'd fail their school exams if they didn't pray every night and go to church on Sunday mornings. And in the end, the two who didn't go to church passed, but the one who attended every week bombed out.'

Thomas hesitated for a second before chancing a snigger, unable to translate the idiom "bombed out" into his native language.

'I'm sorry,' the polyglot backtracked. '"Bombed out" means she failed. Didn't pass.'

This time the young man sounded genuinely amused, although Jeff also detected a slight crisis of conscience. Had his commentary cemented the African's own religious scepticism? He changed the subject, so as not to push him too far too fast.

'Anyway, I do believe there's something each of us has inside that guides us, hence my reserving the right to turn atheist. And I think that force inside... the soul, if you like... has often lived other lives before us.'

'Reincarnation?' Thomas asked, now suspicious.

'Yeah. Sort of,' the philosopher nodded. 'My theory is that some souls are older than others. They've inhabited more people than others. Mine's very, very old, I reckon. Maybe yours is on its first time round. Why am I like I am, and you're like you are? We make our own destiny. That I believe. But I don't believe we set it.'

The gunman sat up straighter again, not knowing if he should be fascinated or wary. 'That is interesting. I never think of this before.'

'Do you like reading?'

'Oh, yes. I would like to read again,' the uniformed mercenary rued. 'I have no books now. They are all in my home.'

'Shame, mate,' the Australian shook his head. 'If the rest of my shit wasn't in a hotel somewhere, I could give you five at once! There's a book that came out in in the late 'sixties called "One Hundred Years of Solitude", by Gabriel García Márquez... a Mexican guy, I think... It ends with something like "Races condemned to one hundred years of solitude did not have a second opportunity on Earth."'

'I see,' the young man appeared puzzled. 'Can you say the line again? I need to hear it slow to understand.'

'Sure,' Jeff smiled, preparing to repeat the novel's final, weighty sentence. 'Sorry, mate. Your English is so good, I forgot to be careful.'

'Second opportunity on Earth,' his captor ruminated. 'Reincarnation. But what does it mean?'

The intellectual chuckled. 'I can tell you what I think it means, but it can mean whatever you want it to mean. When you've read the whole story, 'phone me and tell me what it means to you. Deal?'

'Ha! You send me the book? Then I read it. Good, Mister Diamond. What does this hundred years of solitude mean to you? I like to know, please.'

'OK. I'll tell you like this: who was it who told me to do what I do and not bum around wasting my life?' Jeff posed another rhetorical question instead. 'Plenty of others do, but I can't. Something drives me to do more every day, and that's my idea of God. I have no clue if we're born with our God, or perhaps it chooses you at some point during your life, when you deserve to be chosen. Or even if *you* choose *it*. God's not the same for everyone either, so I can't justify a single supreme being sitting in heaven looking down on us all.'

'Because some people are guided to do good things, and some bad?' Thomas dared to continue the argument. 'So there is a good God and a bad God, like Satan?'

The wise man whistled. 'Hmm... Maybe there is. I think it's up to each of us what we want to believe, and what type of God we want to guide us. I don't rely on it though. My amazing wife and I have two children who make people smile wherever they go. Friends of ours have rude, obnoxious children. Did one God make both sets of children how they are? I don't think so. I believe in a world where you and your God can work together to get things done while my God and I get on with what we need to do. And if you don't work together... like if one of you's bad and the other's good... you go crazy.'

Thomas reached into his breast pocket and pulled out his packet of cigarettes, handing it to the earnest orator. The rock star wondered whose God had planted this welcome seed, or was it the power of telepathy from his addicted mind? Eager for a hit, he helped himself to the gift and paused for a light. Raising its glowing end to his nose and breathing in the smoke, he toasted his companion.

'Cheers.'

'Cheers! Mister Diamond, you have good children because you are good,' Thomas blurted out, causing his own cigarette to slip from his lips before it caught alight. 'You are doing good things for my Africa. I believe God will find you and thank you.'

'That's a nice thing to say, Tom. Thanks,' Jeff smiled. 'But it's pretty hard to believe when I'm stuck here. I should've been on a 'plane to London yesterday. I was meant to open a new treatment centre for traumatised kids. Don't tell me your God didn't want me to go there. Don't you reckon God's a "big picture" kind o' guy, mate?'

Seeing the guard turn his gaze towards the ceiling, embarrassed by the sudden confrontation, the peacemaker backed off and changed the subject again. 'What's happening tomorrow?' he asked, laying back across the couch. 'Is there anything to look forward to here on Sundays?'

'No,' Thomas shook his head. 'Same as today. Perhaps some news for you?'

'Oh, yeah? What sort of news?'

'Nothing for certain,' the younger man hesitated. 'They say they take you to Addis Ababa.'

The hostage played down the effect this welcome dose of optimism served his brain. 'What for?' he asked. 'Who's in Addis Ababa?'

'I cannot tell you,' Thomas clammed up. 'Rasul plans to talk to you in the morning. They think the police knows where you are.'

'Really?'

'Yes. I am sorry to see you go.'

Jeff sat up, private euphoria now tempered by outward concern. Had the ringleader fed his subordinate this information, expecting him to pass it on? Perhaps he was being punished for becoming everybody's friend. A powerful means of assuring a sleepless night, from one psychological manipulator to another.

'So you guys won't be coming with me?'

'No. We stay here,' Thomas told him. 'I think Rasul go with you. There are many more of EPRP men in Addis Ababa. It's a city; our capital city.'

'Yeah. I know. I've been there.'

The performer faked a yawn to dispel a lungful of disappointment. Another long car journey to another unknown destination, and his relationship-building scores would rewind to zero with each new person in his planned chain of custody. The rebel leader was no dunce. Jeff needed to bring things to a head soon. If it were true that the police were waiting to knock on the farmhouse door, there was a good chance he might be smuggled out during the night.

'Please could I make another 'phone call?'

'No,' came a predictably emphatic reply. 'So you can tell your wife where you are going? I get fired for this.'

Fair enough, the Australian thought. Thomas didn't trust his God to keep him in this job, let alone secure him a better one. He would have to resign himself to the night's dark secrets and trust his stock of sublime fantasies to carry him through until morning, when he would run the same question past Femi.

Before too long, the young guard began to doze off. Tonight he had abandoned the dining chair in favour of the bare floorboards, with his machine gun by his side at all times. His slow, regular breathing betrayed his descent into a deep sleep.

Rolling off the edge of the couch and onto the floor not three metres away, Jeff congratulated himself for having taken his shoes off, for he was able to stand up and walk around the room without a sound, by now familiar with its layout. The lamp which had been left on during the last two nights had been switched off, and the thirty-three-year-old stood at the window giving over the front of the property. The road was too far away to make out, and there was no movement in the barren, neglected garden outside.

Were army personnel circling the house, camouflaged by wheat chaff and cow dung, re-enacting an episode of "Dad's Army"? The hostage pressed his fingers round the edges of the window, placing a safe bet that the disused sash frame would sound a squeaky alarm if he tried to dislodge it. He padded across to the other side of the room, peering into the darkness. Two gang members were drinking from cans of beer and smoking at the back corner of the building, and as his senses tuned in, he picked out more voices. The sounds were yet clearer from the rearmost window.

Hoping he was far enough from his sleeping minder, the multi-millionnaire fished a lighter and a packet of cigarettes out of his shirt. He lit one without delay and imbibed the smoke on a direct course for his spinning mind. What had Lynn made of their brief telephone conversation? And good on Gerry for forgoing a wild Saturday night to look after his best mate's wife and kids! He wasn't the Tin Man after all. Although the accountant's heart pumped his lumbering frame round the squash court admirably, its emotional function was as underutilised and immovable as the chipped, cream-coloured window furnishings upon which the celebrity's eyes were now fixed.

In spite of a temporary respite, his dream girl was little better off than before in terms of certainty, but at least she had been reassured that he was in good condition. The call had ended in such a commotion, with Rasul punching one of the others for ignoring the longest hand on his watch and allowing a bonus fifteen seconds.

Placing himself in Lynn's frame of mind, Jeff pre-empted her next steps. Any security operatives crawling around in the undergrowth were equally likely to have been dispatched as a result of her actions as his. If the local authorities had pinned him down to Wonji, assuming the Dibaba family hadn't popped up elsewhere since young Daniel received his music certificate, this also showed someone at the hospital had deciphered the message he had secreted on Dennis' person. Regardless of the source, they were now in a race to ascertain his current whereabouts before he was transported to another city altogether, whence the whole process would need to begin again.

On the bright side however, if his people were hanging out in the bushes, they couldn't help but notice a vehicle containing one white and any number of black men speeding back to the highway. Their route would take them through or round Adama to reach the capital, if the seasoned traveller's knowledge of Ethiopian geography was accurate.

Glancing over at the gangly Namibian, the prisoner toyed with sneaking out of the room to make his telephone call. He had no idea how many guards were on duty at once. Even if this wasn't the most coordinated gang of *guerrillas*, Rasul was intelligent enough to station more than one sentry on the night-shift in such a rambling, old house.

No. Jeff had another change of heart. He wouldn't push his luck. All things considered, he was faring way better than he had expected on first climbing out of the battered vehicle and coming face-to-face with the open end of a gun. He ought to be grateful he was injury-free, not gagged and tied to a chair and sitting in three days' worth of noxious bodily fluids. Shuddering at the unpleasant image, he resolved to be patient and play their game until his next opportunity arose, much as his compulsive urges wished otherwise.

Thomas stirred at a creak from the old couch as it sagged under Jeff's weight. His eyes opened, and an instinctive right hand reached for the gun, which was not where he expected it. Waking with a guttural cry, the young guard panicked for a second or two. The hostage felt sorry for him, choosing to roll over and face the back of the settee so as not to force a confrontation. After a few muttered phrases and the sound of metal scraping across wood, renewed silence gave way to the inevitable snores of a man lying face-up on a hard surface.

The musician rewound his mental video tape to his son's seventh birthday, when the boy and a group of friends had spent a cold winter's afternoon skirmishing on the dunes below *Escondido*. Their fertile imaginations fired up by lunchtime stories of battles won and lost from the dads present, the pint-sized soldiers had fashioned rifles and hand-grenades from dead wood and pine cones retrieved from the beach.

Why were boys so obsessed with fighting? The pacifist had been no different at their age; the perfect candidate for a lifetime of violence and intimidation. So where was the tipping point which turned normal boys into mercenaries? Snoring Thomas had grown up with a God and a mother, yet he had chosen Satan by his own admission. The boy from Canley Vale could have easily made the same choice...

Jeff's mind next wandered to the same beach, beneath the cliffs of Mount Eliza, along which he and his beautiful best friend often walked under the cover of moonlight, in search of a soft, dry spot to make love. He smiled at the wild excuses they would concoct for the children and their nannies the following morning, the mess of their sandy footprints through the kitchen and up the wide staircase having exposed their midnight tryst.

Sleep caught up with the homesick man, and he enjoyed a torrid, passionate dream with Lynn in their favourite *Parisien* hotel. Removing her clothing, piece by enticing piece, their lips traversing the length and breadth of each others' exposed flesh, he uncovered the sexy, black teddy embroidered with tiny red roses he had bought on the way home from his last African *sojourn*.

Caught in the vice of youthful frenzy, a troll-versus-angel moment saved him from losing his load far too soon. She had danced for him, evading his grasp and testing his self-control to the limit, before allowing him to take her to bed and bring her to orgasm with only moments to spare.

As the dreamer lay lost in his dream world and wrapped in the arms of the woman he loved, he became aware of movement behind him. Dark shadows lunged forward and grabbed his neck and shoulders, dragging him onto the floor. The Jaworski brothers taunted and jeered in their special brand of australianised Polish, with his father laughing in the background, somehow in cahoots with the EPRP aggressors. The distraught teenager hiding in the captive's dream repelled their fists and knives, thrashing out at the faceless figures he knew so well.

'Mister Diamond!' Thomas yelled, leaping to his feet. 'Wake up! You are having a nightmare.'

For another thirty seconds or so, the alarmed gunman watched as his charge's crazed eyes focussed in and out of a subconscious world, struggling with invisible demons and fighting for his young life for the first time in many months.

'Jeff Diamond!' the guard shouted again, rocking the songwriter's arm back and forth. 'Wake up! Wake up!'

A string of Spanish profanities rushed out of Jeff's mouth, and he lashed out with his right hand towards the deep voice. The *brouhaha* brought another two men running in from outside, fearing they were under attack. As the door flung open, it slammed into a sideboard behind, the crack of wood against wood conspiring with the metallic slide of a weapon being readied and cocked.

'No! Stop!' Thomas' plea singed the air, raising a luminous palm to prevent his colleague from opening fire. 'Stop! He is dreaming. We must wake him.'

The series of sharp *staccato* sounds pierced the superstar's torpor, a few years of relative peace shattered in an instant. He was returning to consciousness, awareness drifting between past and present tense as terror mounted in the room. His breathing was heavy, and sweat covered his brow and cheeks and had dampened his shirt in large patches. The three rebels stood mesmerised by the disturbing sight, not knowing what to do.

Their hostage let out an atrocious low moan, and then his left hand relaxed before moving up to protect his face from the bright light which shone in his eyes. Crying out once more, he sat bolt upright and swang his legs off the couch until his feet made contact with the floor.

'Jesus Christ!' he swore at the top of his voice, standing up only to flop back down onto the cushions, off-balance from the sudden exertion. 'Jesus fucking Christ!'

Ashamed of his outburst, Jeff's bloodshot eyes scanned from one gunman to the other and grimaced. Levering himself up by pushing on cramped thighs, he tried once again to stand. Thomas walked forwards to help him, only to have his arm batted away.

'I'm good,' the embarrassed man hissed. 'Leave me alone, mate.'

The young mercenary took a step back, eyeing his prisoner with suspicion as he shook the tension out of his cumbrous limbs, still gasping for breath. Loneliness flooded the tortured soul's brain, realising these men had witnessed the same hideous sequence that Lynn used to live through on a nightly basis. Humiliated and devastated that his recurring dream had returned after so long, fury raged inside at having treated his enemies to this mental loophole.

Momentarily depersonalised, Jeff leaned against the window frame at the side of the house and stared out at the sun's first light, sickened and exhausted. 'Sorry, guys,' he spoke after a few moments of turgid silence. 'Panic over. As you were.'

'Do you want a cigarette?' Thomas approached, holding out an opened packet.

Trying not to act like a frightened puppy returning to its owner after a scolding, the showman turned to accept the kindness. Blowing smoke towards the ceiling, he let out another loud roar, and once again the men were put off-guard. The best he could manage under the circumstances, the pathetic reaction made him laugh.

'Thank you,' Jeff's left hand waved the cigarette. 'That hasn't happened in a long while. I'm sorry you had to witness it. Thanks for not shooting me.'

'What were you dreaming about?' one of the other guards asked. 'You were not speaking English.'

'Wasn't I?' the Australian smiled, shaking his head. 'I have no idea. Spanish, I expect. I'm OK now. Go back to whatever you were doing.'

The door to the lounge room re-opened to reveal Rasul in a state of undress. His men stood to attention like schoolboys caught in a wicked act. The rebel leader, skinny and unimpressive in an unflattering pair of white underpants, dismissed their respectful gesture and marched towards the prisoner.

'What's going on?' he barked. 'Why are you all here standing up? You should be asleep, Jeff Diamond. You are our guest.'

The star let out a sarcastic laugh. 'Yes. That would be preferable. As your guest, I'm grateful for your hospitality, Rasul Andrew. These blokes were watching me wake out of a violent nightmare. All good though... It happens. No-one's done anything wrong.'

The semi-naked soldier appeared to wilt a little before aligning his posture with his position of power. 'Nightmare,' he repeated with disdain. 'Me too, I have nightmares. God is punishing us, Mister Diamond.'

'Yeah? Punishing us for what?' Jeff asked, intrigued by the rebel's sudden openness in front of the other men. 'What have we done?'

Rasul turned on his heels, muttering something on his way out the door. He flicked a finger at Thomas, who followed his boss outside into the hall. The dejected songwriter tugged an upright, wooden chair out from under the desk and slumped down onto it. His leg muscles twitched in searing spasms, and the explosive ache in his head brought back a slew of intense suicidal urges.

Never a dull moment, he sighed.

'Mister Diamond,' his guard called from the doorway. 'Please come with me.'

Nonplussed, the exhausted star did as he was told. Where was he being taken now? And why? It must only be five-thirty or six o'clock in the morning. Rasul and the other guards had vanished, leaving him alone with Thomas in the dark corridor. It was clear these men considered he posed them no threat.

The Namibian led his famous hostage into the rear half of the house, through an enormous kitchen not dissimilar to Benloch's. A few more paces took them past a scullery and a basic bathroom, and on into an office which these days served more as a munitions store.

'You can call your family,' the younger man pointed to a telephone on the desk. 'Do not tell them you go to Addis tomorrow. Just say that you are alive. Two minutes only.'

Jeff reached out his left hand to rest it on Thomas' shoulder, rocking it back and forth. His eyes had filled with tears, and he couldn't care less if the guard noticed or not.

'Thank you,' he whispered. 'You're a good man, Tom. I really appreciate this.'

'It is Rasul,' the rebel countered. 'He is a good man now also, you think?'

The rock star smirked. 'Yeah. Guess so. I'll remember to thank him.'

The grateful traveller lifted the receiver, watching Thomas leave the room. What time was it in Melbourne? Sunday afternoon, about two o'clock, he calculated. No guarantee anyone would be at *Escondido*, but he dialled the number anyway. The international exchange responded with a muffled click before connecting, then rang four or five times. Just when he expected the answering machine message to kick in, the line cleared and he heard wheezing and puffing from a child's gallant swipe.

'Hello?'

'Jetto,' the father sobbed, struggling to speak. 'Son, it's Dad.'

'Dad!' the eight-year-old yelled straight into the mouthpiece. 'Mum! It's Dad!'

'Are you guys OK?' the caller asked, his heart buoyed by the happiness in his little boy's voice.

'Kizzy's front tooth fell out.'

Jeff chuckled, amazed at the simplicity of his children's lives, as opposed to the convolution of his own circumstance. 'Whoa! Is that right? That's good. The tooth fairy'll be visiting her as well as you now. Hope she's got enough money.'

The lad cackled. 'Yeah! She'd better. Mum's here. When are you coming home?'

'Soon, son,' the celebrity's voice cracked again. 'Let me speak to *Mamá*, mate, please. I need to make it quick. *Te amo, amigo.*'

'OK. *Te amo, Papá.* See ya later.'

By this time, tears were rolling down the musician's face. Jet never called him *Papá* these days. That was kid's stuff. A subliminal force between their weird parallel universes had made him use the Spanish term, knowing it would mean something special to his father. Sniffing to clear his airway, he heard Lynn thank their son for passing her the telephone and imagined him running off to resume his busy day.

'Jeff, are you there?'

'Hey, angel,' he answered, fingertips itching to touch her, and heart thumping nineteen to the dozen. 'I only have a minute. You OK?'

'Yes. We're fine. What about you?'

'Capital!' he emphasised, hoping his minder wasn't concentrating too hard while watching the seconds count down. 'Christ. It's so bloody good to talk to you. Stirring, in fact. Very stirring. It's driving me crazy being here. I love you so much.'

His wife caught her breath. 'Stirring? Are you talking in code or something? Do you mean you're moving? Where? To Addis Ababa? Is that why you said "Capital"?'

'Yes, baby,' he smiled. 'Jesus! Absolutely. Can't wait to hold you. Take a picture of Kierney's toothless grin for me, will you?'

Thomas appeared beside him and tapped the tabletop with jagged, split fingernails. Their time was up.

'Already have,' Lynn told him. 'Jeff, I love you too. Hurry home. We miss you so much.'

'I miss you too. I'm sorry, but I have to go now. *Adiós*, gorgeous.'

The guard nodded as the call finished, and again the Australian's hand closed around his bony shoulder. Without a word, the pair retraced their steps to the hallway. Doubling back before reaching the living room at the hostage's request for a bathroom break, they climbed the stairs. Jeff shut himself in, stealing a few valuable moments alone with pleasant thoughts of home.

Dawn broke in a glorious blaze of eastern sunshine, not long after the prisoner and his compassionate guard had resumed their positions. Another plate of miscellaneous foodstuffs soon appeared, with its customary side order of tobacco on a saucer, all covered with a dirty napkin.

The motley mob's so-called guest made a jovial comment as to its presentation, which fell on disinterested female ears. He ate and drank without ceremony, wondering how this morning would unfold. Lynn had understood his attempt to communicate their plans, hadn't she? Of course she had.

***

'I think Jeff's being moved,' Lynn updated Matthias Hendriksen.

'Excuse me? Did you say he's been moved? How do you know?'

The young mother recounted her husband's two-minute chat almost word-for-word. Quite apart from the emotional overload both had experienced, she discerned a new calm in his voice this time. There had been no exchange of cross words in the background either.

Busy absorbing these details, the security consultant took a few seconds to respond. 'Well...' he said, taking a deep breath. '"Capital" is obviously Addis Ababa, I agree. They must have told him they were driving him there. I'll pass this information on immediately. Thank you.'

'You're welcome. Anything to get him home. What about the ransom? Is there any update on where that's got to?'

'No,' Hendriksen's mood sounded flat. 'The spokesman agreed to wait until tomorrow. I'll find out first thing in the morning. Someone will ring you. They are taking it seriously. Please don't worry, Lynn.'

'How can I not worry?' the Olympian chuckled. 'But thanks, I suppose. And no intervention from Mister Mehretu?'

'Not yet,' Matthias confirmed, his tone dismissive.

'You don't think he'll act?'

'I hope he does,' the consultant doled out more unconvincing platitudes. 'I think our best bet is to intercept their vehicles on the highway. There's only one decent road out from where they are.'

'If they *are* where you think they are,' Lynn qualified the arrogant man's statement. 'But yes, you're probably right. As long as it doesn't end up in a shooting match. It's also the most dangerous option, I presume.'

Once a soldier, always a soldier, the anxious wife thought. The image of Jeff tied up in the back of a van with bullets raining like a swarm of angry horseflies chilled her blood. He had survived one ambush, and now he was heading for another. Or already slap-bang in the middle of it, for all they knew.

'Of course,' the security specialist acknowledged. 'It will be a confrontational situation. Oh, and I can confirm that Gerry has wired through the transfer.'

'Excellent. Thanks. I expect he has,' the celebrity's reply grew yet colder. 'That's the least important part. If cash helps to oil the cogs, as Jeff would say, then that's a good thing. Is there anything else before I let you get back to bed? I'm grateful for your help, Matthias.'

Lynn put the telephone down and stared again at the iconic photograph above her desk. What an ordeal… There would be outrage on a global scale if those who identified with this handsome do-gooder found out what had befallen him. She let the poster boy know how much she loved him, before leaving the room and returning to her children.

'Is *Papá* coming home?' Kierney asked.

'I hope so,' her mum replied. 'He said to tell you, "*Te amo.*" Jet told him about your tooth.'

'Oh,' the little girl whined. 'I wanted to tell him.'

'You can tell him later. It doesn't matter. And you can show him the real thing when he gets home. We'll book the tooth fairy for after he comes home too, shall we?'

Her daughter giggled. 'OK, *Mamá.*'

***

'Can I make a request before we leave, please?' Jeff asked the rebel leader.

Outside the front of the old farmhouse, three white four-wheel drives, dusty grease caked on with engine oil and ditch water, had been driven around for the journey northwards to Addis Ababa. The songwriter's stomach flipped as nostalgia sent him back to the "Please wash me" episode which had seen the ambitious nineteen-year-old student proclaim his love for a certain smart and stunning sixteen-year-old schoolgirl.

Rasul must have noticed the smile on his hostage's face, becoming incensed. 'What the fuck is funny?' he demanded, nudging the taller man's shoulder towards the entrance. 'Why do you laugh at us?'

'I'm not laughing at you. I was just remembering something, that's all. Please could I have some paper and a pen for the trip? I want to write a song down. It's been marching round in my head for hours. It's driving me insane.'

'A song?' the sour-faced warmonger mocked. 'So you are going to make another million dollars from this time in your life?'

'At least,' Jeff gave him a playful smirk and extended his right hand. 'I'll go fifty-fifty with you if it's a hit.'

This outlandish gesture pacified Rasul somewhat, sealing the deal with a half-hearted handshake. It appeared the Pied Piper of Africa could conquer even the hardest heart. One of the other gunmen pointed to the rear door of the middle car, so their famous passenger opened it and climbed in.

Thomas ran back from inside the house, clutching a squawking walkie-talkie, two or three sheets of paper and a ballpoint pen, all of which were snatched from him without a word of thanks. He span around to return to his post, eyeing the departing convoy as if hoping for a chance to stow away.

Jeff wound down the window and shouted over the gravel expanse. 'Hey, Tom?'

Checking with his boss, the furtive engineer glanced back at the rock star for whom he had gained enormous respect over the last few days, even bordering on affection. He had lived up to his humanitarian image in the young man's eyes, a character described by newspapers and television programmes as a leviathan. Jeff Diamond was indeed a colossus, whose power observed first-hand was inclusive, non-judgemental, and above all, kind.

Thomas smiled and waved. 'Goodbye, Mister Diamond. Good luck.'

'You too, man. I'll send you that book, OK? Keep safe.'

Rasul snarled at the soldier and shooed him back inside. With two men in the lead car and another pair bringing up the rear of the cavalcade, the chief took his place in the passenger seat in front of their hostage. Three further gang members hitherto invisible joined them in the second vehicle, one sitting beside the Australian and sporting a shotgun, and the other to do the driving.

'So write,' the scrawny soldier commanded, pointing to the paper in Jeff's hands. 'Write your hit song.'

'No sweat, mate. Don't go over any potholes, or they won't be able to read my writing if they publish it after I'm dead.'

His dry comment raised a laugh from the man next to him, and the gold-toothed chief turned around to put a stop to yet another smooth attempt to make friends. Suitably reprimanded, the gunman grabbed his weapon and menaced the prisoner. The convoy moved off, leaving the old farmhouse to fade into the distance, shrouded by a cloud of dust.

When one chapter closes, another one opens, the hostage gritted his teeth. *Life goes on.*

Inspiration came thick and fast for the songwriter while the bland agricultural countryside slipped past. The hard-hitting number for "The Black Sheep"'s Act One *Finalé* had so far eluded him, drawing blanks whenever he had first used the onerous task to distract him from the last few days' hardships. However, as soon as the idea took hold, his head became vertiginous with evocative themes, an intricate and interwoven structure and a lyric fuelled by crude emotions.

Throwing himself into the world of the underdog, from which he had risen not so long ago, Jeff fed the hard-luck stories he had heard from his twentieth-century African captors into the mix, along with the harsh economic backdrop of eighteenth-century Europe given life through the classic Balzac novel. Every character in the musical had his or her own challenges and desires, all depending on the others to fulfil their destinies.

From time to time, Rasul craned his neck to monitor the progress of his new gravy train. Sometimes he caught the muscular, dark-haired showbusiness personality deep in concentration, either with his eyes closed or gazing out of the window. At other times however, various lines were being crossed out or re-ordered on the page. The composer never uttered a sound throughout this whole process, even when the soaring chorus rang tumultuous in his mind.

During a rare glance ahead through the windscreen, the peacemaker caught sight of a vehicle on its side and facing towards them. Where were they? On the road to Adama, he presumed. As the convoy whizzed past the stationary hunk of metal, he noticed it had gone up in flames. Its tyres had melted onto the parched ground, and large swathes of paintwork were burned off.

'Was that my car?'

'Yes,' the leader answered. 'You were lucky.'

The superstar rolled his eyes. 'Yeah. Guess so. Have you heard about Dennis? How was he when he got to hospital?'

'Alive,' the gruff voice growled again. 'Shut up.'

'Shut the fuck up. No worries,' the celebrity taunted his nemesis, more confident now that his life would be preserved since the shared rights to this latest composition formed part and parcel of the deal. 'I apologise. I forgot my driving *étiquette*.'

The toothless man in the driver's seat guffawed, receiving a sharp jab from his boss in the soft flesh of his triceps muscle. The three cars rumbled on, following the road-signs for Mojo and Addis Ababa. Jeff wondered whether anyone might be looking out for them after he had passed on his coded message. How he and Lynn would laugh about their separate but shared experience later on, once life had returned to the ordered brand of abnormal with which they had become comfortable.

And how much closer this episode would bring the soul-mates too... Here was yet another fascinating observation about his state of mind: cloud and silver lining had these days swapped places...

On the outskirts of Dishoftu, the convoy came to a standstill. The driver of the vehicle ahead jumped down and strode across the dirt until he reached Rasul's open window, where they exchanged a few words in their dialect. The leader's arm waved the last car up, and it hurried past, stopping twenty or thirty metres further on.

It appeared the first contingent was preparing to split off. Jeff's curiosity piqued as the two remaining drivers spread a map out over the rear window and pinned it down with the wiper blade, each catching hold of a lower corner to stop it flapping in the wind. They examined their route, animating the discussion with plenty of nods and finger-pointing.

'You're too quiet,' Rasul chided, turning round to the Australian. 'Have you finished?'

Jeff nodded. This was a keen observation on the irascible *guerrilla*'s part. Writing an important song always exhausted him, and this one was important on several fronts.

'Yeah. It's finished.'

'Is it good?'

'Doubtless.'

Two rows of yellowed teeth spread into a grin. 'When do I get my money?'

'From October,' the songwriter answered without changing his expression. 'It'll pay my ransom.'

'A handsome ransom,' Rasul quipped in a rare spark of humour.

Jeff laughed. 'Yeah. I'll use that. And some.'

His face breaking into another wide smile, the freedom-fighter rocked back and forth in his seat for a while before buttoning his lip, opening the car door and walking away. The multi-millionnaire imagined this man, similarly afflicted with old ghosts, to be furious at having succumbed to sharing a joke with his hostage. He would have been annoyed with himself too, if the shoe had been on the other foot. Damned *macho* adversarial spirit!

The metaphorical scales tipped in the world-changer's favour. Both men knew who had the upper hand now, and it was not the hand holding the gun...

He was sure this transition hadn't entirely come about as a result of the new song. Whatever the trigger, Rasul Andrew was no longer in control of his own mission.

Once past the village where this dangerous segment of his African odyssey had commenced, the traffic became more congested. It was Sunday lunchtime, and many people were out and about; Christians returning home after church services, visiting family or shopping, while Muslims, Jews and everyone else spent the day working as normal. On this rare occasion when the celebrity was not bothered about preserving his anonymity while travelling in a car, he saw person after person do a double-take through his window, tugging on their companions' sleeves and pointing at the white, utilitarian vehicle disappearing into the distance.

The famous face sat back from the glass, a sudden change of heart upon him. Although not for the same claims, his fame was as rife throughout Africa as it was in the western world. His safety was far less assured if a local resident were to raise the alarm, because his captors might feel cornered and forced into drastic, unplanned action. He wondered if his plight had been reported in the country's domestic press? He hoped not but chose to behave according to expectations.

Lynn and Gerry would have requested a media blackout. Stonebridge Music's many, boring risk management meetings tended to hinge around this mitigation strategy, causing his confidence to wax and wane as the miles slipped by. Rasul had fallen silent, no longer even snapping orders at their other two travel companions. The atmosphere was laden with negative energy, as if an additional, volatile variable had been added into the equation since last night. The captive allowed himself a modicum of optimism that it wouldn't be long before he could exchange more than a few minutes' worth of loving words with his wife.

The depleted convoy was soon within ten kilometres of Addis Ababa. The suburbs were better served with amenities; the lawns were greener and the cars newer. In fact, the sight of four-wheel drives containing dark-skinned men in *khaki* clothing seemed overly conspicuous, and Jeff sensed a little apprehension from his fellow passengers.

They were in unfamiliar territory, and every so often the driver would check the map with his boss. Neither let slip any clues as to their destination. If an EPRP safe-house existed in this neighbourhood, it was unlikely to run as a commune, the intrigued celebrity reasoned. They had arrived in the North African version of middle-classed suburbia, where foreign-educated adults lived in pairs, commuting every weekday into the city and ferrying their sons to football practice and their daughters to dance classes. Kids who grew up here played behind high fences, not among livestock with spears and knives.

The young father slipped off into a daydream. He pictured his gorgeous gipsy girl with a gap in her front teeth. Only last year, Jet had been through life's first, inescapable major humiliation, soon forgotten when two strong, white incisors began to push through his gums to endow "The Boy Who Would Be King" with a whole new *visage*. And how much would Kierney's pristine countenance change with adult teeth? He was in no rush for the little angel to grow up. She was perfect the way she was.

The car lurched into a sudden turn, scarcely slowing down for the corner. The guard to Jeff's right had been asleep, the changing momentum of the vehicle bumping him into the hostage's shoulder. Waking with a start, shock, fear and guilt collided and sent him into a flap while he offered a profuse apology to his colleagues. Rasul twisted round to dole out a mouthful of harsh words, then focussed back on their map.

'Are we there yet?' the celebrity piped up, assuming cultural differences would prevent anyone else but him from being amused.

He was wrong. The man behind the wheel laughed again.

'Ah! So you're a father too?' Jeff seized an opportunity.

'Yes. I have three children. Two boys and one girl.'

Anticipating Rasul's desire to cut this idle chit-chat short, the friendly Australian opted for some sport by testing how long he could keep the banter going. He was under the impression that their journey was almost over, given the regular turns the vehicle was making, well away from the main highway.

'Cool,' Jeff nodded, catching the driver's eyes in his rear-view mirror. 'How old?'

'Twelve, ten and seven.'

'Nice, mate. We all hope our children'll have a better life than ours, don't we?'

'Enough,' Rasul warned, wagging his finger.

The ambiance inside the cabin stiffened again. From his position behind their heads, the songwriter noticed both front-seat occupants continually checking their door mirrors. He swivelled round to look out of the window, where a bottle-green sedan containing four Caucasians in dark suits sat right on their tail. Either they were being followed, or these men were going to a funeral. Or both...

The rebels' nerves were contagious, hairs on the back of the prisoner's neck now prickling. The weapon resting on his companion's knees still pointed in his direction and could be brought to bear in an instant, should anything unusual happen. The four-wheel drive took another starboard tack into a narrow, residential street, slowing to a crawl for Rasul to peer at the brass plaques on each gatepost. The green sedan's indicator suggested it was turning too.

'Over there.'

Making his rear-seat passenger jump, the leader waved at a row of houses on the left, all obscured by high wrought iron fencing. The car swang into a driveway, bouncing over low speed bumps, and came to rest behind a sleek, black Mercedes. Jeff glanced over his shoulder again, not surprised to see their four smartly-dressed followers steer their vehicle sideways across the dropped kerb, blocking the entrance.

The main house was palatial by North-African standards. Its lush gardens were meticulously maintained on several terraced levels, with a sweeping pathway leading to a set of black double doors. Seeing the solid barrier up ahead, the musician wondered if his door phobia might have returned along with the nightmares. There was no time to worry about this now. One of the high-gloss portals had opened, sending three more dark-suited men running down the path. Black Africans on this occasion however...

Whose house were they visiting? And why? At least there were no guns and no raised voices. A bulky plain-clothed heavyweight stepped forward from the green car and grabbed the handle of Jeff's door, pulling it wide open and gesturing for him to step out.

'Go,' Rasul growled, nodding his head towards the light. 'You are free.'

Summoning forbearance from deep inside, the unlikely statesman said nothing in reply. He who was seldom short of words could think of none. Was his ordeal really at an end? To whom had these rebels handed him over? He descended from the vehicle, looking his new doorman in the eyes.

'Thanks. Am I allowed to ask where I am?'

'Headquarters of the TPLF, sir,' the man answered, holding his hand out. 'My name is Hendriksen.'

'Jeff Diamond,' the tall Australian responded, smiling and shaking Matthias' hand. 'But I guess you already know that.'

'Indeed. I've had the pleasure of speaking to your wife at all hours this weekend.'

The relieved hostage chuckled. 'Oh, yeah? You lucky bastard. Looks like I owe you, so cheers.'

While the security consultant accepted the genuine gratitude, Jeff's attention diverted to a shortish Tigrayan tribesman ambling down from the house. Simultaneously, out of the corner of his eye, he noticed his three *guerrilla* companions freeze to the spot. Hendriksen moved to one side and allowed the smiling man to approach the rear door of the car, and again handshakes were exchanged.

'Mister Diamond. Welcome. How are you? It's nice to see you again.'

'I'm fine, Mister Mehretu. It's good to see you too,' the negotiator grinned, distracted along with everyone else by the moment's surrealism. 'Sorry I'm late. I hope you started without me.'

Jemal Mehretu embraced the amiable traveller before stepping out of the way and ushering him forward. Directed to enter the house, the three resident security guards began to scale the steep incline backwards, training their eyes on Rasul and his fellows.

'One minute, if I may, please?' the peacemaker requested of his surprise host, jogging across in front of the filthy vehicle, much to the bodyguards' dismay. 'Rasul Andrew, thank you. And to your men and women. I can't say it's been a pleasure, but you treated me fairly.'

'Jeff Diamond,' the gruff leader responded. 'You are a great man with a big heart. With you, my men learn a lot about being men. They do not learn this from me. Do not forget us when you talk of ending the Derg's power. It needs to happen everywhere. Not only with old men in fine houses and with government officials. It must be with young men too.'

The philosopher nodded. 'And young women,' he added. 'Thanks, and I won't forget. I also need to know where to send your royalty cheque for the song we wrote.'

'*We* did not write it,' the humbled man shook his head.

'Yes, we did. That song wouldn't exist without you and your guys, so we did write it, and you'll receive your money in October. Give one of these guys some way of contacting you, please. You have my word.'

The songwriter extended a hand to his inadvertent collaborator, who shook it harder than either expected. The kidnapping episode was over with all parties left standing. Tapping the bonnet of the dusty car a couple of times, the free man's eyes held those of his former captors before he joined Mehretu and Hendriksen.

Two of the remaining white security detail loitered in the driveway, with a third making his way up the hill to the rear of the property. Jeff was eager to learn what the TPLF boss had in store for Rasul Andrew and his cronies, yet knew it was not his place to ask. His focus must change to the old men in fine houses and the government officials for now, but he wouldn't forsake the disenfranchised youth of this famine-ravaged country.

***

'He never did, did he?' Ryan sighed, closing the photograph album and recalling Fiona's somewhat naïve question. 'Forget the common man and woman, I mean. I find that amazing. I get caught out all the time, but Dad never did.'

Gerry Blake had been surprised to find the captain of the Australian cricket team on his doorstep the day before his sixtieth birthday, having flown down from Sydney with the rest of the squad for a week of intensive training at the Melbourne Cricket Ground. He had brought a new girlfriend with him too, a stunning blonde who bore a striking resemblance to his much-missed mother.

'Mum and Dad always remembered the important stuff,' the younger man recounted. 'Mum was into the detail... the facts and figures of everything we did... whereas for Dad, it was either the cryptic meaning of things, or the funny side. Like "enthusiastiasm", for example...'

'What?' the Paragon Holdings' former Chairman cried out.

'"Enthusiastiasm",' the incumbent repeated. 'I wrote it in an essay, for school homework when I was eight or nine, and it stuck forever. He even extended it to "enthusiastiasmically" just to take the piss out of me in front of all and sundry. He was always good like that.'

Fiona curtailed her laughter, watching Ryan's eyes moisten. 'How's Kierney?'

'Well, thanks. She finishes her stint in Geneva next week. Back next Tuesday for a fortnight, on her way to Beijing. She's desperate to perfect her Mandarin.'

Gerry offered his mate's thirty-two-year-old son a cigar, only to have it declined due to tomorrow's heavy day in the nets. He was becoming more like his father as the years went by; less physical and more cranial, exactly as the great man had predicted. The sporting fraternity had speculated that Ryan Diamond might ditch his bat and ball at the end of the coming tri-nations test season against Pakistan and the West Indies, with his film-making expertise now world-renowned and his place at the helm of the NASDAQ's shining light set in stone.

'So do you think your dad condoned the actions of that rebel gang in Ethiopia?' the Irishman asked, flicking through the album and stopping at a picture of Jeff with Jemal Mehretu.

The sportsman shrugged. 'The word "condone" has an element of judgement about it, in his humble opinion and mine. From what I can remember about that time, he didn't think anyone should judge anyone until they'd walked a mile in the person's shoes. You know that old Elvis song?'

The grey-haired accountant whistled. 'My God, you sound so much like him. It's uncanny. If I close my eyes, I could be sitting here with him again.'

'Oh, yeah?' the Colorado resident smiled. 'That'd be good. I'd like that too. I still miss the cantankerous bastard. Hey…'

His voice trailed off on spying a shot of the helicopter which had been housed at *Escondido* towards the end of the family's tenure at the beautiful seaside *hacienda*. Gerry and Fiona both looked up, wondering what their guest had been reminded of this time.

'Dad kept that damned hangar in absolute lockdown!' Ryan laughed. 'He didn't trust me not to take it for a spin. Pun alert!'

The other's chuckled.

'Rightly so, Boy Wonder,' the older man put on his most pompous schoolmaster's voice. 'I seem to remember your *penchant* for pressing buttons you shouldn't press…'

'Yeah. Alright, alright! Batman couldn't keep his mouth shut, obviously! While he was dealing with some conflict resolution or other, he told me he used to sit in the chopper some nights, when he felt life was kicking him in the balls, so Mum didn't have to deal with him.'

'That doesn't sound right,' Gerry countered. 'I thought they told each other everything.'

'They did. It wasn't her pushing him away. Dad called time on the amount of sympathy she had to dish out, I think. Like when those two women died at the concert in Chicago... Much later though, he told me he used to sit staring through the windshield of the helicopter at the headlights reflecting off the inside of the hangar doors, still torturing himself about payback. And then after Mum died, Kierney said he finished drafting Act Three's *finalé* in the cockpit at Moorabbin Airport, the day before he sold the chopper. He sure got his payback, didn't he?'

'What's this quote?' Fiona jumped in, eager to keep the mood light.

The former corporate lawyer who had married the Diamonds' loyal business manager at the end of nineteen-ninety-six, sat with a second photograph album spread out across her lap. Ryan leaned over to check what she was pointing at. The woman's gleaming, varnished fingernail drilled into the page beside a decorative piece of card which had been inserted next to a picture of Jeff Diamond receiving the Nobel Peace Prize for his significant efforts in securing stability and prosperity in Africa.

'Oh, that!' the young sporting hero smiled. 'Mum put that in there. It's a line from *"Les Misérables"*. It means something along the lines of "It's wrong for a man to leave behind a shadow in his own shape." Humility, in other words.'

Gerry raised his brandy glass. 'That day was tough. The same day he found out he'd won the prize, we also discovered two of "Teachers for Peace"'s longest-serving field workers had been shot by *militia* in Eritrea.'

'Yeah,' the cricketer nodded. 'They told us about that. He used to use this quote when he spoke about being a facilitator rather than a dictator, particularly in response to suggestions that he was a powerful force on the world stage.'

The forthright woman caught her breath. 'Wow! I never knew...'

'Not many people did. The other line's also from *"Les Mis'"*, about the fall of *Napoléon*. Can I borrow the photos, please?' Ryan held his hand out, the strength in his arms bearing the load with consummate ease. 'Yep. That's it. I have to remember the translation Dad preferred. You know how picky he was about getting into Hugo's head.'

'His former self's head, you mean,' the billionnaire's oldest friend sniggered.

The billionnaire's firstborn sniffed, annoyed by the derision in the accountant's tone after all these years. 'Whatever, Blake-san, as someone we know would've said. Oh, cool... The translation's in here already. Kiz must've added it. "That there should be so great a concentration of vitality, so large a world contained within the mind of a single man, must in the end have been fatal to civilisation." Still sends shivers down my spine! It was like a guiding principle, he told us, for whenever he thought the press was putting him too much on a pedestal. He always said he couldn't afford to dominate public opinion if any new idea was to gain broad support.'

'Phew,' Gerry sighed, wiping the back of his right hand across his forehead. 'Too highbrow for this time of night, mate. Haven't you got any ordinary happy snaps in there? You guys went to Bali about that time too, didn't you?'

'Ha! We did. We had an awesome holiday in Ubud. That's where I learned to ride a motor scooter, and where I won my first ever brownie points for sarcasm.'

'Sarcasm. Not you, surely?' Fiona chuckled.

Their guest smirked. 'Are you trying to be funny?'

'Accidentally, I think,' the executive teased his wife. 'Or else it was quite clever, darling. For what did you win your Nobel Prize for, pray?'

'I'm not sure exactly. As far as it was replayed to me, I'd obviously listened to Mum telling us why shopkeepers leave those colourful little trays of flowers and incense outside their doors. So one day, when we were walking along a footpath, I pointed to an empty potato crisp packet that'd been tossed on the ground and said, "Hey, look! A gift to the litter gods. How kind!"'

Fiona's jaw dropped. 'Cheeky bugger!'

'Thank you,' Ryan replied. 'Dad was proud of me that day. My wicked sense of humour was emerging already. I got a "Good on ya, son," for my audacity.'

***

'¿Papá, estás feliz?' Kierney shouted into the telephone.

'Sí, pequeñita,' Jeff smiled. 'Estoy muy feliz de hablar con tigo. ¿Y tú?'

'My front tooth broke off,' the little girl couldn't wait to impart her news.

'¿Verdad?' her dad pretended not to know. 'Right one or left one?'

'The right one,' the high-pitched reply became garbled as a tiny index finger prodded the gap to make sure. 'Creo.'

'Doesn't matter, gorgeousita. Is your brother there, please?'

'Sí,' she giggled.

'What are you laughing about?'

'I was going to say, "One moment, please," like Mamá when she's joking.'

Jeff laughed too. 'So why didn't you?'

'I don't know,' his daughter answered. 'I'm too happy.'

'Too happy to tell a joke? That's weird. We'll have to talk about that when I get home. *Te amo*, baby. Please could you go and find Jetto?'

'OK. *Te amo también, Papá.* See you soon.'

'*Ciao, bella,*' the celebrity spoke into empty space, hearing the tip-tapping of dainty footsteps across the kitchen tiles.

After a leisurely shower and a change, albeit into stiff, new and rather straight-laced clothing which Jeff would never have chosen, an untimed conversation with his family painted the world all the brighter. He listened for his son's arrival, soon rewarded by a quirky wiretap of the boy asking his mother what he should say. The father's imagination had Lynn shrugging and pointing to the telephone, always keen for the children to find their own way through such growth opportunities.

'Hi, Dad. Where are you?'

'Hey, mate. I'm still in Ethiopia.'

'Still?' the eight-year-old whined. 'When are you coming home?'

'Yes, still. I hear you! I'll be home next week. I've got so much to tell you.'

'But that's ages,' Jet sounded dejected.

'I know,' the musician moaned in return. 'It is ages. You're not wrong. I miss you and can't wait to get home. I'm going to meet you from school on Friday *arvo*. Then we can spend the weekend at *Escondido*. You'll have to give me a tour 'cause I've forgotten where everything is.'

The lad scoffed. 'No, you haven't. Stop treating me like a little kid.'

'But you are a little kid.'

'No, I'm not.'

'Hey, Captain?' his father interrupted.

'Yes...'

'I need to say thank you for saying *"Te amo, Papá,"* the other day. It was fantastic for me to hear that from so far away. It cheered me up big-time.'

The eight-year-old's not-so-little chest puffed out with pride. 'That's OK, Dad,' he said. 'I mean, *de nada, Papá.* You were sad, weren't you?'

'I was, mate, 'cause I didn't know when I'd see you guys again. But I'm not sad anymore.'

'So why can't you come home now? You deserve it.'

'Thanks!' Jeff laughed at the innocent statement. 'I'm glad you think I deserve it. Me too, but I've got heaps of important stuff to do. What've you been up to today?'

A loud inward breath vibrated round the globe. 'Cricket training, then homework. And then we had lunch. Um... Then what?'

'I don't know,' his father teased. 'I wasn't there.'

'I know that! Oh, yeah! Mitch came over, and we just mucked around, then he went home and we had dinner and then you rang. And now is now.'

The doting dad nodded. Nostradamus hath spake. Now was now.

'*Excelente,*' he chuckled. '*Muy bien.* Please could you put Mum on the 'phone, mate?'

'Yes. Hang on,' Jet answered, before yelling out at the top of his voice.

'Jeez, mate! Not so loud! If you're going to shout, you have to put your hand over the 'phone. You burst my eardrum.'

'Sorry, Dad. I forgot.'

'That's OK. You're excited. I'm excited too, but I'll be much more excited on Friday *arvo*. I don't know how I'm going to wait 'til then, but I'll try.'

'Me too,' his son dismissed the sentiment. 'Mum's here. Bye.'

'Cool. *Adiós, amigo,*' Jeff laughed.

'*Olá, amigo,*' Lynn's voice sang straight to his faraway heart. 'You alright?'

The young mother stood and waited for an answer to her question, daring to hope her husband was on the road to recovery, even though they might encounter a few bumps along the way. She also guessed why no reply was forthcoming, happy to be patient until he managed to string a sentence together through the emotional rush. Punctuated by the odd sniff, his deep breathing set her own passions vibrating from head to toe.

'I've got the *finalé* for Act One licked,' he told her, gulping down the lump in his throat.

'What? Oh, have you? Fantastic. When did you do that?'

'Today, with what I presume was a loaded gun bouncing around on the guy next to me's knees. It's the finished article, angel,' the songwriter explained through his tears. '*La pièce de résistance,* no less.'

'*Excelente*, I suppose. Sounds awful.'

'Not really, as it turned out. I wrote it in the back of the car while we were driving to Addis Ababa. Parallel worlds colliding, people having to make hard choices and accepting their fate. You'll love it.'

'I know I will. Are you OK though? Really?'

'Yep. But I have to ask you a favour.'

Lynn thought she discerned fearful overtones. 'Oh, yes? What sort of favour?'

The crackle of noisy breath sounded close to the receiver. The image of her sex-god decorating the air with white smoke while they spoke was enticing, but not enough to change the subject. There was a sincerity in his voice which she recognised only too well.

'Something neither of us wants me to do, but I need to do,' the traveller hinted.

'You're not coming home, are you?'

'No.'

Chuckling, the Olympian responded. 'I said you'd do this. To Gerry, when we first knew you were missing.'

'Did you?' Jeff asked, his chest tightening again, kicking himself for assuming the worst.

'Yeah. I said you wouldn't be able to come home straightaway because it'd send the wrong signal.'

'*Exactement, Regala*,' he almost shouted. 'So you don't mind?'

'Well, I wouldn't go that far… Of course I mind, but I wouldn't let you come home either, for precisely the same reason,' the long-suffering wife insisted. 'It's completely the right thing to do.'

'Christ Almighty! I wish I could kiss you,' the tired man whispered. '*Gracias*, angel. I don't deserve you.'

'Shhh,' Lynn murmured. 'Yes, you do. You're a hero, Jeff. My hero, and the kids' hero. I love you so much.'

The caller relaxed, his concerns stubbed out along with the end of his cigarette. 'Jesus! I love you too. And hey, angel… I'm sorry about that first 'phone call.'

'Why? What about it?' she asked.

'They only gave me two minutes, and were literally counting the seconds,' he explained, reconstituting the scene from his recent memory. 'I couldn't talk. I didn't want to lose it in front of six armed and fuck-ugly, twenty-something meat-heads.'

'Oh,' Australia's darling giggled. 'That's a fine string of compliments! All good. I know real men don't cry. I was just so glad you were still alive and not badly hurt. So now will you answer my first question, please?'

'Which question?' her husband laughed too.

'Are you OK?'

'Oh, that old chestnut?' he teased. 'Can't you ask anything more original?'

'No,' Lynn huffed. 'For God's sake, give it a rest for one second! It's an oldie but a goodie. Just answer me, and we can move on.'

Jeff sat back in his chair and began to cry all over again. He was relieved and a little bewildered to find himself alone in a comfortable room, with no guns to be seen and no foul-smelling blokes sharing his space.

'Yeah. I'm fine, angel,' he reported. 'My collarbone's much better and hopefully won't need re-breaking. A few cuts and bruises, and a lump at the back of my head where my undivided attention was summoned with a rifle butt…'

'Ouch! Oh, my God. That's terrible. Why did they do that?'

'Ah, I can't remember. Probably said something stupid. Y'know me... I never know when to keep my bloody mouth shut.'

'Ain't that the truth!' the tennis champion laughed. 'Yes, I do know you.'

'It was funny,' the comedian carried on, now much more relaxed and horny beyond belief, 'the whole hostage situation.'

Lynn feigned incredulity. 'Right! I'd never have used the words "hostage situation" and "funny" in the same sentence.'

'No. Me neither, normally,' her man agreed. 'Except there've been so many beautiful ironies and surreal contradictions over the last few days. It's going to take me a while to process them all well enough to tell you. Anyway, when I was in the care of the EPRP the first time...'

'After the car rolled over?' the amazed listener checked.

'You know about that?'

'Yes. You and the driver, Dennis.'

'How d'you know all this? From Hendriksen?'

'Yes,' his wife's calm voice reassured him. 'But carry on with the story.'

Jeff whistled through pursed lips. 'Yeah. It was weird as all hell... I started asking questions like "Where are you taking us?" and so forth, and the guy next to me holding the gun told me to shut up. Then the head honcho turned round and said, "Shut the fuck up." Straight into my face, just like we were at a Collingwood match.'

The sportswoman's sunny laugh rang out again. 'That *is* funny! Much funnier than being shot.'

'Don't you start,' her husband chided. 'If I'd have said that, you'd have given me heaps.'

'You're right,' the woman admitted. 'I'm sorry. So what are you doing tonight then?'

'Masturbating,' Jeff responded without fanfare.

'Oh, OK,' Lynn sighed. 'More fool me for asking.'

'Sorry, baby. Honesty is the best policy, isn't it? Just that I had the most amazing dream last night. I want to replay it tonight, when I'm not sharing a room with someone called Thomas.'

'Hey, enough! I actually meant with Jemal Mehretu,' his wife brought her distant caller back down to Earth. 'You sex-starved idiot!'

'Right,' the world's greatest lover smiled. 'How disappointing...'

He opted to leave the unwelcome information about his nightmares' return until the pair was face-to-face. The last thing he wanted was to give his dream girl more to worry about; not after everything she had been through in recent days and with all she had done to secure his safe release.

'We're having dinner,' Jeff answered instead. 'He wants to hear about the negotiations. And it'll be good for me to focus my mind on them too. Leave all this shit behind, y'know...'

'Yeah. I bet,' Lynn affirmed.

'And then I'm going to come back to this quiet, luxurious bedroom with a lock on the door and no lumpy seats where the springs have broken through. I'm *gonna* wank myself sore, imagining you touching me all over and my hands on your body, and your gorgeous eyes staring into mine.'

'Hmm,' he heard his dream girl exhale.

'Come to think of it, angel... You got ten minutes to spare? I'm not really that hungry.'

LORRAINE PESTELL

Life's Magic Formula

The weather on Bali in March was perfect for a normal family looking to escape for some fun in the sun. Jeff Diamond's homecoming flight was cut short in Perth, having made a snap decision to meet his loved ones on the peaceful Indonesian island instead of connecting through to Melbourne.

Chasing his breakfast down with the first beer of the day, the free man scanned the local newspaper while cars, vans and scooters crammed through the narrow Semanyak streets, every one on a vital mission. The beard he had cultivated during the final week of his African adventure surrendered after a valiant struggle with three successive razor blades, and his clean-shaven features had met with amorous appreciation when at last he was reunited with his dream girl.

Their lovemaking never sweeter or more satisfying, the famous couple braved the seaside promenade for breakfast with hundreds of fellow Australian tourists. Cathy and her media *machinistas* had managed to keep the hostage ordeal out of the newspapers, leaving the superstars to field the usual trivial questions about touring and their latest hit singles.

'I want us to do that!' Jet shouted, pointing at yet another heavily-laden motorbike, this one carrying bags of shopping in addition to an entire family.

The pavement was still wet after a recent deluge, leading diners at this particular restaurant situated on a busy corner to witness two minor accidents in the time it had taken for their meals to arrive. Lynn's eyes flicked from her son to his dad, hoping his attention might soon be drawn elsewhere, only to have their daughter echo the boy's request.

'I want us to do that too!' the little girl yelled at the top of her voice.

'*Papá?*' their mother turned to her husband.

'I want us to do that too,' Jeff joined in, pointing at the incessant trail of four- and five-ups dodging holes in the uneven road surface. 'Looks like fun.'

'May we do it, Mum, please?' Jet's blue eyes were pleading. 'It *will* be fun. It's not dangerous.'

The ratio of three to one in favour was little surprise for the young woman, whose heart could never resist pleasing her brood even if her head were inclined to overrule. After a sly aside to her dark-haired Adonis concerning his renewed *penchant* for living on the edge, she relented after securing good behaviour bonds from both children.

As always, the waiter's signal to deliver the celebrities their bill also brought a long queue of fans flooding to their table for autographs. Swapping the pen between them, the parents each took a child to the bathroom while the other worked through the line. To anyone passing and unable to identify who sat in the small alcove, it must have looked like payday on the farm at harvest time.

The family extricated themselves from the throng before their collective patience ran out and jogged the short distance to a nearby scooter hire shop. Ten minutes later, they had purchased a full twenty-four hours' worth of sixty-cubic-centimetre Honda for less than an Australian dollar.

'Bargain!' Jeff laughed. 'Best buck we've spent this year. Eh, kids?'

Jet stood on the footplate between his father's long, hairy legs, while Kierney straddled the seat between her parents. The bike lurched forward at a heavy-handed twist of the throttle, nearly sending all four passengers over the handlebars. Amid cries of alarm, the man in charge apologised and set off again at a much more sedate pace.

Trundling downhill, making for their accommodation, the youngest Diamond's initial apprehension turned into whoops of joy. The feeling of tiny hands hanging on to her dad's waist through his cotton shirt sent shivers of pleasure through him. Lynn's lips brushed the skin below his hairline, and her fingers gave his neck a loving squeeze before descending to form a barrier to prevent their daughter from falling sideways as they leaned into the next corner.

What an exhilarating experience for the happy children! With Jet shouting random greetings at intervals, he used the raised speedometer dial as a mysterious source of cosmic energy which allowed him to spring into orbit whenever they encountered a bump in the road. After the upward force of the crown of his head banged the underside of his dad's chin, clamping his tongue in his closed jaws for the third time, the boy reluctantly settled for surviving on his hyperactivity alone.

The two-wheeled explorers stopped to share a bottle of water and admire the view of the steep escarpment below. They could just about make out the coastline way in the distance. Kierney, who had been as quiet as a mouse, content to be *en famille* and to enjoy the outing, pointed to the handlebars.

'Please may I go on the front next, *Papá*? Like Jetto?'

Lynn angled her forehead down to rest on her husband's shoulder, knowing how difficult he found saying no to the adorable miniature. 'You can try, Kizzy, but I don't think you'll like it. You won't be able to see anything.'

'I will, *Mamá*,' the girl insisted with a sweet smile. 'I can see.'

'Listen to *la mamá, pequeñita*,' her father requested.

Already committed to her mission, the little mite jumped off the low wall they had occupied for their drinks break and ran to the scooter's running board. It was propped up on its stand on the footpath, and the superstar lunged towards it, in case it were to fall over.

'Careful, baby. *Vienes*. Let's try. Just a few minutes, *yo y tú*. OK?'

Two huge, dark eyes lit up with glee, and Kierney clapped her hands. Her parents exchanged silent messages of gratitude and love, both lapping up these precious moments of togetherness. Jet thought otherwise however, weighing into the argument as the all-knowing member of the family.

'Kiz, you're too little. You can't do that 'til next year.'

Jeff threw his leg over the seat and kicked the stand backwards to let the scooter settle back on two wheels. Without hesitation, the seven-year-old placed one foot and then the other onto the footplate and made a grab for the rubberised hand-grips. Lynn laughed as she snapped a couple of pictures for the holiday album, seeing her little girl's arms stretched as far apart as they could reach.

The entranced father turned the key in the ignition, and the engine sprang to life. Kierney twisted her neck all the way around like a barn owl, her smile beaming.

'*¿Vamanos?*'

A tiny left hand raised itself high, with an index finger pointing forwards as if she were flashing an *epée*. Taking this as his cue, the driver winked at his wife and carefully released the brake.

'Bye, Dad!' his son yelled. 'Bye, Kizzy!'

Only the very top of the youngster's head was visible, encased by her *chauffeur*'s thighs and the faring around the bike's steering column. Initially, the little girl squealed with delight as her father let out the throttle, accelerating to a respectable speed. The more she fidgeted however, the closer together her protective barriers moved, until she was hemmed in on all sides.

'You OK down there, *pequeñita*?'

The first time he asked, Jeff received another grin and a muted shout of pleasure. Yet by the time they had travelled another fifty metres or so, the diminutive body had begun to sag. He slowed to a crawling pace to find out what was wrong. Sure enough, the mop of dark hair, pulled up into a ribbon in the way she preferred, rotated anti-clockwise by one hundred and eighty degrees to reveal a less than happy face.

'*¿Qué tal*, baby?'

'I can't see anything, *Papá. No me gusta. ¿Podemos parar, por favor?*'

An enormous, empathetic hand swooped down, coming in to land on his daughter's hair, returning the smile to her face in an instant. The matching pair rode in a wide arc to end up in the same spot, where the driver brought the scooter to a halt with a comic jerk. Kierney's head whipped back against his crotch before the loss of momentum pushed them both forwards until his knuckles banged against the instrumentation panel's glass casing.

'Ow, *Papá*,' the child chirped, thinking her daddy must have hurt his hand.

She jumped down to the ground, straightaway turning round and trying to kiss his fingers better. Jeff grabbed her around the waist with a kindly roar and whisked her up to his chest. Heaving himself off the motorcycle, he held his nonplussed daughter aloft.

'*Gracias, pequeñita.* We're here! Did *ya* miss us?'

'Yeah!' mother and son replied in chorus.

'So how was the ride, darling?' the slender blonde enquired, seeing the little girl almost lose her balance while running to join her brother.

'I couldn't see anything,' she repeated. 'It was fun, but Jet can go on the front. I like to sit with you, *Mamá*.'

Her father smiled. '*Bonne idée, gorgeous. Très bonne idée.* You tried anyway. That's the most important thing.'

***

With normal business hours well and truly over, on the Monday evening after the Diamonds' holiday in Bali had come to a close, Gerry, Cathy and Jeff had adjourned from the Collins Street offices to the Supper Club on Spring Street for a quiet drink, forsaking the noisy crowd of familiar faces in Rosati's with express purpose.

A press release had been sent out to coincide with the family's return to Melbourne, and the rock star had flown in to Tullamarine alone at lunchtime to face a large gathering of well-informed journalists and some die-hard fans. While Lynn and the children prepared for the trip back to their seaside abode after the following day at school, he walked the two kilometres between their apartment and the security firm's premises to debrief in secret.

Over an expensive bottle of *Cabernet Sauvignon*, the celebrity's communications specialist and business manager listened in amazement as their boss recounted his hostage experience in intricate detail. One minute they were laughing and the next gasping in horror.

'You have to write all this down,' Gerry told him. 'It's a movie in the making.'

Jeff shook his head. 'No, mate. It's not for me to write. Well, not yet anyway… I need to concentrate on getting these talks happening properly. There's no way I can be seen as distracted by self-serving publicity stunts.'

'But people'll love it,' Cathy objected. 'You've got to put some sort of media release out, at least. We're drowning in the office. Calls are absolutely jamming the switchboard since word got out.'

'Yeah, OK,' her boss capitulated. 'You're right, I guess. Perhaps we should say something. Can you give me a day to think about how I want to play it.'

Gerry nodded. 'Sure thing. Another bottle?'

Jeff checked his watch, guessing his children's bedtime wasn't too far off. 'No. Cheers,' he declined, 'but d'you mind if I bail?'

'Yes! I bloody well do mind. What's going on?' the adamant Irishman exclaimed. 'I'll pay.'

'Come back to the apartment,' his client suggested, laughing at the man's outlandish reaction. 'We can open a bottle there. I just don't want to be away from Lynn and the kids any longer than I have to.'

'Wimp,' the accountant teased.

'That's me,' the thirty-four-year-old was unfazed. 'We're still in the separation anxiety zone. And besides, I quite like spending time with people I love, mate. You should try it sometime...'

Their sympathetic office manager smiled at the men's typical banter, gathering her handbag and umbrella together. Gerry frowned in disapproval and sank his remaining mouthfuls of wine. Reaching across the bar, he slapped a heavy right hand on his mate's shoulder.

'Come on then, Cinderella,' he joked. 'Let's get you back to your domestic splendour. Our company not good enough for you these days obviously.'

Jeff went to swear but changed his mind. The complex emotional toll of the last few weeks had affected everyone, including those who professed only to have feelings for themselves. The two longstanding friends bid farewell to the staff and escorted their colleague to her car through a late evening shower. Cool raindrops bounced off the superstar's face, waking him up a little.

'Don't listen to this cold-hearted oaf. We're really glad to have you back,' Cathy said, giving her employer an over-enthusiastic hug. 'Say hi to Lynn and the kids from me. Sleep well.'

'Thanks,' Jeff responded, kissing her on the cheek. 'You too. Hope the 'phones calm down tomorrow. Sorry for all the extra work. Tell everyone I'm sorry, will you, please?'

His personal assistant nodded and smiled, instructing the smartly-dressed gentlemen to pick up the pace to save their suits from the wet weather. Scoffing at her motherly advice, they continued northwards up Spring Street to the busy corner above which Australia's hottest superstars lived their anonymous city life.

Within five minutes, the lift had swallowed its damp passengers, and they ascended to the sixteenth-floor sanctuary. Stepping out onto the landing, Jeff half expected the Jaworski brothers to come rushing to meet him, old instincts bracing just in case.

'Mate, are you alright?' Gerry asked. 'You look as if you're about to throw up.'

Subtle lighting in the hallway couldn't conceal the welcome atmosphere within, and the householder breathed a huge sigh of relief to encounter nothing but the sounds of youthful exuberance. Slipping his friend a thumbs-up, he tensed his muscles for the second time to receive an incoming small boy without brakes. Jet's feet left the ground as his father wrestled with him, grimacing as eight-year-old fists battered his last few African bruises.

As battle ensued, the visitor wandered into the lounge room to greet Lynn with a kiss, both spectators shaking their heads at the funny spectacle. The big-kid billionnaire had sunk to his knees and was soon rolling on the floorboards with his much smaller opponent, having trouble pinning his flailing limbs down. Jet could hardly fight for laughing, reduced to fits when every time he tried to stand up, his dad would tickle his ribs with penetrating musician's fingers.

'Hey, Daws!' the boy yelled. 'Come and help! I'm getting killed here!'

Dawson Jenner answered his mate's call, having rushed away from the television when the fuss first started. He ran past Gerry like a whirling dervish, ending up walloping himself against Uncle Jeff's outstretched spare hand. Underestimating the backward force of an adult's strength, the older boy ricocheted to the floor with a bump before scrambling to his feet again, even more fired-up.

'Die! Die! Die!' Jet shouted, taking advantage of his assailant's distraction by pummelling his stomach with a barrage of blows.

The heightened level of activity was overdubbed with a symphony of growls and cries, interspersed with the odd groan, while the family's male childminder fetched bottles of beer for the recent arrivals. Gerry stood on the sidelines with Dave, placing bets on which wrestler would come off worst. The smart money was on Dad.

Breathless, Jeff endeavoured to shake himself free of the flyweights. His spine hadn't even had the chance to straighten before he was leaped upon from behind, his neck seized by two persistent hands. The head of the pride let forth a fitting roar, then wheeled around and sent Jet's legs circling high in the air, warning Dawson to duck if he wished to avoid a kick in the face from his best friend's runners.

'Mum, you've gotta help us!' the lad screamed. 'Help! Put me down! Help, someone!'

'No way!' his mother chided. 'You started it. You have to finish it.'

Her husband groaned, sneaking a glance in Lynn's direction. Her only response was to shrug as if to say, "You're on your own, mate!" He dealt her a suggestive wink, sustaining a swift toe in the groin a split-second later.

'Aaaaargh!' the injured man yelled out in pain, bringing Kierney and Irina running from the little girl's bedroom.

320

'Come on, boys,' the tennis champion relented. 'That's enough. Poor Dad. You'd better watch out. He might want to stay in Africa forever next time.'

'No!' their daughter cried. 'Stop it, Jetto. Stop!'

Jeff sprang to his feet, and both lads slithered down onto the floor. All three were red-faced, sweaty and panting like fury. The father offered a conciliatory hand to his son and his ten-year-old playmate, yanking them up to signal the end of the match.

'That's it. I win,' he declared. 'Revenge is sweet. Go cry in your milk, guys.'

With the runners-up deciding to slug it out for second place, Gerry handed the victor a cold bottle of beer. 'Check out your shirt!' he boomed.

To the songwriter's astonishment, one of the boys had bitten through the fabric of his right sleeve, leaving a rip the length of his index finger. On the skin underneath, when he parted the tear to inspect the damage, was a neat, red arc of teeth-marks. The pair of pint-sized wrestlers stared at each other in shock.

'Did we do that?' Jet asked in wonder.

'Well, mate, process of elimination... I certainly didn't do it,' the executive waded in, 'and it wasn't torn like that in the lift coming up.'

'Whoa! Sorry, Dad.'

'No drama, son,' Jeff smiled. 'It could just as easily have been you, Daws. We'll have to get Forensics to match the imprint, to see who's giving up their pocket money to buy me a new shirt.'

The youngsters hoped he was joking. Kierney ran to her father, who picked her up, raising her face to his.

'*¿Qué tal*, my gorgeous, quiet, non-pain-inducing angel?'

'*Muy bien, gracias, Papá*,' the seven-year-old giggled, accepting a kiss on the end of her nose. 'You're all wet.'

'It's raining outside,' the breathless man made his feeble excuse.

'And inside,' she smiled, wiping her finger across his forehead and then on his shirt. 'Yuck.'

Hugging his good-natured daughter to his chest, the tall musician leaned over to place her feet on the floor, ready to move their evening on. Seeing him walking towards her, into the lounge room, Lynn asked Dave and Irina to ferry the three children to their rooms to prepare for bedtime. The men commandeered a couch each, and Jeff patted the cushion beside him for his beautiful best friend to join him. She obliged, pulling a face as she too felt the damp cotton and inspected the wrecked sleeve.

'It's raining outside,' the overgrown teenager whined again. 'Not my fault, *Mamá*. I'll go and take a quick shower. Shall we order takeaway? I'm sorry for another spur of the moment decision, bringing him home with me.'

'It's fine. No,' she countered, smiling at their visitor. 'There's plenty to go round. You're welcome, Gerry. It's nice to see you outside working hours. At least you behaved with some *decorum* when you arrived.'

Her husband sniffed at the favouritism, levering himself to his feet. Scenes such as these reinforced how fantastic it was to be home. He handed the rest of his beer to his business manager and headed along the corridor to freshen up for their meal.

'Is he doing better?' the executive asked, once the great man was out of earshot.

'Comes and goes,' Lynn nodded. 'Better on Saturday than yesterday. I think it's only just sinking in. Bali was excellent for getting the stress out of his system, but being back here's forced him to confront things. The nightmares are back too. He hates it, and that's making everything worse. I've got some good news for him though... news he won't be expecting... so hopefully, he'll cheer up after dinner.'

Gerry's inquisitive expression sought more information, but the rear-end of the Diamond pantomime horse refused to spoil the surprise. Switching on the television and offering the remote control to their guest, she excused herself to say goodnight to the youngsters. On the way to the southern side of the apartment, she put her head round the door of the master bedroom. Music blared from the *en suite* bathroom, so she scrawled a short note on his bedside lyrics notepad requesting a *rendezvous* in the kids' bedrooms.

Over the past two days, every hour or so, the solemn woman had made sure she placed a call to Blake & Partners, checking in with the returned hostage and reminding him their unending love was still very much alive. The violent dreams were every bit as intense as those she remembered from ten years ago, and she was under no illusion that their resurgence would plunge her brave world-changer into another pit of depression.

Jeff's demonic encounters had also woken the children, who had been frightened by their father screaming and shouting in the middle of the night. Luckily, the rest of the inhabitants of their *Escondido* paradise slept far enough away for the noise not to disturb them, yet the parents were concerned about the first overnighter all together in their penthouse haven, with both nannies and one of their drivers due back from their respective nights on the town.

'Come and eat,' Lynn urged, taking her man's hand as he wished Kierney a good night. 'Sleep well, darling. We love you so much.'

Serving dinner into three large bowls, to be eaten on their knees in front of the television, the caring wife breathed a sigh of relief. Jeff seemed more relaxed after his debrief with Mike Maynard and the Lion Security team, dressed in an old sweatshirt and tracksuit pants. An amorous foot played with hers under the coffee table, every now and again wandering higher to caress her calf.

Gerry, by contrast, still wore his tie, although he had loosened his top button once the wine was uncorked and his glass filled. 'You said there was news?' he piped up, finishing a huge forkful of the rich and meaty Italian dish.

'News?' the rock star echoed. 'What news?'

'Did I?'

'Oh, you did indeed,' the indomitable one insisted. 'Don't try that with me, with all due respect, Missus D. I'm not making it up. You definitely said before dinner that you had news.'

'Oh! That news?' the blonde entertainer faked a sudden jog of her memory. 'Yes. I do have news.'

Playing with the men's impatience, she piled a mouthful of sauce and *pasta* onto her fork and proceeded to insert it between her lips with a certain provocative flair.

'Jeez! For fuck's sake,' Jeff jeered. 'How much longer can you drag this out?'

His wife cocked her head, eyebrows raised while she provided an answer. 'Hmm... A very long time, I reckon.'

The songwriter appreciated the beauty's constant attempts to improve his mood, recognising a distinct stir in his lap under the emptying bowl. He groaned and swept his foot along the sheen of his wife's smooth leg, noticing a tell-tale glint in her eye. Tonight was developing into an exceptional night, and he was determined to enter into the spirit, anxious to display his gratitude in the way he knew best.

Turning to his old friend, he lifted his glass off the table. 'Mate, you can leave now. You can bring the plate back some other time.'

'Professor Engelbrecht rang,' Lynn blurted out, reaching her right hand across and resting it on her husband's left thigh, hoping to calm any adverse reflex.

Predictably, the lost boy's limbs cramped up with the shock. She traced her fingertips along his quadriceps muscle, between hip and knee and back again, applying varying amounts of pressure until it relaxed. Setting his fork down, he leaned back on the couch, breathing out through pursed lips and then inhaling through his nose. He had forgotten during their blissful decade how debilitating it was to walk the anxiety tightrope, yet here he was all over again.

'Christ. Piet? Did he? What did he say?'

'Yes,' his dream girl said with a smile. 'He wants you to ring him back.'

'The guy in Cape Town,' Gerry checked. 'The one you wanted to be part of the French negotiations?'

Jeff nodded, feeling his face flush. 'So what did he say?'

'Yes,' she repeated. 'Are you deaf now too? Drink up, mate. You're slipping.'

'Jesus Christ! Are you serious? He's on board?'

'He'd like you to ring him back,' Lynn spelled out to her astounded husband, whose complexion had since paled. 'He found out about the kidnapping. Don't know how... He said he decided after hearing about it that he couldn't not help you.'

Grimacing while he deciphered his wife's deliberate double-negative deception, the edges of the world-changer's mouth curled upwards. '*Excelente. Merci, mon amie.* That is amazingly good news.'

'Don't thank me,' the kind woman smiled. 'I'm just the messenger. He was charming, as always.'

Jeff's left arm rose over Lynn's head and came to rest on her shoulders. By the faraway look in his eyes, she had no trouble imagining the wheels spinning inside his capacious mind, glad to play a part in stoking the fire. She would let the revelation sink in, and encouraged the others to continue eating and drinking, shifting their conversation to more mundane matters, such as Michelle's upcoming wedding, the scheduled opening of "The Black Sheep" in London and the first dress rehearsal which was due to take place within a fortnight.

'Ah, yeah?' her husband tore his gaze away from the televised football match.

'Yes,' his wife shook her head. 'And I spoke to that annoying Welsh guy from DCF in Brisbane, Zac Prior. You remember him?'

'Sure. I wanted to throttle him last time we crossed paths. What did he want?'

'Only reporting new numbers. He's so damned good, so squeaky clean. Too squeaky clean.'

The philanthropist sniffed. 'Yeah. Squeakiness is next to godliness, I s'pose, but it's not being good from the heart, 'specially if people see through it. More like he's good 'cause he knows it's how he's supposed to behave. Maybe I shall throttle him next time I see him, in that case. I don't want to compromise our reputation by having someone who's that one-dimensional, no matter how sincere clean he comes across with the stats.'

'He called you a quiet achiever,' the Olympian added.

This outrageous statement was enough to divert Gerry's attention from the Collingwood-Hawthorn match. 'Quiet achiever?' he yelped. 'You? No-one could call you a quiet achiever, mate!'

'Oh, I don't know,' Lynn refuted. 'What about all the PTSD research? Hardly anyone knows about that, or the technology venture capital stuff which both of you do...'

At ten o'clock, their guest rang for a taxi to reunite him with his BMW, which had been left in the car park behind Blake & Partners' prestigious 333

Collins Street office building. He thanked his delectable host for a lovely dinner and embraced his friend.

'Take it easy, mate. You don't have to rush to set up these talks. Repair yourself and let us take care of some of it in the background. You've been through a fair bit lately.'

'Cheers,' Jeff slapped his overlord on the back. 'I'm fine. Stop treating me like some sort of invalid. It was only a few days.'

Pretending not to eavesdrop, Lynn smiled at the two men carrying on, both mellowed by alcohol and a full stomach. She knew how much her husband treasured the close relationship he had with Gerry. Neither had a brother, so they were each other's. With the lift on its way down to street level, she held her arms out for her man to walk into and was instantly swallowed up into a hungry hug.

The couple turned the lights out in the lounge room and detoured into the kitchen to load the dishwasher. They exchanged observations on the following day's agenda, realising it would be inappropriate to make contact with the professor in Cape Town until late afternoon South African time. Lynn sympathised with her husband's impatience, assuring him their discussion would be all the more fruitful for the extra hours of cogitation.

Armed with two mugs of tea, the sportswoman held out her hand. 'Do you want to take these to bed?'

'Not particularly,' Jeff sniggered. 'I want to take you to bed. Bugger the tea.'

The world-changer's greatest admirer tutted like a schoolmistress, pleased his sense of humour had not deserted him. To her surprise however, once they reached their bedroom door hand-in-hand, he released her fingers and veered across to the living room, guiding her this time by the shoulder. A few steps later, he paused to throw her a quizzical grin. What on Earth was he up to?

The television was switched back on, channels scrolling until something suitable appeared. While a series of diverse voices pleaded with the viewers to keep watching, Jeff pointed to the couch and invited his companion to sit down. She obeyed, sipping on her tea and pondering their fate.

Her lover plonked his heavy frame down by her side and picked up one of their son's science fiction storybooks from the coffee table, leafing through it with his left hand while his right fondled his wife's thigh through her skirt.

Lynn chuckled. 'Are you enjoying that? Since when have you liked books about alien planets?'

'Since about now, in fact,' the comic quipped. 'And yes. I'm allowing myself to enjoy it.'

'You snob!' the aristocrat laughed aloud.

'I know. He takes them very seriously, and I want to talk to him about them.'

Taken by surprise, the young mother's heart fell victim to his guile once more. 'Oh, that's so lovely. You're such a great dad.'

'And you're the greatest *mamá*.'

Sitting in silence on the couch with nothing interesting on television, both superstars drifted off to sleep. The record producer had given up trying to second guess her complex man's motive, preferring to set his mental state back on track. She would coax him to bed whenever he showed signs of security, but for now, this tacit hesitation felt wondrously intimate.

'Is there life out there?' the Olympian asked, brushing one of the spaceship illustrations with a long, elegant finger.

'*Bien sûr, mon amie*. The story says so. That's what I want to talk to him about.'

'OK. So if you went in search of other life-forms, would you come back?'

Jeff turned the science-fiction adventure book over and spread it across his knee, cupping the stunning face with both hands and kissing her lips. '*Bien sûr, mon amie*. Why wouldn't I?'

Downing what was left of his tea, he swivelled himself around until he was laying with his feet over the arm at the far end and his head rested in Lynn's lap. Tears began to stream from his eyes, trickling over the bridge of his nose until they dripped in a regular beat onto the fabric of her skirt. A slight breeze kissed his cheek as her hand passed by to stroke his hair.

'You're the handsomest hostage in the world. You looked so sexy tonight at dinner. I love you so much.'

'Jesus Christ! I love you too, angel,' the songwriter continued to cry, unabashed while soaking in his dream girl's unique brand of compassion. 'I was raging that first night. Fuckin' raging, baby.'

'Were you?' she crooned. 'That's good. From my perspective anyway.'

Jeff chuckled. 'I needed you, like it countered the fear.'

'Hmm... Can I do anything else?'

'No. Well, yeah. Let me rant, I guess. I just can't shut my brain down. Those guys' situations were no different to mine before you came along. You saved me from a life like that.'

The schoolmistress voice refuted, making her star pupil laugh again. 'No, I didn't. You were already destined for great things, so don't take their side, Jeff. No-one expects you to.'

'I expect me to.'

'Well, don't do it, please. What is it you say to the kids? Sympathise with their cause but not their methods?'

'But there's a better way,' the philanthropist persisted.

Still the sensible woman refused to give in. 'OK. Maybe there is, but I can hear you telling them!'

'Don't call my bluff, angel.'

'Why not?'

'Because you're supposed to be on my side,' the lost boy sat up, his eyes drilling into hers.

'Jeff! I *am* on your side,' his wife raised her voice, kissing his forehead and rocking forwards to signify she was about to depart. 'Just questioning your methods, Watson. Let's go to bed.'

Groaning his indignance at having been exposed by a more astute intellect yet again, the peacemaker rose to his full height and offered the stunning star his hand. She accepted with a smile and a curtsey, and the *duo* stood locked together, hands and tongues searching and finding while their heart rates climbed.

'You're perfect,' the caring woman whispered, stroking the side of his face. 'Are you alright?'

'Yep,' Jeff muttered. 'For now. It's not all chivalry, y'know.'

Lynn sighed, aware her charming lover was afraid to sleep in case another nightmare might be lurking around the corner. 'I know. But you're still perfect.'

'No, I'm not,' he countered. 'Can I tell you something?'

'Of course,' she replied, gazing up at the handsome but serious face.

'The more I see of life, the more I appreciate you and the kids, and everything we have together.'

'Wow... Thank you. I know what you mean.'

The thirty-three-year-old's right hand took hold behind his wife's neck, lowering her head towards his. They drew each kiss in for a long time, pausing for breath every now and again, while both sets of clothing were peeled off one by one.

'I'm generating love faster than I can dole it out to you these days,' Jeff murmured.

The beautiful woman smiled, unbuttoning his shirt and sliding her hand across his ticklish obliques. 'Thanks again. That's a lovely image.'

'I mean it,' he sighed. 'It's like our family's an oasis in a fuckin' shit world.'

The billionnaire's abrasive language hung heavy in the small space between their heads as if it were a speech bubble in a comic strip drawing. And as if their bodies were part of a whole different scene, his fingers slipped their mischievous way down to massage her clitoris with enough force to educe a deep moan of pleasure. Her hand closed around the thickness of his shaft, driving him to monopolise her every sense and make the most of their isolation.

'Well, OK... That's what we need to make life all about then,' Lynn said, returning her attention to serious matters upon seeing Jeff's eyes anxious to interpret her meaning. 'We have to give people the power to create their own oases and stop trying to fix the whole shit world. We have to be realistic about what's achievable.'

'You're spot on, angel. I must remember that too. Can we pick this up again later? I need to get my mind in a different place for a while.'

Half an hour went by with both stars immersed in their respective books before the caring wife glanced across and saw her bedfellow's eyes were closed, his breathing having changed a moment earlier. Would she leave him to sleep where he sat? No, she oughtn't. He longed for some semblance of normality in their familial rhythm, so she flexed her leg muscles in an attempt to rouse him. The subtle hint worked a treat.

To signal a return to consciousness, Jeff sidled over far enough to rub his cheek on the underside of his lover's enticing breasts. 'Hey, Thomas... Err, I mean Lynn,' he began, receiving a gentle slap on the chest. 'Sorry, angel. You coming to bed?'

Fevered lovemaking brought to its inevitable climax, the forever friends lay still while moonlight streamed through their bedroom windows. Pulling the sheet over her chilling body, the tennis champion noticed her lover pressing a finger and thumb into his temples, obscuring the nocturnal brilliance from his eyes.

'Headache?'

The world-changer nodded, squeezing out an incoherent murmur.

'How long?' she asked.

'Five minutes, that's all. It's nothing, angel.'

The young woman leaned over and kissed the heel of his hand. 'You've developed an allergy to sex now. Shame.'

'Yeah,' Jeff smiled.

'You'll have to rent me out,' she suggested, shuffling down the bed and tucking her body in alongside his.

'Eh? Not a chance, lady! If I can't get it, you can't get it. I love you. Thanks for joking about it.'

Lynn grinned. 'No worries. I'll shut the fuck up. It's not funny though, is it?'

'No,' her husband exhaled. 'But it's good to talk. Awesome, in fact. I haven't seen you for so long. This'll be gone in the morning.'

'Shhh... Perhaps you're dehydrated from the 'plane?'

'I'm *deLynneated*.'

The young woman shook her head, letting out a deep sigh. 'Be serious and drink something.'

'Sure, but I'm definitely *deLynneated*. I'll be fine. Just don't leave me.'

The air pressure in *Escondido*'s spacious interior shot skyward in an instant, neither bedfellow prepared for such an admission. Silence wrapped itself around them and drew their spirits closer together.

'Wow! After all this time, you're still so intense. You still feel that way?'

'More,' Jeff assured her. 'Much more, angel. Before, it was just selfish, but there's so much more at stake now. Absolutely everything depends on you sticking with me.'

Lynn's eyes filled with tears. 'But I'm here. I *am* sticking with us. There's nowhere I'd rather be, believe me. What do you want to do tomorrow?'

'Stay in bed?' the grateful traveller offered.

'OK. Sounds great actually.'

The amazed songwriter opened one eye, turning his head to find out if his wife was joking. 'Are you sure? Now you're scaring me.'

'Yes! Why not? Once I take the kids to school.'

'Alright, but,' he sat up, imbued with renewed energy, 'I'll take the kids to school. I'd like to. And then I'm definitely staying in bed all day.'

'If you like,' the sportswoman giggled at the zeal in his voice.

'Oh, I like. *Me gusta mucho, señora.*'

***

'Time to ring Piet?'

'D'you mind? It can wait 'til later.'

'No, it can't,' Lynn grinned.

'You're damned right,' her husband smiled back. 'It can't. You know me too well.'

'Excellent! You bet I do. I'll make some coffee then join you in the office,' she instructed, waving towards the door across the hallway. 'The 'phone number's in there. It's his work number.'

Jeff checked the clock. The professor should be on campus by now, probably assisting the long-legged Odette with an assignment. Or something similar... The rock star wondered if he would have still been behaving the same way if Australia's sexiest schoolgirl hadn't come into his life this time around? Damned straight he would!

Before dialling the number, he leaned back on the headboard for a few minutes and collected his thoughts, gaze settling on Kierney's toy rabbit. It had been posed in front of an open atlas on the other chair. He picked it up and sat it on his knee, staring into its golden-brown glass eyes. What did the world have in store for his gorgeous gipsy girl and her conquering hero of a brother?

'Professor Engelbrecht,' the thirty-three-year-old turned on the authoritative charm as soon as he heard the man's voice. 'It's Jeff Diamond. How're you going?'

'Oh, Jeff! You just caught me,' the tenured academic replied. 'Thank you for returning my call. I'm well, sir. But how about you? What the hell happened after you came to visit?'

The caller hesitated, wondering whether it was appropriate to seek sympathy so long after his release. 'It's all good, thanks, Piet. An interesting few days, you might say... Not too hospitable in parts, but everything worked out in the end.'

Lynn appeared through the half-open door, turning to click it shut behind her. The caller pressed a button on the telephone handset, broadcasting Engelbrecht's voice around the Diamonds' office. With her hands massaging his shoulders, the couple leaned into each other while the conversation continued.

'So I hear,' the South African agreed. 'Was it EPRP or rank-and-file TPLF? That lot've been quiet for a while. Just bounty hunters mostly, but still a shock to find out they'd taken you hostage.'

Jeff laughed, squeezing his wife's fingers. 'EPRP, yeah. Bit of a shock to me too.'

'Christ! Don't joke about it, man. Were they rough with you?'

'To start with, yep,' he recounted. 'Lynn's here, mate, by the way. She can hear every word you say.'

'Right-oh! Good day, m'lady. Long time I haven't had the pleasure.'

The stunning woman rolled her eyes. 'Hello again, Pieter. Nor me. Too long.'

'The girls send their regards. So the rebels roughed you up, Jeff? Badly?'

'No. Not too badly. Only at first. Listen, Piet, I'm not in much of a mood to go through it all again, to tell you the truth. Those stories are for a future evening in, over some more exquisite whiskies. My shout next time.'

'You're on!' Engelbrecht agreed. 'I suppose you're calling because Lynn passed on the message about the negotiations?'

Deftly, a playful arm reached around and twisted the tennis player's waist until she lost her balance and tumbled onto his lap. Jeff cupped his hand over the mouthpiece to cover her squeal of objection, before kissing her into submission.

'She did indeed. And thanks a lot. I'm ecstatic you changed your mind, mate. What clinched it?'

The activist heard the professor's leather chair spit under his weight and imagined him squirming at the prospect of putting his feelings into words. Without doubt, this would have been a hard decision for him to make, and equally difficult to unmake if he were still in two minds.

'Several reasons... I'd been giving the whole thing a lot of thought, ever since you left that night,' he explained. 'Your comments about my housekeeper's children being able to apply for the same jobs as my daughter. All that stuff... You're so right. It is what's important. I asked Catherine what sort of Africa she wanted to be an adult in?'

'*Excelente.* And what did she tell you?' Jeff asked, winking at his smiling partner-in-crime, who motioned that she was leaving the men to their business.

'Pretty much the same as you,' Pieter scoffed. 'Firstly, here in South Africa: no more segregation, better understanding of blacks by whites, and vice versa. And elsewhere: no more no-go areas and an end to minority powerbases. Freedom of movement, in short.'

'Smart girl,' the Australian responded. 'Did you talk to Nandi too?'

'Yes. A little. She was the one who told me about what happened to you. She heard from her family that your car had been ambushed and that a militant group was holding you hostage. I didn't believe the story at first, because I was sure if it were true, it would've been all over the media.'

'Nope,' Jeff sighed, gripping his wife's hand. 'Lynn kept it out of the press. Listen, Piet... I'll talk more about it when I see you. It's all a bit too raw just at the moment. Give me some dates when you're able to come to Provence. A three-day stretch is what I'm thinking initially, and then perhaps a couple of follow-ups. Would that be about right, d'you reckon?'

The grateful man scribbled down details of Engelbrecht's availability, and they shared some more ideas on facilitating the delicate negotiations and how they might achieve concord among such a diverse group of people sitting round the one table. Before signing off, they passed a few minutes reminiscing about days and nights spent together at London University with John Francis, both vowing to contact him soon.

'Who knows?' the billionaire ventured. 'He might even come to *Le Castellet* to meet us? That'd be tempting for him, I bet. We could *passer un bon weekend à la Ciotat* afterwards, *n'est-ce pas?* Just the three of us. It'd be bloody awesome.'

'Will Lynn be with you?' Pieter asked.

'No. I doubt it. The kids'll still be at school. We like to keep our interests pretty separate. And we only fly together as a four, if we can help it. You know, in case something happens...'

A shiver ran down Jeff's back, throwing him into a panic as he pictured his beloved family surrounded by the brute, Rasul, and his band of renegades. Their guns aimed once more at his face, the smell of dank, concentrated body odour rushing through his nose and turning his breakfast over. Palms beginning to sweat, his chest tightened around his heart.

At that same moment, the office door opened, revealing his dream girl holding two full mugs. Seeing her husband in distress, she clattered them onto the desk and hurried to reconnect her hands with his shoulders. He leaned back into her body and allowed her to massage the strained fibres beneath the surface as the tremors took hold.

'I was wondering if I should bring Mathilde,' Engelbrecht was saying. 'It'd be nice for the four of us to catch up, but not to worry.'

'Another time, mate,' the peacemaker said, steadying his breath and inviting his senses to order. 'We'll sort something out.'

'Good stuff,' the South African answered. 'She's still most disarming, your wife, by the way.'

Jeff laughed, tilting his head upwards until Lynn's upside-down but smiling face came into view. 'You don't have to tell me that,' he agreed. 'She's the best. She's right here, so I can't say anything else, can I?'

The blonde sportswoman leaned down and planted an inverted kiss on her man's lips, confronted by the emblematic anxiety symptom of lockjaw. His spare hand reached up and grabbed hers, squeezing so tight that she had to shake it free. The instinctive action and reaction reminded her of the old days, which was disturbing yet also comforting. Here again was the tortured adolescent with whom she had originally fallen in love; the one who had lost his way then found it, and now had lost and would soon find it again. Her brain froze when she realised they had constituted this fatalistic prediction in a recent hit song.

'No, he can't,' the beauty answered loud enough for the professor to overhear.

Pieter chuckled. 'I'll let you go, Jeff. I've got an appointment waiting. Keep safe, and I'll talk to you soon.'

'Sure. No worries, and you too. Thanks again for helping us out. It's going to be huge. *Adiós*, mate.'

Replacing the receiver on the hook, the rock star shook his head to rid himself of the tension which threatened to fuse his upper and lower banks of teeth together.

***

The date for the first round of peace negotiations was set for the end of April in rural Provence, some thirty kilometres inland from the Mediterranean, a little over halfway between Marseille and Toulon. Facsimiles flew, telephones ran hot and spirits climbed higher as the Diamonds directed their energies into planning and logistics. With recordings and rehearsals for "The

Black Sheep" scheduled every few days, the couple enjoyed a blissful, uninterrupted month in each other's company.

Unable to shake the trauma's aftermath, Jeff's nightmares continued to persecute them, fierce and unrelenting. All too familiar symptoms of mental exhaustion returned with a vengeance, denting his enthusiasm for the new day and leaving him feeling guilty for disturbing the rest of the family too. As if the need to rely on his beautiful best friend to curtail the unconscious rage and thrashing limbs wasn't disheartening enough, having two alarmed youngsters running into the bedroom to scrutinise the spectacle was totally unacceptable.

On Easter Monday morning however, the breakthrough happened. Lynn had hatched a daring and dangerous plan with their daughter without letting her husband in on the secret. He would never knowingly risk harming the kids, and instinct persuaded her that they were on to a winner.

The Diamonds had reached home after midnight the previous day, having spent two days at Benloch with the whole Dyson clan. The children had slept in the car almost all the way, giving the couple ample opportunity to discuss all manner of adult topics while the Holden Caprice's well-engineered glide made light of the hundred-kilometre homeward journey.

Jeff's mood was lighter than it had been since he returned from Africa, at ease and in tune with life under the circumstances. Bart and Marianna had been genuine in their appreciation for the tireless campaigners' commitment to Africa's future, and the focus of the family's sporting ambitions this year had shifted to Anna's transition from gymnastics to athletics as a welcome change.

Letting themselves in through *Escondido*'s hinged courtyard *portico*, the foursome lingered outside in the dark for a few minutes to play with the dogs, who were excited to have everyone home and safe. Lynn sent Jet and Kierney upstairs to clean their teeth and issued a nonchalant request for coffee and *liqueurs* to be served at the grand piano in the lounge room while she settled them down. Giggling with her mother at their shared secret, the proud gipsy girl clambered into her parents' huge bed as arranged and fell straight back to sleep.

About an hour later, the musicians abandoned a new song under construction and activated the ground-floor alarm. Lynn led her anxious man up the stairs and into the master bedroom, somewhat nervous too.

Jeff disappeared into the bathroom out of habit, deep in morbid contemplation of the night ahead and failing to notice the small bundle wrapped up in the *duvet*. His wife slid into bed and nudged Kierney sideways to make room for her *papá* to fit on the other side. Luckily, the little mite didn't stir, and all was quiet when he returned and lifted the corner of the quilt.

'Oh, no,' the afflicted songwriter mouthed, releasing the cover and letting it come to rest on the motionless mound.

The young mother opened her eyes when she heard the sharp intake of breath, watching his hands cross over each other in objection.

'No, no, no,' he whispered. 'That's not fair.'

Nodding her insistence, Lynn pointed a finger from his head to his pillow with equal emphasis.

Jeff frowned. 'I can't.'

The dejected man sighed and wheeled around, pulling a T-shirt out of the bottom drawer of his bedside table. He threaded his hands through the armholes and tugged the garment down until it covered his torso, the door handle twisting in his grip. Determined not to inflict yet more disturbance on his daughter, he made it to the top of the stairs in the time it took for the athlete to slip out of bed and catch up with him on the landing.

'Hey... Please come back in,' she urged. 'She really wants to help you. She won't wake up.'

Her confused lover sagged against the bannister. '*Ya* think? She will if I start thumping her. It's not fair, angel. Don't do it to her. I don't want Kizzy to be a pawn in our psychiatric games. I'm pissed off enough at what I'm doing to you guys, after all this time without having to deal with nightmares. Please don't make this any worse than it already is.'

'It won't make it worse, Jeff. I'm sure of it.'

'How're you so sure?'

'I don't know, but she's sound asleep. You've climbed into bed when she's been here before, haven't you? Heaps of times.'

The seasoned traveller gave a reluctant nod, his aching legs giving way until he crumpled onto the carpet. 'Sure. It feels different now though. I'm unhinged, angel. How d'you know she doesn't sense it?'

'Listen... Have I been wrong before?' Lynn asked, holding out her hand and tugging his dead weight back towards the open door. 'Just try it. Please?'

Jeff sighed. 'No. I can't do it. Thanks for thinking of the idea, but it's just too risky. I'll sleep downstairs.'

'Well, at least sleep in her bed,' the caring woman begged, disappointed. 'You need to break the cycle the nightmares have created somehow. Start in our bed, and I promise I'll wake you up if you start dreaming, and then you can move to her bed. It's just an idea. If it doesn't work, we can carry her back to bed, and she'll be none the wiser.'

'But that doesn't make sense, baby,' the logician smiled. 'She'll be awake by the time we find out your sneaky plan hasn't worked.'

'Oh, come on...' his wife beckoned. 'Please... You won't let yourself hurt her. I know it. You just wouldn't.'

Unconvinced, the troubled soul surrendered. His guardian angel's theory sounded plausible, and he couldn't think of a better outcome than to banish these evil dreams again. She was correct that ample evidence suggested their daughter would come to no harm. In all the screaming and thrashing of the old days, he had never once dealt his dream girl a damaging blow. Somehow or other, he always managed to avoid landing a direct hit, even though his unconscious self was engaged in a proper punch-up with his adversaries.

Jeff reached out and pulled his saviour towards him, covering her head with his large left hand and holding it against his heaving chest. He kissed her hair, keen to let her know how grateful he was for her constant determination.

'I love you heaps. I just hope you're right.'

'So do I, times two,' she replied, raising his other hand to her lips. 'Come back to bed.'

Slowly and with a good deal of trepidation, the couple made their way into the master suite. With his dream girl circling the end of the bed to slip back under the covers, the nervous father left his T-shirt and boxers on and climbed in, sandwiching the seven-year-old between them. Kierney didn't so much as twitch.

'Goodnight,' Lynn said at almost normal volume. 'Thank you.'

Exhaling with a slight chuckle, Jeff chose not to respond. Within a few minutes, his wife's breathing had slowed to match their daughter's, and he turned onto his side to feast his eyes on the gorgeous pair together in the same bed. It was a beautiful sight, and rare these days; each other's negative side-by-side. His two precious angels. *Regala* had better be right this time, he swore under his breath.

The lyricist played through the sequence in Act Two of "The Black Sheep", for which they were due to begin rehearsals the following day. He tried not to focus on the violent confrontational scenes. It was baffling to the pacifist humanitarian how often his peacemaking efforts attracted all manner of conflict. Perhaps some latent, unspent bitterness inside him was still in need of exorcism. Or perhaps the voice of reason was trying to convince him there was no guaranteed method of achieving the massive non-violent solutions he sought.

Before long, the philosopher felt himself succumbing to the sleep he had been anticipating all evening. The temperature had chilled, and he pulled the quilt up around his shoulders, taking care not to smother the sleeping child. His knuckles brushed her shoulder by accident, giving him a fright when she twisted round to face him.

'Hey, gorgeous,' the tortured soul whispered, his heart in his throat. 'Don't wake up. You look so beautiful.'

'I'm your dream-catcher, *Papá*,' Kierney told him with a sleepy smile. 'Is it working?'

Jeff closed his eyes. Was he already dreaming?

'Yeah. It's working, *pequeñita. Gracias*,' he replied, stroking a soft cheek piping hot from being buried in the pillow. 'Go back to sleep. *Te amo.*'

'*Te amo.*'

Roused by the quiet words exchanged by her neighbours, Lynn remained motionless and listened in. If she had believed in God, she would have prayed for the little girl's wish to come true. Instead, satisfied that no sparks were flying, she let herself drift back into peaceful slumber. Her heart was full of hope for the ensuing hours, while the distant lapping of waves onto the beach below the *Escondido* cliffs lulled them all into the land of nod.

***

Kierney prodded her mother's skin gingerly to see if she was awake. Daylight streamed in through tiny cracks in the shutters beyond the French windows, and the mattress was vibrating behind her with the resonant snores of a lifelong smoker in repose. She was exceedingly excited, requiring every shred of her seven-year-old reserve to hold her tongue.

'*Mamá*,' she murmured, picking up strands of Lynn's long, blonde hair. '*Mamá, Papá*'s still sleeping.'

Her mother awoke, blinking as she felt her daughter's breath so close to her face. It took a second or two to remember why they were in the same bed. Once fully conscious, she rolled over to check for vital signs on the other side.

'Yay! Well done, darling,' she whispered, kissing the excited child on the lips. 'You *are* the dream-catcher. What did you do with them?'

The happy child shrugged and reached both arms around her mum's neck. The two Diamond girls hugged each other tight, delighted with the result of their little experiment. Thinking their stifled giggles might wake the sleeping giant, Lynn suggested a head-start to breakfast, so the stealthy pair slid out of bed and ran downstairs undetected.

It was seven-thirty-five, according to the clock on the kitchen wall. While the young mother waited for the kettle to boil, she rejoiced that each extra half-hour of sleep would raise her lover's happiness score another notch. Jet was already up and outside, practising his bowling in the nets which he and Jeff had assembled a few weeks earlier. He waved to the others, running back towards the house to find out if the devious plan had been a success.

'What happened?' the boy shouted, slapping his hand over his mouth and lowering his voice. 'Is Dad still in bed?'

'Yes, he is,' his mum nodded, bracing to receive the incoming missile against her hip. 'It worked perfectly. No nightmare whatsoever. Not even the start of one.'

'Woohoo!' Jet shrieked. 'He'll be stoked when he wakes up.'

His sister beamed from ear to ear, joining in the communal embrace before being ushered inside to rustle up a celebratory breakfast. The nannies had all been given leave over the Easter school holidays, giving the family some space to enjoy a rare run at being four.

The attentive youngsters sat agog as their mother recalled the first time their dad had slept through a whole night. She told them how thrilled she had been to play a part, like they had on this occasion; so happy that it had been difficult to resist the urge to wake him to let him know he was still asleep! Jet and Kierney laughed aloud at the funny scene this story conjured up, encouraging Lynn to follow it by telling them about when their father hadn't moved from his bed for forty-three hours in one stretch.

'Wow!' the boy gasped. 'That's nearly two whole days.'

'I know,' the sportswoman nodded. 'It was getting quite boring with no-one to talk to.'

'I hope *Papá*'s back to normal now,' the smiling dream-catcher said. 'Shall I do the same thing tomorrow night just in case?'

'We'll see, gorgeous,' her mother advised. 'See how *Papá* is when he gets up. He's scared he might hurt you if he has a nightmare. He doesn't want to take any chances.'

Upstairs, in the half-empty matrimonial bed, the man of the house was beginning to stir. A certain part of his anatomy was leading the charge, publicising the night's yield of healthy rejuvenation. Left hand tracking downwards to join in the fun, he glanced to the right to find an expanse of vacant, dark green satin sheet, a pillow bearing only an indentation and bright shards of morning intruding through the wooden slats.

What was the time? Rolling the other way, towards his bedside table, the songwriter saw ten minutes past nine o'clock. No wonder no-one else was here! Was he late for something? Weren't they supposed to be in the city early to commence their dress rehearsal? Currents of confusion and relief converged to spur him into action, eager to locate the rest of his clan. Had Lynn needed to wrench Kierney clear of the bed to save her from his nocturnal rampage, or did they all enjoy a full night's sleep?

Cautiously optimistic, Jeff jumped straight into the shower. He would remember being woken up screaming, wouldn't he? He had vivid memories from every other recent *réveillé*, when it had taken his wife repeated rounds of shaking and yelling into his ear from point-blank range to break him out of the loathsome perdition re-established by his hostage experience. Through the raised pulse of his rude awakening, the shower's warmth drew out a refreshed calm. Could his dream girl have found the answer yet again? Christ! He hoped so.

The thirty-three-year-old rinsed the shampoo out of his hair and shut off the taps, still stuck in his guessing game. Hearing music in the bedroom however, he jumped as the screen door opened away from him and a towel appeared. He took it and stepped onto the mat, staring into the blue eyes he loved so much.

'Feeling OK?' Lynn asked, waiting for her tall, dark, handsome man to find his tongue. 'You didn't dream, in case you're wondering. Out cold all night.'

'Yeah? Awesome. Thank you,' her husband replied, confronted by a mixture of humiliation, joy and gratitude. 'You were right again.'

'Told you!' the Olympian chided, standing on tiptoe to kiss him hard on the mouth. 'Take me, you hunk of gorgeousness. I want you so badly.'

Despite the mælstrom of emotions drenching the hot-blooded man's senses, there was no point in resisting such a brazen invitation. He wrapped his prize up in the damp towel and hugged her, pressing their bodies together and kissing her neck.

'Where are the kids?'

Shaking her head, Lynn took hold of both ends of the towel, dragging her quarry out of the bathroom. They collapsed down on to the bed in the throes of breathless desire. The door had already been closed, and faint thwacks of tennis balls could be heard from beyond the lawn.

'I locked them outside,' came a nonchalant reply. 'They'll be alright for a while.'

Jeff's lips formed a sexy half-smile, peeling the playful woman's top over her head. 'A long while, I hope.'

Lynn was undressed in no time flat, entangling their limbs in a building frenzy. Lyrics forced their way past the expert lover's lips as he brought her to the edge twice and then a third time, before thrusting deep into her and groaning in pleasure. She moved on his urgent size in slow, antagonistic provocation, her head bowed to kiss the tattoos on his chest. The room's ambiance was laced with the heady excitement of yet another burden having been lifted, both half in wonder and half in disbelief.

'I love you,' the champion cried out, submitting to a fourth orgasm with his fingers' effortless art and the strong, measured movements of his throbbing penis. 'This feels so perfect.'

'Yep. Better than... You are the most beautiful woman in the world,' her husband told her again, this time to her face. 'I'm so damned lucky to have you. Don't ever let me stop telling you that.'

'We're lucky to have each other,' Lynn corrected, pulling back against him and trying to prolong the sensation of his climax for as long as possible. 'We're here for each other, no matter what. That's what makes it so perfect. Today is a good day, and tomorrow...'

Jeff's hand folded over her mouth as she spoke, leaning forward and kissing the sensitive skin in the outer corners of her eyes, unleashing his every last drop of passion. The couple lay together in a blissful silence, cherishing this most special moment of closeness as if it were the only chance life would ever send their way again.

'Jeez, angel. This is too good, but we need to get moving, don't we?' the drowsy man moaned, breaking the spell. 'What time is it?'

'Ten-ish? Why? Where do you think we're going?'

'Ten-ish?' her husband echoed. 'Very humorous. To rehearsals. Aren't we due at the Arts Centre about now?'

His collaborator craned her neck. 'No,' she smiled. 'That's not 'til tomorrow. You're a day ahead of yourself.'

'Christ Almighty! Am I? *¡Fantastico!*' the composer sank back down onto the mattress. 'Another day off? That's pure luxury! Remind me not to quit my job. It's not so bad after all.'

'OK, but you do have to go and commune with a certain Romany princess. She'll be champing at the bit to see you. She's very pleased with herself.'

Downstairs, the children were hungry again. Waiting for their parents to descend after the clandestine and intense lovemaking session, they had become bored with tennis practice and had parked themselves at the kitchen bench in front of the television. Jet had even begun to do some homework, from which he was easily distracted upon seeing his hero appear in the lounge room.

'Dad!' the boy shouted, running across to meet him. 'You didn't have a nightmare!'

'No, I did not, mate. And you, little lady, are my brilliant dream-catcher *extraordinaire. Gracias tanto tanto.*'

Kierney nudged her brother out of the way to climb into her daddy's arms. Jeff squatted on his haunches to hug both children, almost losing his balance when hit by another huge wave of emotion. The positive vibes from his restful night magnified yet further through the concern shown by the two pint-sized lights of his life.

'*De nada, Papá.* I know I am. I'm so happy! Will they come back tomorrow?'

'Hope not,' the grateful father replied, 'but you can sleep in our bed again if you think your job's not done.'

'Depends if they're going to have sex,' Jet jeered, scowling. 'You don't want to be caught up in all that kissing with no undies and stuff.'

The precocious girl grimaced, leaning over and punching her boisterous brother's chest. 'Be quiet,' she scolded.

'That's right, mate. Keep your opinions to yourself. No undies and stuff? What stuff? What d'you know about sex anyway, Captain Marvellous?'

'Nothing,' the boy answered in his usual carefree style. 'I don't want to know anything about it. It's totally gross.'

'Is it really?' his father laughed. 'That's what your auntie Anna used to think too, but I bet she's changed her mind now. What about you, Kizzo? D'you think sex is totally gross too?'

'I don't know,' the seven-year-old answered. 'If you like it and *Mamá* likes it, then how can it be gross? *Mamá* says we'll like it when we're older, but I don't even know what it is.'

'Yeah, well...' Jeff smiled, keen to cut this particular conversation short for now. 'We definitely like it. We like it heaps, in fact. And, you gorgeous kids, you guys wouldn't even exist if we didn't have sex. So there!'

Motioning for the children to head inside for breakfast, the doting dad thumbed his nose at his son and received a smack on the back of his thigh in return. The youngsters followed him through the *patio* doors and found Lynn trying to wipe the grin off her face. Her husband's ardour was reignited the instant he detected remnants of their not-so-secret *rendezvous* being consigned to her private memory banks. He stole a complicit kiss while she distributed their full plates.

'D'you hear that, angel? We have to give up sex.'

'Do we? That's a shame. Why's that?'

''Cause it's gross!' their son cackled, by now playing to the peanut gallery.

'Right,' his mother nodded. 'Whatever you say, darling. What are you two prepared to give up if you make us give up sex? Has to be something you really love, by the way...'

The eight-year-old pondered this deal for a few seconds before blowing into the steam rising from his freshly-cut hash brown. 'Nothing,' he sighed. 'Alright, you can keep doing it. But I'll never do it. It's just so ridiculous.'

Jeff smiled at his wife. 'Ridiculous, eh? I wish we had a tape recorder handy for that proclamation. That'd be an absolute gem to play for all your mates at your twenty-first birthday party. And to your girlfriend, mate.'

Kierney didn't utter a word. Seeing she had stopped eating, Lynn nudged her upturned fork with her wrist, jogging the girl out of her daydream.

'What'*ya* thinking about, Kizzy? You look sad now.'

With a long inward breath, the thinker fought back tears. 'If you and *Papá* give up sex, Jet and I won't exist anymore. That'll make us all sad.'

'Yes, we will exist,' her smarty-pants of a brother sneered. 'That's rubbish.'

'Hey, mate... Don't tell your sister what she says is rubbish, please,' Jeff jumped at his son. 'Did I tell you you were talking rubbish when you said you thought sex was totally gross?'

Suitably reprimanded, the boy fell silent and shook his head.

'*Bueno. Gracias, hijo mío.* Everyone's allowed to express an opinion without getting insulted. Them's the rules. You OK with that?'

'Yes, Dad,' Jet replied. 'Sorry, Kierney, but we shall still exist.'

'But *Papá* said we wouldn't.'

Jeff rested his cutlery on his plate and took the girl's hand. 'I know that's what it sounded like, *pequeñita*,' he explained, smiling at his reticent spouse. 'What I meant was that you two were born because *Mamá* and I love each other and love to have sex with each other. So if we didn't do it, we'd

never've had any kids, and then you wouldn't have existed. If we stop now...
and I hope we don't have to, please... you guys'd still be here, but we
wouldn't ever make any more babies.'

Kierney's expression brightened. 'Oh, good. I get it now.'

'Did Grandpa and Grandma love having sex with each other?' the
inquisitive boy asked, this time with a naughty smile on his face.

'Of course,' his mum affirmed, sneaking another sideways glance at her
partner, 'and I expect they still do. That's how most children are started.'

Again, the conversation was straying into territory best avoided. After
agreeing to be open with their offspring about the birds and the bees, it was
turning into a daily challenge to decide precisely how open. Such bright minds
didn't always make four with a pair of twos...

'Not if you're adopted,' their daughter piped up, throwing one of her
expanding collection of tangential spanners in the works.

'Correct,' Jeff replied, giving the mature seven-year-old a wink. 'How
does that work then, *pequeñita*?'

'*Papá!*' Lynn warned. 'That's enough.'

The Wisdom Of Ages

'Ironic, isn't it?' Jeff raised his eyes from the rehearsal notes.

'What's ironic?' Lynn asked.

'That I'm part of creating an *œuvre* about being a misfit at the least misfitting time of my whole life.'

His dream girl smiled. 'Oh. See what you mean, but maybe not as ironic as you think... What if you have to be beyond that stage to truly make sense of it.'

The librettist stared into space, ruminating on this left-of-centre suggestion. The notion was seductive, despite the unsettling truth therein. The past few days had taught him a good deal more about the power of family and the nourishment a soul stood to gain from striking a balance between giving and receiving. Even though he had written on the topic many times during the musical's construction, he was only now coming to realise the true impact of these messages being channelled through him from wherever songs originated. Reciprocity had been a byword of his for years, yet the theme's potential was finally coming of age in this work.

The star blew a kiss across the table and finished his last tepid mouthful of instant coffee. Standing up, he drew the company together to prepare for their first full shakedown of Act One's *finalé*. His captivating blonde conductor sprang to attention, chuckling at the typical impulsiveness; another approbation issued weightless onto stilled airwaves.

A grateful hand brushed the small of his back as Lynn walked past him towards the orchestra. 'OK, everybody,' she raised her voice. 'Let's run through from bar eighty-three, all the way to *Coda*. We need to hear how the characters' private thoughts end up in the community's rallying cry. We'll take it with all voices first, then stop to pick out individual bits and then finish by whizzing through it again non-stop. Kiley, is that OK?'

The delighted violinist and co-composer waved her bow, turning to count the players in without further delay. Today's *ensemble* was a select complement occupying Melbourne Academy's smaller rehearsal room, yet their sound was expansive enough to set the atmosphere buzzing. After several weeks learning their parts and practising in various combinations, the lead characters were impatient to see the Diamonds' latest blockbuster stage show unfolding in its expected magnificence.

Building from a strict *andante grandioso*, the march gathered speed into its *crescendo*. Mouthing an expletive to the producer beside him when the seat creaked with the sudden relief from his weight, Jeff retired to sit several rows further back. Hiding in the dark to consider the interplay between characters, he lapped up the symphonic sounds, each with their own swirling melody and bolstered by a soaring chorus.

Shivers raced up and down the entertainer's spine, and the lyric's humanity chased a vulgar frost through his shoulders, down his arms and up into the base of his skull. Honoré de Balzac could rest easy, proud of this modern adaptation of a novel which had been so pivotal in the Sydneysider's teenaged political and ideological development. It was about to be given fresh dimensions for a whole new audience.

The songwriter examined the impact of each soloist's lines, scribbling the occasional note to adjust their projection out from the stage to guarantee integrity between the acting and the songs. The piece, which had been designed from the outset to bring the half-time curtain down on an intermission of thoughtful discourse, involved a complex multi-part harmony to weave a number of individual stories into a single plea for the triumph of good over evil.

Hearing the well-honed snippets in their polished completeness, the awestruck songwriter felt himself being transported back to the Ethiopian heartland, where the majority of these words had been conceived. His senses were bombarded with foreign sights and sounds and smells, once more travelling in the rear seat of the bone-shaking four-wheel drive to an unknown destination, alongside a man with a machine gun on his lap.

Recalling the vivid rush of inspiration which had struck him that morning, demanding expression in these most unlikely of circumstances, the billionnaire philanthropist was humbled to the point of self-denigration. These ideas weren't his own, were they? The god within him had furnished them, *per* the peculiar conversation with Thomas, using the old soul's latest human incarnation as the delivery boy.

Had the same power supplied the celebrated French author with the original nuggets of wisdom too? Or was some sort of supernatural chain of command being followed? Regardless of medium, the famous Australian was convinced he was merely the agent, trusted to do the right thing with this heavenly guidance. It had never felt more important that the *avant-garde* rocker from Sydney's western suburbs employ the global phenomenon he and his dream girl had created to fight the good fight into eternity.

The *finalé*'s rousing last line, embellished by a progression of extended chords lingering in the air, rang out around the rehearsal room. With a flick of the conductor's *baton* inciting obedient silence, the collective exhaled, and a ripple of chatter broke out of their midst, their dreamlike mood ascending to the ceiling on the evocative theme.

Lynn span round on her heels to seek a verdict from the show's architect, who stood alone halfway down the bank of stalls seating, clapping hard and whistling. Even she was struck by the omnipotent stance he had adopted, her insides churning with desire at his slow, exaggerated swagger.

'OK! You guys rock! That was fantastic,' he shouted, wending his way back to the aisle and loping down the steps towards the stage. 'Absolutely fantastic. Thank you. And now we're going to do it better.'

His wife smiled at the assortment of sighs, groans and laughs from the soloists and chorus. As much as Jeff had taught her about the emotional appeal of spontaneous imperfections, he had also assimilated her drive for flawless execution!

Anxious not to pour cold water on their emotions, the showman explained himself. 'Guys, ten out of ten for technical excellence, ten out of ten for musicality,' he insisted, resting his hands on his wife's shoulders and leaning on her steadfast frame to counteract the dizziness. 'However, from now on, you've got to do all this, plus act like you're living these people's dreams, pain, joy... Like you can see the opportunities just out of their reach. Does that make sense?'

His wide, brown eyes were met with a mixture of nods, expectant stares and confused, blank faces. Lynn stepped to one side and let him ram his lessons home, well aware that the magic ingredient which turned a Jeff Diamond show from a great gig into a theatrical *extravaganza* was about to be administered by the master himself.

'The whole point of stopping here before the interval,' he continued, putting his crumpled pages of notes down on a chair and starting to pace around, 'is that each character wakes up to the fact that he or she has to change. Right now. No shit! Some of you are mostly scared and some of you are mostly excited, but you all need to convey the perfect combination of both for each character. D'you see what I mean?'

Generating more nods this time, many more smiles appeared, along with a few muted cheers. Kiley Jones had left her position as lead violinist and had joined Lynn at the piano. The world-changer's two co-conspirators in this mammoth undertaking stood arm-in-arm, straining on every word as he spoke.

'That's the key to this show, folks. This is a journey into the unknown, but moreover a journey out of your wretched, downtrodden existences,' Jeff paused long enough to let his words sink in, eager to capitalise on the singers' undivided attention. 'Now before we do it again, I'd like to talk through each part. When I say what I'm going to say, I'm not talking about you as an artist or as a person. I'm talking about your character. So don't get bent out of shape by what I'm going to say, OK?'

Another quake of uncertainty moved through the assembled company.

'Philippe, let's start with you,' Jeff pointed to the strapping figure of Barry Yates, an established star of London's West End who had leaped at the chance to play the elder Bridau brother. 'You're one of life's survivors because you don't have any values to live up to. You're the last century's equivalent of a white Anglo-Saxon male; the world's been made for you. You know what I mean? You hold all the privilege cards and don't give a shit about anyone lower down the food chain than you.'

The actor's chest swelled, and his Cheshire Cat grin put the orator's inner child off-guard, wondering how literally his home truth had been taken. 'No principles guide you, Philippe, so you're all about making life easier for yourself. Who cares how? You have no respect for others or for yourself. You're simply out for everything you can get.'

The philosopher paused to let the sniggering die down around him. 'But the additional dimension to convey on top of all this is that you have no love in you. *Nada, nada.* Not even for your own family. You crave the base things in life. You're all about want, want, want... Who cares about anyone else, eh? The more people fall by the wayside, the greater chance you have to reap the benefit.'

Barry shuffled on his feet, an awakening imminent. The theme was uncomfortable to hear but right on the money. The writer wheeled round and swooped on his unsuspecting wife, holding his hand out to channel some of her strength as he regrouped, while the spellbound audience began to clap.

'Whoa,' Jeff said, eyes shooting to the rafters as a jolt of high-octane adoration nourished him. 'Thanks, guys. Now Joseph...'

Durham Yarra was the youngest of three brothers, all of whom had been through the Melbourne Academy music stables. They had each emerged as promising young stars in their own rights. He stood to attention, keen to learn from a man he admired.

The superstar obliged. 'You're the most conflicted, mate. You want to be true to yourself, to your own motivations, but you know this isn't what makes the world tick. So give us anguish on your face and let us hear it in your voice. You've only just found what you'd like your future to be, and now you have to leave it, not knowing if you'll ever get it back. Jesus Christ! That was me when I first met this exquisite creature! I remember that feeling like it was this bloody morning.'

A collective laugh rang out, morphing into romantic sighs when the company watched the two stars engage in a heart-stopping kiss. The embarrassed soloist shrank a little in the meantime, the words bound to ring true with any hot-blooded male.

'This thing you're all about to embark on...' Jeff continued, casting his eyes around the room. 'This cause isn't about want, it's about need. It's not about you, Joe. It's about us. All of us. *Entendu?* Got it?'

The writer requested the rehearsal pianist play a few bars before Joseph's part came in. Durham sang his heart out for his idol, who stood and clapped, nodding in approval. Lynn and Kiley both cheered their encouragement, and the young man took a sly bow in front of his peers.

'But by contrast, Phil,' the songwriter addressed Barry again, drawing a sharp breath as he was treated to the face of Rasul Andrew behind his eyes. 'You've never been in love. Only lust. You're a boy playing a man's game. You have no sympathy for your brother, although you don't go all out because you're basically a good sort when it comes to pleasing your mum… You serve the ruling classes, believing it'll stand you in good stead. And of all of us, you are the most driven, the most single-minded and, if I have to say it, *naïf*.'

A hush descended on the group. Here was a chilling message, delivered by someone who had lived these concepts on so many levels and had learned the hard lessons well. Even those who knew nothing of Jeff's past couldn't help but feel trapped by the idea of committing wholeheartedly to such a shallow, short-term cause.

The pianist responded to a nod from today's guest director and began to play. Yates, who had travelled from New South Wales to try out for the original cast recording, blew out a lungful of air before hyperventilating a few times.

The actor's performance was lacklustre in comparison to the others, but Jeff didn't press the issue. Philippe's was a role to be filled elsewhere in the future, and they planned to work with Barry on an independent production for the time being. In fact, the Diamonds had confessed to a common desire for the elder Bridau brother's part being played by their son in years to come, should the musical enjoy a long shelf-life.

The charismatic intellectual looked across at his wife, who had fixed him with an equally percipient stare. Jaw set in a characteristic smoulder, he turned to the veteran actor, Colin Steadman. Unbeknown to one another, both he and Lynn had put this man's name forward when they had first written the part of Maxence Gilet, the true villain in Balzac's novel.

'*Monsieur Gilet*,' the strong baritone crooned, hands on his hips and feet planted in a wide stance. 'Max, me old mate… You're determined to prolong your liberty, but your conscience is fucking killing you.'

Everybody laughed, the sudden bad language fracturing the rehearsal's tension. Again, the stunning blonde musician cast adoring eyes at the introvert who claimed not to relish being the centre of attention, thinking how magnificent he was when holding court. He was every bit as imposing as her father, yet Bart Dyson shared but a fraction of this man's unswerving sense of justice. People followed Big D into battle, emulating him to a tee with tried and tested methods. In comparison, this Pied Piper to whom she was married had also orchestrated a crusade all his own, but his armies were invited to bring their own instruments and improvise to their hearts' content.

'You just need a few more days to prove your innocence,' Jeff suggested to Colin. 'You're not like the half-wit, Philippe, who's motivated by the social status that money can buy. You're purely after the money, and it doesn't matter whose money or how much hardship stealing it would inflict on those you deprive. Whatever Jean-Jacques or Agathe may think, none of it matters to you. Make sense?'

'Makes sense, Jeff,' the star of the British West End nodded. 'Right up to the point where I die. Once a desperate man, always a desperate man.'

The boy from Canley Vale grinned. 'Abso-fucking-lutely. Ain't that the truth. Let's have you then, *maestro*.'

Unable to resist, the entire company carried on singing the last few lines of the song. Lynn let them run riot, always on the lookout for interesting accidental harmonies. The atmosphere was laced with excitement as the songs took on deeper meaning, and she wasn't about to compromise her husband's coaching session by bringing them to an early finish.

The attention remained on the petty criminal, Max Gilet, with Jeff marching across the stage. Steadman met him halfway, and the pair faced off less than a metre apart, two prime steers glaring into each others' eyes. A tumid pause unsettled the rest, the sensation of which served to fire up the apparent adversaries still further.

The rock star began to prowl around in a circle like a matador eyeing his bull, and Colin followed his lead. Lynn whispered to Kiley that it reminded her of a *tango*. It was true. The feuding *duo* circled one way and then the other, before the convincing actor shot his left arm out as if he had drawn a knife on the thief. Jeff Diamond had become Joseph Bridau, as he had in his mind since his teenage years.

Dumbstruck, the remainder of the cast gasped in surprise when at last the celebrity backed off with a throaty laugh.

'*Monsieur le bandit!*' he shouted, walking away from his opponent, who drew a relieved hand across a not-so-imaginary fevered brow. 'You'll have to wait 'til after the interval to bring down your nemesis, and it's eating you up inside, isn't it?'

Seeing the actor grin in the affirmative, Jéff clapped, shaking the tension out of his arms and shoulders. 'We like you, reluctantly. Even admire you. But you're still a no-good crim', regardless of the excuses or your unfortunate circumstance. You know you're wrong by the letter of the law, but you also know that in the bigger picture, Joe's the real deal. *Magnifique, alors, monsieur Max*. My blood runs cold. And now, who's next? Agathe.'

Judy Makin, a rising star soprano, had defected from highbrow opera especially to play the role of the Philippe's and Joseph's mother. She gave the rock star a coquettish smile. Her mind told her she ought to be overawed by him, but his devastating good looks bowled her over instead. Jeff had received a merciless ribbing from his co-writers for the way the woman had fawned and flirted around him during earlier rehearsal sessions; so much so that even now the residual embarrassment was hard to overlook.

'Agathe, you think your firstborn's the be-all-and-end-all. He can do no wrong in your eyes. Deep down, you know he knows this too, so be honest with yourself.'

The lyricist once more plunged into his own past, unbeknown to the others, waving an expressive hand at the provincial town walls outside which the cast were collected. Judy stared at the floor while he spoke, ruminating over her character's strident assassination.

'You live in a comfortable house through other people's charity. You have fine clothes, plenty to eat and drink, but you're actually more like Joe than Phil,' Jeff pointed to Durham Yarra who almost choked on his bottled water. 'You know you should've listened to him, not dismissed him as useless. And you also know you should thank him for always putting others first.'

The actress nodded, half smiling and half apologetic. To her delight, the much-loved celebrity wandered over and put his arm around her shoulder. He kissed her cheek, making her blush while the other female cast members regarded the compassionate act with envy.

'Have this thought in the back of your head while you sing, please, Judy. You're not sure if you're putting your trust in the best man.'

Eternally bored with the novel's title role, which he had always thought had the most shallow characterisation in Balzac's story, Jeff moved stage-right to the tiny figure of Annika Clemmets, who had flown all the way from Sweden to audition for the title role of the troublemaker who teams up with Maxence Gilet to swindle the Rouget family. As unlike the stereotypical Swedish woman as one could imagine, Lynn and he had been captivated by the diminutive, mousy twenty-two year old and her haunting waiflike voice.

'*Et Flore...*' he resumed, leaning on the piano. '*Ma pauvre rabouilleuse.* You're insanely jealous of women who marry well; the ones people take care of without a second thought. In fact, you're insanely jealous of everyone.'

Annika laughed. The great man had shared the character's backstory with her before, but it didn't hurt to hear it made public knowledge.

'Agathe's grateful to you but she's never actually expressed her thanks, so you're bitter about this too. She thinks you're beneath her and that you don't deserve an apology, because she's a kept woman and you're not. You know she's no closer to being a real lady than you are. And most important, you also know that all women have the power to be a lady, and the right to be treated equitably. So when's it your turn?'

'When Max arrives,' the young woman answered, proud of her role opposite Colin Steadman.

Seeing his left hand plunge into his pants pocket for his cigarettes and lighter, Lynn knew to expect a cold, semi-autobiographical dramatisation to spring forth from her eloquent leading man. After the unending string of ups and downs the couple had lived through, creating this musical had delivered an intense and satisfying aggrandisement to the abandoned nobody who had turned himself into the most impressive of somebodies. His eyes had witnessed more inhumanity in their thirty-four years than the majority experience in a lifetime, and bringing this cathartic *œuvre* to the stage sent pain oozing from every pore.

'So why does Agathe deserve the finer things in life and you don't? Because she got lucky? Why didn't you get lucky? Why her and not you? Flore, you are the core character of this whole damned story. You're it, baby. You have to sing the loudest because yours is the strongest message.'

The tall, hypnotic man placed both hands on the tiny woman's shoulders. Annika rocked backwards on her heels, requiring his steadying hand to prevent her from keeling over. He winked, and she visibly glowed until the next words brought her back to the here and now.

'And Joe... You, *mon brave*, are insignificant scum; an artist, an introvert and a nice bloke. You really are pretty worthless to those around you,' the celebrity whipped round until his gaze met Durham Yarra's, his insults plain but kindly. 'Why should anyone listen to you? No-one's likely to take you seriously, and as yet you haven't figured out how to change this fact. You're determined you will, even though the world seems a desolate place. You don't care if you live or die, particularly knowing your brother couldn't give a stuff about you.'

Lynn watched several female cast members wiping their eyes. The directorial instructions had been incisive and *à-propos*, leaving everyone in the perfect frame of mind to play the scene henceforth. So after a short break, during which the players were able to let off some steam with the composers and musicians, Kiley Jones took "Act One, *Finalé*" from the top once more.

The rock star's pre-eminent fan walked away in silence and sat down to observe from behind the first block of stalls seating. Across the aisle, her husband took his place in the front row, elbows on knees and staring at the floor while the rehearsal orchestra's contingent of stringed instruments spirited cast and crew back to nineteenth-century Paris.

Superb sounds soared around the auditorium, making hairs on the nape of each actor's neck prickle and every heart beat that little bit faster. The entire throng had changed up a gear. By the final bars of the introduction, all players had become integral to creating a truly extraordinary theatrical masterpiece.

The *fortissimo* accompaniment, stirring enough to vibrate the nails out of the floorboards, rose to a dramatic *crescendo* before fading into its last chord, leaving a deathly vacuum which resonated in everybody's eardrums. No-one moved a muscle, all hanging on the superstar's verdict. The fact that he also stayed statuesque and silent left Lynn in no doubt as to his level of approval. She gave Kiley a sly thumbs-up, and received a knowing nod in return.

Keeping the cast on tenterhooks until he sensed they could bear it no longer, Jeff raised his head and levered himself up to a standing position.

Every dust particle in the atmosphere seemed charged with anticipation, yet still the actors daren't budge. Wondering if they had all stopped breathing, the show's chief architect began to clap, his hands colliding as slowly as the drummer in a New Orleans funeral band.

Tears streamed down his face despite its broad smile. 'Quite good,' he croaked. 'Quite fucking brilliant, in fact.'

The singers and musicians burst into laughter at the anti-climax, confident they had produced something special.

'It was bloody perfect, guys,' Jeff went on, taking languid, arrogant strides towards the stage. 'So damned perfect that I don't want to hear it again until opening night. You're masters, all of you. Thanks heaps. And thanks, Kiley. Thanks, angel.'

'OK! You're welcome. It felt awesome, and that's a wrap!' the redheaded producer stated, giggling as she dismissed the company for the day. 'I've always wanted to say that.'

***

'So did you write this book too?' Lynn asked in the car on their exodus to *Escondido* that same afternoon.

Her husband shook his head, still stunned by the whole experience of seeing their epic endeavour coming to fruition.

'I think you did,' she persisted.

'Madam,' Jeff replied with pompous, West End theatrical affectation. 'That's the most preposterous notion you've ever come up with, but I like it.'

The patient woman in the driver's seat grinned from ear to ear, content to have peeled away yet another layer of her enigmatic stranger's complex personality and revealed more of his unfathomable soul. He stretched his right hand sideways and stroked her cheek.

'Yeah, OK. I have entertained that thought once or twice, in my egotistical madness, over the years. But I doubt it. I don't feel anywhere near as clued in to Balzac as I do to Victor Hugo. Thanks heaps though. It's an amazing compliment.'

Lynn grappled with a feeling of *déjà-vu* while the couple drove for the next few kilometres in silence. Her memory played back a conversation she had shared with Gerry's former girlfriend, Suzanne, only a few weeks after she had met her beautiful black stallion.

'What is it about you?' the schoolgirl-turned-superstar revived questions she had posed at this time too. 'Where do you get your endless capacity from? And your depth of appreciation for everything?'

'Who knows?' Jeff replied, pressing his back into the Caprice's firm leather upholstery. 'I get the impression the world reserves extra dimensions for people like me. Brighter, louder, harder, sweeter or sourer... It's always been this way. As if my senses are more acute, or I just soak things up further. Ancient soul again? I don't have a bloody clue, angel.'

Sighing at her wise man's self-effacing chuckle, Lynn kept her eyes on the road. Here was a man who now lived placidly with the unexplained, ever humble as adolescent fervour receded and made way for mature acceptance.

'Somehow I got extra numbers on the knobs of my life's amplifier. I can tune things more finely, I reckon. I've always used my senses more than other people around me, ever since I was a little kid. What if I've spent time as an animal in another former life, depending on sensory perception for survival?'

'Hmm...' the driver reserved judgement on this latest theory. 'No. I can't see that. Or if you were, it was many, many incarnations ago.'

Provocative eyes flashed at his wife's, which had snatched a curious glance leftwards. 'Am I not enough of an animal for you now? I'll have to up my game.'

The athlete raised her eyebrows. 'Sounds appealing! I imagine you're way more of an animal than Victor Hugo would've been.'

Jeff laughed, rubbing his hands together at the challenge. '*Et comment tu le sais? Viens avec moi, mon amie. Cet après-midi, je t'emmènerais au ciel.*'

Arriving home to an empty house presented a perfect opportunity for the busy romantics to relax and enjoy each others' company in the wake of today's emotional rehearsal. Now Jeff had rationalised the hostage situation well enough for his bouts of nocturnal disturbance to be downgraded to the "bad dream" mark on the Richter scale of nightmares, a whole new chapter of closeness was opening up for the forever family.

Fascinated by her animated passenger's detour into supposed former lives, Lynn fetched a dog-eared copy of "*Les Misérables*" from their lounge room's growing library. She took it up to the master bedroom, changed into delicate ivory silk *lingerie* and a matching robe and stretched out on top of the sheets. She was ready to repay her soul-mate's animal adorations in ways she knew would excite him the most: entwined with illicit European *liqueurs* and before a backdrop of Bonaparte's Second Empire.

***

'*Les Thénardiers* remind me of my gold-digging, classless relatives dancing at my own wedding.'

Lifting her eyes from the heavy Hugo classic, Kierney smiled. 'I didn't think your *rellies* went to your wedding. Apart from Auntie Lena, that is...'

'No. They didn't,' her father affirmed. 'I mean in my head. While we were deciding on the guest list, I was plagued with visions of what havoc they would wreak if my mob had turned up in the swanky setting of the Dysons' ballroom. It would've been horrendous.'

The Diamonds' autobiography was primed for publication, having had vociferous praise piled upon it through a rapid editing process. A mock-up of the hardbound book sat on the office desk, but neither its author nor his children could summon the fortitude to open it in the lead-up to the first festive season without their missing loved one.

'Where's Ry?' the seventeen-year-old mumbled, distracted by a passage in *"Les Misérables"*.

'Some party, I think,' Jeff responded. 'He got all dressed up. Suit and tie; the whole box and dice.'

Kierney laughed. 'Oh, right. Must be a girl involved. I've got a date tomorrow night too, by the way. Are you still going to Gerry and Fiona's?'

'Yeah. Can't get out of it. For someone who would rather have spent the rest of his life on the moon than get married, the old bastard's worse than Bridezilla about everything being planned down to the last second. I'm half-expecting to be issued with wedding socks and jocks before I leave.'

'Ew! That's crazy,' his daughter giggled. 'Fiona strikes me as quite finicky, so perhaps he's only protecting himself from her. I think she'd give me the shits if I had to work for her. Anyway…'

'Jesus, *pequeñita*! You're changing so much lately. Are you OK? Are you angry because of what I'm doing or just exercising your right to be an objectionable adult?'

'*Papá*! Shut up and listen. I'm not angry. Nervous, I suppose. But wait a minute… I read some of *Mamá*'s diary entries from when you were…'

'Who's the date with?' her father interrupted.

'Oh, no-one you know. A guitarist in a band I saw last week. His name's Kye, which'll never work.'

Jeff smiled at his little girl's casual attitude. 'Kizzy and Kye?' he scoffed. 'You sound made for each other, so it's doomed from the start. What's the name of his band?'

'"Stripped",' the teenager replied, unable to stop her cheeks from blushing. 'Actually, he looks a bit like you, so no doubt that's another black mark against any relationship. I don't care if it doesn't go anywhere.'

The forty-four-year-old placed his palms over his ears and scrunched his eyes closed, mental exhaustion squeezing into deepening crows' feet with each passing week. Before Lynn's death, both doting parents had expressed concern at the earnestness with which their daughter approached romantic liaisons. The hapless Dylan had been the first suitor to pass her rigorous test, similarly serious about his checklist. Since then, after a passionate but stormy few months with David Ekwensi, an impressive Melbourne University academic, the young woman's compatibility care-factor had dwindled almost to match her brother's.

'A musician who's like your dad, in a pub band and with a name that's not even a name,' the melancholy man attempted to look on the bright side. 'I'll ask Fiona to keep all her wedding magazines for you.'

'Oh, for God's sake,' Kierney jeered. 'I know what you're thinking, but it's not like that.'

'Ah, yeah? What am I thinking?'

'That I've lost faith in relationships 'cause of what's happened to you and *Mamá*.'

'But it's not like that?' her father teased, offering his packet of cigarettes and preparing to light one for his mirror image. 'Could've fooled me.'

The young woman sighed. 'It's not,' she insisted. 'I've decided to postpone my search for a soul-mate. My mind's too absorbed with other things at the moment. Jet's no different. He still wants to meet someone special, but just not yet. Is that OK, Father? Can I get back to what I wanted to show you, Father? I honour you and seek to please you at all times, Father.'

'Watch it, ma'am,' Jeff mocked. 'Your similarity to me can only earn you so much licence before I call you on it, Miss Diamond.'

Fluttering her eyelids like the best Vaudeville caricature, Kierney capitulated. 'I'm fine, *Papá*. Really. Now look here! *Mamá* wrote in her diary about the bishop in "Les Mis"' being autobiographical, didn't she?'

'Yep. And what of it?'

'Don't make me cry. Well, not yet anyway,' the teenager warned. 'I think I've found the passages she was referring to.'

The widower scuffed his chair closer to his gipsy girl, preparing himself for what was to come. 'Great. I'll be crying along with you, in that case.'

'Here...' his daughter opened the book a few chapters in, flicking up a corner which had served its purpose. '"The bishop overflowed with love." He's you, isn't he? You are the Bishop of Digne.'

'If you say so.'

'Not if I say so, *Papá*. Listen to this bit... "What was this excess of love? It was a serene benevolence embracing all men and extending even beyond them."' Doesn't that sound like you? *Mamá* thought so, and so do I.'

Jeff bit back tears, just as the "JL" tattoo on his chest gave a sharp twinge. 'Apparently so, *pequeñita*.'

'Oh, my God! Was that your tatt'? *Mamá*, are you here too? That's amazing,' Kierney sniffed and wiped her eyes. 'And look at this bit: "He was held to be weak by the sober-minded..."'

'"By responsible citizens and sensible people,"' Jeff quoted from memory. '"Those *clichés* of a tawdry world in which egotism takes its time from pedantry." Jesus! *Je vous aime*, angels. Together, forever, wherever.'

Smoking down to the edge of the filter, the old soul extinguished his cigarette in the ashtray and reached a long arm around his tearful child. 'Repeat after me, gorgeous…'

In unison, the dark-haired pair recited the lines which Lynn had transcribed into her diary in nineteen-eighty-six.

> "Ugliness of aspect and deformities of instinct neither dismayed nor outraged him. He was moved by them and sometimes grieved, seeming to search, beneath the appearances of life, for a reason, an explanation or an excuse. He contemplated without anger, rather in the manner of a scholar deciphering a palimpsest, the chaos that still exists in nature."'

'What's a palimpsest?' Kierney asked.

'A document,' her dad answered. 'Old text. Something like that.'

'So do you think you wrote "*Les Misérables*"? Were you Victor Hugo in a past life?'

'Sure! If *Mamá* believes it, then I'll believe it too. There's no way to prove or disprove any of this, is there? For any of us.'

'So who are you going to be next?' Kierney urged. 'United States' President or the Pope? You'd better come back as someone with influence, or this wisdom of the ages'll be wasted for another generation.'

Jeff smiled. 'Exactly, Kizzo. It's what *Mamá* and I are hoping with this kooky plan of ours, to engineer getting back together in a meaningful way. At our age, soul-wise, we can't leave our futures to random accidents of birth anymore. We've learned that real, lasting change can't happen in a single lifetime. Surely we need to carry more and more forward every time, leaving some disciples behind to continue the good work while we give our next incarnations space to grow up and understand their mission. This time… maybe for the first time, or maybe not… we're doing it consciously instead of relying on the vagaries of the cosmos to dictate our destiny.'

The seventeen-year-old gasped. 'That's amazing! I suppose I'd kind of figured this out, but it's cool to hear you actually say it. How can Ryan and I help you and *Mamá* get back together? How can we know whose bodies you go into?'

The superstar settled further into the leather cushions, his resolve faltering. It was one thing to share fantasies of talking tattoos with the love of his life, but quite another to draw this ambitious law student into his reckless stupidity as well. In truth, he did have a few hare-brained ideas which he intended to leave behind in letters to his children. He hadn't planned to discuss them face-to-face, but perhaps he ought to.

'*Gracias, pequeñita,*' the smoky voice whispered, his lips kissing the soft skin of the teenager's cheek. 'You will play a part in getting us back together. Between us, we'll engineer something. There'll be a whole slew of people pretending they're us though, after reading this book. Your challenge'll be figuring out the two genuine articles from all the fraudsters.'

Kierney sighed. 'Bloody hell! That sounds terrible. Do you know how we'll know? You could be anyone and anywhere. You may even skip a lifetime.'

Jeff flinched and let out a yelp, his right hand shooting inside his shirt to scratch the skin over his left pectoral muscle. A sudden *vertigo* threatening to fell him to the floor, he leaped to his feet before slumping back down and dissolving into a flood of tears. He couldn't bear the thought of his precious lighthouse disappearing further beyond the horizon; not at this crucial stage. And, by the acute sensation above his heart, neither could she.

'I'm sorry, *Papá*,' their daughter cried out. 'And *Mamá*. I hope you don't skip a lifetime. I really do. I want you to be back together now. Are you alright?'

'Jesus fucking Christ!' the grief-stricken man cursed, forcing a smile. 'My heart's taking a real bloody hiding lately, between you two ladies. We need to dust off my old saying: "Hope for the best but expect the worst." Can't promise any of us better than this, can I? Happy, angels? Ease up, for fuck's sake.'

Having scrambled to her feet when her father jumped off his chair, Kierney breathed a sigh of relief and embraced him. His long arms closed around her body, and the pair stood together in silence. This level of anxiety was becoming unhealthy, and both knew it. Ryan was the sensible one, keeping his distance from the celebrity's forthcoming showdown and resisting the temptation to get carried away with what might lie beyond.

'I know you'll do the best you can to stay in our lives,' the young woman sniffed, rubbing the cotton fabric of Jeff's shirt pocket. 'I still feel connected to *Mamá*, so I'll hope for the best that it doesn't fade after you join her.'

'*Gracias*, Kizzy. This whole mad afterlife ambition's got somewhat out of hand, hasn't it? I don't want you seeing me like this; freaked out about the future when I've probably made the dumbest decision possible. You're the reason I'm as sane as I am, so I'm truly grateful for you sticking with me. Your brother's made his choice, and I totally respect that too.'

'Thanks, and it's fine. I know all that already,' the teenager said, stepping back and returning to her chair. 'But do you really think you're communicating with *Mamá*? Honestly?'

Jeff nodded. 'Yep. She talks to me at daybreak almost every morning, otherwise I don't think I'd be able to get up at all. And I'm convinced she wakes me when the nightmares start, just like she used to.'

'Oh. That's so weird. I've gone all shivery. But how?'

'Not sure… One minute, I'm in a dream and sense the background music getting scarier, and the next minute, I'm awake and looking around for her. That kills me, obviously, so I keep thinking I should ask her to let me have the nightmare anyway. The end result's the same when I wake up. She's not here, regardless how high my blood pressure climbs.'

Kierney frowned. 'Yeah. S'pose so.'

***

As part of the ongoing treatment plan instituted after his hostage ordeal, Jeff had invited Sarah Friedman to Melbourne to work on the latest papers, adding to their body of groundbreaking research into depression and Post-Traumatic Stress Disorder. Their brief doctor-patient *liaison* long forgotten, the Diamonds worked hard to integrate some of Bart Dyson's techniques for sporting success into the proven cognitive therapy and recovery planning methods pioneered by The Fellowship.

The combination of Lynn's focus on winning and Jeff's ability to motivate those on the losing side of life soon achieved academic acceptance. This was the vital ingredient for persuading victims of violence or neglect to take greater control over their own progress.

'"Who are your stakeholders?"' Lynn recited from an article the couple had written for an American medical journal. '"For whom is it important you stay alive and in good health? Who runs your life? Who's in your team?" Oh, we should change that to "on your team", I guess, for a US audience. Sarah, do you think this gets the main point across well enough? We have to help patients decide what they want to achieve. They need the tools and vocabulary to sell the concept of recovery on their terms to each stakeholder.'

'It's selling itself as you speak, angel,' her husband grinned. 'Gone are the days when your counsellor or psych' tells you how your life should unfold. Their role now is to convince you that you've got what it takes for everything to come good. And to create a partnership… Your psych' team needs to influence you in how you can and your supporters to all move in the right direction together.'

The professor had moved on from her original research fellowship at the University of Toronto, her career skyrocketing as a result of the collaboration with Jeff Diamond in the nineteen-seventies. She now ran the whole Psychiatry faculty at Harvard University, juggling her time between Massachusetts and another teaching post at King's College in London. This new angle to their research fascinated her, especially hearing Jeff's painstaking dedication to demystifying the human brain.

The inspirational musician's former lover delighted in following his journey from lost boy to commander of all he surveyed. Also grateful for Lynn's acceptance, she learned both perspectives on the couple's tentative attempts to mend such a broken mind, dating back to the first time the Dyson winning formula was added into the mix, during those terrible last few weeks before the sixteen-year-old left for her Californian sabbatical.

For Jeff's part, these informal discussions served as a timely reminder of how hopeless that period had seemed and how hard he had fought with his own unrelenting suicidal inclination. Catching his dream girl's eye in full view of their visitor, his words spared no inhibition in crediting her as the source of his current strength and inspiration for a newfound peak of endurance.

Sarah's amazement shot to yet another new level when he recounted his unexpected adventure at the hands of Ethiopian militants, remarking on how typical it was for the friendly star to establish a bond with his captors.

'It's not something I decided to do consciously, Sarah,' the intellectual remembered. 'When you find out something horrendous is about to happen to you, it's not the facts you react to. At least, not as much as you react to the emotional response you get when you learn something new. Good or bad. Eh, angel?'

His adoring wife smiled, cocking her head to urge him to continue.

'What you see, hear, feel, smell, *et cetera*, is much more powerful than the actual words being spoken. Like when you feel the end of a rifle smack into the back of your skull... Therefore, we believe learning of any kind can be triggered by directing that same visceral response elsewhere, toward something more constructive. You know as well as we do that sensory perception by the subconscious mind can account for ninety percent of one's instinctive responses. So if we can influence this perception positively somehow, through therapy, it should counteract some of the long-term negative effects. D'you think, doc'? Gradual process, of course, so it'd be part of a prolonged attack. But feasible?'

The tennis champion hadn't participated in the prior, lengthy sessions of professional introspection between her husband and the psychiatric expert. This latest round of interviews was the pre-cursor to to a fourth volume of their research, each one building on evidence garnered from the last. Watching this giant of the entertainment world laying himself bare to any and every idea Sarah posited gave Lynn a glimpse into a contradictory facet of his working style: serious but plain-speaking, intent on concentrating on the practical, yet entrusting each plausible conclusion to Doctor Friedman's jurisdiction.

'The brain's just like any other organ and muscle: physiologically programmed to filter on what it's interested in, what it's good at or focused on at any point in time,' the sportswoman offered, her unusually dispassionate tone reminiscent of her father's. 'Focus on what you want, and the brain works to make it happen, i.e. the Law of Attraction. And then it makes sure the action's more repeatable over time and with practice, either through visualisation or embedding motor skills. Do you remember that discussion we had back then, Jeff?'

From his current position on top of the world, the thirty-four-year-old was struck by another inexplicable spiritual maxim bearing out in his bizarre reality. 'Sure do,' he smirked. 'Jesus! Time really does heal, angel, doesn't it? Even a couple of years ago, I would've smarted at revisiting that comment, but now it's almost a fond memory. I wasn't exactly the most willing student that night.'

'Oh, you were, considering...' his saviour refuted. 'I was amazed I retained your attention with that stuff, given how sad we both were. I didn't have much confidence in it helping at the time. I was way more than fifty percent sure you wouldn't still be around on the other side of my trip.'

Sarah sat straighter in her chair. 'That's the reason he was though... The fact you spoke in those honest and non-judgemental terms at crunch-time, as Jeff's called it before in my sessions, played a big part in him sticking around,' she surmised, always staggered by the fortitude this atypical showbusiness pair demonstrated during their turbulent life together. 'You showed an interest in Jeff still being alive when you got back, Lynn. If you hadn't, the result might well have been as you describe.'

Husband and wife exchanged loving glances. These ideas were already implicit in every nuance of their relationship, immortalised in their matching "JL" tattoos.

Jeff steered the conversation full-circle to their emerging formula for minimising the effects of trauma. 'If you focus on all the things that can go wrong, you'll get things that go wrong. ¿Verdad, Regala? As we know, there are two types of motivation: moving away from something to avoid pain, and moving towards something to gain pleasure. This new therapy has to improve the chance of being irresistibly attracted to something worthwhile, like having this piece of human perfection walk back into my life after two years of hell on wheels.'

'That's very good,' Sarah laughed. 'It will. Absolutely. You guys only need me to document this, don't you? You could've avoided my expenses and used a resident psych' from the Royal Melbourne instead! But can we return to the nightmare treatment for a moment? Explain to me again how you think that should work?'

Jeff took a large gulp from a glass of water, needing to redirect his thoughts. 'Yeah, alright. Let's see... Are we all comfortable with the notion that the subconscious doesn't sleep? And that it makes our dreams?'

The two women nodded.

'Well... This gorgeous creature here once told me that if I found a conceptual solution to a problem before going to sleep, rather than analysing problems to death, then I'd stand a better chance of waking up with the makings of a real solution rather than the remains of a huge problem; i.e. dream *versus* nightmare. So, during that night I was held in the old farmhouse, I went to sleep in the midst of wild fantasies of you, angel. It was the most exquisite dreaming experience ever, I reckon; as real as it could be without being real, if you know what I mean. It was a deliberate strategy based on this exact principle. Tough gig, but a man's gotta do what a man's gotta do...'

The red-blooded larrikin grinned, stroking his crotch and regretting the fact that both classy woman hanging off his every word had seen more than was currently on display. 'Of course, after a while, the dream turned to shit anyway,' he continued, 'but afterwards, my strongest memories were of the good bits instead of the bad. When I got home however, I forgot to keep applying the strategy, stupidly thinking nothing could catch me out in the safety of my own family, which was when the PTSD took over and I fell in a fucking heap in grand style. I stopped protecting myself as soon as the clear and present threat was gone. Too soon, as it turned out. Lesson well learned: *ergo*, continuing the treatment is the key. The only question is how long do you keep going in self-preservation mode?'

'Until the nightmares stop?' Lynn suggested. 'Might be ages, I know, unless we develop a way to tell by brain activity. It'd be impossible to tell scientifically 'til then, I suppose. And I think we need to keep making connections between the various levels of consciousness. Thoughts link to behaviour links to results. Convince yourself you're a champion. That's what we were always taught. Go to sleep imagining we'd won the gold, and we'd wake up one step closer.'

'Sure... There's no way you could be further away,' the erstwhile cynic smiled. 'There can be no chance of harm in this case, 'cause the worst that can happen is waking up in the same place. Unless you'd been abducted in the meantime, which'd be a whole 'nother traumatic experience to deal with.'

'For God's sake, Mister Doom and Gloom! We should talk about this angle too, shouldn't we? Not as part of Sarah's work though,' the caring mother remembered. 'And another idea I had, while we're doing these, is for patients to create a list of deliverables. Objectives, goals or whatever... Things they'll need on the way to reaching their goals, like finding someone they trust, getting rid of debts that are stressing them out, outcomes that are significant to their ultimate ambitions. And it should be every possibility imaginable, such as when the kids make lists of what they want to do in the school holidays. There are no boundaries. Anything's possible.'

'¡*Excelente!* Dare to dream,' the world-changer chuckled, closing his eyes and leaning back into the office couch. 'I like that a lot. Maybe not to the extent of "Drive Dad's Aston Martin outside *Escondido* for one kilometre" however.'

Lynn laughed aloud at another of their son's more outlandish wishlist items. 'Hey! I forgot about that. You let him do it though, and he grew from the experience, so it worked!'

'Jet?' the Canadian professor snapped. 'Drove your car beyond the gates of your property, on public roads? How old is he?'

'Eight, going on eighteen,' the young mother sighed. 'Jeff pushed the seat back as far as it would go and sat behind him. He can barely reach the pedals! It was pretty irresponsible of us, but the streets into Mount Eliza are quiet enough.'

'He couldn't see much over the dashboard either,' her partner-in-crime admitted. 'Wasn't that dangerous. The windows are so dark. Someone walking along wouldn't even have noticed he was in front of me. We only saw Jim and Polly, and neither of them gives a shit about that sort of thing.'

'Fortunately,' Lynn sighed. 'Can you imagine the press getting hold of it? No worse than things my dad let us do with farm vehicles when we were young, but that was on private land. Anyway... Is this worth exploring further as a tool? Making achievement lists?'

'Sure is, baby,' the amateur psychologist jumped in at Sarah's invitation. 'Again, you can't be any worse off than staying the same, which is fast becoming a guiding principle for this whole exercise. With this and the stakeholder list, the next steps are, "What do I have to become, and who can I enlist to help me find the motivation to deliver these outcomes?" Y'know, Sarah... We're thinking of setting up a Modern Behavioural Science institute somewhere; ideally here in Melbourne, but it doesn't have to be.'

'That'd be amazing!' the clinician clapped her hands. 'You guys are doing so much. I won't say no to any new facilities, and who cares where they are? Air travel's the norm these days. There's such a wide application for this type of practical research, even for businesses.'

'Yep. I was getting to that,' Jeff grinned. 'Sales training, leadership, organisational change... All that fluffy stuff. Soft skills, they call them, although I don't get the whole "soft" thing. Lynn, all that stuff we used to talk about in London: mimic a millionnaire, play in their world.'

The Olympian checked the time, knowing the children were soon due home from school. 'Yes. I think it all works on some level. And what about learning how not to self-sabotage?' her voice reduced to a whisper in deference to the legendary "elephant in the room", which had been hitherto overlooked in their cogitations. 'I'm surprised you haven't mentioned this yet. It was a huge fear of yours back in those dark days, wasn't it? One of success' scariest side-effects is that failure looks like a mighty long way down. The pressure to to keep succeeding is so huge once you get there. Therefore, it's easier not to succeed in the first place.'

The billionnaire exhaled, his blood pressure plummeting. These were painful memories to drag out, yet vital to paint the complete picture. His guardian angel was tough on him sometimes, always with just cause.

'Definitely,' he sighed. 'From alcohol and drugs to deliberately missing appointments, and pissing off people who matter. And all points in between. I hate how you keep doing this to me, and I love that you do it too. So much. Is that the kids? We'll call it quits soon. Thank Christ!

'Anyhow, can we stop people letting themselves down, Sarah? Trivially or fundamentally? What is it that makes us more likely to let ourselves down when others let us down? Low self-esteem, I'm guessing. If they can't be bothered, I mustn't be worth it... It's almost as if we think we deserve to be let down, when it should be the other way round.'

The researcher turned a leaf in her notebook, now scrawling across the page at speed.

'I'll go and say hello in a minute,' Lynn nodded. 'Dave knows we're busy. We need to turn those self-destructive *scenaria* the other way round. It all goes back to motivation again. You set the goals, discuss how to make them specific and measurable, set a timeframe...'

'And no room to wriggle out of anything,' her husband scoffed. 'You're a killer like that, Lynn Dyson.'

The formidable champion coughed, loading their coffee cups onto a tray in preparation for drawing the meeting to a close. 'And I'm not going to stop.'

'*Bueno, Regala.* You can't. I don't want you to. The ecological argument is paramount too, before we forget. That's well documented. I mean don't set yourself up for something physically impossible. If a person's depressed because he or she's gay and wants to be straight, we can't fix that. But we can drill down to find what it is about being straight that they crave? Maybe it's having kids? That's fixable. They could adopt or do the surrogacy thing. Or maybe it's dressing like a woman, less to do with sex and everything to do with gender? That's fixable too, although I'm not willing to go out in public yet.'

Lynn's mouth twitched at first, as if suppressing a smile, but neither superstar could keep a straight face once shock overruled Sarah's normal professional demeanour.

'You're not going to tell me you're a closet transvestite, are you? My illusions are destroyed! I'll be the first to enrol into this program in this case.'

'No, you won't!' the blonde singer burst out laughing. 'That class'll be oversubscribed multiple times!'

'Jesus, ladies!' Jeff sensed a little competition creeping in between the two women, anxious to dispel any animosity. 'Don't jump to conclusions. It's purely hypothetical, I assure you. I'm perfectly at home with your, I mean, my wardrobe. How do you know I wasn't casting nasturtiums... nasturtia? ...about either of you? Could happen!'

'Oh, shit,' his wife grimaced. 'I've been meaning to tell you, darling...'

'Cool. No worries, angel. I knew anyway. That's better. Rightful places restored, so back to the ecological theme. We need to tie these goals and deliverables to values and beliefs, and something that's a stretch but not inconceivable. And...' the handsome man paused, leaning forwards and pointing a long index finger at the television in the office. 'Christ Almighty! I've just thought of something else.'

'Yeah? What's that?' Lynn asked, seeing a new spark in her headstrong intellectual's eye.

'We need to run a campaign against domestic violence,' he digressed. 'We could call it "Don't beat about the bush."'

After a moment of pure disbelief, both women voiced their outrage at this impish suggestion. The tone's base quality was indicative of looming mania, signalling it was high time they drew this particular workshop to a close. An Olympian right hand delivered a resounding smack to his shoulder, just as Jet and Kierney rushed in to join the fun.

'That's the most terrible thing I've ever heard you say,' the disgusted mother couldn't help but laugh. 'It is funny though. Only you could get away with that, you degenerate!'

Spreading Love

The Diamonds' busy calendar galloped across the first half of nineteen-eighty-six, heralding a number of coordinated famine relief events and the grand opening of "The Black Sheep" in London looming large at the end of the year. The month of May deposited them at Michelle England's wedding to her handsome heart surgeon, Alan Hadley. Best friends since primary school, Lynn was the obvious choice for her matron of honour, a role the superstar accepted with joyful enthusiasm despite her many work commitments.

Kierney was to be a bridesmaid beside her mother, which entranced their legion of fans more than the little girl herself. As her Uncle Sandy had been at an equivalent age, she preferred to be immersed in useful activities rather than parading in public, answering the same silly questions time after time. Her young brain, crammed full of unconventional ideas picked up at the dinner table with her hyperactive parents, brought regular interesting insights home from school as to the happiness abounding in her friends' families.

Consequently, the invitation for the youngster to join a bridal party raised a stream of probing questions. Why did people choose to marry? And why did so many who made these permanent promises end up divorcing and leaving confused offspring behind? Her parents rued this sudden foreshortening of her innocence, having expected nothing less from the intelligent seven-year-old. It was a challenge not to leave collateral damage in the wake of honest answers, neither wishing to sugar-coat their children's expectations nor deny them a fairytale future like their own.

In the public eye, the Four of Diamonds were these days acclaimed as the *epitome* of Australian establishment, Bart and Marianna's rightful heirs. Not only was Junior's brood more deserving, being the Dysons' eldest child and a wholesome role model who had married a sixth-generation Victorian, but Lynn and Jeff's fundamental philosophies also remained at odds with the implications of their status as household names.

By no means ashamed of the hard-edged image he had cultivated as a twenty-something rock star, now in his mid-thirties, the songwriter resisted his slide into orthodoxy with every fibre of his being. With his charitable commitments, outspoken support for youth disadvantage and victimisation, and the couple's investment in AIDS treatment and HIV research all over the world, not to mention all the trails he had blazed for mental illness sufferers, he had transformed from a charismatic orator into every parent's examplar for their teenagers.

The reason for his stubborn forbearance was frustrating in its irony. The shining beauty, whom the boy from Canley Vale had worshipped from his lonely childhood bedroom, had always been Australia's sweetheart. She could do no wrong in his eyes either, then or now. Nevertheless, apart from an initial bubble of disappointment from the true-blue conservatives at her choice of husband, the furphy gnawing at his pride was that the golden-haired angel was all too often credited for elevating Jeff Diamond out of the gutter.

His petty rancour at this injustice was both foolish, since he had sought her out on purpose for free entry into the upper echelons of society, and baseless, given the plethora of testimonials surrounding his work. And with the addition of two adorable children, they were now considered all-round paragons of virtue.

Lynn was all too aware of this misconception, constantly at pains to refute it in public. In magazine articles and television interviews, she used every opportunity to expound the songwriter's passion for improving the lives of underprivileged people. This, among his many attractive features, was often cited as the catalyst for her own social justice agenda.

No matter the origin of their work's momentum, the "Together, Forever, Wherever" *motto* rode high and proud at concerts and public appearances for the second year running. Their devoted team of Diamond Celebration Foundation employees brought the plight of the downtrodden and forgotten to the attention of mainstream Australia, and their special place in the population's hearts was due in no insignificant part to the emotional accessibility of the princess-and-pauper love story.

Why should these factual inaccuracies matter so much, as long as those in need capitalised on the fans' generosity? But they did matter. His own struggle, the songwriter explained to all comers, gave legitimacy to every other second-classed citizen fighting discrimination from the highs and mighties who held them down.

Interviewed for the ABC's "7:30 Report" a few days after Stonebridge Music announced the latest international fundraising event for African aid, Jeff explained himself to the show's presenter. 'The last year or two saw a big shift, I'm told, in people's perception of me. I went from being a singer with a loud mouth to a loudmouth who sings. The "Feed Africa" campaign was the tipping point for this, in that it merged who I am and who I want to be into the same person.

'I've never been interested in money in and of itself, which people find hard to believe when all the 'papers show are pictures of our house, my car, overseas holidays, *et cetera*. But what really turns me on is seeing I have value beyond making ourselves rich and famous. I understand myself very well, and that's a great position to be in when your livelihood depends on understanding others and their situations.

'I get accused of hogging the limelight and only being interested in self-promotion, but there's only a small element of truth to that view,' the handsome celebrity grinned into the camera. 'Yeah, sure... I'll admit I'm not one to hide in the background, but in order to breathe life into issues on the unsavoury fringe of life and hopefully bring about some change, it's necessary to be in people's faces all the bloody time.'

A cheer erupted from the small audience gathered to watch the outside broadcast, which the friendly star acknowledged with a tempered wave.

'And I'm damned well going to be in your face until you no longer want me there. So far, even though folk say they're sick to death of seeing Lynn and me wherever they turn, we're still overrun with invitations to do more. Take your pick, ladies and gentlemen...'

The show's reporter had no choice but to allow the photogenic star to soak up the enthusiastic reception, before labouring a certain notoriety for drug use and alcohol abuse in his early career. She asked whether this side of his personality was now reformed.

Although infuriated at first by yet another attempt to discredit him, Jeff trotted out the well-worn reply. 'Reformed? Yes and no. Sure, I still have all my addictions. Once they take hold, they're reluctant to let go. And part of me doesn't want to lose them either, 'cause they're part of who I am. It's the only me I know, and the only me Lynn's ever known. We don't need to change who we are.

'My wide range of addictions and compulsions are under control these days, and with minimal effort too. While I don't think an addiction, as a human defect, ever leaves you... rather like depression, anxiety and all those other mental issues... I do believe it's possible to replace one addiction with another. Right now, I'm totally addicted to my family, and I don't get enough of them. My dependencies have shifted, that's all.

'We have to take the emphasis off beating addiction outright, to take some of the pressure off ourselves. We should focus on getting stronger than it instead, with the help of those around us. Addicts, largely as a result of misinformed public opinion, put too much expectation on themselves and on their support network, which only screws them up even further when life gets too hard. We all need to learn to live with whoever we've become, whether it's our own fault, someone else's or no-one's.'

On the third of May, the Diamonds suspended their hectic life to celebrate their friends' wedding. Michelle's mother had passed away when the redhead was only eleven, leaving her to be brought up by her father, two brothers and an armoury of amenable aunties. Her lasting friendship with Lynn Dyson had led the celebrities to feel as if they too were on the list as family rather than friends.

'I hope Mish isn't settling,' the chief bridesmaid mentioned as the singers rehearsed for the upcoming reception. 'I think she is, don't you?'

'Settling for Al?' her husband frowned. 'Wouldn't think so. What does settling mean anyway? That she reckons she'll never find the perfect match? He's a good bloke, and they seem pretty close. They're not as old as we are, angel. Perhaps they don't even know they're each others' one and only yet... Did *you* settle?'

'What?' Lynn cried out, wondering if he were joking or if his persistent lingering insecurities had motivated the question. 'Sure.'

A broad smile broke out on Jeff's face, standing up from the piano stool to plant a heartfelt kiss on his wife's forehead. 'OK, cool,' he replied. 'I'm going to start charging you rent then.'

'Rent as well as mortgage? That's not fair.'

'Basic economics, baby... I'm in high demand. You said so just the other day,' the comedian scoffed.

The tennis champion flexed her spine and stretched her long legs, gaining an appreciative whistle for her provocative stance. She pushed her arrogant partner's advances aside and groaned. The pair had been holed up in *Escondido*'s recording studio for four hours, and her muscles were beginning to cramp after a tough training session that morning. Refilling their wine glasses, she lifted her collaborator's glass and passed it his way.

'So how do you propose you'll charge this rent?'

'Oh, in the usual way,' he grinned, toasting the humorous banter.

'I might find a housemate to share the costs in that case. Do you want me to share you?'

Jeff burst out laughing. 'Why not? There's an interesting proposition!'

'Time share?' his wife teased. 'Been there, done that, I seem to remember, my former sexual mercenary.'

'Fuck! That hurt, you bitch. Lucky I'm in a generous mood, or I might evict you.'

'Seriously though,' the blonde's voice tapered off, hugging her man's strengthening frame. 'Michelle has sort of settled, I think. She wanted a good father more than she wanted a hunk in bed. I get both in the same package, so even if you evict me, I'll just sit outside the gates for the rest of my life in case you change your mind.'

Lynn's duties in the bridal party saw her drive away from their city apartment before eight o'clock on the day of the wedding, with Jeff enjoying a fun-filled breakfast with his children. He was under strict instructions to deliver them to the church, all scrubbed up and shining, at one-thirty in the afternoon. Their rambunctious mood, magnified by an absence of childminders, promised to make this a distinct challenge.

Childish excitement was infectious indeed to a man with an addiction to his family and who had missed out on such life-affirming circumstances during his youth. His hostage episode had seen the rock musician embrace parenthood with even more conviction than before, and its positive effect on Jet and Kierney was noticeable to whomever spied them together.

Confident that nothing had been forgotten, the youngsters were treated to an *impromptu* shot through one of the new automatic carwashes which had sprung up in Melbourne's suburbs. After threatening to lower a window while the brushes were spinning above the roof, the father soon got his comeuppance when Jet leaped into the passenger seat and began to open the door. After imparting a thorough admonishment and entering into a pact not to tell Mum, the metallic grey paintwork sparkled in the late morning sunshine as the family's Victorian-made sedan glided through the leafy streets of Toorak towards St John's Anglican Church.

The celebrity allowed the kids to let off steam with Michelle's nephews, looking forward to a sly cigarette or two. Their ceremonial attire remained protected inside the car while he wandered around the grounds, enjoying the therapy of lilting birdsong and eavesdropping into the children's exuberant and imaginative games. As expected, it didn't take long for his dark-haired gipsy girl to tire of innocent pursuits and weave her way through the decaying gravestones until she found him.

'*Papá*?' Kierney looked up, slipping her hand into his. 'How long 'til Michelle comes?'

'How should I know?' he smiled, trying to yank his right hand upwards, weighed down by a small human being. 'I can't see what time it is.'

The seven-year-old giggled, grabbing her father's wrist with both hands and twisting it around to reveal his watch's face. 'Quarter-past-one,' she announced, swinging their joined arms. 'When do I get changed?'

'Soon, *pequeñita*. Ten minutes. Come and have a look at these...'

Jeff led his curious daughter across the mossy ground and pointed out some of the headstones' inscriptions, obscured by lichens and rendered indistinct by the passage of time. 'This is where they used to bury all the local people who died. These are so old. Look... Eighteen-eighty-six, Kizzy. That's a hundred years ago. People can't get buried here any more 'cause they ran out of room.'

'How did they die?' Kierney asked, glancing from side to side at the higgledy-piggledy rows of graves.

'Can't tell,' the old soul replied, crouching down and resting a hand on his daughter's tiny shoulder. 'This is Arthur Mitchell. See? He died in nineteen-forty-two. He was seventy-three, which was pretty ancient in those days. How d'you think he died?'

'Born on eighth of April eighteen-sixty-nine,' the young girl read, tracing the weathered engraving with her fingers. 'He's part of history.'

'He *is* part of history. *Exactement,*' the philosopher agreed. 'We'll all be part of history at some point, gorgeous. He was an early settler. Life would've been pretty tough for his family. No carwash, no TV or cinema, no swimming pools. He did well to reach seventy-three. Don't you reckon?'

Kierney and Jet had both inherited their father's fascination with death, for some strange reason that neither parent understood, and Jeff guessed the little girl would be keen to explore the graveyard. She smiled at the list of twentieth-century luxuries. Her brother had been given a lecture by their mother only the other week about learning to play musical instruments rather than sitting on his backside and listening to records.

'Arthur Peter Mitchell,' she read out. 'You didn't need a carwash because you didn't have a car. How did you die?'

Jeff leaned over until his mouth hovered behind Kierney's left ear. 'Hello, pretty lady,' he whispered in his ghostliest voice. 'It's Arthur. Pleased to meet you.'

'Hello, Arthur,' Kierney giggled, her frame turning rigid for a couple of seconds, not prepared to turn around in case it wasn't her daddy playing games. 'Pleased to meet you too. How're you going?'

'How'm I going? I'm not going at all actually. Would you like to know how I died?'

The graceful girl nodded, standing stock-still and staring at the deceased man's grave. The messenger's back was beginning to ache from stooping so far over, but this was too priceless an opportunity to miss. He loved discovering how the little prodigies might cope with new ideas.

'Well… I was very sad one day, because my dear, old wife passed away. She was a lovely woman; gave me twenty-three children.'

'Twenty-three?' Kierney danced with delight, no longer frightened.

'Yes, my dear. Twenty-three. So many birthday presents to wrap. Anyway, when she died, I was so sad, so I went to the doctor, and he gave me some laughing medicine.'

'What's laughing medicine?' the girl shot back, a wavering left hand reaching back to touch her father's face as he spoke. 'Did it work?'

'Oh, it worked alright,' Jeff kept the story going. 'The bottle said to take five millilitres, but I didn't have my glasses on, and I thought it said to take five litres.'

'Five litres?' she exclaimed again, whipping her head around in surprise.

Pretending he was but another witness to this news, the showman mirrored his daughter's astonishment, his eyes bidding the youngster to turn back to the headstone and wait for Arthur's tale to conclude.

'Yes, indeed,' the shaky voice answered. 'I should've been more careful, shouldn't I? I died laughing.'

The littlest Diamond shrieked. '*Papá!* That's so funny! How can someone die laughing?'

'Don't ask me!' her father yelped in reply, standing up and lighting another cigarette. 'Don't you believe old Mister Mitchell?'

'It wasn't Mister Mitchell. It was you,' she insisted, punching her dad's thigh. 'You told the story.'

Jeff shook his head. 'Hey! That hurts! She doesn't believe you, Arthur. *Tant pis*. What about this one, *pequeñita*?'

The joyous pair moved to a burial site that was even further in ruins. Again, Kierney ran the fingers of her left hand along the chiselled letters.

'Elsie Anne Bright,' she enunciated. 'That's a nice name. I think she was a teacher.'

'Could be,' her dad nodded. 'Great name for a teacher. How did Elsie die then?'

The child stood for a few moments, hanging on to the leg of Jeff's suit pants. His right palm alighted on the top of her head and began to sway her from side to side.

'Hey! What are you doing, *Papá*?' Kierney asked, determined not to topple over.

'I'm putting you in touch with Elsie Anne Bright's spirit,' a sonorous tone floated downwards. 'Can you tell me how she died, Miss Diamond?'

The little girl fixed her eyes on the crumbling headstone and took a deep breath. 'Elsie Bright was a teacher at a nearby primary school,' she tried to emulate her dad's creepy characterisation. 'One day, her class was so naughty that she had to shout to make them be quiet, and so she was very angry by the time she left school. And her throat was sore too.'

'Yeah,' her spellbound audience frowned. 'All that shouting would certainly make her throat sore. Poor Elsie. So what happened next?'

'Well… She had to buy some milk for her cats, but the shop was busy, and she was in a big hurry. She wouldn't wait in the queue, so she found some poison in her handbag and threw it over three children and an old lady in front of her.'

'Alright. That was a bit drastic. So Elsie Anne Bright, how did *you* die?'

'She went to a trial, and the judge was a cat. And the judge told the court, that was made up of all cats too, that Miss Bright would have to die because she's a murderer.'

'Whoa!' Jeff tugged on Kierney's hand, enthralled by the youngster's rule of law. 'Are you sure about that? Do cats believe murderers have to die?'

'Yes,' the precocious advocate confirmed. 'Because she didn't say sorry, and she was cruel and impatient. They made her eat cat food for ten days, straight out of the can, and it killed her 'cause she was allergic to fish.'

Chuckling, her dad checked his watch again. 'Okey dokey, folks. Enough already! We'd better go back to the car, Madam Tipsy Tall-Tales. Awesome story, by the way. I hope I never get into trouble with cats. Shall we get you into your bridesmaid's dress, so you can put away all those dark thoughts.'

'No. Not yet,' the girl objected, pouting and waving her hand. 'May I do one more, please?'

The billionnaire took a quick look around the churchyard to locate the boys before turning back to pleading eyes, far too interested in hearing her next gruesome *scenario*. 'Yes yet, but OK. Who's your next case? Find one quickly.'

Skipping on ahead a few paces, Kierney pointed to a crumbling vault-like structure behind Elsie Bright's last resting place. It belonged to John Godfrey McDonald, who had died in nineteen-eleven.

The bemused man held out his hand. 'C'mon. Tell me about old McDonald while you change, angel.'

'John McDonald was a farmer,' she declared on their way up the path towards the car park, his fate set to emerge from its spooky past.

'A farmer in Toorak?'

'Yes. There were farms all over Victoria in the olden days, *Papá*,' his daughter defended herself, raising her hands above her head as if to ask how he dared to pick holes in her historical account.

'*Bueno*,' the father allowed. '*T'as raison, bien sûr*. Carry on, *señorita encyclopædia*.'

Jeff opened the Caprice's rear door to allow Kierney to climb inside. Her dress lay on the back seat in its clear, polythene cover. She didn't miss a beat while removing her jeans and jumper, with her dad standing in the doorway to block anyone's view. He leaned in as her elaborate story unfolded, thinking how grateful he was that his children felt so safe and secure in their tiny worlds.

'The farmer was in trouble too, *Papá*. He never cleared up all the horse poo from his farm, and it got so smelly that the neighbours complained. But he didn't get rid of it, and just put more and more all over the place.'

'Eugh!' her dad laughed out loud. 'Is that right? This is a better story. What did the neighbours do about it?'

'They called the police, but they couldn't help. Did you know it's not a crime to leave horse poo on the ground?'

'Isn't it? Did *Mamá* tell you that? Perhaps it ought to be. Sounds pretty disgusting!'

'Yes, it was disgusting,' Kierney giggled, pulling the long dress on, her head angled into the roof as she struggled to straighten its soft, slinky panels. 'Anyway... Is this right? Like this?'

'Yeah,' her *papá* tugged the skirt down until the bodice sat smooth across her shoulders and chest. '*Es muy hermosa*. Turn round, and I'll tie the ribbon. So what happened to farmer John?'

Retrieving tiny satin shoes from their box, the intrigued chaperone clopped the two soles together to recreate the sound of horses' hoofs. 'Did he get trampled by all his horses?'

'No! *¿Puedo poner los zapatos, Papá, por favor?*'

'*Sí. Certo,*' Jeff smiled. '*Sientate.* I'm going to put them on like in Cinderella.'

'Yay! Are you Prince Charming?' Kierney laughed, flopping down on to the wide bench seat of the Caprice.

'No,' he shook his head at the fanciful suggestion. 'I'm the Fairy Godfather, and I'm going to do some black magic if you don't tell me how old McDonald popped his clogs.'

The pretty bridesmaid-under-construction sighed, much preferring the idea of Prince Charming to an evil fairy. She slid off the leather seat and dropped down onto the bitumen, then stepped aside to show herself off by twirling around in two full circles. Jeff whistled. He still remembered Lynn behaving the same way, and he was gripped by an intense pang of longing.

'You, Kierney Lynn Freedom Diamond, are the most beautiful bridesmaid in the whole wide world,' he praised, before dropping the act and painting on his best enquiring face again. '*Allora... ¿Qué pasa con John, pequeñita?*'

While the seven-year-old checked her reflection in the tinted windows, her father lifted another bag out of the boot. It contained his son's wedding outfit. Transforming a twisting tornado into a church-ready cherub was bound to be a far less pleasurable experience. He also furrowed around the rest of the family's usual paraphernalia for anything else they might need for today's engagement.

Slotting the wide-toothed comb his wife had left in Kierney's shoe-box into the inside pocket of his suit jacket, the superstar slammed the car door and made sure it was locked. He held out his hand to his elegant miniature companion, and they walked towards the church to find the other children. Quite a number of guests had already arrived, among whom Jeff recognised various faces belonging to the bride's extended family.

Flouncing her long skirt with each proud stride, Kierney was intent on finishing her story. 'So, *Papá*. Farmer John... What was his other name again? Oh, yeah. John Godfrey McDonald. All the neighbours put more and more money into a box until they had enough to rent a gigantic tipper truck to take away all the horse poo.'

'OK. Gigantic tipper truck, huh? Good idea. But how did he die in the end?'

The seven-year-old huffed. 'Hold on! I'm getting to that part. It's a long story.'

'You're not wrong! It's a bloody long story,' the kind man chuckled. 'Get on with it, please.'

Trying to keep a straight face, Kierney reeled off a rapid *dénouement* to her noxious plot, disclosing the unfortunate John McDonald's demise. 'When the truck was nearly ready to leave his farm, he ran after it, yelling to the driver. He tried to stop the truck from driving away, but instead the driver reversed up to him and tipped the horse poo all over Mister McDonald.'

'Oh, my God!' her dad exclaimed, pinching his nose with his fingers, his eyes wide with alarm. 'What a terrible way to go! Did it kill him stone dead there and then, or did he die slowly from the smell?'

'Oh, very, very, very slowly,' Kierney laughed. 'He *suffocaked* in poo.'

Jeff bent down and grabbed the naughty storyteller round the waist. Hoisting her up in his arms, he planted a big kiss on her lips.

'You mean suffocated, not *suffocaked*, but that's an excellent end to the story. Well done, Kizzy. Suffocated is a ten-out-of-ten word. Congratulations. You win the prize of being Michelle's *specialest* flower-girl. OK! *¿Dónde está tu* bloody *hermano?*'

'*¡Allí!*' the happy child pointed towards a bevvy of boys bunched up, with only their backs on view from the bushes. '*Voy a buscarlo.*'

'*Gracias, pequeñita,*' Jeff nodded. '*Pero lentamente, por favor.* You can't get yourself dirty now, remember?'

The celebrity followed the princess in dainty satin shoes as she skipped away, the white dress with its pale yellow ribbon reminding him of Anna on his own wedding day. His thoughts were soon interrupted however, finding himself swallowed up into a crowd of bridal relatives. Kisses and handshakes appeared from all quarters, requiring him to be on duty once more. The same, tired twenty questions circled, seeking the inside scoop about his music, the African charity work and various other trials and tribulations which came with being the country's most notorious notable.

'I can't believe how much Kierney's grown up,' Michelle's aunt cooed, seeing the little girl depart on her errand to repatriate her brother from the jungle.

'It happens,' Jeff agreed. 'She's nearly twenty-one already. It's scary.'

The throng broke out into a chorus of titters, gasps and sighs, only dying down in time for a second round when a storm of approaching footsteps became louder. Jet ploughed straight into his father's legs, as he always did.

The star performer groaned on cue, repelled his son with a gentle push and pretended to straighten the tie which was still folded in his pants pocket. 'Jeez! Watch it, mate,' he requested, flipping up the collar of his shirt and threading the missing item into place.

'How old are you now, Kizzy-Jo?' Aunt Belinda asked, lacing a strand of the girl's long, wavy, dark hair through spindly fingers.

'I'm seven.'

'And was that your big brother outside running around?'

Jeff shot his daughter a sympathetic wink, knowing she would consider these questions so juvenile these days. He and his beautiful best friend never worried about their children letting them down in social situations, yet this type of false friendliness was enough to test anyone's patience.

'Yes,' Kierney answered. 'Jet has to get dressed now, so I hope he doesn't run off and get messy afterwards.'

'Hmm… So do I,' her father added. 'Lynn'll linch me if you guys are less than perfect when the cars arrive. Come into the church, kids. We'll find a bathroom where we can make ourselves completely pristine. Catch you later, everyone. Enjoy the service.'

'What are we doing now, Dad?' the eight-year-old asked, waving to the sea of faces. 'What service?'

'The wedding ceremony's often called a service, mate. And getting changed is what you're doing right now. Need to be ready for action. Look lively, Kizzy-Jo!'

'*Papá*! Why did that lady call me Kizzy-Jo?' the girl bleated, trotting along beside her brother.

Jeff shrugged. 'No idea, *pequeñita*. Old ladies are weird sometimes. Just smile and nod. Always the best move.'

'Who are all those people anyway?' his son asked. 'Michelle's family?'

'Yeah. And Alan's, I s'pose,' his dad responded with a chuckle. 'I don't know most of them. Did you have fun with Tim's kids?'

Jet nodded. 'I'm so hot. Do I have to put my suit on now?'

''Fraid so, *hijo mío*,' Jeff smiled. 'We need to hose you down and douse you in after-shave, or Mum'll suspect something fishy.'

'Yuck!' he scowled. 'I don't want to smell of after-shave. It's like perfume. The boys'll laugh at me.'

'It *is* perfume,' the rock star laughed at him, ruffling his sweaty fringe. 'It's only called after-shave to convince men to buy it. Too bad, mate. Sorry. You and I have to smell the same for a change. Is that so terrible? It'll have worn off by the time you see the lads next.'

A musty odour hung in the air inside the gothic landmark built in the nineteenth-century on a corner of Alfred Ross' "Orrong" property. The bells in its single spire pealed in an irregular rhythm, as if one of the ropes had been shortened in a campanologist's prank. The musician marched his two charges in a correspondingly wavy line towards a small, unassuming door near the pulpit, in accordance with Lynn's instructions.

Sure enough, a kindly church elder was behind the scenes to receive them. She showed the chipper *trio* into a large dressing-room, the choir's habitual home prior to Sunday masses and carol services. Kierney sat frozen like one of the ageing marble sculptures they had filed past on their way through the knave, while Jeff cracked the metaphorical whip over his son. Time was running out for the boy to wash and dress, leaving his protests at being too warm to wear a suit to fall on decidedly deaf ears.

Wielding the after-shave bottle with a maniacal cackle, the father sprayed with wild abandon as Jet's bare-chested body darted around the room, doing its best to avoid contact with the fine mist. 'Wise up, Captain Marvellous. The more you fight, the more I'll put on you!'

Common sense prevailed, and as the family's antics quietened down, they could hear female laughter from the other side of the door. Embarrassed, the eight-year-old stalled to fasten a crisp white shirt over his fragrant chest and neck. Jeff knotted his son's tie out of haste before bending down to do the same with his shoelaces, all the while putting off the final battle of the morning: the head of thick hair their girl-child had inherited from both sides of the family, its tangles impossible to comb without tears.

'D'you want to do it yourself?' he asked, seeing his daughter tense up as the familiar implement hovered overhead. 'I can't do it like *Mamá* can.'

'No,' the little girl whimpered. 'It's OK. You do it.'

Eventually, this time with Jet under orders not to move a muscle, the bridesmaid's knotted locks were unravelled and combed sleek and glossy down her back. The mirror returned a wide smile, agreeing that her father had made her look lovely, complete with a yellow ribbon to match the sash on her gown. Having her hair swept off her face revealed a striking resemblance to Auntie Madalena, the likeness strong enough to be recognised even by her big brother.

'Cool?' Jeff croaked, tears brimming in his eyes as he blew the pocket beauty a kiss. 'You are the prettiest girl ever, ever, ever, Kizzy-Jo. *Te amo, todos los dos.*'

Kierney nodded, swivelling around on the stool to give her dad a hug. '*Gracias, Papá,*' she giggled, wiping a droplet off his cheek and licking her finger. 'Oh, that's salty. *Te amo.*'

'*De nada, pequeñita,*' he sniffed, running the comb through his own mass of dark waves. '*Vamanos. Mamá*'ll be here any minute. Nearly showtime!'

After guzzling the contents of a bottle of water between them, the proud father snapped a few quick photographs of his dapper offspring. They let themselves out of their private hideaway and ran the gauntlet through an inspection committee of ladies, all several decades older than the average Jeff Diamond groupie. He reminded the youngsters to walk with poise, as if they were on stage, guiding them to the grand organ with its three keyboards and a pedalboard at floor level.

Jeff explained how the organist controlled the timbre, pitch and volume of sound which was pumped all the way through the walls of pipes on either side of the choir stalls just by pulling out or pushing in a combination of stops. The children gaped in wonder on hearing how small boys were drafted, in the days before electricity, to pump bellows of compressed air to power the mighty instrument.

Noticing the number of guests beginning to swell at the back of the church, the celebrity allowed Jet a few seconds to climb the pulpit steps, unable to stifle a laugh when only the very top of the curly, blond head showed above the lecturn.

'You're not ready to become a priest yet, I'm pleased to tell you,' he said, striding closer to stop the lad jumping up and down in an effort to reach the microphone. 'Come down before you break something, please, mate.'

All three Diamonds stood at the top of the aisle, a hymnbook's throw from the altar. Jeff's imagination again journeyed back to his own marriage ceremony, flooding his head with blissful memories. How nervous and excited had he been to sense Lynn arriving at his side! An occasion he never would have predicted in a million years, two lovers with matching tattoos standing ready and willing to cement the rest of their life singular into this traditional and rather peculiar institution.

Today would be an emotional day for the England family too, the empathetic man concluded, bringing himself back to reality. Lynn had told him how Ron struggled through a short speech at Michelle and Alan's engagement party, one of the many social events he had missed due to his hefty travel schedule. His conscience delivered him a guilt-trip on behalf of Bart Dyson, forced to acknowledge how difficult it must be for a father to give away his daughter.

A surge of power billowed through the ancient stone building as the altar and outer aisles were illuminated. Seeking to prolong the wondrous expressions on his children's faces, the rock star described who sat where in a wedding: the bride's family and friends on one side and the groom's on the left. He told the wide-eyed pair which parts their Uncle Gerry and Aunties Madalena, Anna and Michelle had played on the first of January nineteen-seventy-six, enacting a comical sketch of a vicar marrying a couple.

'So if people promise to stay together until they die, how come they get divorced?' Jet asked, confounded by such a breach of straightforward logic.

'All kinds of reasons, Jetto,' his dad replied. 'Things just change for some people, and they realise they don't love each other anymore. Sometimes it's someone's fault, like if they sneak off and have sex with another person, or if they hit their partner or behave like they don't care. That stuff really hurts 'cause it's like you can't trust the person who's supposed to love you, so it makes people fall out of love.

'And sometimes people simply grow apart from each other. Y'know, like at school when one boy or girl's your best friend for a while, and then you find you don't have so much in common with them anymore... You start hanging out with other kids instead, and your mate doesn't understand why. It all depends. Adults make life way too complicated, I reckon.'

Both kids nodded, hanging on his every word. Jeff sneaked a casual look at his watch and presumed the bridal cars would turn into the driveway at any minute. His invisible elastic connection had struck a distinct, demanding resonance, spoiling to see his *regala* return the favour which Michelle had afforded them on their return from London.

'Do you think that'll ever happen with you and *Mamá*?' Kierney asked in a sad tone.

'Get divorced? Definitely not, angel,' Jeff responded without hesitation. '*Mamá* and I are together, forever, wherever, remember?'

Smiling at the familiar slogan, the dreamy bridesmaid repeated the three magic words, raising and lowering her hands in time with the cadence. 'Together, forever, wherever, and nothing's ever gonna change it.'

'Nope. *Nada, nunca, pequeñita.* And let's hope Auntie Michelle and Uncle Alan won't split up either.'

'Please may I go over there?' Jet asked, spotting his playmates milling around at the back of the church.

'Sure, if you like. But don't go outside again, please. Promise you'll stay exactly like you look now: handsome, clean and smiling. OK?'

The clown prince grinned, standing to attention and saluting his superior officer, who reached over in an attempt to flick the top of his head. The boy's reflexes were far too quick these days however, the Dyson inheritance honing his agility. His father was outsmarted, left with only words of warning.

'Walk, Jet, please, and watch for the limo',' he shouted after the curly-haired streak of lightning, offering his hand to Kierney. 'Hey, Kizzo. Come and sit at the back here. We need to be close-by when *la mamá* and Mish arrive, so you can take your place in the procession.'

The youngest Diamond was not usually interested in the glamorous side of their celebrity, preferring quiet days at home. Musical instruments, books and exhaustive debate were her pastimes of choice, yet this maiden ceremonial role had kindled her feminine imagination far more than her parents had expected.

'*Papá*, why do some people have weddings and some people don't?'

'Heaps of different reasons, same as for getting divorced,' Jeff replied, sitting down on the end of the rearmost pew and drawing his daughter's attention to the altar, where the vicar and his assistant were making their preparations. 'Some people, like *Mamá* and I, want to show the world they're so happy about spending the rest of their life with their favourite person. Whether you're religious or not, marriage is a special way to tell everyone how much you love each other. But then others don't want to do this and are quite happy to keep love as a secret between them. They don't have to tell anyone they're in love except themselves.'

The tiny sage nodded. 'Does Uncle Alan think Auntie Michelle's the most beautiful woman in the world?'

'Ah, yeah. I hope so,' her father smiled.

'But she can't be, 'cause *Mamá* is,' the authoritative bridesmaid refuted, cocking her head.

The intellectual chuckled, having been well and truly boxed in by a seven-year-old. 'Yep. She is, but that's just what *I* think.'

'And it's what *I* think too.'

'*Bueno, pequeñita,*' the showman responded. 'We think *Mamá*'s the most beautiful woman in the world because we know how gorgeous she is, inside and out. But really, there's no easy way to measure beauty. Who says one colour of hair or eyes is more beautiful than another, for example? Or tall people are more beautiful than short people?'

The dark-haired gipsy girl shrugged, discomfited by these choices. It was her dad's turn to make a point, and a natural competitiveness born of the Dyson genes left her straining against her opponent.

Jeff steered her out of her dilemma. 'Kizzy, you're the most beautiful girl in the world to *Mamá* and me. And someday, when you're all grown up, some lucky man'll say you're the most beautiful woman in the world, just like Uncle Alan when he asked Auntie Michelle to marry him.'

'Will he want to marry me?' the primary school student's excitement was conspicuous.

'In a freakin' heartbeat, gorgeous!' her father exclaimed. 'They'll be fighting each other on the streets to marry you. And you need to want to marry him too, 'cause you don't have to if you don't want to.'

Kierney's eyes glazed over while suppositions in her far-off future bombarded her wide-open mind. The wise man beside her had no trouble relating to these unspoken thoughts, his own childhood impressions of marriage frequently defiled as a result of the atrocities to which he had borne witness. Indeed, with the divorce rate climbing each passing year, he had confided in Lynn not so many months ago that the age-old institution might well be worthless and inconsequential by the time their children reached majority.

'You could stay single or live with the man you love without getting married,' he continued. 'It's totally up to you, *pequeñita*. Two people can be head over heels in love and never ever get married. As long as they're happy, it doesn't matter. Have you heard the expression "Beauty's in the eye of the beholder"?'

'Yes.'

'Well, it means that when someone says, "She's the most beautiful woman in the world," something magic's happening between them. It's like when your eyes lock, and all your insides jump up and down in an unexpected but really cool surprise.'

With her dancing, dark brown eyes fixed on his, the true romantic poked his daughter in the ribs, making her giggle. 'That's when you know if you love someone. You feel all safe and happy, like you've come home to a warm house with your favourite person ever in the whole wide world.'

Again the youngster's face gave away some concern. 'But I love *you*, *Papá. You're* my favourite person. And *Mamá* and Jet too.'

'*Gracias, angelita,*' Jeff smiled, claiming her tiny hand and planting a chivalrous kiss on its pale, smooth knuckles. 'And I love you too, *tanto tanto*. But you won't always love me the most.'

'No! I will, I will!' she whined, jumping to her feet on the wooden pew and almost ending up on the stone floor, the slick soles of her brand new bridesmaid's shoes slipping on the polished surface. 'I really will.'

The showman lunged to catch his falling angel, laughing at the startled expression on her face. 'Shhh! Careful, *pequeñita*. We don't want you limping up the aisle. I hope you do always love me most, in a way... But I bet you fifty thousand kisses that's not how it'll end up. You'll meet a boy, or maybe more than one, and someday you'll turn round and say, "*Papá* who? Never heard of him."'

Disgruntled at the absurd idea, Kierney was torn between smiling and frowning. 'No, I won't.'

'I reckon you will,' Jeff hugged the precious child, tears pricking behind his eyes at the thought of having to give her away. 'That's what's supposed to happen, baby. And then maybe I'll be the proud dad taking you to a wedding as the bride instead of the bridesmaid.'

This did the trick. The little girl's expression lit up with the idea of wearing a long, white gown similar to the one Auntie Michelle had tried on when she and her *mamá* had visited the tailor for their dress fittings. Envisaging many changes of heart ahead, her father cemented her approval with a silent hug.

'Grandpa!' Jet's voice rang out from behind the last row of pews.

Jeff turned around to see Bart Dyson's apparition in the dusty sunlight streaming in through the church's main entrance, accompanied by his elegant wife. He stood up and waved for them to come over, and Marianna's face beamed at the sight of her granddaughter all dressed up and looking so pretty. Jet left his friends and ran over to meet the new arrivals too.

'Hello, Jeff,' the lady said, angling her face upwards to receive a kiss on the cheek. 'How are you? Don't you look gorgeous, Kierney, darling?'

The musician had to steady the little bridesmaid as she gave another twirl, dizzy from all the attention. He glanced at his watch again, assuming the limousines ferrying the bridal party must be about to turn the corner. Also having spied the Dysons' arrival, one of Michelle's elder brothers approached all three generations of the Melbourne dynasty and requested they take their seats.

'You guys go on,' Jeff encouraged his in-laws, 'I just want to stay in the background, thanks. Jet and I'll stay back here so we can enjoy the view without causing a stir. OK, kids! Come with me, please. We'd better wait outside. Time for you to join the circus, Kizzy-Jo.'

The precocious flower-girl grimaced at her father's use of the silly nickname while camera shutters clicked from all sides. '*Papá*, that's not my name,' she objected.

'Isn't it?' her dad feigned surprise. 'Sorry. I'll try and remember who you are in future. Coming, Mary-Ellen? Patty-Sue? Yoko Ono?'

Jet's face was a picture, staring at his father as if he had gone stark raving bonkers. Marianna gave a polite titter too, without the slightest idea what the comedian was up to either; simply carrying out her grandmotherly duty to find things funny. The Diamond *trio* walked outside into the bright sunshine at the exact moment when an enormous, rheumatic white Rolls Royce Silver Shadow turned into the gravel driveway, decked out with white ribbons and garlands of roses spread over the rear parcel shelf.

'Hey! Mum's here!' Jet whooped, peering into each window in turn. 'Where is she? Where? Mum!'

The boy began to race towards the car, remembering only at the last minute that he had promised to be on his best behaviour. Slowing down to a brisk walk, the two excited children waited for everyone to alight and arrange themselves into formation, as they remembered from the rehearsal. A *chauffeur* in a grey suit and a peaked cap opened the door behind the driver's seat, and out stepped Ron England, the father of the bride. Jeff caught the youngsters up and stood between them, gripping a quivering shoulder with each hand.

A second white car followed, from which Lynn Dyson Diamond and Michelle's fifteen-year-old niece were helped out into the sunlight. The handsome onlooker felt a whole different kind of pride, his loins responding to the sight of his beautiful best friend dressed in a stunning, pale lemon, full-length, satin dress, off-the-shoulder and figure-hugging.

His wife had left the apartment this morning in sports clothes, with her hair thrown up in a ponytail after a hurried romp, and now stood in her finery, exuding the type of casual self-assurance which accentuated her radiance still further. Regardless of the *persona* her chameleon career forced upon her, this woman couldn't look anything but sizzling hot!

The young mother gave her family a quick wave before darting over to help straighten out the voluminous train so it was ready to follow the blushing bride. Jeff had to force his eyes to focus on the lady in the white dress, but when he did, he found her happier than he had ever seen before. What was it about weddings which made women so happy? Despite the growing *furore* over women's liberation, it appeared there remained an innate desire to give themselves to their chosen man. The exact same joy had graced his new wife's face too, a whole decade ago. And to this day, it had seldom faded.

Nudging Jet and Kierney forwards, the thoughtful comedian approached the bridal party. Michelle grinned like a lunatic on speed at his lascivious gestures, glancing at her reflection in the car window. Evidently pleased with what she saw, she blew a kiss to her best friend's glorious husband.

'Ms England, you look absolutely fantastic,' he responded, greeting the bride's father with a fortifying handshake. 'Doesn't she, Ron? Proud moment for you.'

The retired banking executive nodded and smiled, his eyes permanently close to tears. It wasn't hard to fathom that marrying off one's only daughter would inflict a certain loneliness on the man who was still grieving the loss of his wife.

Satisfied Michelle's accessories weren't about to cause any mishaps, the chief bridesmaid walked over to where her patient little ones stood. 'You two are perfect. Very smart. Ready to smile for the cameras? Thanks, Jeff. Not a hair out of place, either of you.'

'I stink of after-shave,' Jet moaned. 'Dad put it everywhere!'

Lynn leaned down until her nose hovered next to her son's neck, stealing a sneaky kiss. With the official photographer buzzing around, the boy's vocal dissent made everyone laugh, which only further embarrassed him.

As he turned to take his place in the church, still playing up to the crowd, the dashing showman made a grab for his lover's waist, angling for a parting peck. 'Not *gonna* check my after-shave too, gorgeous?' he teased, being pushed away by Olympian arms lest he smudge her make-up.

'Later,' she whispered. 'You're fantastic too. Thanks for getting them ready. They look lovely.'

Much to the bridal party's amusement, Jeff suddenly dropped down onto one knee on the warm shingle and asked the stunning matron of honour to marry him. No-one was more astonished than the woman herself, a rush of adoration evident on her face.

'Get up, you idiot!' she laughed. 'I'm already taken.'

'So what? He's an arsehole,' the pleading Romeo persisted. 'Run away with me. I'll show you a good time.'

This was the grand gesture he had decided to omit on that magical afternoon in Edinburgh, now filling them both with nostalgic elation. Not wishing to steal the spotlight from today's happy couple, they dismissed the significance of this stolen opportunity until they noticed how bewitched their audience was with the overture. Trust Jeff Diamond to turn a selfish act into the show's winning opening number!

'But *he* shows me a good time,' Lynn shook her head.

Standing up and brushing sand off his trouser leg, the tall man refused to back down. 'Ah, yeah?' he scoffed, clutching his heart in both hands. 'You can bring your kids.'

The blonde singing star sighed. 'OK. Perhaps I shall. Ask me again after nine o'clock, but make sure my husband doesn't see you. He gets very jealous.'

With an arrogant smirk, Jeff closed his eyes and raised them to the cloudless sky. '*Merci, mon amie*,' he whispered, fanning his fingers as if they had been burned by the searing heat of Lynn's touch. 'On *ya* go, or you'll be late. Alan'll have fallen asleep. Enjoy the ceremony, Kizzy. And mate, come with me... Let's go inside and let these guys do their thing. You all look amazing.'

In the preceding few seconds, taking its cue from the ushers, the magnificent organ had begun to play the Bridal March. The vicar's assistant was beckoning for the procession to start. Ron gripped his daughter's left hand, and everyone else fell into line.

Kierney stood alone behind the bride and her father, holding a cute basket of freesia and iris. She was followed at a respectable distance by the two adult bridesmaids. Her deportment picture-perfect, she held her head high as they passed Jeff and her brother. Lynn smiled, seeing pure pride in her man's eyes.

He shrugged and bit his lip. 'Don't they scrub up well, Jetto?'

Taking hold of his son's hand, the songwriter whistled at Michelle and then at his precious girls again. His sight was blinded for a moment, having beaten a hasty retreat out of the bright sunshine, and by the time he and Jet found a spare pew, the others had reached the entrance steps. The groom and best man, who had been loitering in the knave, talking to old friends, jumped to attention when the famous pair hurried inside.

The rock star extended his hand to Alan. 'Good luck, mate. They're here, and she looks amazing. You're a very lucky bloke. Get going!'

Doctor Hadley and his university buddy sprinted around the groom's pews to take their place at the front. The vicar had slipped his robe on, out of sight of the congregation, and now stood holding a large, fabric-bound prayer book adorned with gold tassels. Hoping he could make himself invisible for the next half-hour, the superstar slotted himself and his son into a vacant section of the second-last row.

A sedate and dutiful Kierney walked up the red carpet, eyes forward and concentrating on keeping her stride steady in her slippery shoes. The emotional father urged Jet to pay attention while he fast-forwarded to the momentous milestone when he might give his gorgeous gipsy girl away to her very own life partner.

What sort of day might this be for him? And for her? He hoped the innocent giggles and lively, inquisitive eyes to which he had been treated today would be replaced by a smile of rational inclination similar to the one that had greeted him in the ballroom at Dyson Administration. It was his and Lynn's duty as parents to cultivate the necessary worldliness and pave this path, whether their daughter chose to follow it or not.

Ron England seemed chuffed to the extreme, caught up in the drama of the occasion at last. Putting himself in the elderly man's place, Jeff wondered if he would feel the same pride? Yes, without question. But also somewhat orphaned too, he suspected. Was it possible for a child to orphan a parent? He didn't see why not. The way he felt about the mini version of himself right now, there was not a man walking this Earth who could love her as much as he did. Impossible.

To the celebrity's annoyance, a brand new song began to compete with the organ processional, assaulting his ears with the resultant jarring disharmony. His old soul saw fit to warn him of the inevitable difficulty of accepting another significant male in Kierney's life. *A good thing too*, he congratulated himself, committing the musical gift to memory so his mind would be free to relax and refocus on the present time, safe in the knowledge that wisdom accumulated now would serve him well in years to come.

Jeff smiled to himself, shoving his misplaced melancholy to one side. A microphone suspended over the altar clicked and fed back into the speakers as the vicar addressed his flock. Hearing hushed voices murmuring his name on all sides, the famous father put an arm around the squirming boy's shoulder and hugged him in against his hip.

These were good times, the musician acknowledged. His dark heart was too quick to withdraw from happiness, still unable to dodge the fear of everything crashing down. He longed to catch Lynn's eye and imbibe her boundless positive energy, but only the tall, slender lines of the body he worshipped and the back of her shining blonde head were visible.

A jolt of shame caused the world-changer to shiver, listening to Ron England saying the two immortal words which sealed the transaction between father and groom. Time was indeed a powerful teacher. He ought to have cut Big D more slack in those days. He now knew that surrendering a daughter was no easy thing, particularly for a control freak! An apology was in order for whenever he and the great man next found themselves together.

The vicar signalled for quiet and asked the congregation to be seated. Whisked off on another whirlwind tour of his past, the dreamer let the monotony of the traditional service wash over him. The overpowering smell of incense reminded him of the many stale, tedious sermons he had endured as a teenager, along with Gerry and his sisters and under the ever-watchful eye of Celia Blake.

Kierney stood in front of her mother, whose idle hands toyed with the long locks of dark hair which fell down her back. Jeff hoped someone would snap a picture of his two favourite females, the best substitute being to commit the fabulous footage into his own memory banks. During the couple's vows, Lynn cast a furtive glance behind her at the rest of her tribe. Their son jumped at the sudden attention, which gladdened the thirty-three-year-old's heart. He was pleased to know that even riotous future cricketers were inexplicably drawn to their family.

'Slip through there if you want a closer look,' the songwriter suggested, his finger mapping out a route through the sea of bodies. 'Say, "Excuse me, please." If you stand to one side, up there on the left, you'll see everything but you won't be in the way.'

The boy nodded, executing his dad's master plan. Australia's favourite music star smiled in gratitude as others in their row let the lad through, receiving a few swooning sighs from women who experienced a disturbance of a whole different nature. Now free to slide into his daydream again, he sat back and waited for Lynn to take centre stage while the newlyweds signed the register.

Michelle had chosen the hymn "My Song Is Love Unknown" for her lifelong friend to sing, more for her father than for herself. It had been one of her mother's favourites. Apart from the obligatory Christmas carols, the darling of Melbourne's establishment rarely made anthemic music, unlike her husband, who used the rallying power of a gospel chorus to splendid effect in his live shows.

Struck once more by the command his wife's stirring rendition exerted over those assembled, her effortless *contralto* voice soaring to the buttresses and resounding above the organ's rich tones, the atheist rocker imagined Ron England fighting with his self-control. When the accompaniment finished, loud applause broke out and the long-haired billionnaire tearaway found it hard to resist the temptation to wolf-whistle.

Momentum Building

As the month drew to a close, the world's happiest couple flew to London again to host another sequence of focal events in the "Feed Africa" campaign. Having left the children at home in Melbourne, Lynn and Jeff ran a half-marathon, spearheading the field and receiving tumultuous applause from onlookers lining the streets. Television cameras followed them for all twenty-one kilometres, capturing them signing autographs and posing for photographs in exchange for donations of coins or notes.

That same evening, the Diamonds boarded an aeroplane bound for New York, where they attended the *gala* dinner for a United Nations special session on the African famine, elated at having pulled off yet another enormous feat of logistics and generosity. The music industry didn't fail in its support for the *duo*'s tireless endeavours either, with many of the most popular artists and bands contributing performances to a video that would be released at the end of the year.

Once this latest batch of hysteria had subsided and the megastars had repatriated to *Escondido* to connect with their children, a chart-topping British band took the commercial theme for "The Black Sheep" to Number One in twelve countries, in advance of the musical's *première*. Yet more millions of dollars were banked for the causes to which Lynn and Jeff had devoted their physical and emotional energy for nearly two years.

Predictably, after all the hype and adulation, the globe-trotting songwriter plunged into the depths of another anti-climactic depression. His guardian angel was not worried for his recovery this time however. She and the children had seen their beloved figurehead rise above the chronic affliction after his hostage experience, and together they hatched a fitting plan to reset his equilibrium at record-breaking speed.

Long, lazy mornings sequestered within the walls of their Mount Eliza fortress were at the top of the list, and wrapping up warm for beach walks with the dogs as a close second during the winter school holidays. And once Term Three commenced, weekends were kick-started with cooked breakfasts on the deck, setting the family up well for all sorts of crazy sports or board-games in the face of inclement weather.

Spontaneous musical acts and plays enlivened the early evenings, often entertaining enough for the complement of childminders to abandon their usual Saturday night jaunts into the city. Throughout the afternoons and sometimes long into the night, Jeff hid himself in the office, writing and recording, writing and recording. Not only did he find setting his thoughts to music therapeutic, but there seemed to be no end to new ideas for novels, films and songs flooding into his mind, the pace of invention increasingly outstripping his capacity to bring them forth and cash them in.

And as if the Diamonds' profile were ever in need of boosting, Jet and Kierney's return to school allowed the couple to accept an invitation to attend talks with the General Secretary of the Soviet Union's Communist Party. The USSR was uncharted territory for both peacemakers, and they were quick to dismiss Gerry's ardent reservations about harming their relationships with loyal capitalist governments.

Mindful of the risks, the musicians and their advisers seized the opportunity to show the world that their work transcended all political and social boundaries. Here was a chance to prove to everyday people that humans were motivated by the same basic values, no matter where they came from and how they lived their lives.

Mikhail Gorbachev had begun several significant reforms in his all-powerful role, including a massive reconstruction program dubbed "Perestroika". The Diamond Celebration Foundation's work in supporting African agriculture initiatives had caught his eye, along with the exalted status Jeff had attained in the global arena.

Conscious of the gratuitous photo-opportunities the ambitious politician was engineering, the travellers received a personal tour of Red Square and the Kremlin when they arrived in Moscow, and later travelled to Leningrad, spending four full days soaking up Russian culture and arts.

The trip was a resounding success. Despite unavoidable criticism from certain quarters, Jeff and Lynn were applauded for their openness and acceptance of Gorbachev's gesture of co-operation. Before heading on to London for rehearsals of their long-awaited West End show, they stopped off in Warsaw. It was time for the Polish Jew to test whether the last ten years had mellowed his original reaction to the birthplace of his paternal grandparents.

They hadn't. Even touring with an interpreter and chatting to local dignitaries and fellow musicians failed to impress the stormy intellectual; the city and its people avowed no familiarity for the thirty-four-year-old.

Throughout the days and nights stuffed full of stressful meetings and boring dinners, the lovers never exchanged a cross word. Their work brought them closer together every day, until they realised each was quite confident in predicting the other's preference in most circumstances. This useful addition to their lengthening *répertoire* of skills enabled them to divide and conquer, and thereby accomplish even more.

Lynn penned a song entitled "Mighty Shadow" during the flight home to Melbourne, to acknowledge the humility she saw in her husband. Jeff never took anything or anyone for granted, and each time his mood crashed close to the danger zone, he somehow found the will to pick himself up and keep the show on the road. She dared to think it might be getting easier to shake off the blues, having become so practised at riding the deceptive rollercoaster. Seeming to demand less of everyone lately, it was as if he were reaching a level of peace with the world which had been hitherto unattainable.

After listening to his saviour's new composition in their lounge room, understated in its combination of luxury and comfort, with its sumptuous white leather sofas, the deep-pile, welcoming rug and the imposing grand piano taking pride of place. Heavy curtains, tailor-made in a shade somewhere between champagne and cream to soften the clinical whiteness of the room's furniture, were drawn against the wintry gales which blew in off Port Phillip Bay, at times threatening to take the roof off with their force.

'This is not my fault, y'know,' Jeff gritted his teeth as he smothered the singer into a thankful embrace. 'It's largely your fault, where we are now.'

Lynn shook her head. 'Thanks. Partially maybe, but you still have to get up every day. I'm not the one who's making the ultimate decision. That's a hundred percent your own work.'

The hot-blooded man began to kiss the side of his wife's neck, working round to her mouth. Hearing her sigh, he backed away until her smiling face was at arm's length. Her radiance dimmed somewhat, encountering the same voracious sex drive which had been extinguished only an hour ago, the crumpled rug, pushed half under the couch during their undulations, bearing testament to the recent activity.

Compassion replaced desire in her husband's covetous grip. 'It's fine, angel. We don't have to. Being hungry for you is a perpetual state for me. It'd be no different if we did it again, so just ignore me. I'll try and ignore me, so you can too!'

The couple had commissioned a set of twenty photographic prints from a cameraman who had travelled with them on various aid missions. The A2-sized pictures depicted boys and girls from the Omo River in Ethiopia, tribespeople who adorned themselves with plants and fruit and daubed their skin with natural make-up in a most artistic way. The first four in the collection had been hung on two sides of the lounge room wall, bringing vivid colours and warmth to the *décor*. Some of the faces frightened Kierney a little, but her father couldn't take his eyes off them.

During filming for another series of the Diamond family's long-running documentary, the presenter opened the interview by asking the good-looking pair what life was like now they had been married for ten years. The crew had set up a number of cameras in the house, and they had caught the weary traveller arriving home in the morning after an arduous transpacific flight.

He sat at the kitchen table with the kids while they were getting ready for school. Lynn massaged his shoulders as they made smalltalk about his latest *sojourn* in the northern hemisphere before starting to press into the small of his back, homing in on an unyielding muscle next to his kidneys.

'Jeez, that's really good,' Jeff squirmed to maximise the effect. 'How did you know I needed that?'

'Because you always need it!' she laughed.

'Ah, yeah. S'pose so. Can we buy a rack?'

'A rack?' Jet screeched, having developed a recent obsession for weapons of torture.

His mother lifted her index finger to her mouth to quieten the boy down. 'Yeah, Dad,' she repeated. 'Where would we put a rack?'

'I don't care. Just hang me from the top.'

'By what?'

Seeing his son's filthy mind react, Jeff pulled a pained face at both children before turning to the lens. 'My wrists! Christ, woman! It's a good thing I let *Mamá* have her marish head with this torrent of marauding language.'

Sally-Anne Crosby, the TV presenter assigned to follow the Diamonds in this latest string of episodes, stood dumbfounded at this statement, unsure of having grasped its true meaning. 'What goes through your mind, for example, Jeff, when you see Lynn's naked body on the big screen in a movie, alongside a hot male actor?'

'Blind fury?' the musician snapped, beating a melodramatic fist on the arm of the chair. 'No. Only kidding, folks... I enjoy it for what it is, as long as it's only my eyes that have to share. To be honest, I tend to be more jealous of guys she has lunch or dinner with. They get to see her smile directly at them, feed off her sharp wit... We're comfortable with what's real and what's fake, on both sides of the bed.'

'Aren't you ever tempted, like other celebrities are,' the journalist asked the confident star, 'by the new, young things clamouring for the limelight?'

The handsome man shrugged, a glint in his eye, relaxed and reigning supreme in front of the cameras. 'Of course I am! I might be married but I haven't been castrated. Yet anyway! But look at my wife and my kids... Look at my house... Look at what I do for a living! How much better could this get?'

The cameraman panned around the sumptuous scene, taking in the bold artwork and the enormous picture windows which drenched the room in sunlight. Coming to rest on the presenter and her subjects, he filmed her capitulating smile before panning full-circle.

'Nope,' Jeff confirmed with an arrogant smirk. 'The grass on my side just keeps getting greener. This perfect piece of womanhood helps me make the most of life every single day. Sure, I'm not blind to other women, but they're for my viewing pleasure only. Sometimes I see someone attractive within easy reach and think, "Whoa, she's damned hot," or "That'd be a bit of fun for a while." Then pretty soon after, my conscience'll remind me how much I'd be giving up, how much I'd be risking. It doesn't exactly take a master's degree to realise I'd be a bloody idiot to take things any further. Lynn's no different, are you?'

The elegant blonde shook her head, placing her hand on her husband's twitching thigh. 'No. Well, not quite so lecherous, I hope! But yeah, there's temptation wherever we go. People want to be seen with us, and some make it extremely difficult to say no. It's the nature of our profession... sport or music... and it's no wonder that so many showbiz folk fall victim to infidelity. We're determined not to be casualties though, because we mean too much to each other.'

'Bloody oath, angel! To talk stereotypes for a second, it's just that men tend to take the fantasy further than women do,' Jeff explained in all seriousness, sitting the palm of his hand on top of his wife's and squeezing it. 'Women keep it at fantasy, whereas men push their luck. Too far, a lot of the time. But for me, taking things any further's certainly not on my playlist. Why would I? Would you?'

The affable Sydney native's last question was directed at the cameraman, who twitched the lens from side to side. Again, the pair's antics resulted in perfect television. True star quality was no match for petty mud-slinging.

'I rest my case,' the songwriter declared, raising his arms in triumph.

'Bringing our kids up is a rewarding process too,' his wife pushed the interview on from this dead-end smear campaign. 'That's another thing that keeps us grounded.'

'Absolutely,' Jeff agreed. 'Y'know, Lynn taught me ages ago about the three steps to success: setting challenging goals, reaching them and then enjoying the fact you've reached them. One without the other at any point in our life or our kids' lives won't work. And not forgetting that you have to fail sometimes too. We apply these principles to being parents, and it's working a treat so far. We're fairly instinctive with it all. We react on a balanced combination of our brains, our hearts and our senses. Our kids are the same, most likely not by accident.'

Sally-Anne let the proud father continue, receiving a thumbs-up from the producer.

'Throughout both our childhoods and teenaged years, Lynn and I were lucky enough to undergo significant self-awareness training; hers through sport and the Dyson movement, and mine as part of a sustained period of psychiatric treatment. So, quite independently, we turned out pretty robust, and we can easily recognise and compensate for strengths and weaknesses in ourselves and each other. It's an invaluable skill worth passing on to the next generation, without their having to live through all the negative factors that go with that sort of learning.'

The interviewer swapped topics, keen to cover the making of "The Black Sheep" and the couple's collaborative relationship with Kiley Jones. The show revealed the extreme level of commitment the couple gave to children from all walks of life, not simply to their own. In an earlier segment, the outside broadcast crew had followed the stars to Melbourne University and into a workshop run for The Good School, from which the violinist and composer had been one of the first graduates.

'Here we mentor the students to capitalise on their existing capability,' Lynn told the camera. 'These are already high-achieving young people, but they don't know what they don't know. That's what we're here for. We've got so many useful experiences we can share, and a whole heap of hard lessons too. So much knowledge to pass on to these guys, hopefully to make them better decision-makers in their chosen careers. We have one life, so let's use it well. We encourage all the young people who come through the program to think widely and challenge convention, but with patience and humility.'

'These students won't have the kind of childhood I had, where I needed to fight the education system's bias over and over again,' Jeff insisted. 'This year we're running the "Cool To Be Smart" campaign. Students from this program and in other cities go out into their schools or to any clubs they belong to... footy, cricket, choirs, *et cetera*... and spruik the power of becoming a philomath, i.e. someone who loves gathering knowledge.'

Jet and Kierney featured heavily in the remainder of the scene, describing how their parents helped other primary school children too. Through Childlight, pupils from wealthier schools visited their counterparts in less affluent suburbs where the future may not have seemed so bright.

'Mum and her friends are mentoring girls, to stop them measuring themselves by how they look,' the confident nine-year-old sports nut let on. 'And to stop boys thinking girls aren't as clever as them.'

His sister nodded in agreement, standing on tiptoes to reach the interviewer's microphone. '*Mamá* speaks to all the girls, to discourage them from thinking the only way to act like a grown-up is to have a baby, and it's good to think about what you want to do with your life. Having a good job and making the most of your talents, such as going to uni' or something.'

Proud of their two trainee ambassadors, Lynn took up the commentary with a loving hand rubbing each child's back. These next generation Dyson-Diamonds were fast fulfilling their destinies, and with any luck, this innocent enthusiasm for life would soon rub off on their peers around the country. Even around the world.

'That's exactly right. Thanks, darlings. We encourage students to take responsibility for their future and to pay attention to the impact they have on their surroundings: being kind to other people, the natural environment, taking care of their possessions, and so on. Sometimes it can be hard to avoid gender stereotypes because there's no escaping them in the media, or in books and movies.

'Boys and girls *are* different, of course. Some are more different than others...' the young mother laughed, seeing her son pulling grotesque faces in the mirror. 'We all need to stop trying to make everyone equal. Equal opportunity doesn't mean everyone needs to be treated the same. It means we need to appreciate, value and make the most of each person's differences to an equal extent.'

Jeff strolled into shot, draping a lazy arm around his wife's shoulder. 'Absolutely. That's such an important message. Kids aren't always good at everything, but we're teaching them that most are good at something. Whether it's maths or music, science or sport, everyone's got their talents and skills. You just have to be smart enough to recognise what you're good at; the thing that makes you cool.'

'Isn't this man amazing?' the blonde athlete changed the subject again. 'Family's what grounds us, more than anything. We're both intent on raising happy kids, and this requires us to stay in love. Which is no hardship, I might add!'

Her husband grinned. 'Yep. I echo that sentiment! Jet and Kizzy were deliberately conceived and utterly wanted. Two boxes ticked by default in life's checklist. That kind of start sets you up for life, I figure.'

'I remember coming home from some record industry cocktail party not long ago,' Lynn continued, 'having been forced to listen to another married couple bickering. I could hear every word they were saying, even though I was engaged in another conversation. Quite apart from our lifestyle and everything we've become, I don't envy any of our friends' relationships.'

The presenter's eyes switched to the swarthy, devillish rock star, moving the microphone in his direction.

'Me neither,' he affirmed, reaching for his partner's hand. 'Not even close, so don't go away, will you?'

The young woman pounced to catch the dark heart's slide and save his embarrassment. 'Oh, I'm not going anywhere.'

'*Gracias, Regala,*' he shrugged. 'Just checkin'. Y'see, Sally-Anne, we've got heaps of first-hand data supporting the way we're bringing up these little guys. I know what didn't work about my parent's way of relating to kids, if I can even give them that much credit... And that's also why we've poured so much energy into "The Black Sheep". Here... Let me read you something insightful from the nineteenth century, if I may.'

On cue, both Diamond children rolled their eyes. As another priceless moment in time was captured for posterity, the songwriter left his chair and ran to fetch his dog-eared copy of Balzac's novel from the office. In response to a question about the plot, Lynn filled in time by describing the ageless fable.

'It's about two brothers who represent good and evil,' she smiled. 'Philippe, the older one who serves in Napoléon's army, and Joseph, who's a painter. The moral of the story is not to confuse good and evil with strong and weak. They're totally different scales which can bisect each other at any point.'

'*Absoluement,* angel,' Jeff agreed, willfully taking up the commentary. 'Joseph, the younger brother, didn't understand who he was until he was thirteen. We don't want this to happen to these guys. This sentence here explains it a bit: "His instinct was making itself felt, a sense of his vocation was stirring within him."'

The world-changer's audience sat in silence, both behind and in front of the camera, knowing there was far more to come.

'Angel, d'you remember the feeling of walking up to a piano or into a studio and being totally at home?'

Lynn shook her head. 'No. It wasn't like that for me. Mine was all practice, practice, practice.'

Unbeknown to the others, her husband had prised this fact from his stunning sidekick some years ago. She was not, as he suspected, a great artist at heart; at least, not in the tradition of noble European literature.

'"A great artist is a king,"' he read on, motioning a quick aside to modernise the text. 'Or queen, I should add on his behalf! It's a bugger for these dead authors, not being able to moderate their idioms to suit current times. Anyway... "In fact even greater than a king: to begin with, he is happier, he is independent, he lives as he feels inclined; better still, he reigns over the world of the imagination." Somehow we need to bridge the gap between great artists and people like Lynn... and probably Jetto here, if early signs are anything to go by... who understand the power of art and the power of making things happen even if they're not born artists. And *vice versa* of course.'

The second episode of the series caught a private moment of grief which gained a whole new *cadre* of fans. Merak's health had deteriorated while his original owner, one of the family's drivers, was away in Vanuatu with a girlfriend. The film crew captured the veterinary surgeon's late-night visit, and then the adults' bowed heads as they debated whether to ring George and spoil his holiday with the sad news. They had cut the shoot before making the decision to leave the ailing dog's sedated until the morning, with the hope he might rally in the peace and quiet.

'Your heart's so heavy,' Lynn sighed, brushing her lover's cheek as she pulled the quilt over her shoulder. 'The bed's tilting.'

The couple had inflated a camping mattress downstairs, positioned opposite the hallway alcove where the German Shepherd had plonked himself down some hours ago. Neither could bear the thought of missing him struggle for breath or try to make for the garden if he needed to.

'Cheers,' came the sullen reply.

'We're doing the right thing. You're a great man.'

The thirty-four-year-old turned over and cupped his wife's sad face in his hands. 'And you too? What are you?'

'I exist for you, in our perfectly perfect life singular.'

A passionate kiss swallowed the well-worn phrase. 'No, don't say that. We exist for each other. You'd do no differently if I weren't here.'

'Yes, probably,' the young woman nodded. 'Our path's the same, Jeff.'

'Sure. But we need to modify the whole "perfectly perfect" thing. I've thought that for a while now actually. With hindsight, it's not really what we want.'

'Isn't it?' Lynn stared into doleful eyes. 'What do you mean?'

'Just that "perfectly perfect"'s not who we are,' the intellectual explained. 'I'd much prefer "perfectly imperfect". That's much more in line with our general message, don't *ya* think?'

'Oh, yes! It is. I love that idea,' his soul-mate agreed. '"Perfectly" because we're comfortable with imperfection, as long as we're working to make things better.'

'*Exactement*, angel. "Perfectly imperfect" it is then. Minute that!'

Merak let out a weak bark, his front feet twitching as if enjoying a run across the meadow in his dream-world. Both Diamonds sat up, only to relax again on the resumption of peaceful snoring.

Jeff closed his eyes, exhaling after an onerous and protracted evening's vigil. 'Jesus! I like that sound.'

'Can you make it?' his wife asked.

'No,' the caring man chuckled. 'Doubt it. Not yet.'

As if his guardians' succour triggered a reminder of his frailty, the creaky dog chose this moment to wake in distress. They jumped to their feet, running from either side of the mattress to meet in front of the patient's mat. Jeff sat down beside him and lifted the greying muzzle until it rested on his thigh, opening up his windpipe as wide as it would go. With Lynn's hand brushing the length of the old boy's spine with slow, firm strokes, the pair remained silent until he descended into slumber again.

After five minutes or so, they crept back and settled under the *duvet*.

'Fuck,' the man of the house cursed.

His wife sighed and repeated a similar pattern of reassurance on her human patient, running her thumb along his tense jawline.

'Whoa! Feels amazing. You should go and do this to him too.'

Wrapping their bodies together for warmth beneath the covers, the forever couple didn't notice Jet walking in on them, rubbing his eyes.

'Mum, Dad... Is Merak OK? I heard him panting.'

His mother popped her head into the cold hallway air, its high cathedral ceiling misappropriating their body heat. 'From your room?' she asked. 'Could you really hear him from upstairs?'

'Yes,' their son insisted. 'I did hear him. Coughing and spluttering too.'

Jeff held out his arms, inviting the nine-year-old into the bed. 'I think you must've been dreaming about him. Sit down, mate. We're keeping him company.'

'Is he really dying?'

His father frowned, sneaking a quick glance across to the sleeping German Shepherd. 'I think so. He's alright for the moment. We won't let him live with pain, Jetto. That wouldn't be fair, would it?'

The boy's head moved from side to side, and he wiped tears from his eyes.

'He's alright now,' Lynn carried on. 'Better than before.'

'You don't get better before you die,' Jet whined.

The man with the death-wish drew the youngster onto his lap, wondering how many of his unconventional opinions he should surface to one so impressionable. 'Maybe you do. Like you're peaceful; ready to go.'

The three attendant night-watchmen changed the subject, talking about cricket and what was on at school the following week. After a series of wide-mouthed yawns, Jet agreed to hunker down under the spare blanket, using two couch cushions as a mattress and another for a pillow. He fell asleep mid-sentence next to his parents.

'We just need Kizzy to wake up and we can all sleep on the floor together,' the young mother whispered, grinning at her favourite troublemaker.

'She won't wake up. I love you so much. This is a horrible night, but somehow one of the best nights of my life. Is that a disrespectful thing to say?'

His wife kissed his cheek. 'For you, no. I understand what you mean. We're here together, making something bleak a little bit more bearable. I know you didn't have that as a child, and I totally get that you want us all to have it now. At the risk of repeating myself, Jeff Diamond, you are a great man.'

Lynn squeezed the hand she had been holding, hoping her beautiful black stallion would drift off to sleep. She let him know she was awake, realising his deep breathing signalled a raging hard-on. As if on autopilot, they turned to face each other on the unstable mattress, jogging them out of their passionate escapism. Jeff tried to push the glorious body away.

Without a word, the Olympian used her strength to flatten the strung-out parent onto his back, lowering his shorts and taking his full erection in both hands. Her head slipped into the darkness of the quilt, hoping the lack of oxygen wouldn't cause her own laboured breathing to rouse their son. Surrendering to the divine favour, the lost soul came in her mouth with dog and boy sound asleep at their side.

Along with "The Black Sheep", Jeff Diamond's first novel since the children were born hit the shops in October nineteen-eighty-six. "Kindred Spirit" gave its readers a glimpse into the mind of a man living two parallel lives in two vastly different eras. His son's growing interest in science fiction had inspired the futuristic character, blessed with the unquestioned ability to dictate his other life in the nineteen-thirties.

Consistently defending the individual's right to free expression, the author raised many critics' eyebrows through his assumption that the general population would take the necessary leap of faith with this unnerving psychological thriller. Mirroring the celebrity's own irrepressible drive, the twin protagonists harboured a fervent belief in the power of love and sex and identified a distinct purpose to their lives. Most controversial however, was their healthy respect for people who wished to die at a time of their own choosing.

Lynn was overjoyed to receive the first autographed copy, inscribed with the simple message of "Thank you. I love you." A bookmark had been slotted in somewhere near the middle, and she opened the book to find an underlined quote: "My heart kept beating despite the melancholy of the previous night. Pursuing my people's freedom leaves me no choice but to abandon the one who gives my life meaning."

Admiration for this new work shone through in the next instalment of the family's weekly television programme, when Australia's favourite mother described the novel's storyline to her children. With Jet on her right-hand side and his kid sister on her left, she mimicked a tennis umpire while the important lessons sank into their sponge-like minds.

'An easy decision isn't always the right decision,' she told them. 'Just because you might want to do something, it doesn't mean it's the right thing to do. Aitken knows he's going to be really lonely without Zaria, but his knowledge about the future makes him the best man to go and help change history.'

'And Zaria understands,' Kierney pipes up, ''cause she knows sometimes heroes have to leave. And she already has enough: Aitken's love.'

'That's right,' Lynn nodded. 'And she's confident he'll come back whenever he's done what he needs to do.'

Jeff went on to explain in a later segment of the same episode that his own belief system was tending towards some mysterious entity which recorded every piece of sound and vision in some kind of universal video footage through time, preserved for all to learn from. Laughing at how absurd this theory seemed when put into plain English, he added to the magic by linking the idea with an unearthly omen he had received as a child that Lynn Dyson would be the one to shepherd him through his odyssey.

'As Paulo Coelho wrote in "The Alchemist", we can't make gold if gold's the end-game. He uses the term "personal legend" in the way Lynn and I use "odyssey". It's the part we're cut out to play in the eternal script. The goal should inspire us, rather than the reward. My goal is spreading happiness and wellbeing more evenly across the world, and my reward is Lynn calling time and telling me I succeeded.

'I believe that if we don't learn who we are from the journey we take, we won't get another shot in this lifetime. We'll need to wait until our next go-round to try again. The most powerful lesson I've learned during this peculiar life is that its main purpose is the endless pursuit of love and wisdom. Nothing more and nothing less.'

***

'Repeat and fade,' the songwriter grabbed his sexy blonde around the waist and span her round. 'You look stunning, and I'm as horny as all hell.'

'Is that right?' Lynn smiled, kissing his lips. 'And you think I can just drop everything and follow you upstairs?'

The thirty-four-year-old frowned. 'No. We can stay down here. I'm not fussed.'

In a flurry of activity, the pair shed their clothes on the spot, with the ground floor of the house deserted. Irina and Dave both had university assignments to complete, and their employers suspected they had shut themselves into the young man's room to study. Or perhaps not to study…

'Repeat and fade,' Jeff began again. 'That's where we are in our life right now. I just want to keep doing the same stuff forever.'

'Mmm…' the record producer murmured. 'Come here. Let's explore that a little further. I love having you here during the day. This couch needs a workout.'

A meaty Stratocaster riff blasted at full volume through the speakers on either side of the studio, putting the ardent lover right off his stride. Kneeling on the floor and staring in wonder at the exquisite female form stretched out beside him, he grabbed his penis in a dramatic burst of air guitar, leaving them both laughing and short of breath.

'Can't say I was expecting that!' Lynn panted, holding her hand out. 'Better than the Nutcracker Suite, I suppose. Shall I turn it off?'

Her husband nodded, usurping the vacant space on the sofa while the naked sound engineer took care of the background music. 'D'you know what Kiz said to me this morning?'

'No. What?'

'She said, "I couldn't sleep last night. I couldn't switch the light off in my eyes." Isn't that magical?'

Lynn straddled the muscular body, taking his fading erection in one hand while tracing the "JL" tattoo with the other. 'Yes. Very sweet. Sounds like you.'

'I know,' the philosopher smiled. 'That's what I told her. I said, "I know exactly how that feels, *pequeñita*," and she was chuffed. But enough of such diversions. Get this inside you. I love you so much.'

The last few days had been so busy that the happy couple felt as if their marriage had been downgraded to passing each other in *Escondido*'s splendid hallway, one leaving as soon as the other returned home. Snatching these brief encounters added a dash of extra spice to what was already a perfectly imperfect existence, which in turn was doing wonders for the children.

'She also told me she'd invented a new word with you,' Jeff continued, his breath keeping pace with their rhythmic movement.

His wife laughed. 'Oh, yes! I forgot about that. "Screaping".'

'"Screaping",' her lover confirmed. 'Because when I have nightmares, I spend more time screaming than sleeping. Jesus, this is so good, angel. Who said men can't multi-task? Doing this is a real turn-on. Takes the edge off the urgency for a few seconds.'

'So tell me something else then,' the athlete teased, rising high enough off his lap to leave the sensitive tip of his penis poised in the opening of her vagina. 'I bet you can't come up with anything on the spur of the moment...'

Undaunted, strong legs heaved her *paramour*'s hips upwards, leaving her no choice but to swallow his entire length. 'How much?'

'Oh, my God, Jeff! I don't care how much! Just do that again.'

A precipitous orgasm ripped through the ecstatic woman, taken by surprise by the forceful act. Eager to prolong his wife's pleasure, the expert lover dropped sideways onto the couch until they lay facing each other. His back resisted against the cushion to push as far inside her as possible, until his own climax burst forth.

'*De l'argent provocateur*,' he growled in her ear, pinching her earlobe in his teeth and running his tongue over the post of her earring.

Lynn's face creased into a frown, sniffing at this novel play on words. 'What? What's that all about?'

'The guy from the Premier's office who came to see me and Gerry yesterday morning. It's what he offered me.'

Their bodies still entwined, the couple relaxed down into the sofa. Jeff brushed a few stray strands of golden hair out of the beauty's eyes, encouraging her head forward into a long, loving kiss.

Neville Wran's Labor government had been playing hardball with Paragon Holdings over their plans to build a state headquarters building on Sydney's western fringe. The prime piece of real estate had proven too costly for the New South Wales government's hospital rebuilding fund and had undergone a sudden re-zoning when the celebrities and their powerful machinery had shown interest. However, having realised their sly ruse had been rumbled and the high-profile buyers were backing away, a sizeable donation to The Fellowship had been brought to Gerry's attention.

'I've no idea if *l'argent* is masc' or fem',' the billionnaire continued, 'but I'm going with masc', otherwise my phrase doesn't fly.'

'Provocative money?' the flushed woman translated.

'Yeah. Kind of. But more active than that: money as the provoker. Provoking.'

Lynn sat up. 'You mean he tried to bribe you?'

'*C'est possible,*' her humble world-changer raised an expressive eyebrow.

'Wow! *Qu'est-ce que t'as fait donc?*'

'Well… With no premeditation whatsoever, he and I were walking across the gardens from Parliament House to that *café* on the corner of Martin Place and Hunter Street, and we passed a homeless guy begging. I opened my wallet, took out three green ones and slapped them into the undersecretary of *minutæ*'s hand and said, "Do the right thing with this, John. This Stones Road worm's not for turning."'

The tennis champion leaned forward and planted a kiss on her beloved's lips. 'Congratulations! I wonder what the guy did with the three hundred dollars!'

'The biggest hit of his life, I expect,' her husband laughed. 'And lunch too, hopefully.'

'Wow! You're so amazing. How did the official react? Was he annoyed?'

'*Na,*' the philanthropist sneered. 'He's one of those types who are constantly surprised by life. Never likely to think of the consequences.'

His wife giggled. 'He should have that on his tombstone. Here lies Nigel Smallacre. Died fifteenth of September. Last words: "Well, that was a surprise!"'

Jeff exhaled as emotion poured in torrents through his veins. The gentle, forgiving soul who strove to see the good in everyone had the capacity to turn up the vitriol when warranted, and he appreciated the show of support. As they pivoted their naked bodies off the couch and went in search of their scattered clothing, she reminded him of a heated telephone conversation he had shared with someone earlier that morning. She hadn't wanted to interrupt the flow, yet there was no denying the familiar desperate pull on their invisible elastic connection.

'You're so self-sufficient in every aspect of your life except with me,' she recounted.

'I know,' Jeff nodded, 'and I have no real clue why. It's always been that way, angel. You're the key to everything. You're like the final piece in the puzzle to unlock all this latent potential. Without you, I feel like I'd just fall in a useless heap.'

***

'Mate! Good to see you,' Gerry shouted, grabbing Jeff's hand and shaking it with his usual vigour. 'Are you back to normal?'

'Back to normal?' the superstar scoffed. 'I doubt if I'd recognise normal if it spat in my face. Weak and feeble, but getting there. How was Christmas in the Blake household?'

'Oh, same, same. You were missed, my friend.'

'Cheers,' the recovering patient smiled, raising his beer bottle to the party animal and sensing a level of boredom. 'It was a blast here too. So what's new?'

The traveller had brought malaria back to the family from Africa for the festive season. He had passed the first three weeks of December schlepping around the northern half of the continent, holding talks with all manner of people in the strangest of places. He had shown no symptoms during the trip, right up until boarding the homeward leg in Singapore, when the sweat began to pour out of him as if the airport's humidity had followed him into the aircraft.

After the extraordinary success of the opening months of "The Black Sheep" in London, the Diamond family had forged separate paths for most of October and November. Lynn had spent time in Los Angeles and New York, presiding over the American *premières* and accepting a bunch of music industry awards for albums she had produced over the year.

The stalwart diplomat had also held meetings with representatives of the various United Nations organisations with whom the Diamond Celebration Foundation had partnerships. In the meantime, Jet and Kierney were ensconced in their Melbourne apartment with their childminders, finalising the school year and preparing for concerts and sporting carnivals galore.

Their father's temperature had shot sky-high by the time he landed at Tullamarine Airport. He telephoned his wife from the Qantas lounge, making the reluctant decision to divert to the nearest hospital. Isolated immediately on admission, he was subjected to a slew of tests, hooked up to machines and filled with disappointment. His mind had been dominated for the whole flight by pleasant thoughts of *Escondido* and being with his three most favourite people.

'It was bloody torture,' the billionaire explained to his manager. 'I couldn't touch Lynn and the kids for a week, after having been away for three already. That's enough to drive anyone crazy, not to mention it was Christmas too.'

Gerry sniggered, feigning sympathy with no success. 'No festive nookie? I concur, old boy. Pretty tough going, even for an old bloke like you.'

'What d'*ya* mean? Yeah, well... Whatever. I didn't completely go without,' Jeff confessed. 'We did manage to sneak in some minimal contact sport a couple of times, but it knocked me around. The nurses caught on to the coincidental jumps in the mercury pretty fast!'

'Alright! Now this is more interesting,' the lecherous executive raised one eyebrow. 'Are they up for it?'

His old friend shook his head. 'Not with them, you bonehead! Although it certainly crosses one's mind over those long nights... But get this, mate: it's no bad thing when your wife drops your kids off at their friends' place wearing nothing but a trench coat and high heels, then speeds to the hospital to treat you to scarlet *lingerie*. You can dine out on that one during your next tedious Finance Committee meeting.'

Gerry whistled. 'That's pure gold indeed. I've got to hand it to you, sir... How did you make such a minx out of Australia's favourite girl next-door?'

'Ah, y'know,' the dark-haired rocker grinned. 'She knows what I like, and I know what she likes. Reciprocity, mate. That's all it takes. You should give it a try.'

The self-absorbed accountant tutted, changing the subject. 'So I heard the gig was hard going the other night. Was it?'

'Shit, yeah!' Jeff groaned and leaned back in his chair. 'You heard about that? From Lynn?'

'No. From Cathy from Lynn.'

'Jesus Christ, mate. It was a complete bloody nightmare. I couldn't bring myself to cancel on them. There were so many people depending on us performing, but I was dead on my feet. Fevered and nauseated and weak as hell. I even snorted cocaine to get me through the second half.'

'Shit! Did you really?' Gerry exclaimed. 'Don't tell me that. I don't want to know.'

The reformed bad-boy chuckled. 'I shouldn't have taken it in the first place, let alone tell you I took it. It was the thing that saved me though. My engine was sputtering all the way through the first set, and I even had to run off the stage and chuck up.'

'Right. Too much information, but it sounds dreadful.'

'It was fucking dreadful. I ended up scooping handfuls of ice from the beer esky into the sink so I could stick my head in it! I was boiling and dehydrated, and pretty sure I wasn't going to be conscious for too much longer if I didn't do something drastic. Definitely didn't have the strength to do the songs justice.'

His manager frowned. 'I guess the show must go on. We need to find you an understudy, mate!'

'Sure. Sounds great actually. Time to retire and exploit someone else for the rest of my career. I'll leave that to you. Anyway, the band couldn't believe the sudden transformation, and Lynn was bloody furious when she found out!'

'You told her? What possessed you to pull this ridiculous stunt?'

'Of course I told her. You know us… I can't not tell her stuff. There was nothing she could do about it by that time. She hates those hardcore drugs, even though she understands why I needed to take it. The roadies and the blokes in the band were hailing me as some kind of martyr for going on to deliver such a spirited performance, until I showed them the syringe and told them, "I'm no bloody superhero, guys. I'm high as an effing kite! And tomorrow, the world'll make me pay for my sins." Then I came home to shake and sweat for five hours, waiting for the shit to flush through my system along with the malaria.'

'Jesus, Mary and Joseph! So what was it like?' the conservative Irishman asked. 'I have no idea what high as a kite feels like.'

'Fuckin' amazing, mate. Like you're invincible; limitless energy, ready for anything. But it doesn't last long. That's why it's so addictive. I didn't get a chance to revel in it this time though. I had a job to do, and it got me to the end of the program, by which time I was pretty much down to ground zero again.'

'What happened then? What's it like taking a drug like that?'

'Ah, you don't *wanna* know, mate,' Jeff scowled. 'You're too old to start getting curious about this shit. It wasn't pleasant for any of us. I pushed my luck that night, I can tell you. And that's no exaggeration.'

'God Almighty! With Lynn, you mean? In what way?'

'In every bloody way,' the rock star answered, full of shame. 'It was a dumb idea, and I'm surprised she didn't throw me out. By all accounts, I said some pretty ugly things and behaved like a real arsehole.'

'Worse than usual?'

'Yeah, you bastard,' Jeff shook his head in mock frustration. 'And that's saying something. I spent the next twelve hours in a coma, so remind me never to do it again. Lynn was petrified. I'm not putting her through that twice. And thank Christ the kids didn't see me.'

The Irishman was torn between laughing about the episode in hindsight, giving his client a professional scolding or sympathising with the trail of misery. 'Fuck,' he muttered, opening his briefcase and sliding out a box of slimline cigars. 'You're right. We're far too old for that shit. I bet there's no nookie for you for another month now.'

Jeff stood up to buy another round of drinks. 'That's what I deserve,' he shrugged, 'but mercifully, not what I got. *Noch einer?*'

Gerry nodded back. '*Jawohl.* You get away with bloody murder, Diamond. Someone up there likes you.'

403

'Tell me about it,' the billionaire smiled. 'And then, on top of everything, my darling daughter sits on the end of my bed and spins me outrageous yarns all afternoon. I *gotta* tell you, mate, I'm the luckiest fuck in the entire world.'

While waiting for the barman to uncork a dusty bottle of Grange Hermitage which the pair had requested from the cellar, the celebrity cast his mind back to the previous day and to Kierney's storytelling. He had asked if she concocted them in advance and stored them in her head or if she heard the story develop as she was telling it. Her response hadn't surprised him at all: a bit of both.

'She's so like me,' the proud father recounted, raising his glass.

'Kizzy?'

'Yep. But she's also like her *mamá* 'cause she cares enough to sit and talk to me when she could be elsewhere having fun. Some of her stories are set back in time, which is most disconcerting. She told me one about a princess and a soldier, which I'm sure is based on Lynn and my story. Loosely at least... And then some of the others were sci-fi, inspired by her brother's epic universe-hopping adventures. She came up with the idea of a spaceship in the shape of a *mange-tout*.'

'A what? What's a *mange-tout*?' the accountant screeched. 'Isn't that some sort of vegetable?'

'Yeah. Snow peas,' his old friend laughed. 'She asked me which way up it should fly? Vertical or horizontal? For a while there, it was as if I were still under the influence.'

Gerry grinned. 'Streamlined aerodynamics either way, so good choice of veggies. She should send the design to NASA. A single-flight, biodegradable spaceship. Hey! I forgot to mention you've been summoned to the White House again. Both of you.'

'Oh, yeah? What for?'

'Don't rightly know, sir,' the buffoon attempted an American southern drawl. 'The Republican president who used to be an actor wants to talk about ending the Cold War with a liberal songwriter who gives his millions away. Clearly, the world's gone stark, raving mad.'

'OK,' Jeff was pleased. 'That makes me happy. We can trade showbiz drug experiences. Why didn't Cath tell me about this earlier? Does she know?'

'I thought she did,' his manager replied. 'Maybe not. You'd think we'd remember something like this, but once we get on a roll, everything else just goes out of our heads. I saw it scribbled on the notepad on my desk. Perhaps Cathy wasn't around when the call came. I don't know. I'll ask her to ring you in the morning. What are you doing tomorrow?'

'Staying in bed. We've got a lot of catching up to do. Lynn's my highest priority over the coming few days, if you know what I mean... We're going to Benloch for the weekend for Jet's cricket coaching, then she's in the studio next week with Steve Christie. Last chance to relax for a while.'

Testing Resilience

Nineteen-eighty-seven was a year for growing up, as the Diamond household's forward plan foreshadowed. With another summer of intense cricket training behind him and celebrating his tenth birthday just before the winter school holidays, Jet seemed to grow up overnight. He had invited three friends to stay at *Escondido* for the weekend, and the boys had been messing around with the security barrier which his parents had installed after the hostage situation.

The idea for this innovative measure had been inspired by homes the dogged wanderer had visited in Johannesburg and Pretoria, where families' bedrooms were often protected by reinforced steel lattice. It was the only way their occupants could sleep soundly, safe in the knowledge that their lives and those of their children were out of reach, even if their houses were ransacked by looters.

The couple commissioned an engineering company to construct a roll of ingenious interlocked posts in the attic. Similar to a garage roller-door, the mechanised contraption was rigged up to a motor to unwind through an aperture sliced in the ceiling whence it would drop all the way to the landing's floorboards at the push of a button.

On this particular morning, while his father was flying home from yet another international trip, Jet decided it might be a good lark to surprise his mates by trapping them behind the sturdy fence and legging it down to the ground floor.

Lynn had been training in the gymnasium when the alarms began to blare, setting the whole house vibrating. She ran upstairs to find the four lads in hysterics, playing a raucous game of *limbo* while the steel cage ascended and descended. She was livid, wasting no time in dispatching the three friends outside to play football while she berated her son without holding back. The severity of her reaction completely knocked the boy sideways, never having experienced such brazen anger from his mother, who was normally one for reasoning with her intelligent children.

And then, when Jeff returned in the evening and learned of their son's antics, he had been no less irate. The tennis champion's account ended with her threat to punish Jet by moving his possessions into a guest bedroom, beyond the *grille*'s perimeter. She had watched the shock register in his mind when the truth hit home: if ever an intruder were to break in, the others would be saved but he would not.

This forfeiture affected the man of the house almost as deeply, waning energy depleting as he listened to his frustrated wife. He headed straight for the ten-year-old's bedroom, expected to give him a tongue-lashing of equal intensity. Yet his own rampant fears rendered his message far less damaging. His plan was to remind the lad that the security bars were there to protect him and those he loved, hoping the wake-up call would serve its purpose.

'It's not a toy, mate,' the passionate family man stressed to the youngster. 'Remember John Lennon? JFK? What'd happen if someone were to lay siege to this house tonight, while we're asleep? If you'd blown the power supply, we'd have flicked the switch and nothing would've happened. Think about it for a while, eh? Mum and I made sure we'd never be in this situation, and you and your mates might've screwed us completely.'

The trauma inflicted on him by his own father prevented Jeff from unleashing at full bore. He didn't want to risk freaking Jet out by hearing the same proposed fate for a second time. Instead, he vowed to remain the voice of trust who enriched Lynn's voice of reason rather than augmenting it.

Later on, the empathetic man opined to his dream girl that she had been too hard on their son. Letting him think she would consider leaving him outside their safe haven was a step too far. Nevertheless, both agreed a lesson had been well learned by all. Jet never played with security equipment again, and Lynn came clean months afterwards that she couldn't have gone through with her threat.

The lad cruised through the entrance examination for Melbourne Academy, following in the Dyson tradition, leaving him with only one term remaining at primary school. The family flew to Los Angeles at the end of September, where all four Diamonds joined forces with a batch of promising Californian musicians to experiment with video and audio technology. The end result surpassed all expectations, concluding with a special message for kids all over the world.

Lynn's reputation as an album producer was also recognised as second-to-none, now counting a decade of experience with A-list artists queuing up to book time in her busy schedule, supplemented by Jeff's endless stream of song ideas so easily moulded into instant hits. "Generation Share" was the collaboration's first saleable product, starring one Jet Diamond and featuring Lynn and Kierney as extras. With more than a passing *homage* to Spielberg's "ET", the science-fiction fan played the part of a schoolboy on a globe-trotting journey.

The music video's theme was the importance of celebrating the diversity in the world's population, and its release was greeted by huge media acclaim at the end of a year plagued with economic uncertainty and delicate peace. Not only did the production company win almost every award available, but with the help of their worthy collaborators, the groundbreaking partnership had conquered yet another entertainment *genre* in one fell swoop.

Confined to Melbourne's environs in January nineteen-eighty-eight for the new year's training camp, the couple attended the formal opening of a brand new arts precinct in the city of Frankston, down the road from *Escondido*, financed from the previous few years' Diamond Celebration Foundation surpluses. They had long intended to give something back to the townsfolk, many of whom had lived through some tough times at the hands of a turbulent state government.

A foreshore picnic was hosted by the town's famous residents on Australia Day, originally meant for those involved with the ambitious project. They also wished to remind their neighbours that they had chosen to live in Mount Eliza because of the proximity to a regional city boasting many cultures and socio-economic *strata*, into which they could immerse their children. The town had been kind to them in return, allowing the celebrities to come and go in peace for the most part, with shops and *cafés* welcoming their instantly-recognisable patrons with open arms.

That morning, Jeff had left home early to drive two recent Sudanese immigrants to the international stores on Sydney Road in Brunswick, looking to buy spices to cook up an authentic African feast. He caused his usual stir walking around the market, conversing with the men in a mixture of fluent French and passable Arabic. Later, he manned the barbecue himself, much to the joy of local female members of the community.

Dressed in board shorts and a short-sleeved shirt open to reveal his hairy, muscular torso, and sporting a simple pair of thongs on his billion-dollar feet, the superstar was the picture of contentment while chatting to stallholders and customers about sport, politics and local news, a cigarette and a bottle of beer in one hand and an oversized meat fork in the other.

Jet and Kierney played ball games on the sand below the parkland, meeting up with friends whom they had rarely seen since leaving the nearby school. They were monitored from a distance by security staff kitted out in beachwear. To allow them to blend into the scene as far as possible, the guards had been encouraged to bring their families along too, and their partners were wide-eyed to find themselves eating and drinking alongside their idols.

At one point, standing round the entertainment area, a Mount Eliza dad nudged the man next to him and made a lewd gesture. The testosterone-charged group was powerless to resist the refined sensuality of Lynn Dyson and a friend strolling up from the beach. The tall, blonde athlete looked breathtaking in a bikini covered only by a long, unbuttoned linen shirt. Heading towards the assortment of amateur chefs, the beauty shook her head and smiled as Jeff whistled his appreciation.

'Man, you are one hell of a lucky bloke!' Mario piped up. 'You can have sex with that whenever you want.'

Seeing red at the crass comment, the beauty's husband took a breath before correcting the owner of one of the town's popular Italian restaurants. 'D'you mind, mate? The lady's no "that". And it's whenever *we* want, by the way. But yeah, I guess you're right, basically!'

This summer's day spent in touch with their fans in a normal, Aussie pastime inspired the song "Cruel Game", which was to become the highest grossing single of all time. Intent on filming a raunchy video to accompany its suggestive lyric, Jeff and Lynn took the children to the Caribbean for a holiday at the end of the year, where they shot the clip featuring a rather *risqué* lovemaking scene on a beach of pure white sand and lined with date palms. The songwriters had confessed to reporters that the visual *extravaganza* was their chance to thumb their noses at the ageing process.

'We want to give people the idea that anything's possible,' Lynn explained. 'Love and sex aren't solely the domain of twenty-somethings. Make the best of your life, your relationship and everything. We do, and shall continue to do so.'

The Diamonds' Midas touch continued unabated into the final year of the nineteen-eighties, when they found themselves celebrating their daughter's double-figures *début*. By now, Jet and Kierney were at home in front of the cameras, and the family's loyal public expected them to play their parts.

'What's all this about "Baa, Baa, Green Sheep"?' Jeff asked an audience of schoolchildren while shooting a special television show about acceptance and tolerance. 'It doesn't make sense to me. So today, we're here to talk about "isms". We're going to convince ourselves we can do without "isms" in our lives. OK? Who's ever seen a green sheep? Anyone?'

The kids gave an enthusiastic cheer, latching on to the serious message behind the programme's debate.

'Racism, sexism, ageism... You guys know what I'm talking about. How come we can't say black and white any more?' the world-changer asked. 'That's not racism. It's a label. Shorthand, if you like. People instinctively understand what it means, for better or for worse. Come on... No-one's white. We're either a fleshy pink colour, or a brown colour, or a darker brown colour, or in Billy Connolly's case, a blue colour.'

Again, everyone laughed at the reference to the madcap comedian who had toured Australia in the recent past, performing to sell-out crowds.

'Billy reckons all Scottish people are blue, so what's in a label? If someone said to you, "He's the black sheep of the family," you might even be a little bit proud of yourself. It shows you're getting noticed. You stand out from the crowd. A bit left of centre, but there's nothing wrong with that. But then if we start saying, "He's the green sheep of the family," you're going to feel like a total freak, because there ain't no green sheep. Am I right?'

Another two-hour documentary made in January of the following year chronicled Lynn Dyson and Jeff Diamond's world-famous life singular, complete with the "Together, Forever, Wherever" slogan and their "JL" emblem. The camera crew crawled all over *Escondido*'s house and grounds, pursuing the couple with relentless verve as they went about their business and capturing metres of priceless footage of the family at work and play.

'Funny how everyone looks busier in the kitchen when these guys are here,' Jeff laughed, his dark eyes zeroing in on the lens and transporting himself directly into the viewers' living rooms. 'Big brother is watching you! We should have you guys here all the time. Things'll get done much faster.'

Lynn nodded, standing next to the son whose head reached his mother's shoulder these days. 'Yeah. That's why we all need bosses, to make sure things get done.'

'Who's your boss, Dad?' Jet chided.

'Mum and I are each other's bosses,' his father responded without missing a beat. 'We're all each others' bosses. The difference is we're doing it because we care about each other and respect each other. That's the key, son. So get movin'!'

This particular episode also featured the family's first set of mobile telephones, bulky and not too easy to master. Jeff and Gerry took delivery of the long-awaited consignment, placing their first call in front of the cameras. Paragon Holdings had funded several research programs to bring cellular telephony into the hands of everyday people, starting with carphones and now graduating to smaller, lighter handsets which didn't require a battery the size of a house-brick.

'Hey, angel!' the billionnaire greeted his wife at home, grinning from ear to ear. 'Get this! I'm standing on the steps of 333 Collins, and everyone thinks I'm a lunatic, talking to myself like this. Henceforth, no more need for our invisible elastic connection. I'll be able to ring you from wherever I am. Well, nearly wherever. Eventually. Yeah. Long live the Internet, huh? Just think what we can do with this in Africa...'

The documentary series concluded with a private and somewhat poignant moment where Jeff spoke to his children about the sheer grace their mother had exhibited during public appearances when he had first met her, at only sixteen years of age. He told them how much he had learned from the way she carried herself and her style of interaction with total strangers, by maintaining an appropriate balance between arm's-length diplomacy and in-the-know amiability.

'The trick is to always take that little bit longer to do things than you normally would,' he advised. 'Walk slowly, talk slowly, and even think slowly. It makes you look like you're in control, and being in control means nothing rushes you. That's the impression you want to give.'

***

'I said, "I love you,"' Lynn smiled, turning over as her husband slid under the sheet beside her.

'Sorry, angel. I was in another world.'

'That's OK.'

Jeff sniffed, gathering the naked body into his arms. 'Why is it OK?'

'Because I know what you're thinking about, and I know how much you care. Are you ready to talk about it?'

'Ah, yeah. But I also care about you. I don't want to neglect you just because I've got a shitload on my mind.'

The pair had received a telephone call earlier that day from the Head Teacher at Melbourne Academy, in an absolute panic. A staff member had stumbled across one of her students huddled in a dark corner of the music room with a bottle of vodka and a plastic container of razor blades.

Fortunately, the busy peacemaker was not far from the city, at Benloch enjoying a peaceful afternoon writing songs and hanging out with the children while Lynn and her siblings succumbed to more of Bart Dyson's torture. After listening to the distraught principal's story, he had called the boy's parents, dropped everything and jumped into the car. He hoped the poor lad wouldn't be ferried off to the nearest psychiatric hospital before he arrived.

Roderick Germany, the promising young musician who had sung at Sandy's funeral, had come to the Diamonds' attention for a whole different reason at a songwriting workshop. Lynn had engaged him in conversation during the recess, worried by the gloomy lyrics she had helped him put to music, recommending that he meet with the Childlight counselling service.

The fourteen-year-old's parents refused to admit their son might suffer from depression, despite referring him to a string of credentialled psychiatrists and pædiatricians. They interpreted the aspersion as an indictment on their parenting, citing the many luxuries they had ladled on their three gifted and good-looking offspring. Therefore, no amount of gentle cajoling from the school and its high-profile patrons caused Rod's symptoms to improve.

'You're not neglecting me,' the compassionate woman insisted. 'You're in my bed.'

'Oh, I'll always be in your bed, lady. Whether I'm here or not.'

Lynn stroked her *paramour*'s forearm, fingers skimming over tense muscles. 'You're not blaming yourself for what happened, are you?'

'Nope.'

'Good. So how did you leave it with them?'

Jeff sighed, kissing the tanned skin stretched over her knuckles. 'I'll go back tomorrow morning and speak to him, to check where his thoughts went overnight. I warned his dad that I'm not who he wants his son to talk with.'

'Why?' his wife yelped. 'You're exactly who he should talk to.'

'Thanks, gorgeous, but I don't think they'd see it that way. They don't know my views on suicide. They're staunch Christians, *Hochkirche* folk. Rod told me this a few weeks ago. It's a sin not to value your life, and all that crap. He said he'd been struggling with it all his life. His parents have convinced him he's a bad person because of it, which is hardly going to help his recovery.'

Spinning round to face her magnificent old soul, whose anger simmered below the polished exterior of an exceedingly wise man, the Olympian kissed his tense jaw. His own deeply-held beliefs on this contentious topic led to counsel dispensed with the utmost care, especially when it pertained to under-eighteens. They had both learned this lesson at the Abbotsford Convent, overseen by nuns on Good Friday while she ventured into the same uncharted territory as a sixteen-year-old.

'It sounds like you think Rod's mature enough.'

'Oh, he is, but the law still protects him. I don't want to have to lie to him to comply with the law, when all he needs is to hear an honest opinion. He's convinced it's all his fault. His parents are upset he's lost interest in life, and that makes him feel even worse.'

'Hmm… Sounds familiar. Can you speak to them first?'

'No. Not yet. I don't think it's the right time. If he agrees to keep trying, it's a discussion worth having once everything calms down. I told him, in front of his mum, "You're not a bad person because you want to kill yourself, mate. A bad person is one who takes a rifle into school and kills everyone else before turning the gun on himself. You'd never do that, would you? Remember this when anyone tries to tell you otherwise."'

Lynn sighed. 'Wow. How did Renate take it? Was she embarrassed?'

'Yeah. A little. Oh, yeah… Did Kizzo tell you about what happened this morning, by the way?'

'When? I don't think so.'

The strung-out father shook his head, shivering at the recent memory. 'Firstly, I ran down to the stables with the kids, to make sure they got kitted out for their ride. They wanted me to come with them, begging… I said, "To be honest, I feel too much for the poor horse with my weight on its back. Why should he carry me?"'

The farmer's daughter was shocked at such a heartfelt explanation. 'I had no idea you felt that way.'

Jeff shrugged. 'Neither did I until the words came out of my mouth, and then I was hit with a profound sense of relief. Almost like something had been trapped inside my head for so long and then managed to fling itself headlong at the outside world.'

'So did they stop begging after that?'

'Sort of, yeah. It gave me a chance to turn around and walk away,' her lover replied. 'And secondly...'

The sportswoman giggled as her husband began to stroke the ticklish skin underneath her right breast. 'Yes. Why are you trying to distract me?'

'I'm not. I'm practising multi-tasking.'

Lynn grabbed his hand as it wandered across her abdomen. 'Liar! Don't try that one on me. What's secondly?'

Was there no end to the minor revelations her lover's complex mind uncovered as it let go of its insulating layers? She could tell he was crying but chose not to acknowledge his distress. Half his strength came from being forced to confront these memories head-on.

Jeff coughed. 'Secondly was in the stables, waiting for them to rub the ponies down after their ride. A full-blown panic attack engulfed me when I saw Kierney with her hands in a feed bucket, almost up to her elbows. She looked up when she heard me scramble to my feet and start running towards her. She said I'd gone as white as a ghost.'

'But what for?' his wife asked. 'What was wrong?'

'Nothing. That's just it. Another flashback, but it fucking floored me. I did the same thing at the Blakes' once. I wanted to feel how the flakes moved round my fingers. Y'know, sensory input addict, *et cetera*.'

'Yes, I know. So what happened? Something horrible obviously.'

"Jesus! I didn't tell the kids until we were walking back, but I remembered sticking my hands into the trough and rummaging around, and then I was bitten by a bloody great rat. Gorging itself on the mix. Christ, it stang again like it'd only just happened. The bugger's front teeth went all the way through my hand...'

The tormented man clenched his fingers round Lynn's hand, pinching the muscles between the fine bones that ran from her knuckles to her wrist. 'Like this... It was still hanging on when I jumped up. Jack and Tammy both screamed the house down.'

'Yow! Stop!' the young woman cried out, wrenching her hand free. 'That does hurt. I believe you! How horrible. What did Kizzy say when you told her?'

'She went a bit white too,' Jeff admitted. 'Anyway, better out than in. That's enough about my ongoing weirdness. Come here and let me take your pain away.'

The sportswoman relished the sensation of her husband taking hold around her ribcage, offering no resistance to his attempt to lift her on top. She was content that sufficient verbal therapy had been administered, more than ready to balance it out with the more corporal kind. They laughed as they recreated another, much more amusing moment in a Japanese restaurant earlier in the week, when the couple had quite coincidentally turned up for separate lunch appointments.

'You having an affair too?' the handsome philanthropist had asked, seeing his wife's host shrink in fright.

Lynn nodded, game to play along at the poor journalist's expense. 'I didn't know you'd be here. How are you?'

Jeff slapped his male companion on the back. 'It's not how it looks. We're just friends.'

'That's perfectly fine,' the blonde issued a dismissive smile and resumed eating. 'See you at home.'

By now, the whole restaurant had tuned into the public encounter. Whispers surrounded them as the songwriter bent down to share a passionate kiss.

'Don't wait up.'

'The look on Mark's face!' the breathless woman gasped. 'Did you already know him? I've never heard you talk about him before.'

The couple kissed, being overtaken by a wave of passion which claimed their attention in the most pleasurable manner.

Paragon Holdings had advertised for a state manager to run their Western Australian operations, and the conglomerate's Chief Executive Officer was meeting Mark Wainwright as a courtesy before they made him a written offer of employment.

The unusual introduction had solicited the candidate's latent homophobia, a trait frequently undetected or overlooked by Jeff's trusty offsider. Two hours later, after a litre of *Sake* and many a wise word from Australia's richest man, the recruit had changed his opinion on white, heterosexual male supremacy, and his new boss had enjoyed another fierce debate on diversity and inclusion.

***

'Have they gone?' Lynn asked her husband, spotting a sickly expression on his face.

Jeff had emerged from the office at *Escondido* after a long telephone call, closing the door with a quiet click. Deep in thought, he lifted his eyes to find his beautiful best friend walking towards him, her hands held out as if she needed a hug as much as he did. The lovers embraced, their sombre mood pervading the atmosphere enough to worry the unflappable Janey.

'They've gone,' a serious voice confirmed, ruffling the fur behind the dog's ears. 'About half an hour ago apparently.'

Fighting back tears, the young mother turned away, heading for the lounge room. She had only managed a few paces before being swept into greedy arms again. For a fleeting moment, she wondered if her conflicted man sought to use their combined angst to assuage his infinite sexual desires.

Lynn held her breath, in two minds whether to give in to his compulsions. The old Jeff would have exploited their time alone in the house, without question, and the recollection unleashed uncharacteristic antipathy. But the new Jeff? Chastising her cynicism as soon as she clocked the intensity in his eyes and tasted the rasping desperation, she realised with relief that her initial conclusion had been unwarranted.

'Did they go quietly?' she asked, leading the way down the corridor and into the kitchen to make some coffee. 'Who were you speaking to?'

'Ian Mills. And no, not at all quietly. Good on 'em, huh?'

Lynn grimaced. 'Oh. Poor things. I hope this is worth it.'

Neither parent could settle over the next few hours. They mooched around the house like zombies, avoiding eye contact for fear of weakening and calling the exercise off. Finding no inspiration at the piano nor in the newspaper, Jeff excused himself and sought refuge in the garage. There, he found George tinkering with the Harley Davidson he was in the midst of restoring.

The family's second driver ignored his employer's restlessness while he completed three circuits of the barnlike building in search of a manly pursuit to distract his attention. One by one, both sports cars and the ageing Caprice were backed out, soaped up, rinsed and polished with a *chamois* leather until they sparkled. Watching him move on to repeat the process on the battered station-wagon which had been bought for shuttling sodden, sandy shepherds back from the beach, the retired policeman stopped him and proffered his cigarette packet.

'Sorry, boss,' he scoffed. 'Not clean enough for you? We'll do better next time.'

The men stood smoking together while Jeff explained the latest lesson in personal security the couple had administered to their children. The two loyal transportation consultants had been informed of their plans in advance, under strict instructions not to share the information with anyone, in case it were to reach the press. Even the childminders were not privy to the youngsters' curious adventure.

Too discreet to utter an opinion, the former officer nodded his understanding. 'They'll be right, mate. They're tough cookies, those two.'

'I'm sure,' the songwriter agreed. 'But what are they going to think of us when they find out it was all our idea?'

George slapped the doting father on the shoulder. He had gained considerable respect for the Diamonds in the five years he had spent in their employ. They had achieved so much, and as a law enforcement officer who had seen far too many innocent children turn into criminals for all the wrong reasons, he appreciated the way in which these celebrity parents conducted themselves.

The day had started in an everyday fashion, with the mad Monday morning rush into the city after a busy weekend entertaining other chart-topping musicians who had descended on Melbourne to take advantage of Lynn Dyson's record-producing skills. At this moment, the amiable sixty-three-year-old felt protective towards the serious-minded musician so intent on preparing his little gems for any eventuality.

'How's Lynn bearing up?' he asked, waving another cigarette under his nose.

'Ah, y'know her...' the songwriter chuckled. 'She's nervous. We were driving each other crazy in there. She's made of tough stuff too though. Old man Dyson did some pretty extreme things with Lynn and the others when they were kids, so she thinks it's a fantastic idea. And so did I to begin with. Right up until I got the 'phone call to say they'd put up some resistance when the guys pushed them into the car.'

'Was the school in on it too?'

'Only the head and one student counsellor. We needed to keep it as real as possible. The counsellor was on hand to make sure none of the other kids got scared. The plan was to tell the rest of the kids that it was just a test, as soon as Jet and Kierney were clear of the grounds.'

Jeff stubbed out his cigarette on the brick outer wall and tossed the butt into a nearby bin. A dose of healthy male bonding was helping him through this latest stressful episode, but his mind was also preoccupied with his dream girl. No matter how resolute and single-minded his stoic Dyson maiden purported to be, he was still remiss for leaving her alone in the house. She would benefit from some caring and sharing too.

Thanking George for his comforting words, the superstar headed back inside, promising to provide an update before the end of the day. The driver's interest warmed his heart. In fact, their entire household adored the young Diamonds, and these feelings were reciprocated in spades. He smiled at his lingering socialist objection to commissioning so many people to take care of his family's whims, knowing his children were growing up happy, safe and stimulated in their weird extended family of paid helpers.

The devoted *paramour* found his wife deep in conversation, with the telephone receiver pressed up against one ear and doodling on a sheet of manuscript paper. He draped his arms around her shoulders and kissed her cheek. Grateful blue eyes flashed their thanks, and he sat next to her while the call continued for another few minutes, deducing that the party on the other end of the line was someone from Diamond Celebration Foundation's Manhattan office. The couple's charitable interests were big business these days. Over the course of the last two years, they had opened regional offices in Sydney, London, New York and Los Angeles, with others slated for Vancouver, Paris and Barcelona.

Watching the delightful rear-end of their pantomime horse at work, the frontman began to piece together their children's predicament. If everything was proceeding to plan, their current location was an unleased floor of an empty office building between Little Collins and Bourke Streets, around the corner from the Southern Cross Hotel. He imagined them both to be reserved and compliant, anxious not to upset their captors, hoping they were at least confident enough to speak to each other.

The couple had taken advice from their contracted security experts on how best to equip Jet and Kierney for a kidnapping, today's event being their money's worth. In hindsight, the situation was ghastly, Jeff rued, for all involved. The plan had been for three men dressed in black suits to turn up at Melbourne Academy's music department during choir practice, on the pretext that the junior Diamonds had been summoned to the airport to join their parents on a last-minute trip to Sydney.

The elaborate ploy was designed to be improbable yet not outlandish. As Lion Security had indicated in the earlier call, their son had been vocal in his objections. The men must have convinced everyone after a while, resulting in the boy's teacher rushing to round up his sister and allowing them to be bundled into a black Ford Fairmont and driven out of the school gates at high speed.

'You OK?' Lynn hazarded, once her call had concluded.

'Yep. You?'

'Sort of,' she smiled. 'I wonder if they're alright? How long should we leave it?'

Jeff's gaze lifted towards the clock on the wall above their desks: four-fifteen. 'Half past?' he suggested with a smirk.

The young mother shook her head. 'You can't cave, Jeff.'

'I can. Don't you want to?'

'Of course I do,' his wife shot back. 'I was thinking more like twenty past.'

Pleased that the stalwart was not quite as hard-nosed as he had intimated to George, the musician lunged for the telephone and passed the receiver across the table. 'Call 'em then,' he teased, 'cavewoman.'

Caught in a simultaneous dose of distress, the pair rose out of their seats and hugged each other close. Both knew they needed to remain focussed on the end-game, otherwise there was no point in staging the mock abduction at all. One of the kidnappers was to issue a ransom demand by telephone to Gerry's office, within earshot of the children, and they were to be denied any contact with their parents for at least another two hours. Staff at Blake & Partners and Stonebridge Music had not been made party to this information, with the exception of the chief himself, who had chosen to leave early that day for a haircut or some other lame excuse.

'Jet'll be beginning to brave up about now,' Lynn ventured after a few minutes.

'D'you think?'

His wife nodded. 'He'll start asking questions. Where are we? What are you going to do with us? He remembers every detail of your Ethiopian stories. I still hear him bragging to his friends about it. He's very proud of you, so I'm sure he'll try to emulate you.'

'Cool,' Jeff muttered. 'I guess. And what about Kizzo? She'll be asking questions too, but maybe only to herself at this point.'

Lynn slumped down again, despondent at this thought. 'Perhaps we should've had them taken separately. That'd mean Kierney couldn't rely on Jet's lead.'

'No way,' the lost boy snapped. 'She's only eleven, baby. Don't you reckon she'd take the lead if she had to. And maybe she will this time? We'll have to wait and see who's the stronger.'

Bart Dyson's daughter frowned at her troubled Catholic Argentinean Polish Jew, as ever coming to the defence of his dark-haired gipsy child. She decided not to retaliate or apologise, and neither was she about to press the issue. It was important to stay united during this pretend ordeal, which was proving excruciating despite both parents' confidence that no harm would come to their precious children.

'I can't feel anything from them,' Lynn lamented after a few more minutes' contemplation. 'Can you?'

Jeff shook his head. 'Were you reading my mind?'

'No,' his soul-mate let out a gentle laugh. 'That's what I mean. We've had this peculiar telepathic thing between us for all these years, but try as I might, I can't put myself close to the children. Can you even with Kiz?'

'Nope,' the father agreed. 'I don't want to analyse it now either 'cause it'll make me feel inadequate. But at the same time, I'm kind o' glad there's still something that separates our relationship from all the others. Is that wrong?'

The singer was taken aback. 'Wrong?' she repeated. 'No. Why's it wrong. You hear of twins being able to sense each other, but that's more about how their genetic similarities process life in exactly the same way. I don't think they can actually feel what each other's feeling; just what they'd feel in the same situation.'

Jeff nodded. 'Sounds eminently sensible, angel. But I still feel inadequate that my own genetic similarities aren't serving me well. More coffee, or a real drink?'

The celebrities brought a fresh brew out onto the verandah and took turns to make their outstanding telephone calls. Both struggling for concentration, they scolded each other light-heartedly every time they checked the time. The sun lingered for an absolute age, finally sinking over the cliff-top trees, and they were glad when mosquitoes began to gather in swarms over the pool. The humid summer's day was turning into a magnificent Melbourne evening, yet neither artist was much inclined to laud its arrival.

'Did I ever tell you I thought I was pregnant when you'd been taken hostage?' Lynn mentioned, attempting casual conversation.

Straining her ears across the moonlit expanse of water to where Jeff was tidying toys which the children had left strewn everywhere after a fun-filled weekend, it was clear she hadn't.

'If you did, I forgot,' he shouted back. 'Was it wishful thinking?'

'Subconsciously perhaps,' his wife shrugged, 'although I remember feelings of exhaustion at the thought of nappies and all that effort needed to make them fall asleep. Or making them wake up, or feeding and whatever. I don't miss that side of it, do you?'

'No. S'pose not, but I'm sure we'd adjust if we had to do it all over again,' the thirty-eight-year-old countered. 'We had a lot of help, angel. Most people do it way harder than we did. And at least their stuff's smaller and lighter at that age.'

Lynn chuckled at the sight of her husband feigning a sore back from lugging plastic containers crammed with pool toys into their rightful places. He was correct on all fronts. They had rarely experienced prolonged periods of a typical daily parental grind.

The telephone rang during the couple's oddly peaceful dinner, startling them out of their stupor. Jeff answered it, swallowing his mouthful with a corybantic gulp before the lump in his throat threatened to cut off access to his stomach. One of the fake kidnappers, no longer in character, supplied the nervous pair with a full update on how the youngsters were faring.

By all accounts, Jet had smelled a rat from the moment his teacher informed him that he was to go to the airport, and it had taken their considerable powers of persuasion to convince him to grab his school bag and jump into the waiting vehicle.

Kierney was similarly untrusting, even having expressed polite frustration at why no-one had warned them this morning that there may have been a chance of having to fly anywhere. It was most unlike their super-organised mother to spring something on them like this, they had both insisted.

After much cajoling and false promises, the Diamond *duo* had agreed to go with the men. The clincher was the production of identity cards sporting a logo which Jet recognised as belonging to his parents' regular security firm. However, no sooner had the car deviated from the familiar drive northwards out of the CBD to Tullamarine, the caller reported, than the children had become animated, exchanging feverish whispers.

'Bill, were they arguing?' Lynn interrupted.

'I couldn't hear,' the plain-spoken man replied. 'I could just about see the tops of their heads in my rear-view mirror. I'd say they were supporting each other more than arguing.'

Jeff sighed. 'That's a gold star, mate. They're collaborating, which was half the point of staging this bloody nightmare. Good result, thanks.'

The young mum reached for her husband's clammy hand and squeezed it, while the consultant continued. Apparently, Jet had asked all sorts of suspicious questions once he realised they were heading back into the city. He had raised his voice but hadn't acted petulant or angry, and Kierney had been content to let her brother speak for her. Both children had tired, their faces turning pale, eventually becoming fearful when ordered to disembark in front of a foreboding black door in a small laneway.

'Shit,' the father muttered under his breath. 'I detest this commentary. Be careful what you wish for… Eh, angel?'

His wife nodded, also queasy. 'Bill, did they attempt to get away?'

'No, Ms Diamond. We had their bags. Your daughter kept looking at hers, which was in my colleague's hand, and then at your son. But she couldn't catch his eye at that point.'

'Hmm… Interesting. If they'd managed to make a break for the street, they would've easily been able to work out where they were. Did you threaten them?'

'Yes, a little,' Bill replied, his tone softening. 'Only in so far as they were told if they behaved themselves, they'd stand a better chance of being treated fairly. Jet reacted forcefully when I grabbed his shoulder to pull him out of the car, but it wasn't a serious attempt to hurt me. They're both pretty controlled individuals, aren't they?'

'Yes,' their mother replied without hesitation.

Jeff frowned. He wasn't so sure "controlled" was the best trait to deploy under pressure, preferring free expression in any normal circumstance. Nonetheless, he exercised unnatural control at this juncture and refrained from offering an opinion. His mind traced back to his own interaction with genuine kidnappers and how it had taken time for him to be in a position to express himself freely. As long as his children's level of control was unforced, he supposed Lynn to be right to be erring on the side of caution.

'I can't wait to ask them what their strategies were,' he relaxed and gave his beautiful best friend a kiss on the cheek. 'I wonder if they realise they won't be able to get into the apartment?'

'Hmm...' she nodded. 'They could go to the Jenners' or to Admin. They'd have no problem finding their way to either place.'

'They'd expect to be chased though,' her husband grimaced. 'Probably think they'd be caught pretty quickly, and then they'd only end up where they were being taken anyway. To face unknown consequences...'

'Good risk management,' the sensible woman chuckled. 'So what next, Bill?'

***

The very ladylike watch Kierney had received on her birthday told her it was after eight o'clock. She had guessed as much since the sky was darkening outside. The famous siblings sat on two battered couches, in the middle of a large, vacant floor of a disused office building. She had seen a sign saying "Level Six" as they stepped out of the lift, now noticing how few taller buildings were visible from the centre of the floorspace.

The eleven-year-old was only partly confident that she had recognised the narrow street where the car dropped them off, and her brother had also drawn a blank at this detail. The labyrinth of magical laneways connecting *café* kitchens and bathrooms and leading to freight access and utility areas for larger commercial buildings were largely indistinguishable one from the other.

'Where are we, please?' she asked the smartly-dressed men, who stood in a huddle on the other side of the big area.

'You don't need to know, love,' he barked back. 'You're in Melbourne.'

Jet huffed in indignation. 'We know we're in Melbourne. Where else could we have gone in five minutes' drive?'

'Shut up,' Kierney hissed. 'Don't get cocky. That won't get us out of here any faster.'

The junior cricketer shrugged. 'May we take a look out of the window, please?'

A shorter, more menacing man with tattoos and a prominent, hooked nose pointed at the young girl. 'She can. You stay put, mate.'

Initially, the littlest Diamond's courage deserted her, baulking at leaving her brother's side. Jet flicked his hand to encourage her to go. Keeping her eyes fixed on their captors, the soles of her shoes scuffed the floor as she paced towards the bank of metal-framed windows, which appeared freshly painted in a clean cream colour. The observant child also ticked off the room's high ceilings and the sight of St Paul's Cathedral spire in the distance. These windows faced south, she was sure. The river was in this direction too, and Flinders Street station…

Standing on tiptoes, the thoughtful girl found she was tall enough to see all the way down to ground level, yet was unable to identify any landmarks; only dustbins and lock-up sheds in tiny yards, with the occasional car parked in a tight space. Craning her neck leftwards, she thought she could make out a line of mature trees marching in an easterly direction, adorned with masses of light green leaves. The Paris end of Collins Street, as it was known, where she often went shopping with her mother and grandmother.

Sirens wailed outside, sending the youngster's heart into her mouth. She wheeled round in alarm, finding her brother had reacted with excitement instead. Had their mum and dad found out by now where they had been taken and called the police? She hoped so. Were their parents even alright? What if people from the same gang had captured them too, with a similar elaborate story?

Glancing to her right to complete her furtive survey, Kierney saw the tops of several prominent buildings her *papá* had pointed out while on their many walks through the city, whether trudging back from the Dyson Administration building or running away from fans gathered outside Gerry's office. Instead of gawking in shop windows, he usually encouraged the children to look up and admire the architecture. He always said it was impossible to compare their hometown's edifices with the classical and modern architecture they had seen in his favourite, ancient European cities.

Taking the girl by surprise, the austere fluorescent tubes overhead, minus their diffuser covers, flicked a few times, then bathed the empty space in brightness. The men laughed as their hostage jumped, her view over the built-up landscape disappearing behind an unkind flare of refractive artificial light. What was left of the daylight had been obliterated at the flick of a switch, and she dropped back down onto despondent flat feet.

Her heartbeat was racing, and with the sirens fading into the distance, the eleven-year-old retreated to the couch and sat next to her brother. Seeing her apprehension, he took her hand, like his parents had a hundred times over, to soothe their frightened babes. Under her breath, Kierney relayed her best guess as to their position: somewhere just north of Bourke Street, next-door to the *art deco* building she remembered as "Capitol House".

Jet listened with interest. The name certainly sounded familiar. As far as he recalled, it was an ugly building in need of renovation, on the corner of Swanston Street. Wasn't there a theatre in the middle of it, accessed between the shops, where the family had held a few rallies? His sister nodded. They had been amazed that such a ritzy cavern was hidden inside what amounted to a boring old office block.

'Do you think *Mamá* and *Papá* are OK?' the younger child whispered. 'They might've been taken prisoner too. Should we ask them?'

Tears welled up in Jet's eyes, and he fought to suppress them. He hadn't felt too scared before this latest suggestion. These men weren't brandishing rifles or knives, like their dad had described in his Ethiopian *post mortem*. Neither was any other weaponry on display, and their guards were more reminiscent of characters from "The Blues Brothers" than of rebel soldiers. Yet now, with the image of their parents holed up in another location, the boy's mind began to run wild.

'Excuse me?' he shouted over to the three men. 'Please may we ask you a question?'

The tallest of the *trio* rested his mug on the windowsill and marched over to the vacant couch. His knees cracked several times as he sat down, and the children listened to him swearing to himself. He stared at the two faces he knew so well from the years of saturated media coverage surrounding the famous family. They were not ratbags, unlike other rich brats whose families demanded safeguarding. These kids looked him in the eye, used polite language and then waited for a response.

'Of course. What would you like to know?'

'If our parents are OK, please,' Kierney answered. 'Have they been kidnapped too?'

'I don't know, young lady.'

'Please could you ask the others?' the budding sportsman urged. 'They might know.'

'None of us know,' the kidnapper retorted, frustrated at the boy's insinuation that certain information had been withheld from him.

'Oh,' the young girl sighed. 'None of you knows.'

'That's right. We don't know where your parents are.'

With her brother glaring in dismay, the primary school student thought better of pointing out the flaw in the man's grammar for a second time. 'OK. Thanks anyway. What are your names, please?'

'Our names? Why do you want to know our names?' he sneered, his smile patronising. 'You don't need to know who we are.'

'Our mum and dad always ask people how to address them, sir,' Jet reinforced his sister's question. 'It's easier to communicate. I'm Jet, or Ryan, and this is Kierney.'

The foul-tempered man guffawed, drawing the others' attention. 'Yes. We already know that! You're prime targets, kiddies. My name's Nigel.'

Kierney's mouth almost broke into a smile, but she managed to stop herself, daring not to catch her fellow hostage's eye. It was funny to think of a criminal with such a nerdy name! This man's parents mustn't have anticipated their son's chosen career when they decided upon a name for him.

'Thank you, Nigel,' the twelve-year-old replied, using his own bright smile to greet their newly-dubbed friend. 'What about the others? What are their names, please?'

'Or are you all called Nigel?' Kierney couldn't resist, caught in a sudden brave and mischievous impulse. 'Nigel's Kidnapping Service.'

Her brother could scarcely believe his ears. Had his kid sister flipped her lid? His face struggled not to reveal concern, only magnifying further on noticing she was no longer fazed by her situation. Instead, she gave the guard one of her cutest shrugs.

Hearing the banter from the other side of the room, the stocky, bearded man who behaved as if he was in charge picked up a walkie-talkie and sauntered over to the children. 'What's going on?' he asked his sidekick. 'What do they want?'

The guard sitting opposite the youngsters continued to snigger, which annoyed his nameless superior. He went to sound off at his colleague, but then thought better of it.

'I'm sorry, sir,' the courageous girl offered. 'I made a joke, that's all.'

'A bad one,' her brother added, not wishing to miss out on the credit for lightening the mood.

'Did you now, Miss Diamond? So, young man, what was your question?'

'We'd like to know if our mum and dad are OK,' Jet repeated. 'It was my sister's question, but I want to know too.'

'I see,' the deep voice grunted. 'It's nice that you're asking after your mum and dad. You're good kids. I'm sure they're fine.'

Kierney smiled, clenching her thighs together as she was hit with a sudden urge to urinate. Once comfortable, she stepped backwards to sit on the couch in case she were caught out again. The children's self-defence instructor had warned them of such relaxing impulses taking over in stressful situations, when heightened emotions played tricks on one's body. The awkward phenomenon reassured her in a strange way.

Meanwhile, her brother had sneaked another glance at Nigel. He had told them only moments ago that none of their captors knew anything about their parents. Had he lied or was he kept out of the loop for a reason? Whichever the reason, he appeared most displeased at having been exposed.

'Have you asked for money for us?' the little girl enquired. 'I heard you on the 'phone. Please could you tell us if you were speaking to our mum or dad?'

'It was a woman called Cathy,' Nigel piped up. 'Who's she? Your maid?'

Hardly, the affronted youngster bit her tongue. 'No. If you mean Cathy Lane, she runs our parents' management company. Please tell us your names. I don't want to be rude.'

'Bonnie and Clyde,' the stooge sneered, impatient. 'He's Clyde, and she's Bonnie.'

His finger first pointed in the direction of the man who behaved like their leader, and then at the remaining kidnapper, who was on the telephone on the far side of the echoing space. The pair of immortalised folk heroes rang no bells with either child.

'He's not a she,' Jet called him to account. 'Have you got guns? AK47s or semis?'

Again Nigel flinched, embarrassed to disappoint the astute youngster. 'Not up here. Why? Do you want a gun pointed between your eyes?'

The boy's courage waned, receiving a withering glare from his sister. 'No, thanks. It's OK. I'm a bit hungry actually. Please could we have something to eat? I haven't had anything to eat since breakfast.'

Kierney nodded. 'Me too. That would be nice. Please, sir, have you asked for a ransom?'

The chief smiled. Despite being unfailingly polite, these mini-celebrities were also quite prepared to stand up for themselves. He was impressed; unable to imagine his own offspring bearing up so well. It was difficult to believe all the glowing praise lavished on this prominent Melbourne family, yet these two were holding up well under pressure.

He shouted across to their remaining colleague, who was no longer on the telephone. 'Callum! They want feeding.'

The children tried to hide their surprise. The gruff phrase had made them sound like animals. Again searching back to his father's catalogue of hostage recollections, the boy pictured their dad being served huge plates of bacon and eggs by armed soldiers. The prospect was so appealing that he began to salivate. What might kidnappers dressed in suits conjure up for dinner? Hungry Jacks would be his first choice, and if his sister had pinned their location correctly, the nearest one was only round the corner.

The third man reached under a table and dragged out a blue coolbox, which he lifted with a groan and brought over to the couches. Placing it on the floor next to his superior, he stood back and waited for him to open it.

'Please may I use the toilet?' Kierney asked. 'Is there one?'

'Ha!' Nigel sneered again. 'You hope!'

'Be quiet, Nige,' Callum snapped. 'Yes, young lady. I'll show you. Jet? You too?'

The boy nodded and jumped to his feet, thankful his sibling had raised the subject first. They were led down a set of stairs, midway between two floors, where they found a door marked with a recognisable symbol.

'That's the ladies',' Jet stated the obvious. 'Where's the gents', please?'

'Just go in there with her,' their chaperone ordered. 'I'm sure you'll work it out.'

Kierney pushed the door, her eyes beckoning for her brother to follow her in.

'And be quick. Thirty seconds, and that's it. No talking.'

The children scurried into a cubicle each and locked themselves inside. With a wall between them, it was impossible to decipher each other's frantic whispering, and they expended more effort hissing "Pardon" and "I can't hear you" than sharing useful information. Both toilets flushed at the same time, the doors opening to reveal pink, flustered faces.

'This is bloody terrible,' Jet mouthed to his sister at the wash-basins. 'What can we do?'

'We need to ask them to let us ring *Mamá*,' Kierney replied, on the verge of tears. 'I'm glad you're here. I'd hate being here without you, Jetto.'

The big brother put a comforting arm around her shoulders and squeezed, emulating his father once more. The gesture had the desired effect, signalled by a grateful peck on the cheek. Flicking off the girl-germs in disgust, Jet poked his tongue out and grinned, before yanking the door handle towards him and ushering his tormenter out ahead of him.

'All done?' the guard asked. 'Feel better now? Come on then. Let's eat.'

The cricketer sprinted up the single flight of steps, with the more graceful young lady trotting after him. Their guard followed behind, letting them back into the empty space. Filled rolls sat on the couch cushions which the children had vacated, selected from a bag on the floor between the other men.

Callum issued his next command, waving at the two foil-wrapped bundles. 'Help yourselves. Want a drink?'

'Yes, please,' the youngsters answered in unison.

'Beer or wine?' quipped the only one without a name.

'Whisky and dry ginger for me, please,' the twelve-year-old saw the leader's humour and raised it. 'With ice. And Kierney'll have a vodka and tonic.'

'Oh, you will, will you?' Callum exclaimed. 'We don't have any of that here. We have Coke or water.'

'Just water, thank you,' the girl requested, though the sugary fizz of Coca-Cola would certainly hit the spot. 'May I have some Coke later too, please? How long will we be staying here for? It'll be getting dark soon.'

The three men stared at each other in a combination of wonder and dismay. They had been instructed to remove two schoolchildren and had somehow ended up having a picnic with two measured conversationalists.

'So how long are you going to give Mum and Dad to come up with the ransom money?' Jet asked the leader. 'Sorry. I still don't know your name.'

'It's Bill,' came the reply, through a mouthful of ham and cheese roll. 'We'll reissue our demand in the morning, if we haven't heard anything. Then the price goes up. You better hope they think you're worth it! What makes you think they're going to pay?'

The youngest Diamond choked on her food. What alternative was there? She kicked herself for not thinking this through more carefully. Their parents had often aired their principles when it came to capitulating to threats against their safety or demands for money, always keen to state that paying people whose causes were unaligned with their own ought only ever to be a last resort. How long would she and her brother need to stay imprisoned before this option reached the top of the list?

'What do you need the ransom for?' the pre-teen dared, puffing out his chest. 'Our mum and dad'll want to negotiate first. My dad was taken hostage last year.'

Before their captors had a chance to respond, Kierney interjected. 'It was two years ago,' she spoke in clipped syllables. 'Don't talk about that, Jetto.'

The boy shrugged but did as he was told, causing laughter to ripple across from their couch. Bill proceeded to explain that they wished to raise money to start a new political movement in East Timor, to train the locals. They needed funds to set up a headquarters and buy vehicles. Nothing violent, as his brief had specified.

The two littlest Diamonds paid attention to the story, uncertain whether to believe it or not. They had heard of East Timor and knew it as a dangerous place often featured on news bulletins, but they were unaware of any involvement from their family or its charities over there.

Kierney reached forward to take hold of the Coca-Cola bottle, her eyes seeking permission from those around her. 'May I, please?'

Receiving no objections, the girl separated five plastic beakers from a stack lying on the table, and poured the brown, sparkling drink into each, taking great care not to let the bubbles overflow.

'Please could we ring our parents?' her brother asked, emptying his cup straightaway. 'They'll be worried about us.'

'You think so? Are you sure about that?' Nigel snapped. 'If they're that worried, why haven't they called us?'

Both children noticed his colleagues shoot a reprimanding glance at the bad-tempered guard, catching each others' eyes in amusement. The tallest of the three was also the most immature, Jet observed. Perhaps he had sacrificed a hot date tonight after receiving orders to take part in this stoush? Searching his vast knowledgebase on the subject, he surmised that going without sex would render any man grumpy.

'You can 'phone them at ten o'clock,' Bill consented, 'if you're not asleep by then.'

Ten o'clock? That was late, Kierney's heart sank. Although she didn't yet feel tired, she expected the situation might well be different in a few hours' time. The prospect of missing out on an opportunity to speak to *Mamá* and *Papá* made her determined to stay awake at all costs.

The View From The Top

'Jesus Christ!' Jeff snapped, cursing how the pace of one's life had a habit of varying in the opposite direction to one's heart rate. 'I'm getting mighty sick of this waiting game. Are you?'

His wife glanced up from the sheet music she was annotating and nodded. 'Hmm... Just think of how horrible it'd be if it were for real.'

The billionnaire rose to his feet and stretched his hands up towards the ceiling, full of regret that his own disappearance had caused so much heartache. Lynn knew precisely how horrible the real version of this waiting game was, and he loved her even more for never apportioning any blame to his incessant and perilous excursions.

Crossing to where she sat, he leaned over and planted a kiss on the crown of her head. 'I get it, angel. And I'm sorry.'

'Oh, I didn't mean that,' the patient woman smiled. 'It's a different kind of worrying, I think. You were much more capable of standing up to people than they'd be in a real kidnapping. I wonder if they're asleep, poor things? Do you think they can take care of themselves?'

'Hope so,' her husband muttered. 'We'll soon find out. I'm going to hide in the gym'. Need to let off some steam. Come and get me if anything happens, please?'

Another half-hour dragged by, the clock's hands as heavy and immovable as Jeff's feet as he pounded the treadmill. He had flitted between pieces of equipment, bored by each within no time and unable to purge the pair of precious, pristine *petits* from his mind. At least they were safe abductees, he consoled himself, hoping they might even be enjoying the positive aspects of their adventure, such as an evening free of homework...

At one minute after ten o'clock, the songwriter picked up the sound of footsteps in the corridor, approaching at a fast pace. The door to the gymnasium swang open seconds later to reveal the blonde singer, excited hands motioning him to follow her. He dropped the dumbbells on the nearest cradle, grabbed a hand-towel and ran after her, rubbing his sweaty palms dry on the way.

427

'Hey! Leave me alone!' he jeered, as the sexy sportswoman brushed her fingers across his chest, sending beads of sweat flying through the air. 'Are they on the 'phone now?'

She nodded, holding the office door open while her husband lurched towards the telephone.

'Hello?'

'Mister Diamond,' a man replied.

'Yep. Who's this, please?'

Eager to hear what the caller had to say, Lynn pressed a button on the base unit to activate its loudspeaker. Jeff waited for the red light to illuminate before setting the receiver back down, then rolled a chair nearer to the desk for his wife to perch on. He heaved himself onto the polished mahogany surface, still wiping perspiration from his bare upper body.

'We have your son and daughter here, Mister and Ms Diamond,' the gruff voice announced. 'They're unharmed but concerned they haven't spoken to you since this morning. I'm prepared to give you a few minutes to speak to them before we insist they get some sleep.'

'Thank you,' the young mother replied, the circulation in her right hand constricted by the grip of one much larger. 'We're on speaker-phone, so we can both hear the conversation. Can you do the same at your end?'

'No, ma'am. One at a time. Two minutes per kid.'

The world-changer raised his eyebrows at the prescriptive language. Their agent sounded convincing enough, so he imagined the children to be well and truly hoodwinked. He rested his free hand on an Olympian shoulder, trusting their little gems had managed to remain amicable during their ordeal.

'Mum, Dad!' Jet shouted into the receiver. 'Are you there?'

'Yes, Jetto. We can hear you,' Lynn replied with a similar level of energy. 'Thank goodness you're alright. It's great to hear your voice. We've been worried sick. Are you both OK?'

The dazed parents exchanged amused glances to acknowledge the entertainer's acting prowess, only to be brought straight back to reality by a series of rapid sniffs. Somewhat crestfallen, tears welled up in the mother's eyes too, picturing their brave little boy unwilling to betray how upset he was.

'We're fine, thanks, Mum,' the lad responded in a forthright tone, as befitting the captain of the Under-fifteens. 'Is Dad there?'

'Yeah, son. I'm here. Where are you?'

'Not sure. Melbourne city somewhere. Kiz looked out of the window,' the young boy's voice became more subdued, presumably given an instruction to change the subject. 'We had ham and cheese rolls and Coke.'

'Did you? For dinner? Excellent!' the rear-end of the Diamond pantomime horse took over. 'We love you, Jetto. Are you both comfortable enough?

Warm enough? And what about sleeping? We're trying to get you out tomorrow morning. The police are looking for you everywhere.'

'Good,' their son's intonation was now monosyllabic and abrupt, as if counting down valuable seconds. 'I don't want to stay here much longer. There's nothing to do here. Just chairs and floorboards, and one table. It's worse than after-school care.'

Jeff couldn't help laughing. 'Whoa, son! That bad?'

The couple detected male voices in the background, followed by the lad's anxious goodbyes. They envisioned the receiver being prised out of his hands and transferred to their daughter's. After a short pause, they heard the much quieter and typical poetic lilt of the dark-haired gipsy girl.

'Hey, *Mamá*. Hey, *Papá*. *Amo mucho a los dos*. Are you OK?' Kierney launched into her allotted time.

'*Gracias tanto, pequeñita*,' her doting father replied. 'We love you too. Speak in English. The guys might get suspicious that we're talking in code. We miss you so much. Did you eat your food, baby?'

'Yes. We're going to sleep on the couch. It's not too bad here, but we want to come home.'

The eleven-year-old was also crying, though concealed to good effect by her usual understated demeanour; a perfect combination of the distinct personalities she had inherited. Calm but expressive, introspective and measured. Her brother, by contrast, was singleminded and imaginative, usually unflappable but always excitable. It was strange how both children bore traits of each parent, yet each was demonstrated in such a distinctive manner.

'Where are you, Kizzo?' Jeff forced the little girl to regroup. 'D'you know?'

'Yes. I think so,' she hesitated, her plan to use Spanish to transmit their secret exchange having been thwarted. 'Near the capital house, but not Canberra. Other side of the crossroads. You know? I saw through the window, *Papá*.'

'*Excelente, gorgeous*,' the proud father smiled, tears trickling down both sides of his face. 'You are a smart girl. *Tanto, tanto, hija mía*. And tell Jet he's a hero, will you, please? You're both fantastic for sticking together.'

'*Gracias*. We're taller than other buildings.'

The diminutive detective received a sharp dig in the back. She span round to scold her big brother, who had extended all five digits of one hand plus his other thumb, pointing downwards and out of their kidnappers' view.

'Six, we think,' Kierney added. 'I'm so tired. Are you going to pay the money? They said they need it for East Timor.'

'East Timor?' her mother repeated. 'Did the men tell you that? You know more about them than we do, Kizzy, darling. We're going to carry on talking to them tonight. Hopefully, they'll release you without us having to give them any money.'

'*Bueno*. That's the best answer.'

'We'll have you home by tomorrow, gorgeous,' Jeff added. 'We promise.'

A torrent of obtuse words burst through the telephone line. The adult celebrities assumed the junior hostages were being told to finish up.

'Bye, Mum and Dad,' their son yelled into the receiver. 'Don't worry about us. Except get us out soon! May I have Hungry Jacks tomorrow, please?'

Lynn laughed. 'Of course. Take-away, let's hope! What would you like, Kierney?'

'Oh, I don't mind. Hungry Jacks too. Whatever you guys want.'

'Hope you sleep well, darlings,' the tearful woman urged. 'You're doing really well. Just stay brave. Talk to you in the morning. We love you.'

'*Adiós, amigos,*' their father appended, fearing the line would be cut.'

'*Adiós, Papá,*' Kierney returned. '*Te amo, Mamá, Papá.*'

'Right-oh,' Bill snatched the telephone from the sorrowful girl and raised it to his mouth. 'Mister and Missus Diamond,' he barked, keeping up the act. 'Are you assured that your children are in good health?'

'Yeah. I guess so,' Jeff replied. 'I wish they were here though. Please keep them safe and ring us back in an hour, if that's OK. We need to speak to you as soon as possible.'

'Maybe. We'll think about it,' the chief chuckled, before terminating the call and turning to the children. 'What was that foreign language stuff?'

Kierney's neck bristled with fear. She hadn't counted on having to explain herself to this frightening man.

'Kizzy always talks to our dad in Spanish,' her brother came to her aid. 'It's their special father-daughter code.'

'Oh, I see,' Callum nodded, relaxing a little. 'And what did you tell him in this code?'

The young girl gulped, also unaccustomed to lying. In fact, she couldn't remember the last time she had. She remembered her father's advice though: sometimes it served the situation well to lie, as long as no-one was harmed as a result. This must be an example of such a time, she concluded.

'I told him I was fine and that we were safe, and that there were three of you here with us,' she explained. 'Then I said I was looking forward to going to Canberra. We're going there next week, I think.'

The three guards appeared satisfied with the girl's cautious excuses. Callum leaned across and ruffled her brother's curly locks. If Jet could have reached to pat his sister on the back, he would have thumped her right at this moment.

***

The superstars went to bed in a mood of restrained consolation, safe in the knowledge that their children had not buckled under pressure. Impressed by the inventiveness they had shown when communicating their whereabouts, the parents saw no point in prolonging anyone's anguish. Being left to fester in the empty office building for much longer would only cause them to lose their faith in humanity; a far worse outcome at their tender ages.

'It's the boredom that'll wear them down, I reckon,' Jeff said, as they both lay staring out at the multitude of stars suspended over *Escondido*'s cliffs. 'If there's unpleasant shit going on around them, we shouldn't leave their minds to exaggerate it out of proportion.'

Lynn rolled over and kissed his stubbly cheek. 'They could always do their schoolwork,' she teased. 'I assume they have their backpacks with them... I seem to remember you were pretty productive during that time.'

Chuckling at her reference to the song he had written while held at gunpoint in the back of a battered Toyota, which had gone on to earn his captors seven-digit royalties, her husband slid out of bed and disappeared into the bathroom.

The tennis champion heard the shower splashing and figured he was not quite as relaxed about the youngsters' welfare as he made out. Was the complex intellectual angry at subjecting Jet and Kierney to this unusual life-lesson? Or was his intention to coerce her into dispensing her special brand of therapy? Whichever, the devoted mother was not immune to her own anxieties. She followed him in and climbed under the cool water, immediately engulfed into a slippery embrace.

They vented their combined frustrations, testosterone-fuelled blood pulsating through his body and on into hers. Jeff Diamond was still a magnificent animal when all wound up, and his beautiful best friend found herself succumbing to the ultimate pleasure once, twice and then three times until he slammed her back against the tiles and came with an almighty roar.

Lynn screamed as the thrill of simultaneous orgasms ripped through them. 'Oh, my God! That feels so fantastic, you sex-god!'

Turmoil temporarily chased away, the thirty-eight-year-old chuckled at the oft-used silly nickname. He lowered his wife down until her feet made contact with the tiles, locking their mouths together in a deep kiss. More than a minute must have gone by before he pushed the screen door aside and invited his very own goddess to step out and grab a pair of towels.

'Whoa,' Jeff sighed. 'I really needed that. Sometimes one's just not enough.'

The next morning, the new Range Rover that had been delivered less than a week ago swung out of the Mount Eliza driveway and opened its throttle to the maximum, bound for Melbourne at a furious rate of knots. Music rang through all six speakers, an overture to greet the day.

The eager parents had arranged to meet Bill at Gerry's office for a debrief of the night's events, before being taken to the environs of "capital house, but not Canberra", just as their clever daughter had encrypted. The two remaining kidnappers had been instructed to supervise the children's homework and make sure they were fed and entertained in their leader's absence.

At a few minutes before eleven o'clock, a pair of anxious faces looked up at the sound of raised voices in the lift lobby. The high volume of a talkback radio station prevented them from decoding what had triggered the sudden flurry of activity. However, all was revealed as the door unlocked and in walked Bill with the conspiring celebrities, and the overjoyed family was reunited in the bare, sixth-floor surroundings.

'Oh, I am so proud of you guys!' Lynn gushed, nestling the squirming bodies tight against her. 'We're not letting you out of our sight all weekend. It's so good to see you're alright.'

After picking up the promised burgers and fries from Hungry Jacks across the road, Jeff drove his three favourite people back to the apartment to chill out for the afternoon. The couple had debated on the trip up from the coast whether to confess to the hoax sooner or later, opting for sooner with negligible hesitation. They owed it to the poor mites.

'No way!' Jet's screeching exclamation pierced the others' eardrums, as he jumped to his feet in the restaurant and postured at his father like a lion cub angling for honours. 'I can't believe you'd do something like that! To us? Your prides and joys? It's not fair!'

'Jetto, please don't shout at your dad like that,' his mother scolded, hoping they weren't going to attract too much attention.

'It's OK, angel,' her husband laughed. 'I appreciate the venom, and I agree, mate. I wouldn't do it again. It was bloody stressful for all of us.'

'But don't you feel proud of yourselves now?' Lynn encouraged.

'Yes,' the boy murmured, the worst of his anger dissipating. 'But it was Kiz who found out where we were. I wish I'd thought of it.'

'I had to lie about what I'd told you, when they asked me what I said in Spanish,' Kierney piped up from opposite, all the while hanging on to her father's arm with her free hand as she tucked into her juicy burger. 'I thought we might get punished for it.'

'Thanks. It's good you realised that. It's the chance you take in those situations, *pequeñita*,' Jeff nodded. 'The lesser of two evils. Or risk management, as the boffins say.'

His son had recovered his confidence, now with his feet spread and hands gripping the edge of the table. 'So Bill was in on it all the time? May I swear, please?'

'Swear?' Lynn echoed. 'If you must!'

'Yes, I do must. Bastards!' the boy shouted with a broad grin on his face. 'Bloody bastards!'

All eyes turned to the source of this outburst. Their fellow patrons were bemused by the surreal scene, wondering where the television cameras had been hidden. The songwriter let out a smoky laugh, prising himself away from his daughter's clutch and pouncing on the unsuspecting lad. He wrestled him to the floor, amid screams of protest, absorbing untamed punches to every part of his body. Kierney and her mother sat back, cuddled up against each other, and surveyed the battle from the table, shaking their heads in dismay.

Patent to both parents was the fact that their kids were far from babies anymore. They knew how to modify their behaviour and language to suit the occasion, with enough nous to engage their adversaries to achieve a peaceful outcome. They were also well in tune with their own emotions and had proved themselves equipped to deal with whatever the world might throw at them.

Over dinner, the parents dissected and scrutinised each step of the kidnapping process and checked for any collateral damage. They all deliberated on the way the scenario might have played out if there had been a real ransom demand or if their captors had been less civilised.

'Do you think there *is* someone somewhere who wants to take us hostage?' Kierney asked.

'We don't know,' Lynn answered. 'We hope not, but you never know who might take offence to something we say or do. There are folks out there who believe in a completely different set of values to ours, or they're really angry about something, and somehow we push them to extremes. People who have money and power... or just want to express a strong opinion... are often targeted by other, jealous people who're bitter about what they think is unfair. It helps to get them noticed too; their picture in the 'papers and on television. I suppose it's a chance for them to feel like someone's actually listening to them for a change.'

'Yeah,' her husband agreed. 'That's usually half the battle, guys. You know what they say: even bad publicity's good publicity. If you can shut off their avenues to the general public and stop them enlisting a whole bunch of new sympathisers, they may lose interest in you. Hopefully, anyway...'

Jet thumped the table. 'OK! So how much money would you have paid for us?'

His father scoffed, slamming the palms of his hands onto the hard surface too. 'Ah, mate, I don't know. Couple o' hundred dollars.'

'Two hundred?' the grumpy boy echoed. 'That's not very much.'

'Lucky you were able to give us all those clues then, wasn't it?' their mum joined in, rubbing her son's back to reassure him. 'Otherwise you might've been waiting a long time for your burger and fries.'

'*Mamá!*' Kierney objected. 'That's not a very nice thing to say.'

'Sorry. It wasn't,' Lynn acknowledged. 'I was only joking.'

'Right. That's it!' their son declared, pointing a threatening finger at his dad. 'If you're kidnapped again, I'll tell them two hundred's my limit. *Tómelo o déjelo*, OK?'

'OK. Sure thing, mate,' Jeff chuckled, tossing his wife a sly wink. '*Capisce*. I'll just tell 'em if they released me and kidnapped you, then I'd pay four. See where we went from there. Deal?'

The young sportsman's mental agility came up too short to deliver an adequate comeback for this new angle, so he gave up, flopping back down onto his chair. He was tired after the last two days of unscheduled excitement, looking forward to the normalcy of cricket training the next morning. It was a pity he couldn't share these experiences with his friends, but he understood why. What if someone known to his mates were one of these freaks, as their mother suggested? Having had a taste of imprisonment, he was in no hurry to tempt providence.

That night, after exhausting every slice and dice of the children's ordeal and its pursuant happy ending, Lynn and Jeff tumbled into bed. They had judged it best to spend the rest of the evening at opposite ends of the house. Determined not to mention the subject for a few days, the songwriter had shut himself in the family's cavernous playroom, where he sang and played his heart out in soundproofed isolation.

His wife, on the other hand, with the US Open tennis championship only weeks away, had thrown herself into an arduous, late-night session in the gymnasium. She showered on ground level so as not to wake the rest of the family, and padded up the grand staircase to find the dark-haired, handsome man already stretched out on top of the bed, sporting a full erection and an inviting smile.

'Hey! You look happy. Did I miss something?' the naked woman asked.

'Jesus, I'm so damned lucky,' the joker replied. 'She's only just left.'

Lynn lifted the sheet and climbed under it, her hand ironing the surface of the mattress in jest. 'I wondered. You look a bit guilty, come to think of it. And the bed's still warm. How long've you been up here?'

'Oh, hours. Had to 'phone for some company, y'see. It was pretty relaxing though. Shall I show you what we got up to?'

'Well... What if I were to say no?' his wife teased. 'Did you look in on the kids lately?'

The world's greatest lover dropped his act for a moment to humour the lithe nymph. 'Yeah. A while ago. They were *sparko*, so I just came to bed.'

'Did you? How un-Jeff-like!'

'Jesus!' the rock star exhaled. 'You're so amazingly beautiful.'

Lynn shrugged, flopping down onto the pillow and staring lovingly at her biggest fan.

'But you're right. They don't need cossetting so much now. They wouldn't have noticed if I'd stayed with them. Besides, I've been waiting for you.'

The athlete frowned. 'With the girl who just left?'

'Yeah. Didn't want to get lonely. Christ! You're unreasonable sometimes too, woman.'

'Fair enough. That's more like the Jeff I know.'

Lynn groaned as she made herself comfortable, doing her best to ignore her man's gentle advances. Her muscles were tightening after a tough night's training, on top of their day of driving to and from the city when she should have been loosening up on the tennis court with her practice partner.

'You'd think with all the money invested in sports science, they'd have come up with a cure for lactic acid build-up,' Jeff smiled.

'They did,' his dream girl countered. 'It's called getting up early and going for a run. Shall we set the alarm? Back to normal, you said.'

'Did I? Fuck that!'

***

'You sound worried, Cath. What's up?' Jeff stopped his publicist mid-sentence. 'Is everything OK over there?'

'Yes. Everything's fine. We're busy, that's all.'

The widower twisted in the chair in Kiley Jones' boxroom of an office, elbowing the door closed. Having taken up residence in the violinist's New York apartment while filling in a few blanks with some of his dearly departed's closest friends and musical colleagues, he had been called to the telephone during the children's supper time. Their Chinese nanny had been inveigled into teaching them some amusing phrases by the incorrigible superstar, and his sudden departure made him rather unpopular!

Despite her denial, the office manager and the billionaire had been working together far too long for any metaphorical wool to obscure his view for more than a sentence or two. Her team had been given strict instructions not to bother their grieving boss while he was overseas, but this was unlikely to be the reason for her reticence.

'*Na*,' the celebrity scoffed. 'I don't buy that. It's obviously important, or you wouldn't have rung. And it's not diary- or money-related, 'cause you'd send an e-mail about that.'

'Oh, you're such a bastard!' Cathy sighed. 'I wish you weren't so perceptive.'

'Sorry. So that means it must have something to do with Lynn. Am I right?'

'Yes. Of course it does.'

It was her boss' turn to sound disappointed. 'Right. Where am I going? What do I have to do? You can give me a straight answer. I can handle it.'

The woman chuckled, coughing her fraught emotions into some semblance of businesslike equanimity. This man never failed to provoke her profoundest emotions, either reducing her to tears or cracking her up into fits of laughter. Jeff Diamond never did anything by half-measure, which was why she loved him so much.

'Are you sure?' she countered. 'How are things going with Kiley and Guy? Are you sick of babysitting yet?'

'No. It's cool. We've been learning Mandarin today. Such useful phrases as "My toy train is stuck in the toilet," and "Triangular cookies are the tastiest." All stuff I'll find utterly indispensable when I next go to Beijing. I can teach you, if you want.'

The prospect of attending another tribute event had deflated the songwriter's mood too, evident to Stonebridge Music's most senior employee by the series of lame one-liners being fired into the telephone.

'No, thanks,' Cathy replied. 'Maybe save it for our staff end-of-year party. I feel a new game coming on: translate your favourite sayings into another language and get everyone to guess what they are.'

'Hey! That's not a bad idea. Like an international version of *charades*... Write that down, Missus Lane. Now... What've you signed me up for?'

'Diana Godfrey from the agency organising next year's Grammy Awards 'phoned yesterday. CBS has asked her to sound you out.'

'Ah, yeah?' Jeff's heart sank a little lower. 'They want to know how much they can rip companies off for commercials during the show? That figures.'

'Yes. The idea is to give Lynn and you a joint Special Merit Award, like a lifetime achievement thing, I suppose... In recognition of your contribution to promoting live music in schools. Everybody knows "The Black Sheep"'s bound to take out "Musical of the Year" and probably a bunch of other stage-show gongs. They also told me Lynn's nominated for "Producer of the Year", and there's no doubt she'll win. Di wants to know if you'd accept them in person.'

The marketing specialist's voice trailed off, anticipating the ire brewing in a certain Upper East Side apartment building. She was only too aware that the first anniversary of his wife's fatal shooting would derail the celebrity's recovery through the inevitable heartbreak of reliving the event in the public eye. Gerry had corroborated her fears in advance of the call, recounting a similar conversation *vis-à-vis* the Academy Awards in Hollywood.

'Christ Almighty!' the decorated music industry veteran cursed. 'Can't you go instead?'

'Me? Don't be ridiculous! No-one'll buy advertising if I accept on your behalf. Lynn'd want you to be there, I'm sure.'

Would she? The old soul cringed at the number of lies and false promises he was destined to concoct over the remaining months of the year. In normal circumstances, his beautiful best friend would undoubtedly have insisted they alter their schedules to accommodate such a prestigious occasion, not to mention the opportunity to promote their latest charitable projects to the world's *glitterati*.

By the sharp twinge in his chest, rendered all the more intense when he pinched the skin where their "JL" tattoo had been etched more than twenty years ago, it was apparent that Lynn sent her ethereal regrets. The lovers were double-booked, having already given their RSVP for a much more private reunion, on the other side of the globe from Madison Square Garden's hallowed stage.

'Who's the host next year?' Jeff asked, fumbling for a delay tactic.

'Ellen. You like her, don't you?'

The world-changer laughed. 'Sure. Absolutely. But it doesn't make me want to say yes. What's the date?'

'Oh… I haven't written it down. End of Feb', isn't it, usually?' his office manager guessed. 'Hang on… I'll find out.'

'No!' the rock star jumped in. 'Cath, don't stress. The date's not important. I just don't want to commit myself to anything so far ahead. Same goes for the kids, by the way. Christmas and the New Year'll take a toll on them, and then it'll be a year…'

A lump rose in Cathy's throat, hearing the great man falter. He had been almost upbeat before leaving for The Big Apple, making solid progress on their life-story and heartened by Jet and Kierney's fruitful resumption of normal duties.

The flow of tribute records had steadied at last, for which the whole Stonebridge crew was grateful. The first six months since Lynn's death had been a veritable nightmare, managing a dozen offices filled with wailing females whose dream jobs had been forgone in favour of daily counselling sessions with fans, fellow artists or even with each other. The onset of another summer had brought optimism and cheer, allowing ordinary tasks for their extraordinary stars to take precedence over their collective loss.

'OK, Jeff. I get it. Shall I say you'll get back to them in a couple of weeks? They're looking for an answer sooner than that, but I'll try and stall them 'til you're back. I'll tell them your calendar's not fixed yet for the first quarter of next year.'

437

The philosopher couldn't help but laugh. 'No. That's perfectly true. Sounds good. Extenuating circumstances or something to that effect. Or "The man's a basket case, Diana." I can hear you already!'

The kind employee grumbled. 'Oh, for God's sake! If I didn't know better, I'd think you were teasing me. You never change…'

'Yeah, yeah, yeah! Come on… Speak your mind. You've got no idea how Lynn put up with me for so long,' her boss appended his own self-deprecation.

Cathy snorted, not sure whether the bereaved husband was angling for sympathy or a little light relief. 'No, I certainly do not. Don't try that one on me, or I'll cancel your ticket home. Is there anything you need from us by the weekend?'

'No, thanks,' Jeff humoured her. 'I do.'

'You do what?'

'Know how she put up with me.'

'Something to do with sexual attraction, I'm assuming,' his publicity officer mocked. 'I can't compete. I wish I could, and you know it very well. You were her magic man, Mister Diamond. And I'm not saying that just to boost your deflated ego. Far from it. You're everyone's magic man, but you outdid your magician's powers when it came to your forever lady.'

The superstar's brain froze, his attention stolen by a piercing sensation underneath his shirt. Even the photograph of Kiley in full flight, taken from one of her stellar *concerto* performances at Carnegie Hall, seemed to flash him a momentary knowing smile from the wall in front of him. Such unsolicited praise from the consummate professional was rare, regardless of how tongue-in-cheek it may have been, stemming from a mutual sense of grief. Here was a topic worthy of its own chapter in the couple's maturing autobiography, since this paradox had emerged even before the two medical students had perished at one of his concerts. The greater the liability an aggrandised sense of self-importance became to their mission, the more the fans seemed to view it as an asset.

Indeed, this incongruous blessing did not apply to him alone. Lynn had also developed an immunity to the Antipodeans' favourite pastime of taking pot-shots at those perceived to have done well, immortalised by the curious expression "Tall Poppy Syndrome". No matter how the Diamonds had tried to play down the happiness of their marriage, it remained a subject of fascination which nine out of ten interviewers and popular commentators sought to interrogate.

'Thanks, Cath,' the humble widower replied. 'Good of you to point it out. I don't feel quite so magical right at this moment, but you never know. Anything else going on back there?'

'No. You're welcome. We miss you, and everyone's worried about you.'

The Chief Executive Officer chuckled. 'No change there then!'

'Oh, there *was* one other thing…'

'Yeah? Fire away,' he invited, seeing the shimmering shapes of approaching children on the other side of the study's frosted glass door.

'Craig's class at school's doing a sponsored event. A new idea someone's thought up called "Forty-hour Famine", to raise more money for Ethiopia. Can I put you down for thirty dollars, please?'

'Sure,' Jeff laughed with much more enthusiasm this time. 'You're asking me to pay for your kid to starve himself? Now that's irony at work! D'you want to enroll them into a program while you're at it? Is Jamie doing it too?'

'Oh, trust you to see it that way!' the caller chided. 'And no, Jamie's not doing it. It's only the older kids.'

The study door burst open, and in barrelled Rhapsa and Tok Kahn, the elder pair of Kiley and Guy's three children. Their meal devoured and cleared away, they had gone in search of their entertainment coordinator, who had been missing for twenty minutes by now.

'Hey, Cath. Gotta go in a minute,' the forty-four-year-old raised his voice, letting the youngsters know he was still busy. 'Chinese classes are over. I'm on duty again. But listen… Are we still matching when people fundraise?'

The philanthropist was referring to the team-building initiative that Lynn had instigated at Stonebridge Music a few years ago, whereby the company subsidised employees whose children participated in charity events to double the amount raised. Another attempt at masking their own generosity, he admitted, which had a habit of backfiring, since most parents couldn't wait to reveal the source of the additional money.

'Yes, we are,' Cathy affirmed. 'You mean I can match whatever Craig's class raises?'

'Absolutely. Triple it. Go for your life!'

'Thanks heaps, Jeff. That's great. You'd better get back on duty. Say hello to Kiley from me. Hope you're still getting plenty of time to write. Is it going OK?'

The author smiled. 'Cheers. I shall. She's in her element in NYC. They both are. And yes, I'm writing plenty. Got a huge download from Janis and the boys yesterday. They're all so bloody good to me, I've gotta tell you. I feel very welcome here.'

'That's great news. Just think of all the times you guys entertained them at *Escondido*… They're only giving back. What are you writing at the moment?'

'The *bar mitzvah* on steroids. I started a chapter on it today, and it's going to take another session or two to get it all out through my fingers. That was such a stupendous weekend, Cath. A real step-change in our relationship. There's a wealth of good content to commit to perpetuity.'

'Fantastic! I'm really looking forward to reading it. Are you planning to give any of us a sneak preview?' the marketing *guru* hinted. 'Apart from Jet and Kizzy, of course.'

The study door and the songwriter's privacy were breached at last, and in barrelled Kiley's eight-year-old daughter. Privileged beneficiary of the name "Rhapsody Diamond Kahn" for reasons known only to the musical couple whose independent careers had blossomed on a global scale after graduating from The Good School, she tugged on her handsome visitor's sleeve. Raising a hand to request a minute more of her patience, her favourite pseudo-uncle was inclined to agree. He had spent way too long on the telephone.

'You can read it anytime you like, ma'am,' Jeff told his loyal staff member. 'You've lived through it all, from sex, drugs and rock'n'roll to sex, decadence and acclaim. And drugs and rock'n'roll... Who am I trying to kid? You're the perfect fact-checker, in fact. I'll almost be afraid to hand it over. You'll find inaccuracies I mightn't be keen to correct.'

Cathy giggled. 'No doubt! I'd love to. Enjoy the rest of your stay. I'll send you an update overnight, OK?'

'Thanks. You too. Say something encouraging to the troops from me, please. And buy the Craigster an extra serve of chips tonight. He's gonna need 'em!'

***

After a low-key Japanese dinner, the superstar parted company with his hosts on the doorstep of their apartment building and continued along First Avenue for half a dozen blocks. He stopped in at a convenience store to stock up on cigarettes and cigars before turning right towards East End Avenue, his leather jacket buttoned against the stiff breeze.

'You with me, angel?'

The songwriter's spirits had been lifted for a few hours by general New York trivia from his imported hosts, yet despair caught up with him in a rush as soon as he found himself alone. Lynn had traced his whereabouts last night, when he had shared fine wine and sweet memories with Richard Kerr and his partner at a popular gay hang-out. So far however, she hadn't shown up tonight.

'Come for a walk in the park,' the charmer suggested to his wife's ghost. 'I need to talk to you about Jet's *bar mitzvah*. I don't want to exaggerate its effect on him just because it left such an impression on me. Does that make sense?'

Six lanes of traffic thundered along the twin layers of FDR Drive underneath Carl Schurz Park, all other sound drowned out by its unremitting monotony. The wandering minstrel unwrapped the cellophane from the pack of cigars, stuffing it in his pocket until he found the next trash can. Gracie

Mansion stood out among the rest of the neighbourhood, lit up in celebration of mayoral splendour.

Jeff recalled with particular *ennui* a dinner he and his beautiful best friend had attended at the Federation-style stately home as guests of Ed Koch, in the same year their son had turned thirteen. They had been invited for a second time only the previous February, in the depths of a severe cold snap shortly after Rudy Giuliani had taken office. Lynn's inbred rightward leanings had been correct to expect good things from the incoming mayor. He had since done wonders to eradicate petty crime in the city, irrespective of how far the couple riled against their fellow diners' hubris and paternalism after the successful Republican incursion.

Australia's most influential public figure continued walking, soon reaching the end of Eighty-ninth Street. The sporadic positioning of lamp-posts cast pale, white spotlights onto the winding pathways, leading him down to the statue of Peter Pan. Winter had stripped the twigs naked, leaving the boy who never grew up with precious little cover.

Kiley's children had brought their special guest here earlier today, darting under the archway to listen to their voices echoing around them. He had forgotten how much energy young kids possessed, and then how easily they tired and transformed into ratbags.

It put the father in mind of his gorgeous gipsy girl, with whom he would soon *rendezvous* at the United Nations headquarters, only a couple of miles further down-river. While her brother had exhibited strong ratbag tendencies on a regular basis as a child, Kierney had always drifted between a two and a three on the same scale. Or perhaps time and grace had discounted this number...

After a few minutes, Jeff adjusted to his new surroundings so well that the constant thrum of tyres bumping over joins in the highway below no longer registered with his shrewd senses. Yet once the sound finally infiltrated his busy mind, it dulled his focus for a split-second, allowing his emotions licence to interfere *via* the same incision. He climbed the curved, stone staircase out of the hollow and headed away from the road until he stood gazing out towards Astoria and beyond, at the growing skyline of Queens. With memories swirling round his head, he took solace in the East River's blackness.

'Why do I make things so fucking complicated, angel?'

To his relief, a pleasant tingling acknowledged his question and stole his breath away. He re-lit his extinguished cigar, the flame from his lighter leaping several centimetres higher than usual in the freezing night temperature.

'Anyone else'd just wallow in grief and loss until time healed the worst, then pick himself up and start again. Don't you think?'

His tattoo itched again, supplemented by a fevered melody blaring in his ears. What did this mean? Was Lynn annoyed with him for not being honest with Cathy? Or was she wondering why he wasn't in more of a hurry?

Whatever the reason for her mixed messages, the widower had never experienced such an undeniable pull towards the raging river…

'Be patient?' he guessed, soaking up the sting but without the accompaniment this time. 'Me be patient, or you?'

Another sharp jab, more intense. '¡*Excelente!* Now I get it. I can't tell any more people, can I? Gerry's the only one who can be party to any secret suicide business, and even he's asked for no details. I can't implicate people. You know that. Anyway, how're you going? Have you flown over Cambridge lately? How's the new sex-god? I'm about to write about our trip to Bathurst, baby. That'll be effortless writing…'

'Excuse me, sir,' a man's voice caused the celebrity's heart to miss a beat. 'We couldn't help noticing how much you look like Jeff Diamond.'

'Hi. Do I?'

'Yeah. Man! You know… Australian Jeff Diamond.'

Turning on his heels, the dark-haired rock star smiled. 'Hmm… Him again? Yep. I've heard that before.'

A couple in their early thirties had approached from the star's left, now quite agitated at having stumbled upon someone famous strolling through their locality in the dead of night. While their inquisitive Maltese Terrier sniffed his shoes, they stared more intently, unsure if they had picked up the twang of an accent which would give him away.

'You are him, aren't you?' the woman asked. 'Mister Diamond? We've been fans of yours since forever. It's unbelievable to find you in our local park! What are you doing here? Sorry. I'll stop jabbering now. Oh, wow! I can't believe it! And oh…'

The musician paused halfway through extending his hand, knowing the chatterbox had been about to apologise for his loss, *comme d'habitude*. 'It's OK,' he sighed. 'I am Jeff Diamond, yeah. And thanks.'

'Thanks for what?' her companion butted in. 'I'm Aaron Coleman, and this is my wife, Vania. It's fantastic to meet you.'

'You're correct, and thanks for being fans. Good to meet you too. D'you live around here?'

'Yes,' Aaron replied. 'We often walk this park on a Wednesday. We teach a night class at the synagogue a few blocks from here. Hebrew School. Are you staying somewhere round here?'

Jeff nodded, pointing overhead in the general direction of First and Eighty-fourth. 'I'm staying with friends who don't smoke, so I'm sucking enough poison into my system to last me 'til morning. Sit down. Would you like one?'

The pair shook their heads, being invited to join their idol on a wooden bench on the other side of the path. The widower took a cigarette out of the open packet, lit up and slipped the remainder back into his inside pocket.

Before his owners could stop him, the Colemans' pint-sized dog hopped onto the celebrity's lap. Horror spread over both faces, and they shooed him off with all four gloved hands, scrambling to make sure the famous man's clothes hadn't been soiled.

'Don't worry about it,' he laughed, bending down and making a fuss of the little animal. 'I love dogs. Really. I also exude melancholy, and dogs tune into that. What's his name?'

'This is Jesse,' a relieved Vania gasped, despairing as the dog continued to crave attention. 'Are you going to be in a new movie?'

The celebrity was taken aback by the question. 'No. Hey, Jesse. A movie? What've you heard?'

'Heard? I'm not sure what you mean.'

'Only that I'm wondering where you got your information from,' Jeff explained. 'I get signed up for a lot of things without my knowledge!'

Aaron came to his wife's rescue. 'Oh, it was only an assumption. You looked like you were rehearsing your lines.'

'Ah, OK! No, I wasn't. Just sounding off at an angel. Looking for a second opinion on something.'

These cryptic answers lent nothing to the two New Yorkers' understanding, having arrived during a one-way conversation. Since ploughing the majority of his energy into writing, the world-changer had ceased to regard his reclusion from the rest of civilisation as strange. It mattered little whether his fellow human beings considered him deranged. They were correct in all likelihood, and regardless, he only had to endure a couple more months before he could set himself free.

'Shit!' Jeff swore under his breath as another spasm twinged through his pectoral muscle. 'I'm writing a book; an autobiography, in fact. I'm collecting inspiration from all over, which is why I'm in New York. Some of Lynn's closest friends live here now. People who knew her before I did. It's important I capture all that early stuff.'

'Oh, wow!' Aaron crooned. 'We'll definitely get a copy. It sounds amazing. When does it come out?'

'Sometime in the New Year. The plan is to finish it for a January release,' the author responded. 'It's all about the backstory, as far as I'm concerned. If I'm going to give Lynn the credit she deserves, I've got to focus on the things that matter. Our life together wasn't what people saw on TV or read in trashy mags. Our universe was no different to yours or anyone else's on the face of it. Good things happened, and we gloated for a while. Other stuff went wrong, and we fixed it. Repeat and fade. You know how it goes.'

The scripture teacher was once again in awe. 'I read "The Runner" again recently. That's an amazing book. I think I've read it three times. You've read it too, haven't you, Vanie?'

His wife nodded, still preoccupied by the dog, who had calmed down enough to become obsessed with licking the superstar's fingers. 'Oh, yes. I loved it. The movie was more frightening than the book. I like those psychological dramas that keep you in suspense.'

'Cheers,' Jeff said. 'That's good to hear. I wrote it under the influence of some pretty hard-core drugs. There's more backstory for you! These days I'm writing under the influence of fine red wine and plenty of these...'

He retrieved the cigarette packet from out of his jacket, turning away from the others to light another. 'And the odd joint here and there. Mostly there, in case someone catches me.'

Vania giggled, cupping her hand to her mouth even though they had the park to themselves. 'I smoked pot in college! Our parents would kill us if they knew. I love how you don't care about those pointless barriers. As if people who get a few things wrong in life can never turn things around. They showed you on TV after your trial, talking to the shooter's wife...'

The intellectual sniffed. 'It wasn't my trial, by the way, but I know what you mean. Nothing I said to that woman was going to change the facts that her husband was getting locked up and my best friend'll never come back. I didn't give a shit about convention then either.'

'Well, I'm definitely buying your autobiography as soon as it's released,' Aaron repeated, standing up and lifting Jesse into his arms. 'We'll keep an eye out for it. We should leave you in peace.'

'Thanks a lot. That'd be cool,' Jeff smiled. 'Here... Take this. It's my marketing manager's. I can guarantee I'll forget otherwise. Are you on e-mail? Send her a message to say you met up with me. That way, you'll actually stand a chance of receiving something.'

The New Yorkers both made a grab for the tendered business card, unable to read it in the dim light. Nonetheless, they were ecstatic at having encountered one of the most revered men of the late twentieth century on their route home from the temple.

'Oh, wow! Thank you, sir,' the young man raved. 'We'll make sure to get hold of a copy. It'd be extra special if you signed it. You are going to sign some, aren't you?'

The celebrity paused. He hadn't ventured this far yet. Planning to launch a book after one's demise was on a par with a posthumous seat at the Grammies ceremony! He resolved to have some sort of commemorative insert typed up in the next few weeks, to serve as a vehicle for inscribing personal messages to the book's waiting list. Another thing that Lynn would have already taken care of...

'No worries, Aaron. I'll make it so. *Leil Selichot* to you both.'

Grateful recognition spread across the Jews' faces. 'May God forgive your sins,' they chanted in unison.

'Of which there are many,' the Melburnian chuckled. '*Mazel Tov*, guys.'

444

He imagined the orthodox pair had been preparing their students for the holy month of October, signalling a new year in the Jewish calendar. Starting with *Rosh Hashana*, passing *Yom Kippur* and ending up with a celebration of the *Torah*, the writer deliberated on the spiritual coincidence which saw him cross paths with these devout followers just as he was about to embark on a retrospective of his son's sacrilegious coming-of-age weekend, recognised at the most secular of modern-day festivals.

'*Mazel Tov* to you too, Jeff.'

'*L'chaim*,' the comedian raised an imaginary glass. 'There's a cocktail for that.'

Two puzzled expressions strained to make sense of the revered man's oddball comment, their sheltered upbringing obfuscating the nastier side of life. The seasoned traveller marvelled at another manifestation of blind ignorance from supposedly well-educated Americans living in this most cosmopolitan of cities, so often magnified by clerical devotion.

'*Mazeltov* cocktail?' he tried again, still eliciting no visible recognition. 'They're banned on the West Bank?'

Now sporting an asinine grin, Aaron turned to his wife, neither wishing to be rude.

'No worries,' the wordsmith shrugged. 'Call it Aussie humour. D'you guys put on a big family shindig for *Rosh Hashana*?'

Vania laughed. 'Oh, my goodness, we have the works! This is my first year as a married woman, which means I'm under a lot of pressure to make a good impression on the Colemans.'

'That's right,' her husband interrupted, as if the penny had finally dropped. 'You have some Jewish ancestors, don't you? Didn't your grandparents come from New York?'

'Sure did. Came here from Poland after the second World War. My dad's side of the family lived here until the end of the 'forties. I don't know much about them though, I'm ashamed to say.'

'So you don't observe the traditions?' the young woman asked.

'Nope. Traditions never were my thing, regardless of their origins,' the intellectual smirked. 'That's kind of why I'm standing out here this late. I'm staying with strict Catholics, and somehow their home stifles me with its pious purity! Coming to New York, as I have regularly over the years, I'm always surrounded by in-your-face religious beliefs. More than anywhere else in the world, strangely. And it's especially poignant at the moment, when I'm questioning my own beliefs in a much less personified and poorly-understood faith; that of the atheist who'd like to believe in something but he's not quite sure what.'

This time, the lack of comprehension was tempered with an element of compassion from the teachers, whose role included expunging any vestiges of doubt from such enquiring minds. Surely Judaism was an obvious choice... A

445

God followed by the Jewish people for almost fifteen hundred years prior to the Common Era, who could stamp out pestilence and raise taxes in a world created in time for the Sabbath, had as strong a pedigree as any other deity to shepherd the human race into the next century.

Jeff carried on, warming to the couple's innocent zeal. This dogged attitude was not unlike the one he often adopted at the table with cynical politicians and apathetic government operatives, if he were honest.

'I'll tell you where I'm staying, if you promise not to broadcast it everywhere. I'm staying with Kiley Jones and Guy Kahn.'

'Oh, my God! Are you really?' Vania exclaimed. 'They're so talented. I didn't know they lived here. I see posters all over, advertising her concerts. And Guy Kahn's Big Band Sound. That is him, isn't it?'

'Yeah. Their styles are pretty much poles apart. Kiles hates Jewish fiddle music… y'know, *Klezma*…' the songwriter was confident this subject would be understood. 'So we made a bet that I could get her to dance the *Hora*. She's determined she won't do it. We're going to a Gramercy Park venue tomorrow night to see if I can't change her mind. You're welcome to come along and watch.'

Aaron's face lit up. He handed back the business card for the noble celebrity to write the details on its reverse side. As Jeff reached into his leather jacket for a pen, he winced in pain when a seismic shock raced through his heart. His dream girl approved of this gesture too.

Vania paused, listening to her husband saying their farewells. 'I'm sorry for your loss,' she babbled, talking over the others.

All three were caught in a moment of awkwardness. Struck by a shot of anger at having failed to escape the encounter without reference to the gaping void in his life, the Australian stood back and breathed deeply.

'Thank you, Vania.'

'It must be rough going,' the woman added. 'I lost my grandmother just last month. I can't imagine losing someone so close.'

'Yep. It is rough going. Losing anyone's hard. I'm sorry for your loss too, in that case. Have a safe walk home.'

'You too,' Aaron replied, steering his wife away with a clumsy sidestep, the fidgeting dog now tucked under his arm. 'We may see you tomorrow night. It was great to run into you. Good luck with the book.'

'Cheers, mate. G'night. Have a happy New Years.'

'You too,' the younger man repeated.

'Oh, I shall. Not for a while, but I'll drink to that. *Adiós*.'

At the top of the stone staircase, Jeff Diamond turned one way while his fans turned the other. With only a single pair of shoes resonating through the deserted park, he guessed they had only taken a few paces before stopping to watch him walk out of sight; another common occurrence which had remained a mystery throughout his career.

He reached the river in no time at all, planning to track southwards in the direction of the Jones-Kahn residence, when he spied a gathering of overcoats and parkas huddled together with their eyes raised to the skies. Torn between satisfying his boundless curiosity and wishing to remain anonymous, he stopped at the railings under the sign marking John Finley's Wall, whence he could eavesdrop on their chatter while pretending to gaze in wonder at the Triborough and Throg's Neck Bridges illuminated in the distance.

The philosopher smiled and rubbed the itching tattoo through his clothing, scolding his mind for its insistence on finding connections between events where perhaps there were only coincidences. This location appeared to be a meeting place for Manhattan's astronomers, which explained the elevated level of geekiness pervading the atmosphere.

A stream of condensation carried the wanderer's lonely lament out over the wall. 'I was rehearsing my lines. Wasn't I, *mon amie*? Just rehearsing my lines.'

Ambling in a wide arc around the stargazers, one of Planet Earth's biggest and brightest skirted away until he could safely continue along the Riverwalk without being identified. All this talk of new years had unleashed a fresh sense of urgency. On the one hand, his confidence was boosted that each day took him closer to his *nirvana*, while on the other, it frightened him to think of everything he needed to finish beforehand.

'Dancing with Kiles tomorrow night. D'you remember that wager we had? I'd far rather dance with you tomorrow night though, angel,' Jeff swallowed his rampant emotions and put on his best Yiddish accent. 'By whosoever God, my life already. Come back and show Kiley how it's done, will you?'

The muscle behind his shirt sang; a comforting lullaby which assured him Lynn would wait as long as it took. The wind rippled the water's surface, washing miscellaneous pieces of litter and foliage on their own nocturnal outings. Were it not for its pungent motion and the glint of lamplight on empty, discarded drinks cans, the river itself might well have been absent too.

The lost boy gripped the rail with both hands. After the strength and endurance training his taskmaster of a son had put him through in recent weeks, he had no doubt that a deep knee-bend and a flick of his wrists would generate sufficient thrust to propel himself clear of the wall and into the choppy current. Were it not for the buoyancy afforded by his twentieth birthday gift until he managed to shake it off, the weight of his heart would be enough to drag him under the surface pretty rapidly.

'Jesus, baby! What I'd give to feel your arms around me,' Jeff snarled, shaking his head to banish this destructive obsession. 'I want to taste your kiss again. Hear you sing... Fuck! I miss you more every damned day.'

A swirling swathe of strings flooded through the sad poet's ears, materialising from nowhere but stamped with a hallowed trademark. His wife's spirit had heard the plea and was determined to focus his mind onto a more positive incline. The description of atheism, which had tripped off his tongue with minimal premeditation during his conversation with the Colemans, had begun to steep his morbid thoughts in an eccentric form of optimism.

'You liked that?' he asked his departed saviour. 'Can't even remember what I said. Something about wanting to believe in something no-one can clearly define? Am I craving a faith, or is faith trying to recruit me? What d'you know, now you're on the far side, *Regala*?'

The music softened in his head, and the dull ache of sleeplessness eased for the first time that day. Was he descending further into delusion, or was his trust in being reunited with his soul-mate based on something more valid which he wasn't supposed to comprehend until he arrived?

Had he, who presumed greater knowledge would direct him towards a more cynical, reasoned view of the world's intangibles, chosen the scientific over the spiritual for too long? This new brand of wisdom was the rude awakening he needed to remain vital to the end of this current incarnation, designed and delivered by the one whose selfless devotion endured through the ages.

Picturing his grandparents and five-year-old father preparing to leave this crazy city for their western Sydney backwater, the billionnaire mongrel gave thanks for everything that had happened in between, barring a single, fateful day when his charted course had made its premature and immutable alteration. Clearly, as it may well have done in lifetimes past and with equal probability for those to come, their hypothetical supreme being had only to turn his back for the briefest moment in time.

'*Merci, mon amie*,' Jeff whispered. 'I'll meet you at the dam on New Year's Day, as planned. You're right, as usual, and there are no words for how amazing it'll be to be together again. "Perfectly imperfect" just doesn't come close anymore. What d'*ya* reckon? Our souls'll be so red-hot, we'll set the whole damned world on fire.

'I should've learned my lesson when Anna's Victoria was born. After all these years, and after all the success we've had together, somehow my brain still catastrophises. It worked out OK before, so it'll work out OK again. I'll do my best to stay patient, and I hope you can too.'

Tears blurred the view across to Queens until the songwriter could no longer gauge from the landmarks across the water how far away from Eighty-third Street he had strayed. Lynn always caught him before he fell, so many times and in so many ways. His thoughts turned to Jet and Kierney. For their sakes, he vowed to put his trust in this mysterious power for the remaining months.

'I just wish I knew why we came crashing down too soon,' he cried, standing with his back to the railings and taking in the enormity of the Upper East Side stretching to the endless expanse of dark cloud. 'Things were really shaping up, angel, weren't they? D'you think we could've avoided that bastard and his petty jealousy? It's so fucking frustrating to know we've got to start again from scratch. That's what freaks me out the most. Not knowing where each other's going to pop up. I bloody hope we'll have some kind of an inkling at least? Or are we oblivious to our prior existences when each generation starts out, not even able to second-guess destiny for the umpteenth time? I s'pose it's too much to ask for something to be easy!'

A new melody crystallising in the musician's head began to soothe his fretful conscience. *No worries, mate.* His saviour had friends in high places. Her forty years as Lynn Dyson Diamond had been spent in a state of perpetual certainty. The stinging both within and outside his heart reassured the soul she left behind that she had their future covered as well.

'Hey, angel? I've had another whacko idea: I'm going to write a song, seal it in an envelope and leave it with Kizzy for safekeeping. Then if my next incarnation writes it, she'll find out who I became. Reckon that'd work?'

Jeff lifted his eyes to the heavens as blind fury ripped through his core yet again. 'Yes, of course it bloody will. And if that outrageous notion's true, how the hell do I figure out who you are? I guess you never had the chance to engineer such elaborate contrivances! You've got to help me find you. Or the new me, I should say... It'll happen. Who knows what this nonsense is all about? I have no damned clue, angel, but I believe in you and me. Maybe that's all it takes.'

End of Part Five

If you enjoyed reading this book, please take the time to tell your friends and leave a review on Amazon and Goodreads.

Book 6 in the series, "A Life Loved", was published in December 2016. Full details can be found at http://lorrainepestell.com.

Lynn Dyson and Jeff Diamond had become the celebrity couple with the Midas touch. With their son showing signs of fulfilling his sporting destiny and a daughter who was already driven to right the world's wrongs, they were showered with accolades and adoration from every corner of the globe.

How had this nobody from the wrong side of the tracks got so lucky? With his dream girl by his side every step of the way, the superstar's multi-faceted career knew no bounds. Politicians clamoured for photo-opportunities, the press fed well on each persuasive controversy, and the success of their business empire funnelled millions of dollars into worthy causes.

No wonder they had become an assassination target! Jeff's autobiography foretold this omen with twenty-twenty hindsight, his open wounds smarting with each obvious opulent and outspoken occasion. "The higher you climb, the harder you fall." The tedious cliché rang true for the father as he captured his teenagers' many exploits for posterity. He and Lynn had dared to scale enormous heights, paying the ultimate price far too soon.

Had it all been worth it? The book held these secrets, all painstakingly transcribed by a man who couldn't wait to find out what was to come. Whether taken from his lover's journals, the children's memories or the cataclysm of poetry pouring from his lonely heart, the months leading up to his latest challenge legitimised every decision the forever couple had ever made.

He only hoped the same good fortune would hold true in the next lifetime.